Warrior of Light

Warrior of Light

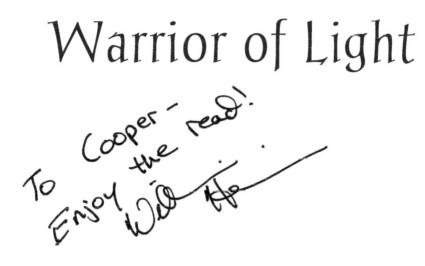

WILLIAM HEINZEN

Copyright

Book cover design by Dane Low at CreativIndie.

ISBN-13: 9780692769058
ISBN-10: 0692769056
Library of Congress Control Number: 2016913675
William Heinzen, Mandan, ND

Dedication

For my parents, who bought me my first journal

Acknowledgments

Writing this book remains one of the greatest adventures I've ever had, and many people helped along the way. My first reviewer was my father, who wasn't afraid to write "bull—" in the margin where he saw it (the mark of a great editor is being direct when necessary). Next, I owe thanks to three who provided a great deal of assistance during my early drafts of this novel at the University of Jamestown: Sean Flory, Myra Watts, and Bette Nelson. Other early readers were Barb Heinzen, Todd Muth, Elizabeth Cronin, and Jolene Brink. I'd also like to offer my gratitude to Kelly, Tom, and the other staff from the editing team for a superb job. Last but not least, thanks to Tim Tobin, who will tell you he was the first Kyrlod.

One

Boblin Kule shivered. Around him, the icy wind whipped through the confines of the Kaltu Pass without mercy. That was fitting, for the North was not a merciful place.

"What do you think, Kule?" Wayne asked him.

"Fresh," Boblin said, crouching down and running his hands over the markings on the stony ground before him. Malichons had been this way only hours ago. That wasn't unusual; malichon patrols often roamed the Kaltu Pass, and by now Boblin and his fellow elion scouts had traveled several miles from the safety of the Fort of Pellen. The scouts had no reason to think these malichons in particular were planning an attack on the Fort. More than likely they were just making their presence known to harass the elions, to keep them on their toes.

It didn't mean Boblin had to like any of it.

Another burst of wind whipped up a swirl of dust from the ground in front of them. On either side of the two elions, the sparse clusters of shrub vegetation rocked from the gust's onslaught. Yes, if nothing else, one could at least count on malichons *and* wind out here. Boblin wasn't exactly a fan of either.

"What do you suppose Desh will make of it?" Wayne asked.

"I don't particularly care what Hedro Desh makes of it," Boblin replied quietly. As it so happened, he cared for Hedro Desh even less than he cared for malichons or wind.

Wayne replied with a tight smile. "He's not that bad, Kule. He means well. And he's quite handy in a fight."

"He doesn't win by fighting," Boblin said. "He stands on a nearby rock, and the radiance of his insufferable ego turns everything around him to stone."

Wayne choked back a laugh.

Boblin stood up, dusting off his kneecaps and adjusting the sword at his belt. The hilt had been digging into his side, sort of like the way Hedro's personality dug at him.

Still, after two years in the Patrol—eligible elions were allowed in at sixteen years of age—Boblin had to admit that Hedro was quite capable with a sword. And with a quarterstaff. And with a bow. And with female elions.

In fact, Hedro was quite capable at just about everything.

An impartial observer might have called Boblin's sentiments jealousy. An impartial observer would have been partially correct. Boblin wasn't in the business of lying to himself, after all. But his dislike stretched back much earlier than their days in the Patrol. It stretched back to—

"Well?" Hedro asked. He had come from beyond the ridge to their west, clambering first up the far side and then down into the narrow gulley where Boblin and Wayne now stood. He wore his sword strapped across his back, presumably because it allowed him to puff out his sizable chest and flex his not inconsiderable biceps while remaining ready for an inevitable clash with enemy troops.

"Malichons," Wayne said.

"Obviously," Hedro replied.

"They were probably here this morning," Boblin said. "I assume they traveled north. They weren't making for the Fort. They're just letting us know they're here."

Hedro looked at the tracks. "We'll have to report it."

Boblin imitated Hedro's tone. "*Obviously.*"

"Settle, gentlemen," Wayne murmured.

They often dispensed with the regular formalities of rank when on patrol. Hedro was technically in charge here, and should it come to actual combat, Boblin and Wayne would obey him without hesitation or question, but in the meantime, the three had conducted patrols like this together for long enough that they could get away with throwing around a few figurative punches to ease the pressure of an arduous and unforgiving duty.

"What do you suppose Commander Jend will say?" Boblin asked.

Hedro shrugged. "'Stand fast.' 'Keep the watch.' Those sorts of things."

"It's about five hours until sunset," Wayne said. "Any reason to think they'll come back this way?"

"I'd rather not stick around and find out," Boblin said.

"Scared?" Hedro asked, a faint smirk hanging on his lips.

"I like being alive," Boblin shot back.

"Fine then," Hedro said. "Circle up."

The Kaltu Pass stretched west to east for two miles, serving as the gateway to the Fertile Lands, a small delta of vegetation fed by the waters of the Pel River and the only area in the North that had escaped the blight of Dark Lord Zadinn's presence.

The Fort of Pellen, the last free dwelling in the North, sat nestled in the stone peaks at the western end of the Pass. But freedom had a price, as the soldiers of the Frontier Patrol knew. Zadinn did not let them live unmolested. The only things keeping the elions safe were the Fort's walls and the skill of its defenders. The Frontier Patrol scoured the Pass day and night without pause, always vigilant.

However, every elion also knew that Zadinn had never fully committed to destroying their home. If the Dark Lord were to send the full might of his malichon army to their doorstep, the elions of the Fort were doomed. But the Fort stood far south of the Deathlands, and Zadinn didn't find the elions worth the effort. The Fort housed a mere three hundred citizens—hardly a pressing matter to the Dark Lord.

Of course, the members of the Fort still fought their battles. The North's grim lifestyle required an elion to give up much if he wanted to remain free. Boblin had killed his first malichon at only twelve years old. On that day, he'd been playing with other children just outside the Fort's walls when a pair of malichons managed to slip past the guards and capture the children. Boblin and a few others fought back.

Every elion in the Fort grew up with one rule ingrained in his or her mind: *A malichon will show you no mercy, so you must show it none. If a malichon attacks you, you must kill it. You must kill to survive.*

Boblin had feigned unconsciousness. Then as one malichon was binding him, he surprised his captor by stealing the creature's knife. Boblin stabbed the malichon in the heart, and his friend Celia killed the other.

He killed his second time four years later, within his first weeks of training with the Patrol. Boblin and his fellow recruits, Hedro and Wayne among them, encountered a malichon division surprisingly close to the Fort. It had very nearly been a fight for their lives, and Boblin took no shame in admitting that only the arrival of Commander Jend and the more seasoned fighters had saved them from that predicament.

During two years since, in many long days and nights on the Patrol, Boblin had encountered more malichons than he cared to admit, and the scars of his very first kill were replaced by the ability to do what was necessary. Skirmishes with malichons were by no means frequent, but even an encounter once every ten patrols added up over time.

He didn't like any of it, but it was the law of the North. *You must kill to survive.*

*   *   *

The remainder of the patrol passed uneventfully, and at the close of day, the scouts returned to the Fort of Pellen, which stood against the base of a stone peak at the head of a narrow path. The trail to the main gates could fit three or four elions abreast at most, thereby forming the Fort's first and most basic line of defense. No matter the size of the army, the Fort's enemies would have to approach the gates in small groups, leaving them to the mercy of archers on the battlements.

As the Fort came into view, Boblin felt a glow of comfort at the sight of its stone walls. Those walls were *home*. Stout and unyielding, they held back not only enemy troops, but also wind, rain, and snow. Behind the Fort, the land sloped upward at a steep angle, reaching its summit far above their heads. The Fort wasn't just home. It was a bastion of hope set against a stark backdrop of gray rock and cloudless sky.

As they reached a nearby summit, Boblin saw the wooded expanse of the Fertile Lands west of the Kaltu Pass, where the fresh waters of the Pel River and the wildlife of the forest sustained the Fort's livelihood. If he turned, he could see the Durin Plains to the east and the dead Erdrar Forest to the south, both bare in contrast to the Fertile Lands, offering nothing but emptiness.

The current peak on which the three elions stood sloped down to the main path, which then led back uphill to the Fort's main gates. Boblin recognized Hugo and Ken Rindar standing atop the battlements in the distance. Second in command to Jend Argul, the Rindar brothers were the Fort's most highly respected soldiers next to the Commander himself.

The sun slipped down into the west as Hedro led Boblin and Wayne back to the Fort. As they dipped into the narrow path toward the front gates, they gained shelter from the ever-present wind, traveling the last stretch in silence, footsore and ready for the day to end. When they reached the portcullis, Ken saluted them from atop the battlements, and each of the three elions returned with a modified salute, left hand instead of right, the standard code to let the guards on the battlements know all was clear in the Pass. After they gave the signal, the portcullis in front of them rose, gears creaking and grinding as the spiked gate lifted high enough to allow them entrance to the grounds within.

"You're up for ailar training today, Kule," Hedro said. "Wayne, you're free for the evening."

Wayne gave Boblin an apologetic glance before nodding and splitting away from the group. Most likely Hedro just wanted an opportunity to drop somebody to the ground ten or twelve times so he could work up an appetite for dinner. But Hedro *was* good with ailar, and Boblin would grudgingly admit he could learn a few things from the other elion.

Besides, Boblin was sure Celia Alcion would be training in the court as well. That would not disappoint him in the least, as long as he could prevent himself from an outright embarrassing defeat underneath Hedro's instruction. Of course, Hedro probably had the same inclinations as Boblin where Celia was concerned, meaning it wasn't at all coincidental that he wanted to conduct a training session at this time.

Boblin acknowledged Hedro with a nod, and the two stepped into the Fort together. In all, five buildings stood inside the grounds, one in each of the four corners and a tower in the center. The building closest to the gatehouse was the barracks for the Frontier Patrol, two other corner buildings served as housing for families in the Fort, and the last was a ward for the sick and injured.

The tower in the grassy center of the Fort's lawn soared above the heights of the surrounding battlements, a lone bell tower at its peak. Pellen Yuzhar's private chambers were in this tower, along with the Council's meeting rooms and the Floor of History, which preserved memories of the North as it had been over two hundred years ago before the Dark Lord came to power. The tower's floor held a large dining hall for community gatherings and feasts. The elions committed to celebrating seasonal festivals to remind themselves that remaining free meant more than just keeping malichons at bay. Freedom was about *living*, about enjoying the crisp night air and celebrating their right to smile and laugh.

A smaller courtyard, surrounded by low wooden walls, stood in front of the barracks. There the Patrol members practiced not only with swords, bows, and quarterstaves, but also ailar, the art of hand-to-hand combat that Commander Jend stressed above all else. The Commander's creed held that, when deprived of every other weapon, every member of the Patrol would still have his or her hands and feet available, and would therefore be able to continue fighting until the last breath.

Only elions lived at the Fort. Humans and dwerions had once lived with them, but according to the histories in Pellen's archives, a vicious plague swept through the Fort a century ago. The sickness did not afflict any elions, but every human and dwerion at the Fort had died.

Boblin read as much as possible about the other races. Scholars speculated that humans, dwerions, and elions were initially all one species, but that over time their descendants split into three distinct groups. Boblin thought it a sun-baked idea, but scholars frequently held such notions. He supposed humans had enough in common with the other races, but elions and dwerions bore practically no resemblance to one another. Elions were tall and slender— Boblin himself stood over six feet, and there was nothing extraordinary about his height—but dwerions were short and stocky. One might as well compare a willow to a stump. Dwerions were respected for their brute force, but elions were known for nimble agility and speed.

"Care to wager a pint before we start?" Hedro asked.

Boblin would have rather poked himself in the eye with a rusted nail than buy Hedro ale, but vocalizing such sentiments would be counterproductive at best, so he simply shrugged. "Why not two?"

"Indeed, why not?" Hedro agreed. "Very well then. Let's head inside."

* * *

"Defend your flank," Celia Alcion said to Ana, who stood in front of her. Ana was a good recruit, and two years ago Celia herself had been in her shoes. Sixteen, fresh to the Frontier Patrol, Ana was eager to make a good impression. Tough, but inexperienced. Again, no different than Celia had been at that age.

The North would change that soon enough. It changed everyone once they left the safety of these walls and ventured out into the Pass, where malichons were much less forgiving than training instructors.

Ana stood in a traditional ailar stance, hips square and forward, a diagonal line from her left foot in the back to her right foot in the front, fists up in front of her face. Left forearm to block, right fist to strike. Basic, fundamental ailar— if one's opponent was attacking from the front.

"You need to be able to shift your stance," Celia said. "Malichons are trained to attack in groups of three. One keeps you occupied, while the other two attack your flank. So you need to defend it." Celia assumed a stance. "Like so." Instantly centering her gravity, she turned ninety degrees, striking with her right arm in a diagonal block while her left hand remained ready for the attack. "See?"

Ana nodded and followed suit by repeating Celia's movements. Ana was an elion of few words, and Celia appreciated and admired her attention to detail. She would make a fine soldier. This was good, for the Patrol had precious few to guard against the ever-encroaching malichon army.

Without warning, Celia struck. She ducked in low and fast, coming beneath Ana's guard and seizing her wrist in a fluid motion. Celia dropped to her left knee, swinging her right hand in a counterclockwise motion and bringing Ana with her. The momentum carried Ana forward, flipping her onto her back and to the ground.

Celia allowed herself a taut smile. The maneuver hadn't been fair, but this war wasn't fair. Besides, Celia had lost count of the times Jend Argul or the Rindar brothers had sprung such tricks on her when she was in training. There were lessons to be learned here. To survive, one must expect the unexpected and adapt to the unadaptable. It wasn't easy, but it was the way of the land.

"You got me on that one," Ana said.

"It works on everybody the first time," Celia replied. She released Ana, who rose to her feet and beat the dirt off her training pants.

"I don't intend to let it work a second time," Ana said, favoring Celia with a smile of her own.

"Good," Celia said, rising off her knee and brushing her own pants as well.

"What's it like out there?" Ana asked. "On patrol?"

"Hopeless," Celia said, "but that's not the point."

"What is the point?" Ana asked.

Celia turned to the recruit, arching an eyebrow. "I think you should know the answer to that. Otherwise, you don't belong out there."

"It's what we have to do," Ana said, shrugging. "If we didn't fight, we wouldn't be who we are. It's the answer that's always worked for me. I wanted to know what answer works for you."

It was a fair enough question, and one that deserved an honest response. "We won't win this war," Celia said. "Not by ourselves, not in this generation. But if we can buy the next generation enough time, then maybe they *can*." She clapped a hand on Ana's shoulder. "That will be all. Hedro Desh has the training grounds next. You did well."

Celia led Ana across the training yard. The grass underfoot was mostly brown and lifeless, with just a hint of green here and there. The wind cut across them as they walked. This was the Fort of Pellen, and as Ana had said, this was what they did. They trained every day, constantly honing skills to defend their homes. It was the only life they had ever known, the only one they expected to know.

"Hi, Celia."

Celia stopped on her way out of the grounds and into the Fort proper. Boblin Kule knelt in the entryway to the training area, lacing up his boots before entering the grounds within. On the far side, Hedro Desh was shedding his chain mail patrol shirt for a lighter leather jerkin.

"Hello, Boblin," Celia replied. "Ailar training?"

"My favorite," Boblin said, in a tone of voice indicating it was decidedly *not* his favorite. "Explain this. How, when a malichon attacks you, is it practical to attempt a flying kick as the primary means of defense?"

Celia couldn't help but smile. Humor, the ever-present defense mechanism of the one and only Boblin Kule. "It's about the *principle*, Boblin. Did you skip that lecture?"

"I skipped a lot of lectures," Boblin said.

"I know," Celia said. "I was there."

"In the lectures, you mean," Boblin said, "not skipping with me."

"No," Celia said, "not skipping with you. I wouldn't dream of such a thing."

From behind Boblin, Hedro Desh entered the training grounds. The big elion towered over both Boblin and Celia, his face set in its typical glower. He was likely upset about something and ready to take it out on Boblin. Nothing unusual about that; Hedro was always upset about something, and Boblin was always a good target.

Hedro handed Boblin a second leather jerkin. "Kule, training pattern twelve. Okay?"

Boblin gave a wry smile. "Yes, sir," he said. "Okay indeed." Before passing into the training ground, he turned back to Celia and nodded. "Have a nice day, Celia." As he said it, a faint flush crept into his cheeks, barely perceptible unless one knew to look for it—and Celia did.

She smiled back at him, seeing his flush deepen as she did so. "You, too, Boblin."

She turned and left the training grounds. She called it the "Boblin blush." It was as reliable as clockwork, and she knew exactly what it meant. She wasn't ignorant. But she'd let Boblin Kule work that out on his own time—no need to do that for him.

It was the *principle*, after all.

* * *

Muscles aching, considering the pros and cons of pounding his head against the nearest wall in a form of self-induced punishment, Boblin climbed the battlements at the western edge of the Fort. Unsurprisingly he now found himself indebted to Hedro Desh in the form of two pints of ale, payable at Hedro's discretion.

Boblin didn't over- or underestimate his own abilities. He knew enough ailar to train any recruit on his own, but Hedro was simply bigger and faster than him. He *had* managed to land a few blows of his own, no doubt about that, but Hedro gained the upper hand by spinning him through the air and dropping him on his back once, twice, and thrice. Not being inclined to meet the Maker this evening, Boblin conceded the duel.

He now climbed the battlements, enjoying the subtle sensation of the lengthening evening before him. Sitting atop this wall and watching the sunset always soothed him. He could see the Fertile Lands from the western edge of the battlements. In the distance, beyond the Lands, the sun's fiery orb turned from orange to blood red, tingeing the treetops with its dusky hue. It was a breathtaking sight. Even the North, a wasteland of stone and rocky outcrops, had a certain beauty when the multihued rays of evening light touched it. Boblin raised his face to the sky, feeling the sunset's warmth.

"A sight in which even the young can find solace," a voice said.

Boblin started and turned as Pellen Yuzhar took a seat beside him. The Fort's ancient, white-haired leader was the best elion Boblin knew. He was the reason the Fort continued to exist, the reason they remained free. No one else had his wisdom and charisma. Sometimes it seemed Pellen's willpower alone held the malichons at bay. No one knew how old Pellen was. Boblin's late grandfather had claimed Pellen was old even when Boblin's grandfather was young. As for Pellen, he simply said he was much too old to die.

"Good evening, sir," Boblin said. He removed his cloak and put it around Pellen's shoulders, but the elion shrugged it away.

"You will need that more than I," Pellen said. "Your bones have more to lose than mine from these frigid elements."

"Sir, you'll become ill."

"The last time I became sickly, I was your age," Pellen replied. "That, I assure you, was quite a long time ago. I believe I will last for one more night."

"Very well, sir." The two sat in silence for a while, enjoying the last hour of warmth. Nights in the North were exceptionally cool.

"You served on patrol today, outside the Fort," Pellen said.

"Yes, sir," Boblin answered.

"Did the day meet your expectations?"

"It was rather uneventful, sir," Boblin replied.

Pellen turned to him. "Do you wish for adventure on these excursions?"

Boblin shook his head. "No, sir. There is no adventure here—only freedom and those who wish to protect it."

Pellen fell silent again. Then he said, "Well put, Boblin Kule."

For a compliment from Pellen, Boblin would willingly suffer a thousand insults from Hedro. "Thank you, sir," he replied.

They did not speak again until the sun had set. Then, as the sky darkened and the stars began to shine, Pellen stood. He turned and pointed north.

"Do you know what lies in that direction?" he asked.

"An ugly rock," Boblin replied.

"The Deathlands, my son. And who dwells there?"

"The Dark Lord," Boblin said.

"Yes," Pellen said. "My son, that man's soul is the most evil thing to ever touch our land. We have lived free of him thus far, but the time will come when he arrives and breaks these walls. When that happens, our people will survive only through unity. He will not care what arguments exist between you and an elion named Hedro Desh. And on that day, neither will you."

Without another word, Pellen turned and left the battlements, leaving Boblin sitting alone as night fell.

Two

Boblin awakened with a start. He'd just had an extremely bizarre dream in which he watched a group of people travel through a swampy marsh with hazy mists engulfing their path. He counted four travelers: three humans and one dwerion. One human, the youngest, seemed especially…important. A bright aura surrounded his body, cutting through the vapors of fog.

Never mind that. It's cold *in here.*

Boblin lived on the third floor of the Patrol barracks at the Fort's outermost edge. His quarters consisted of a cot, mirror, washbasin, and desk. The blank stone walls bore no decor, and he could cross the entire room in six strides. One small window, set above his cot, provided the room's sole exterior illumination as well as a view of the battlements outside and the gatehouse below.

Soft moonlight streamed into his quarters, casting a mysterious hue on the walls and desk. He'd left his window open to let in the springtime air, but the temperature had dropped and the breeze now chilled him. Boblin sat up on his mattress and reached forward to close the window. As he did so, he paused to look at the grassy lawn near the gatehouse. After a moment, he frowned. He saw no guards on the battlements.

He looked left and right. The Frontier Patrol rotated the night watch weekly. The sentries could be making a circuit of the walls, but it would be a serious violation of protocol. Even when making a circuit, at least one soldier kept watch at each section of the wall. Under no circumstances were they to leave the wall completely unattended.

He waited a few minutes, expecting to soon see a sentry reappear, but the walls remained empty. He stepped back from the window. Something was wrong, and he should probably head outside to investigate. Of course, if he did that, some foul creature would probably seize him with its claws, drag him into the shadows, and devour him.

Then again, Boblin occasionally suffered from an overactive imagination.

Imagination aside, night was a very dangerous time in the North. It was unlikely anything had made it inside the Fort's walls, but creatures *did* lurk in the darkness outside. Zadinn's presence had birthed all manner of strange things across the land, and one did not want to encounter such beasts without a sizable army at his back.

As Boblin tried to decide whether this imagined creature ate its prey alive or dead, he spotted a lantern bobbing near the gatehouse. One Patrol member, Kaiel Tulak, stepped into view. A stranger—an old human with unkempt gray hair and a greasy beard—stood at Kaiel's side. The newcomer wore tattered brown robes, and yet stood tall in spite of his aged body. *But what kind of man travels about at night? And why has Kaiel brought him into the Fort?*

The two walked purposefully toward the central tower, drawing Boblin's gaze toward the tall building. A light was glowing in one of the third-floor windows.

On the lawn below, Kaiel held one hand on his sword as he escorted the stranger. The signs were apparent, but subtle. This man was not a guest—perhaps not a prisoner, either, but anyone who approached the Fort under cover of dark was a potential threat. As the other guards remained conspicuously absent, the nighttime breeze faded into an unnatural stillness. Boblin liked this less and less. There was *always* a breeze in the North. This dead, unresponsive air lacked its customary sharpness.

Then the old man turned and looked straight at Boblin. He knew the stranger couldn't see him—Boblin's quarters were dim and stood a good fifty yards away—and yet Boblin *felt* the man looking at him.

Follow us, Boblin. Not all is as it should be.

The voice rang in Boblin's head with astonishing clarity. He staggered back from the window and sat down hard on his cot. Looking around, he fixed on the washbasin. He strode over and splashed icy water over his face and neck, trying to clear his numbed mind. Talking to himself was no problem, but a foreign voice in his head was something else entirely. An elion should be all alone upstairs, thank-you-very-much.

He stepped back from the basin, feeling colder and more alert, but the compulsion to follow the old man remained. Boblin dried his face and contemplated his options. *Well,* he supposed, *life in the North is short. I might as well spend it doing something interesting.* He donned his lightweight patrol cloak and left his room without a sound. He walked down the hallway, carefully listening for any suspicious noises from other rooms, but he heard only his neighbor snoring and nothing more.

He traveled down the stairs and stepped outside. The gatehouse stood a dozen yards to his right, and from there a path led to the central tower. The tall, imposing structure jutted high into the sky, entirely dark save for the light emanating from the third level.

For now, Boblin decided to stay in the shadows of the barracks. Until he better understood what was going on, he preferred to remain unseen. He pressed himself against the outer wall of the building and walked toward the gatehouse until he saw the light of Kaiel's lantern. The guard and the stranger were still on the path, almost near the tower.

When Boblin reached the corner of the barracks, the old man glanced over his shoulder. It was a fleeting look, but enough to freeze Boblin in his tracks, pry open the corners of his mind, and sear his soul. It was a *knowing* glance. This stranger knew many things about days long past, as well as those yet to come.

The moment lasted only a heartbeat before the stranger turned and continued following Kaiel. *That's it. If this fellow is going to continue taking up precious space in my already too-little brain, then he'd better have a karfing good reason.* Boblin stepped behind the building's corner and counted to fifty before sprinting across the lawn toward the tower. *Still no guards on the battlements.*

The doors to the main floor remained permanently open. Since armed soldiers guarded the exterior walls of the Fort night and day, there was no reason for anything on the inside to be locked. Boblin peered through a window, checking to ensure the vast dining hall stood empty before moving inside. The large room was bare except for several rows of tables and benches left behind from the spring feast two weeks ago. Unlit torches filled sconces along the wall, and soft moonlight illuminated the rest of the floor.

Boblin wasted no time. He walked across the hall as quietly as possible, wincing every time his footsteps echoed. When he reached the opposite end, where a flight of steps stretched ahead of him, he waited for another count of fifty.

The stairs led to the Floor of History, which held relics from before Zadinn's reign. The next floor held Council meeting rooms, and above that, Pellen's living quarters. Kaiel and the old man were most likely on the third floor near the meeting rooms, where Boblin had seen the light. Boblin gritted his teeth and climbed the steps.

So what am I going to tell anybody who catches me at this?

Don't worry. I'll just tell them I'm following the voices in my head, and everything will be fine.

As in the dining hall, moonlight bathed the Floor of History. This place held impressive pieces: ornate vases, decorations from the old palace in Galdon, and weapons from the Invasion. Boblin was especially fond of the enormous broadsword on the western wall. Several elaborate tapestries covered the room's sidewalls. Most depicted the North in times before the Invasion, though one portrayed the great battle itself. The Floor of History preserved memories of a long-lost age of peace and contentment.

Boblin approached the next flight of steps and listened. So far it was still silent. He climbed to the third floor and found himself in a long hallway lined with closed doors. A thin sheen of lamplight glowed underneath the crack of a door on the corridor's far right. Boblin tiptoed toward it until he heard voices, and then stopped.

"…will do you no good," a soft-spoken voice, the same one Boblin had heard in his head, said slowly.

"Old man, you underestimate the situation." This was Elson Tulak, Kaiel's uncle. "You came here for a purpose. The Kyrlod do not simply appear on a lark."

Boblin frowned. Elson was a Council member, and the Kyrlod—well, they were supposed to be dead. *What is this about?*

A long pause followed. "Ah," the stranger replied, "well deduced, my friend."

Boblin heard a sneer in Elson's tone. "We are one step ahead of you, due to a certain associate of yours. My master tells me your comrade was quite helpful regarding certain matters."

"Your master?" the stranger said. "Tell me, Elson Tulak, when did the elions of the Fort begin selling their souls to Zadinn Kanas?"

Boblin felt his chest grow tight. The accusation was ludicrous. *Elson Kulak, a traitor?* And yet…he edged closer to the door and placed his eye against the crack. The old man stood in the center of the room, facing Elson with a desk between them and his back to the door. Elson sat with his hands folded on the table. To Elson's right, Kaiel stood in the corner, one hand on the hilt of his sword.

Elson's face ordinarily had a kind, gentle appearance…but not tonight. Furrows of contempt creased his brow, and his black eyes gleamed. In response to the stranger's question, Elson smiled. "When the pay became good enough," he said, affirming the stranger's accusation with a tone of apathy.

Boblin's knees went weak. He stepped back from the door, placing his hand on the wall as his heart pounded against his chest. *No.*

The Fort of Pellen had been betrayed.

"What do you know of Malath, Elson Tulak?" the stranger asked. "There is a place there for elions who betray their comrades."

"Enough," Elson said. "This digression is pointless. My question remains. You came here to speak to Pellen Yuzhar. *Why?*"

Boblin looked back through the doorway to see the old man shrug. "As I said before, the information will do you no good. It is nothing of which Zadinn does not already know. But if you must, my name is Nazgar of the Kyrlod. I've come to speak to Pellen about the Warrior of Light."

So the stranger is *a Kyrlod.* It made no sense—scholars assumed Zadinn had killed off the last of these ancient prophets long ago. But Boblin had also assumed it would snow in Malath before any elion, let alone a member of the Council, betrayed the Fort, so in light of Elson's treachery, the return of the immortal Kyrlod after two centuries was nothing.

"The Warrior of Light?" Elson asked.

There was a smile in Nazgar's words. "How does an elion know his standing with Zadinn? It is in the information his master allows him to know. Let this be a lesson: if you were truly important to the Dark Lord, you would know of the Warrior."

Nazgar's attempt at aggravation proved successful. Elson stood up, placed his fists on the tabletop, and stared into the Kyrlod's eyes. "Be assured the only reason you survive right now is because of the information you bear," he said.

"And because you fear me," Nazgar replied softly, meeting Elson's gaze.

"Fear? No, I think not. I know of the Kyrlod. You will not raise a hand against me without further provocation."

"You just threatened my life," Nazgar said, voice calm and even.

"And for all your fabled powers, you sit and do nothing," Elson shot back.

Boblin again turned from the doorway to lean against the wall. He closed his eyes, trying to still the tremor in his body. His breath came in short, quick gasps. He needed to do something…but what?

"Kaiel!" Elson snapped. "What was that?"

Oh, hisht. They had seen him move.

Boblin had nowhere to run. He had one chance to remain hidden, and a feeble one at that. If Boblin stayed behind the door when Kaiel opened it, he could crouch in the shadows and—he hoped—remain unseen. *Karfing brilliant plan—do I truly expect Kaiel to miss me?* But he had no other option.

Kaiel opened the door and stepped into the hallway. Boblin pulled back and watched through the slits between the hinges. It would be easy for Kaiel to see him. A trickle of sweat dripped between Boblin's shoulder blades.

Kaiel looked up and down the corridor before starting down the stairs at the far end of the passage. After peering at the floor below, he headed back toward the room, every step bringing him closer to Boblin, who steeled himself. He could fight Kaiel, but his chances of winning were slim; Tulak had been in the Frontier Patrol for at least ten years. Boblin clenched sweaty palms, preparing to do his best regardless.

When Kaiel reached the door, he looked straight through the hinges at Boblin. The game was up. But then Boblin noticed the soldier's eyes had a glassy, vacant appearance. Kaiel stared not at Boblin but *through* him. Turning away from the crouching elion, Kaiel reentered the room and closed the door.

"It's clear," he said.

Boblin expelled his pent-up breath, wiping beads of sweat from his brow. After counting to fifty once more, he peered through the door, still numb from the shock of the close encounter. Elson and Nazgar continued to talk, but he could not hear their words. Instead Boblin found the old man again staring straight at him. The noise of the outer world faded to a mere buzz, and a sound like rushing water filled his head.

I cannot intervene for you again, Boblin. You must go. Travel south, find the Warrior, and save us all.

The entire world seemed to solidify around that moment—and then it shattered. Elson turned. He saw Boblin and shouted. Kaiel spun around, unsheathing his sword in a fluid gesture, but Boblin was already running. He heard Nazgar utter an obscure phrase, and the entire floor shook, knocking Boblin to his knees. Behind him, Kaiel and Elson shouted. He heard glass breaking, and the hallway plunged into blackness, accompanied by the noise of splintering wood as a table fell over.

Boblin struggled to his feet and looked over his shoulder. The moonlight silhouetted Kaiel's tall figure as the soldier staggered into the hallway. Kaiel snarled, his sword in the air, and ran toward Boblin. Boblin leaped down the stairs and plummeted to the Floor of History. Nazgar's command rang in his mind. He had to get out of the Fort. The Kyrlod could take care of himself.

Boblin ran across the second floor and vaulted again to the bottom floor. He had a good head start, and the distance between him and his pursuer was steadily increasing. *Kaiel must be wounded.* Boblin paused on the main floor to drag a table across the foot of the stairs. In the dimness, Kaiel would not see the obstacle until he had fallen over it. Boblin raced through the hall and out onto the Fort's lawn, headed straight for the gatehouse. He looked about for other guards and still did not see anybody. *Has Kaiel killed them all? No, Kaiel couldn't kill all his fellow guards without raising an alarm.* The traitors must have created a diversion to distract the other members of the Patrol. Fortunately, their plan worked to Boblin's advantage. Unhindered by questioning sentinels, he burst into the gatehouse, taking a moment to catch his breath.

He risked a glance through the window. Twenty seconds passed before Kaiel appeared, moving with a noticeable limp. The table had done its job well. Boblin dropped out of sight, moving to the opposite side of the gatehouse.

The portcullis stood open. Boblin slipped through the shadows and into the night beyond, setting a quick pace down the narrow path away from the Fort. The darkness felt deadly, the air cold. Sharp rocks rose and fell in front of him, and he watched his footing carefully. An elion could break a leg or a neck in the Kaltu Pass at night. However, strangely enough, these jagged hills now offered him a safe haven the Fort could not provide. The world surely stood on its head tonight.

Boblin selected a nearby outcropping and climbed up a short way to crouch behind a boulder. Moments later, Kaiel appeared from the Fort. He ran down the path and stopped, surveying the area. Boblin waited while Kaiel made a cursory examination of his surroundings. The nighttime air leeched into his bones as Boblin shivered. Soon enough, Kaiel gave up the hunt and turned back toward the Fort. Before he passed through the gates, though, Kaiel turned and shouted into the night.

"The North will kill you far more quickly than I would, Kule!"

This time, the cold Boblin felt had nothing to do with the temperature. Kaiel was right. The land Boblin was now in could be deadly and unpredictable. *And here I am, stranded outside the Fort with only the clothes on my back and weaponless to boot. Well, I always did say I liked challenges.*

Boblin rose from his hiding spot. No, his chances were not good, but they were better out here than back at the Fort. At least this way, he could die respectably at the hands of some monster, rather than have his throat cut while sleeping. After all, when an elion died, all he had left was to do the deed with honor.

South, Nazgar had said. Boblin wasn't sure what he was meant to find there. He would reach the Kavu Hills soon enough, and after that…

The Barricade.

The massive, seamless wall stretched across the entire continent, towering high into the sky. Nobody knew what lay on the southern side. It could be the edge of the world, for all Boblin knew. He certainly hadn't heard of any Warriors in that region. If anyone *did* live over there, he or she was surely lucky. Because chances were, they had never heard of Zadinn Kanas, or of the troubles of the North. Boblin envied them already.

Boblin Kule turned south and began his trek across the hostile wastes, seeking a savior for them all.

Three

Tim Matthias wiped his brow of perspiration. Outside his cottage, the young man balanced on a stump while holding a practice sword made of thin, tightly bound sticks. He wore no shirt, and the overhead sun had turned his skin to a tender shade of pink. Streaks of dirt and sweat ran across his torso.

His father Daniel stood below him, also shirtless and wielding a practice sword of his own. Tim didn't like their respective positions one bit; Daniel had stable footing, while Tim teetered on the narrow redbark stump. Tim was also at a distinct physical disadvantage. Though father and son, the two had very different builds. Daniel was a large, broad-shouldered man with a respectable beard, but Tim was short and lean, more like his mother—and no beard, even at eighteen years old.

Consequently, Daniel's approach favored sheer power while Tim had to rely on nimble footwork. At the present moment, Daniel's position allowed him to make the most of his strength, whereas Tim's compromised his sole advantage.

Daniel nodded, giving Tim the courtesy of a warning before striking with his bundle of sticks, clenching his muscles as he applied force to the blow. Tim did not block in time, and the wood smacked against his rib cage. He grunted in pain, tumbling from his perch and landing on his back.

As Daniel stepped forward to claim a victory, Tim kicked out, catching his father's ankle and knocking the bigger man to the ground. Daniel hit the earth as Tim rose to his feet. His feet firmly on the ground again, Tim moved with lithe grace, a sapling to Daniel's oak. He whirled his practice sword in an arc before closing in on the fallen man.

But when Tim came forward to disarm his father, Daniel moved with a speed that belied his bulky frame. He brushed Tim's stick aside, grabbed his son's sword-wrist, and yanked him onto the ground. Daniel rolled, using his superior size to force Tim underneath him, and pressed the edge of his blade against his son's throat. The two stared into each other's eyes—Daniel's brown, Tim's blue. After a moment of silence, Daniel spoke one word: "Good." He relaxed his grip and helped Tim to his feet.

They stood side-by-side, chests heaving as they regained their breath. There was no better time to practice sword work than during an early spring morning. The sun cast a blanket of light on the small clearing behind their cottage, and around them leaves on the trees of the Odow Forest budded into existence as they emerged from winter hibernation. A wisp of smoke rose from the chimney of their log-and-thatch cottage, the sole homestead in this stretch of the Odow.

Daniel leaned against the brown fence that stretched across the yard toward the stable, crossing his thick arms over his chest. "What was your mistake?" he asked.

Tim sat in the bed of an empty wagon, brushing a few strands of black hair away from his eyes. "The stump," he conceded. "I shouldn't have jumped onto it. I thought the higher ground would give me an advantage, but instead I sacrificed my footing."

"Exactly," Daniel replied. "You had to fight from an unfamiliar level. At your standing height, you know where to strike. When you are two feet higher, you lose your sense of direction and balance." He took the bundle of sticks from Tim, and the two walked toward the cattle stable at the edge of the clearing.

"And yet," Daniel continued, "you gained an advantage from the ground, which is not easily done. You're more than ready to go to Vonku next year."

The two men entered the stable, where Daniel hung the sticks on the wall. Tim picked up a pair of brown jerkins, tossing one to his father and keeping the second. He pulled the shirt over his head, carefully avoiding the sore spot on his ribs. However, even the simple motion of raising his arms made him wince in pain. Daniel said it was a disservice if learning swords didn't hurt as much as a real fight. Tim shrugged the shirt into place, tying its leather laces and fastening the buttons. "What was it like when you were there?" he asked his father.

"Vonku? Desperate. There was a rebellion on the Icor Peninsula, and King Aras needed soldiers. The Alcatune Army didn't ask many questions; all a man had to do was walk up to the city gates, find an officer, and swear to serve. A fortnight later, they had you on the Peninsula. You just kept your sword close and prayed you'd find yourself marching back in another fortnight."

"The Rebellion lasted much longer than expected, though. Isn't that right?"

"Aye, it lasted nigh on two years. Some say we're better for it today. We've had peace in the South ever since, and no man would call that a bad thing." Daniel grabbed a ladder and dragged it over to the hayloft. "Up you go."

Tim climbed up the ladder, keeping his head low once he entered the loft. A shaft of sunlight filtered through a window to his left, lending the room a dusky yellow glow. Dust motes danced in the air, swirling in tiny spirals as Tim moved toward the bags of feed at the far end of the loft. On the stable floor below, the cattle made soft, complacent noises.

This was Tim's last harvest before departing to join the Alcatune Army, to train in the city of Vonku just as his father had done twenty years ago. But peacetime or not, Tim wasn't sure he was ready.

He picked up the first bag of feed and carried it over to the ladder. After passing the bag off to Daniel, Tim took a breath. "Why did you do it?"

Daniel cut the sack open with his knife. "Do what?"

"The Icor Peninsula is a long way from here. When all is said and done, the war had nothing to do with Alcatune. King Aras only sent soldiers because of his alliance with Icor."

Daniel did not reply immediately, but instead turned to pour grain into the nearest trough. He handed the empty bag back up the ladder to Tim. "I could ask you the same. You become a soldier this fall. Why are *you* doing it?"

Tim picked up another sack. "That's part of the reason I'm asking you. I'm not sure I know."

"A man doesn't choose lightly to become a soldier, Tim." Daniel paused. "What's more, he doesn't do it for another man's reasons. He does it for his own reasons."

As Tim handed him the next bag of feed, their eyes locked. "In a man's life, two decisions are his and his alone," Daniel said. "We can't justify them using another's reasons. *You* have to know why you are joining the King's army. I can't tell you that." He paused again. "When you are ready to tell me why you are becoming a soldier, I will tell you why I became one."

Tim climbed down the ladder. "What's the *other* decision?"

Daniel frowned. "You act as if I already told you the first."

"Well, you did. Being a soldier, right?"

"You're not really asking about being a soldier."

"No," Tim said. Without meaning to, he glanced at the practice swords hanging from the wall. Boys at play were no strangers to "killing," so long as it involved imaginary enemies. But a time always came when the imagination faded, the luster died, and reality was all that remained. Lately when Tim practiced sword work, he wondered how he would cope when the swords weren't wooden but steel, not flat but sharp.

"The battlefield is a hard place," Daniel said, "and when you come to that moment, when another man's life is in your hands, you have the ability to choose what to do with it. Know this, Timothy Matthias: if you choose to kill that man, you must live with your actions. Do not let someone else make the choice for you."

As Tim filled the remainder of the feeding troughs, Daniel walked over to the watering well and wound the crank to lower its bucket into the hole.

"So?" Tim said.

His father looked back at him. "So?" he replied.

Tim sighed. Daniel was playing games with him. "So what's the other decision?" he asked. Daniel chuckled at his son's aggravation.

"Someday you might find a woman worth spending the rest of your life with." Daniel nodded toward the cottage. "Choose her well, and treat her well."

Tim looked toward the cottage as well. "And if you hadn't joined the King's army," he said, "you'd never have met her."

"No, I wouldn't have," Daniel said, "and my life would have been far emptier." His lips curled in a mischievous smile. "You know, I've always had a theory. Your mother and I met while we were both fighting against the rebels. I think that's why she likes her rules so much—because the rebels stood against the rules, and she stood for them."

Tim smiled. Rosalie Matthias had precious few rules, in fact. But that didn't stop Daniel from making jokes every chance he got.

"My rules aren't that difficult," his mother's voice said. Rosalie stood in the doorframe of the stable with a bemused grin. Daniel turned to face his wife with a smile of his own. Locks of cherry-red hair framed her face and landed on her shoulders in gentle waves, contrasting the beautiful blue in her eyes. She arched an eyebrow, feigning irritation. "Besides, they're good for you."

"That's what you keep telling me," Daniel said.

"It's worth it though, isn't it?" she asked.

"Always," Daniel replied.

Rosalie looked at Tim, and then at the practice swords on the wall. "Did you teach your father anything this morning?" she asked.

"Always," Tim said, imitating Daniel's inflection.

"I didn't say it like that," Daniel objected. He turned to Rosalie. "Do I talk like that?"

Rosalie leaned against the side of the door and crossed her arms. "Always," she said, lowering her voice an octave.

Daniel raised his hands in mock surrender. "Very well then." He raised a bucket of water and handed it to his son. Tim poured it into the drinking trough, careful not to splash any of it.

"If I may ask," Rosalie said, "what have you planned for this fine spring day?"

"A question that could have many answers," Daniel replied.

"Oh?" she said.

"One might ask what we would *like* to do, or one might ask what we *should* do." Daniel paused, a twinkle in his eye. "Suppose I said we were planning to spend the afternoon at the tavern in Raldoon?"

Rosalie raised a finger. "I would say that's one reason I make rules for you."

Pouring another bucket of water into the trough, Tim grinned. This was typical of Daniel and Rosalie's banter. They did it often, though such feigned "arguments" never carried a hint of actual anger.

"Well put," Daniel acknowledged. "Timothy, your mother insists we be productive. What do you say?"

Tim shrugged. "I was thinking of checking the traplines in the Odow. If nothing else, I'd like to see if we should move them into new territory."

"Not a bad idea," Daniel agreed. "Some spots near the ravine aren't producing as much as before."

Tim handed his father the empty water pail. "Would you like to come?"

"I'll stay here. It's a good day for cutting firewood."

"Your favorite thing," Tim said with a wry smile. "Not mine." He went to a shelf and picked up a redbark bow and quiver of arrows.

"One day you'll learn to appreciate firewood," Daniel replied.

"You keep telling me that," Tim said.

"I promise you," his father said. "You'll wake up one morning and realize you miss the feel of the ax between your hands, the rise and fall of the chop, the satisfaction of a clean split. It's a job to be proud of."

Tim chuckled as he left the stable. "I don't want to rob you of the satisfaction."

"Be careful," Rosalie said.

Tim winked. "Always," he said.

"You two aren't going to let that alone, are you?" Daniel asked.

"No," Tim and Rosalie said in unison.

* * *

The Matthias family hadn't always lived in the Odow Forest. Until recently, they'd lived in Vonku, the very city Tim would return to this fall.

At the close of the Icor Rebellion, Daniel Matthias took a position in the Royal Legion of Vonku, King Aras's most elite group of soldiers. The family had lived in the city for the better part of Tim's life. Then at the close of the previous winter, Daniel retired from the Legion and moved with his wife and son to the countryside.

Raldoon, a dwerion village, was located a half-day's walk from their cottage. In the Alcatune Army, Daniel had served alongside a dwerion named Quentiin Harggra. While dwerions were a short, quiet folk who preferred the peace of the forest, Daniel once told Tim that Quentiin was worth three other soldiers when a battle-ax was in his hands—despite the fact he stood no taller than four feet. Besides, Quentiin made up for his height with a broad-shouldered, massive frame. Daniel owed his life to the dwerion more than once.

When Daniel sent word to his old friend that he was leaving the service, Quentiin told him the land in the Odow was ripe for tilling. Good farmland could be hard to come by in the South, so Daniel and Rosalie built their home near the outskirts of the village.

Aside from the Matthias homestead and dwerion village, the Odow Forest remained largely unpopulated. Few wanted to dwell this close to the Northern Rampart, the vast wall stretching across the land's northern border. The Rampart wasn't dangerous. In fact, living near it was a good deal safer than living in a city, where one could fall victim to thieves and footpads. But it was a forbidding landmark to have on one's doorstep. No one knew what was on the other side of the enormous wall. At over two hundred feet high, it proved impossible to scale, and in spite of numerous attempts, nobody had ever discovered a way through it.

Tim had never seen the Rampart, but one night at the tavern in Raldoon, Quentiin described it to him. "The Odow is a good place, laddie," the dwerion said. "An' when it comes down to it, that wall ain't bad at all. But we can't see it from the village, an' that makes all the difference. There's just somethin' about the Rampart. Ye can't put words to it, but when ye walk up to it ye'll understand. It was meant to be left alone."

Here, nearly two days south of the Rampart, the Odow was far from menacing. Tim walked into the forest, the trees forming a gentle canopy over his head, their green foliage glowing in the morning light. A mixture of redbarks and blueleafs marked the territory directly to the north, and a thicket of steely gray aspwards stood near a shallow bog to the west. Tim left the clearing behind and pushed ahead, staying on the meandering path. Not all the trees had leaves yet, since spring was still in its early stages. Shafts of sunlight landed in small pools, and motes of pollen floated along the beams of light. Tendrils of moss crept up tree trunks, vying for a position in the world. Tim and Daniel had made this trail when they first arrived in Odow. No bigger than a wildlife trail, the path traveled in tandem with a winding stream.

The snares along the stream yielded plenty of results early on, as every animal needed water at some point, but of late they had turned up empty. It was time to move them somewhere else—no sense in depleting the wildlife from one area. They could pull the snares out, let the area rest a bit, and perhaps return next season.

Tim searched the banks of the ravine, looking for animal signs to track. It didn't take long before he came across a deer trail that ran east to west across the water. He crouched near the ground, noting several hoofprints. He picked up a few crumbs of soil and rubbed them between his fingers. They fell apart easily, meaning the tracks were fresh.

Tim followed the path deeper into the woods, eventually leading him into the aspward swale. Such swales were generally thick stuff, but deer liked them because it covered them from prying eyes. Tim stayed with the path, squeezing through the tight spaces between the thin, brittle trunks. His course took him around the bog to the other side of the swale, from which he traveled up toward a nearby ridge.

Absorbed in the passage of the trail, Tim did not notice the thick clouds accumulating on the horizon. There had been no trace of clouds when he first entered the Odow, and the speed with which they gathered would have confounded even the most experienced woodsman. He continued on the path, across the ridge and around another bog, deeper and further into the woods, every so often stopping to kneel and check the tracks in the dirt. By the time Tim noticed the chill in the air and looked up, a blanket of gray and black clouds already hung over his head, shifting and growing more massive with every passing minute. All too soon, a jagged streak of lightning flashed in front of him, followed by a peal of thunder.

How in Malath did things turn so bad so fast?

He was at least an hour, if not more, from the spot where he had veered from the stream. A gust of wind rattled the treetops, and Tim shivered. This would be a cold springtime storm, one in which the water wanted to turn to snow but temperatures wouldn't allow it. *Wonderful. This is just what I need.*

Tim looked around but didn't recognize any landmarks. Having lived in the Odow for only a short while, he wasn't yet familiar with the entire forest. Though a capable woodsman, Tim could still make mistakes, and he had made one today. He could follow the deer trail back toward the stream, but he needed to move quickly. If the rain came down hard enough, it would wash away the path's tracks. Tim set a brisk pace, walking back toward more familiar territory.

Thunder and lightning struck again, and then the dark clouds unleashed the rain. Tim grimaced as freezing droplets of water spattered his skin and soaked his clothes. The winds grew stronger, and stinging shards of hail descended among tree trunks that swayed in violent, jerking motions.

As he'd feared, Tim soon had trouble distinguishing the deer trail from surrounding vegetation. He saw several potential routes, but was unsure which path to take since the cloud cover prevented him from obtaining any sort of direction. The noise of the rain drowned out all other sounds, and his soaked clothes began weighing down on him. Rivulets of water ran over the earthen floor, pooling together wherever pockets of empty space existed.

As little as he liked it, Tim's best choice was to find cover nearby and stay put until the skies cleared up. Then he could move in the general direction of the cottage until he found more familiar territory.

He came to an area where a large, uprooted redbark tree stretched across the ground, a yawning cavern in the space where its roots had once been. Tim moved toward the tree, boots slipping across the slick ground. He flexed his fingers, which were growing numb in the cold weather. Pray to the Maker, he hated being wet and freezing. Tim clambered underneath the redbark's roots. Once out of the wind and rain, he found the temperatures more tolerable. He wasn't exactly comfortable, but he would be fine waiting out the deluge.

After huddling in the small cave for about ten minutes, he noticed something strange. A hundred yards in the distance, a light bobbed through the trees, slipping in and out of sight between the trunks. A few feet behind the first light, a second light appeared, following the same meandering path. It had to be a pair of torches. But it made no sense. *Who would be out here in the woods in the middle of such a storm?* Then again, *he* was out here in the storm. Not that this served as a resounding endorsement of his most recent decision-making skills, but facts were facts.

Tim knew a dirt road leading to Raldoon ran from south to north through the Odow—it was made for travelers to the dwerion village. He had thought he was far from the trail, but in his confusion he could have easily blundered closer to the path than he realized. Though *that* would be quite embarrassing, if he were to learn he'd huddled underneath a fallen redbark with the road to the village only a few strides away.

Tim climbed from his shelter and made his way toward the source of the lights. Soon enough, he figured, he'd come to a break in the trees and find the path, on his way to being warm and dry. However, the break in the trees never came. As he neared the lights, the skin between his shoulder blades prickled. These travelers were not on any path at all. Instead, the two hooded figures, each with a torch in hand, walked through the middle of the Odow, far from any village or house. Each had a sword buckled around its waist. A mule pulled a wagon behind them, struggling as it made its way across the slippery ground.

Tim halted behind a blueleaf tree, slowing his approach. Something about this just felt…wrong. In front of him, the wagon became stuck between several roots on the forest floor, and one of the strangers tried to wrestle it free. As the figure did so, Tim caught a glimpse of its face.

And it wasn't human.

Tim drew in a sharp breath. The creature had gray skin, angular cheekbones, and a bald head. Perhaps most disconcerting of all were its eyes. They smoldered with a dull, red light as the creature went about its task.

Tim crouched down, trying to reduce his visible profile. The second creature turned to aid the first. He heard them curse a few times as they heaved and pulled to free the cumbersome wagon. Their voices had a steely, raspy quality. The wagon at last pulled forward again, and the travelers continued on their original course. Tim slowly and steadily drew back from his hiding place, keeping low and out of sight.

However, the creatures must have sensed something, because as soon as he moved, they turned in unison toward him. The one on the right hissed and stepped forward, drawing its sword from its sheath.

Tim turned to run and collided with a third creature, which had crept up behind him. The thing moved like a snake, seizing Tim by his tunic and lifting him from the ground before hurling him through the air. Tim landed and rolled across the muddy earth. Droplets of falling rain struck his eyes, and he blinked to clear his vision. As he did so, he felt a sharp prick against his neck and looked up to see the creature standing above him with its sword at his throat. The blade was forged of pure, black steel.

The creature smiled, baring a pair of triangular, pointed teeth.

"You're coming with us," it said.

Four

Rosalie Matthias fought against the wind, pulling wooden covers over the outsides of the stable windows to protect the glass from incoming hail. The ground beneath her feet had turned to mud, running up against the sides of her boots and causing her to slide as she moved from window to window. Daniel struggled to latch the twin stable doors as the rain pounded down around them. Inside the stable, the cattle made noises of discomfort—they didn't like this weather any more than Rosalie and Daniel did.

Rosalie covered the last window and moved toward the cottage, her husband following close behind. Even though their home was only thirty paces from the stable, every step was a battle. Jagged streaks of lightning shot across the yard, and the full brunt of the wind made it hard to breathe.

Rosalie pulled her cloak around her shoulders, trying to protect her skin from the bite of the cold air. She climbed the doorstep, shouldering the front door open, and entered the warm, dry interior of the cottage. She pulled her cloak off and hung it on a peg as Daniel staggered in behind her and slammed the door. The noise of the storm instantly cut back, changing from a roar to a steady drumbeat on the roof.

Against the cottage's far wall, a fire snapped and burned underneath the stove, lighting up the log walls with its dancing flames. A wooden table, which Tim and Daniel had made last winter from the smooth wood of a blueleaf trunk, served as the room's centerpiece. Daniel walked over to the fireplace and placed his chapped hands over the flames, rubbing his fingers. Rosalie stepped up to a window and peered out, trying to see through sheets of falling water.

"Tim will be fine," Daniel said, addressing her unspoken concern. "He's been in the woods before."

Rosalie looked at her husband. "I know," she said, voice soft. "But a mother's instinct never changes."

"No," Daniel replied, "I suppose it doesn't."

"I think about the Peninsula a lot more now," Rosalie said.

Daniel held his hand out to her. She took it, and he pulled her in to place a kiss upon her lips. "It wasn't all bad."

Daniel had fought one kind of battle during the Icor Rebellion, but Rosalie, serving as a Healer, had fought another. The two met on the Peninsula, after Daniel's battalion suffered heavy casualties and Daniel nearly lost his leg from an infected wound. Thanks to Rosalie, all he had to show for the wound was a faded scar on his thigh.

"Tim asked me today why I'd joined the Army," Daniel said.

Rosalie looked up at him. "Did you tell him?"

"Not yet. I want him to understand first."

Rosalie closed her eyes and leaned against her husband. Being a Healer had not been easy. In the middle of battle, a soldier's blood ran hot as time ran slow, creating an unprecedented wave of vitality that propelled him forward from one moment to the next. A Healer, on the other hand, dealt with the aftermath of the battle, after the bloodlust had worn off and left the men shaking, injured, and often near death. A soldier surrounded by enemies on all sides could hack and slice his way to freedom, but a Healer surrounded by the cries of the wounded had no such opportunity. She had to ignore all but the wounded man in front of her, do her best to save him, and then move on to the next. When not all could be saved—and they never could—she had to do what all Healers must do: make the terrible choice of who lived and who died.

"I think Tim already does understand," she said. "He just doesn't realize it."

"I think so, too," Daniel replied.

Rosalie left his embrace and turned back to the window. Rain hammered against the glass, creating tiny rivulets of water that ran from the top of the sill all the way down to the ground below. "He'll come home safe today," she said.

"But next spring, he may not," Daniel said, finishing her thought for her.

Rosalie looked into the yard and saw a shape emerge from the woods to the west and walk toward the cottage. *Tim.* "I can't protect him forever. Much as I might like to."

"You taught him well," Daniel said. "That's as much as anyone can ask for."

"*You* taught him well," Rosalie replied. "As much as I can ask for."

Daniel smiled. "*We* taught him well. I suppose that's all there is to it."

Rosalie supposed that was true. But as she'd said, a mother's instinct never changed.

In the yard, a second shape emerged from the woods, followed by a third. Rosalie frowned. *Who has Tim brought back with him?*

"What is it?" Daniel asked, still standing by the fireplace.

Rosalie stepped closer to the glass, straining to get a better look at the newcomers. As they approached the cottage, her stomach twisted. *What in Malath are those things?*

None of the arrivals was Tim at all, in fact. They weren't even human, as far as she could tell, and they weren't dwerions either. Rosalie had seen many parts of the South in her lifetime, but had never seen anything like these strange beings. They had bony, ridged faces, muscular bodies, gray skin, and smoldering red eyes. All three carried torches, and as Rosalie watched, they threw them toward the cottage. Two torches landed on the roof, and the third flew straight at the window.

"Down," she said.

"What?"

She didn't have time to explain. She immediately dived to the side, pushing Daniel onto the ground with her. Her husband uttered an oath of surprise as they hit the wooden floor together.

The window above them shattered as a flaming torch crashed through it.

* * *

Tim's captor leaned forward, pulling Tim onto his feet and slamming him against the side of the wagon. "What is your name?" the creature asked, raising his voice over the noise of the pounding rain.

"Benjamin," Tim replied with a straight face. "Who are you?"

The creature responded by punching Tim in the stomach, and it didn't stop there. It lifted its sword and smashed the hilt against Tim's face. As pain blossomed in Tim's nose, a trickle of blood ran down his chin. "I will ask the questions," his captor said. "Understand?"

Tim realized defiance would not get him very far. "Yes," he replied.

"Is Benjamin your father's name?"

"Yes." Tim didn't see what was so important about names, but he had no choice except to go along with it.

"Where is your home?"

Here, the truth worked to his advantage. "I'm lost."

The creature grasped him by the throat and squeezed tight. Tim struggled against the chokehold, feet slipping over the muddy ground. "It's true!" Tim said, fighting to speak coherently.

"Krinzen!" one of the others interrupted. "Remember our orders!"

"The Overlord won't mind if we kill one here or there," Krinzen replied. "What is one human less?" In spite of his words, though, he loosened his grip. "Do you live in the village of Raldoon?"

"Close enough to it," Tim answered.

Krinzen nodded and lifted Tim into the wagon, where he shoved the young man facedown into the empty bed. Above them, thunder boomed and lightning flashed as Krinzen tied Tim's hands behind his back. Tim wriggled back up into a sitting position. Try as he might, Tim could not stop shivering. His clothes were completely soaked from the deluge, and the wooden wagon bed was hard and cold.

"In that case," Krinzen said, "do not worry. We will visit your friends and family very soon." He slapped the mule's rump, and the cart jerked into motion. The other two creatures smiled at Tim before they all continued into the woods, one placing his torch into a sconce on the cart's side.

Tim's earlier bravado faded. Whoever these creatures were, they moved purposefully and confidently. They had a plan, and they were executing it perfectly. These were not everyday road robbers or bandits, who would have either stripped him of his belongings or killed him outright. Instead they had taken him alive, presumably to bring him to Raldoon. Why they were doing this, he did not know. What would happen when they arrived, he did not know. But he *did* know he had to get away.

Tim always kept a spare blade inside his boot. As long as he was careful, he could probably reach it. He surveyed his captors to make sure they weren't watching. Krinzen walked ahead of the group, paying no attention to any of them, while the other two walked in front of the cart, entirely focused on the forest ahead.

Tim twisted until his fingertips brushed the lip of his boot. The storm drowned out the noise of his movements. He clenched his teeth in concentration, straining until he felt the smooth hilt of his knife by his ankle. He managed to just barely grasp the handle between thumb and forefinger, grimacing from the effort.

The cart bounced across the forest floor, jarring his movements with every step. He lost hold of the handle and regained it two more times before getting his palm fully curled around it. Slowly and carefully, Tim drew the blade from its sheath. He lay down on his side, hoping to keep his profile low should one of his captors happen to glance back. Tim ran the blade over his rope bonds. The knife probably wasn't as sharp as he should have kept it, and the twine was wet and stringy, but it would have to do.

The three creatures kept moving into the woods, only giving an occasional glance toward the cart. Tim kept his back against the side of the wagon, concealing the blade and his escape efforts, uttering a silent cry of success each time a strand snapped free. As Tim worked, he scanned the forest for familiar landmarks. Escape would only get him so far if he didn't know his whereabouts. Though, he decided quickly, he would gladly take being lost and free over being lost and captive.

The twine loosened around his wrists as he made progress with the knife. Every rut and rock they bounced over made the task more difficult, but he had to bide his time. The cold and rain moved to a distant part of his mind as he focused all his effort on cutting just one more strand, and one more after that…

Climbing a mountain may seem an impossible task, Rosalie Matthias was fond of saying, *but all it has ever taken is one step at a time.*

When the rope finally snapped free, Tim took a long, deep breath. He turned just slightly, looking first at Krinzen and then the other two creatures. All three remained focused on the task of navigating the forest's wet and muddy terrain as best they could. Tim tensed his muscles and lowered his body as close to the floor of the cart as possible. The walls on the side were not that low, but they kept him just out of sight. When the wheels hopped across a series of roots, he used the momentum to his advantage, rolling toward the back of the cart a few inches at a time.

Patience, he cautioned himself. *Patience.*

As the cart continued over the uneven terrain, Tim moved himself even closer to the back. Soon enough, he'd be able to roll off and tumble to the forest floor.

However, one of his captors spoiled his plans. The creature, pausing to catch his breath, looked back toward Tim, who tried to hide his freed hands but not quickly enough.

The kidnapper shouted a warning and Tim leaped into motion. He rose, grabbed the torch from its sconce, and tossed it into the hay-covered wagon bed. Flames shot to life around his feet, causing the mule dragging the cart to rear with a terrified squeal. As the frightened animal bolted forward, trying to outrun the flaming contraption strapped to its back, it knocked Krinzen's companions into the mud. Tim did not wait to see how they fared, but instead jumped to the forest floor and took off in a sprint.

Puddles of muddy water splashed under his feet, and branches slapped his face and sides. Several times he slipped on wet roots and almost fell. His breath came in gasps as he glanced over his shoulder. He had only gained a few precious yards. Though two of the creatures were preoccupied with the flaming wagon, Krinzen had sidestepped the catastrophe and begun pursuit in earnest, snarling as he slashed his way through the underbrush.

Tim pushed himself into an aspward swale, using his smaller size to his advantage. The thick foliage would further delay and frustrate Krinzen. Tim made his way through the gray, whip-thin trunks, every so often reaching behind to push a branch or sapling into his pursuer's path. Wind howled through the trees, and sporadic bolts of lightning lit up everything in flashes of white. Tim's lungs burned as he gulped for air, and he repeatedly wiped a hand across his face to clear his vision. His palms became streaked with dirt and bark as he pushed through the forest, brambles cutting into his arms and leaving angry red welts on his skin.

Before he knew it, he stumbled upon the original ravine, bursting from the aspward swale and skidding to a halt on the banks. Water rushed and gurgled below him, flowing over the shallow streambed as raindrops pattered down. Tim slipped on the muddy embankment before righting himself in the direction of his cottage. Without missing another beat, he took off running again. Behind him, Krinzen slashed his way out of the trees and resumed the chase.

As Tim raced through the trees, his stomach lurched when he saw a cloud of smoke rising into the sky from the direction of the cottage. It was not the smoke of a cooking fire. It was much too thick.

Daniel and Rosalie were in danger as well.

He did not have time to think or change his options. Krinzen was close behind, and Tim would rather reach familiar ground before making his stand. He put on an extra burst of speed, racing down the banks of the ravine toward a clearing at the edge of the woods. He dodged several traplines, hoping they would ensnare Krinzen, but no such luck.

Ahead and to the left, he saw a familiar tree that marked the clearing. For better or worse, he was almost home—to meet whatever fate was there. He balled his hands into fists and pumped his arms, lengthening his stride as much as possible. He tried to regulate his breath—in and out, in and out—steeling himself for the impending conflict.

He emerged from the trees and into his yard. The entire cottage was in flames, giant orange tongues of fire licking at its sides and reaching for the sky. A column of smoke spiraled toward the clouds as rain pounded down. Rosalie and Daniel Matthias stood near the barn, back to back, each with a sword in hand. Two more red-eyed creatures, doubtless more of Krinzen's companions, surrounded his parents, circling as they made a joint attack.

Tim had no time to enter the fray. Instead, he stumbled over the body of a third assailant, who lay in the mud with one of Daniel's arrows protruding from its throat. Tim rolled across the ground and pulled the sword from the dead creature's hand. Using his leverage, as Daniel had taught him so many times, Tim came back to his feet, spinning as Krinzen attacked him from behind. Their blades clanged together as a peal of thunder rolled across the clearing.

"You are a young and healthy boy," Krinzen said, his voice a hiss, "fit for many years of service to my kind. It would be a shame to slay you."

"Who are you?" Tim asked.

Krinzen smiled, displaying his pointy teeth. "You and your brethren shall know soon enough." The creature struck, moving his sword with a swift, fluid movement. Tim parried, the hilt of his sword wet in his hands. His pulse pounded, and his vision narrowed. This was not practice with Daniel.

He stayed light on his feet. Krinzen tried to trap him inside a flurry of attacks, but Tim had none of it. He sidestepped the creature's circling movements, fighting defensively but not desperately.

In the thick of battle, you will find your mind flows differently, Daniel had taught him. *It will want to survive. It will make you quick and frantic. It will feed you a thousand details in the space of a second, hoping to give you a chance to survive. Your duty is to stay ahead of the raw, animal instinct of survival. Use what it gives you, but regulate yourself. Keep your breath even, your eyes open, your hands still. Bide your time, but strike when ready.*

After a minute of parries and thrusts, Tim had his chance. Krinzen stepped in front of the other creature's body, and Tim shifted from cautious defense to all-out attack, forcing his opponent backward. Krinzen, focused on the fight, did not see the body behind him. He tripped over it, landing in mud.

Tim closed in, dropping to his knees and slamming the hilt of his sword against the creature's skull. Krinzen's eyes rolled back, and he sank into unconsciousness. Tim rocked back onto his feet, breath coming in gasps, and looked for his parents.

A single opponent remained between them, Rosalie on one side and Daniel on the other. As Tim ran toward them, Rosalie drove a sword into the creature's chest. It fell backward, and Rosalie pulled her sword free from the body as she and Daniel turned to Tim.

There was no opportunity to speak. The roof of the cottage caved in with a large crash, and a cloud of embers rose to the sky before falling back in a hailstorm of blazing pellets.

"Get water from the stable," Rosalie said. She knelt and dug up handfuls of wet mud. "Quickly!"

Tim nodded and ran to the stable, shoving the door open and grabbing two empty water pails. Breathing heavily, he raced to the well and lowered a pail into the water. In spite of his efforts, he knew the cottage was lost. The only purpose now was to ensure the flames did not spread. After filling both buckets, Tim ran back outside. Daniel and Rosalie were frantically digging a trench in the mud, trying to build a break around the flames. Tim emptied both buckets onto the fire and immediately returned to the stable, filling the pails and repeating the process.

The rain aided their efforts, soaking the surrounding ground so the fire had nowhere to go. As the three poured mud and water onto the conflagration, the fire faded from an all-out blaze to a low sputter, while the storm subsided to a slow, steady drizzle.

Tim and his parents stepped back from the cottage in silence. After a few minutes, Tim turned to his father. "How many attacked you?" he asked.

"Three," Daniel replied. "What happened to you?"

Tim pointed toward Krinzen's unconscious body. "They took me while I was in the woods," he said. "I got away, but that one followed me. Two others were with him, and they're still out there."

"What do they want?" Rosalie said.

"Prisoners," Tim answered. "They didn't steal anything, and they didn't mention money. One told me I look 'fit for many years of service.' I think they are slave drivers, and they're headed to Raldoon."

Daniel knelt next to one of the bodies, turning it over to look at it closely. "They may be slave drivers, but they are also soldiers. If they've targeted Raldoon, the attempt will not be sloppy."

"We need to go," Rosalie said. "We have to warn the dwerions."

"Aye," Daniel agreed. "We don't have time to lose." He turned out the pockets of the creature's trousers, searching for anything to identify it, but turned up nothing.

"We have dry clothes in the stable," Rosalie said. "If we leave now, we can make the village by nightfall."

"Aye," Daniel said. Raindrops hissed and sizzled as they landed on the smoldering ruins of the family's home. Later, Tim supposed, the reality of the situation would settle in. But for now, events were moving too fast. The dwerion village was likely in terrible danger, and they had to do something about it.

Daniel led the way to the stable, holding the door open for Tim and Rosalie. Inside, the cattle shuffled, disturbed by all the commotion. As Daniel opened chests that held dry clothing, Rosalie and Tim moved among the cattle, hushing them with gentle words and pats.

"Keep your swords close," Daniel said.

Tim nodded in agreement. They moved quickly and quietly, exchanging soaked clothes for dry attire and donning traveling cloaks. Tim buckled his sword around his waist. A cold wind gusted through the open doorway, causing him to shiver.

"Time to go," Rosalie said. They made their way across the clearing, then into the woods for a short way toward the main path to Raldoon. Upon reaching the path, they turned north, keeping close watch on the surrounding forest.

After the first hour on the path, the misting rain ceased as the sun returned. Drenched trees—tall sentinels against the backdrop of the Odow—reared high on either side of the path, wet leaves glistening in afternoon light, while dripping water pattered throughout the forest. Few animals moved, and all remained still.

After a long while, Daniel spoke. "You were faced with a choice today," he said to Tim.

"Yes," Tim replied. There was another silence. Rosalie glanced at the two of them, her face impassive.

"Which did you choose?" Daniel asked.

"He's still alive," Tim said.

Daniel did not ask why. He was true to his word—the choice, and reasons behind it, remained Tim's alone. He simply nodded and looked into his son's eyes, a weary, distant look in his own. "Then you still have something I lost long ago."

Five

Quentiin Harggra was walking to the inn when the first raindrops came. Though he stood four feet in height, the dwerion was half again as wide as a full-grown man—a stature not unusual for his kind. Quentiin wore a long, red coat that fell past his knees to meet the tops of his leather boots. As he pulled up his hood, he tugged on his beard—a thick, white mass encompassing the lower half of his face—and grumbled.

Early spring storms were the worst. He'd learned this campaigning beside Daniel Matthias back in 662, the year of the Icor Rebellion. Nothing made a platoon more edgy than being slowly soaked overnight and waking up to a breezy, gray dawn by morning. Quentiin was glad when Daniel moved near Raldoon. The former Legion man clearly saw the sense in moving toward fertile farmland.

After all, the Odow was a nice place during spring—the game was ripe, the plants were healthy, and it was the gentlest forest a dwerion could ask for. *Except when a bloody storm comes pourin' down on yer head. Then it's time to tuck tail an' head fer the nearest rooftop, preferably one with a spot o' ale underneath it.* The raindrops grew heavier, signifying the arrival of hail. Quentiin sighed. Raldoon had precious few cobblestone roads, and this would certainly turn the village's pathways into a muddy mess. He pulled his cloak a bit tighter and quickened his pace—not that his short strides put on much speed.

The Hungry Wanderer marked the center of the village. The inn, a full three stories in height, contained enough food and ale to satisfy even the most famished dwerion. Lights glowed from at least half the windows, and a pleasant buzz emanated from the common room. Quentiin entered to join his fellow villagers, who sat on benches and toasted one another with mugs of dark ale.

Quentiin had visited several taverns in the city of Vonku. Most were bigger, many had more people, and some even served better beer, but none was half as *good* as this place. The *Wanderer* was not a drunkard's tavern with straw-covered floors, bawdy songs, and bile on the tables. Yagglem, the innkeeper, wouldn't stand for such nonsense. The *Wanderer* was a place for friends to come together, be social, and enjoy the taste of finely brewed beer.

Quentiin looked over the heads of the patrons until he saw Jolldo Graff at a corner table. Jolldo was delving into a well-seasoned roast, an empty mug waiting to be refilled in front of him.

"Jolldo Graff!" Quentiin said, voice booming across the room. Jolldo looked up and grinned, gesturing to an empty seat. Quentiin stepped up to the wooden bar where Yagglem stood and slammed down a fistful of coppers. "Two pints an' a chessboard," he said.

"Aye, laddie," the innkeeper acknowledged, turning to draw ale from a barrel.

Quentiin walked to Jolldo's table and sat on the bench opposite his friend. "It's goin' to be a good long drizzle outside, mate," he said. "We ain't foolin' around this time, d'ye ken?"

Jolldo stabbed his knife into the roast. "Bring on all ye got," he replied. Yagglem approached from the side, carrying the ale and chessboard. Quentiin took the proffered mug and drained one-third in a single swallow.

"Don't drink too fast," Jolldo warned. "Ye'll need yer wits about ye this afternoon."

"This beauty here enhances my wit." Quentiin gestured toward the mug

Yagglem placed the chessboard on the table and chuckled before turning away. Jolldo swiped a pair of pawns and put his hands behind his back. "Choose," he said. Quentiin pointed to Jolldo's right hand. Jolldo opened his fist to reveal a white pawn. "Yer move, brother."

Quentiin arranged his pieces carefully in front of him. *How to start? The Korrlian Gambit, perhaps?* It was a bold strategy, as it involved sacrificing two pieces early on, but it had the advantage of boxing in his opponent's queen, often before the other player realized what was happening. Quentiin grinned. He hadn't become the village's most formidable chess player by being shy. All that time spent evaluating battle plans in the Alcatune Army—the lessons and strategy—would stick for the rest of his life.

"What are ye smilin' at, laddie?" Jolldo said. "I'll give ye reason to weep soon enough."

"Ye will, eh?" Quentiin countered. "We'll see about that."

Just then, the inn's front door slammed open and another dwerion staggered inside, followed by a gust of wind and rain. The newcomer stumbled forward a few steps before collapsing against the side of the bar. It was Galldo, the village blacksmith. Rivulets of blood streamed down the side of his head. He grasped at the edge of the bar, trying to steady himself as all heads turned toward him. The common area fell into unnatural silence while Yagglem rushed to Galldo's side, righting the injured dwerion and placing an arm under his shoulder to support him.

"What in Malath happened?" the innkeeper asked.

"Attacked," Galldo said, gasping, "Me an' Vellgo…were ambushed in the woods. They're comin' with more, lots more."

Yagglem eased the dwerion into a chair and wiped the side of his head with a rag. "Who's coming?" the innkeeper asked.

A light flashed, and Quentiin looked out the window in time to see a nearby house erupt in flames. Seconds later, two more buildings followed suit in a blaze of red and orange. Quentiin stepped up to the glass, peering through the misting rainfall to the street, and saw three gray-skinned creatures with swords in hand.

"They're already here," he said darkly.

The other patrons scrambled to their feet, standing shoulder to shoulder to stare out the window. On the village outskirts, more creatures materialized, all bearing torches and swords. An uneasy murmur traveled through the room, and one dwerion started for the door. "We've got to get out o' here!" he said. "We need to protect our families!" A chorus of voices rose in assent.

"Hold fast!" Quentiin shouted, holding up a hand, and the tavern fell silent again. The Icor Rebellion might be two decades gone, but some things never changed. Quentiin was still a soldier, and the others knew it. "We can't rush this. We'll be more use to our families if we play our hand right." He looked out the window again.

The creatures at the edge of the village moved past the houses one at a time, systematically torching each one. He swallowed hard as he realized what he was seeing. The invaders were making a ring of fire around Raldoon, starting with the outermost homes and working inward. It was a neat, simple trap from which none could escape.

"What have ye got for defenses, Yagglem?" Quentiin asked the innkeeper.

"Just what ye see here," Yagglem replied in a grim voice, pointing to an assortment of weapons on the walls. "They're decorative, but they'll draw blood."

Ye need to go outside, he told himself. *Assess the situation. Learn their strengths. Learn their weaknesses.*

"Pass 'em around," Quentiin said in a low growl. Yagglem nodded, and Quentiin addressed the remainder of those in the common room. "Take Yagglem's longbows an' man the windows. Those sons of goats are goin' to come at us with everythin' they have, an' we're goin' to show 'em we have some teeth." He looked at Jolldo. "How would ye like to take a stroll outside, laddie?"

Jolldo nodded. "Seems like a bloody good day for it, mate."

"Aye, then. Ye an' I are goin' to move into the streets to see what we're up against. Along the way, we'll gather as many folks as we can an' bring them back here. If we keep our wits about us, we can hold the inn against those creatures."

Jolldo grunted in affirmation. Around them, the dwerions in the common room took action, following Quentiin's instructions to line up beside the windows and prepare a solid line of defense. Quentiin took a sword Yagglem offered him.

"Hold the line, laddie," he said to the innkeeper.

"Aye," Yagglem agreed. "Send as many villagers back to us as ye can get. We'll move 'em into the cellar an' keep 'em safe."

Jolldo took a second sword from Yagglem. As Quentiin and Jolldo moved toward the door, the innkeeper passed out longbows to the defenders at the windows.

"Be careful," Galldo said, still holding the rag against the cut in his head. In his other hand, he held a long staff, as ready to do battle as anyone else in the room.

"The same to you." Quentiin nodded. Then, with Jolldo at his back, he pushed the door open and stepped into the street.

A gust of wind blasted their faces as shards of hail cut the air, hitting the ground like tiny pebbles. Quentiin's red coat whipped in the breeze. "Stay low, and stick to the corners," he said to Jolldo. He'd much prefer an all-out assault, but he knew it was out of the question. They were outnumbered and out-matched. He had to play defensively, just like in chess; gather quick information and get back to the inn, where he'd be more effective.

The houses in Raldoon were arranged in concentric circles, *The Hungry Wanderer* at their center. Mayor Billian Briiga's house stood across the street from the inn's eastern wall, and one street past the mayor's house was the Village Hall. Everything except the Hall was made of wood, so the fires would spread quickly.

"Do we risk movin' everyone to the Hall?" Jolldo asked. They could see the top of the stone building just past Mayor Briiga's house. "It's the one place they can't set afire."

Quentiin grunted. "I intend to find out. If there's a safe way to get inside, we can hold the Hall better than the inn." He ducked and ran across the street to the mayor's house, Jolldo behind him. Muddy puddles splashed beneath his feet. He kept a hand around the pommel of his sword, ready to draw at a moment's notice.

On the other side of the street, Quentiin ducked and rolled under the eaves of the mayor's home. He stood, flattened his back against a wall, and crept toward the house's northwest corner. The entire outer ring of Raldoon was burning, as were most of the inner houses. Any hopes of escaping the village were gone. These creatures knew their business, and they performed it well. Everywhere he looked, flames billowed and plumes of smoke rose. They didn't have long before the invaders arrived on the front steps of *The Hungry Wanderer*.

When he reached the corner of the mayor's house, he squatted and peered around the corner to the Hall. The Hall was truly the most defensible building in the village, but one glance told Quentiin they would not be going there. Two wagons stood in front of the Hall at an intersection, and homes on all sides of the stone building were ablaze as the gray-skinned invaders roamed all around. They dragged struggling dwerions through the mud, throwing them into the carts one at a time before turning back to gather more prisoners. Quentiin growled. They were taking his friends, and he was helpless to do anything about it.

A single house, belonging to Veeron Yiila and his family, stood directly north of the mayor's home. As Quentiin assessed the scene in front of the Hall, the sound of shattering glass turned his direction toward the house, where an invader pulled Veeron out of a broken window and into the street. The creature stood only twenty strides away from where Quentiin crouched in the shadows, its back to him and Jolldo.

Now *this* was something he could deal with. Quentiin raced across the open space, drawing his sword with a rasp of steel. The creature glanced over its shoulder just as Quentiin slammed into him. Veeron tumbled out the window as Quentiin tore his attacker away. The creature moved in a circle, drawing its sword, but Quentiin had already closed in. He sliced into the creature's chest, driving it up against the wall of Veeron's home. In its death throes, the creature attempted a downward stroke with its blade, but Quentiin blocked the blow by clamping his hand against the attacker's wrist and pinning it to the wall. As his opponent slumped away, dead, Quentiin pulled his sword free and helped Veeron to his feet.

"Inside," Veeron gasped.

Jolldo leaped through the open window and roared a battle cry. Quentiin followed into a narrow space where three creatures had seized Veeron's wife and their three children. Behind Quentiin, Veeron clambered back through the window. These were close quarters, and Quentiin had to take care to avoid harming the innocent. He upended a table in the middle of the room and shoved it toward the attackers to delay them; then circled to the far side to block the door.

Jolldo closed in on the first creature, which had both its hands on a child. In the narrow space the creature could not draw its sword quickly enough Jolldo used the pommel of his sword to force the creature to the floor, freeing the children, who ran to their father as Jolldo plunged his blade into the invader's heart.

The other two attackers came at Quentiin simultaneously, one on either side. Quentiin ducked, sweeping his leg out and dropping a creature to the floor. As he rose back to standing, he held his sword perpendicular to his head to block an attack from the other creature. A *clang* of steel rang loudly in the tight space. "Get 'em out o' here!" Quentiin shouted to Jolldo. "Back to the inn!"

Jolldo complied, helping Veeron's family out the window one at a time. Quentiin and his opponent parried as the last assailant regained his feet. But Veeron had stayed behind, and as the creature ran toward Quentiin, the other dwerion intercepted. Kitchen knife in hand, Veeron tackled the creature and stabbed its neck, causing a spray of blood to shower on the floorboards. "Leave my family alone," Veeron growled.

In the close quarters, Quentiin had an advantage on his taller attacker. He moved in circles, keeping the creature constantly on the defense. Quentiin had his moment when they came to a dwerion-size doorframe, which Quentiin ducked through just as his attacker delivered yet another sword stroke. His attacker's blade buried itself in the wood of the doorframe, and splinters showered onto the floor. Quentiin did not hesitate. He moved back into the open and took the creature's head off in one stroke.

Veeron stepped forward to thank him, but Quentiin waved him aside. They needed to move. The two dwerions went back out into the street, where Jolldo kept Veeron's wife and their three children close. As Quentiin and Veeron emerged, Jolldo pointed east toward the Village Hall, where a creature on horseback led yet another wave of invaders thundering toward them.

"Run!" Quentiin shouted, waving the dwerions toward *The Hungry Wanderer*. He sheathed his sword and scooped up one of Veeron's children in each arm. As they neared the inn, a pair of arrows shot past them and toward their pursuers. *Good dwerion, Yagglem.* The innkeeper was buying them much-needed time. At the entrance of the inn, Quentiin let the children down and waved them and their mother up the steps. Veeron and Jolldo went next, and Quentiin last. A creature on horseback fired a crossbow bolt at Quentiin, but it missed and planted itself in the wood of the inn. The door slipped open a crack to let Quentiin inside, where he slumped to the floor to regain his breath.

Yagglem came over and crouched next to him. "It's bad, isn't it?"

"Aye, laddie," Quentiin said between gasps. "It's bad."

He struggled back to his feet and stood next to the windows. Outside the inn a dozen creatures had formed a line of attack, each holding a fire-tipped arrow fitted to a bow. The dwerions defending the windows unleashed more arrows, but the creatures hung back as the shafts landed harmlessly in the mud. Then, as the inn's defenders paused to reload, the attackers rushed forward, coming just within bow range to launch a volley of flaming arrows. The fiery barbs thudded against the sides of the inn from all directions.

"Water!" Yagglem yelled. A group of villagers, standing by with buckets, doused the flames while the archers at the windows unleashed another pair of shots. Quentiin looked outside; the intruders had immediately retreated, keeping their distance, out of the way of retaliation. Quentiin knew something didn't add up. Only a small number of creatures stood in front of the inn. That meant others had moved elsewhere, and he needed to find out where.

He had his answer when he heard several telltale *thunks* behind him. Quentiin turned around and swore as the rear portion of the inn caught fire. The attackers in front had been simply a diversion to keep the villagers occupied while the rest of the creatures struck from a different direction.

The dwerions were now running out of buckets of water, and chaos mounted as they scrambled to beat the rising flames. They knocked over tables and chairs in their haste, glass mugs shattering against the floor as panic took over. The creatures in front fired new arrows, and Quentiin knew they were doomed. Smoke stung his eyes as the heat rose. *The Hungry Wanderer* was made of good, dry timber, and the fire was rapidly consuming its fuel. Quentiin's skin scorched while the other villagers ran from the building, succumbing to the danger outside rather than risk being burned alive.

The wall on Quentiin's right shuddered and buckled. Quentiin's mind raced through his options. Trying to regain control of the situation was pointless. Each dwerion had to take care of himself now, and Quentiin faced the same dilemma as the rest. He could either die now or try his luck running. But *where?* There had to be something left, some final trick to save himself and his companions.

Quentiin heard a loud groan and saw the timbers sagging above his head. The beams groaned, shifting their weight against the already unstable wall. All the pressure teetered on a corner beam, which supported both the wall and ceiling.

Oh, no…

The beam snapped. Sparks showered. Quentiin glanced at the table with the chessboard. As the inn's outer wall collapsed and the roof crashed down, Quentiin dived under the table, hoping it would withstand the ceiling's crushing blow.

It didn't.

The table's legs snapped as falling timbers struck its top. Chess pieces flew in all directions. Quentiin curled into a ball, raising his arms over his head. The combined weight of table and roof fell on top of him, and he was struck senseless.

Around him, the inn burned to the ground.

Six

The Matthias family arrived in Raldoon just before nightfall. The village was a smoldering ruin, most of its buildings reduced to charred skeletons, though a few still burned with crackling flames. The flickering fires created bursts in the twilight. A handful of stone buildings stood out from the rubble, lone monuments of survival, but their presence only punctuated the surrounding desolation.

The moon came into the sky as the three travelers approached the village, its soft light caressing the wreckage. No sign of life stirred, and a fragile silence hung over everything. *We've come too late.* Tim's heart pounded, becoming heavier with each passing step. "Did they take all the dwerions?" he asked in a whisper.

"I don't know," Daniel replied. "If any remain, they will be in the Village Hall."

It did not look promising. The windows were barred shut, and no sounds floated toward them. A ring of ashes surrounded the stone building. Daniel walked toward the Hall, his family behind him. As they crisscrossed over fallen beams of burned wood, navigating by moonlight, the night enveloped them in a cool embrace.

Tim had been to Raldoon numerous times, and more than anything else he remembered the warmth and welcome Quentiin and the others had shown him. Now the raw, abrupt reality of the village's broken remains clashed with those memories. To his left, the blacksmith Galldo's anvil stood amid a pile of fragmented logs. To his right, all that remained of Tarrdin the weaver's shop were a few upright timbers. Directly ahead, a light wind blew a shredded tapestry across the ground.

They walked down a street, once filled with shops and homes, which now only offered collapsed, hollow buildings, every one a shell of its former self.

Wreckage littered the ground. They came upon a muddied doll that had been trampled by many passing feet. Rosalie picked up the doll, brushed off as much grime as she could and placed it in her pocket.

On the village green, wagon ruts ran across the lawn, leaving gaping furrows of earth. The previous year Quentiin had brought them to Raldoon's Midsummer Festival, held on this very green. How could a place of such happiness now feel so cold?

Then, as they walked past the green, a figure materialized from the shadows and leveled a crossbow at them. "Halt!" he ordered, his voice cracking the air. "Show me yer hands!" The three stopped midstep, raising their hands to show empty palms. The figure, a dwerion with ashes smeared over his body for camouflage, stepped forward. As forceful as his voice might be, he could not conceal a tremor in his disposition. He looked at the newcomers, eyes sharp with distrust. "What brings ye here?"

"We came to help," Daniel said.

The dwerion took another step forward, appraising the family. As he did so, he partially lowered his crossbow, relaxing just a hair. "Daniel?" he said. "Yer Quentiin's friend, ain't ye?"

"Yes, sir," Daniel replied. His brow furrowed as he searched his memory for a name. "Herrdra, right?"

"Aye, laddie," the dwerion affirmed, lowering his crossbow the rest of the way. "My apologies fer the cold welcome, but as ye can see…" he gestured back toward the remnants of the village.

"They attacked us, too," Daniel said.

"I ain't surprised," Herrdra replied. "When did it happen?"

"This morning," Rosalie answered. "Three of them burned our cottage, and three more attacked Timothy in the woods. How many came here?"

"At least forty," Herrdra said. "They took almost all of us."

"Did anyone recognize them?" Daniel asked. "I've never seen their likes before."

"Nor I, laddie. There ain't a one of us who knows where they came from. Fer all I know, they're from Malath itself."

Daniel acknowledged this with a grim nod. "Are the others in the Hall?"

"Aye, those who remain, at least. Come with me inside. The out o' doors is a little too dangerous for my likin' right now."

Herrdra led them to the Village Hall, relaying events as they walked. "It was early afternoon when they came. Most of us were at the *Wanderer*, waitin' out the storm. They made a circle 'round the village an' then hit us all at once, burnin' everythin' as they worked from the outside in." He pointed toward the remnants of the inn. A few small fires still flickered, casting an orangish glow over the surrounding ashes. "We held our defenses there. Quentiin rallied us at first, but everythin' went straight to Malath after they torched the inn. Things got out o' hand real quick after that." He spat in the dirt.

Before they made it another dozen paces, though, they heard a moan from the ruins near the inn's eastern wall. Herrdra swore. "Another survivor," he said. "We thought we had 'em all. Hurry!" They turned and ran through the tavern's gutted remains, dodging fallen timbers and splintered beams, broken tables and shattered mugs, looking for the source of the noise.

When they reached the far wall, Tim heard the moan again. He turned to the right, squinting his eyes to gain better focus. He had only moonlight and firelight to go on. He took a few careful steps forward, eyeing the wreckage closely. Then, near a plume of dancing flame, something shifted under a collapsed table. Several rooftop beams lay crisscrossed over the tabletop, creating a precarious pile of unstable weight.

"Over here!" Tim said.

The others ran over, Daniel reaching him first. The body underneath the table stirred again and the beams rolled to the side, risking further injury to the dwerion.

"Don't move!" Daniel said to the injured figure. "We need to get the weight off you."

Gesturing to Tim, he stepped toward the first beam. "Go slow," Daniel told Tim, who nodded. Taking utmost care not to upset the rest of the pile, they lifted the log together and removed it from the wreckage. Behind them, Rosalie and Herrdra arrived. Each took a side of the beam, and they carried it a safe distance away from the pile.

"Matthias," the injured dwerion said, his voice a muted groan. "Did ye come for the ale?"

"Quentiin!" Daniel said. He knelt next to the table. "Are you hurt bad?"

"It tickles a little," the dwerion mumbled.

"Hold on," Daniel said. He and the others removed the wreckage one delicate step at a time. When at last they lifted the splintered table, Quentiin

Harggra raised a hand in feeble greeting from his position on the ground. A long, bloody gash ran along his head, and a bruise marked his left cheek. The dwerion's long red coat was blackened and torn, but he had no apparent injuries on his torso.

Rosalie squatted by his side. "Stay still," she said, examining the wound on Quentiin's skull. She carefully tilted his head up to inspect it from all angles. She exhaled softly, a sigh of relief. "It's not deep. Can you move?"

"What is this—the elderly ward? 'Course I can move." Quentiin sat up and held a hand out to Tim. "Don't stand there like that unless ye're plannin' to draw a canvas portrait, laddie. Help a chap up."

Tim took Quentiin's hand. The dwerion's gruff demeanor was reassuring. It was Quentiin's way of telling everyone he was okay. He helped Quentiin to his feet, and then both he and Daniel wrapped the dwerion's arms around their shoulders. They walked through the ruins to the Hall, supporting Quentiin between them.

Upon reaching the Hall, Herrdra led them up the steps and into the building. Roughly two dozen dwerions stood inside, gathered in loose clumps—some sitting, others lying down, some crying, others dry-eyed—but all with the same blank eyed look on their faces. At least half bore injuries—wounds ranging from cuts and scrapes to broken bones. Many were females and youngsters. They at least had been spared whatever horrors the kidnappers intended for their captives. A few dwerions, like Herrdra, had covered themselves with ashes, and all carried weapons. At the far end of the hall, flames blazed in the massive fireplace, but the fire did nothing to lighten the survivors' somber mood.

Tim could understand their pain. Aside from physical injuries, these dwerions had lost homes and loved ones in a single night. It was bad enough that his tiny cottage was gone, but that was nothing compared to what this group was enduring. Beside him, Rosalie quietly took in the scene. A mixture of emotions filled her blue eyes, compassion for the villagers mingling with anger at the injustice of their plight.

In the corner, a young dwerion sat on a stool, thumb in her mouth, looking at the newcomers with wide eyes. Grime and soot covered her once-white dress, and ash streaked her blond hair. Upon seeing her, Rosalie walked over and crouched at eye level. "Hi," Rosalie said. The dwerion said nothing. Rosalie reached into her pocket for the doll from the street and held it out, but the dwerion turned away from Rosalie, burying her face in her stained dress.

"Shh," Rosalie said. "It's okay."

She slowly reached out and touched the child's wrist. The dwerion jerked, but only a little, keeping her face in her dress. Rosalie waited a few moments, and then took one of the dwerion's clenched fists and opened it. She placed the doll in the youngster's hand.

"It's okay," Rosalie repeated.

The dwerion lifted her face again, eyes still wide, and accepted the doll. She clutched it against her chest and put her thumb back in her mouth. Rosalie leaned forward and placed a kiss on her forehead. When she stood back up, she turned to Herrdra. "Who's tending to the injured?"

"Anyone who can," Herrdra replied helplessly. "The Healers are either dead or captured. We're doin' what we can."

Rosalie nodded. "Do you have any supplies for healing?"

"Precious few," Herrdra admitted. "We need a lot more."

"There's oak root and yew leaf in the Odow," she said, picking up a lantern and a knapsack. "I'll gather some."

"It might be dangerous out there," Herrdra said.

"These dwerions need proper help," Rosalie said. "And I won't be alone." She looked at her son. "Tim will come with me." Potential danger didn't matter to Rosalie. The red-eyed, demonic invaders could be surrounding them on all sides, leaving no way out, and Rosalie would still go out there if the villagers needed the supplies. It was what she did.

Tim helped his father lay Quentiin on a stone table, ignoring the dwerion's protests. Quentiin might feel fine now, but if the cut on his head were left untreated, it would soon become infected.

"Stay close to your mother," Daniel said to Tim. "I'll remain here with Herrdra. We need to decide how to protect the Hall if another attack comes."

Tim nodded. "We'll be fine."

"Good. Be careful."

Tim looked into his father's eyes. "Always," he said. He joined Rosalie and the two stepped outside, once again making their way through the ruins of Raldoon. The village looked ominous in the ghostly moonlight, jagged edges of broken buildings casting fragmented shadows. Out here, the real horrors of the day had turned into the imaginary dangers of night—or perhaps not so imaginary. Rosalie led the way, directly west, past Mayor Briiga's ransacked home.

Like the Hall, the stone building still stood in one piece, but the windows were shattered and the oak door in splinters. A bloodstain ran across the doorstep.

The Overlord won't mind if we kill one here or there, Krinzen had said in the woods.

Briiga was a good mayor—all of the dwerions were good—but Tim hadn't seen Briiga among the survivors. Had he met his death on this very doorstep? Had the invaders dragged his body over the same path Tim now walked?

"I saw many villages like this in Icor," Rosalie said. "I prayed I'd never have to see anything like it again."

"Do you suppose the attackers came from the Odtune Mountains?" Tim asked. The mountains spanned the western border of Alcatune. When Tim lived in Vonku, he received education at the hands of the city's public instructors. A student in his classes, an older man named Jalen, claimed to have lived in the mountains for a year. Jalen told many stories about the Odtune, tales ranging from giants twenty feet tall to wraiths in the caves, and Tim hadn't believed half of them. But now, in the gloom of night in the ruins of this once-peaceful village, the stories no longer seemed so far-fetched.

"No, I doubt those creatures are from the mountains," Rosalie said. "If anyone's right, it's Herrdra. They came straight from Malath."

Rosalie followed the tree line along the edge of the village, holding her lantern high as she searched for herbs. Every so often, she paused to pull a leaf from a branch or a root from the ground, placing each in her knapsack. They stayed close to Raldoon, avoiding the deeper parts of the dark forest. As Rosalie searched, Tim watched for signs of danger. His mind turned every twig and leaf into a red-eyed invader, but he quickly reprimanded his overactive imagination. Jumping at shadows served no purpose.

When they were halfway across the western length of Raldoon, Tim saw moonlight glinting off a metallic object in the bushes. It was probably nothing, but he was not taking any chances. He put up a hand to halt his mother.

"There's something over there," he said. The moment he spoke, the bushes rustled. Tim gripped the hilt of his sword, and Rosalie loosened her weapon. They held still for a few moments, and the movement stopped. Tim counted to twenty and then carefully approached the bush. Rosalie followed him.

There was a sudden snarl and flash of movement. Tim brought his sword up just in time to deflect the blow aimed at him. As he knocked his assailant's blade away, the figure staggered and fell backward, its sword clattering as it fell from its fingers. Whatever it was, it did not have much fight left. Tim kicked the sword away, stamping down on the stranger's wrist and placing the tip of his weapon at the attacker's throat. Two red eyes glared back.

Rosalie lifted her lantern. The creature was badly wounded. Its helm was shattered, dried blood plastered the side of its head, and an arrow protruded from its ribs. It would not be alive much longer.

"What is your name?" Tim asked.

The slave driver responded with a scornful laugh. At the end, it coughed a spatter of blood. "I do not answer to lesser races," it said. "You have no authority over me."

Rosalie Matthias was the most gentle, loving woman in the world, but she had no tolerance for injustice. In a single fluid motion, she unsheathed her sword and stepped forward, kicking the arrow in the creature's side. It howled in pain.

"I'll make you a deal," she said, leveling her blade at its throat. "Tell us who you are and where you come from, and I will put you out of your misery."

Its red eyes sharpened. "I am one of the higher blood," it said. "I come from a place you know nothing about. But you will know all too soon—you and the rest of your friends. Your kind will wither under my master's might."

"Who is your master?" Rosalie asked. She got no response, even when she pressed her sword uncomfortably close to its jugular. "Where does he live?"

The creature looked briefly toward the north and then back at Rosalie. "Beyond," it said, sneering.

"Beyond?" Rosalie asked.

"Beyond," it repeated. It laughed, a dry, rasping sound, accompanied by a spattering of blood from its lungs.

Tim looked toward his mother. Dread welled up inside of him. "Does he mean…?"

North. It looked north. There was only one thing in that direction. *Beyond.*

"We have to get back to the Hall," Rosalie said.

"Indeed," their captive said. "Tell them, so you can cower in fear as the day of your bondage approaches."

Rosalie removed her sword and looked at the fallen creature with disgust. There was no need to stay here. The creature's wounds were mortal, so it wasn't going anywhere. It just wanted to mock them while it still breathed.

She and Tim headed back toward Raldoon. They had enough herbs to care for the wounded, and it was imperative they tell the others what the creature had said.

"Do you think it's lying?" Tim asked.

"Perhaps," Rosalie replied. "But I think not."

When they reentered the Hall, Rosalie gathered a few dwerions to help her prepare salve from the herbs and roots. Meanwhile, Tim approached his father, who stood next to Quentiin. Herrdra joined them.

"Well?" Daniel asked, noting the look on Tim's face.

"We found one at the edge of the village," Tim said. "It was dying, but it talked a little, and I think I know where they came from. These creatures don't belong in the South. I think they come from the other side of the Rampart."

"The North?" Herrdra said. "That's nigh impossible, laddie. There ain't any way to cross the Rampart, not from either side."

"Apparently that ain't true," Quentiin countered in a rumbling voice. "If anythin', it makes the most sense. The beasts appeared from nowhere, burned everythin' in their path, an' disappeared. If they're comin' from the other side o' the wall, that explains a lot."

"All except how they got past the Rampart," Daniel replied. "It may be true, but how?"

"There's one way to find out," Quentiin said. "We follow their trail."

Herrdra swallowed hard. "We should discuss this with the others before making any plans." He cleared his throat and called for attention. It grew silent, and Tim told the villagers of his encounter and his suspicions regarding the Rampart. The dwerions regarded his conclusion with understandable skepticism, their expressions ranging from shock to numbed acceptance. A few voiced doubts, which in turn sparked debate.

Tim looked to his companions, feeling an underlying tension in the air—not because the dwerions disbelieved him, but because of the opposite. They feared that what Tim said might be true, and if these creatures were powerful enough to cross the Rampart, something that had never been done, what else were they capable of?

Quentiin Harggra struggled into a sitting position, raising his voice above the others. "We won't know if this is true unless we travel north an' investigate ourselves," he said. "The Rampart is a day's walk from here. With every hour we twiddle our thumbs, those sons of goats take our brothers farther from us.

It also wouldn't surprise me if they plan to come back lookin' for more of us. A group of us needs to follow their trail, which may or may not lead to the Rampart. While we do that, another group needs to travel south to alert King Aras. He needs to know what happened here."

In response, the Hall again buzzed with rising arguments until Daniel raised his hand for silence. "Your village has always shown great hospitality to my family. I will find out who has done this. At first light tomorrow, I will set out." He paused. "And if I know anything of my wife and son, they won't let me go without coming along."

"Nor I, laddie," Quentiin said. "I took a blow to the head an' no more. I'll be shipshape by the morrow."

"Not without this first," Rosalie said, lifting her bowl and applying a sticky, white substance to the cut on Quentiin's head. He winced in discomfort, but she seized his head and held it still.

"I'll go to the Royal City," Herrdra said. "Another should come with me. The rest must stay here and keep our village safe."

A dwerion named Yuulin volunteered to make the journey with Herrdra, and that ended the matter. The Hall settled into a ragged silence as the survivors prepared for the evening. A group made a meager supper—not much more than boiled vegetables and a few chunks of meat—while Rosalie and others tended to the injured.

By the time the villagers finished eating, they were exhausted. The dwerions stretched onto the floor, most falling into fitful sleep within minutes. Tim rolled up his cloak and lay close to the fire, while the activity in the Hall died down. He felt just as tired as the rest of them, but at the same time, his mind remained vibrantly alert.

The fireplace, the only illumination left, filled the room with its dim orange light, shadows dancing on the ceiling. In them, Tim saw the shapes of the creatures that had burned this place.

It wasn't only the dying soldier's suggestions that drew Tim's thoughts north. Tim could *feel* the land on the other side of the Northern Rampart, almost as if it were waiting for him, wanting him to arrive—and at its heart he felt something more, something darker. He could almost see it: a cold pit with frost-tinged edges and evil in its depths.

The land wasn't the only thing waiting. Something was alive over there, something that should be human but no longer was. The sensation chilled Tim to his marrow. He told himself to relax, to stop imagining things. He eventually fell asleep, but it brought him no comfort.

Seven

Isanam, the malichon Overlord, was pleased. The foray into the South had gone just as planned. Zadinn could now proceed with the next phase of his objective. And when Zadinn was content, Isanam was also content.

Astride his horse, the Overlord led two-score malichons and their prisoners into the rise and fall of the Kavu Hills. The desolate North, a barren and frigid wasteland of rock and tree, surrounded them. The sun set in the west, but its dying rays offered no comfort to the captives.

A sharp wind knifed across the traveling brigade. Some shivered at its touch, but Isanam rode on unperturbed by the elements. A black cloak hung from his shoulders, rippling with the sudden blast of icy air. A cowl enshrouded his head, and within the hood a mask fashioned from a human skull covered his face. Isanam never lowered the hood in public. What lay beneath was not for others to see.

It was almost time to speak with Zadinn. The Dark Lord wanted to know when the scouting force returned, and Isanam had much to share with his master. Even better, he had the dwerions. They could glean many precious facts about the South from these captives, though Isanam planned to leave the finer aspects of interrogation to Zadinn. Watching the Dark Lord at work was beyond fascinating. Zadinn could inflict the most exquisite pain without drawing a drop of blood—most intriguing.

Isanam directed his malichons to a cove of sheltered hills. Night came fast in the North, and they needed to make camp soon. Being servants of Zadinn did not exempt them from nighttime's dangers. As they approached the area, all was silent save for the grinding of wagon wheels and the clatter of horses' hooves upon rocky ground. A handful of sparse trees dotted the hillside, their roots tangled among the nooks and crannies of the stone-covered earth. The wind gusted down the hillside, causing pebbles and shale to slide from the site.

Upon arriving at the cove, Isanam dismounted from his horse. He didn't just drop to the ground—he *flowed* down in one sinuous, uninterrupted movement, robes billowing out and in again as he landed. At full height, the Overlord reached nearly seven feet, a full head taller than his subordinates. His stallion bucked and pawed, nostrils flaring. Isanam placed a hand on its neck, conveying authority through the barest touch, and the animal quieted.

"Make camp," he said, handing his reins to Commander Neebra. His voice sounded like a file drawn across wet stone. "I am not to be disturbed tonight."

Neebra nodded as he took the horse and called out orders. The stallion nipped at his hand, but Neebra readily avoided the bite. He'd seen plenty of malichons lose fingers to the Overlord's mount.

Isanam walked past his troops as they busied with the tasks of making camp—lighting fires, raising tents, and preparing food—all in complete silence. As Isanam approached the wagons holding the prisoners, he stopped to survey the dwerions. They clustered in their cages, huddling for warmth, seeking what small comfort they could find in one another's company. It was just as well— the remainder of their lives would not be pleasant. Their clothes were shredded, their faces grimy, their eyes blank. Some cried, and others remained silent, but none spoke.

A few shrank back—wise, and not entirely unexpected—as he approached. They saw what he had done yesterday, when a captive tried to run away and failed. Isanam made the rest of the dwerions watch as he lowered the would-be escapee into a pot of boiling oil. Slowly. The prisoners did not eat well *that* night. However, there was no need for such a demonstration today.

Isanam continued past the prisoners and traveled uphill to a nearby rise. He saw the brittle trees of the Erdrar Forest, a dark mass on the surface of the landscape, just a few leagues from the hills where he now stood. The aging woods groaned and creaked as evening winds blew across them. The endless expanse of the Durin Plains stretched north of the Forest, shining in stark radiance under the white light of a rising moon.

The Overlord faced the horizon, gathering his thoughts and preparing his energy. It would take considerable effort to make contact with the Dark Lord. Isanam grasped his sword, which gave an oily rasp as he pulled it from his sheath. The blade, running a full meter in length, was obsidian black. It glistened in the dusky evening glow.

Isanam curled the fingers of his left hand around the blade, positioning his grip until satisfied, and then clenched his fist. The sharp edge bit deep into his flesh, but Isanam did not so much as flinch. He breathed just as evenly as if he were on an afternoon stroll, all the while running the blade across his skin. Blackish-red droplets of his blood splattered the ground. The pain had the desired effect. Isanam's mind locked into focus, and the world dimmed to shadows. Power welled up inside of him, rolling and surging with its might. The very fiber of his being tingled. He sighed and tilted his head back, raising his cowled face to the sky. He closed his eyes, using the pain to empty his mind, and reached *out*, stretching his thoughts across the vast landscape of the North.

Many ages ago, men in the North learned how to unlock the mystical energies binding the cosmos together. They called this power the Lifesource, and they named themselves its Advocates. For centuries the Advocates of the Lifesource used their gifts to guard and protect the common folk. That time was gone, lost in the fires of war. Zadinn Kanas was master of the Lifesource now, and he had taught Isanam how to harness this power, too. No one else knew how to use it. The Advocates were gone, and the few who happened to be born with the gift soon found themselves dead at Zadinn's hand.

I have returned, my lord, Isanam said in his mind. *I come bearing news… and gifts.*

* * *

The message traveled across the bleak wilderness in the space of a mere instant, passing across the Kavu Hills, slipping through the dead trees of the Erdrar Forest, whistling around the Kaltu Pass, and singing across the Durin Plains. It reached the Deathlands in the moment of a single breath.

Years past, the landscape of the North had been markedly different, but it changed after Zadinn's armies overthrew the old empire. This reaction was not instantaneous—it happened over time. Every year the wilderness perished a little more, a slow death of the natural world, a disease brought on by the Dark Lord's mere presence. Signs of affliction were everywhere, but the true corruption resided in the Deathlands.

While the rest of the North shivered from lack of warmth, the Deathlands languished under intense heat from a blazing sun. Streaks of orange, purple, and red ran across the stones on the ground, and jagged cracks spread over the surface of the landscape. The dirt between these cracks was sharp and precarious, like desert sand.

A slight plateau stood at the center of the Deathlands, rising thirty feet above the rest of the landscape. Sheer, impenetrable walls surrounded a dark city perched at its top, and an oily moat surrounded the fortress. Guards patrolled the rampart above, their spear tips glinting in the red light. A drawbridge led across the moat's restless waters and passed through the walls underneath the fangs of a portcullis.

Behind the battlements, the sound of metal on stone echoed from a deep valley of obsidian rock. Known as the Pit, here slaves of every race labored to cut and shape stones for the buildings and palaces within Zadinn's city. The Pit's steep edges dropped down a chasm, sloping toward a lake of fire. Plumes of lava periodically shot into the sky, raining droplets of fiery ash upon the workers. The slaves in the Pit were forced to work on narrow, cramped ledges underneath the whip of Veldor the Slavemaster.

Zadinn's palace, a black citadel of swooping curves and steep angles, loomed from the city's center. It formed a dome, all its walls arching toward one central peak, where a single pointed spire jutted high into the clouds. Its exterior windows were opaque, which was just as well for those who lived in the city. Evil things happened behind those walls. Most who went into Zadinn's citadel did not come out, but everyone heard their screams.

In the heart of the palace, Zadinn Kanas sat on his monstrous, twisted throne atop a raised dais in the middle of the room. His chair was a warped amalgamation of obsidian from the Pit and bones from human skeletons, fused together to form a seat of sharp, angry contours. The throne was liable to draw blood from the one who sat in it.

All around Zadinn, smoldering torches lit his ruling chamber. Vents on either side of the room emitted eerie green light, and strange, multicolored vapors filled the air. The mists covered the ground in fog, here and there reaching up with tendrils to clutch at the air. Ledge upon ledge of human skulls surrounded the entire area, each appearing to scream in pain.

Zadinn Kanas was over two hundred years old but did not look more than thirty. His smooth, unwrinkled face and solid black hair remained untouched by signs of age. His skin held the pale color of a creature that had sat in darkness too long, away from sunlight. He wore long, billowing robes, which remained eerily impervious to their surroundings no matter the circumstances—when wind blew, they stayed still; when rain fell, they stayed dry. He cradled a gnarled staff in his lap, a single black stone inlaid at its top. Occasionally flashes of white light erupted from within the stone's depths.

Zadinn sat with eyes half closed, breathing in and out in even increments. He felt Isanam reaching out toward him from the southern boundaries of his kingdom, from near the Barricade that had tried and tested him all these years. But not much longer now—it was as he'd been told.

What do you know of the South? Zadinn asked.

Isanam's response came immediately. *It is ripe for the taking, my lord.*

And what of the other?

They do not speak of him. I believe he has yet to realize his potential.

Zadinn nodded. Isanam had been given three orders upon departing for the Barrier: First and foremost, remain unseen. Second, bring back prisoners. And last, but most important, find out what the Southerners knew of the Warrior.

Apparently none of the prisoners Isanam interrogated knew anything of this Warrior. The Kyrlod had spoken truth. Good, it meant there was still time to act.

Are you prepared to begin your next mission? Zadinn asked his servant.

Without a doubt, Your Majesty, Isanam replied.

Send the prisoners north with Neebra. A force in the Fertile Lands awaits your orders.

It shall be done, my lord.

Zadinn opened his eyes. The South was ready for the taking, but according to the Kyrlod, he had to complete one final task before the way was open. Zadinn left the dais and walked across the room toward a giant cauldron. A pale, yellow-green liquid flowed inside the basin, and a moaning emanated from its depths. The Cauldron of Souls was true to its name, for hundreds of spirits suffered within its waters.

Zadinn stood at the Cauldron's edge, careful not to let the waters touch him. Those trapped inside would gladly drag him into its depths and devour him, but as long as he remained untouched by its waters, he was master of those spirits within. The Dark Lord raised his staff, and shadows circled inside the stone at its top. The vapors spread, moving down the length of the staff like freshly grown vines.

Zadinn held the tip of the staff over the waters in the Cauldron, and the liquid swirled. The moans within the Cauldron grew stronger as a small whirlpool formed at its center, erratic lights flashing within the depths. The pool inverted to form a cone of turbulent green water. A thin trickle of fluid stretched from the tip of the cone and touched the black stone. The air above the Cauldron shimmered before coalescing into the shape of an old man: Ragzan of the Kyrlod.

"Take me back to where we began," Zadinn whispered to the spirit. It moaned softly, and the memory came.

* * *

The Kyrlod arrived a year ago. On the day it happened, Zadinn sat in his throne room, musing over the Fort of Pellen. The beginnings of an idea were forming. He'd had one or two in the past, but none quite like this one. It had an appeal like few others.

When Isanam entered the throne room, Zadinn pushed the thoughts aside and turned to face his servant. The Overlord carried an air of hesitation, which did not happen often. Something was different.

"My lord," Isanam said. "I am sorry to disturb, but someone is here to see you."

"Who?" Zadinn asked. Strangers did not just walk through the Deathlands and into the city without his leave.

"He does not give his name, Your Majesty, but he has significant influence."

"What do you mean?" Zadinn sensed a sharpness in the air. A hundred years ago, he might have suspected a rogue Advocate. There'd been a few foolish assaults on his city in those early days. He quickly introduced them to the Cauldron of Souls, though not before relieving them of things like eyes and fingers. But Zadinn could not imagine any of those sorcerers still lived.

"It is best if you see for yourself," Isanam answered. "Forgive me, but I think you should come outside."

Curious, Zadinn followed his lieutenant into the hallways of the citadel. They passed row upon row of cells, some occupied with the living, many with the dead, and others open for new tenants. At the palace's main entrance, flames blazed in the arched doorway, a design of Zadinn's that covered all entrances—and exits. Zadinn waved his hand, the fires died, and he stepped outside. At the head of the citadel's steps, two stone gargoyles watched over the entryway. Isanam followed Zadinn, and the fires leaped back into life behind them.

The entire city was suspended in time, every inhabitant immobilized. Some had their hands raised over their faces; others had weapons halfway drawn. One malichon was stuck on the verge of falling over, its body suspended at an awkward angle a few feet above the pavement. All the victims wore expressions of wide-eyed shock.

An old man, crooked-limbed and bent with age, stood unaffected at the base of the steps. The stranger observed the flames behind Zadinn with a look of mild curiosity. He had long, oily hair, and a beard sprawling down to his chest. Worn robes, whipping in the wind, covered his gnarled, stick-figure frame.

Zadinn surveyed the man and the city around him. He had to admit he was impressed. All in all, this was a most intriguing display of skill.

"Well," he said, "is there a purpose to this demonstration?"

"I've come to help you," the intruder replied.

"I do not need help," Zadinn said, flicking a hand to dismiss the man's spell— but nothing happened. Zadinn watched the stranger closely. "The usual counterspell appears to be ineffective," he said dryly.

"Of course it is," the man replied, meeting Zadinn's gaze.

"I would be much obliged if you gave me your name," the Dark Lord said.

The old man smiled, his eyes glinting. "I am Ragzan of the Kyrlod," he answered. "To be accurate, formerly of the Kyrlod. I was banished for inappropriate practices."

"Oh?"

"Let me explain." Ragzan looked at one of the frozen malichons. The malichon's muscles twitched, and its body sprang back to life. Free of the spell, the malichon stood up straight and looked around, taking in the scene with bewilderment. It turned in circles, staring at its comrades before coming at last to face Zadinn.

The malichon's nostrils flared, and it breathed heavily. Its eyes darted in panic. "Your Majesty—" it began, but stopped as it fell to it knees. Ragzan continued staring at the creature. The malichon screamed in agony, and Zadinn saw droplets of blood form at the corners of its eyes. Meanwhile a thin trickle of red flowed from its ears. The malichon shrieked even louder as the hemorrhage steadily increased, until it was literally drowning in a pool of its own blood. After a few brief moments, it shuddered and fell on its back, lifeless eyes staring at the sky.

"Fascinating," Zadinn said. *He didn't trust the Kyrlod, not one bit. But one didn't need to trust people in order to use them.*

* * *

"Enough of this," Zadinn said to the spirit. "Tell me about the Warrior again."

* * *

On an evening in midwinter, Zadinn and Ragzan stood together in Zadinn's throne room, discussing the brotherhood that banished Ragzan.

"How many of the Kyrlod are left?" Zadinn asked Ragzan. The books said the world had begun with twelve, but most had to be dead by now.

"Only one lives that I know of," Ragzan replied, his tone full of spite. "But he is naïve and weak. He has committed himself to a lost cause."

"What cause is that?"

"The Warrior of Light," Ragzan answered.

Zadinn looked at the prophet, narrowing his eyes. "The what?" he asked.

"The Warrior of Light," Ragzan repeated.

"I know nothing of any Warrior," Zadinn said. "Tell me more." He half suspected a trick, so it was best to tread carefully.

"The Warrior only exists because you exist," Ragzan said. "When you came into power two hundred years ago, the Maker realized the Demon Lord had chosen you as his surrogate, so he prepared a surrogate of his own. A new Advocate of the Lifesource has been born, and his potential is great. The prophecies speak of a coming conflict that will be both great and terrible. It will shake the very foundations of the world. The balance between Harmea and Malath is shifting, and the battle between you two will decide which way the scale tips."

"This... Warrior is more than just an Advocate then?" Zadinn said. "This is about the War, the Ancient War."

"Yes," Ragzan confirmed.

Zadinn lounged back in his throne. So the Demon Lord had not told him all when he left Agrazab. That was hardly surprising. Zadinn liked his secrets, but Uklith liked his own secrets even more. The Ancient War was more than a simple battle. It was a conflict as old as time, fought between two spiritual kingdoms: Harmea, the realm of light, and Malath, the realm of darkness. Every so often, their rulers—the Maker and the Demon Lord—waged this battle with human surrogates.

Ragzan spoke, cutting into Zadinn's thoughts. "The Demon Lord did not believe the Warrior would be born. He knew the Maker was preparing to select a champion, but he did not heed the signs of the Warrior's arrival. Besides, the lord of Harmea made an unexpected move."

"And that was?"

"The Warrior is on the other side of the Barricade."

"Then what good is he to anyone? Or what threat is he to me?"

"Because there is a way through the Barricade."

* * *

Zadinn stepped away from the Cauldron and rubbed his tired eyes. At first, Ragzan refused to tell him more about the Barricade. The Kyrlod insisted he would reveal everything in due time, but Zadinn would have to be patient. So Zadinn waited.

Far to the south, an enormous wall stretched across the entire length of the continent. It was made of sheer stone and reached so high that it could not be scaled by any means—nor were there any weak spots in the stone. Zadinn had tried plenty of ways to bring it down, but not even the Lifesource affected the Barricade. Its stones simply *absorbed* the magic.

Now Zadinn knew why. It had taken steady, persistent work to coax the knowledge from Ragzan, but eventually Zadinn received the answers he needed.

Ragzan's spirit gave a low cry and faded away. Zadinn sighed and reached his staff toward the phantasm. The spirit shuddered as Zadinn denied him the ability to leave. Even in death, the man's eyes sparkled with malice.

"I would like to refresh my memory once more," Zadinn said.

* * *

Ragzan finally revealed the truth a fortnight ago. "The South does not know of the Warrior," Ragzan told Zadinn, "nor does he have business there. It is not his land. This battle will take place in the North. I will tell you the secret of the Barricade, but with a warning.

"Thus far the Barricade separates you from the Warrior. Once that wall is crossed, however, the end game begins. The Warrior will find his way into the North, but the Barricade will seal once more behind him. And then, the only way to reopen the passage will be by your death…or his."

Zadinn remained quiet for a long moment before finally speaking. "I have waited long years to destroy that wall," he said. "If I must fight one more battle before the way is open, so be it."

Ragzan nodded. He knelt forward on his staff, and Zadinn was acutely aware of how ancient this man was. The Kyrlod had walked this world for over millennia, and did not involve themselves in events upon mere whims.

"The world," Ragzan said. "We will remake it. You know this?"

"I would not have it any other way," Zadinn replied.

Ragzan looked beyond the walls of the citadel and toward the south. "So it begins, Nazgar," he said in a voice no more than a murmur. "But do you know how it ends, as I do?" He turned back to face Zadinn. "My comrades and I raised the Barricade one thousand years ago, summoning it from the depths of the earth and setting it high into the sky so none could pass through, around, or above it. To pass through the Barricade, you will need a door and a key. You already have the key — it is the Lifesource. But that key is nothing without the door, and a door can only be fashioned from the blood of a Kyrlod."

Zadinn shrugged. "Then let us prick your finger and be done with it."

"It is not that simple," Ragzan said. He reached into his robes and pulled out a short, thick vial. "We must take the blood from beneath the layers of his skin and put it in here. He cannot die until we have collected all we can. It must be the blood bonded to his life force. In essence we must exchange his life for the power it contains. Only this will give us the strength to penetrate the Barricade."

Zadinn reached for the vial, but Ragzan made it disappear inside his robes with a casual, nonchalant gesture. "We must find a Kyrlod, then," Zadinn said, "and skin him alive."

"I gladly offer my brother," Ragzan said. "It should be no trouble to capture him, and I would find the process exceedingly enjoyable."

Zadinn remained very quite for a minute, carefully considering his options before making his final decision. The time was right—he had waited long enough. "I agree," he said, "but first I have one more question."

"Yes?" Ragzan replied.

"When I have defeated the Warrior and taken the South, why should I share my kingdom with you?" He waved with his staff, a negligent gesture of dismissal. At the same time, he unleashed his magic and lifted Ragzan into the air, slamming the Kyrlod against the wall with violent force. Ragzan's muscles stood out as he struggled against the invisible forces holding him.

"Don't bother," Zadinn said. "Retain your dignity." He made a crooking motion with the forefinger of his left hand, and the vial appeared from within Ragzan's robes and floated across the air toward him. Zadinn would need it for the task in front of him.

"You forgot something," Ragzan hissed. "I am more powerful than you." He closed his eyes and relaxed, muttering a silent incantation.

"Forgive me for deceiving you," Zadinn said.

Ragzan opened his eyes. They bulged when he realized, to his despair, that his efforts were futile. Zadinn's power still held him captive. Ragzan snarled and Zadinn felt him reach through the Lifesource to cast a vicious spell. Zadinn promptly deflected the magic, and Ragzan stared at him in shock.

"You can't be stronger," the Kyrlod said. "Your counterspell, the day we met—it didn't work!"

Zadinn held the Kyrlod's gaze. "I pretended."

It had suited him much better to do so. As long as Ragzan thought he had the upper hand, Zadinn remained free to probe and examine the Kyrlod's motives. And it ultimately made undermining Ragzan much easier.

Ragzan's face filled with fear. As it should have. Zadinn was about to peel his skin off and let him bleed out a slow death. Zadinn wrapped his hand around the vial, which almost tingled in his palm. As Ragzan had said, this would be exceedingly enjoyable.

"Do you think you can fight the Warrior without me?" Ragzan asked.

"Yes," Zadinn replied. "The last time I fought an Advocate, I turned him into a crater. Now if you will excuse me, I need something from you."

As per instructions, Zadinn skinned Ragzan. Alive.

The entire city heard Ragzan's screams.

* * *

Zadinn smiled as he relived the prophet's final torment. Upon procuring Ragzan's blood, he fed the Kyrlod to the hungry souls inside the Cauldron. He planned on dealing with the remaining prophet when the Warrior arrived. It had been refreshing to work with Ragzan—the Kyrlod possessed a diverse array of talents—but on the whole, he was better off without the challenge to his throne. Ragzan's death had been inevitable. So the pieces were in place.

Zadinn did not yet know where the Warrior was, but that would become clear. He would keep his eyes and ears alert, and when the Advocate's presence manifested, the Dark Lord would be ready. Meanwhile there was work to be done in the Fertile Lands, a canker to be eradicated.

Zadinn smiled. All was going well.

Eight

Tim woke up early. Red dawn light filtered in through the windows, the early spring air pervading the Hall. His breath misted in front of him.

Some of the dwerions were up and moving about. A group of them carried logs to the fire, which had burned down to embers during the night. Tim rose from his bedroll and tied his boots before going over to assist the villagers with their chores.

Daniel and Rosalie were also on their feet, helping with preparations for the meager morning meal. The scene felt surreal. To the casual observer, it might have appeared to be a public gathering for a large spring breakfast, perhaps a festival of sorts. However, the disposition of the participants spoke otherwise. Everyone present was missing friends and family. It would be a long time, if ever, before a sense of normalcy returned to Raldoon.

For the large part, Tim knew only a few of the dwerions. He'd visited Raldoon often enough and could name a fair number of villagers, but when it came right down to it, he did not *know* many of them besides Quentiin. Acquaintances, yes, but companions? No.

Just yesterday, Tim had asked his father why Daniel involved himself in a war that had nothing to do with his family. And yet, Tim realized, the same could be said of the trip he was about to undertake. Raldoon was not his village. His family was safe, and they had a farm to care for. Why leave? Why travel north? Would it not be better to turn back?

No, it would not. The burned buildings, the shattered lives—none his, but all of which were *somebody's*—deserved respect. They deserved closure, at the very least, and justice, if it could be obtained. Tim needed to be a part of this journey. He could not state a tangible reason as to *why*. There was no logical explanation, no way to describe what drove him. But he also realized that this didn't need to make sense. It just *was*.

"Mornin', laddie," Quentiin said to Tim, slapping him on the back. The dwerion's limp was barely noticeable. His injuries had been, in the end, merely superficial. By the time they reached the Rampart, Quentiin would be ready to fight every one of the kidnappers singlehandedly. And that was how he probably wanted it.

"Morning," Tim replied, warming his hands over the fire. "Ready to set out?"

Quentiin growled deep in his throat. "I'm always ready," he said. "I could run to the karfin' Rampart."

"Don't run too fast," Tim advised. "You'll need your breath when we catch up to this army." Quentiin chuckled at that, and Tim continued. "What do you suppose we'll do when we find the others?"

"That depends on whether or not those chaps are still on this side o' the Rampart," Quentiin said. "If they're still over here, things ain't goin' to be a problem. We're deep within the King's realm, and that group ain't a match for the Royal Legion. But if they've gone to the farther side, things become a little more confusin'. First order o' business will be to find out how they got across the Rampart. Then we need to alert the King immediately. Goin' over to the other side would be a dangerous business indeed. I ain't averse to the danger, but we'll want soldiers at our back if we have to cross that wall."

Tim swallowed, thinking of the night before. Maybe it had been his imagination, but he had felt something, a hideous presence waiting on the other side of that wall. The Rampart had always held a sense of mystery, but now the feeling was stronger than ever. What if the creatures *had* come from the other side? What if the way were open, and that *thing*, whatever it was, could get through?

"Are ye all right, laddie?" Quentiin asked. "Ye've gone all pale."

Tim shook himself. "I was just thinking about the cottage," he said. "They took my home. They took *our* homes. It's wrong."

"Aye," Quentiin said, "but we're breathin' today, all of us here, an' that's what matters the most. Some grub'll fix ye up." He pushed a bowl of porridge into Tim's hands, and Tim ate gratefully. The soft meal warmed his insides. Dwerions were talented cooks, and this porridge was a true testament to their skills. Even with their homes burned and supplies thin, they managed to cook a delicious, filling meal.

Beside him, Quentiin attacked his own bowl. Being a member of this race of culinary masters, he was more critical of the food than Tim. The dwerion grimaced. "My apologies, Tim," he said dourly. "It ain't bad considerin' the circumstances, but this ain't a real breakfast."

Tim shook his head. "Dwerion cooking, friend. It's all good."

Quentiin grumbled, but regardless of how he felt about the meal, he still ate twice as much as Tim did.

After the villagers finished eating, they helped Tim and the others prepare for their departure. While Daniel made arrangements with Herrdra to care for the cattle at the Matthias farm, the dwerions assembled knapsacks of food, clothing, and other supplies.

The sun came into the sky as the four travelers—Daniel, Rosalie, Tim, and Quentiin—left the Village Hall. At first the kidnappers' trail was difficult to find among the signs of chaos. Wagon ruts crisscrossed the village, some trailing into it and others trailing out. Most of the ground was still muddied, but some spots had dried to a hard crust. Charred bits of wood lay strewn across the path, and much of the wreckage still smoldered. After circling the perimeter, the companions finally found a location that indicated a departure. From there, it was easy to follow more definitive tracks north.

As they traveled into the Odow, Tim felt the forest around him awakening from its winter hibernation. The woods were notably active in the wake of the prior day's thunderstorm, many of the smaller forest animals emerging to skitter about on the earthen floor. Today was nothing out of the ordinary for these creatures—their homes were intact, and they didn't have kidnappers to chase.

Tim watched the woodland creatures come and go between the trees. It could be easy to forget oneself in this place. The leaves were green and full of fresh morning dew, and the overhead sun shone through the foliage and illuminated their path. The beauty of the morning stood in contrast to the ugliness of the previous afternoon.

The day held no surprises. As expected, the path led consistently north. It would be only a matter of time before they reached the Rampart. In the sky, the sun inched past its noon zenith, while below, the travelers continued in silence, preferring to cling to the peacefulness of the woods.

As the day slid into afternoon, and afternoon faded to dusk, they stopped to make camp within a cove of blueleaf trees. While the low *thrum* of evening life replaced the brighter sounds of daytime activity, Tim and Daniel gathered wood for a fire and Rosalie and Quentiin prepared the meal. Marsh frogs sang their evening chorus in the distance. The foursome ate well, a hearty stew of vegetables and roots, finishing the meal with a side of dwerion bread—good stuff that stuck to the stomach.

When night fell, the four posted rotating guard duty, with Daniel on first watch. After the others went to sleep, Tim joined his father at the edge of the camp. The two men sat on a pair of stumps and looked out into the surrounding woods. Nothing stirred within the trees.

"I realized something last night," Tim said to Daniel.

"What is it?" Daniel asked.

"I know why I'm doing it—becoming a soldier, I mean."

Daniel looked at him. "That was quick."

"So was the attack on Raldoon," Tim replied.

At this, a distant look came into Daniel's eyes. "You're right. It was quick."

"It's the same reason we're here," Tim said. "I can't put it into words, but you were there, the same as me. You saw Raldoon and the creatures that attacked us. Do I know these dwerions? No, but I'm still here."

Daniel remained silent for a long time. Tim began to think that his father wasn't going to speak, but then Daniel began. "I first heard about the Icor Rebellion from a refugee in a camp. The man had his home near a junction in the rebels' supply lines. The rebels couldn't afford this. He was in the way, so to speak, so they ambushed him at his farm and made him watch as they hung his wife and children from the trees. They hung him, too, but his noose broke and he survived. It was too late to save his family." Daniel turned to look at Tim. "I joined the King's Army the next day."

He sighed. "All men have the responsibility to care for their fellow man. Everyone feels this call. Some ignore it, and some even act against it. Very few—a handful, really—follow it. Those who do, make it their duty. They make it their life."

This time, it was Tim who fell silent. Neither man spoke again, and after some time, Tim went to get some sleep. When he closed his eyes, he saw a man hanging from a tree.

* * *

Early the next day, the travelers came within sight of the Rampart. They topped the rise of a hill with an undulating expanse of fir-leaf treetops on the far side. They could see the Rampart at the edge of the landscape. The wall was a sheer, impenetrable expanse of gray stone, stretching east to west without end. Mists of cloud obscured the wall's top, which rose far into the sky above. Still following the path, the companions descended into the sea of fir-leaf trees. The trail rarely meandered, leading directly north from Raldoon.

By midday they arrived at the edge of a bog. The trail skirted around the murky water, while the trees thinned out. Moments later, they left the forest and entered a meadow, which extended for perhaps two hundred yards before ending against the stones of the Rampart. At last Tim understood why few people came this close to the wall. The mere presence of such a titanic object caused him to feel small and insignificant. A foreboding sensation emanated from its very stones.

When the sun was right, the Rampart cast a shadow that encompassed the entire meadow. The grass grew right up to the edge of the wall, but no vegetation grew on the stone itself. The wall's blank, unmarked face remained completely untouched by passing years. The Rampart had been present throughout recorded time, putting its age at very close to a thousand years, but its history was shrouded in the unknown. *Who built this wall? Why is it here?*

Scholars had long speculated about what lurked on the other side. Some contended it was another world entirely, with its own history and peoples, its own language and customs, none of which would be recognized or even understood by those who dwelt in the South. Others claimed it was the gateway to the afterlife, to the kingdoms of Harmea and Malath, and that at death all souls would cross this divide. Still others professed there was nothing beyond these stones but the edge of the world and a black abyss.

The gray-skinned slave drivers had clearly crossed the meadow, evidenced by the trampled swathes of grass leading to the structure, but their path ended abruptly at the stones of the Rampart. The four companions walked across the grassy field until they were close enough to touch the wall. Neither Rosalie nor Daniel had ever come this close to the Rampart. Quentiin claimed he had been here once when he was young, but after that he had no desire to return. The wall felt strange, like it was pushing him away.

"In the name of the Maker," Rosalie whispered, "what is this?"

No one answered her. The question couldn't be answered.

Tim reached out and brushed his fingers against the stone. He had expected the wall to be an interlocking structure of bricks and mortar, but that was not the case. The face of the Rampart was completely seamless.

"Men couldn't have made this," he said in awe. "You would see evidence of their work. But this is one sheer piece of stone. It wasn't *built*. It simply exists."

"The formation is perfect," Quentiin added. "This wall is here for a reason, laddie. Maybe men didn't build it, but *somethin'* did. Perhaps it was the Maker, perhaps another bein', but this ain't happenstance or nature."

Tim's fingers tingled as he pressed his palms against the wall. The sensation made him imagine a latent energy running beneath the surface of the Rampart, waiting to be unlocked. He stepped closer and put an ear against the stone. A gentle breeze rustled around the party, parting the grass softly. Tim thought he heard voices riding on the tails of the wind, speaking in whispers. They were trying to tell him something, to give him important instructions, and they steadily became more persistent. At the same time, the tingling in his hands intensified and spread throughout his body.

"Do you hear that?" he said, turning to his family. They looked at him blankly.

"Hear what?" Daniel asked.

The voices abruptly fell silent, and the prickling sensation ceased. Tim lowered his hands and stepped back from the Rampart. "Never mind," he said. "The wind was just playing tricks on me. There's something about this place— it's strange."

"Aye," Quentiin agreed.

"But there is a clue here," Daniel said, idly kicking the wheel marks left from the wagons. "The creatures' trail ends here. Somehow they made it to the other side of the wall. There is a way through, and we can find it."

"Yes, we didn't travel a day and a half to go back empty-handed," Rosalie agreed.

The idea was intriguing, but the task less than exciting. And it felt depressingly fruitless. The slave drivers' trail ended at the wall, and that was where things stood. The creatures could not have climbed the wall, and nothing indicated they had gone *under*, so the only other option was *through*, but there was no sign of a doorway. The group spent the afternoon traveling the length of the wall for several miles in both directions, and in the end gained nothing but sore feet.

"Maybe it was magic," Tim said as the travelers settled down to rest. The sun was beginning to set, and everyone was tired and frustrated.

Quentiin shook his head. "Magic ain't fer real, laddie. It's all tavern tricks."

"Haven't you ever heard of the Lifesource?" Tim asked.

Quentiin snorted. "Of course I have, but the holy books say its use is exclusive to the Maker an' the angels."

"Don't forget the other side," Rosalie said darkly.

"Aye, I suppose the demons of Malath are part of it, but humans and dwerions don't get to touch it."

"Supposedly some can," Tim said. "My instructors in Vonku talked about it. Scholars have evidence that such magic exists. Yes, the books say only spiritual beings can touch it, but this power runs through everything that lives. So perhaps every few generations, there comes a person who can actually sense and manipulate its power."

"Ye know how those academics got their jobs?" Quentiin asked. "They weren't worth their hide when it came to *applyin'* their knowledge, so they got stuck feedin' their students a load of goat hisht."

In the background, Daniel chuckled quietly. Tim shrugged, dropping the topic. There was no point—it was only an intellectual exercise, and everyone's tempers were on edge after their lack of success in penetrating the wall's mysteries. Pushing the issue would only lead to an irrelevant argument.

"So where do we go from here?" Rosalie asked.

Daniel crossed his arms and leaned back. "In the broadest sense, we have two options. We stay here, or we turn back."

"Turn back?" Quentiin said, arching an eyebrow.

"I'm not saying we should, but it's an option," Daniel replied. "Fact is, we spent all afternoon looking for signs of a crossing, and there is *nothing*. The trail ends here, and that's that. We were all hoping there'd be some evidence of what happened here, but there isn't.

"Say we do turn back," he continued. "It might feel like we're giving up to turn around so quickly, but we might make better use of our time returning to the village to meet with the King's soldiers. We can lead them back here to continue the search."

"How much energy d'ye think Aras will really devote to this, laddie?" Quentiin asked. "It's a tragedy, t'be sure, but the King has an entire nation to care for. He'll extend his condolences, but will he send his men to pursue a group of kidnappers that just disappeared? Besides, that ain't his kingdom over there." Quentiin waved at the Rampart. "What good will it do him?"

"We have evidence it's possible to cross the Rampart," Rosalie said. "We can make King Aras the man who discovers this. How do you think that will affect his standing with other nations?"

"Aye." Quentiin approved. "Ye make a good point, miss. It can be done."

"What about time?" Tim asked. "Every day we spend on this side of the Rampart, the kidnapped villagers likely get farther away from us."

"All too true," Daniel said. "We have no way of knowing. We could spend three days here at the wall, searching for signs, or we could spend three days getting word to the King. Either way we lose three days."

They sat in silence. The truth was aggravating, but since the wall yielded no clues, they had few options.

"I say we sleep on it," Rosalie said. "In the morning, we see where things stand. What happens, happens."

"Wise as always, m'lady," Quentiin said. "I'll agree to that."

Above them, the sun went down and the Rampart's looming shadow passed over them. Tired, sore, and disappointed, the travelers made camp. A gentle wind crossed the meadow, and the stars began to shine. The four took turns standing watch and sleeping.

And the Rampart waited.

* * *

Tim had the last watch. When he took his position, a faint gray sliver of dawn showed in the east, though it would still be some time before the sun rose. He sat at the edge of their camp, noting the uncomfortable silence of the surrounding area. Even the animals of the Odow stayed clear of the Rampart. He contemplated the wall once more. Here, in the night with the moon shining down, the stone shimmered. Shadows rippled across its surface, running around the wall's smooth face. These currents of light and darkness made the Rampart look alive, like it was breathing. In they went, out they came, and in they went again.

The Lifesource runs through everything that lives, Tim thought, thinking of the earlier conversation. *It's in me, it's in the woods around me, and it's in that wall.*

It's in that wall.

He recalled the tingle he felt when touching the wall earlier that day. Later when he called the Rampart "magic," he wasn't really being serious. It was a dry joke, made to soften the sharp edges of disappointment everyone felt. Yet now his mind shifted over these thoughts, rearranging them, and an idea formed. *Quentiin called sorcery a "fairy tale," and perhaps he's right. But all fairy tales stem from nuggets of truth. This wall defies all things natural, but what if there were men and women who could use this power ages ago? Could they have raised a wall with it? Would it look like this?*

Tim stood up. The rippling shadows on the surface of the Rampart beckoned him, and right on cue another breeze ghosted across his face. Something whispered in his ear, and then it was gone. Another whisper followed, and another after that, as a chorus of voices rose up around him. Speaking in a tongue long lost, they told him to go forward.

Timothy Matthias stepped up to the Rampart and, as earlier, put his palms on the stone. It felt warm now, like an animal's pulsing blood, like the latent energy underneath its surface. There was a door here, one that needed a special key, and it waited to be unlocked.

Tim's fingers prickled again. The current beneath the stone sought him out, rising toward his touch, while around him the whispering grew so intense that it drowned out the rest of the world. Tim breathed in cadence with the wall's pulse, and in his mind's eye he imagined a nimbus of pale yellow light surrounding the Rampart. A tendril of the light crept away from the stone, wrapping around him and enveloping him in its soft aura. He no longer felt the ground beneath his feet or heard the sounds of the night. It was just Tim, the wall, and the light.

The energy wants to leave the Rampart and move into me. Tim inhaled, focusing all his attention on the thriving current, pulling it toward him. The power flowed into his body, filling his very core with its quiet potency. Tim allowed the energy in as much as he could, until he hung suspended halfway between pleasure and pain. Then he exhaled, gently but forcefully releasing the power back into the wall.

Tim opened his eyes. The gentle shape of an archway etched itself into the wall in front of him, burning against the stone with a bright white light. Coruscating ripples of multihued color spread from his fingertips, each creating its own pool of radiance. Then came a sudden moment of intense, blinding radiance, and Tim cried out as the Rampart grew scalding hot. He fell away from the wall, landing on his back as his companions awoke. By the time Tim hit the ground, the others stood with swords in hands, looking about for the threat.

Instead they saw the scene unfolding before them. All four travelers stared in awe as the archway became more defined on the wall's surface. Each pool of light left by Tim's fingers rushed deep into the stone. There was a grinding noise, and the area inside the arch's outline shifted. The innermost portion formed itself into cubes, and the cubes folded in on themselves to form a tunnel. It started on the surface of the stones and burrowed in, traveling deeper into darkness. The travelers stepped forward and peered through the resulting doorway, watching with mouths agape as the Rampart opened to the world beyond.

The passage beckoned. Daniel raised his torch, and they peered into the tunnel, which stretched for about sixty feet before opening on the far side. They saw nothing beyond the passage other than a few vapors of mist. An entire new land waited for them, reaching forth with fingers of destiny.

"What happened?" Daniel asked Tim.

"I'm not sure," Tim said. It was the truth. "I was walking next to the wall, touching the stone, and suddenly this light appeared all around me. Something changed in the wall, but I don't know what."

The companions stood side by side in the morning light, gazing into the tunnel before them. Around them, the world hung still.

"Well," Rosalie said, "we can't turn away now, can we?"

"No," Tim said. "We can't."

Holding his torch to light the way, Tim took the lead. Behind him, the others shouldered their knapsacks to follow, entering the passage one at a time.

* * *

In the center of the tunnel, the travelers unknowingly crossed an invisible line. When they did so, an undetectable tremor started miles beneath the earth and raced across the expanse of the North.

Isanam, the malichon Overlord, standing with a detachment of his best troops at the fringe of the Fertile Lands, felt the tremor only as an uneasy chill that caused him to shudder.

Boblin Kule, making his way through the rise and fall of a treacherous valley, felt it as a sensation of strange and indescribable warmth spreading through him, though he could not explain what it was or from where it came.

Deep in the cells below the Fort of Pellen, bound in rusted shackles, Nazgar of the Kyrlod rested his head on the prison floor and gave a knowing smile.

The tremor continued traveling north. The stones of the Deathlands gave the barest of trembles, and then it struck the citadel, where Zadinn Kanas resided. The walls shuddered and creaked, and a violent wind rose in his throne room. Flames erupted from the vents in the floor, and noxious fumes stirred about. Zadinn felt the quake rumble around him, but sat unperturbed. He did not even flinch when the water in the Cauldron of Souls suddenly exploded skyward, or when Ragzan's image flickered into view. The dead prophet glared at him.

"The Warrior of Light has entered the land!"

Zadinn smiled. "Come to me, my enemy."

Nine

Tim was quite aware of the enormity of this situation. He and his family were traveling through a tunnel in the center of the Rampart—the giant, impassable wall that had stood for centuries. Countless explorers had attempted to achieve this very feat and failed. Even more daunting was the fact that he was crossing a line separating two worlds. North and South existed a mere hundred yards apart from each other, but because of this wall, they had developed as separate entities. And in just a few more paces, Tim and the others would bridge that gap.

Faint vapors at the end of the tunnel obscured the land beyond. Tim stayed in the lead, holding his torch to illuminate the way. The walls of the passage were bare and smooth, with no trace of grime or cobwebs. Even the tiniest of animals remained loath to enter this place. Within minutes, the travelers neared the end of the passageway. Tim felt the significance of the moment swell within him. What they were doing was irrevocable—it couldn't be undone. At the head of the group, Tim looked back at the others.

"Here goes," he said, taking a deep breath before stepping out of the tunnel to the other side of the Rampart. Rosalie followed him, Daniel came next, and Quentin arrived last. The mists gently touched Tim's face before dissipating, and he found himself standing at the summit of a small rise, gazing at the land before him.

Nighttime was fading into early dawn. In the east, the sun's first rays spread bloodred fingers across the horizon. The hill where they stood formed a gradual slope toward a gray terrain filled with dirt and stone. The valley was all sharp edges and angles, with a few sporadic patches of brown grass poking up between cracks. Save for a handful of stunted trees, the landscape remained bare and silent. A cold, harsh wind blew toward the travelers, bringing a faint, dusty scent along with it. Tim felt uneasy. The place was dead. Perhaps life had once thrived here, but it had withered.

"Well, this place ain't agreeable," Quentiin said. "D'ye suppose there's anythin' *alive* out there, or is it all like this?"

"Your villagers are certainly alive," Daniel said, pointing. Plenty of tracks covered the ground, leading straight north in an uninterrupted continuation of the trail from the southern side of the Rampart.

Rosalie crouched next to the markings, picking up some earth and crumbling it between her fingers, testing for freshness. "We're still quite a bit behind them," she said. "I don't doubt we're moving faster, but they had a head start and probably didn't spend an afternoon twiddling their thumbs on the southern side of the wall."

Tim knelt next to his mother. "I'd say our options are the same as before, except now we're on the other side of the wall. So do we keep going forward, or do we return for the King's soldiers?"

"I'd like to say we keep going forward," Daniel said, "but the farther we get from the King, the farther we are from any aid. Without knowing what we might come across out here, prudence dictates we return for assistance."

"Time dictates we stay on track," Quentiin grumbled.

"I know, friend," Daniel said, nodding, "but we didn't set out to take on all these creatures single-handedly. We set out to prove they came from across the wall, and we've done so. Four against forty will not end well."

"Ye speak truth, laddie," the dwerion replied. "But—"

He never finished the sentence. All around them, the ground started shaking violently. Caught off balance, Tim fell to his knees. His father shouted, but Tim could not make out the words. The wall groaned, and they watched as the stone around the tunnel shifted. The edges of the archway crept toward each other, the cubes of stone moving back into place. Tim pushed himself onto his feet and ran to the Rampart, but the tunnel shrank fast. He put his hands against the stone, trying to seek its power, but to no avail.

"Stop!" Tim shouted, pounding against the surface. Whether or not it heard his command, the wall ignored him. The Rampart shuddered as the stone locked back into place, sealing the opening with alarming finality. After only a few moments, no trace of the arch remained. The surface of the wall was again seamless stone. Tim slumped against the wall, panting in desperation.

The others ran up to the Rampart, also pushing against the spot where the arch had been, but nothing happened.

When the noise ended, the resulting silence felt very loud indeed. The four travelers looked at one another, trying to comprehend this turn of events.

Finally, Quentiin coughed. "Well, this makes the decision easier. Unless we get this karfin' passageway back open, we're stuck."

"What did you see on the other side, when the tunnel appeared the first time?" Daniel asked Tim.

Thinking about the power in the wall made Tim feel uneasy. For all he knew, it could have been his imagination and nothing more. There were certain preconceived notions regarding men who heard voices on the wind, and he didn't want to bring up that particular subject.

"I was thinking that if one couldn't go over or under the Rampart, then the only other way is to go through," Tim said. "I thought the creatures might have discovered a passageway, so I touched the wall to look for anything unusual. As I put my hands against the stone, the Rampart grew so hot it hurt. Then the light appeared, and the tunnel opened."

Daniel shook his head in confusion. He believed his son, but it didn't make the situation less bizarre. "We're dealing with a force we don't yet understand."

"Can you find the spot again?" Rosalie asked. "Was there anything special about it?"

Tim walked up to the Rampart and placed his palms on the stone. "It was here," he said, "but this place doesn't appear any different than the rest of the wall."

He closed his eyes and concentrated, seeking the power, but the tingling sensation was gone. The stone was cold and lifeless, just like the brick of an ordinary city wall. He opened his eyes and stepped back. "I'm sorry. I just don't know how it happened."

"There ain't anythin' to apologize fer, laddie," said Quentiin. "It ain't yer fault."

"I know," Tim conceded, "but it makes no sense."

"If I didn't know better," Rosalie added, "I'd say the Rampart has its own will."

"In which case," Daniel said, "the Rampart *wants* us on this side, and won't let us back through."

"Like I already said," Quentiin told them, "it makes the decision easier. We ain't goin' back anytime soon. I say we keep followin' the trail."

It was either that or sit at the base of the Rampart, so the travelers picked up their gear and set out across the harsh landscape. The wind picked up, cutting across them with its sharp edge. Tim shivered, for the air was uncomfortably cold for spring. Nothing stirred as they moved through the valley. Sharp inclines and declines filled the hilly terrain, making for hard going. The sky remained gray and overcast most of the morning, and the few patches of sunlight shone through provided little warmth.

This leg of their journey formed a sharp contrast to their trek through the Odow Forest. The Odow had streams, while the North had steep gullies and ravines. The Odow had songbirds and squirrels, while the North had ravens and crows. These birds, the only signs of wildlife the travelers saw, perched in the crooked stems of trees, taking flight whenever the four came near. In the Odow, they'd had little fear of their rations running out, but meals here would be slim.

As day progressed, the sun and warm temperatures rose higher. It didn't count as "comfortable," but it was better than the bite of early dawn. The stony ground made it harder to follow the trail but not impossible. Enough grassy patches and dirt-strewn areas remained to provide clues. But the going was tiring, every hill a struggle. The terrain was decidedly treacherous, with many steep gullies where one could easily twist a leg or break a neck. Despite frequent breaks, by the end of the day, they were worn out and sore.

When evening fell, the air grew frigid. They stopped, choosing a shallow cave in the side of a gully to make their camp. Tim went to a patch of gnarled trees to gather wood, but Daniel grabbed his arm and halted him. "I don't think we should make a fire," Daniel said. "I don't like the way this place feels. Let's not give away our presence so soon. We need to find out what else is out there."

So they ate their meal cold. Reality had a harsh bite—this journey had seemed like a grand time on the other side of the wall, but traveling wasn't all about moonlit nights, warm firesides, and full stomachs. The others had experienced it before, in the Alcatune Army, but to Tim the notion was quite new.

At the very least, the cave kept them out of the wind. *If this is what spring is like,* Tim wondered, *what is winter like?* As he prepared for sleep, he put as many extra coverings over his bedroll as possible.

That night, he dreamed he was standing next to the Rampart again, but this time the entire wall was ablaze with white light. He was meant to touch that power, to control it, but each time he stepped forward, the energy scalded him with its intensity. It was too much for one man to consume. He kept stepping away from the power and then toward it again, only to be driven back repeatedly by the heat. *There has to be a way.*

Still dreaming, Tim watched a shadow pass over the wall. It rippled through the bright light, staining it with evil. The darkness morphed into a hideous, serpentine creature before coiling around Tim. It squeezed, and Tim struggled uselessly. He could not escape, and he felt his life draining away. He reached toward the white light, knowing he could live if his fingertips touched it, but it was still too hot.

The morning dawned gray and cold. The surrounding countryside remained as empty as ever, and Tim wondered if the entire North was a hilly wasteland. The travelers set out once more, speaking little as they walked.

At noon they came to a large, rocky outcrop. Tim and Daniel climbed the hill for a better view of the land. The rise gave them a decent view for several leagues, and they noted that the hilly terrain ended in front of a line of dead and decaying trees on the northern horizon. They'd probably reach the deadened forest by nightfall. Tim didn't like the looks of the woods any more than he liked the jagged edges of the current landscape, but it wasn't like he had any choice in the matter.

"What now?" Tim asked.

Daniel had no chance to reply. A sudden clatter of pebbles caused both men to turn around. They had just enough time to recognize one of the now-familiar red-eyed creatures before it attacked. Tim shouted, reaching for his sword. As the creature jumped forward, Tim raised his blade to block the oncoming blow. Daniel unsheathed his sword, too, and another attacker materialized from behind a nearby rise of stone. The creatures' gray skin and drab armor made for good camouflage against the bleak landscape. Daniel stepped in to deflect the second attack, and the two fought savagely back and forth, the *clang* of their steel echoing loudly in the emptiness of the wasteland.

Tim landed on his back, his assailant on top. The creature pulled a knife from its belt, but Tim grabbed its wrist and kept the blade at bay. He pushed upward, forcing himself and his opponent into a roll. Their momentum caused both to tumble down a hillside, accompanied by a spray of soil and rocks. As they bounced across the sharp stones, Tim slammed the creature's wrist against the ground, trying to dislodge its knife. His attacker held onto the knife for quite a while, but eventually the creature succumbed to the pain and opened its fingers. The weapon fell free as both combatants landed at the base of the out-crop. This time Tim was on top. He delivered a sound punch to his attacker's face.

Tim stood and backed away from the creature. Sword in hand, he waited for the creature to rise, risking a glance toward Rosalie and Quentiin, only to see that they, too, were under attack from four more gray-skinned slave drivers. On the hillside, Daniel and the other creature still sparred over the rocky landscape.

Tim's nemesis stood, drawing his own sword. *I should have killed him when he was down.*

Tim faltered. Seeing this, his assailant took advantage of the opening and rushed in, swinging its sword straight at Tim's exposed neck. Tim blocked the creature's attack, narrowly saving his own life. He fought savagely, parrying his opponent's rapid thrusts, but even so the creature made it past his guard several times. Each time his attacker scored a new mark in Tim's flesh, Tim felt a bubble of fear rise from deep within his stomach. The sensation was entirely new to him. He'd sparred with a number of opponents in his time, but none of those battles had contained the raw, visceral danger Tim felt now. Street thugs in Vonku wanted to take one's money and dignity, but this creature wanted to take Tim's life.

Nearby, Daniel managed to gain the upper hand in his duel. He drove his sword into his opponent's stomach, and the slave driver's body fell to the ground with a solid *thump*. Two more red-eyed creatures immediately descended upon him, attacking from both sides, and Daniel spun in a circle to defend himself. He moved incredibly fast, blade flashing in a blur of motion, but one man could only do so much against two.

Tim narrowly ducked another blow, and the creature's sword *whisked* through the air above his head. The blade passed so close that Tim felt a whisper of air rush across his scalp. Tim pulled back, raised his blade again, and the fight resumed. As time passed, Tim's hands grew sweaty, his efforts more labored. The pommel of the sword started slipping in his grip.

Tim noticed how far the two of them had moved during the fight. They now stood near the center of the camp, along with the other combatants. Tim realized their attackers had deliberately choreographed their efforts to achieve this position. The creatures now surrounded the four travelers on all sides, enclosing them in a circle from which there was no escape.

* * *

Boblin Kule sat down on a boulder and let out a deep breath. He'd found a tiny stream of cold water, and this was a fine place to take his noon break. The going was tough in the Kavu Hills. He'd managed to work up a sweat regardless of the cool air and sharp wind. He wiped perspiration from his face, fumbling in his pocket for a few scraps of meat—all that remained from the squirrel he'd caught the previous morning.

Boblin had been traveling for the last two and a half days with only the clothes on his back. He'd gathered what little food he could find, not enough to fill his stomach but plenty to survive. He downed the strips of meat, wishing he had more. He'd have to hunt again before nightfall. When done eating, he knelt by the stream and drank the water, which had a refreshing bite.

I really hope that I am able to come up with a stalwart plan. I traveled south like the old man said, but so far all I've got to show for it is a deeper appreciation of the exotic scenery around here. Still, he'd take this over staying in the Fort with Elson and Kaiel. But he couldn't move south indefinitely. In just one more day, he'd come to the Barricade, and he had no idea what to do at that point. *That's the price I pay for listening to crazy old men.*

He stood back up, telling himself to be quiet. That was when he heard voices shouting and swords clashing.

Boblin tensed, hand instinctively reaching for his sword, which was *not* buckled at his waist. In the North the sounds of battle only meant one thing: malichons. He didn't know whom the malichons were fighting—the Frontier Patrol didn't scout nearly this far—but a malichon's enemies were Boblin's friends.

He pulled his cloak around his body and ran up a nearby hill, keeping low. Soldiers of the Patrol knew how to stay quiet and unseen, one of the few advantages they had over malichons. Boblin glided across the ground without disturbing a single pebble as he reached the rocky summit. Once there, he paused and peered over the edge into the valley.

Four travelers—three humans and a dwerion—were locked in combat with no less than six malichons. The strangers were clearly winded, barely holding their own against the enemy's superior numbers. All bore wounds.

A flood of questions poured into Boblin's mind. *Who are these people? Where did they come from? Three humans and a dwerion, by the Maker!* But he pushed the thoughts aside. No soldier of the Fort looked the other way when malichons were about.

Boblin pulled back down and moved to a different point on the hill, closer to a pair of malichons. He looked over the side again, noting that both of Zadinn's troops had their backs to him. *Excellent.*

Boblin vaulted over the side of the hill and threw himself into the fray.

* * *

Tim saw a flash of movement from the north. A young elion leaped down the hillside, landing in a graceful fighting stance behind one of the slave drivers. He moved so fast that Tim barely had time to register his presence. Armed with only his hands, the elion darted in low and fast, getting so close to his opponent that the creature did not have enough room to swing its sword. The tactic took real nerve, but it was effective.

The elion brought his opponent to the ground in less than a second. In one smooth movement, he swiped the creature's belt knife and stabbed it in the chest. Without pausing, the elion jerked the nestled blade free and faced the other direction, throwing the knife as he completed his turn. The blade flashed through the air and buried itself in the back of Rosalie's enemy. At the same time, Daniel disarmed and beheaded his own opponent. The creature's body tumbled, blood gushing from the stump of its neck.

Tim's assailant turned left and right, watching its comrades fall, but instead of backing down it redoubled its efforts. It snarled, launching an all-out attack on Tim and driving him away from the rest of the group.

The creature managed to unleash a ferocious onslaught without sacrificing one degree of skill. Tim's defenses became faster and more frantic to keep up with his opponent's renewed savagery.

What happened next was an accident more than anything, but it changed the course of the fight. The creature delivered a calculated strike at Tim's neck, but when Tim tried to block the blow, he missed the blade. The sword instead struck the creature's wrist, severing the limb in one clean sweep. Tim's opponent shrieked in pain and rage. Its lifeless hand hit the ground, fingers still wrapped about the sword.

Tim blinked, barely able to comprehend what had happened. A part of his mind managed to lock into focus, to stay in the fight, and he leveled the tip of his sword against the creature's neck. He could not, however, keep his hand from visibly trembling.

"Yield," he said, voice cracking with fear and tension.

Tim had every conceivable reason to believe his opponent would let it end here. The creature had lost both its weapon and the hand that held it; the fight was finished, and that should clearly be the end of things.

But it was not. Using its remaining hand to pull out a long knife, the slave driver knocked Tim's sword aside and jumped toward him. The knife's blade flashed in the cold sunlight, not nearly as powerful as a sword but every bit as deadly. A knife in the heart killed the same as any broadsword to the neck. Tim knocked the creature's blows aside and, in spite of his superior weapon, found himself on the defensive once more. Tim didn't understand. His opponent was finished. Why didn't it yield?

And then Tim understood. *He's not finished until I finish him.*

Aim for the chest.

Tim risked a glance toward his companions. All of their enemies were dead. The entire party, except for Tim, had killed their opponents. The creature continued its onslaught, stabbing and slashing with the knife, defiant to the last. If Tim were to take the creature's other hand, it would make no difference. The slave driver would continue to fight right up to the moment Tim ended its life.

Something deep within Tim flexed, buckled, and broke. Giving a cry that was part fear, part desperation, Tim knocked the creature's weapon to the side and stepped in close, driving his sword into the slave driver's chest. The blade made a crunching noise as it broke through mail, flesh, bone, and finally into his enemy's heart. Blood sprayed from the chest cavity and onto Tim's face, as the creature shrieked in agony. The slave driver gave a gurgling rasp before sliding off the end of Tim's blade and thudding to the ground.

Tim staggered back and dropped his stained blade. Blood covered him, all over his face, hands, and soul. It could never be wiped away. The deed was irrevocable. Tim stared at his father. Daniel Matthias returned the gaze and solemnly nodded. Tim knew he had done the right thing. It didn't stop him from feeling like he'd never be whole again.

"Welcome to the Northland," the elion said grimly.

Ten

Tim fell onto his knees and vomited. All he could think of was the sickening *crunch* his blade had made when he killed the creature. He could smell every drop of blood that had splashed on his body. It carried a nauseating, metallic scent. His world blurred in and out of focus, and he began shaking uncontrollably. As the tension left him like a rushing waterfall, leaving him cold and shivering, a hand touched his shoulder and he turned to see the elion who had joined the fight with them.

"Follow me," the newcomer said.

The elion couldn't have been any older than Tim himself, but his eyes spoke of a tough youth. A trace of sympathy on the elion's face said he knew what Tim was going through. He'd killed two of the creatures without a flicker of emotion, indicating that fighting wasn't an unusual experience for him, but it was also clear that he neither wished for such experiences nor enjoyed them.

Tim stood and wiped his mouth. He followed the elion up and out of the valley, then down the other side, where a cold stream trickled through the rocks.

"Here," his guide said, "you can clean yourself up." Tim rinsed out his mouth to get rid of the vile aftertaste of vomit. Then he plunged his hands into the water, splashing it over his face and chest, wiping away every drop of blood he could find. The memory would remain, but at least he could remove the physical stain.

The elion sat on a rock, watching Tim silently. At Rosalie's urging, Daniel lay next to the stream so she could tend to his wounds. While Rosalie rummaged through her bag for herbal salve, Quentiin tore strips from his shirt and dabbed them in the water. The dwerion placed the cloth over Daniel's gashes and rubbed the dirt free. Daniel winced but said nothing. Tim sat back as his shuddering subsided.

"When I first killed a malichon," the elion said, "I was twelve years old. I had nightmares for two weeks after."

Tim looked at him. "How old are you now?"

"Eighteen. Six years makes a difference." He paused. "It's easier to kill them now, but it isn't any more pleasant."

I could barely hold a sword when I was twelve. Imagine killing somebody. The thought made Tim want to vomit all over again.

"Is that what you call those things?" Rosalie asked. "Malichons?"

"You aren't from the North, are you?" the elion said.

"Well spotted, laddie," Quentiin growled. "Now answer the bloody question."

The elion stirred. "Pardon me. Yes, ma'am, they are malichons." He stood up. "My name is Boblin Kule. I'm from the Fort of Pellen."

"The fort of what?" Quentiin asked, arching an eyebrow.

"By the Maker, show some respect," Rosalie said to Quentiin. She turned back to Boblin and continued. "Forgive us, my friend. As you said, we aren't from the North."

"I know," Boblin replied. "So how did you get here?"

"I wish I could tell you," Rosalie said, "but we don't know. We live on the southern side of the Rampart."

"The Rampart?" Boblin asked.

"Aye, laddie," Quentiin said. "A great big wall, so high ye can't see the top. I thought ye might have noticed it by now."

"Ah," Boblin said. "We call it the Barricade." He chuckled and looked down. "Nobody's ever crossed the Barricade before. I shouldn't believe your claim so quickly. But...these days, I'm more willing to accept the incredible."

"Where is this Fort of yours?" Rosalie asked.

"It's two days' walk northwest," Boblin replied, "but it's not a very good place to be right now. I'd appreciate it if you took me to the Barricade. I'd like to see how you came across."

"That's not possible, my friend," Rosalie said. "Just over three days ago, those creatures—malichons—attacked our village. They took our friends captive, and we followed their trail to the Rampart. There was a tunnel in the wall, but it closed behind us after we came over here."

"It closed?" Boblin repeated.

"True enough," Quentiin said. "We ain't tryin' to put a charade on ye, laddie."

Boblin laughed—a dry, humorless, desperate, amused laugh. "This could have happened to somebody else," he said, "but no. It happened to me, of course. *Karf.* I found an abandoned camp yesterday, and it's likely the malichons made that camp. I'd put their number close to forty. Whether you like it or not, you won't be any good against that many. They're taking your friends to the Deathlands. I wouldn't recommend following them any further. Traveling to the Deathlands means…well, there's quicker ways to die, but it's definitely one way to go."

"Ye're speakin' sensibly, laddie," Quentiin agreed, "but I ain't just goin' to abandon my village. What d'ye suggest we do from here?"

"I'd suggest you find a way to turn back time so that you never came here," Boblin said. "But that would be a waste of effort, since I don't know any way to do it. Instead…" He stopped for a moment, clearly wrestling with several decisions. He picked up a rock and fidgeted with it while muttering under his breath. At last he dropped the stone and looked back up. "I'm taking you back to the Fort."

"I thought you said it wasn't safe there," Tim said.

Boblin looked at him. "You're in the North, mate. Nowhere's safe anymore."

*   *   *

Boblin wasn't entirely happy with his decision, but it was the best option. Besides, he told himself that going back to the Fort wasn't so dangerous. If he arrived at the gates in broad daylight, Elson and Kaiel would be powerless to do anything. They still had to act from the shadows, and the other elions would protect Boblin long enough for him to speak with Pellen. These travelers virtually guaranteed Boblin a private audience with the Fort's leader. Boblin would produce the visitors and request to speak to Pellen in person. Accusing Elson of treason would be outrageous, but now Boblin had evidence that Nazgar was telling the truth. He didn't know what had happened between Elson and the Kyrlod after he fled from the Fort, but he would bet Nazgar was still alive.

There was one thing he still hadn't told these people, though. He recalled his mysterious dream from the night Nazgar arrived. There had been three humans—two men, one woman—and one dwerion in the dream. And that just coincidentally happened to describe the group he now had with him.

"I hope your South is a more agreeable place than this," Boblin said to Tim. He hoped he could take the man's mind off killing the malichon.

Tim nodded. "You could say that indeed. Is the entire North like this?"

"The terrain changes depending on the location, but yes, it's more or less like this—not much alive. There's one spot near the Fort we call the Fertile Lands, and it's the only area that hasn't wasted away. You see, it wasn't always like this. Two centuries ago, this place was no doubt as prosperous and lively as your side of the Barricade."

"What happened?"

Boblin looked around to be sure the others were listening. They, too, would want to hear this. They'd be much better off the sooner they understood their circumstances.

"The North used to consist of three separate countries—Irsp, Ardrein, and Kaevun—all ruled by a single emperor. The last emperor was Ladu Jovun III, exactly two hundred years ago." He stopped and gave a humorless laugh. "You picked a good time to visit. This summer is an anniversary of sorts, though you'll forgive us if we don't celebrate it. Two centuries ago, a malichon army from the Western Desert invaded the old empire. According to legend, there is a city in the Western Desert, and it's the site of a portal between our world and Malath. The man leading the malichons called himself the Dark Lord Zadinn Kanas. He was a former Advocate from the Academy. Do you have Advocates in the South?"

The four travelers looked at him blankly.

"An Advocate is someone who can use the Lifesource—a sorcerer. You've encountered them before, right?"

A look passed between the members of the group. "They're a myth," Daniel said. "We've heard stories, but all who claim to use the Lifesource invariably end up exposed as charlatans."

"I'd have to see it to believe it," Quentiin added in his rumbling voice.

"You're the one who saw a tunnel appear in the middle of the Barricade, not me," Boblin told him. "Anyway, Zadinn Kanas *can* use the Lifesource. We had Advocates to defend us, but they could only do so much against such large numbers. The malichon army had nearly half a million troops when they first invaded. It isn't nearly that big anymore—perhaps fifty thousand remain—but they still control everything. After taking over the emperor's palace in the capital city of Galdon, Zadinn enslaved almost everybody.

"A small group of refugees, my ancestors, banded together and built the Fort of Pellen. Thus far, it's the only place that has managed to remain unscathed over the years. There aren't many of us, and to be honest that's probably the biggest reason we *are* still here. Zadinn doesn't find us worth the trouble. Also, the Fort's built into the side of a mountain, meaning we have defenses to hold out against a much larger force.

"Zadinn is the reason the land is dead. You say you have to see the Lifesource to believe it? It's at work all around you. Zadinn's dark magic has powerful effects on the world. At any rate, that's our history. Once we're at the Fort, there are elions who can explain matters to you in greater detail. I would do so myself, but I tended to fall asleep during history class."

It took the rest of the day to walk across the Kavu Hills. While they traveled, Boblin explained the geography of the North. They would reach a place called the Erdrar Forest at nightfall, and after that the Durin Plains, which were open and exposed like the Kavu Hills but flat. However, they would not have to cross the Plains. After a day and a half in the Erdrar, they could turn west toward the Kaltu Pass. From there it was another half-day's travel to the Fort of Pellen.

"Why did you tell us the Fort is dangerous?" Daniel asked.

Boblin sighed. The recent knowledge that the elions had been betrayed by one of their own was constantly on his mind. His thoughts did not make good traveling companions. His guilt vied with his anger, his anger vied with his sadness, and all three left him drained. He'd always viewed Elson as a kind elion and Tulak as an honorable soldier. If it had been a ruse, what was the point in trusting *anybody*? When good folk fell under the sway of Zadinn's influence, then the battle for survival in the North was truly lost.

He related his experiences to the travelers, taking no joy in recollecting his last night in the Fort. What he didn't mention was this apparent Warrior of Light. He had his own suspicions about that last bit, but for now he wasn't going to voice any of it. Boblin expected he'd see Nazgar again soon, and he would gladly leave such matters to the prophet. And, if Nazgar evidenced displeasure with Boblin's progress, then Boblin would politely tell him he could only do so much with an obscure instruction like *go south*.

They stopped at the edge of the Erdrar to make camp. Boblin leaned back against a rock and kicked his boots off, flexing his toes in relaxation.

"How dangerous is that place?" Tim asked Boblin, pointing toward the line of stunted trees that formed the Erdrar Forest's border.

"It's nowhere near as bad as its cousin," Boblin said.

Tim looked at him quizzically.

"There's another forest, but it's a long way from here," Boblin explained. "It's called the Korlan, and I wouldn't go through it unless I had no other choice. The Erdrar—well, it's not bad in the daylight. There's nothing there except jackrabbits and squirrels. I wouldn't go in there when the sun is down, though."

"Why not?" Tim asked. "What's in the Erdrar?"

In answer to Tim's question, a keening wail rose into the air. It sounded like some poor animal having its blood sucked out…slowly. The Southerners all turned and stared at the woods, faces pale.

"No idea," Boblin answered. "And I'm not too eager to find out."

"Should we move camp?" Daniel asked.

"No, we're better off here. If it wants to get at us, it will find us regardless of where we are. And, from right this spot, we've determined we can hear it— meaning if it chooses to attack, we'll at least have a warning, and I count that a good thing."

"An' if it *does* come fer us?" Quentiin asked.

Boblin shrugged. "Then I hope fighting the malichons didn't dull your swords too much."

The travelers fell silent, preparing for sleep—not that rest would come easily after the noise from the woods. Though Boblin had treated the matter nonchalantly, he was just as concerned as the others. He prayed the creature didn't come closer, but worrying about it was pointless. Either the creature would attack or it wouldn't. He had no power over that; he could only react to it. Stoicism was yet another form of survival in this place.

Daniel, Rosalie, and Quentiin climbed into their bedrolls, but Tim joined Boblin at the edge of the camp while the others fell asleep.

So this is the Warrior of Light? Boblin thought. *Probably.* His instincts said so. He felt sure Timothy Matthias was the young man from his dream, but Boblin would let Nazgar handle that matter. He definitely wasn't about to tell Tim about the Kyrlod's prophecies.

"Is it always like this?" Tim asked.

"Pretty much," Boblin answered. "You get used to it."

Tim shook his head. "It's hard to believe. One wall stands between our worlds, and yet I can't imagine any two places more different. I haven't been here long, but still—this place is completely different than the South. Here, there's an undercurrent of danger everywhere. I didn't even see those malichons until they attacked us. The same could happen again at any moment, couldn't it?"

"You learn fast," Boblin replied.

"And that forest in front of us—I'd think nothing of going into the Odow at night, but there? You heard that sound. Is anything safe here?"

"No."

Tim pointed south. "On the other side of that wall, people across the South are asleep right now—calm, comfortable. They have no idea what's over here."

"That could change," Boblin said. "If the malichons have found a way across, it won't be long before they take over the South. And if you think malichons are bad, their leader is worse. I'd kill myself before I came within a hundred leagues of Zadinn Kanas."

This was why Boblin had decided to stay quiet about this Warrior business. If Tim were the one Nazgar spoke of, then the Dark Lord would be very interested in him—and not in a good way. Zadinn would want to personally kill Tim, to eliminate any threat to his reign.

Boblin continued. "There's also Isanam, who commands Zadinn's army." No elion had ever fought the Overlord and lived. Even Commander Jend said running away was the best defense against Isanam.

"How many times have you fought malichons?" Tim asked.

"How many times have you become ill?" Boblin asked with a chuckle. "I could have counted if I wanted to, but it's not a pleasant experience, and I'd just as soon not keep track."

"You fought empty-handed," Tim said. "No weapon. That takes real nerve, I'd say."

Boblin suppressed a second chuckle. Fact was he'd almost soiled himself after the first malichon nearly took his head off, but such reactions were more common in battle than one might realize. "It's called ailar," Boblin said. "Hand-fighting."

Tim remained silent for a long minute before speaking again. "He wasn't going to stop, was he? If I didn't kill him, he'd have killed me."

"Yes," Boblin said, "the malichons know only death." *You must kill to survive.* The rule never changed.

After another period of silence Tim stood up. "I'll go get some rest. My watch is next."

Boblin waved him farewell and turned to face the night. Thankfully the Erdrar remained silent. The danger had probably passed, but Boblin didn't let that ease his vigil. One couldn't get too relaxed out here.

*   *   *

The following day, Boblin led the group into the emaciated forest. Vegetation grew only sparingly behind the veil of trees. Brown leaves littered the ground, so it was easy to see a good distance. So far, Boblin wasn't too worried. They'd have to survive for one night out here, but he knew of some higher ground where they could stay above the tree line and probably remain safe.

As they traveled, Tim told Boblin about his life in the South: growing up in the Royal City, his education under the public instructors, the family's subsequent move to the village of Kaldoon, and his intentions to become a soldier. He couldn't fathom the simple beauty of Tim's youth—living in a city without danger, able to choose his profession, and moving to a place of his family's choosing. Relocating outside of Vonku's protective walls seemed like a dangerous idea to Boblin, but Tim explained that living *in the city* could be more dangerous than living abroad, as thieves and brigands clung to the more populated areas. Boblin found the concept of men who stole for a living completely abominable. In the Fort, no one stole anything. They depended on one another too much. At least, that was the case before Elson's treachery.

In turn, Boblin told Tim about the Fort's history and also about Pellen Yuzhar. Boblin had yet to meet an elion he respected more than the ancient, white-haired leader of the Fort. He described the Frontier Patrol and Commander Jend Argul, the soldiers Hugo and Ken, and his comrades from youth—Celia and Wayne and Hedro.

Boblin was glad to find the higher ground before day turned to dark. It was a small foothill, deep within the Erdrar. From its summit, the travelers had a clear view of the surrounding area. Most of the creatures that lurked in the night preferred to stay underneath covering and were reluctant to venture beyond the trees, Boblin figured. He hoped he was right.

Fortunately, the night passed without incident, if not without noise. The keening wails returned, this time more prominent, and for one tense hour the travelers heard a group of creatures circling the base of the foothill. The companions stacked stones along the hillside to create a line of defense, but no attack came. The last few hours before dawn, the cries receded, and once the sun rose, the eyesore travelers packed their bags and set out.

At about midday, the foothills Boblin called home came into view. As they approached the steep cliffs, he formed a plan of action. He couldn't afford careless mistakes. Once Elson and Kaiel learned he had returned, they would do everything in their power to stop him from reaching his destination.

"I'd prefer to avoid any scouting members of the Patrol," Boblin said to the group. "We can't risk Elson and Kaiel learning of our arrival."

"How d'ye propose to avoid the scouts, laddie?" Quentiin asked gruffly. "I certainly hope the men defendin' yer Fort are skilled."

"They are," Boblin said, "but I know their routes and when they cover each area. It's never exactly the same from day to day, but I can make a good guess of where they'll be." Somehow, hiding from the Frontier Patrol made Boblin feel like *he* was the traitor.

Boblin led the travelers up into the rocky Pass. The going was tough at first, but grew easier once things leveled off. The wind, however, also became more pronounced. Boblin was accustomed to the cold, but his traveling companions winced at its brutality. Boblin kept to the outer edge of the hills, knowing the patrols made inner sweeps of the Pass before pushing outward.

They had gone perhaps a mile when Boblin spotted the first division of elions. Unsurprisingly it consisted of Hedro, Wayne, and a soldier named Vern. Boblin felt bad for Vern. He was a nice fellow, and doing duty with Hedro had to be irritating. Boblin led the others into a sheltered nook, where they remained very still. The scouts, however, never came closer than a hundred yards to their hiding place. All was going well so far.

The group came within sight of the Fort at midafternoon. This was good. Boblin did not want to risk approaching at nighttime, when Elson and Kaiel could get away with their treachery. Nazgar, after all, had arrived at night. In daylight, though, the traitors had no chance to touch Boblin or his companions. Despite the danger, Boblin felt a rush of gratitude upon seeing the Fort's walls. Inside those walls were his home, his sanctuary, his life. When at the Fort, he felt at peace. This place provided a small beacon of hope in the middle of the Dark Lord's night.

A beacon in danger of being snuffed out, he reminded himself. As they neared the Fort, hiding no longer served any purpose. Boblin saw a trio of guards on the parapets, and they could doubtless see him. He knew they had their longbows trained on the group, because the travelers were still too far away for the defenders to recognize him, but soon enough they would lower their weapons and raise the portcullis. Boblin led the others up the narrow stone path, while to their right, the sun began setting. The stones of the battlements glowed faintly in the late afternoon light. The wind had mercifully abated, and for a few brief moments, things felt peaceful.

It was too good to last, of course. An arrow *whizzed* from the battlements, landing just a few feet from Boblin. Taken aback, the young elion halted. A few more arrows followed, making a line in front of the group, and Boblin shouted in surprise. He hadn't expected them to break open wine caskets in celebration of his return, but neither had he anticipated hostility. Perhaps it was Turn-Boblin-into-a-Pincushion Day. Maybe there was even a feast involved.

The portcullis lifted with a foreboding *creak*, and three elions emerged: Jend, Hugo, and Ken. All three held their swords drawn. Boblin glanced at the battlements, realizing the sentinels had not yet lowered their longbows. *This reception is only getting better!*

"Drop your weapons," Jend said.

"What is this?" Daniel murmured.

"I don't know, but you should do as he says," Boblin replied. Ironically, he was the only one unarmed. Boblin raised his palms, showing that he was weaponless, and the others dropped their swords to the stony ground. Beside him, Quentiin grumbled in discontent.

"Pardon me," Boblin said to Jend. "Is there a misunderstanding of some sort?"

Hugo spat at Boblin's feet. "You've got a lot of nerve coming here, Kule."

"Stand down," Jend said to Hugo. "Show him the civility he did not show us."

"Was I supposed to leave a note before I left?" Boblin asked dryly. "I didn't mean to be impolite, but I was in a rush."

Hugo lunged toward Boblin, but Jend raised a hand and halted him. "We're escorting you back to the Fort, Kule," Jend said. "You can face your charges there. Run, and the archers will not hesitate to slay you. The same goes for your companions."

"Charges?" Boblin said as Hugo and Ken flanked the group. He didn't like where this was going. *If I didn't know any better, I'd say that Elson and Kaiel have been hard at work slandering my name.*

When they passed under the portcullis, Boblin saw the entire community waiting on the grass. They stood in a nearly perfect semicircle, some looking at him in shock, others in disgust, but the majority in rage. He spotted Celia first. He could not discern the look on her face. *Surprise? Confusion? Anger?*

His father stood there, too, alongside his mother. Mandar and Jess Kule looked upon their son, faces set as though Boblin had shamed them more than ever possible.

This is not good.

"You captured him." It was Hedro, back from patrol with Wayne and Vern.

"Aye," Ken said. "We did."

The only person Boblin did not see was Pellen, and then the crowd parted. Boblin expected to see the white-haired elion, but instead he saw Elson and Kaiel. Boblin's stomach turned.

"Boblin Kule," Elson said gravely. "You are charged with the murder of Pellen Yuzhar. Six nights ago, our friend and leader was pushed from his quarters in the Fort's central tower. On that night you disappeared. We found this among your possessions." He threw a sack at Boblin's feet, and a few gold coins tumbled out. "You will have a chance to speak for yourself on the morrow. For now, you and your companions are going to the dungeons." He turned and walked away in a swirl of robes.

Boblin collapsed. *They killed him. Those karfing sons of goats killed Pellen, and they framed me for it.* Kaiel approached him with a coil of rope, and a wave of rage seized Boblin. Elson was not strong enough to push Pellen from his window, so Kaiel must have been the murderer. Boblin twitched, nearly launching himself at the traitor, but half a dozen crossbows immediately pointed toward him. Any such action and today really *would* be remembered as Turn-Boblin-into-a-Pincushion Day. There probably wouldn't be a feast, though. Boblin seethed as Kaiel bound his hands.

"Kaiel?" Boblin said, mildly surprised by how calm his voice came out.

"Yes?" the elion replied, almost nonchalantly.

"I'm going to kill you," Boblin said matter-of-factly. It was not a mere threat. It was a promise. Kaiel had killed the best elion in the North.

Kaiel smiled, showing his teeth. "Say what you like, Kule. You'll be hanging from a gibbet by this time tomorrow."

Eleven

Neither Tim nor his companions resisted as the elions bound their hands. There was no point, not with all the armed soldiers standing guard. Besides, Tim was still numb with shock. Things had turned about so fast. Pellen—the person Boblin thought could help them—was dead, and the elions thought Boblin to blame. What would this mean for the travelers? Trial? Death?

Hugo, Ken, and Kaiel escorted the prisoners across the lawn toward the giant tower in the middle of the Fort. Everyone remained silent, except for Quentiin, who grumbled to their captors about making accusations without proof.

"Here's how it is," Ken said, interrupting the dwerion. "Someone murdered our leader, and it's quite clear Kule has been in the pay of Zadinn Kanas. Kule vanished the night of Pellen's death and returned with four strangers, so we must assume you are allied with him. You will have a chance to speak your piece on the morrow, and we'll give you a fair hearing. Until then, you're prisoners."

"You're bloody awful hosts," Quentiin shot back. "Kule told us things were bad on this side of the Barricade, but I didn't guess how bad." For all his bluster, Quentiin was quite clever. He'd chosen his words carefully, and his comment had the desired effect.

Ken stumbled. "*This* side of the Barricade?"

"Keep moving," Kaiel interrupted.

Ken continued forward, but Quentiin had achieved his goal. Ken would spread word of the dwerion's claim, generating interest and controversy among the captors and allowing the travelers time to exonerate themselves.

The tower bell tolled out the afternoon hour as they approached. In the lead, Ken opened the door to the tower's base floor. The room inside was nearly empty, its walls blank and gray. Rows of empty tables and benches filled the hall, but nothing else decorated the interior.

"Watch out for that table, Kaiel," Boblin said, pointing at a long counter at the far end of the room. "It's a nasty one to trip over." Kaiel gave the other elion a look of loathing but remained silent. Hugo and Ken ignored the comment.

At the other end of the room, a large, broad stairway led to the next level. At the base of the steps, an oak door was set into the wall. Ken opened it with a large iron key, the frame groaning in protest as he did so. Damp air wafted up from the tunnel as they started down a set of broad steps to a second door, this one made from stone, at the bottom. A foul-smelling puddle of green scum covered the floor. Ken used a different key to open this door, which revealed a long hallway with lines of prison cells on either side.

The elion took the prisoners all the way down the hall, where more green ooze dribbled across the ground. Eventually the passage opened into a larger chamber with shackles hanging from the walls. The room already held two occupants: a white-haired elion and an aging, bearded man. Grime covered their faces, and ragged clothes hung over their bodies.

Upon seeing the prisoners, Ken, still in the lead, halted in surprise. "Pellen?"

At that instant, a trio of malichons materialized from the shadows. Ken swore. He drew his sword, glancing back toward Kaiel and Hugo. But Kaiel had been waiting for this moment. The instant the malichons appeared, he'd unsheathed his sword and stepped behind Hugo. Before Hugo had a chance to react, Kaiel grabbed him from behind, placing the blade against Hugo's throat and grabbing his wrist, preventing the elion from drawing his weapon.

"Stay still," Kaiel said.

"What in the name of Malath is this?" Ken demanded, weapon in hand.

"The truth," Boblin said.

"Hand your sword over to the malichons," Kaiel ordered. "I would not like to cut your brother's throat."

"You need to protect Pellen," Hugo said urgently to Ken. Kaiel pushed his blade a little harder against Hugo's neck, silencing him.

"Encourage him," Kaiel said to the malichons.

A red-eyed creature stepped over to Pellen, kicking him onto his back and stepping on his chest. The malichon unsheathed its sword, placing its tip at Pellen's throat. "Disarm yourself and the old one lives," the malichon hissed.

Faced with threats to his brother and Pellen, Hugo slowly lowered his blade before stepping back and looking at Kaiel. "Apparently Boblin wasn't the one receiving Zadinn's money," he said.

"You are so easily manipulated," Kaiel replied, sneering. "Elson tells everyone Pellen has been murdered, his body mangled beyond recognition, and you believe him. Next time, ask for proof."

The malichons shackled the prisoners to the wall. Hugo and Ken glared at the malichons but reserved their most hateful looks for Kaiel. The traitor, however, ignored them.

"Interestin' politics ye have at this Fort," Quentiin said.

"Silence," a malichon said, kicking Quentiin in the ribs for emphasis.

Kaiel looked to his malichon comrades. "These two soldiers are Commander Jend Argul's best. With them down here, the battle will be over much more quickly."

"Then you have done well," a malichon replied. "Let us continue."

Kaiel faced the prisoners. "I am loath to leave such good friends in the dungeons, but I have a Fort to betray. If you will excuse me, I must open the doors for Isanam."

Hugo, Ken, and Boblin threw themselves against their chains. "Do you think Isanam will reward you for this?" Ken said. "He'll burn the Fort down and enslave you in the Pit! Malichons do not respect other races!"

Kaiel did not respond as he and the malichons left the dungeons. The captives slumped against the wall, contemplating how to free themselves from their predicament.

"Do not give up hope," Pellen Yuzhar said, breaking the stillness. His calm voice carried a soothing tone. "We still live, my friends. An hour ago you believed me dead, but I live. Who knows what may change in the next hour?"

After a long silence, Quentiin cleared his throat. "All well an' good," he said. "For once, though, would somebody tell us what in Malath is happenin'?"

The other prisoner, the bearded man who had not yet spoken, raised his voice. "Direct and to the point, my friend, and I agree. It is time you learn the truth of things. I am Nazgar of the Kyrlod, and it is I who sent Boblin Kule away the night Elson Tulak imprisoned me. I believed Boblin would find a way to bring hope to the Fort."

"Instead, he found a bunch o' wanderers from the South," Quentiin said. "Sorry to disappoint ye, laddie."

"Do not underestimate the power of serendipity, Quentiin Harggra," Nazgar replied. "You come from a land where the Dark Lord holds no sway. Do you not think such a place, by its mere existence, would bring hope to these people? At any rate, you deserve to know who you fight against. I don't have time to give a detailed account of our history, but I must tell you of the Advocates.

"Nearly a thousand years ago, a man named Isar Naxish discovered he could touch the Lifesource. The power nearly killed him, but he learned to harness it. Isar searched the land for others who also had this gift, and he gathered these people together in the capital city of Galdon. There he founded a place of learning, the Academy of Naxish. Those who graduated from the Academy were named Advocates of the Lifesource.

"The Academy prospered for hundreds of years. Imperial families came and went, but the Academy remained. Then, during the Jovun dynasty, a student named Zadinn Kanas arrived. When Isar first charted the methodologies of the Lifesource, he also unlocked a…darker…aspect of its nature. The Lifesource is like a giant lake fed by two rivers: the first river flows from the Maker in Harmea, but the second stems from the Demon Lord of Malath. The power itself is not corrupt, but the men who use it can make themselves so. Zadinn Kanas learned remarkably fast, but one night he vanished. Few men know what transpired next.

"There is a great expanse of desert to the west. Long ago, even before the founding of the Academy, the Demon Lord of Malath forged a portal between our world and his. He entered the world of mortals, manifesting as a human named Uklith and arriving at a city in the Western Desert. He conquered this place and enslaved its inhabitants. Uklith named the metropolis Agrazab, which translates from the ancient Homdee language into City of Darkness. Zadinn Kanas sought out the City in order to serve Uklith. In human form, the Demon Lord remained bound to the portal and therefore could not leave the boundaries of Agrazab. Consequently, he wanted a man to be his hand in this world. Zadinn Kanas decided to be that man.

"After reaching Agrazab, Zadinn learned the secrets of Malath. He was able to make a second portal to the underworld, but it was weak and temporary. Working with Uklith, Zadinn summoned the demons of Malath and clothed them in flesh. Those demons are malichons. Zadinn led this army back east, invading the North and overthrowing Emperor Ladu Jovun III." Nazgar folded his hands, and that was when Pellen Yuzhar spoke.

"The time has come for me to reveal matters that have long been secret between Nazgar and myself," the elion said, taking a deep breath. "I was twenty-one when the Invasion began."

Boblin's eyes widened. "But that was two hundred years ago!"

At that moment, Pellen Yuzhar looked older than ever. His face became a weary mask, bearing centuries of pain and loss. "I have been blessed with a long life and cursed with an unbearable responsibility. Know that it was my choice. I grew up in the country of Ardrein. When Zadinn's armies came out of the Western Desert, they fell upon the empire without warning. At first all I knew of the war were stories from refugees.

"As they told it, one night the guards on Irsp's western border saw a great cloud on the horizon. Initially they thought it was the thunderhead of a storm, but it was the first wave of Zadinn's army. Thousands of malichons hammered the frontier, laying waste to everything in their path. By the time word of the Invasion reached the emperor, Zadinn's armies were halfway to the capital. Ladu sent a messenger to the opposing forces, demanding to know their intentions, and the man returned with a simple message: *I am the Dark Lord Zadinn Kanas. There will be no bargaining. Surrender or die.*

"Emperor Ladu ordered every last soldier to the frontier, but the malichons cut them down. Every man in the empire, young or old, poor or rich, traveled to Galdon. We dropped our plowshares and took up swords. The emperor's own son went with us and fought at our side. Ladu always said that our land remained free as long as the people drew breath. But on that battlefield, I learned the meaning of despair. Nothing could stop this army. The Advocates, who normally took vows of peace, unleashed the full strength of the Lifesource in a desperate attempt to save the empire."

Pellen drew in a shuddering breath. "Watching the Advocates fight was terrible. The last week of battle, they used the Lifesource as a raw weapon, all elements of nature at their command. Sheets of lightning scored enemy ranks, and the very ground opened up beneath the malichons. Yet they still kept coming. For every one of theirs that perished, ten of ours did. Then Zadinn Kanas himself came onto the battlefield." A haunted look came into Pellen's eyes. "I've never seen a human wield such terrible power. It was like the Demon Lord himself had arrived. He burned our best Advocates to naught but cinders, until he came face to face with the head of the Academy, High Advocate Herdar Ashan.

"Herdar was our best hope. No enemy could touch the High Advocate. He alone slaughtered malichons by the dozens. And when he and Zadinn faced each other, the battlefield fell silent. The destruction wrought by the Advocates was terrible, but it was nothing compared to this. For over an hour, the skies rained fire while the earth shook around us. We could barely see the combatants amid flashing lights, and the thunder of the battle drowned out all other sounds. Yet when it was over, Herdar's body was a black corpse, burning on the ground.

"At that point, our hearts broke and we lost hope. I retreated with my battalion, fleeing south while Zadinn took Galdon without opposition. My crime was abandoning the empire when I could have fought for it. For this reason, the Kyrlod chose me to carry out a terrible task. I had been gravely wounded in the fighting, and one night an old man came to me in my tent. I thought he was a Healer—and he was, of a sort—but he was much more. This was the first time I met Nazgar of the Kyrlod.

"Nazgar said his brotherhood had selected me to be leader of the remaining free people. He accused me of failing my emperor and of answering to fear. On that night he granted me both a curse and blessing: to live far beyond the years allotted to a normal elion. It is my task to keep our people safe, to pass on knowledge of times before the Invasion, and to keep the light of hope alive.

"We hid in the Fertile Lands for ten years, while Zadinn solidified his hold on the rest of the North. After the land began decaying, we needed a place where we could defend ourselves, so I founded the Fort. I have waited these long years for Nazgar to return. Today, that time has come."

It was a lot of information to take in during one sitting. The historical account had taken nearly a half hour, but it had held Tim's attention. This land had both a great and terrible history—nothing anyone in the South could have fathomed. The urgency of the situation was clear.

"Good history lesson," Rosalie said, voicing everyone's thoughts. "But what do we do *now*?"

* * *

Elson Tulak sat in Pellen Yuzhar's quarters, looking out the window at the Fort of Pellen. Even though the elions were still distraught over their leader's apparent death, a sense of peace hung over the place. It was high time for that peace to be disturbed. No, not disturbed—*shattered.*

He bore no ill will toward his fellow elions. He did not hate them, and he was not looking for vengeance. His motives were far more basic. The situation in the North had grown very bleak, so he felt the Fort was bound to fall sooner or later. Why continue to resist Zadinn then? It would be more profitable to join him.

The elion turned from the window and lifted a lantern from the wall before leaving the room. He walked down the hallway until he arrived at a life-size portrait of the long-dead Emperor Ladu Jovun III. He slid the frame aside to reveal a tiny spiral stairway behind it. The passage had been built in the event of emergencies and crises, allowing one to move about unseen.

Elson traveled down the stairway, which took him to a tunnel beneath the tower proper. To the left, the tunnel led to the dungeons, and to the right, it stretched into darkness. Elson hung his lantern from a hook on the wall and waited. This tunnel, built to save the Fort—an avenue of escape, a last resort for the Fort's citizens—would instead bring its doom.

After a few minutes, another light appeared in the distance, and Elson's heart quickened. He'd dealt with ordinary malichons before, but someone else now approached. He wondered if the stories were true. He felt a cold breeze float down the corridor. Something stirred in the depths of the tunnels, and a pair of red eyes flickered in the dark. Elson swallowed as a cloaked figure emerged from the passage, gliding across the ground like a disembodied apparition. The air frosted around the newcomer's profile.

The elion lifted his lantern before the cloaked form of Isanam, the malichon Overlord. The lantern's meager glow revealed a skull-mask within the void of Isanam's hood. A double line of malichon troops, numbering perhaps eighty, stood behind Isanam.

A much larger force of enemy troops approached from the Kaltu Pass above, but Isanam planned to use this small group now in the passageway to infiltrate the Fort and take command of the gatehouse. The Fort's excellent defenses would do no good if the enemy commanded the portcullis.

"My lord," Elson said, trying to prevent his voice from trembling. He failed. Swearing allegiance to Zadinn's servants was much easier than meeting them in person. If Isanam were to be displeased, Elson would not be alive for long.

"Elson Tulak," Isanam replied in his grating voice. "I trust you have completed your duties."

"The entire community believes Pellen Yuzhar dead. He is in the dungeons, as my nephew Kaiel can show you. The Kyrlod is with him." Isanam's messengers had stressed the importance of keeping the prophet in chains. Nazgar's presence could ruin the whole ambush. "There is also a new development. Boblin Kule returned to the Fort today, with a group of Southerners."

"Interesting," Isanam said. "I trust they, too, are in the dungeons."

"Yes, my lord. The Fort is ready to fall." Elson gestured to the left. "This leads to the dungeon entrance. From there, a stairway will bring you to the main floor of the tower. It should not be hard for you to take the gatehouse, where you can open the doors for the rest of your troops."

"Well done, Tulak," Isanam said. "You shall be rewarded in a way that befits your position. You may have the honor of leading us into your Fort."

Elson smiled at the thought of striding into the open with a malichon army at his back. No more hiding. The looks on the elions' faces would be well worth remembering. *They brought this on themselves,* he thought. *Why resist the Dark Lord when an alliance is more profitable?* He turned to lead the malichons through the secret doorway, but as soon as he faced the other direction, a white-hot pain exploded in his back. His limbs spasmed as he fell onto his face.

Elson tried to move his arms but could not even twitch. The agony that overpowered him was even more unbearable because he could not respond to it. He felt Isanam's boot near his face, and the Overlord turned him over with a rough kick.

Isanam stood over Elson, casually holding his sword in one hand. "As promised, I present you with a reward befitting one of your race," Isanam said. "It is the only reward your kind has ever deserved. Know that you have earned my gratitude."

Elson Tulak realized, much too late, that Pellen Yuzhar had been right all along. The malichons did not bargain with other races. Isanam drove his sword into Elson's stomach. The pain was excruciating. Blinding light flashed in front of Elson's eyes, and he shrieked in spite of himself. The Overlord pulled his weapon back out, its black blade drenched in blood. Elson rolled his head back, watching through dimming eyes as Isanam turned away and the malichons passed by. He'd heard it took hours to die from a stomach wound. That in itself would be bad enough, but he soon realized it would get worse.

All elions grew up afraid of the dark, because the shadows of the night belonged to Zadinn Kanas. Some elions overcame this fear, and others did not. Elson Tulak was among the latter. He'd have picked almost any death over the one that now befell him. Because after the last malichon passed by, the light of Elson's torch slowly waned until it sputtered out completely.

And so Elson Tulak died alone. In the dark.

* * *

Tim heard footsteps in the corridor, and the prisoners went silent as two malichons entered the dungeon. The red-eyed creatures strode purposefully over to Pellen Yuzhar, ignoring the rest of the group. "Greetings," one said. "We received some special *permission*, from the Overlord himself."

Pellen looked up at them but said nothing.

"The two of us have been underneath the Fort for some time," the other malichon said. "We've been helping Elson Tulak with his…duties." It pulled a long knife from its belt, testing its thumb on the blade. "In either case, this is a roundabout way of saying the Overlord is rewarding us." The malichon suddenly and viciously kicked Pellen in the ribs. The old man fell over onto his pack, grunting in pain as he landed.

The other malichon stepped forward, bending over and seizing Pellen's tunic. It smashed the elion's face against the stony floor before jerking him back upright. Pellen faced them on his knees, blood trickling down his nose, the expression on his face never wavering. A surge of rage erupted inside Tim. Beside him, Boblin and the twins screamed curses at the two malichons, but Pellen's tormentors paid no heed.

One malichon licked its knife. "The Overlord said we must leave you alive for your journey north, but he also said that it did not matter if some pieces were missing."

"So be it," Pellen said. He spit in his captor's face.

The malichon turned to the side, wiping a hand across its face. When it turned back, its red eyes blazed with anger. "I'll have your tongue for that," it said, "but first we'll take your eyes." Its companion grabbed Pellen's white hair, jerking the elion's head backward. The Fort's leader did not struggle.

"Let him be!" Boblin shouted.

The malichon with the knife turned to the other prisoners, acknowledging them for the first time. "I don't believe you're in a position to stop us," it said. "Don't worry. I'll make sure everyone has a good view." It turned back toward Pellen, raising its knife again. The elion did not flinch, remaining serene even with blood on his face and a blade in front of his eyes.

"Do you want to hear me beg?" Pellen asked. "Because you will be sorely disappointed. You'll get no pleasure from this."

"Oh? I think you are very wrong." The malichon leveled his blade. Tim threw himself against his manacles. The malichon took its time, drawing the blade across Pellen's cheek before going near his eyes.

"I am still a free elion," Pellen said, blood streaming down his cheek.

"Not for long," the malichon said, placing the tip of its blade beneath Pellen's eye as it prepared to drive the point in.

The anger inside Tim came alive, transforming from emotion to raw energy. His body tingled all over. Tim roared, throwing himself against his chains again, and the power erupted from him. His shackles ripped free from the wall in an explosion of dust and stone. He landed on his knees, face to the ground.

The malichon with the knife stopped and stared at the young man. Tim met the creature's gaze. Then, without warning, the malichon shrieked as its body burst into black, oily flames. It fell, writhing in agony as its skin cracked and peeled.

The other malichon released Pellen's hair and backed away from the prisoner before turning to run. It did not make it far. Tim *thought* the flames at it, and the second malichon also caught fire. In less than a minute, only charred husks remained of their captors, and as soon as it began, it was over.

The power left Tim, and he collapsed. He forced himself into a sitting position. He stared at the charred corpses and shivered. *What did I just do?* He looked at the other prisoners. The four elions' eyes were wide, mouths slightly parted. Quentiin stared at the corpses, his jaw clenched in a firm line. Nazgar of the Kyrlod remained perfectly still, watching everybody and nobody, his face impassive.

Tim glanced at his father. Daniel met his son's gaze but said nothing, instead giving a firm nod of acknowledgment. Rosalie, the one closest to him, placed a hand on his arm. He turned toward her, looking into her gentle blue eyes.

"It's okay," she said.

Tim glanced at the corpses. *This makes three—one on the plains, two in the dungeon.* It would happen again, he realized. Three would become four, and four would become five. This was not the South, where he could knock Krinzen unconscious and walk away. Things had changed, and the rules were different. "I know," he said.

A massive gong sounded above their heads, breaking the silence. "It's begun," Hugo said.

Tim looked up the stairs. The gong sounded again, followed by shouts and cries. Running feet pounded against the ground, and soon the sharp, fresh *clang* of steel on steel filled the air. Glass shattered, fighters screamed, and bodies fell. Unseen but not unheard, the battle for the Fort had started in the tower above them.

"Quickly, Matthias," Hugo said. "The Fort must be saved."

Tim nodded, stepping away from his mother and toward the charred corpses of the malichons. One still held a knife clenched in its fist. Tim knelt next to the body, prying its blackened fingers open and pulling the blade free. Ashes flaked to the dungeon floor. One at a time, Tim used the knife to pick open the locks of the prisoners' chains. Once free, they stood in a tight circle and spoke quietly.

"We need weapons," Daniel said. Each dead malichon had a sword, but that only gave them two blades, hardly an arsenal.

"Can ye do that thing again?" Quentiin asked Tim.

"I don't know," Tim said. "It just…happened. Now it's gone." He pointed to Nazgar. "But you can, can't you?"

Nazgar shook his head briefly. "I can, but it would be unwise. Zadinn killed a Kyrlod not long ago, and he now has access to the man's mind. The Kyrlod are all connected in consciousness. If I use my powers, I will open my mind to Zadinn. The risk is far too great. I must only use the Lifesource as a last possible defense of our lives."

Hugo wrapped a chain around his fist and swung the manacled end through the air. "This will do just fine," he said. Ken nodded approvingly, preparing a makeshift mace of his own. Tim shrugged and picked up another pair of chains. He'd feel better with a sword, but Daniel and Quentiin had taken a blade apiece. The elions could hold their own unarmed, using the art of ailar. Of the Southerners in the group, Daniel and Quentiin were most skilled with swords.

The group left the dungeons, moving slowly as they approached the stairway leading aboveground. Tim trembled as he looked up the steps to the door at the top. When he crossed the line, it would happen. Three would become four. Four would become five. But he wasn't ready.

No, he *had* to be ready. The penalty was death. *Welcome to the Northland.* Tim's heart hammered.

"Ready?" Ken asked, taking the lead. "Then let's do this."

They charged up the steps.

Twelve

The comrades burst through the door leading out of the dungeon and found themselves in the midst of complete chaos. In front of them, elions and malichons battled in a sea of bodies and weaponry, both sides vying for control of the central tower. A similar battle took place on the outer lawn, and it didn't take much to ascertain that the elions were vastly outnumbered. Tim could only hope the gatehouse still held. If not, the Fort was most certainly doomed.

"Charge!" Hugo bellowed. The group surged forward, save for Tim. He froze, gripping his chain so hard his knuckles turned white. There was so much *death*. Everywhere he looked, he saw elions maimed and mauled by their opponents. Noise filled the air, weapons clashed, and combatants screamed in rage and pain. The room stank of blood, sweat, and fear. As Tim stood transfixed, his companions slammed into the enemy's flank.

Everything happened so fast. Hugo and Ken moved first, attacking a pair of malichons in tandem, catching the creatures between them and cutting them down. Farther down the line, a malichon struck at Daniel with a halberd, but Daniel dodged the blow and plunged his sword into the creature's guts. Beside Daniel, Rosalie attacked with her chain, wrapping the links around a malichon's neck and bearing it to the ground. Quentiin, positioned at the corner of the flanking maneuver, took on two malichons at once, rolling between them and slicing with his sword left and right as he let out a bellow of rage.

Tim breathed heavily, deep and fast, adrenaline surging through his veins so quickly he felt dizzy. Despite his best efforts to move, he remained locked in place, heart pounding against his chest, unable to take so much as a step forward. The world spun at a sluggish, surreal pace as combatants of all races vied back and forth in a grisly dance of death.

Then an elion's body flew past Tim, startling him into motion as the elion slammed against the stone wall in a splatter of blood and bone. As Tim jumped back from the gruesome scene, he found himself face to face with none other than Krinzen.

The malichon from the Odow Forest grinned, eyes narrowing as its lips pulled back from its teeth. "We meet again, boy," Krinzen said.

Luck, more than anything else, saved Tim. As Krinzen lunged forward with a blade, Tim jerked back, clumsily whirling his chain in defense, swinging the links upward and spinning to the side. Krinzen's blade sliced through empty air where Tim's chest had been, mere inches from skewering Tim against the nearest wall. Though Tim completely missed hitting Krinzen with his chain, when he pulled it back in for a second attempt, the links wrapped around Krinzen's sword. Krinzen's eyes widened in surprise as Tim reacted instantly, yanking down on the chain *hard*, for dear life, using the unexpected momentum to rip the sword from his enemy's grip.

Tim was barely aware of what happened next. He was an observer, outside his body, watching what followed. He threw his chain in a circle, slamming it into Krinzen's head and crushing the malichon's skull. A spray of blood struck Tim in the face as Krinzen's mangled corpse slumped.

Four.

Surrounded by malichons, Tim swung his makeshift mace in every possible direction, hoping to stay alive one moment to the next. He had no time to know whether or not his blows were successful. There were so many enemies and so few allies that he was constantly in motion, blocking sword thrusts from all directions, retaliating whenever possible, arms growing heavy as the nightmare of blood and violence continued.

His next close call came when a malichon emerged from the side and swung a sword toward his stomach, the blade coming so close that Tim felt a rush of air across his navel as he stepped backward. And then Tim tripped over a long wooden table, landing back-first on the countertop, exposed and undefended while the malichon brought its sword down in a second attack. Tim rolled to the side, and the malichon's sword landed in the table's surface, spraying fragments of wood in all directions. Without pause the malichon jerked its weapon from the tabletop and struck a third time. Tim held his chain crosswise, one end in each hand, raising the links just in time to stop the blade from splitting his face.

Then the malichon stiffened in front of him, and Tim saw the tip of another sword protruding from the creature's chest. His attacker gasped and fell to the side, revealing Boblin Kule, standing in the midst of the battle with weapon in hand.

"Come on!" Boblin said, reaching a hand to help Tim up. "We're moving to the stairs!" Behind Boblin, another elion held off the advancing enemy, fighting enemies from all directions.

"We have to move, Kule!" the other elion shouted. A second later, a malichon beheaded him.

Boblin swore, pushing Tim toward the stairway. "We'll die if we get trapped down here. Move up to the next level!"

"What then?" Tim asked.

"We'll decide when we get there," Boblin said. "Let's get to higher ground first, worry about tactics next. Move!"

Tim needed no further urging. He nodded and climbed to his feet, following Boblin up the stairs three at a time, the enemy hot on their heels.

* * *

On the far side of the room, Rosalie saw Tim and Boblin running up the broad stairway, putting distance between themselves and the malichon horde. *Good,* she said to herself. *At least some of them will make it out of here.*

Daniel stood twenty yards away, but it could have been a mile for all the enemies between him and his wife. At least Rosalie now had a sword she'd retrieved from a dead elion, hoping it would serve her better than it had its former owner.

The enemy troops had systematically separated the defenders into four groups, forcing them toward each side of the room to trap them against the walls. Rosalie swung her sword, downing an opponent with each stroke. Daniel had taught her well, but regardless of her skill, there were too many malichons and too few elions. Even as her attackers fell, more closed in, continuing their ceaseless assault.

One malichon struck with enough force to knock Rosalie's own sword out of her hand. Now weaponless, Rosalie dodged the next strike by ducking to the left. Instead of killing her, the blade only sliced her shoulder. She winced as blood flowed from the wound, but she did not have time to give in to the pain. She feinted right and then rolled backward, hitting the floor as the malichon's blade passed through the air above her head. She tilted her body, landing on her good shoulder and using the momentum to roll away from the creature's next attack. Her sword lay just a few feet away. Rosalie came back up in a crouch, lunging for the weapon, as the malichon stepped forward and delivered a kick to her ribs. The blow knocked her back several more feet, where she landed in a tumble, skidding across the tower floor, wounded and unarmed.

* * *

Tim gasped for breath as he ran. At least a dozen malichons raced up the steps behind him and Boblin, bristling with weaponry and very much intent on killing them.

"Do you have a plan for dealing with those malichons?" Tim asked.

"No," Boblin replied. Side by side they emerged onto the Floor of History, a room filled with relics inside glass cases. Massive tapestries hung from the walls, each a masterpiece, but Tim had no time to admire them. As soon as he reached the top of the steps, he blocked an attack from behind, raising his chain and knocking aside a malichon's sword. Tim's attacker stumbled backward, colliding with several others in a tangle of limbs.

Another malichon came at Tim from the side, grabbing his tunic and throwing him across the room. Tim slammed into a glass case, which shattered beneath his weight. As he rolled off the pedestal, he saw a sword, which had been in the case, now lying on the floor among fragments of broken glass. *At least something has finally gone right.* He dropped his chains and picked up the weapon. The sword was plain and unadorned except for a green pommel stone—a piece of junk, really, but Tim didn't care. It was a real weapon.

He came up, weapon in hand, and met the malichon blade to blade.

* * *

Sliding across the ground, Rosalie reached for her weapon, which lay just inches from her grasp. She strained to reach just a bit farther, her fingertips brushing the pommel. The malichon advanced slowly from behind her, savoring the moment. As Rosalie curled her fingers around the pommel, hoping to draw the hilt into her palm, she risked a glance toward the malichon. She wouldn't have enough time to—

Quentiin Harggra emerged from the mass of enemies, landing in front of Rosalie's prone form, baring his teeth and growling as he drove his sword into the surprised malichon's bowels. The malichon stumbled back, weakened but still able to raise its sword for one last attack. Quentiin, however, caught the malichon's wrist in hand, halting his opponent from further movement.

"Go back to Malath," Quentiin said, pulling his weapon free from the malichon's stomach before plunging it straight into the creature's heart.

Rosalie struggled to her feet, weapon back in hand, and smiled at the dwerion. "Thank you, friend."

"Nothin' to it," Quentiin replied with a lopsided, cocky grin. They charged into the fray where they stood with their backs to each other, dealing death to all who came close. All the same, Rosalie doubted it could last for long. The malichon troops continued pressing forward, pushing the defenders toward the wall once more. Though committed to drawing as much blood as possible, Rosalie simply did not know how much longer they could keep this up.

Quentiin knew it, too. He pointed. "See Daniel over there?" Rosalie's husband stood with Hugo and Ken, similarly fending off a fresh wave of enemies.

"Yes," Rosalie answered.

"Can ye make it to him?"

"Through *this*?" Daniel was still no more than twenty yards away, but plenty of malichons, and a whole lot of swords, stood between them.

"Don't worry about the malichons," Quentiin said, as if reading her thoughts. "They're about to become preoccupied."

Rosalie tensed. "Don't," she said, shaking her head. "You'll never last."

Quentiin ignored her. "Give my regards to Daniel and Tim, d'ye ken?"

Before she could stop him, Quentiin roared and charged into the malichons. The unexpected, half-mad onslaught caught the enemies by complete surprise. Quentiin moved between them, staying so close that they remained too entangled by their own comrades to effectively retaliate—for the moment at least.

Blast that stubborn dwerion. Well, she wasn't going to make his sacrifice meaningless. It was only a short distance to where Daniel stood his ground with the elion fighters. Rosalie turned and ran toward her husband, sword held over her head.

Behind her, Quentiin disappeared into the swarm.

* * *

Daniel Matthias knew the situation was rapidly becoming hopeless. The tower's main floor was a deathtrap. Hugo and Ken stood guard over Pellen and Nazgar as the small group made its way ever so slowly toward the exit doors. They *had* to get outside for any hope of surviving. The malichons had surrounded them in an efficient pincer maneuver. Daniel reflected that the rebels on the Icor Peninsula would have fallen before such deadly enemies in half the time it had taken King Aras's soldiers to quell the resistance. Of course, Daniel noted, an entire *empire* had fallen before a malichon army—a fact that did not bode well for this day's outcome.

In front of him, Daniel's opponent overextended on its next thrust. Daniel went for the opening, striking the malichon's wrist and cleaving the creature's hand straight off. Shrieking, the malichon fell, blood pooling across the floor to mingle with that of other combatants, as Daniel finished him with a thrust to the chest.

A *whisk* of air rushed past his ear, and Daniel stepped aside just in time to avoid a strike from another malichon's ax. The creature snarled and whirled its weapon for another attempt. Daniel turned around all the way, bringing up his sword to block the next blow, but he tripped on a corpse and fell. The malichon grinned, stepping forward to strike again…and lost its head to Rosalie Matthias, who'd leaped out from the surrounding battle.

"Do you *always* need someone guarding your back?" she asked, holding out a hand to her husband.

"It's good to see you too," Daniel said, taking her hand. "Where's Tim?"

"He went up the stairway with Boblin," she replied.

"Good." Tim would have a better chance if he could fight from higher ground. "And Quentiin?"

"Gone."

"Dead?"

"Not yet," Rosalie replied bitterly. "But perhaps soon."

* * *

Quentiin was far from dead. He ran straight through the malichons, scattering them in all directions. The creatures barely had time to regroup before he rounded on them. Battle fire raged through his veins, and he slew two malichons before the others even began to fight back. In spite of his initial success, Quentiin knew he was greatly outnumbered. However, he had not entered this fray with any intention of winning; he just wanted to divert the enemy from his friends. If the malichons remained focused on him, then Daniel, Rosalie, and the others had a chance to get away.

Quentiin leaped over a long countertop, putting the table between himself and his opponents. He pushed the table toward the oncoming malichons, forcing them to slow down. A long rope, attached to a chandelier overhead, hung in front of him. Knowing an opportunity when he saw one, Quentiin slashed the rope with his sword, and the gigantic ornament crashed down.

The malichons saw it too late. The chandelier made a beautiful explosion on impact, erupting into a thousand fragments as it crushed two malichons and drove glass spokes into the neck of a third.

Quentiin turned and found himself up against the stone wall yet again. The nearby door to the dungeons hung askew from one hinge. Quentiin grabbed the massive oak door and heaved, muscles bulging as he ripped it free and threw the door at his last two opponents, knocking both over.

Quentiin heard a snarl behind him and turned in surprise. Another contingent of malichons charged up the steps, arriving from the tunnel below. *Karf. Now they're gettin' in from underground!*

Neither Quentiin nor the approaching malichons had any room to swing swords in the tight space. Quentiin slammed his shoulder against the first malichon at the same time the malichon seized his neck. The malichon pulled Quentiin off balance and hurled him down into the shaft. Quentiin rolled down the steps and slammed into the stone floor. His head cracked against the stone, and he sank into oblivion.

* * *

Tim and the malichon fought across the floor, maneuvering between glass cases and wooden pedestals that surrounded them. Every so often, a stray blow struck a case so it shattered, and soon jagged shards of glass lay strewn across the floor alongside the overturned pedestals. One misstep could mean death for either combatant.

At the head of the stairs, more malichons surged forward onto the Floor of History. Boblin took up position behind a pedestal, pulling a crossbow from the wall and taking aim. He fired twice at the approaching troops, and as the first two malichons fell dead, the others retreated, taking cover behind the lip of the steps. The only sound in the room was the clash of steel as Tim and his opponent fought. A bead of perspiration dripped in front of Tim's eyes. Momentarily distracted, he blinked it away, and the malichon struck. Tim brought his sword down low and fast, deflecting the blow and slamming his shoulder into the malichon. As the creature fell against a glass case, Tim stabbed it in the heart, fingers shaking as he did so. *More blood, so much blood. Will it never end?*

Tim looked at Boblin. The elion wiped sweat from his face, too, holding the crossbow fixed in place, still aiming at the edge of the stairs as Tim joined him behind the pedestal. "How many arrows do you have?" Tim asked.

"I *had* two," Boblin replied.

"You're out, then?" Tim asked.

Boblin raised an eyebrow. "I see you're good with numbers."

Tim glanced at the malichons. "How long before they realize?"

"I don't plan on staying to find out. I was only covering you. Let's go."

Something dark *whizzed* through the air and Tim pulled back as a throwing star, tipped on all sides with wicked spokes, landed on the pedestal in front of his face.

Boblin eyed the star. "Interesting," he said. "*They're* short of arrows, too." He dropped the useless crossbow and seized either side of the wooden platform, hoisting it up into the air like a shield in front of them. "Walk backward," he ordered as another pair of jagged stars *thudded* into the pedestal.

At the head of the stairs, the malichons resumed their inexorable advance. Tim counted eight of them spreading evenly across the floor. He looked about for other defenses but saw nothing useful. Then, eyeing the wreckage, he had an idea. "Move toward the tapestry," he said to Boblin.

"Why?"

"I have an idea," Tim said.

Boblin complied, and they moved toward the wall, where a large tapestry hung. The tapestry displayed green pastures and thick woods, indicative of a time much more pleasant than the immediate moment.

Tim cut the tapestry from the wall, and it descended to the floor in waves of woven fabric. "Numbers time is over. Hand me the pedestal."

Boblin handed him the rectangular box, and Tim threw it into a pile of other broken cases the tapestry had covered. As soon as the two lowered their defenses, the malichons charged, but Tim moved quickly, seizing a torch from a wall sconce and tossing it on top of the tapestry. The threads blazed into fire, and the pedestals—all made of good, dry timber—flared up almost immediately, creating a blazing wall of flame between them and the malichons.

Boblin, taking the hint, turned and ran for the next flight of stairs, Tim right behind him. The fire would fend off the malichons for a short time, but not forever. Tim heard them stamping out the flames behind them. He and Boblin continued upward, floor after floor, while the malichons continued their pursuit. Tim and Boblin made a brief stand at each level, some lasting longer than others, but the malichons always pushed them up to the next level, until at last they came to the top floor, a long, narrow passage with a single room at the end.

"Well, this is it," Boblin said. "We've no other options from here."

Tim heard the malichons coming up the steps, boots pounding. "What now?" he asked.

Boblin pointed to the closed door. "Fortify the room and last as long as we can."

They ran to the end of the hallway and into the room. Boblin slammed the oak door shut and lowered a large beam across it to hold it in place.

"Where are we?" Tim asked, looking around. Dust and cupboards filled the room, and the only source of illumination came from a single large window, which provided a view of the ground far, far below. He noted a trapdoor in the ceiling, which undoubtedly led to the roof.

"This," Boblin said, "is a glorified, oversize attic. The trapdoor leads to the bell tower. We could go up there, but there's no point. All we could do is make music, and I'm not feeling artistic right now."

They dragged cupboards across the floor to further reinforce the door. Their best defense—their only defense—was to keep the malichons from coming in. If the troops got past the door, Tim and Boblin were surely dead. They could not fight a group of malichons while boxed in by four walls.

Boblin kicked the cabinets open, looking for something they could use to their advantage, but they had precious few options. At last Boblin found something and paused before turning back to Tim. "How good are you with heights?"

Tim peered out the window. They were at least two hundred feet in the air, and the fighters on the lawn looked like toy figures. He swallowed hard. "Not very good."

"Me neither," Boblin said, holding up a length of coiled rope. "Not good at all." Outside, the malichons snarled and pounded against the door, causing the frame to shake from blow after blow. Boblin pulled more rope from a box. Several large iron hooks were mixed in with the assorted junk. "We can attach a hook and throw the rope from here to the battlements. Then we can slide from the tower to the walls below." He looked at Tim. "Feel like facing your fears today?"

Tim looked out the window again. The plan was crazy, but—provided the grappling hooks held—it would work. He looked back to Boblin. "Are you serious about this?"

Boblin glanced at the door, which started to bend inward as the malichons beat against it. "Do you have a better idea?"

In response, Tim helped Boblin secure the hook. They had more than enough rope for the job, but it would be hard to attach the grappling hook to the far battlements.

Tim turned as a definitive *crack* sounded. A fissure appeared in the center of the door, and several large slivers of wood fell onto the ground. "Boblin—"

"I see it," Boblin replied, fastening the knot. "Done. Now just one more thing." He picked up another piece of rope, measured a few handspans, and cut a piece. He took the two ends and tied them together, forming a loop.

"We each get one of these," Boblin said. "We'll wrap them around the main line. See? It makes a loop you can hang onto as you slide down the line. Otherwise, you'll burn the skin right off your hands."

The doorframe shook, sending dust and splinters into the room. "Time to go," Boblin said, bringing the grappling hook to the window. Tim shattered the glass with his elbow and cleared the shards from the sill. Boblin hoisted the hook over the ledge, stopping its fall about halfway down and letting it rock like a pendulum. Using this momentum, Boblin swung the rope toward the far battlements, but the hook clattered ineffectually against the stones. The door shuddered again, and a fresh wave of cracks spider-webbed across its oaken face.

Boblin swung the rope again, to no effect. "Everything works on the third try," he said, leaning over and putting extra effort into the swing. The hook caught for a brief moment, but then fell free.

"I guess not," Tim said. The cracks in the door widened, and the cupboards barricading it budged forward. With the next blow, Tim saw the tip of an ax protrude from a fissure. The malichon on the other side pulled the ax free before slamming it against the door once more, and a wave of oak fragments cascaded into the room.

Tim turned from the window, facing the doorway with his sword in both hands, palms clammy with sweat. He had to be ready to fight as soon as the defenses failed. The beam holding the door closed tumbled free. They had only seconds left.

"Got it!" Boblin said exultantly.

The door exploded inward.

Thirteen

Tim had no time to hesitate. By the time he turned around, Boblin was already out the window. As malichons swarmed into the room, Tim put his sword behind his belt, grabbed the loop of rope with both hands and climbed atop the windowsill. His stomach lurched when he looked at the dizzying drop directly beneath him—two hundred feet to the ground—and the tiny figures fighting on it.

May the Maker help me.

He heard malichons converging behind him and knew it was now or never. Without so much as a glance backward, he gripped his hands around the loop, fitted it over the line, and vaulted off the ledge. Wind rushed past him as he slid down the line, which swayed in an appropriately terrifying fashion. He felt sure the rope would break at any moment, causing him to plummet to the lawn. Ahead of him, Boblin struck the battlements and tumbled unceremoniously onto the fortifications. Seconds later, Tim himself slammed into the stone parapet with jarring impact.

Boblin reached over the edge to help Tim up and onto the wall. Tim slumped against the bulwark, heart pounding, hands trembling, and an unusual juxtaposition of fear and relief surging through his body.

Boblin caught his own breath in staggered gasps. "Of all the karfing, sun-baked ideas...." he said. "But it worked. Ha!"

"I do not suggest we ever do it again," Tim replied.

"Noted," Boblin said. "But I make no promises."

At the tower window, two malichons leaped onto the rope. After only a brief hesitation, the malichons grasped the rope and descended hand over hand toward the parapet, moving quickly.

"Stubborn sons of goats," Tim said.

"Aye," Boblin concurred, "but I can give them something to think about." He unsheathed his sword and sliced the rope free from the parapet. All four malichons tumbled from the line, screaming all the way down.

"That takes care of that," Tim said.

"But not *that*." Boblin pointed toward the gatehouse, where a fierce battle raged between elions and malichons. "It's Kaiel. We can't let him take the gatehouse. If he does, he'll open the doors for the rest of the malichon army."

"Then let's do something about it," Tim said, unsheathing his sword as he spoke.

"Yes, indeed," Boblin replied. "Time to go."

Without another word, the two companions raced across the battlements and toward the raging battle. The gatehouse *had* to hold. If they lost this battle, the Fort died.

* * *

Celia and Ana had been standing atop the western battlements when the first sounds of battle came from the tower. Ana had hesitated, turning toward the center of the Fort as voices cried out and steel clashed, but Celia was already in motion.

"Malichons," Celia said, unsheathing her sword in a rasp of metal.

Ana turned back toward her, mouth half open, eyes wide. "How?"

"No idea," Celia responded. No time for wondering—the Fort was under attack, and that was all they needed to know. "Training is over, I'm afraid."

Ana responded perfectly. She smoothed her face over, blanking out all evidence of shock and surprise, and drew her own sword. "No time to lose, then."

Celia replied with a tight nod. She took off at a full run, Ana behind her, making for the north-facing battlement. The other guards moved into high alert, some shifting attention to the immediate threat inside the Fort, while many like Celia moved toward the presumed threat outside. Neither flank could go undefended, whether the enemy struck from within or without. Besides, the attack was likely coming from both.

Celia's mind raced as she ran. Something was wrong about all this, beside the obvious fact that a malichon assault was underway. The seeming conclusion was that the traitor Boblin Kule had returned to the Fort to orchestrate the attack. But he was *Boblin Kule*, whom Celia had known for as long as she could remember, and, while he could barely even look at her without turning redder than a crimsonflower in full bloom, he simply had too much honor to betray his own. But the evidence spoke otherwise, and Celia could not decide what to make of it.

However, that wasn't the most pressing issue at the moment. Regardless of how, or at whose hand, the Fort was under attack, and she had to defend it. Celia led Ana to the battlements above the gatehouse, where Kaiel Tulak stood looking toward the Kaltu Pass beyond.

"We're in trouble," Kaiel said to the two approaching elions. Celia followed his gaze to the north, her chest tightening. Scores of malichons marched rank and file toward the gate, armed with bristling weaponry, stamping against the ground in unison as they bared their sharp teeth and raised swords above their heads in a war chant.

On the other side of Kaiel, Illion Neldis approached the trio at a dead run, a quiver of arrows at his back and a longbow in his hands. Easily one of the Fort's best bowmen, Illion could drop an enemy from five hundred strides without breaking a sweat.

"We'll need all the archers we can get," Illion said. "Alcion, Tulak—both of you are better on the ground. Get in front of the gatehouse and defend it with everything you've got. If the malichons breach it, not even all the longbows in the Fort can help us."

"This must be Kule's work," Ana said. "He meant to get captured all along, so he could carry this out."

"If you see him, cut his throat," Illion said, notching the first arrow to his bow.

"With pleasure," Kaiel said.

One look at Kaiel's eyes said it all. Celia reacted instantly, pushing Ana to the side a second before Kaiel attacked. Kaiel struck in a circle, his sword flashing through the air and toward Celia's head. Celia ducked underneath the blow, bearing Ana to the ground and covering her in a protective maneuver.

"Illion!" Celia shouted. Kaiel completed his circle, driving his weapon deep into Illion's neck. Bright gouts of blood spurted in all directions as Illion dropped his bow and fell to the floor of the battlements, his sightless eyes wide in surprise.

"Boblin Kule was a decoy," Kaiel hissed. "Albeit a useful one."

Celia was already moving, rising into a crouch and lifting her sword, but she wasn't fast enough. Kaiel caught her in a turning sidekick, driving his boot into her gut and knocking her against a back wall. Kaiel looked from Celia to Ana, apparently deciding he could not take on both at once, and turned to jump over the battlements onto the roof of the gatehouse.

Ana seized Illion's bow and fitted an arrow to the string, drawing back and taking aim. Below them, Kaiel rolled off the gatehouse and to the ground below, running toward the tower. Ana released an arrow, but the shot went wide and landed in the ground in a quivering finish.

"Leave it," Celia said to her. "The other archers will be here soon enough. Illion was right—we need to get on the ground."

Following in the traitor's footsteps, Celia leaped off the battlements to the gatehouse roof, rolling forward with sword in hand. Ana followed, while in front of them a horde of malichons streamed forth from the central tower and into the Fort proper. On all sides, elions rushed to meet the new wave of attackers. Celia drew her sword and let loose a battle cry with Ana beside her, and rushed forward into the conflict.

* * *

Daniel Matthias cursed. Just when things were getting under control, everything went straight to Malath. For a brief time, Quentiin's diversion had allowed the elions to reorganize, clustering in a line of defense and pushing the malichons back. As the scattered elions came together, slowly but steadily gaining the upper hand, more malichons arrived from within the tunnels to renew the invasion with a vengeance. In moments, the elions had gone from an inkling of victory to again fighting with their backs against the wall.

Daniel stood beside Hugo, fending off attacks from all angles, while farther down the line, Rosalie and Ken held their own, protecting Pellen and Nazgar from the encroaching enemies. Dead bodies littered the ground, where puddles of blood oozed across the flagstones and cries of the wounded filled the air. Never before had Daniel felt so thoroughly trapped, not even during the darkest days on the Icor Peninsula. All around him, elion soldiers fell, their lives silenced at the bite of malichons' steel.

"How far is it to the door?" Daniel asked Hugo, his voice tense.

"Sixty feet," Hugo replied. "It's our only chance. If we remain here, we fall."

An elion tumbled in front of them, skull crushed, blood pouring down his face. Behind the fallen soldier, another elion took a sword through the chest and collapsed, lying atop a malichon's body as his weapon slipped free from lifeless fingers.

We are too few against too many. Daniel drew in a deep breath. "Get us to the door. I'll take the rear. This place is lost. Our only hope now is to hold the gatehouse." Hugo nodded, and Daniel steeled himself for the charge. Under ordinary circumstances, sixty feet did not seem far, but these were hardly ordinary circumstances. A flurry of swords, axes, and malichons blocked the way, so they would be lucky to make it through alive. But they had to try.

Just as Hugo prepared to dive into the seething mass of bodies and weaponry, the windows on every wall shattered, glass exploding and raining tiny fragments. Before Daniel fully registered what was happening, a volley of arrows *whizzed* into the room, striking the red-eyed malichons from all directions and bringing them down.

"Duck!" Hugo shouted, pushing Daniel to the floor as another hail of arrows passed above their heads. The main door burst open, and a score of elions surged into the room with weapons drawn, charging straight for the malichon flank. Daniel and Hugo climbed back to their feet, joining with Ken, Rosalie, and the rest in lending assistance to the newly arrived fighters. Bolstered by the arrival of the reinforcements, the elions of the Fort resumed the battle with a renewed sense of hope.

Before long the tide of battle turned, this time in the elions' favor, as they reclaimed the tower floor. As the fighting gradually ceased, the Fort's defenders barricaded the doors while archers took up defensive positions at the windows. Meanwhile, a new arrival from the reinforcements saluted Pellen.

"Sir," the elion said. "I am glad to see you well."

Pellen nodded at the newcomer. "Commander Jend, your timing is quite… appropriate. We owe you our lives."

"It is good to see everyone alive, sir. It's hard to believe the Tulaks betrayed us."

Pellen shook his head. "Corruption can exist beneath even the most perfect surfaces, Commander. Elson and Kaiel took advantage of our trust, and it will take time to come to terms with that. But for now, we fight on."

Jend looked toward the windows. "The situation is bleak, sir. The gatehouse did not hold, and we cannot stay here much longer." Daniel followed

Jend's gaze and saw malichons laying waste to all in their path. The blood-drenched tower floor seemed clean in comparison to the carnage outside.

Pellen took a deep breath. "Then our hand is forced. We have no choice but to sound the final retreat. Commander, you know what to do."

Jend nodded. "I understand, sir. We knew this day might come. The Fort lives in its citizens, not in its walls."

"Then we shall go and do our duty," Pellen acknowledged. "Signal the others, Commander."

"Aye, sir." Jend delivered a salute and then turned away, running up the stairs to the higher floors of the tower.

"What is he doing?" Daniel asked.

"This is our last weapon," Ken told him. "Some time back, we discovered a combination of herbs that has a profound effect when set on fire. We have filled the walls with lines made of this powder, so we could deliver a final blow to our enemies if absolutely necessary. It is time for us to go, Daniel Matthias. The Fort has little time left."

* * *

Commander Jend knew that Pellen was right, but it did not lessen the heaviness of his heart as he ran up the stairs. How had Tulak fooled them? The elion was out there right now, cutting down his fellows without a shred of remorse. If Jend ever saw Kaiel again, he'd show no mercy. Kaiel had murdered a fellow scout, used the body to fake Pellen Yuzhar's death, and then blamed it all on Boblin Kule. Jend had seen Boblin on the battlements, fighting to reclaim the gatehouse, at the same time Kaiel raised the portcullis for the enemy. It was difficult to believe any elion, let alone Tulak, would betray the Fort. In the future, everyone would divide time into two categories: before the fall of the Fort and after the fall of the Fort. Nothing would ever be the same.

Jend climbed level after level without slowing. As he ascended, he saw signs of the battle everywhere. The Floor of History was virtually unrecognizable, with bodies of elion and malichon alike lying among shattered glass, torn tapestries, and overturned pedestals. Small fires burned amid the wreckage, soot from the smoke blackening the walls above the smoldering flames. It appeared a small band of resistance had taken its battle upward, one level at a time, with the malichons following. Jend was not eager to discover the outcome of the conflict. He'd seen too many of his soldiers dead today, and he prayed to the Maker that this one battle had seen a better ending.

When he arrived at the top floor, he saw the door to the storage attic was shattered inward, hanging by a single hinge. The defenders had undoubtedly made their last stand here. Jend ran to the room, bracing himself for the inevitable sight of more dead elions.

Surprisingly, the room was empty. Cabinets lay on their sides, and fragments of wood littered the floor, but he saw neither blood nor bodies. The far window had been broken open, shards of glass lining the sill. Jend stepped up and looked out at the lawn below. Had the defenders climbed over the edge to safety? He acknowledged it was possible but unlikely, and unfortunately he had no time to investigate. His mission lay elsewhere.

Jend opened the trapdoor and climbed to the top floor, where the great bronze bell hung above the rafters. Jend grabbed the bell cord and paused for one long moment, gritting his teeth in reluctance. There was no going back from here. But the decision was made, and he had to do his duty. Closing his eyes in regret, Jend pulled down hard on the bell cord, sounding the alarm.

* * *

Tim and Boblin never made it to the gatehouse. As they ran toward the conflict, they saw Kaiel Tulak on the lawn, leading an arrowhead formation of malichons toward the embattled elion soldiers. In a final, vicious strike, Kaiel and the malichons pressed into the Fort's defenders, breaking through the lines by sheer weight of numbers. The elions, fighting to the bitter last, fell in swathes before the invading force. Moments later, the portcullis yawned open, slowly but surely, admitting a fresh horde of malichons into the Fort. And with that, the gatehouse had fallen.

Boblin swore, skidding to a halt on the battlements. "Fall back," he said. "We need to regroup at the tower." He and Tim turned around, doubling back the other direction, while the remaining elions on the lawn also retreated toward the tower.

Tim's stomach twisted. The last he had seen either Rosalie or Daniel, they had been in the tower, surrounded on all sides by malichons. He had no idea if either still lived, and could only hope he would see them again before this was all over. As he and Boblin rounded a corner, they stopped their run once more. A contingent of malichons had swarmed onto the rampart perhaps a hundred yards away, moving forward at a brisk march.

"That's not good," Tim said.

"No," Boblin concurred. "Back the other way." They turned around and saw yet another group of malichons, identical to the first, marching toward them from the opposite direction, effectively trapping Tim and Boblin between the two groups of advancing enemies.

"Tim?" Boblin asked.

"Yes?"

"Have you ever heard of Turn-Boblin-into-a-Pincushion Day?"

Tim glanced at him, bewildered. "What kind of a question is *that*?"

Boblin shook his head. "Never mind. I just thought I'd ask."

Above them, the bell at the top of the tower rang out, rising above the battle with vibrancy and clarity as it sounded. "Well," Tim said, "at least we'll know what time we died."

Boblin's brow furrowed. "No, that's not the hour. It's a message."

"What kind of message?"

Boblin ignored him, instead running toward the edge of the parapet and peering at the ground below. He nodded once to himself, curtly, and turned back toward Tim. "Walk that way," he said, pointing toward the first group of malichons.

Tim shrugged. "I suppose it's one or the other, right?"

"Fast," Boblin said, reaching out and pushing Tim forward. "Now stop!"

Tim halted. "Would you mind telling me what this is about?" He eyed the approaching malichons, now only half the distance away.

Boblin shook his head. "No time. Just brace yourself."

* * *

"We'll retreat through the tunnels," Pellen said. "They will lead us to the Kaltu Pass, and from there we can escape into the Fertile Lands."

"What about Tim?" Rosalie asked.

"Your son is alive," Commander Jend told them. He had returned from the bell tower and now organized his elions for retreat, directing them into flanking positions to guard the survivors on their way out of the Fort. "I saw him on the battlements with Kule. They'll hear the alarm, and Kule knows what to do."

Daniel put a hand on his wife's shoulder. He didn't like leaving Tim alone, but it was out of their hands. They were in the tunnels, and Tim was on the walls. Tim would have to take care of himself. The same held true for Quentiin. Nobody had seen the dwerion since he'd charged into the swarm of malichons. The tide of fighting had carried Quentiin elsewhere, as such things went. Right now, Daniel and Rosalie's mission was to help the elions escape to the Pass, and they would do it to the best of their ability.

As the elions filed down the passageway, traveling in even columns, Daniel took a rear position next to Hugo and Ken. The tunnels remained empty for now, but the malichons' pursuit could begin at any moment.

As Daniel stepped into the darkness, Jend Argul touched his arm. "You might be interested in seeing this," the Commander said. He stood before a massive door in the side of the tunnel, one with a rusted padlock across its handle. Jend produced a large key from his pocket, handing a torch to Daniel and fitting his key into the lock.

"Be careful with that in here," Jend said, gesturing to the torch, and Daniel held it back cautiously. As Jend pushed the door open, Daniel hesitantly looked inside. A single lone barrel sat in the center of the room with six black cords, reminiscent of steel yarn, leading out from its sides and trailing into thin holds in the walls. A seventh cord curled from the top of the barrel, hanging over the lip and dangling about halfway to the ground. Jend stepped into the center of the room, gesturing for Daniel to join him.

"There's no going back from here," the Commander said, taking the torch back from Daniel and touching the flames to the wire at the top of the barrel. The cord ignited with a brilliant, white light as Jend rushed Daniel out of the room, slamming the door shut behind them. Moments later, an explosion sounded on the other side of the door, rocking the oak frame with the force of its blast. A deafening silence followed, and Jend opened the door once more.

The keg was gone. Husks of wood lay scattered across the floor, and the six cords burned with fire that vanished into the walls, each thread traveling to a separate destination.

"We call these the breakpoints," Jend said. "Each breakpoint has a keg like this, and is connected to six more fire lines. Every time a breakpoint explodes, six more start."

"How bad will it be?" Daniel asked.

"We're below ground, so we aren't in danger. And every elion in the Fort knows where the breakpoints are, so they'll be safe. But the malichons are about to get a nasty surprise."

* * *

"Brace for what?" Tim asked.

He held his sword in sweaty palms, standing back-to-back with Boblin as they faced malichons advancing on both sides. Before Boblin could reply, the wall in front of Tim erupted in a shower of earth and stone, accompanied by a pillar of flame shooting skyward. Tim threw up a hand to shield his face as the concussion knocked him over.

The malichons, however, did not fare so well. As large chunks of the wall blew outward, a maelstrom of shrapnel engulfed the red-eyed creatures, the force of the blast throwing them from the edges of the battlements. Clusters of malichons clung to the parapet's edges, trying to pull themselves back to safety. Another segment of the wall detonated, throwing them to the ground below as rubble cascaded down.

Tim ducked, dodging sharp pieces of rock flying through the air, and Boblin pulled him beneath a lip of the parapet as a series of several more explosions rocked the battlements in quick succession. Boblin grabbed Tim's arm and pointed to a spot where the wall had shifted and formed a pile of rubble sloping all the way to the ground. Boblin leaned close to Tim's ear, yelling over the sounds of the explosions. "Let's go!"

Tim followed Boblin out and onto the broken wall, half running, half sliding down the treacherous wreckage and onto the ground. Malichons covered the stone hill, some crushed to death, others merely dazed, but they made no move toward Tim or Boblin. They were too busy trying to escape the destruction themselves to pay attention to fleeing enemy soldiers. Tim and Boblin hit the earth and took off running.

Behind them, the eruptions grew more frequent and more destructive, section after section of stone ramparts blowing skyward and coming back down in jagged fragments. Other elions fought free of the wreckage as well, all running away from the Fort and into the Kaltu Pass. Boblin took the lead, running northwest, and Tim followed him up, out, and away from the battle, while behind them the Fort of Pellen blasted itself to pieces.

* * *

Isanam's sword descended, cleaving a stray elion in two. The Overlord pulled his blade free from the tumbling body without giving it a second glance. A tingling, a warning, flashed in the back of his mind. His abilities in the Lifesource heightened his sense of awareness in battle. He could predict his opponents' moves, dividing the time between each parry and thrust into minute increments. This allowed him to determine when a threat approached from behind, as was the case now.

Isanam remained still as the elion crept up behind him. At the last moment, he stepped to the side and seized the elion by the neck without even looking back. He lifted the elion into the air and closed his fist in a crushing grip that caused the bones in the elion's neck to *crunch*. After the soldier's body fell limp, Isanam shoved the dead body out of the nearest window.

The Overlord turned away and continued forward. His malichons had secured the first two levels of the tower, and the elions were in full retreat. Zadinn would be quite pleased with this day's events.

Suddenly a deafening blast sounded across the entire Fort, causing the tower to shake beneath him. Isanam staggered, but only imperceptibly, and immediately regained his footing. As he turned to the window, he saw the battlements exploding outward, bodies of malichons flying in all directions, some whole, others in pieces. Stone wreckage cascaded down, crushing clusters of his troops and wounding many more. Isanam narrowed his eyes, admitting a grudging respect in spite of his anger. Pellen's people fought until their last breath, and they had managed to strike a spectacular final blow. It would not be enough though, and both sides knew it.

The tower shook again, much more violently this time, and Isanam felt a massive shock run through the floor, right before the boards beneath him opened up into a gaping maw. Isanam tumbled through the hole as debris cascaded down all around him. He quickly summoned the Lifesource, calling a shield of protective air into existence around his body, and when he struck the ground floor, it felt as light as a child's jump. Above him, the tower collapsed in a spectacular cloud of glass, wood, and stone.

Isanam strode through the carnage unmolested, wreckage glancing off his invisible shield. Around him malichons lay crushed and maimed by the catastrophe. He did not raise a hand to help any of them. If they could not save themselves, they were worthless to him.

After the dust settled, Isanam took charge and tallied his surviving forces. He'd attacked with three hundred malichons, but only one-third remained. Yes, the elions fought hard.

Of course, not all elions had escaped. The malichons did a fair job of taking captives, and on the morrow, Isanam would take the prisoners north to the Deathlands to serve their new master. He smiled beneath his mask. The Fort of Pellen had fallen at last.

"Sir," one of his captains said, approaching him from the rubble. "The resistance has ceased, and the remaining elions are retreating into the Kaltu Pass."

Isanam gave him a cold stare, and the captain faltered. "The *remaining* elions?"

"Yes, sir, a band of survivors fled from the Fort."

"Perhaps you do not understand," Isanam said. "The Fort of Pellen is to be destroyed. Utterly. Go into the Pass and track down these refugees. Kill or capture every last one. This victory is to be complete!"

Fourteen

Boblin and Tim ran a full mile before finally stopping to rest atop a plateau. In the distance behind them, smoke wafted up from the ruined battlements. Small figures scurried over the rubble as the malichons tried to gain some semblance of order. For the moment, nobody pursued the refugees, but Boblin knew this respite would not last long. He leaned against a flat rock, recovering his breath. Beside him, Tim did likewise.

As Boblin sat, chest rising and falling with deep gulps of air, the truth hit him. The Fort of Pellen was gone. The beacon of hope, which had survived long years under the Dark Lord's blight, was no more. Boblin stared at the remnants of his home, numb with shock and sorrow.

Ever since he had fled the Fort, he'd believed he could save his home. That belief drove him south toward the Barricade, following a prophet's voice in his head. He'd demonstrated pure faith, and his reward was the destruction of his home. *An elion can pray to the Maker all he wants, but it doesn't mean the prayer will be answered. The Maker blinks, and our lives pass by.*

Surely other refugees had made it out alive, so Boblin would prepare to lead Tim to the designated rendezvous point. Pellen had always known this day might come, so he'd put contingencies in place. But no amount of plans made coping with the current reality any easier. Boblin wondered who would be among the survivors. His parents could be dead in those ruins. Pellen Yuzhar might have been slain. That would be a cruel joke, for Pellen to be deemed dead and then discovered alive, only to die an hour later. It would fit with Boblin's pointless journey toward the Barricade. He'd discovered a group of Southerners and nothing more. It certainly hadn't saved anyone.

Boblin did not see any other elions nearby, but he knew anyone who had escaped would also head for the rendezvous. He looked at Tim, wondering how this second battle had treated him. Tim looked fairly well, given the circumstances, bearing nothing more than a few bruises and scrapes. "How are you doing?" Boblin asked.

"Terrible," Tim replied dryly, "but I'll survive."

"We need to make it out of the Pass," Boblin said. "There's a place we're supposed to go if the Fort is ever in danger. Once we've gathered there, we'll head to an outpost in the Fertile Lands. Maybe we'll be able to build something from this mess."

"Are *you* okay?" Tim asked.

Boblin sighed, feeling a pang of sorrow. "I should have known better," he said. "*We* should have known better. The Fort was too good to last. Zadinn let us gain a false sense of security, and then he took it from us."

"I didn't expect this when I crossed the Rampart," Tim said, shaking his head.

Boblin looked at him. "If you did, would you have come?"

Tim met his gaze. "We can't ever know that, can we?"

I suppose that wasn't a very tactful question, Boblin told himself. *One doesn't just run around and challenge a man's sense of bravery.* "Let's go. The sooner we get to the rendezvous, the better."

At that moment, pebbles clattered behind them and they both unsheathed their blades in a rasp of metal.

"I'm disappointed," Celia Alcion said, stepping from behind an outcrop. "You should have heard me approaching two minutes ago."

Boblin tried to think of something to say, but his mind was a vacant bubble. All he could muster was, "Sorry." It sounded idiotic the moment he said it.

Behind Celia, Ana Teldin stepped into view, joining Celia and the other two as they huddled in a circle in the relative shelter of the Pass. "We don't have much time," Ana said, looking over her shoulder. "The malichons are already organizing a pursuit."

Boblin looked at Celia. "The rendezvous point?"

Celia nodded. "We'll have to be quick."

"Were you at the gatehouse when it fell?" Boblin asked.

Celia nodded a second time. "Not many made it out. There were too many malichons."

Boblin stood and adjusted his sword so he could run quicker. "It's up to us to salvage what we can." He pointed west across the rise and fall of the Pass. "No time to lose."

"Boblin," Celia said. He turned back to her. "We were wrong. I'm sorry."

"Don't be," Boblin said. "I'd have thought the same as you."

Without another word, Boblin led the group in a run across the hills of the Pass, staying as low as possible. It would not do to give their presence away to the nearest malichon pursuit. The journey passed quickly. The companions had no trouble traversing the smooth corridors of the Pass.

Boblin and Celia knew these hills better than any malichon, and they used that knowledge to their advantage. Tim kept pace with them, but not without effort. The rendezvous point was located in a small clearing between two opposing foothills. A small cluster of elions was already there, waiting for other refugees to arrive. They came across a pair of scouts first—Wendel and Vern—before entering the clearing. Wendel waved the new arrivals through, remaining at his post while Boblin and the others passed into the clearing.

Boblin looked at the refugees. There were not many, but they'd have to be enough. He looked for his mother and father first. Mandar and Jess Kule stood in the middle of the cluster, near Pellen Yuzhar and Commander Jend. It was good to see their leader still lived. Hugo and Ken had done their jobs well. Boblin was happy to see even Hedro Desh, unscathed and no doubt quite impressed with himself and his recent prowess on the battlefield.

Ah, and there stood Daniel and Rosalie Matthias. Both had proved themselves quite capable in the fight, and it was good to see them unhurt, for their sake as well as Tim's. Upon seeing his parents, Tim left Boblin and joined them at the edge of the encampment.

Though there was much to be thankful for, a somber mood clouded the gathering. In all, only thirty-eight elions were present, with far too many faces unaccounted for. Save for this small group, they would have to presume everyone else was either dead or captured.

"Commander," Boblin said, walking over to Jend. "I saw malichons leaving the Fort. They could be here as soon as nightfall."

"Then we do not have much time to waste," Jend said. He walked over to consult Pellen. As the two conversed, Boblin spoke with his mother and father.

"Forgive us, son," Mandar Kule said. "We should not have turned on you as we did."

"No one should have to ask forgiveness from me," Boblin said to his father. "I would have trusted Elson and Kaiel Tulak to the day I died. People might say that Zadinn Kanas destroyed our Fort, but it isn't true. Our own brothers brought death upon us, and that's something we will never forget."

* * *

Tim embraced his parents, relieved. It had been a mere handful of hours since they had last seen one another, but it seemed like much longer.

"Well done," Daniel said to Tim. "You've made me proud."

Rosalie nodded her assent. "It's good to see you, son."

Their praise was the best of all; these two meant the world to him, and he admired each more than words could portray. From the moment they had separated in the Fort he'd felt a tightness in his chest, a knot of apprehension formed by the knowledge that either of his parents could be dead. "Did Quentiin make it out?" Tim asked.

"No," Daniel replied. "We didn't see him fall, though. He might still be alive, but he did not escape."

If he were still alive, the malichons would take him and enslave him in the Deathlands. If that were the case, the malichons had captured one more dwerion from Raldoon, just as they had destroyed the last free dwelling in the North. Zadinn Kanas extinguished hope one home at a time.

"Friends and allies," Pellen Yuzhar said, speaking above the refugees' voices. "We cannot tarry long. Isanam has sent pursuit after us, and they will not show mercy. We must ensure freedom continues to thrive, and to do so, we flee to the Fertile Lands. This is a difficult hour for everyone present, but we must stay strong. There will be time to grieve later. For now, it is time to live."

There was truth in Pellen's words. The elions organized into a defensive formation as they prepared to leave. If it came to battle, the malichons would pay with blood. Daniel and Tim joined Hugo and Ken, who took the rear guard.

The sun dipped beneath the western horizon as the group departed. Stars appeared above them, twinkling in a blanket of sky, and the rising moonlight tinged the ground with a pale hue. The shadows of night flowed across the unnatural landscape, lending a sense of unreality to the moment. As they ran, Tim felt like he was floating through a ghost world, an observer rather than a participant. If someone had told him a month ago that he'd be crawling through a wasteland of shattered rock, pursued by followers of a dark sorcerer, he'd have laughed in their faces. It showed just how little one understood the turns of fate. *Imagine what the next month will bring.*

As they crested the next rise, rocks slid down the hill to the east behind them. Tim turned and saw the first malichons coming into view. One of the malichon troops raised a crossbow and fired at the refugees. The bolt hissed through the air, narrowly missing Hugo and clattering against the stony ground. Hugo cursed, shouting for the exiles to hurry ahead. Cold fear stirred in Tim's stomach.

A hundred yards ahead of the fleeing group, the walls of the Pass grew narrow to the point that the elions in front had to split up and begin squeezing through a crevice in groups of three and four. This could prove to be their best chance of escape; if the group made it through the gap quickly enough, the rear guard could hold the gateway to the Pass while the refugees escaped into the Fertile Lands.

As they approached the gap's opening, the space around them grew tighter, and several more crossbow bolts fell upon them, striking an elion between the shoulders and dropping him. "Push through!" Ken called out, urging the refugees on as he, Hugo, Tim, and Daniel remained behind to guard the entrance to the crevice. "We can hold this," Ken said to Daniel. "You and your son should get to safety."

Daniel glanced at the approaching army. "I cannot allow you to remain here alone."

Things happened too quickly for Tim to fully comprehend what followed next. As soon as Daniel finished speaking, he grunted and staggered backward, the feathers of a crossbow bolt protruding from his stomach. Daniel grabbed the wall for purchase, holding himself up as he snapped the end of the arrow off. He dropped the broken shaft and unsheathed his sword.

"It's all changed now," Daniel said grimly, speaking through clenched teeth. On the hill below, the malichons were approaching. Tim joined his father, unsheathing his sword with trembling hands as he turned to face the enemy.

Daniel looked at Hugo and Ken. "I have to ask you a favor. It is not right of me, but it is all I have left. Tim needs to live. Please."

Hugo and Ken nodded gravely. Then, as one, they seized Tim, each taking an arm and pulling him back from the battle. "Your father's wound has changed matters," Ken said. "He must stay behind. We will take you to safety."

Tim threw himself against their grip. He knew what they were saying, but he didn't accept it. "No! We can't leave him here alone!"

"He won't be alone," Rosalie said, emerging from the crevice to stand by her husband's side. "I'll be with him the whole time."

Tim wouldn't accept this either. There had to be another way. He tried to pull away from the brothers. "You can't do this! I have to stay with you!"

"Timothy!" Daniel said. "The elions need every able-bodied man to help them in their cause. You have to go. *Now*."

Tim broke free from the brothers' grip and knelt by his father. "No," he replied.

"Timothy Matthias, you will do this because you must," Daniel said. "There are many things I would like to say to you, but a lifetime is not long enough for a father to tell his son the things he must. You will have to learn some on your own, as all men do."

He put a hand on Tim's shoulder. "Never back away from what you know is right. Do not hesitate to help someone in need. When you give your word, keep it. And when you find a woman who is worth committing your life to, treat her best of all, always and forever. If you do not do these things, you are not really a man. Now go."

Their eyes remained locked, even as Hugo and Ken once more dragged Tim up into the Pass. In the faint distance, someone screamed. It took Tim a moment to realize it was himself.

* * *

Daniel Matthias exhaled, closing his eyes and allowing himself to relax as the elions took Tim away. All would be well. Tim was safe and in good hands, while Rosalie, the truest companion in the world, stood beside him. After counting ten heartbeats, he opened his eyes and looked at the star-studded sky, thanking the Maker for what had been a long, blissful life.

"We had a good time, didn't we?" he said.

"Yes," Rosalie replied. "We did."

Putting aside the pain from the crossbow shaft in his ribs, Daniel struggled to his feet and embraced his wife. As they separated, both drew their weapons and stood side by side to face the malichon horde. For a moment, time slowed and Daniel allowed himself to smile. If there was a way to leave this world, this was it.

Nearly a hundred malichons descended upon the Kaltu Pass. Daniel and Rosalie stood in front of the opening of the crevice, the narrowing walls forcing the approaching malichons to attack in pairs of two. Husband and wife held a near-perfect formation, blades glinting off the moonlight, moves graceful but deliberate as they built a pile of dead to hinder the living troops behind. Daniel pulled his blade from each corpse in a spray of blood, while beside him, Rosalie did likewise, standing on the balls of her feet as she moved to the rhythm of battle.

Though the sounds of combat filled the air, to the defenders it seemed no more than a dull drone in the background. Daniel heard only the beat of his own heart and that of the woman next to him. Nothing else mattered, because nothing else existed. For a time, everything remained beautiful, and Daniel even entertained the illusion that they would survive this hour.

And then, as Rosalie felled a malichon that had come atop her, another volley of arrows flashed through the air and Daniel felt a sudden, hot flash of pain in his thigh. The immediacy of the pain pulled him from his dreamlike state and he stumbled to the side, clenching his teeth as he looked down at the bolt protruding from his leg. It hurt like Malath, but it was hardly a mortal matter.

Then another arrow struck Rosalie directly in the chest. Daniel looked up to see the force of the blow drive his wife against the wall of the Pass. Her mouth opened in a gasp, and a bright trickle of blood dribbled down her chin. *By the Maker, please make it not so.*

Daniel stepped toward Rosalie, but a malichon pushed between them Daniel didn't even calculate his next move. He just raised his sword high and brought it down into the malichon's skull. Blood and brains splattered the ground. Daniel felt a rush of air behind him and spun around, slashing another attacker across the chest.

He turned back to Rosalie. She sat against the ground, hand resting weakly on her sword's hilt. Blood now covered her chin and chest, and the light of pain burned in her blue eyes. But when she met his gaze, she smiled.

"Rosalie," Daniel said, a sob in his voice as he knelt beside her.

"What?" she said, and Daniel suddenly realized how much he loved the way her freckles stood out on her dimpled cheeks. "You didn't expect anything else, did you?"

Of course Daniel hadn't expected anything else. But whether he expected it or not, living it was something else entirely. "Not you," he said. "Not you. It should be me!"

Rosalie grunted and leaned forward, pushing past him and lifting her sword to strike at something behind him. Daniel heard the blade pierce chain mail and turned to see a malichon behind him, impaled on the point of Rosalie's blade. The lone troop had managed to climb its way past the dead bodies of its comrades to where husband and wife knelt. Daniel shoved the slain malichon away. The malichon fell back, its body adding to those blocking the Pass, but Daniel knew they had only a few moments before the others arrived.

"Just you?" Rosalie said. "I fear the Maker has called both our names, my love."

Tears stung Daniel's face as he grasped strands of her hair. Oh, how he loved that hair. The soft light of the moon made it glow with gossamer radiance. His hands trembled as he twirled coppery locks around his fingers.

He had wanted to die before her, to fall and save her. And yet, she was right. The Maker had called them both, so perhaps this way was more fitting. Had he died first, Rosalie would have had to face the horde without him by her side. Now, though, she had someone to hold her at the last, and Daniel could face his own cold, dark death alone. *Yes. Far more fitting, far more proper.*

"You are my world," he said.

She grabbed him with renewed energy and pulled him forward, pressing her lips against his. Daniel tried to hold on forever. He wanted it to be forever.

When she released him, she still had a smile. In spite of everything, she would not give that up. "Daniel," she said. "I love you…*always.*" Then she sagged over and the light went out of her eyes.

Daniel bowed his head, placing a hand on her eyelids to close them. Then he climbed back to his feet, turning around as a fresh group of malichons clambered into the Pass. He launched himself at the malichons with sword held high, blade flashing in all directions, as he cut malichons down left and right. For a second the attackers shied away, terrified by the fury of this solitary warrior.

But he was one, and they were many. Besides, he was wounded badly and faltering. As the malichons pushed further into the Pass, Daniel's foot snagged on a dead body and he stumbled, losing his guard for the briefest of moments—and that was all it took.

Something cold bit into Daniel's stomach, and the world around him went silent. He stared at the blade in his guts, feeling everything slow to microseconds. The malichon holding the hilt of the blade smiled and twisted its weapon. Daniel staggered, but he would not succumb easily. He pretended to fall and, at the last second, brought his sword back up to behead the malichon, leaving a corpse with blood spraying from the stump of its bare neck.

With the malichon's sword still in his stomach, Daniel swung at another attacker. The closer he came to death, the slower time moved. His enemies surrounded him in a circle, striking him one after another. Daniel saw their blades descending, moonlight flashing from the dark steel as a dozen sharp points pierced him and brought him to his knees. He managed to drag a malichon down with him, puncturing the creature's throat with his knife before falling away and rolling onto his back. He gazed up at the sky as the remaining malichons pushed past him into the crevice of the Pass. *There are still too many. They will still get through. The refugees will not survive. Tim will not survive.*

Daniel tried to rise once more, but a passing malichon kicked him back. From the corner of his eye, Daniel saw his own blood pooling across the ground. Then all sensation except sight ceased. Daniel could neither hear nor feel; he could only watch as the malichons continued to march by. But then, even as all other sensations faded, a new one began—something profound, entirely beyond anything he had ever experienced, an unfamiliar but soothing power that infused his veins and caused his entire body to tingle.

He knew without question this was the fabled Lifesource—that which gave birth to all things. When men died, they melded back into its embrace once more, and now, as Daniel Matthias lingered on the border between two worlds, for a few brief seconds he felt himself a part of both. His soul, trapped in his dying body, held the Lifesource.

It would not last for long, but it would be long enough. Daniel felt the power flow through him, and he reached out with it, delving deep into the earth below the walls of the Kaltu Pass.

The landscape trembled. The malichons in the Pass looked up as the cliffs quaked above them. Daniel seized the roots of the walls and *pushed* them together. The walls of the Kaltu Pass collapsed, stones tumbling down to bury the entire malichon pursuit. Daniel saw rocks descending upon him, filling his world with darkness, and knew he had succeeded. He was at peace.

Daniel's body was buried next to his wife under tons of stone, but his spirit soared up to the kingdom of Harmea, where good souls dwell in contentment for all eternity.

* * *

Tim felt the ground rumble as the Pass shuddered. Hugo and Ken held him by the arms, dragging him forward toward the rest of the refugees. As the earth shook, Tim pulled free from them. His mind knew what was happening—what had most likely already happened—but his heart did not want to accept it. As he turned around, the rumbling reached a crescendo, and the walls of the Kaltu Pass caved in. The sound of stones crashing down was deafening, but it seemed quiet compared to the blood rushing through his ears and the scream of his voice.

Daniel and Rosalie had been in the Pass. The Pass had collapsed. Daniel and Rosalie were dead. The thought seared Tim's mind, digging hooks into his brain, taunting him with all it implied. Dead meant *gone*. He would never again hear his father's voice, or feel the warmth of his mother's smile. He would not laugh with them, or sit by the fireside, or harvest the crops in the South. It was all gone, robbed from him in a few seconds.

Tim looked at the rest of the refugees. The elions stood dumbstruck, staring at the catastrophe behind them. Well, what had they expected when they left his parents back there? Had they thought Daniel and Rosalie would just kill a handful of malichons and catch up with them? Now here the elions stood, free from danger, but it felt so *wrong* to be safe when others had just died.

Tim put a hand on the pommel of his sword. He didn't have to stand here like the others. He didn't have to let his parents' sacrifice mean nothing. The malichons in the Pass might be dead, but many more still lived at the Fort of Pellen. Tim could go there now and seek vengeance. He turned toward the rubble in the Pass and the plains beyond. He would find the malichons and kill as many as he could, until his own life ended. He did not care. He just wanted to slaughter malichons until he could achieve the blissful rest his parents had just received.

"Matthias," Hugo said.

Tim stopped. Hugo had the audacity to speak to him *now*? If not for Hugo and Ken, Tim would still be with his mother and father. "Stay away from me," he said. "I have malichons to kill."

"This is not what they died for," Hugo replied.

"They died because *you* left them!"

"Many of us lost families today," Ken said, stepping to his brother's side.

"Leave me alone!" Tim said. "It's not your choice!" He felt a savage, potent anger growing inside of him, but that was good, that was okay, because anger gave him something to cling to. It grew like a living thing inside his body, coursing through his veins and pulsing with his heartbeat. The sword in his hands throbbed, and as Tim lifted it higher, he saw black fire—the same fire he'd used to kill the malichons in the Fort. It had returned, seeping from his fingertips and swirling around the blade.

Nazgar of the Kyrlod stepped forward. For a brief second, he looked at the sword with a gaze so piercing that Tim almost released the weapon. But when he looked at Tim, his face turned smooth and his eyes remained calm. "Stop," the ancient man said. "This is folly."

"I don't have time for your riddles," Tim replied. This conversation was over. These people could not stop him. They saw the blade afire, and it scared them.

"Your parents' death was necessary," the prophet said, and that *did* stop Tim.

He turned to the Kyrlod. "Necessary?" Tim raised his sword, and the power rose to a boiling crescendo. If he could use it to open the Rampart, if he could use it to kill malichons, then he could certainly use it against the Kyrlod. "Necessary? How in the name of Malath do you know what is necessary?"

"Cease!" Nazgar shouted. He seemed to grow in height, overshadowing the group. Tim had been in the act of moving forward, swinging his sword, but Nazgar's sudden change in demeanor made him falter.

"You know nothing of this world, young man!" Nazgar said. "But you *will* learn, all too soon, whether you wish to or not. You want to know of these powers you have? You want to know why you can touch the Lifesource? You are a figure of prophecy. You are the Warrior of Light, and you will not throw away your life tonight!"

Tim's anger returned. All the riddles and fragments meant nothing to him. He didn't care what schemes the Kyrlod had contrived. His parents were *dead*.

"I don't know what in Malath you are talking about," Tim said, gathering his energy to strike.

"I deny you," Nazgar said, pointing at him. Tim felt something slam into him, and all his powers vanished. In its wake he felt a weariness that consumed everything, weighing down on him like the collapsed walls of the Pass. Tim staggered as the world around him spun.

"Rest," Nazgar said, and Tim felt the weight press down even harder. He could not resist. He fell to the ground and passed out of consciousness.

Fifteen

Tim opened his eyes. He lay on his back on a cot inside a tent. Pale yellow sunlight seeped through the canvas fabric. The world around him was silent and dull. Everything felt dampened and surreal.

But reality was *exactly* the problem. The events of the prior evening returned to him in a rush, from Daniel and Rosalie's stand in the Pass to his encounter with Nazgar at the end. He closed his eyes again, willing it all away, praying to the Maker he had imagined it all. But he received no answer.

Tim sat up. Rosalie had told him of losing warriors in her care, Daniel of losing comrades on the battlefield, so he would know exactly what he was getting into when enlisting in the King's army in Vonku. He now found that, in spite of his previous assertions to the contrary, he'd been woefully unprepared.

"I lost my cousin when I was sixteen," Boblin Kule said. "Malichon ambush." The elion stood in the entryway to the tent, sunlight framing his tall frame. He stepped all the way inside, letting the flap fall closed behind him.

"Does it get any easier?" Tim asked.

Boblin shook his head. "No."

Tim appreciated the honesty. "I didn't think so," he said.

Boblin jerked his thumb toward the exterior of the tent, to the camp outside. "Out there, they'll tell you tomorrow will be better, and they're right, but you've still got to make it through today."

"Where's the Kyrlod?" Tim asked.

"There's something you need to understand about Nazgar," Boblin said. "I expect Kyrlod are as fallible as any of us, but Nazgar *saved* the Fort. Without him, we'd likely all be dead."

"I know," Tim replied. "I'd still like to see him."

Boblin paused before lifting the tent flap. He stepped outside, Tim behind him. The elion refugees had made camp in the Fertile Lands. They were deep in the woods, trees and vegetation surrounding them. They had cut back just enough brush to make a tiny clearing. A small number of tents, spaced at irregular intervals, comprised the tiny camp. Cooking fires were noticeably absent, doubtless to conceal their location from malichon pursuit.

"We built this place long ago," Boblin said as Tim stepped in front of him into the opening. "Two supply towers are a short distance to the west. Should the Fort ever fall, we knew we would need an outpost from which we could regroup. It might not look like much, but it will allow us to prepare for whatever comes next." He pointed to a tent that was slightly larger than the others and located in the center of the clearing. Hugo and Ken Rindar stood outside the tent, protecting the privacy of those within. "He's in there."

"Thank you," Tim replied. He strode across the camp, ignoring the glances the other elions sent his way. He'd rather they ignored him altogether, rather than making him feel like something between a stray dog to be pitied and a leper to be avoided.

"Matthias," Ken said as he approached.

"I'd like to speak with Nazgar," Tim said.

Ken nodded. "Of course." He and his twin stepped aside, letting Tim into the tent.

Nazgar of the Kyrlod and Pellen Yuzhar sat inside, each atop a stool on either side of a small table. Charts and documents were scattered across the tabletop, man and elion hunched over their work and speaking in low tones. Both turned toward Tim as he entered. The three formed a triangle, Nazgar and Pellen on either side of the base and Tim at the apex, looking at one another in silence.

"Necessary?" Tim asked.

Nazgar leaned back on his stool and faced Tim squarely. Tim's anger simmered at the Kyrlod's complacency. *How can he sit there, calm and collected, when so many have died?* Perhaps Nazgar didn't care. He was immortal and therefore untouchable.

"That's what you told me last night," Tim said. "After I watched them die."

"I know," Nazgar said. "I foresaw their deaths."

Rage coursed through Tim. He felt his latent powers return, strong but unpredictable, tingling in his fingertips and humming in his bones. He stepped forward. "You *foresaw* it? And yet you did nothing?"

"It is more complex than that," Nazgar replied.

"It seems fairly straightforward to me," Tim said.

"This war is not a forgiving one," Pellen Yuzhar said. "I don't expect that knowledge to return your parents to you or ease your pain. To expect that is to deny what makes you human. In his final hours, your father made a valiant choice, a choice that sets him apart from countless other men, and your mother joined him. Out of respect for them, for the choice they made, allow yourself to understand *why* they made it."

Tim's initial reaction was to snap. He knew Daniel and Rosalie Matthias far better than the others in this tent, and it was far from their place to educate the son on the nature of his parents. He *knew* Daniel, and they did not. He *knew* Rosalie, and they did not.

And yet—

Tim had seen elions slaughtered yesterday. He's seen their mangled bodies, their broken bones, and their bleeding faces. He'd watched them get stabbed, beheaded, and gutted. Every person in this camp had lost someone the day before. More than that, these elions lost brothers and sisters every day in this war they could not win. As Boblin said, it never got easier. He could not march in here and demand justice as if he were the only one suffering.

His loss was neither more nor less than anyone else's. That didn't stop it from cutting at him, from shredding his heart, but he could learn something from these people. He could learn how to endure.

"So tell me, then," Tim said. "Why did they make their choice?" The power inside him subsided slightly. It still roiled beneath the surface, prepared to spring forth, but it had lessened. Tim realized he had balled his hands into fists, and so he unclenched them, feeling his muscles gradually relax.

"If I may suggest," Pellen said, tone emphasizing he was choosing his words with great care, "You knew them best. Meaning—"

"That *I* should tell *you*," Tim said, noting Pellen had voiced Tim's own previous thoughts. Neither Pellen nor Nazgar responded, so Tim spoke again.

"I think we all know," he said. "The crossbow bolt that hit him was likely fatal anyway. So it simply didn't make sense for anyone else to stay behind." It was cold. Logical. It was also the truth.

"As Pellen noted," Nazgar said, "many men, even knowing the truth of their situation, would not have made the choice to stay. It is human instinct to survive, to hope for a way to avoid death. Daniel Matthias was a great man, Rosalie

Matthias a great woman. Every elion in this camp owes them their lives, and they all know it. So do not go forward with a heavy heart. Go forward knowing your mother and father proved themselves to be among the best mankind has to offer."

"So what now?" Tim asked.

"We must forge on," Nazgar said, "or else their deaths will have been in vain."

Pellen nodded toward the maps on the table. "That is the task in front of us."

"But now is not the time for that discussion," Nazgar said. "We will speak of it later. There are other matters to discuss, things that have gone unspoken until now."

There was no doubt in Tim's mind where this conversation was headed. One thing had brought him to this point, from the far side of the wall into the North, into the dungeons of the Fort and beyond.

The power. The Lifesource. He knew what it was the instant he used it to open the doorway in the Rampart. Now he wished he'd never heard of the Lifesource, much less touched it, because then they would still be on the south side of the Rampart, and his parents would be with him.

And everyone in the Fort of Pellen would be dead. Dwelling on what might have been served no purpose. "How does it work?" Tim asked.

"I will show you," Nazgar said, "tonight after the sun sets. For now, rest. Your body and soul have been sorely tested in the last twelve hours, but it is nothing compared to what now lies before you. So take your respite. Recuperate before we start down this road together."

He certainly knows how to lift a man's spirit. Without another word, Tim returned to his tent and slept. He was afraid of what might come next, but he'd face it anyway. Just as his parents had.

*   *   *

Tim sat up when Nazgar entered his tent. The Kyrlod stood in the entryway, a silhouette set against the moon beyond. The sounds of night floated through the open flap, a soft chorus of wildlife carried on the tail of a gentle breeze.

"It is time," Nazgar said. Tim stood and followed him outside. Most of the activity in the camp had died down, a string of short tents enveloped in the blanket of nightfall.

Nazgar led him across the camp, past a pair of sentries, and into the woods beyond. They walked into the depths of the Fertile Lands, surrounded by trees and muted moonlight.

After a hundred paces in, Tim caught sight of the two supply towers Boblin had mentioned. The short, squat buildings sat no more than ten feet off the ground and were made of rusted steel. They did not clear the treetops, serving the purpose of concealment. A ladder beneath the base of each tower allowed for entry and exit. Nazgar took Tim past the towers and into the woods beyond. He skirted around the edge of a small swamp and headed to a small knoll on the other side of the waters. Two oaks stood at the base of the hill, a pair of woodland sentinels guarding the gateway to another realm. The companions passed through the trees and arrived at the summit of the knoll, above a small valley of coniferous trees. Nazgar sat on a fallen white-bark, and Tim settled next to him.

They remained silent for at least ten minutes before Nazgar finally spoke. "The Kyrlod only see glimpses of the future," he said quietly. "Too much of it changes from moment to moment for us to be sure of what will happen. Man's free will bends events beyond our sight, and exceptionally willful men like you have futures that are uncertain at best. When I come across a man with a weak spirit, I see his fate with perfect clarity, because such a man does not have the strength to influence his own life—he lets others dictate it for him. Your destiny, Timothy Matthias, is almost incomprehensible. Though I can see stops along the road, I know nothing more. Your parents' fate was just as uncertain, and only during that final hour did the rest fall into place."

"How did that make it necessary?" Tim asked. "If willpower matters so much, why did they have to die?"

"It was the least destructive course," Nazgar said. "The future breaks down into thousands of fragments. Every chance event, such as that arrow that struck your father, creates several possible outcomes. Some possibilities are more likely than others, but all reveal themselves. Men have asked me to tell them what I see before, but I do not let them know. One can become obsessed with changing the visions and might unwittingly turn away from a better course of action. You must be free to choose, otherwise you make yourself a mere puppet of prophecy. Your father and mother *chose* to make that stand. If I had intervened, they would have acted on my visions instead of their own free will. However, the ability to make your own choices is the most precious thing a man has.

"I call the fragments of the future 'shadows.' The shadows I see clearest are those that are most likely. I saw more than one future at last night's crucial juncture. I saw a future in which Rosalie and Daniel did not make their stand and died anyway—along with you and everyone else, because there was no one to hold back the malichons."

"Was that other future a certain thing?" Tim asked. "The only other option?"

"Of course not," Nazgar said.

"So is it possible everyone could have lived last night?"

Nazgar looked at him sorrowfully. "You do not understand, Tim. Your parents *might* have held off all the malichons in the Pass and still survived. It was a possibility, because the number of futures is infinite. This is why it is useless to interfere with visions involving people of a strong spirit. They change the course of their destinies at every junction. The irony of the situation is incalculable. Because *I* see the future, I am rendered useless by the forces you call fate. Those who cannot see it, however, are free to shape it as they wish. Create your own destiny, Tim."

The two sat in silence for some time as Tim contemplated Nazgar's words. Suppose there *were* truth in what Nazgar said. Tim imagined the future, an intricate framework of patterns and people, branching in all directions in front of him, intersecting via meetings and chance occurrences, the effects of each encounter rippling far forward. Every time he made a choice, the possibilities shifted like a constantly changing puzzle, each interlocking piece creating a new set of images. Tim sat on one side of the chessboard and fate on the other, each move creating new possibilities.

"Then what do we do now?" Tim asked. "Boblin says there are thirty-six of us in the camp. How do we fight Zadinn?"

"Pellen Yuzhar was not the only one who fled from the battlefield all those years ago," Nazgar replied quietly. "Another group of soldiers escaped in a different direction, and while Pellen led his group south, the other went north. They had something precious with them, the last hope for the people of the Empire. His name was Prince Ladu Jovun IV, son of the emperor.

"Before the armies broke, the last of the surviving Advocates sealed Ladu in a block of sorcerous crystal, protecting the Prince's body from harm and putting him into a deep sleep. The remnants of Ladu's personal guard withdrew north to the Korlan Forest, which sits at the edge of the Northern Mountains. None have ever crossed the Mountains before—in this, the Mountains are very much like the Rampart. Before Ladu's time, many Emperors sent forces into the Mountains, hoping to discover what was on the other side, but none ever returned."

"Do you know what happened to them?" Tim asked.

Nazgar's face was impassive. "The Rampart and the Northern Mountains are akin in more ways than one. Both have effectively sealed Zadinn Kanas between them, preventing his corruption from seeping into the rest of the world. A forgotten sorcery enshrouds the peaks of the Mountains, and one can only pass through them with a talisman of protection. The magic preserving Ladu also gave the men guarding him the ability to cross the range. I sent them into the Mountains, and if the Maker wills it, they are somewhere on the other side."

"What's over there?" Tim asked.

"The prophetic texts speak of a mystical army that will come to the aid of those in need," Nazgar said. "But it is also written that they lie far beyond mankind's reach and that only the worthy may call them forth. They are the Army of Kah'lash. In the Ancient Tongue, Kah'lash means *Those Who Wait*. I have never been allowed into the Mountains, for I do not have the necessary protection, but now we turn our sights in that direction."

Tim shook his head. "Prophecies? Talismans? A mystical army? I don't know what any of this means, or if I should even believe you."

"Are you willing to follow me and find out for yourself?" Nazgar asked.

"You say we need a talisman of protection to enter these Mountains. What will keep us safe?"

"You will, Tim. The Warrior of Light is our talisman."

Tim sighed. This was the third time Nazgar had called him that name. "I've never even heard of the Warrior of Light. I don't think you picked the right man."

"I did not pick you, Tim. You just *are*."

"You tell me my parents had to die; you tell me there's a magical army on the other side of these Mountains; you tell me I am the Warrior of Light. What will you tell me next?"

"That it will ultimately be you, alone, who must face Zadinn."

"I thought you couldn't see my future."

"I said your destiny is *almost* incomprehensible to me. That does not mean I can't see anything. You do not have to be the Warrior or face Zadinn, but you can choose to be the man who does these things, both of them, and even more."

Tim snorted. "How long before I have to choose?"

"It's the choice that matters. The time you spend before the moment of the choosing means nothing."

Though the situation was more than serious, Tim couldn't help but chuckle wryly. "You're not one for clarity, are you?"

"The matters I deal with are rarely straightforward," Nazgar explained, "but if you wish to make a choice of a simpler nature, I ask you one thing. Do you want to know how to harness this power of yours?"

"Is it really the Lifesource?" Tim asked.

"You've known this to be true ever since you opened the doorway in the Rampart," Nazgar answered, once again echoing Tim's earlier thoughts.

"I feel like I brought this all down upon us," Tim said.

"You did not," Nazgar said. "That blame lies with Zadinn Kanas."

Tim knew hindsight mattered little. There was no going back from here. "Does Zadinn believe I am the Warrior?" Tim asked.

"Yes, he does," Nazgar said.

"And does he know I'm here?"

Nazgar nodded. "He's known it ever since you crossed the Rampart."

Tim massaged his temples and sighed. "It doesn't matter if I believe or not, does it? If he believes, he'll want to kill me. If I want to live, I have to learn."

Nazgar's face was a blank, unreadable slate. "I agree. But it is still *your* choice."

Tim looked at the Kyrlod. "Then I choose to learn."

"Very well." Nazgar stood up. "Let us begin. You've already used the Lifesource, albeit poorly and with lack of control." He snapped his fingers, and a tiny blue flame danced above his fist. He flicked his hand and the fire streaked in front of Tim's face, stopping short of his nose and bursting into shattered fragments of sparkling light. "We of the Kyrlod also possess this power. For the moment it is not safe for me to draw upon it to any great extent, but *you* are another matter. You are the Warrior of Light, and not even the Dark Lord can penetrate your thoughts. He will feel your power and know it grows, but your mind will remain sheltered. In the days of the Academy, students spent long weeks in meditation, learning to touch the Lifesource and using their bodies as its vessel. It took years to reach the rank of Advocate. However, we do not have the luxury of time. In one week you must learn what initiates learned in one year.

"The Lifesource exists inside of you. To reach it, you must clear your thoughts and find it. Distraction will be your downfall. Close your eyes."

Feeling like he was in a seer's booth at a village festival, Tim did as he was bid. *How am I supposed to completely empty my head? It's impossible.*

"Imagine a room filled with clutter," Nazgar's voice said, floating in on the night air. "Slowly and deliberately empty out everything in the room, until nothing is left but a thin veil on the far side."

In his mind's eye, Tim envisioned the cottage he and Daniel had built in the depths of the Odow Forest. The building was gone, destroyed by malichon invaders. Tim would never return to this place. At first, it had seemed a simple matter of time and effort to rebuild their home, but that could never happen now. Daniel and Rosalie were dead, and he was trapped in the North. *I am not doing very well at clearing my thoughts.*

Tim slowly emptied his home, erasing the table, chairs, and cupboards from his memory. He tossed away the trappings of his former life—the markings of a happier time. They were gone, committed to dust and rubble, and all that remained was a thin veil covering the fireplace.

He could not hold the vision. Daniel's well-constructed shelves kept returning to scar the scene, his bed kept flashing back into existence, and the dining table returned. He growled in frustration and opened his eyes.

"You're concentrating too hard," Nazgar admonished. "Clarity of mind is not achieved by struggling with detail. You must relax and let the room empty itself."

"How long were my eyes closed?" Tim asked.

"About ten minutes."

Tim started. "It felt like ten seconds."

"You lose time when you slip into meditation," Nazgar said. "That, at least, is a good sign. Do not become overly frustrated tonight. No Advocate ever touched the Lifesource in one day."

That last statement calmed Tim. This wasn't a matter that could be pushed. He settled into a sitting position, and this time he let the memory shape itself. He slowly exhaled, loosening his muscles.

"Is the room empty?" Nazgar asked.

"Yes," Tim said, his voice sounding distant.

"Walk toward the veil. Do not rush. Move as slowly as you need."

Tim did as he was told, floating through the empty room while the veil fluttered tantalizingly. He did not know where the breeze came from, and he did not care. "I'm there," a voice said. He supposed it was his.

"Carefully and gently pull the shroud back. If you do this too forcefully, you will be overwhelmed."

Tim reached out, and his fingers touched the fluttering curtain. The fabric was thin and transparent. He could *almost* see what was on the other side—

And then everything disintegrated. Tim opened his eyes. "I was close that time," he said.

Nazgar looked at him in awe. "Very close," the Kyrlod said. "To have gone that far on only your second attempt—your abilities will be enormous, perhaps even terrifying."

They tried the process three more times, taking up the space of an hour. To Tim the experience felt like being a thirsty man with a cup of water at his lips. All he had to do was tilt the cup to drink a substance both blissful and refreshing. But he dropped the cup every time and had to watch the precious water pool away into nothingness.

"We have done much tonight," Nazgar said. "It is time for our rest. Tomorrow we will try again."

They made their way back to the camp, silently acknowledging the sentries on guard.

Tim ducked into his tent to discover two additional cots had been placed inside, Boblin on one and another elion on the other. Because Tim had passed out in a dead faint the previous night, he'd been given the privilege of personal space, but that luxury was no longer necessary. Tim stretched out on the mattress, closing his eyes and settling to sleep. After his hypnotic sessions with Nazgar, he immediately slipped into a semiconscious state. As he hovered in the world between sleeping and waking, he found himself back in the empty cottage. Wind ghosted through the bare room, rippling across the shroud.

I'm going to open it this time, he thought.

A soft light glowed on the other side of the veil. He stepped toward it, taking his time. Nothing disturbed his peaceful foray across the empty room. The light on the other side of the curtain emitted faint, comforting warmth. Tim gently touched the veil, afraid the light would burn him, but it did not. He pulled the fabric back. An enormous well of light waited on the other side of the curtain, shining with a dazzling radiance. Tim held his breath and stepped forward, immersing himself in its essence.

Tim opened his eyes and was back in the tent, lying on his cot, his entire body tingling as energy coursed through his veins. He sat up, *holding* the power inside him, and lifted his fists in front of his face. He willed the energy forth, and two balls of green flame appeared, dancing above each palm.

Tim stood and walked out of the tent. Nazgar of the Kyrlod sat alone in the starlight, watching as Tim stepped outside. Tim flicked his hands and sent the fire toward Nazgar, just as Nazgar had done to him. The balls stopped in front of the prophet's face and disintegrated.

Nazgar stroked his beard and looked Tim straight in the eyes. The Kyrlod smiled faintly.

No Advocate ever touched the Lifesource in one day.

But I just did.

Sixteen

Tim awakened before dawn. Boblin still slept on one of the other two cots, but the other elion in the tent, one Tim hadn't met yet, was up and about. Tall even by elion standards, he currently had his back to Tim as he crouched over and laced his boots. When he turned around, Tim caught the faintest hint of a glower on his face.

"Good morning," Tim said.

"Good morning." The elion nodded in curt acknowledgment before buckling a sword at his waist and ducking outside. The morning air cut into the tent through the open flap, and Tim saw a glimpse of frost outside.

"That was Hedro Desh," Boblin said, sitting up on his cot. "He has a very advanced opinion of himself."

"He seems to be in a bad mood," Tim said.

"Not necessarily," Boblin replied. "He always looks like that, and he only talks if he feels the need to impress you."

"I see," Tim replied.

"I'm told he's not bad in small doses," Boblin said, "but I tend to disagree with the general consensus on that point."

"Noted." Tim reached for an undershirt to pull over his head.

"You were out late last night," Boblin said.

"Nazgar came for me."

"The Lifesource?" Boblin asked.

Tim faced him. "Is it that easy for you to accept?"

Boblin shrugged. "It's a part of this world. I'll be a sun-baked lizard before I understand it, but that doesn't mean I don't respect it."

"It's a myth in the South," Tim said.

"It's no myth here," Boblin said. "The Advocates are part of our history. Granted, the talent has all but died out, but Zadinn Kanas is proof enough."

"And what about this Warrior of Light?" Tim asked.

"That's not for me to say," Boblin replied. "Though I admit, even if I don't understand Nazgar, I *trust* him." He hopped off his cot. "Come on. There's work to do."

Tim joined him outside the tent. Many elions were already working at various tasks in a bustle of activity. It was clear a departure was underway. Some elions struck down tents, while others traveled from the tree line, carrying supplies of clothing, weapons, and food—items from the supply towers to the west.

"Hmm." Boblin watched Hedro, who carried a bundle of heavy coats, emerge from the nearby woods. "Wool. Are we expecting snow in midsummer?"

Tim shrugged. "There's always snow in the Northern Mountains, I suspect."

Boblin turned toward Tim. "The Mountains? Do you know something I don't?"

"I told you Nazgar came for me last night," Tim said. "We fellow Lifesource users share everything with one another."

Boblin arched an eyebrow. "Did he share the fact that nobody has ever returned alive from the Mountains?"

Tim held his hands up in mock defeat. "You're the one who says you trust him."

Boblin groaned. "There are so many more pleasant ways to die—fall on a sword, jump off a cliff. Does it have to be this complicated?"

Tim snapped his fingers. "Move along. As you said, there's work to be done. Let's get to it!" He turned and started walking toward the tree line.

"I take it back," Boblin called after him. "The Lifesource clearly altered your mental state in unfavorable ways yesterday evening. I highly suggest we reconsider."

"Relax, friend," Tim said. "Thank the Maker for your blessings."

"I'll thank the Maker for shoving his steel-toe boot up my rear end," Boblin replied, biting off each word. He followed Tim into the woods and to the supply tower, grumbling the whole way.

* * *

As the sun peeked over the treetops, the refugees assembled for a morning meal. The fresh air and presence of food, even if cold from lack of a proper fire, caused Tim's stomach to rumble in appreciation. A faint rime, sure to dissipate as the sun rose steadily higher, covered the windward-facing sides of the evergreens and the earthen floor of the encampment.

Tim and Boblin sat near their tent, eating bowls of porridge. The meal did not have much flavor, but Tim didn't even notice. It was good, solid food that would last him throughout the long day's march.

Moments later, Celia Alcion joined the two. The first time he'd met her, Tim hadn't had time to truly appreciate her beauty. She moved with unconscious grace, sitting down next to the two friends and balancing her bowl on her knees. The sunlight gave her dark hair a deep, rich luster, and her skin held a subtle glow.

Tim noticed Boblin tense ever so slightly at her arrival. After a moment of conscious effort, his friend's muscles relaxed and he turned to face the other elion. Tim had to look toward his bowl to suppress the smile that tugged at the corner of his lips.

"Hi, Celia," Boblin managed.

"Hi."

A long moment passed. "Looks like a nice morning," Boblin said.

"That it does," Celia agreed, nodding.

Tim wondered if he should go somewhere else, but he feared leaving Boblin alone at the present moment. In his nervousness, Boblin might stab his fork into his own eye by accident.

"Is Pellen speaking today?" Hedro asked, settling cross-legged to join them.

"I imagine he speaks every day," Boblin replied dryly. "I know I certainly do."

"At great cost to the rest of us," Hedro said. "Enough jokes, Kule. Is he or not?"

"No idea," Boblin said. "Celia?"

She shrugged. "I expect something to happen. We're burning time by staying in one spot too long, so we'll need to leave soon."

Around them, the other elions clustered in groups, speaking in low tones to one another. Tim knew exactly what Celia meant. A low tension hummed through the camp, pulled taut by the events of the last few days and hanging at a breaking point. Unlike Tim, however, few actually knew the plan at this time. He wondered how they would take it.

Hedro finished his meal first, taking his leave as quickly as he had arrived. Celia lingered a moment longer, and then returned to her own tent. Tim scraped the last of his bowl clean and placed it to the side. Then he turned to face Boblin.

"So," Tim said.

Boblin looked at him. "So what?"

"Celia Alcion," Tim said.

"What about her?" Boblin said, his nonchalant tone betrayed by the color of red seeping into his face.

Tim chuckled. "You're not fooling anyone, mate."

Boblin turned back to his porridge. "Go boil your head in a pot of water."

"And miss out on *this* fun?" Tim said with a smile. "Never."

At the center of the encampment, Pellen Yuzhar stood up to speak, cutting off all further conversation. Jend and Nazgar stood next to him, and the refugees fell silent.

"Friends and companions," Pellen said. "Not two days ago, the forces of darkness dealt us a devastating blow, and we escaped by no more than a hairsbreadth. We've lost our families and comrades—some dead, others enslaved—and the Fort we called home is no more. It is an evil hour, my people, but we still draw breath. That is our blessing."

He looked over the heads of the elions. "Yesterday was a time for recovery, but today is a time to move forward. We cannot stagnate forever, thinking only of what we have lost. For the past two hundred years we have survived by defending ourselves behind walls, but now those walls have failed. We can no longer live in passive resistance. Evil struck us down, and we must strike back."

He paused again. A fragile silence hung over the camp. "We've come to a turning point in this war. From this day forth, there is no going back. We will taste freedom, or suffer obliteration." He pointed toward the edge of the encampment. "The Fertile Lands lie all around us, and one can carve a good life from this soil. We have always been free people, and all are welcome to do as they will. Any elion who does not wish to take part in what follows should leave now and build himself a home in these pastures. You are entitled to the happiness it will provide."

Tim watched the elions, wondering if any would leave. Surely there were some whose hearts faltered after the fall of the Fort, but not a single one stirred.

"The Fertile Lands will fall, just like everywhere else," Boblin murmured. "There's no refuge here. If we're going to die, we might as well make it worth the pain."

Pellen's lined face slowly split into a weak smile. "I am proud, my sons and daughters. We will forge our futures together, however bright or dark they might be. Now, it is time to set our course.

"Many of you have heard of the Kyrlod. Most believed these prophets were only of myth, but they are quite real. Two hundred years ago, when the Invasion succeeded and resistance failed, Nazgar of the Kyrlod visited me."

A stir ran through the elions. Tim and Boblin exchanged glances. The dungeons below the Fort had been the first place Pellen revealed his age to anybody. It certainly was a shock to the others, but Pellen did not let the disturbance deter him. And, in spite of their leader's incredible tale, none of the elions appeared to doubt him. The North was indeed a different place from the South. In the city of Vonku, men and women would have scoffed at such a claim, calling it the ravings of a lunatic—but to the elions it was only a minor curiosity, certainly a surprise, and an unusual one at that, but nothing to get ruffled about. When Pellen finished speaking, he stepped aside and Nazgar took his place.

"I will not allow Pellen to give me undue credit, and I will not deceive you," Nazgar told the refugees. "Today we travel for the Northern Mountains to find the Army of Kah'lash. This journey will be perilous, and there is no guarantee we will find the Army. Long ago the Maker gave us a gift, but it came at a cost. The gift was free will, the most precious thing we can ever possess, but it also means we must take responsibility for our own destinies. The Maker will not save us by sending the Army to us—we must save ourselves by finding the Army. So we will travel north and cross the Mountains. But this is not all, because though the Army of Kah'lash will provide the manpower to fight Zadinn's malichons, it will not provide a means for fighting the Dark Lord himself. That responsibility rests on one of us. He stands here now, a stranger from the South. You welcomed him into your fold and allowed him to fight at your side. In time he, not I, will guide you. He is the Warrior of Light, and his name is Tim Matthias."

Because of the previous night, most of the elions already knew this, but Tim felt uncomfortable with the announcement nonetheless. "Nice of Nazgar to let me fade into the background," he said with a touch of wryness.

"There was no way around it," Boblin replied. "Better to get the truth out so everyone knows what we are up against."

When Nazgar finished, the group prepared to leave. They did not take long, since aside from clothing and weapons, there was little else to bring. They'd have to gather most of their food as they traveled, and they needed to be able to move fast. In just over an hour the refugees departed, traveling west while the sun reached its peak.

In spite of everything that had happened, Tim found himself able to relax in the peace and beauty of the Fertile Lands. The soft ground underfoot made the going easy and comfortable. They did not see much wildlife, other than an occasional bird or squirrel, and the forest was quiet. Every so often they came across tracks of larger animals, but nothing threatening appeared. Again, Tim was amazed that no elion had taken the chance to make a new life in this area. The temptation to slip into serenity, here under the trees of the Fertile Lands, could be strong. Then again, it was impossible to forget what had happened at the Fort. Every elion had been robbed of what mattered most to them, and no one would let it be forgotten. They could not just fade into the trees and dismiss the wrongs Zadinn Kanas had inflicted.

"Enjoy the Lands while you can," Boblin said, cutting into Tim's thoughts. "In three days we'll arrive at Lake Pel. A day after that we'll be back in the wastelands. And I'm not talking about a change of scenery. We're *safer* here. There are…things out there."

"What 'things'?" Tim asked.

Boblin shook his head. "I don't really know. They only come out at night, and everyone who has ever seen them ends up dead. A corpse can't give a description of its attacker, especially when that corpse is lying in several different places."

At nightfall the company made a new camp in a protective copse of trees. Tim was exhausted; he'd never walked so far in his life, and his muscles, inflamed by the full-day march, ached all over. After helping Boblin and the others raise the tents, he headed for his cot with every intention of falling asleep. But when he stepped inside his tent, he found Nazgar sitting on the bedroll with his hands folded in his lap. The Kyrlod looked at Tim serenely.

"You touched the Lifesource last night," Nazgar said. "Are you ready to do it again?"

Tim ran fingers through his hair. "I'm exhausted."

Nazgar stood. "When Zadinn's malichons attack tomorrow morning, will they care if you are exhausted? Time is short." He pointed outside. Tim sighed and dutifully followed. They again traveled beyond the circle of sentries, walking until they found a small clearing with thin, tall grass. There, the two men sat on a pair of blueleaf stumps at the edge of the trees. There was no moon tonight, only dark sky interspersed with stars.

As Nazgar led Tim through the same exercises from the previous night, Tim quickly realized his earlier success would not necessarily allow him to accomplish the same now. For the first half hour, he became frustrated time and again.

"Reexamine your effort," Nazgar said. "When you held the Lifesource yesterday, it was upon the cusp of sleep. You must return yourself to this state. Let go of your hold on consciousness, and *float*."

Tim decided he would lie down, and instead of focusing directly on Nazgar's instructions, he simply tried falling asleep. His muscles gradually slackened, and his breathing slowed. As his mind drifted, he found himself back in his family's cabin, its interior completely empty save for the glowing veil over the fireplace. Everything was as it should be. Tim took a step forward, repeating every move from the night before—the way he'd walked, the manner in which he hesitated, his gentle touch on the veil—and grasped the thin fabric. He pulled it aside, and an incandescent waterfall of light washed over his body, tingling as it settled into the pores of his skin.

"Amazing," Nazgar breathed.

Tim stood and opened his eyes. Holding the Lifesource felt like grasping a wet log in the middle of a large river. He could cling to it with his fingertips, but it was slippery and could pull away at any moment. "I have it," he said.

"I know," Nazgar replied. "Do something."

"What?"

"Anything you wish. Just ask for it."

Tim turned toward a fallen redbark tree. He funneled the Lifesource toward it and felt phantom arms reach from his body. He wrapped imaginary figures around the trunk and *lifted*, raising his hands into the air as he did so. He could sense the weight of the tree on his arms—not as heavy as it would be if he'd actually held it, but weight nonetheless.

The tree trembled, its roots shaking as the trunk dislodged from the earth. Clumps of dirt slid from the side of the bark as the redbark rose into the air— first two feet, then five, and then ten. It hung suspended, and Tim stepped toward it.

His boot brushed a root lying across the ground. Tim tripped, the Lifesource slid from his grasp, and the redbark fell, setting off an explosion of soil. Tim lowered his arms, breathing heavily, and wiped the sheen from his forehead. "I did it. In a manner."

"It took the most talented Advocate ever six months to master levitation," Nazgar said. "You did it after two nights."

"I might actually have a chance," Tim said. *I'm doing it. I'm becoming an Advocate of the Lifesource.*

Nazgar nodded. "The North has waited two hundred years for this, and I do not think it will be disappointed. But we must not celebrate too soon, for it would be a mistake to underestimate the might of what we are up against."

Tim asked, "How long did it take Zadinn to master levitation?"

"Six months," Nazgar said. Tim picked up on the tone in Nazgar's voice. "Do you mean—?"

"Yes," Nazgar said. "The most talented Advocate ever."

The pride of success turned sour quickly. Every game of chess had two players, each white knight matched by a black knight. Tim looked north. The other player waited there for him, surrounded by the desolation of the Deathlands and shielded by an army from Malath. No, they could not celebrate too soon. They had to contend with the darkness first.

Seventeen

Quentiin Harggra slowly opened his blood-encrusted eyes, shivering uncontrollably as wind knifed across his body. An empty expanse of clear blue sky hung high above him, and his head ached *horribly*. Every time the blood vessels in his brain pulsed, a surge of pain shot through his skull. When a fresh wave of agony coursed through him, he realized he was rocking on a bare wooden surface. Then the structure lurched, slamming the back of his head against a plank. He wanted to howl in anguish but could not summon the strength.

A pair of hands steadied him. "He's awake, Kevin," a voice said.

Quentiin gathered enough effort to turn his neck toward the sound. An elion knelt next to him, holding Quentiin's shoulders still while another pair of hands tilted his head up to place a soft cushion underneath. The world bounced again, and Quentiin saw raised metal bars on all sides. It looked like he was in a cage—*no, a wagon*. The links of a heavy chain slid across his stomach. Quentiin grasped it and lifted the object to eye level. An iron manacle was clamped around each wrist, the chain connecting the shackles together. Flashes of memory returned.

He recalled fighting at the Fort, falling down the stairs, grappling with the malichons. He'd tried to fight them off, but the memory went dark after that. His next recollection was of somebody dragging him across the ground and hoisting him into the back of a wagon. "Where are we?" he asked.

"Easy," Kevin said. "Give him water, Grendin." The other elion lifted a tiny cup to Quentiin's lips and Quentiin drank gratefully, not caring that the water was dirty and lukewarm. He licked cracked lips and forced a smile.

"Isanam's troops have captured us," Kevin said quietly. "They're taking us to the Deathlands. We've been traveling nonstop since the Fort fell."

"How long ago was that?" Quentiin asked.

"Last night," Kevin said. "You've been senseless for nearly eight hours."

"I think I was better off that way," Quentiin said.

"Aye," Kevin replied. "These chains might be on for good."

"They say we're going to the Pit," Grendin added, voice quavering. "Zadinn's slave pen."

The dark irony of the situation made Quentiin chuckle and break into a wheezing cough.

"What's so funny?" Kevin asked.

"I crossed the Rampart to find my friends," Quentiin said, "to save 'em from bein' turned into slaves, an' now I've become one myself. It's karfin' *hilarious*." He laughed again, but it hurt too much.

The elion looked at him in shock. "You really are a Southerner then?" Grendin asked. "We thought that was just part of Kule's story."

"Kule wasn't a traitor," Quentiin said. "I thought ye might have noticed that."

"Right, but things were chaotic at the end. We weren't sure what to believe."

Quentiin sat up gingerly. The pain in his body wasn't going away anytime soon, but everything seemed superficial. He'd been lucky twice—first in Raldoon, and now at the Fort. *I'm bloody tired o' hittin' my head.* "Yeah, I'm from the South. Malichons attacked my village an' took my people. I'd never seen their kind before. The Rampart is just as mysterious in our land as in yers. A group of us followed the malichons' trail, an' it led us to the wall."

"How did you cross the Barricade?" Grendin asked.

"I can't explain it," Quentiin replied. "A doorway opened. That's all I can tell ye. It closed behind us, an' we couldn't go back, so we went forward."

"And found Kule."

"Aye, but the malichons found us first. Kule came through fer us in a tight spot, though. He pulled us right out o' the fire. He's a karfin' good fighter, too." Both elions looked away, refusing to meet his gaze, and Quentiin immediately regretted his accusatory tone. The Tulak family had framed Boblin with quite convincing evidence, so no one was to blame for believing them.

Quentiin had experienced betrayal one other time, when a soldier deserted his regiment during the Icor Rebellion. Quentiin and the others had just lost a battle and were retreating through enemy-held territory, the most stressful week of Quentiin's life—until now. On the way out, the regiment endured a ceaseless string of attacks. Then right before they reached safety, they walked into an ambush. Apparently the man who deserted had turned to the rebels, betraying the regiment to save his own life. Two-thirds of Quentiin's regiment was slaughtered.

The man had sold out his comrades to preserve himself. In the end, this fact damaged the survivors more than the deaths of their friends. Soldiers could cope with death because it was an unavoidable fact of war. Strangely enough, there was often little malice between opposing armies. The color of the uniforms was different and that's all there was to it. Realizations like this did nothing to abate the horror and pain of battle, but it preserved one's mental integrity.

Betrayal, however, completely undid an individual—whether man, elion, or dwerion. When in battle, a soldier derived courage in knowing others stood beside him—that they were in it *together*. When that trust was stripped away, even the bravest warriors' legs trembled. Then *he* might retreat, betraying the others lest they betray him first. A philosopher might call that self-preservation, but Quentiin Harggra called it cowardice.

The elions would suffer the same effects his regiment had, but this would be worse. Quentiin and the others had been able to recover in the safety and security of the Alcatune Army, surrounded by friends, but the elions had no such luxury. They'd have to cope with the betrayal while in captivity.

"Aye, laddie," Quentiin said, "there will always be folk willin' to turn in their own mothers for a bit of gain. Ye can't escape it, but ye *can* fight it—by not bein' one of 'em. That's what gives us hope—that there are those of us who stand against evil."

"Couldn't be said better," Kevin replied. He ran a hand through his hair and leaned back against the wagon. A nasty gash ran across the elion's right forearm. Given a few weeks, it would form a respectable scar.

The companions settled into silence, and Quentiin surveyed his surroundings. A dozen wagons, pulled by worn-down mules and filled with prisoners, rolled across the rocky landscape. Sharp, gray stones marked the horizon, and the only sounds were howling wind and creaking of wagon axles.

A score of mounted malichons surrounded the wagons, and a tall, cloaked figure rode at the very front of the group. Cold evil radiated from this lone rider. Even the other malichons gave him a wide berth. This could only be Isanam,

Overlord of the malichon armies. As Quentiin watched, the Overlord raised a hand and the moving wagons ground to a halt.

As dusk tinged the landscape, several shadows rippled at the edge of the group, and Quentiin realized a pack of wolves had gathered near the encampment. Neither wolves nor malichons seemed disturbed by the other's presence. One wolf stepped forward, baring its teeth at the wagons, and then retreated into the dark.

Isanam dismounted and faced the prisoners. Twin red eyes burned behind the empty sockets in Isanam's skull-mask. Quentiin did not feel fear very often, but he did now. As the other malichons made camp, Isanam walked toward the refugees, stopping just a few yards from Quentiin's wagon. Quentiin felt the urge to hide behind the edge of his cage, but he fought the compulsion, quashing it. It would take more than Isanam's mere presence to shatter his will.

"You measure the time between the Fort and the Deathlands as a distance of two weeks," Isanam announced. "We will not set such a leisurely place. My master has plans for you, and we will not keep him waiting. Soon you will come to realize that those who died at the Fort were fortunate. Most of you will be sent into the Pit, to build the Dark Lord's fortress, though a few might be selected for…experiments. We will travel all day, stopping only when necessary, and in six days we will reach the Deathlands. During your travels, you are not to speak—at all. The consequences will be fatal."

Quentiin glanced at his companions. Grendin widened his eyes and coughed, shattering the stillness as effectively as breaking glass. The elion doubled over, sides heaving as he wheezed, trying to stop but failing.

"What is this insolence?" Isanam asked, striding over. "I tell you to be silent, and you immediately disobey my wishes. I will not tolerate such disrespect."

Grendin continued to hack and heave. Kevin put a hand on his comrade to steady him.

"Cease!" Isanam said, and Grendin finally managed to quiet himself. He looked up at the Overlord, fear etching deep grooves in his face. Worse, flecks of red covered his chest, and more dribbled from the corner of his lip. He had coughed up blood.

Isanam looked at Grendin. Any expression on the Overlord's face remained concealed behind the cold, impervious features of his skull-mask. "You must be greatly injured," he said. Then, without warning, he reached out and grabbed

Grendin's neck, violently pulling the elion up against the bars of the cage. "The Dark Lord has no use for a slave with poor health."

Grendin reached up, feebly trying to pull free of the Overlord's grip, but his attempts were futile. His eyes bulged as he gasped. Isanam squeezed tighter, and Grendin's face turned purple. The elion shook as blood filled his mouth. Soon the blood overflowed, running down the front of Grendin's chin, and his eyes grew wild in panic.

Rationality left Quentiin. He leaped up and grabbed Isanam's arm, tearing Grendin free and shoving the Overlord back. Grendin tumbled to the bottom of the wagon, still panting for air.

Isanam's response was immediate and brutal. He surged forward, seizing Quentiin's tunic and slamming the dwerion forward against the metal bars of the cage. Quentiin's headache, which had subsided, returned in a flash of sparks.

"Your impertinence displeases me," the Overlord said—and then, to Quentiin's surprise, he released him. Quentiin slid from the bars as Isanam walked to the back of the wagon and opened the door. Isanam reached inside the cage and grabbed Quentiin's ankle, dragging the dwerion from the cart onto the stony ground.

Quentiin did not cry out or resist. Instead, he met the Overlord's gaze and stared back. Isanam was almost certainly going to kill him, but no amount of pleading would change that, and Quentiin was not about to give him any pleasure by doing so.

Isanam lifted Quentiin onto his feet, pulling him so close their faces almost touched. Quentiin felt the Overlord's hot breath on his cheeks. Yes, he was afraid, but he forced himself to meet those burning red eyes. Isanam released him once more, and Quentiin fell back.

"You have a strong spirit," Isanam said. "If I kill you now, we will not have the pleasure of breaking you in the Pit, and *that* will be infinitely more enjoyable. I can, however, still make an example of you."

Isanam turned back to the wagon and seized Kevin. "No!" Kevin shouted as Isanam wrenched him into the open.

The other malichons laughed as Isanam held Kevin in the air so that the prisoner's feet dangled six inches above the ground. "What is your name?" Isanam asked as Kevin frantically tried to break free. "What is your name?" the Overlord repeated.

"Kevin Delnar," the elion replied, and Isanam pulled a long knife from his belt.

"Leave him alone," Quentiin growled.

"Silence!" Isanam said, kicking Quentiin in the stomach. A pair of malichons stepped forward to restrain the dwerion. "You, not I, brought this upon him."

"Please," Kevin said to Isanam, who held the knife against his throat.

"Do you have a family?" the Overlord asked.

"Yes."

"Wife? Children?"

Kevin's voice trembled. "Yes."

"Are they here right now?"

Kevin's eyes flickered toward the prisoners, and he licked his lips. "Yes."

"Good," Isanam said, and shoved his knife into Kevin's throat. Blood sprayed from the wound as Isanam tossed the elion's body down. Quentiin shook with anger. He could not speak as Isanam shoved him back into the wagon. "I hope you've learned something from this," the Overlord said.

Quentiin had indeed. This was not the Icor Rebellion, for that petty war did not hold half the horrors this one did. Isanam had killed Kevin for sheer entertainment. Quentiin turned to his remaining comrade, but Grendin was stiff in the corner, sightless eyes still open. Quentiin reached forward and gently closed the elion's lids.

The wolves at the edge of the camp moved forward, converging on Kevin's body, and Quentiin realized this was why the pack had followed. The wolves knew what to expect when malichons were near. The animals approached the elion's body, bending forward and sniffing the growing pool of blood. Somewhere among the prisoners, Kevin's family was watching.

"Feeding time," Isanam said.

Eighteen

Zadinn Kanas sat in his throne room, deep in thought. Mists spiraled inside the chamber, filling the air with poisonous fumes. Zadinn closed his eyes and breathed in the vapors, letting the toxins sear his lungs. He counteracted the poison by cycling the Lifesource through his body, healing the damage as soon as it began. There was nothing quite like the taste of death. Zadinn leaned back against his chair, settling into the grooves of the interlocking bones beneath him, and curled his fingers around the tips of the armrests.

Zadinn had last heard from Isanam two days ago. The Fort of Pellen had been destroyed, and the prisoners were on their way north. It would be good to have unsullied bodies to put to work. Of course, Zadinn would keep his usual portion of newcomers. He only selected from new arrivals, because he needed his subjects fresh. There was no use dissecting the body of a slave who'd been worn down over years of labor. He'd learned much about the body and its functions over the course of many years, but there was always more to discover, new experiments to test, higher thresholds of pain to be breached.

Well, it was no matter. He had other priorities for the time being. It had been a week since Ragzan's spirit announced the Warrior's arrival. But though Ragzan knew *of* this Warrior, he did not seem to know his whereabouts. This was not a matter of disobedience on Ragzan's part—of that Zadinn was certain. The souls in the Cauldron were compelled to serve the Dark Lord without question, whether they wished to or not. Ragzan simply did not have the knowledge Zadinn sought.

Since the Warrior's arrival, Zadinn felt the flickering impression that signaled a new presence in the Lifesource. However, the sensation was weak and intermittent, like waning candlelight. It never lasted long enough for Zadinn to pinpoint the location of its user. It led him, however, to a satisfying conclusion, something Ragzan possibly omitted. These were not the efforts of a practiced

Lifesource user. Zadinn had assumed the Warrior was the South's equivalent of an Advocate, but this new information indicated he was nothing of the sort. By Academy standards the Warrior would barely be an initiate. This also meant he was young, because the power would have already fully manifested in an adult. If Zadinn was correct, the Warrior was merely an untrained boy.

But there was a contradiction in all this. Aside from these weak flickers of power, Zadinn had felt an additional, *massive* surge in the Lifesource just two days ago—strong enough to level an entire city. Zadinn had not felt anything since, but it still made him wary. The presence of a seemingly "weak" Advocate could be an illusion, a trap to entice him to lower his guard, and Zadinn had no intention of underestimating his opponent.

No doubt this sudden surge in the Lifesource was tied to Isanam's account of the catastrophe in the Kaltu Pass. Such an incident was *far* too fortuitous to have occurred by random chance, but only someone strong in the power could achieve a feat of that magnitude. Perhaps it had been the Kyrlod's doing, but this was unlikely. Nazgar would not expose his consciousness to Zadinn unless absolutely necessary.

There was a way to investigate all of this. It was not something the Dark Lord would do lightly, but it had to be done. He needed to burn this tree before it bore fruit.

Zadinn stood, grasping his staff in one hand. Certain spirits lingered very close to the border between Malath and the physical realm. Every so often, one crossed the border, resulting in tales of ghosts and monsters. Zadinn did not have the strength to access the heart of Malath, but he could reach one of these spirits near the border and prompt it to cross. Zadinn had called upon such a spirit in the past, and it had served him well.

It was time to bring back his old friend. Zadinn ran his fingers over the black marble atop his staff. He'd trusted this demon before, and he could do it again. But he would have to wait until nightfall.

* * *

Zadinn waited on the parapet outside his citadel as the sun set, watching the bloodred orb dip below the horizon while shadows around him lengthened, stretching out their fingers to claw the edge of the landscape. Zadinn looked up at the darkening sky and raised his staff. An eerie white light flashed from within the depths of the staff's pommel stone. A wind gusted past him, whistling through the streets of the city, while a boiling mass of clouds gathered above his head.

The malichons in the city avoided the citadel tonight. All felt the touch of dark magic upon it, and they had no desire to remain close. In the depths of the Pit, the slaves shivered in cages, squeezing their eyes shut and praying for death, the only escape left to them.

But Zadinn Kanas merely smiled, relishing the fury of the oncoming storm. The clouds swirled and split, revealing a yellowish-green sky. The converging vortex moved toward the palace, the clouds gradually forming a funnel that reached down to envelop the citadel's spire.

Zadinn turned and left the parapet, walking to his palace as savage winds whipped his robes. It was almost time, for he felt the barrier between the two worlds grow thin. Zadinn disappeared into his palace just as the storm unleashed its might. Jagged streaks of lightning shot across the sky, and booming thunderclaps shook the city's foundations. Moments later, a deluge of rain descended. The water fell so thick that anyone outside could barely see more than a few paces.

A frigid breeze arose when Zadinn entered his chambers. The moving air swirled, circling the room, and the candles on the surrounding ledges died, leaving only the glowing nimbus emitting from the vents to light the chamber. The air steamed and misted, leaving wet drops upon the ground as the stones beneath Zadinn's feet trembled.

He had to establish his control over the spirit immediately. Dark fire lanced from the tip of Zadinn's staff, and he directed the flames to the floor, where he scored a blazing circle. The circle complete, he stepped into its center, raising his arms toward the domed roof and beginning a string of incantations. Obscure words rolled from his tongue, flawlessly and without pause. The slightest mistake here meant death.

As the spell grew more intense, a spinning ball of light appeared in the middle of the throne room. A ring of pure white bordered the edges of the sphere, but its center was a void of black. The sphere gradually grew larger as a tunnel formed within the void. Zadinn was yelling now, pausing neither to breathe nor moisten his lips. Outside, the storm ripped shingles from rooftops and knocked doors off hinges. Shards of hail shattered windows, and flashes of lightning streaked.

In the throne room, the whirlwind spun violently until Zadinn pounded his staff against the ground, screaming a final order. The vortex slowed, coalescing into the shape of a demon astride a horse. The figure's eyes were yellow, but it smiled to bare a set of glistening white teeth.

This was the Hunter. It dismounted and knelt at Zadinn's feet. "Master," it hissed. "What do you desire?"

"A new Advocate walks the land," Zadinn said, "and he is a threat to my reign. Travel toward the Fertile Lands, where a group of elion refugees is hiding. I believe this Advocate is with them. One of the Kyrlod might be among them, too, but for now the prophet dares not use his powers."

"And when I have found this Advocate?" the Hunter asked.

"Kill them all."

The Hunter bowed before mounting its steed. The winds picked up and the Hunter became a cyclone of shadows, vanishing down the corridor. The demon could travel only at night—sunlight would destroy it—but it would catch its prey soon enough. Nobody eluded the Hunter.

Zadinn did not have the ability to read the Warrior's mind as he could the Kyrlod's, but the Hunter would track this enemy for him. The Warrior could not hide, and this conflict had two possible outcomes. The Hunter could succeed in killing the Warrior, and the matter would be done. Or the Warrior would kill the Hunter and, in doing so, reveal himself to Zadinn. Either way, Zadinn won.

Nineteen

Boblin Kule stepped from his tent into the morning light, his breath forming misty vapors in the air. A gray, overcast sky hung above faint tendrils of fog that covered the surface of the Durin Plains. Rime lined the edges of the tents in the camp, which formed a lonely sight, a tiny bastion of habitation set against the stark backdrop of the wastes.

The elion refugees had left the Fertile Lands just yesterday, putting the vast expanse of Lake Pel behind them to forge north. They were now back in the open, exposed to harsh weather and darkness. Boblin didn't entertain any foolish notions about reaching the Mountains unscathed. The travelers would have to pass through the Korlan Forest first, and only the Maker knew what might befall the elions in that haunted place. They could avoid the Korlan if they traveled east, but that would take them straight into the Deathlands, and Boblin would gladly take his chances in the Korlan over *that*.

As the first rays of sunlight rose, the refugees traveled north. Moving across the Plains was easy, but the flat expanse came at the expense of harsh wind, which bit into the travelers without mercy. Boblin felt his cheeks and lips grow raw from the constant barrage of cold air. The group spread out as they walked, Jend and the twins at the very front, other Patrol scouts rotating the rear guard.

The trudge and grind of the day-to-day march did not have much to offer. The hours slowly blended with the refugees' steady, unwavering pace. In truth, though, no one wished for anything else. Every day that passed without incident, without malichons, was a worthwhile day and a day to be thankful for.

Along with Wayne and Hedro, Boblin served time on scouting patrol as well as nighttime guard duty. They all also partook in the task of making and breaking camp. If nothing else, they had good cause to sleep hard and deep every night.

But if Boblin was tired, Tim Matthias was flat-out *exhausted*. The young man left with Nazgar of the Kyrlod each evening, wandering into the night to practice with the Lifesource. Though Boblin had learned much about the Advocates, he'd obviously never seen a man using the Lifesource, and—truth be told—the whole subject unnerved him. Nazgar claimed it was a natural process—harnessing the power of the earth, as he put it—but Boblin thought that sentiment a load of sun-baked dung. *If it were natural, everybody would use it every day, right?* No. Boblin figured if he were going to fight, he'd take good steel any day. *That* was natural.

For what it was worth, Tim seemed to value Boblin's opinions, to the extent he'd asked the elion to teach him ailar, and Boblin had willingly obliged. In the brief time they'd known each other, the two had formed a strong bond. After all, companions didn't pass through captivity and battle together without becoming the best of friends. So Boblin showed Tim the art of hand-fighting, and though the skill was clearly not Tim's forte, Boblin saw that he nonetheless enjoyed it.

After three days on the Durin Plains, the refugees arrived at the Irsp Valley. They could see it well before they actually arrived, but it wasn't until they stood at its edge that they truly perceived its majesty. The Valley stretched for miles, a slope that slowly but steadily increased its grade until it bottomed. The surface of the basin was impeccably smooth. Not a single pebble marred its surface, and when the light hit it right, the Valley took on a glossy hue, like the surface of a polished gem. The elions halted at the edge of the enormous crater, unwilling to step inside the Valley. A surface this perfect was out of place in the otherwise stunted landscape.

Tim stepped up next to Boblin, staring at the spectacle before them. "What is this?" he breathed.

"The Irsp Valley," Boblin replied.

"I know, but what *is* it?"

"Do you remember Herdar Ashan?"

"He was the High Advocate who fought Zadinn on the battlefield."

"Well, this was *where* they fought." Boblin swallowed. "Only at the time, the crater wasn't here. The history books say this was the most destructive battle ever recorded between two men using the Lifesource. The conflict tore the land apart in all directions. When Zadinn struck his last blow, this was the result."

He instantly hated himself for relating this story. Every word was true, but he wished Tim had not asked him. After all, Tim was to fight Zadinn, the man who had caused all this. Boblin supposed he could have lied, but Tim would have found out the truth from someone else regardless.

The look on Tim's face confirmed Boblin's thoughts. When the elions stood at this valley, they felt a mixture of emotions—respect for Herdar's sacrifice, awe for the power of the Lifesource, and fear of Zadinn Kanas— but when Tim Matthias looked at it he saw the implacable truth of his destiny. Tim alone had to face the man who had caused this savage, unabashed destruction.

"Herdar was the most powerful Advocate of his time, wasn't he?" Tim asked.

There was no use skirting around the truth there. "Yes," Boblin said. "He was." But only in a manner of speaking, because after all, Zadinn Kanas had turned out to be the most powerful Advocate of the time. Boblin turned toward the rest of the group, where the elions were preparing camp, but Tim stayed behind, staring out at the expanse of the Irsp Valley.

* * *

At noon of their last day on the Plains, Tim saw a thin, dark line of trees to the north. At first the Korlan did not appear much different from the Erdrar, but as the refugees approached, Tim realized the two forests were dramatically different. The trees of the Erdrar had been thin and spread apart, but the Korlan was a thick tangle of trunks and limbs. Brambles and leaves choked the roof of the forest, coming together in an intricate cluster that blocked the sun at all times of day. Even at the height of noon, it would be like night underneath that canopy. The Korlan *felt* dangerous, too. An oppressive sensation emanated from the depths of the gloomy forest. Tim almost thought he saw the landscape breathe, as if it gradually swelled up and down with an unseen pulse.

The elions assembled camp in grim silence, no one eager to talk. They might as well have been next to a graveyard. Jend ordered double the usual number of sentries for the night, and Tim thought he might even get a reprieve from Lifesource training. He was wrong.

Nazgar came for him after dinner, and the two wordlessly departed camp. They did not travel as far as on other nights, because even Nazgar did not want to stray too far from the firelight. They settled on a rocky outcrop near a cluster of stunted bushes facing the forest. Again Tim thought he could see the woods swelling in cadence to a hidden beat.

"Why are the elions afraid of the Korlan?" he asked Nazgar.

"They fear it because they do not know it," the Kyrlod replied.

I should have known better than to expect a straightforward answer. Tim closed his eyes to focus on the Lifesource. He knew no amount of questioning the Kyrlod would procure a satisfactory response, so Tim was surprised when the old man spoke again.

"When Zadinn Kanas conquered the North, he did so in the name of the Demon Lord," Nazgar said. "Uklith is trapped in Agrazab, but Zadinn is his conduit to this world. As you know, the Lifesource is present in all living things. When you hold its power, you are drawing on the resources of the natural world. For example, the Lifesource now runs through the stones beneath your feet. If you touch the magic tonight, you will use power that moves through those stones. When you held the Lifesource in the Fertile Lands, you used the power coursing through the trees and soil. Wherever you are, there is a reservoir of this power to draw upon.

"There is a malevolent side to these energies, though. The Dark Advocates do not draw upon the Lifesource in its natural form. The Lifesource itself is not corrupt, but some men and other beings are, and evil actions have consequences. The natural earth, mother of the Lifesource, rebels at such mistreatment of her child. This is why the North has become a wasteland.

"But land is meant to thrive, not die. So things grew here at one time, but Zadinn's evil warped them. The trees of the Korlan now have minds of their own, only wanting to draw other living creatures into their fold. Once you step inside the Korlan, the forest will make every attempt to prevent you from leaving."

"Is this really better than going east?" Tim asked, recalling Boblin's warning.

"Neither path is safe, but going through the Deathlands is infinitely more dangerous," Nazgar concurred.

"Don't ever try being a Healer, Nazgar," Tim said. "You don't have a knack for making people feel better."

"The truth is not always reassuring," Nazgar replied.

Tim closed his eyes and returned to his meditation. The process of seeking the Lifesource was getting easier, and now the empty room manifested almost immediately. Tim faced the veil as the familiar breeze glided across his face.

Nazgar had said these steps would become instantaneous with time, but for now Tim had to move slowly. He'd tried rushing the process several times, but this always caused the room to disintegrate.

It might have taken him a minute, or it might have taken him an hour—he did not know—before he finally stood in front of the veil. He cautiously brushed the silken fabric aside and stared into a well of incandescent brilliance. He moved toward the light, the light moved toward him, and they were one. His entire body tingled. But then an oily, black presence loomed up through the Lifesource, appearing first as a faint warning, next as a tidal wave of shadow that slammed into Tim and enveloped him in its dark arms.

Tim tried to pull away, but it clung to him, seeping over him, drowning him with its foul sensation. It filled his mind, clutching and grasping with tearing, clawlike fingers. Tim cried out and fell. He couldn't breathe, couldn't move. He tried to open his eyes, but they remained shut. The darkness coiled around him, latching into his soul and draining his life.

"Tim!" Nazgar yelled, and Tim opened his eyes. He was lying on his back, the trees of the Korlan stirring nearby. He thought he heard a low moaning, barely perceptible, coming from the trunks. Tim struggled to a sitting position, wiping his brow with trembling fingers.

"What was that?" he asked.

Nazgar helped him sit up. "The forest," he said. "It wants you."

"It's nice to be loved," Tim said, trying to lighten the situation, but Nazgar did not laugh.

"You must rest," the Kyrlod said. "You'll need all your energy if you are to see the other side of that forsaken glen."

*　*　*

Night set on the Irsp Valley, and a light breeze arose. A vaporous shadow appeared in the midst of the swirling air, gradually gaining in size and substance until the form of the Hunter appeared. The demon's horse pawed the ground, nostrils flaring with hot white light, and the Hunter patted the creature's neck to calm it. The Hunter narrowed its yellow eyes as it surveyed the Valley, observing the signs of the refugees' passing.

Any other tracker would have been at a complete loss. The landscape of the North remained harsh and unyielding. With the naked eye, it was impossible to tell if anyone had come this way. Feet did not leave prints in solid stone. But the Hunter could see things others could not. To it, the path of the refugees appeared as a blazing trail of light etched into the ground. The Hunter had followed this path without fail from the Fertile Lands, and tonight the gap was narrowing. Though it could move only at night, the Hunter traveled three times as fast as the elions. The pursuit would end tonight, and the Hunter would reach the party's camp at dawn. Though it could not attack then—sunrise would be too close—it could hide within the Korlan.

In a way this would be much better for the Hunter. After the refugees entered the shadows of the Forest, the Hunter could track them at its leisure. When the time was right, it would attack. Those it did not kill, the Korlan would swallow.

Twenty

The sun hung in the sky as the elions moved into the Korlan Forest, but as soon as they stepped under the trees, they entered a world where darkness took over. The forest floor remained suspended in perpetual twilight, with only the barest trace of solar rays filtering through the branches. Tim could not identify the species of trees in this place. The closest he could compare them to were redbarks—that is, if the redbark were to develop an infectious disease that warped its branches, blackened its skin, and gave off a musty odor. *It's like we are back in the Fertile Lands, except that while we were away, the trees took a bad fever, and now they aren't getting better anytime soon.* The absence of animal life was not surprising.

A half hour in, someone cried out from the front of the group, followed by a bustle of commotion. Through a crack in the crowd, Tim saw Vern struggling knee-deep in a mound of mud and sinking fast. *How in Malath did that happen?*

"Hold!" Jend called out.

Hugo and Ken reached out to steady Vern, and Tim noticed they stayed as far back as possible, deliberately avoiding the ground around the partially buried elion.

"Lie back," Ken commanded. Vern took a deep breath to steady himself and placed his backside on the ground. Meanwhile, another elion fashioned a rope to tie around Vern's waist.

"Do you have quicksand in the South?" Boblin asked quietly.

"I've heard of it," Tim said, "but it's down on the Icor Peninsula. I thought sinkholes only occurred in much warmer places."

Boblin gave him a bemused look. "What made you think the weather patterns up here are natural?"

Up front, the going was steady but slow. Vern remained as still as possible while the other Patrol members wrapped the rope around his waist. Working in unison, the soldiers dragged Vern backward from the pit. Dirt and mud peeled back from his torso with a *sucking* sound as his comrades pulled him free one inch at a time. At last Vern clambered onto the safety of solid ground, covered in muck and breathing heavily, an ashen hue to his face.

A pair of scouts located a route around the quagmire, and everyone stepped more carefully. They skirted the bog a good hour before turning back north again. Thankfully the morning held no more surprises. As the day wore on without further incident, the refugees grew more relaxed; no flesh-eating hordes materialized from the shadows, no malichon army appeared from the east, and the way in front of them remained safe.

Near midday, they discovered a clearing where grass stood knee-high and sunlight filtered through a break in the treetops. The forest created a steady windbreak, and for the first time in weeks, the elions rested in the sun's warmth without the harsh offset of wind.

At Commander Jend's request, Tim and Boblin departed from the clearing to gather sticks for a fire. They didn't want to travel far from the group, but they had no need for concern. A hundred yards from the edge of the clearing they found a copse of good dry wood. With a hatchet apiece, the two friends chopped and split logs. Tim found the process a soothing break from the exhaustive effort of seeking the Lifesource. Here, he could slip into the steady rhythm of the ax's rise and fall as his mind entered a comfortable, relaxed state.

One day, you'll learn to appreciate firewood, he heard his father's voice say, the very words Daniel had spoken to him the morning Tim ventured alone out into the Odow. *You'll wake up one morning and realize you miss the feel of the ax between your hands, the rise and fall of the chop, the satisfaction of a clean split. It's a job to be proud of.*

You were right all along, Tim thought. Funny how things turned out.

"Hand me that piece," Boblin said, interrupting Tim's thoughts and pointing to a thick length of wood to Tim's left. Tim turned away from Boblin to oblige, but when he looked back, Boblin was gone.

"Boblin?" Tim asked. He'd only turned away for a second.

"Right here," the elion said. Boblin now stood on the other side of him.

"You were just standing *there*," Tim said, gesturing over his opposite shoulder.

Boblin eyed him askance. "I've been here the whole time," he said.

Tim shrugged. "Okay," he said. He then tried to hand Boblin the log, but found his hands were empty.

"Are you going to pick it up?" Boblin asked. Tim turned. The log was back on the ground, this time to Tim's right instead of his left.

"Something's not right," Tim said.

"Agreed," Boblin said. "You're standing there like a sun-baked lizard while I do all the work."

Tim picked up the log one more time and then turned back to his left. Boblin was gone again.

"Over *here*," the elion said. This time, he was on Tim's right.

"Pick it *up!*" Boblin said. Tim glanced down at his hands, empty once more, the log back on the ground in front of him. Tim looked at the piece of wood. Things felt very strange right now.

"It won't bite, I promise," Boblin said.

The log *flickered*. Tim hissed in suspicion. "Did you see that?" he asked.

"See what?" Boblin replied.

Tim slammed his hatchet into the log. The wood certainly *felt* solid.

"What are you doing?" Boblin said.

Tim ignored him and instead reached for the Lifesource. The instant he cleared his mind, the surrounding Korlan—and Boblin—shimmered. *It's a karfing illusion.*

He lost any control he might have had over the Lifesource, but it didn't matter. The spell was broken. The world around Tim warped and buckled. Boblin Kule's image no longer spoke but merely stood, a prop with a blank expression on its face. The ground shook and Tim fell forward, landing on his knees as the dirt quaked.

The world snapped back into place as the Korlan fought back, trying to reassert the illusion. "Tim?" Boblin's image asked.

"No!" Tim shouted. "You're not here!" He raised the hatchet and threw it at Boblin's face.

* * *

Tim sat upright, sweat running down his face and back. The world around him hung dark and silent. He lay on the forest floor, alone in the Korlan, unable to tell if it was day or night, because darkness always reigned inside this place. He looked up at the canopy of trees. The elions could never have entered a sunny field. This forest *had* no fields.

The Korlan trapped us—and we didn't even know it. But Tim wondered *when* the group had first fallen under the spell. Where had reality ended and illusion begun? In the end, it didn't matter. The group had been separated, and that was all there was to it. Tim stood up, his nervous heartbeat unnaturally loud in the surrounding silence. He had no idea where to go. The elion refugees could be anywhere. He settled on a small knoll to his left, walking to the top so that he could get a better view of the area. *If everyone fell asleep at different times, that means we are spread out one by one across the entire forest.*

Tim started walking. In spite of being a knowledgeable woodsman, he did not like this situation. The Korlan was a far cry from the Odow. It was one thing to know your way about the woods, another entirely to escape from a place that wanted to kill you. Even now the Korlan was probably working to bring him back within its grasp, to ensnare Tim and draw him into the darkness forever. He glanced left and right at the trees looming all around him, and placed a hand on the hilt of his sword. *Stop it. Don't panic like this.* Tim tried to clear his mind and tap the Lifesource. The process eased his breathing and settled his pulse.

It took him a quarter of an hour to reach the top of the rise. The hill provided a good view of the immediate area, but the gloomy corridors of the forest made it hard to see very far. As far as he could tell, no elions were close by.

"Hello?" he called. The dead trees absorbed his voice, and Tim visibly flinched. *I shouldn't have done that.* The Korlan demanded silence, and he feared he might wake something best left undisturbed.

Leaves rustled to his left. Tim looked down the slope, where shadows rippled at the base of the knoll, and the blackness of the forest floor gave way to something even blacker. He crouched, keeping his profile low, and then heard a rhythmic pounding. *Hoofbeats.*

At the base of the hill, a horse-shaped wraith emerged from the trees, pawing the ground as wisps of smoke flowed from its nostrils. A rider, formed from the same vapor as its steed, sat astride the mount, scanning the territory with keen, yellow eyes. The rider looked toward the hill as the wraith-horse stepped forward, no doubt having heard Tim's earlier shout.

Though it had not yet seen him, it would soon if Tim remained in his current position. While still positioned low, Tim turned away from the horseman.

The moment he moved, the horse cried out, a sound sharp enough to cut stone. The rider had spotted him.

Abandoning any desire to stay hidden, Tim stood tall and ran at full speed. Ahead of him, the knoll narrowed into a steep ridgeline as trees filled the slope on either side of him. He raced into the Korlan, knowing his pursuer was gaining ground behind him. His only hope was to run as far and fast as possible—but to where?

And then a hand reached from the bushes on the side of the ridge, grabbing him by the ankle and pulling him into the darkness below.

* * *

Boblin Kule turned in circles. *This is a most excellent situation.* He'd awakened at the base of a thick tree, alone in the gloom, completely unaware of what had happened. *Stopped for a snooze, did we? Karfing good work, mate!*

When all was said and done, Boblin liked spending time in the woods. After all, it provided a nice change of scenery from the dreary monotony of the Durin Plains. An elion could only take so much dust and stone in his lifetime—but Boblin would rather his forest be peaceful and scenic, not dark and haunted. He could research prospective summer homes *later*, but right now he needed to find a way out of this mess.

Well, at some point I left the group and ended up here. I had to leave a trail behind, right? Boblin looked for signs he might have left. Most likely, he'd fallen under the Korlan's spell and gradually wandered from the group. If he could find a trail, he'd follow it back to the other refugees. The Forest likely had everybody spellbound. The other elions were all out there somewhere, probably slumbering together in one big mound, an enormous Fort of Pellen Sleeping Festival, held at this time every year in an evil forest of choice.

It hadn't taken Boblin long to figure out the Korlan had a spell on him. *When Celia Alcion kisses me* that *passionately, it's bound to be an illusion, and a karfing mean one at that.*

After circling the area several times, Boblin found a trampled swathe of brambles and shrubs along with his own footprints. *Excellent.* He picked up his knapsack, which he'd dropped in his stupor, and followed the path. The trail was clear in some areas, more muddled in others, but it left enough evidence to point him in a consistent direction.

Boblin soon gave up any hope that this might be over quickly. His trail led him across the bowl of a valley before traveling up a ridge, the going slow and tedious, meandering through the Forest rather than following any sort of straight line. After a half hour, Boblin at last arrived at a place where the trees thinned out. Here, he allowed himself a few moments of rest and sat on a fallen tree, pulling a flask of water from his bag for a few brief swigs. It was necessary to conserve water. He didn't know how long he'd be out here, and even if he found a stream in the Korlan, he wouldn't drink from it. The water was liable to birth a strange creature in his guts.

He considered making a torch but hesitated, concerned it would draw unwanted attention. On one hand, he hadn't seen any dangerous wildlife, so maybe the Forest was empty. On the other hand, lack of observation didn't mean lack of existence. On the third hand, he might be safer with fire than without. He didn't want to use a fourth hand, though, so speculation stopped there.

That was when he heard the scream.

* * *

Celia Alcion cautiously stepped forward. The quagmire surrounding her seemed to stretch for miles, and she was in no hurry to repeat Vern's previous predicament—certainly not all by herself. She had been walking through the Korlan for the last quarter hour, making her way across the quagmire by using mounds of solid earth as stepping-stones, one small island at a time. There was no room for error. The process was painstakingly slow, and Celia would have preferred to travel *around* the quicksand, but there was no visible way around the expanse.

It did her no good speculating about the spell that had entranced the party members or fretting about what other dangers the Forest might harbor. She simply had to move forward, and encounter any predicaments as they came.

Upon awakening, Celia had climbed the nearest tree to get a bearing based on the sun's position. She had no idea where her companions might be—not Ana, not Boblin, not Hedro—so, after using the sun to gain a compass bearing, she traveled due north as quickly as possible. There was only one way out of the woods—walking—so she got to it. Anyone else with any sense would travel the same direction, and if that meant crossing a quagmire, so be it.

Four mounds remained between her and the safety of the far bank, but the next step was a bit of a stretch. *Well, nobody said this would be easy.* Celia jumped, landing on the patch of earth as lightly as possible—but the second her weight touched the island, it collapsed beneath her. *Hisht.*

The ground opened for a second and then closed again, engulfing her up to her thighs. Her muscles initially tensed with fright, but Celia forced herself to relax by breathing deeply. Struggling would only make her sink faster. The North killed those who panicked.

A vine dangled above her, hanging from a tree branch. Celia strained to reach the lifeline. Her fingertips brushed the foliage, but she did not gain any purchase and the effort cost her. The more she moved, the more she sank, and soon the quagmire had risen up to her waist.

This was a fine predicament. The vine was close, but not close enough, and if she tried to reach it again, she'd only sink faster. She needed something to lengthen her reach. Celia reached underneath the shifting sand and undid her belt buckle, her sword sliding free. Celia did not want to lose the weapon, but she had no choice. The blade fell away from her and began sinking into the mire.

Celia reached back and flicked the belt up toward the branch. The belt coiled around the vine. She pulled hard, holding to the belt with one hand and reaching for the stem with the other. She squeezed, bringing the stem down enough to grasp with both fists and hoist herself upward. Muck slid from her body, and after a few minutes, she was free of the sand. Clutching the vine, she breathed rapidly, but she was safe.

Then the leaves on the far end of the bank erupted skyward, causing Celia to start in surprise. A scratching sound followed the explosion, and the forest floor at the edge of the quagmire opened wide, revealing a subterranean passage. A clawed hand reached out, grasping at the edge of the hole. Moments later a hunchbacked beast clambered from its lair, walking toward the quagmire on its forward knuckles and hind legs. A wicked ridge of spines ran down its arched back, and drool slavered over its fangs. The creature looked at Celia and screamed at her.

Then came another explosion, and a second monster appeared behind the first. Both advanced toward Celia, hissing from their throats. The leader of the two bunched its hind legs and jumped onto the first mound of dirt between the bank and Celia. In spite of its bulky size, the creature easily retained its balance atop the small island.

Celia met its gaze and gritted her teeth. Her only escape route was up. With the help of the vine, she pulled herself above the ground, moving toward the relative safety of the branches above.

The beast coiled and leaped again, leaving only one mound between her and it. Predator and prey stared at each other for one long second before the monster launched forward, pouncing off the last mound straight toward her. It moved in a blur, streaking toward her face with claws outstretched.

But Celia was faster.

She twisted, holding the vine with one hand and reaching down toward the quicksand with her other hand. Her fingers grasped the hilt of her sword, and she slid the blade free, bringing it from the mire in a single smooth motion. The monster impaled itself on the outstretched weapon, its talons flashing in front of her face before it fell away. Black blood sprayed in all directions. The monster's muscles slackened as she pulled her sword from its dead body, and the creature sank into the sands.

Celia looked to the bank for the other beast, but it was gone. She might have had time to ponder this mystery further, if the vine holding her in the air hadn't snapped.

She fell back into the sands.

* * *

Tim turned to strike his attacker, but something knocked his sword away. A hand seized his shoulder, drawing him close, and in the gloom he discerned Nazgar's grime-streaked face. The Kyrlod raised a finger to his lips and pulled Tim farther into the shadows, motioning him down onto hands and knees. The two crawled through the undergrowth as the thick of the trees closed behind them, concealing them from their pursuer. When they reached the base of the ridge, Nazgar signaled for Tim to stop.

"We cannot run from it," the Kyrlod whispered.

"What is it?" Tim asked.

"It is a Hunter from the border world. Zadinn summoned it, and you are its prey."

"Can it find us here?"

"It can find us anywhere."

A mere heartbeat later, the Hunter and its horse burst from the foliage fifty paces away. More vapor than substance, the edges of its body trailed away into wispy nothingness. The demon exposed its white teeth to them as its steed let out a cry and reared on its hind legs.

"Light," Nazgar said tersely.

"What?"

"Can you touch the Lifesource?"

Tim paused, the answer apparent in the doubt on his face.

"Then we need more time." Nazgar raised his hands. "Run!" Jets of blue fire shot from the Kyrlod's fingertips, slamming into the ground in front of the Hunter to create a blazing wall. Both horse and rider shied back from the flame, unwilling to look at it directly.

Tim fled into the woods, Nazgar right behind him. "You will need to seize the Lifesource," Nazgar said, voice relaxed and calm even as he ran at breakneck pace. "I cannot open my mind to Zadinn again."

How can he be so composed? "I need to be standing still," Tim protested.

"That is not an option."

The horse-wraith neighed in the background as it skirted the flames and resumed its pursuit. Tim gritted his teeth, trying to clear his mind, but he had only ever seized the Lifesource under controlled, safe conditions—nothing like this. This would never work.

*   *   *

Celia landed on her side this time—not a good position. It didn't give her as much time to figure a way out of the sand. She lifted her head clear of the quagmire, breathing deeply as she settled into the murky depths once more. She couldn't stay up indefinitely, but she could at least slow the process. A sound on the bank caught her attention, and Celia raised her head further to look back at the shoreline.

Something moved through the shadows. The second beast must have returned, and it gave her an idea. If she were to coax the monster into charging at her, she could drive her blade through it when it was close enough. She could then use its body to climb from the sand to another mound. *Perfect.* She whistled, hoping to draw the beast to the quagmire.

"Celia?" a voice said.

Celia sighed with relief. It wasn't the creature after all, it was another elion. Hedro Desh emerged on the bank. "Stop!" she called. "It's quicksand."

"I know," Hedro said, dropping his knapsack to the bank. He pulled out a length of rope, uncoiled it, and knotted the end for weight. He then tossed it to her, and she easily caught it. Bracing himself, Hedro steadily pulled her forward. Once she reached the first mound of solid earth between her and the bank, Celia released the rope and pulled herself onto the outcrop, taking the last few steps to safety herself. Only then did she allow her nerves to take over. She slumped onto the ground, feeling a tremor in her body. She closed her eyes and thanked the Maker for Hedro's timely arrival.

The big elion offered his hand. She took it, fingers intertwining in his, and he helped her to her feet. Hedro put his arms around her. Celia hesitated at first, but eventually relaxed and returned the embrace.

* * *

Boblin surveyed the valley. It wasn't hard to pinpoint the source of the scream, and what he saw made his gut clench—two monsters on the bank of a quagmire. The monsters didn't terrify him—it was the fact that he recognized their prey.

Celia. And he could not get to her in time. The first beast leaped toward her as she clung to a vine, halfway out of the quicksand. Boblin saw Celia move impossibly fast, dipping down into the mire and coming up with a sword. The blade flashed, and blood sprayed. *That takes care of one of them.*

But not the other. It streaked toward its downed mate, preparing to exact revenge. Boblin did not delay. He hefted a nearby stone and hurled it at the monster, striking it in the back of the head. The monster caught him in its gaze and gnashed its teeth. *This was a good plan. Now what?*

The creature's clawed feet tore long furrows in the soil as it leaped toward Boblin, its corded muscles rippling with the motion of its limbs. Boblin stood atop a thin ridge, with the quagmire in front of him and the swale behind. He unsheathed his sword and dropped into a low, defensive stance. *Well, it's not even noon and I've already gotten myself into more than a day's worth of trouble.*

The creature crossed the distance in seconds, launching itself into the air. Boblin brought his sword up in a sweeping movement, preparing to gore it through the jugular.

The monster slammed into him. Too late Boblin noticed the thick hide protecting the creature's throat. His sword glanced off its neck, not leaving so much as a scratch. The beast collided with him, propelling Boblin backward with its momentum. As Boblin fell backward down the ridge, out of sight of the quagmire and Celia, the creature sailed above him, its rear claws raking long gashes across his chest. Elion and beast tumbled down the hill, rolling into the base of the valley. Boblin's sword flew from his hands, landing in a pile of leaves several yards away.

The monster was back up before Boblin had time to collect himself. When it stood at full height, its head came to Boblin's chest level. Its massive jaws could probably crack him like an eggshell, but it ignored him. The creature turned and ran back up the hill to aid its mate. *Romance in the Korlan. There's probably a ballad about it.*

Boblin had to move fast. He unsheathed his boot knife and whipped the blade through the air, aiming for the soft, unprotected flesh of the creature's underbelly. His aim was true. The blade buried itself inside the monster's abdomen. The creature stopped in its tracks. Though loath to leave its mate alone, it couldn't let such a challenge go unaddressed. Boblin dived for his sword, rolling and coming back up with the weapon. The creature halted several yards away, front paws scraping the ground. It did not jump yet, gauging a plan of attack. After a moment, it shuffled to the left. Boblin turned with it, and it shuffled the opposite way. *It's trying to throw me off balance—*

The creature feinted left again and then charged. Boblin swung his sword downward, deflecting the monster's snapping jaws, and fell onto his back again. He lost his hold on his blade once more, and the monster pounced. Boblin brought up both hands, trying to protect himself from teeth and claws. He was *definitely* avoiding this karfing swale when he came to build a vacation home in the Korlan.

Boblin held the creature's front legs at bay with his left forearm. He shoved his right fist directly underneath the creature's chin, effectively preventing it from opening its lethal jaws. This standoff was only temporary. The beast was heavy, and sooner or later, it would rip and tear its way to victory. Already the claws on its legs sank into the flesh of Boblin's arm, drawing red droplets of blood. Dying was a job someone had to do, and Boblin was not one to walk away from a job, but if he gave in, Celia would be in danger, and he could not allow that.

His knife still protruded from the creature's side. Boblin never enjoyed risky endeavors, but he wasn't in a position to be picky. He pulled his fist out from under the creature's chin, drawing back far enough to deliver a hefty punch to the side of the monster's head. When the creature reeled back, Boblin grasped the handle of his blade from its belly and pulled it free, black blood spurting from the empty wound.

The creature lunged for Boblin's throat again. Boblin, knife in hand, shoved his fist into the creature's open jaws and drove the blade up through the roof of its mouth and into its brain. More blood rained down on him, but the creature's muscles immediately slackened. *Hard to wound, quick to die. Heavily armored, but fragile inside.*

Boblin pushed the dead corpse off and stood up. There was no time to delay. Celia was still in the quicksand. He practically flew to the top of the ridge—and came to an immediate stop. Celia was no longer drowning in the quagmire. She stood at the edge of the bank, locked in a deep embrace with Hedro. Neither saw Boblin. Boblin swallowed hard and retreated to the other side of the ridge. He felt like the monster had ripped out his entrails and used them to write insulting messages on the ground. *Were they kissing?* He hadn't looked long enough to know. He didn't want to know.

Boblin looked down at the slain creature, deciding Celia couldn't know what had happened back here. Boblin wiped blood off his knife and sword. After covering the creature's body with dead leaves, he walked to the other side of the swale and picked up his knapsack, using his waterskin to wash the cuts and scrapes from his skin. Last, he put on a fresh tunic, leaving no evidence that he had fought the beast. Somehow, this felt right.

Boblin breathed deeply. *I faced the monster, so I can face this.* He shouldered his knapsack and returned to the ridgeline, cautiously eyeing trees for one ideal enough to hang himself. *No such luck. I'd probably tie the knot wrong anyway.*

Boblin reached the top of the ridgeline. Hedro and Celia, no longer embracing, stood close together, talking in low voices. *Probably discussing where to go next, or maybe making sweet exchanges of poetry. Celia and the elion who saved her from the swamp.*

Hedro turned as Boblin approached. "Kule," he said. "Where did you wake up?"

"Back over there," Boblin replied, pointing to the other side of the ridge. "I heard your voices."

"Did you see anything out there?" Celia asked.

"A lot of trees."

Hedro whistled softly. "You're lucky, Kule. If you'd been here ten minutes ago, you'd have become a noon meal."

"For what?"

"There were creatures out here," Celia said. "I killed one. The other is nearby." She looked at both of them. "I don't suggest we wait for it to come back."

"If it's furry, I might want to scratch its ears," Boblin said.

Hedro shot him a look. "Your jokes aren't that funny, Kule."

"They make *me* laugh," Boblin said.

Hedro rolled his eyes. "Let's go." He walked up the ridge behind Boblin.

"Aye," Boblin agreed, "but you won't find anything over there. The scenery is terrible, and there's no place for my summer cottage."

"Besides," Celia said, pointing to a different ridge, "North is that way, and so is the other side of the Forest." Without waiting for either elion to acknowledge, she started walking in the other direction.

"Very well then," Hedro said. "Kule?"

"Right behind you," Boblin said. "Let's make a picnic of it." He followed the other two elions deeper into the forest, hoping they'd make it far enough to see the sun again.

* * *

Tim and Nazgar pushed through the foliage and into a small clearing. The Korlan's canopy still sheltered them in gloom, but relatively few trees stood in the immediate vicinity, leaving a large expanse of empty space between the trunks. This, however, was not a good thing. As soon as the Hunter emerged from the brambles, it would have no trouble closing the distance between them. Tim put on more speed, running as fast as he absolutely could. Behind them, the Hunter materialized from the foliage.

Tim glanced over his shoulder, seeing the horse double its speed. He attempted to clear his mind once more, but did not succeed. The Hunter rapidly gained distance, closing the gap to only a few strides, and raised a hand with fingers spread wide. An incandescent net of glowing yellow fibers shot from the Hunter's palm, falling over Nazgar and ensnaring him like a spiderweb.

"The Lifesource!" Nazgar shouted as he fell, enmeshed in glowing fibers. The Hunter raised its hand again, and another net flared out, jerking Tim onto the ground. He landed with his face in the earth. Wrestling against the bonds, he rolled onto his back.

The Hunter stopped astride its horse, its dark form outlined against the even darker backdrop of the Korlan. The steed stamped, a blast of foggy air erupting from its mouth and nostrils. The Hunter dismounted, patting its horse on the neck, and walked toward Tim, smiling as it circled its defenseless prey, eyes narrowed to slits.

"Focus!" Nazgar shouted. For the first time, his voice conveyed a hint of panic.

The Hunter drew a long knife from its belt. The blade's metallic edge gave off a dull gleam. Tim fought to hold back a rising wave of terror. Panic would ruin any chance he had of saving himself.

No Advocate ever touched the Lifesource in one day, but I did. That means I can also do this. Tim exhaled, his breath leaving his body in a gasp. *I have all the time in the world.*

With that last thought, the empty room sprang into clarity inside his mind. However, instead of finding himself on the far side of the room as usual, he now stood directly in front of the veil. A shadow brushed the edge of his shoulder and the room trembled, but Tim *pushed* the shadow away, quickly but calmly stepping into the light.

He opened his eyes, feeling the Lifesource surge through his entire body. The Hunter moved with vicious force, in the act of bringing its blade toward Tim's heart. Tim directed the energy from the Lifesource outward, creating a bubble of air that threw the demon on the ground in a hiss of surprise. Tim next directed the energy toward the glowing net. It took only a single thought for the cords to disintegrate. Free from the snare, Tim stood tall and faced the Hunter.

The Hunter snarled and the ground shifted, vines growing unbidden from the forest floor, ensnaring Tim's legs and arms, holding him immobile. The Hunter's hands blurred, replacing the knife with a full-length sword. It made a rasping noise, faintly reminiscent of laughter, and swung the blade at Tim's neck.

Tim used the Lifesource, causing the vines to retreat from his legs, and unsheathed his own sword. The two blades met. The Hunter retreated and Tim swung his sword through its midsection, but the blade passed through the demon without encountering the least resistance, leaving only twirling vapors in its wake. Unhurt, the shadow-creature laughed again and resumed its attack.

"Steel will not aid you!" Nazgar called out. "You need light!"

Nazgar's voice surprised Tim, and something terrible happened—or so Tim thought. The Lifesource left him.

But it flowed *into* the sword.

The hilt awakened in Tim's hands as the green pommel stone flared with spectacular brilliance. Blinding light enveloped the entire blade, consuming the sword in green fire.

All of this happened while Tim was still swinging his weapon to counter the Hunter's strike. This time when the two swords met, the Hunter's blade shattered into countless glittering shards. The demon staggered, and Tim detected a hint of fear from it. *Light,* Nazgar had said. Surely light was the quickest way to destroy a shadow.

The Hunter retreated as Tim pointed his blade toward it. A bolt of fire shot from the tip of his sword, over the Hunter's head and into the ground, and a sheet of flame blazed up, cutting off the demon's escape.

Tim commanded the fires to rise, surrounding them with a blazing green ring. The Hunter turned in circles, searching in vain for a way to defend itself, but it had nothing. Tim drove his sword into the Hunter's chest. The flames jumped forward, hungrily biting the edges of the shadow, consuming it with blazing brilliance. The Hunter screamed again as its silhouette shattered into wispy fragments. Near the trees, its horse bucked and reared before disappearing into a smoky whirlwind.

Tim let the sword fall from his hands as he collapsed. The fires of his blade winked out, and the ring of green flames died. Nearby, the glowing net dropped away from Nazgar's body. The prophet stepped over to help Tim up into a sitting position. He held a waterskin to Tim's lips, and Tim took several grateful gulps.

"Well done," Nazgar said.

"What happened to the sword?" Tim asked.

"It was not the sword," Nazgar replied. "It was the stone. It is a focusing point. The Lifesource runs throughout the natural world. Once a man's hands alter an object, that item can no longer hold the purity of the Lifesource, but unscathed, natural items always retain this inherent power. The Advocates found certain items containing…reservoirs…of the Lifesource. Anyone who knows how to touch the power can awaken the latent energy within these objects, and so the Advocates called them focusing points."

Nazgar reached into his pouch and pulled out a small blue marble. "This is another focusing point. Few exist in forms that can be easily carried, but such weapons are immensely powerful. Once an Advocate harnesses the energies of a focusing point, that Advocate can command those powers to his will."

Tim picked up his sword, running his hands over the pommel stone. "You gave this sword to Pellen," he said.

"Pellen was to protect the sword until its rightful owner claimed it," Nazgar replied. "That time has come."

"Why didn't you tell me before now?" Tim asked.

"A focusing point is easier, quicker…and much more dangerous. Becoming dependent on a focusing point will only hurt your training as an Advocate. Besides, if you had used it before you were ready, it might have killed you."

Tim eyed the weapon warily. Like the sword itself, the focusing point had two edges—it could protect him…or cut him as easily as an enemy. He gathered his powers again—it was easier now—and funneled them toward the stone. The blade glowed with green light as Tim moved through several sword forms. The weapon felt like a melded extension of his body *and* his mind.

Tim withdrew the power from the focusing point. The fire fizzled out, and the blade became an ordinary sword again. Tim's fingers tingled as he sheathed the weapon.

"What now?" Tim asked. "We need to find the others."

"I will leave that dilemma to you," Nazgar said, pulling an apple from his sack and polishing it against his shirt. He bit down on the fruit with a deliberate crunch.

Sometimes, his ceaseless calm can be infuriating. But Tim was learning to play Nazgar's game. The Kyrlod was baiting him into frustration, and Tim would not give him the satisfaction. So Tim also took out an apple and sliced it into sections. He looked at Nazgar, raised an eyebrow, and began eating, wordlessly imitating the Kyrlod's motions.

"The Korlan operates by controlling the minds of those in its landscape." Nazgar paused to take another bite. "What hinders can also help."

Tim stopped to consider Nazgar's words. If the Kyrlod was correct, then the Korlan Forest was nearly a living creature. Perhaps, then, Tim could locate its presence within the Lifesource. Tim closed his eyes to seek the power again. There was no longer any need for long hours of meditation. After having drawn the Lifesource in the presence of the Hunter, the power now came to him instantly. He probed outward, delving into the heart of the Korlan, and felt the entire world around him: Nazgar beside him, the earth below him, and the trees surrounding him. But the vegetation of the Korlan felt abnormal. An oily taint covered the length and breadth of the Forest, and Tim as expanded his reach, he realized the corruption originated from a single location.

The evil presence waited, pulsing, throbbing in time to an infernal heart-beat. Spite and malevolence rolled from it in waves. It was the same presence Tim had felt when holding the Lifesource the night before entering the Korlan— something malicious, a mind that wanted to ensnare all who came before it. He did not know where it had been birthed, only that it existed. It reached out for him with claws, as it had the other night, but this time Tim was ready.

He staved off the assault by holding up a barrier of willpower and pulling back. A series of tendrils trailed from the source, locked into the minds of the elion refugees, the connections faint but apparent. Some links felt stronger than others. Two trails led back to Nazgar and him, and Tim assumed a strong connection indicated an elion still under the spell, while tenuous links meant others who were free of the illusion.

As Nazgar said, Tim could use the connections to his advantage. Tim moved back along the path to the source, and struck before it could grab him. He forced his presence deep into the black orb. A slippery vortex wrapped around him, and for a moment Tim feared he had gone too far too fast. But he gained his purchase before the void could drag him away, and then he placed a message deep within the orb: *We are here.*

Tim envisioned the clearing where he and Nazgar stood. The message passed from him into the orb and then back out along the tendrils. It traveled to the elions, urging the refugees to come to him. The black presence lashed in retaliation, but Tim pulled away before it could draw him in. After he was safe, Tim released his hold on the Lifesource and opened his eyes. "Now we wait," he said.

* * *

Within the course of an hour, all thirty-six elions had gathered in the clearing. Several parties had encountered beasts in the forests, but by sticking together they remained unscathed. Thanks to Celia, the refugees gained a bearing on a northerly direction and retraced their steps back to the ridge, traveling in tense silence. Everyone was still slightly unnerved from the close call, but the Korlan did not attack them again. In a way Tim sensed the forest was now leery of *them*. Tim had invaded its mind, turned it against itself, so for now it merely observed the group in wary silence.

As gloomy as the Korlan already was, it became gloomier as night fell, and the group moved faster. They wanted to get out of the Forest as quickly as possible. They emerged on the other side, beneath the peaceful light of a three-quarter moon. For once the sight of the North's harsh landscape was welcome. Tim breathed in the night air. The breeze out here was fresher, cleaner, safer...untainted.

After the last elion stepped from the trees, the entire group visibly relaxed. The danger was past, and they were back in the open. That is, *one* kind of danger was past, but another loomed in front of them.

The base of the Northern Mountains waited a league away. Its jagged, snow-capped peaks jutted into the night sky with primeval majesty. Tim recalled the awesome presence of the Barricade, but that was nothing compared to this. The Barricade was a dwarf, the Mountains a giant.

The stars twinkled down on the company as they camped outside the Korlan. They had been allowed to survive thus far, but Tim knew that the Mountains waited, just as the Korlan had waited, to test their mettle, bravery, and skills. Two hundred years ago, the remnants of Ladu Jovun's imperial army had vanished into these heights. Now it was time to see what had become of them.

Twenty-One

The week it took to reach the Deathlands passed in a blur for Quentiin. After the deaths of Kevin and Grendin, the malichons placed him in a wagon with six other elions. At first Quentiin tried to speak with his companions, but the malichons reprimanded him for these efforts. Soon Quentiin had scars and lash marks all over his back. The wounds stung every time he tried to lie down.

Because of the forced silence, the prisoners communicated with looks and glances. Shifting eyes one way meant someone wanted to trade places; shifting eyes a different way meant someone had to relieve himself. The prisoners weren't allowed to leave the cages, even for this minor necessity, so they were required to use a corner of the wagon.

These silent talks became a way for the captives to hold on to their sanity. The elions had already lost their home, and now the malichons were stripping away their humanity. The presence of other prisoners was a minor comfort, but comfort nonetheless.

In spite of everything, Quentiin took heart from what he saw in the faces of the elions. One might expect the cages to be full of blank-eyed, mute prisoners—people who'd lost everything and had no hope for the future—but this was not the case. Though one could not deny the bleakness of their situation, every prisoner bore a fierce but quiet resolve, a silent proclamation of dignity that they had not been conquered yet. Walls were not the only reason the Fort of Pellen had survived over two hundred years. Its elions had a spirit that could not be taken away. Isanam had meant to weaken their spirits when he murdered Kevin, but instead, he had awakened their wrath. Anger, though it gnawed at the soul in other ways, was a tangible emotion that could be reached out to, touched, and clung to. It was a lifeline.

The ceaseless rhythm of their travels across the landscape soon grew tiresome. Hour after hour, day after day, the wagons rolled over the rocky terrain, climbing hills and bypassing gorges, while winds howled over them. The sky never varied; it was a never-ending slate of blank gray from horizon to horizon. Quentiin tried envisioning the green and rolling fields he'd seen on the tapestries at the Fort, but the image would not stick. He couldn't replace this dying wasteland with a land of health and growth, even in his mind.

Without the regular intervals of stopping for the evening and starting in the morning, time no longer held meaning. There was only the journey and the destination, nothing in between. On the last morning of the last day, Quentiin noticed something markedly different. The wind stopped, and the air became so still it felt surreal. The hue of the stony earth also changed, taking on a reddish hue, and the outcrops across the landscape became even more jagged and pronounced. Though all terrain in the North was harsh, this was even harsher. The stones of the Durin Plains might chafe and rub a traveler's feet, but these stones would *cut* feet.

There was no doubt about it—they were in the Deathlands. As the sun rose, Quentiin felt warm for the first time in weeks. The temperature steadily rose to an unbearable level, and without any shade, Quentiin's skin would burn—if not blister—by the end of the day. The dry air sucked moisture from his skin and lungs, searing him with unrestrained viciousness—a different savagery than the winds but no less potent. The malichon guards did not seem affected by this change in elements, and Quentiin recalled Nazgar's tale from the Fort. Of course the heat did not touch them—they had been bred in the fires of Malath.

A plateau stood in the distance, a ring of battlements at its top. On the other side of the bulwarks, a single massive spire jutted into the sky. Beyond this obsidian pinnacle, a fountain of flame shot into the air, raining down sparks and ash. Clangs and shouts echoed across the landscape, coupled with screams of anguish. This was the core of Zadinn's realm. The plateau's slopes made the citadel even more strategically sound than the Fort of Pellen. Any attacking army would have to fight an uphill battle, with defenders holding higher ground from all sides. To make a potential assault even more difficult, an oily moat enclosed the sheer battlements, a single drawbridge providing the only passage in or out.

The wagons tilted as the malichons began their ascent toward the city. As the wagons crested the plateau, the drawbridge descended, opening the way into the fortress. The massive battlements cast a shadow upon the captives, providing temporary respite from the sun, but such shade did not really provide any solace.

The malichons waited for the sharp spikes of the portcullis to rise, then led the wagons through the cavernous doorway. As Quentiin's cart passed into the fortress, he caught sight of a hunchbacked figure in a brown, hooded cloak manning the drawbridge. The creature clutched the portcullis crank with bony hands, saying nothing as the carts passed into the fortress. Once all were through, it wordlessly lowered the gate behind them.

Drab, identical buildings made of dull stone and thatched roofs lined the cobblestone streets. The entire city was orderly and spotless, without a speck of garbage. In the center of the city, Zadinn's domed palace waited, lined with opaque windows on all sides. The spire at its top was even more daunting up close. At the head of the citadel's broad, stone steps, a pair of stone gargoyles flanked either side of the entryway. Massive flames, fueled from an unknown source, danced and raged in the arched doorway. The malichons brought the wagons to the base of the steps and halted. Even with three wagons between him and the flames, Quentiin felt their heat.

At the head of the group, Isanam dismounted and walked toward the entryway. As Quentiin surveyed the scene, he noticed none of the other malichons placed so much as a foot upon the citadel's steps.

As Isanam approached the fiery entrance, a disembodied voice spoke from within: *"Who goes there?"*

"It is I, Isanam," the Overlord replied. "His Majesty expects me."

There was a momentary silence before the voice spoke again. *"Enter, and speak with my Master."* The flames disappeared, revealing a dark corridor. Isanam stepped forward, cloak swirling about him, and vanished into the passage. As soon as he passed through the archway, the fires sprang back up behind him.

"Horrors," a malichon said, spitting. One of his comrades looked at him sharply. The malichon swallowed hard and glanced back toward the entrance. Quentiin watched the exchange in silence. There was much to learn of this place, and none of it would be good.

The assembly remained still as minutes ticked by, and Quentiin soon felt cramped and uncomfortable. He looked around, but no one else so much as twitched. This oppressive, suffocating lack of *anything* irritated him. *Is there a karfing taboo on movement here? First no talking, now no moving?*

This place had fiddled with his nerves a bit too much. It was time to change things up a bit. He visibly coughed and stood up, raising his chained hands above his head in a stretch. He gave his entire body a good, healthy shake to loosen things up.

"Seat yourself!" a malichon said, holding up a whip.

Quentiin wasn't about to push things too far. He wanted to make a statement, but he had no desire to be whipped, so he settled back to a sitting position. His back felt fine now, all the kinks worked out to satisfaction. He sighed loudly and relaxed, lowering his eyelids. Until something important happened, he meant to get a bit of shut-eye.

The peace was short-lived. Seconds later, a ripple of disturbance ran through the assembly. Quentiin sat up as the flames in the palace doorway shuddered and extinguished, revealing a black void in their absence. Silence pressed down on the group as they waited, breath suspended, for the next turn of events. The seconds stretched...and then, each and every captive heard the distinct heel-toe rhythm of a single pair of boots, walking toward them one step at a time.

Thump. Thump. Thump. Prickles ran up and down Quentiin's skin with unrelenting speed. He knew he did not want to be here when whoever, whatever, was approaching arrived. Moments before, he'd been relaxed—even cocky—but now his heart hammered without pause.

A man stepped out of the passage and stood at the head of the steps. He was tall, over six feet in height, and wore a loose robe that covered him in folds of darkness. Black, slick hair covered his head, and in his hand he held a gnarled staff. He had a strikingly youthful face, smooth and unlined, but his eyes—a pair of glacial orbs that assessed anything and everything in their path—were far from young. Quentiin almost expected to see crystals of frost forming in the air around this man. He suddenly wanted to drop behind the edge of the wagon, out of sight, and stay there forever.

"Welcome," the man said, his voice cutting the air more sharply than the North wind ever could. "I am Zadinn."

Quentiin wouldn't have thought four such simple words could instill so much fear. He fought the urge to bury his face in the straw of the wagon.

"I've wanted to meet the elions of the Fort for some time," Zadinn said. "Pellen Yuzhar is not with you today, a fact I find disappointing. But fleeing the scene of a battle is nothing new to your leader. Two centuries ago, Pellen fled to the hills, much as he did on this most recent day. You should also know that he and those with him have been cornered and slain in the Kaltu Pass."

The prisoners bore this news in silence. Quentiin was not sure whether to believe this tale or not. The man in front of them was deceit clothed in human flesh. The elions could still pray Zadinn's tale was a lie.

Zadinn raised his arms. "Your days of luxury are at an end. Veldor the Slavemaster is your new lord. He holds the leash around your throats. I will not delay you any more than necessary, but there is one thing I must see to." He walked toward the front line of the wagons, narrowing his eyes at the captives as if he were examining slabs of meat at a butcher shop. The difference, though, was Zadinn wanted live meat—meat that still ran red—so he could hear it shriek as it roasted over the fire.

"You," Zadinn said, pointing to a wagon. "And you. And…you…are mine." He turned to the malichons. "Gentlemen!"

The malichons seized the three elions from the wagons. The captives kicked and screamed. One prisoner even managed to break free of his captor's grip and stagger to his feet. The malichons watched, bemused, as he ran back through the cluster of wagons.

"No," Zadinn said in gentle admonishment. "No, no, *no*." He gestured toward the fleeing prisoner with his staff, and the elion's legs suddenly locked together. The elion fell facedown onto the cobblestones. He raised his face and reached forward, grabbing the stones and dragging himself away from the citadel. Blood streamed from his nose, running down his lips and chin.

"You go from amusing to pathetic in the space of a heartbeat," the Dark Lord said, flicking his staff again. An invisible force jerked the elion's legs back and pulled him across the ground, all the way up the steps of the citadel toward the hallway beyond. The elion scrabbled in futility, trying to stop the inexorable force dragging him into the shadows. He let out a keening wail that made Quentiin clench with rage. No elion should be forced to lose his dignity like that. The screaming prisoner vanished into the hallway, and his cry instantly died.

Quentiin saw shapes moving within the dark passage, rippling like a giant liquid wave. The elion screamed again—and if his first cry had been awful, then this next was unbearable. The shriek went on and on, interrupted only by agonized gasps of torment. The noise tore and ripped at Quentiin's nerves. Something inside of that place was breaking the bones in the elion's body, one at a time, and sucking the blood from his veins. And then the air went blissfully silent, but Quentiin knew those sounds would return to him late at night.

He turned to see one of his companions had vomited in the cart. The elions of the Fort, stouthearted folk all, had encountered a level of evil they were not yet capable of contending with.

"Carry on," Zadinn said to the remaining wagons. The malichons directed the prison carts toward the northwest corner of the fortress. Once past the rigorously defined streets and houses, they arrived at an area enclosed by a ring of wooden walls. On the other side of the barricade, a jet of fire and sparks shot into the sky—the sight Quentiin had witnessed while traveling toward the plateau. Cracking whips and resultant screams emanated from the enclosed area.

The malichons led the wagons single file through a doorway, where a single guard stood watch. *A suitable lack o' guards, but ye can bet yer hide there's a reason they ain't worried about escape.* After what he'd just witnessed on the steps of the citadel, Quentiin didn't have to speculate much about that.

Once inside the walls, the outer world slipped away. The slave pens did not possess the rigorous elegance of the rest of Zadinn's city. Here, rows and rows of straw-lined cages ran along the walls to Quentiin's left, leading to a rectangular stone building.

Everywhere Quentiin looked, he saw only signs of endless torment. A stream of work carts traveled up a broad path toward the newcomers, filled with large chunks of obsidian. They were pulled by slaves, not horses—elions, dwerions, and humans, old and young, male and female, all shackled to the reins of the carts. Sharp gravel lined the path, over which the prisoners walked barefoot. Though blood ran from their feet, the drivers pulled onward, while malichons stood along the path and laid whips to their backs.

The work carts veered off to an area on Quentiin's right, where other slaves worked side by side to unload the carts. A third group of slaves worked beside the second, chisels in hand, chiseling rough chunks of stone into smooth blocks. Every captive was worn and emaciated, some more so than others.

And Quentiin recognized several of them. Billian Briiga, mayor of Raldoon, pulled at the yoke of a cart. His beard had grown long and greasy, and bleeding scars crisscrossed his back. Nearby, Yagglem the innkeeper sweated and strained, chiseling square stones to perfection, his hands chafed and peeling. Farther down the path, Galldo the blacksmith staggered toward the fiery pit, shackled to a young man beside him.

Quentiin Harggra had come home…in a manner of speaking.

Upon seeing Quentiin and the new arrivals, one malichon walked toward them. He wore a cape over his shoulders, fastened around his neck with a golden chain, and held a snake hide whip in his hand.

"Welcome, people of the Fort," he said. "My name is Veldor, and you are now my property. You will work all day, every day, until your miserable bodies expire in the dust."

The mules strained against their reins and again pulled the prisoners' wagons forward, taking them past the rows of cages. They halted alongside the rectangular building to face a small pool of gray water. A malichon unlocked the back of Quentiin's wagon. "Stand up!" the malichon said.

Quentiin did as he was told. He wasn't against digging his heels in every now and then, but a lad had to be wise about things like that. "Step out one at a time," the malichon ordered. Quentiin went first.

As soon as he landed, a second malichon grabbed Quentiin's arm in a cold, tight grip and pulled him to the murky water. Quentiin's short legs could only move so quickly, and the malichon took big strides as the dwerion stumbled to keep up. "Ye can take the speed down a tick, laddie," he grumbled. "I'm in here fer the rest of my life, didn't ye hear? Might as well enjoy—"

The malichon released its grip, backhanding Quentiin across the mouth. The blow cut Quentiin's lip and knocked him to his knees.

"Silence!" the malichon said. It jerked Quentiin back up and resumed its pace. Blood ran down Quentiin's chin. *An' didn't I decide, just a minute ago, to keep my jabber-flapper shut for a wee bit?*

They continued walking toward the water, but the malichon did not stop at the edge of the pool. It held a grip on Quentiin—two hands this time—and deliberately marched into the waves.

It was freezing cold. Quentiin gasped in shock, marveling that there was not a sheet of ice on top of the pool. All around him, other malichons did the same with the rest of the prisoners. When they reached waist depth, the malichon put a hand on top of Quentiin's head and shoved the dwerion beneath the surface. Quentiin went under, his mouth still agape. *Bloody karfin' son of a three-legged goat!*

The malichon pulled him back out. Quentiin nearly doubled over as a fit of hacking coughs seized him. Water spluttered out of his mouth. Just when he thought his lungs were clear, the malichon pushed him back down. Quentiin thrashed. This time, the malichon did not immediately pull him back up, and as seconds stretched, Quentiin felt the need for air slowly overcome his chest in a burning trickle. He thought it meant to drown him this time, but the malichon pulled him out just the same.

The malichon then dragged Quentiin back through the water to the shore. Quentiin shivered. The Deathlands might be hot, but being doused in the remains of a melted glacier would give anyone gooseflesh. His long beard dripped, and Quentiin suspected it resembled an icicle. They traveled uphill, past the rectangular building to the cages. The sun was setting, illuminating the slave pen with a bloody hue.

"You are fortunate today," Quentiin's captor said. "There is no need to begin your work until tomorrow." He undid the latch on an empty cell and booted Quentiin's backside, propelling the dwerion onto the straw-lined floor. The malichon closed the door and firmly snapped the lock into place. As he sat there, Quentiin reflected that most of his time in the North had been spent imprisoned. His hands remained shackled; the chains had not come off once during the entire journey in the wagons. Quentiin had hoped that their captors would at least remove the chains upon reaching the slaves' quarters, but it didn't happen. On the brighter side, though, he could finally get some shut-eye without jouncing along in the back of a wagon, where every bump and crevice in the ground jarred his entire skeleton.

However, *that* brief hope also proved groundless. The malichon returned with a partner, and stood by the cage, hands clasped behind its back. It smiled at Quentiin with pointy teeth.

What is he smilin' at? Are we goin' to the inn for a pint, or somethin' o similar value? But something as wholesome as finely brewed ale would likely turn a malichon's entrails inside out. *Ye can't put a good thing into a bad bein' without some sort o' consequences.*

The first malichon opened the cell door. "Stand up," it said. Quentiin did, glancing toward the other cages to see the other newcomers also receiving visits from pairs of malichons. "Hold out your hands," the creature said.

Quentiin complied, and the malichon unlocked his chains. *There are blessin's in Malath after all.*

"Now turn around, and spread your arms out. Hold on to the bars of your cell."

Quentiin continued to follow orders. The malichon refastened the shackles onto Quentiin's wrists, chaining the dwerion to the wall of his cell with arms outstretched and backside exposed. After it finished binding Quentiin, it stepped back and spoke.

"We cleansed you—at least, to the best of our ability, because the lesser races can never be fully pure. Now we will condition you. We do this as a favor. Those who learn their place quickly are apt to survive longer."

The other malichon unclasped its hands and uncoiled a whip. The guard cracked it once, flexing it, and then hurled the length of cord forward. It scored into Quentiin's back, leaving a blazing trail of pain. Quentiin surged against the bars, grunting in pain.

"One," the malichon said.

The whip struck Quentiin again. "Two." Around him, Quentiin heard the other elions crying out as they received similar treatment.

"Three." A few, like Quentiin, schooled themselves to silence. He expelled a grunt every time the whip landed, but he did not scream.

"Four." The malichon continued counting. By the time it reached *six,* Quentiin was seeing sparks. He did not know how much longer he could cling to consciousness. They gave him a dozen lashes before stopping to unshackle his wrists. Quentiin remained standing as his tormentors departed.

His back throbbed as droplets of blood ran past his spine, but only after the malichons had left did Quentiin allow his legs to buckle. He collapsed, careful to do so face-first. If his back were to touch anything, it would elevate his pain to an unbearable level. Before, Quentiin had thought he was going to pass out, but now that the beating had ended, he thought he would never sleep. While in such pain, who could?

As darkness descended, the temperature fell. Blazing hot during the day, the Deathlands at night were as frigid as the rest of the North. Quentiin realized he was dripping wet, and as the cold overcame him, he shivered. His back felt like fire and the rest of his body like ice—a painful juxtaposition of sensations. Quentiin Harggra did not sleep much that night, and he supposed that was the malichons' objective.

Conditioning. What a karfing euphemism.

Twenty-Two

At daybreak, when Quentiin's pain had settled to a dull throb in cadence with his heartbeat, the malichons returned. Quentiin had settled into a light doze, but when he heard the lock *snick* open, he jumped awake. He noted through bleary eyes that this was not the same malichon that had escorted him the previous evening. *Good, I've had enough of that foul-smellin' chap. Then again, unless I've hit a stroke o' luck, this bloke here ain't likely to be much better.*

The malichon reached into the cell, pulling Quentiin onto his feet and marching him out along the path. Quentiin had never won any awards for intellect, but he had a good guess as to where they were headed.

The water in the pool was even colder during the morning. A faint mist clung to its silvery surface. The malichon did not flinch as it waded in waist-deep, pulling Quentiin along. Apparently cleanliness was a matter of high importance around here. Being forewarned, Quentiin took a breath before the guard shoved him beneath the surface of the water.

I've been here less'n a day, and I've already met three malichons I'd like to kill. Make that four. This laddie here, the two from yesterday, an' the Slavemaster 'imself. Imagine how many I'll wanna kill by this afternoon.

When the malichon pulled him out of the water, Quentiin noted that most of the slaves who'd been here for some time did not have malichon supervision. These other prisoners waded in, faces devoid of expression, scrubbing themselves in the icy waters.

"We will not coddle you like this for long," the guard said, noticing Quentiin's glance. "When you are ready to take care of yourself, you will be allowed to do so."

When finished, they did not return to the cells but instead headed to the drab stone building. A thin trickle of smoke rose from its top. The malichon led Quentiin inside to a long hallway with rows of tables and benches. At the end of the hall, a line of slaves stood near a window, where they received bowls of sludge-covered gruel. "Eat," the malichon said to Quentiin, pointing to the line.

Quentiin glanced about and walked over to the serving window. A faint murmur filled the breakfast hall. Apparently talking was allowed in this place, and for that, Quentiin was grateful. The forced silence of the last week had nearly driven him mad. When it was his turn, Quentiin got a closer look at the food. On the other side of the counter, a young girl numbly ladled a scoop of gruel into a tin bowl. It dropped with a soft *plop*, slowly oozing to fill the contours of the bowl as steam rose from it.

The girl handed the food to him, and Quentiin looked at her face. Strands of dirty blond hair hung over her eyes, and she could not have been more than nine or ten years old. Rage coursed through Quentiin's veins. *She should not be here. She should be playin' underneath the mornin' sun in a grassy field.*

He lifted a cup of water and sipped it, turning his lips at the musty taste. Then, after turning from the line, Quentiin saw him—and for the first time in two weeks, his spirits truly lifted.

"Jolldo Graff!" he said, smiling in spite of the circumstances. The dwerions at the breakfast table started, looking up at Quentiin, and his eyes widened in surprise.

For a moment Jolldo even looked happy, but soon the light faded from his face and his demeanor grew solemn. "Quentiin," he said, putting down his fork. Quentiin noticed Jolldo's hands were badly chafed, soil lodged firmly underneath his fingernails. "How did they get ye?"

Quentiin seated himself on the other side of the table. "Because I followed 'em."

"Ye got on the other side o'…o' the Rampart?" Jolldo asked.

"Same as ye did, laddie," Quentiin replied.

"Ye should've traveled northwest. They say there's a safe place there."

Quentiin spat. "It ain't safe anymore."

"What d'ye mean?"

"I went there…and so did the malichons. It's called the Fort o' Pellen. One o' their own opened up the gates and let the malichons in."

"The Fort of Pellen?" an elion asked. He sat a few places to Quentiin's right. "You were there?"

"That's what I'm sayin'," Quentiin said.

"How long was it before the malichons retreated?" the elion asked.

"Ye ain't *listenin'*, laddie, "Quentiin said. "It's *gone*; the whole karfin' place blew itself up."

The elion swallowed hard. He had a spoonful of gruel up to his lips but immediately put it down, hand trembling. "The Fort can't fall. The Fort *doesn't* fall!"

"I didn't *fall*—it blew itself to little pieces. Left a big karfin' hole in the mountain, too."

The elion's voice was hoarse. "Where are the survivors?"

Quentiin pointed to a group of elions clustered at the end of the breakfast line. "Right there, laddie."

"No…no!" The elion stumbled to his feet and walked toward the group, limping noticeably on his left leg. "Where's Pellen?"

The question—*Where's Pellen?*—spread through the slaves the way a bad cough spreads. Quentiin heard a rustle of discontent, and it reminded him of dry tinder. So he'd lit a match to a fire, one that would burn the foundations of hope. He realized he'd done a terrible thing. These prisoners clung to the knowledge that somewhere in the North, some folk awoke to a free dawn after sleeping in their own beds in a real home. They didn't expect the Fort to rescue them—several hundred elions were no good against an army of malichons— but *knowing* freedom existed somewhere, even for a small community, was reason to go on. The arrival of the new slaves now took that away. Perhaps he shouldn't have spoken up, but the story had been bound to emerge sooner or later.

"This ain't good," Jolldo said.

"Aye, laddie," Quentiin agreed.

Many longtime slaves, former members of the Fort, recognized the new-comers as the news continued to spread. By breakfast's end, every slave would know it.

Barely a quarter of an hour later, the malichons arrived and the crowd went silent. "Assemble!" one of the guards said. The slaves responded by standing, and the malichons walked up and down between the tables, issuing orders to each slave.

"Quarry. Cart detail. Shaping. Cart detail. Quarry. Shaping." After each order, the slave in question departed for the doorway.

A malichon approached Quentiin and eyed him up and down, curling its lip as he did so. "You're new."

"Aye," Quentiin replied.

The malichon backhanded him. Quentiin staggered, and the cut on his lip, which had healed overnight, reopened with fresh blood. "Quarry," it said, and looked at Jolldo. "You teach him."

"Aye," Jolldo replied, bobbing his head in a brief bow as he grabbed Quentiin's forearm. "Let's go."

As they walked away, Quentiin wiped his lip. "Son of a three-legged goat."

"They'll do that to ye for about a week or so," Jolldo said.

"I know." *Conditioning.*

Quentiin followed Jolldo outside, where prisoners milled back and forth to their assigned destinations. A row of carts lined the rocky path, each wagon's yoke resting on the ground in eager anticipation to close upon the shoulders of the newest group of slaves. A few elions were already harnessing themselves to the shackles, while nearby a handful of malichons strode up and down the road, lashing their whips whenever they felt compelled to do so. "Keep things moving!" one called out to Jolldo and Quentiin.

"Aye, sir," Jolldo answered, bowing again. Quentiin acknowledged with a much more cursory nod. He wondered if he would get away with it. He did. Jolldo led Quentiin down the path, which took a steep turn down toward a massive hollow.

After they started their descent, Quentiin got his first glimpse of the quarry, an enormous hole that took up almost the entire valley. Walls of jet-black stone surrounded it on all sides, and at the very bottom, hundreds of feet down, an enormous lake of fire raged. As the two dwerions walked forward, jets of flame shot into the sky, arching high above their heads.

Gigantic plinths of obsidian dotted the quarry, sticking up from the fire like long fingers. A network of bridges stretched over the fiery chasm, each bridge leading to a separate plinth. Slaves moved across these bridges, harvesting stone on precarious ground while lava boiled far beneath them. A narrow ledge of stone, filled with more laboring slaves, enclosed the hole. "Welcome to the Pit, mate," Jolldo said.

They walked to a wooden shack at the edge of the quarry. Here, a line of slaves waited for the malichons to place chains around their waists. Each belt was linked to a belt on a second prisoner, so they moved in pairs of two. Each slave also received a hammer and chisel. When they reached the front of the line, Quentiin recognized the malichon from the previous night—and apparently the malichon recognized him, too.

"Does that hurt, mate?" it asked, pointing at Quentiin's lip.

"No," Quentiin replied. He wasn't about to add a *sir* to that, even if Jolldo did. Quentiin didn't object to the word—he'd used it often enough in the Alcatune Army—but by the Maker, the one hearing the *sir* had to earn it.

The malichon swung its fist through the air, connecting dead center with Quentiin's face. Quentiin's nose erupted in a spray of blood. *I'm goin' to be bleedin' a lot today.*

"It does now," the malichon said. It placed a chain belt around Quentiin's waist and gave a good, hard pull. Another malichon performed a similar service for Jolldo, minus the slug to the face. The two dwerions, linked together, walked toward the Pit. Quentiin felt the heat of the flames, even at this distance.

"Do me a favor, laddie," Jolldo said to Quentiin as they neared the first bridge. "Don't fall."

Quentiin looked at him. "Does that happen much around here?"

He'd meant it as a joke, but Jolldo did not respond, and that was answer enough. He carefully followed Jolldo onto the wooden bridge. He did not like the looks of this structure. The planking swayed as he stepped onto it. Waves of heat wafted up from the lava below. Quentiin placed a hand on the roped side rail, palms clammy with sweat, and stepped forward. The planks stood several inches apart from one another, which left numerous gaps across the length and breadth of the walkway.

The bridge sloped down to the first plinth of obsidian, where several groups of slaves clustered to chisel chunks from the stone's side. Others had the task of carrying the blocks up the bridge and to the wagons. By the time Quentiin reached the other side, his legs felt like rubbery ju-fish.

Once the process of work began, the hours passed quickly but not easily. The hammer and chisel rubbed at his palms, and his wrists ached and throbbed. The weight of each stone wore into the small of his back until it felt permanently twisted. The hard ground scraped the soles of his bootless feet, and his skin grew streaked with sweat and dirt.

For the first time in his life, Quentiin felt grateful to see a malichon, because the creature gave them permission to take a respite. It was not a long rest, no more than five minutes, but it was a chance to stop and breathe. When the same malichon returned, announcing it was time for the noon meal, Quentiin almost wanted to thank the guard, and that sentiment scared him more than anything he'd experienced so far—because the moment he began feeling gratitude toward his captors would be the moment he'd been broken.

Lunch was the same sloppy gruel served in the same bare room. Jolldo took Quentiin to a table lined with dwerions. Quentiin knew all of them: Vellgo, Yagglem, Galldo, Greebla, Briiga, and many others.

The prisoners in the Pit could be almost entirely identified by two distinct groups—remnants of the Fort and remnants of Raldoon, one for the South and one for the North. These two worlds, having grown apart so long, were now thrust together in the same depraved nightmare. In addition to the elions and dwerions, there was also a scattering of men and women, no doubt descendants of those taken prisoner many years ago, a generation born into captivity.

Between spoonfuls of gruel, Quentiin told his friends what had happened since the night of the malichon invasion.

"What d'ye suspect the others will do when ye don't come back?" Briiga asked.

"Herrdra an' Yuulin traveled to Vonku," Quentiin answered. "By the time they return to Raldoon with the King's soldiers, they'll know we ain't comin' back. I expect the soldiers will travel to the Rampart."

"Ye said the tunnel closed after ye?" Greebla interjected.

"Aye, an' it's better that way," Quentiin said. "That wall is the only thing keepin' Zadinn Kanas from gettin' into the South."

"D'ye really think so? If he got the malichons through once, he can do it again."

"It don't add up, laddie," Quentiin said. "Zadinn only sent a small group through, an' now they're back on this side o' the wall. He ain't shy. If he had a way o' sendin' more malichons through, he would'a done so already. Somethin's holdin' him back."

"Aye," Jolldo concurred. "The older slaves say there's been a different feel to the place these last couple o' weeks, like its pulse is out o' rhythm. There's more urgency to build, build, build, an' the usual number of guards in the slave pen is down by half. That means they've been sent elsewhere. He's preparin' his forces for somethin'."

"Fewer guards," Quentiin said. "That's somethin' we can make use of, d'ye ken?"

In that instant, everyone else at the table found something else to look at. Not one dwerion met Quentiin's gaze. He laughed. "Don't get ju-fish in yer stomachs, mates! I ain't goin' to put a kink in yer plan." They stayed silent. "Ye have a plan, right? Ye've been here nearly a month. Ye've got to have somethin' worked out by now!"

"Plan for what, Quentiin?" Jolldo asked.

"Escape, ye goat-brain!"

Yagglem stood up. "I've got to get back to work, laddies." He carried his half-finished bowl to the counter, walking with jerky, strained movements.

The other dwerions, save for Jolldo, mumbled similar comments before dispersing. No one glanced back, as they left Quentiin and Jolldo alone. The two friends stared at each other from across the table.

"Clam yer big jaw shut," Jolldo said. "I don't want to hear that talk again."

"What? Escape?" Quentiin asked. "Why don't ye clam *yer* trap? I'll say it if I want! I'll say it eight times a day, laddie!"

Jolldo's face transformed to a snarl that was part anger, part fear. "Shut it! Shut yer trap right now!" He grabbed Quentiin's tunic, whispering his next words. "The first night we crossed into the North, Jiira tried to get away. They caught him before he made it a hundred strides. An' then they brought Jiira before *him*—Isanam, the Overlord. Isanam strung Jiira up by his arms over a pot o' boilin' oil an' *lowered* him into it. He went slowly, twelve inches every ten minutes. It took an hour, Jiira screamin' the whole time.

"When we got to the Pit, another group tried to run off. Ye've seen that last row o' cages? Well, they made it *half* that distance before the guards had 'em. Veldor told 'em he was feelin' merciful, an' for their penance all he wanted them to do was dig a hole an' fill it back up. So they dug a hole, a karfin' deep one. When they said they was ready to fill it up again, Veldor pushed 'em in an' said they'd do the fillin' part with their own bodies. They were stuck down there, the walls steep an' no way back up, an' then Veldor emptied a wagon-full of vipers into the hole."

Jolldo pulled Quentiin closer, snarling. "*So don't ever karfin' say 'escape' again.*"

Jolldo released him and Quentiin was silent. He knew this was a bad place, but he hadn't realized *how* bad. The atrocities weren't what unnerved him. The

malichons' savagery no longer surprised him. It was what this place did to a
dwerion on the inside. The Jolldo Graff in front of him was not the Jolldo Graff
from three weeks ago.

Quentiin took his thoughts of escape and locked them deep and secure
within his soul. He wasn't abandoning the thoughts, no, he was consciously
putting them in a place the malichons could not touch. Jolldo Graff had given
up hope, as had some of his other friends—but Quentiin wasn't giving *his* sense
of hope away.

The first day passed, and so did the next, and again the next after that.
Quentiin received "conditioning" every night for a week. After that, the malichons did not drag him to the water pool every morning; instead, he dragged
himself there. The malichons told him it was because he'd learned to be respon-
sible, that he'd shown he could be trusted. That's what they told all the new
prisoners, that they had been given their rights and independence back.

And that was the irony of it all, because they'd been given nothing back.
The fact that they walked to the gray pool every morning was not a good
thing—it was evil. A free man would have kicked and screamed all the way
before letting a malichon throw him into the pool. But the malichons no longer
had to do this, because they had taught the prisoners *how to do it to themselves.*
The resolve Quentiin had seen in the elions during the early part of captivity
steadily evaporated with each day. This was how Quentiin knew the elions were
no longer free.

That part of himself he'd locked away—Quentiin awakened it every night,
in the cages, and that was how he kept his spirit. Oh, he walked to the pool
every morning, putting on the numb, senseless face, but underneath he nurtured and soothed those pure feelings hope brought. They were secret, but they
were very much alive.

* * *

Zadinn Kanas considered his next move.

The Hunter was dead. Last night, Zadinn had felt the clash of the two
forces—Hunter and Warrior. The demon had not survived, but that was of no
consequence. Zadinn had gathered the information he needed.

Ever since unleashing the demon from the border world, Zadinn had
felt Hunter and Warrior move closer to each other. Up until the conflict, the

Warrior's presence remained faint, and even after the two combatants began fighting, the Warrior's strength was feeble. But at the very end, the Warrior's candlewick flame erupted into a bonfire. The Hunter hadn't stood a chance before that tidal wave of magic.

Clearly the Warrior was still a novice, just learning to use the Lifesource to its full potential. Only luck, nothing more, had saved him. However, from the previous night onward, the Warrior's presence in the Lifesource no longer wavered, now steady and consistent. The boy would become stronger with each passing day. Zadinn had started things, and now he needed to finish them. But though he felt the Warrior more strongly than ever, Zadinn still could not pinpoint his precise location, which meant it was time for another decision.

"My lord?"

Zadinn looked up to see Isanam at the entrance to the throne room, and he waved the Overlord to him. Upon reaching the steps of the dais, Isanam knelt and raised a hand to lift his cowl, directing his face to the floor as he removed his skull-mask.

"You requested my presence," Isanam said.

"Yes," Zadinn said. "The Warrior has defeated the Hunter."

"Is he strong?" Isanam asked.

"Yes," Zadinn said, "but not strong enough. Follow me."

Isanam lifted his face, and the Dark Lord looked upon the commander of his armies. The Overlord had a rotting, desiccated visage, one containing both malichon and human features, because Isanam himself was of both races. He had the angular, sharp teeth of a malichon, and his eyes burned with their characteristic red color, but his gray skin did not conform to the bones of his face, making his features twisted and unnatural.

"We are going to visit the prisoner, my son," Zadinn said. The title was more than just a figure of speech. Isanam was the only malichon who possessed the Lifesource, because he was the only malichon Zadinn had fathered.

Zadinn led the way from the smoke-filled room, running his hand over the skulls on the walls. He strode down the passageway with slow, deliberate steps, momentarily pausing by each cell he passed. Every time he stopped, he relished the sense of fear from the prisoners on the other side. They knew *he* was out there, waiting, and they dreaded that he might come to them.

Zadinn walked to the very last door in the hallway, close to the flames at the citadel's entrance. The door had no lock, just a barely perceptible seam in the wall. The opposite side of the wall, the prison side, was inevitably covered with streaks of blood. The captives, seeing no lock and no latch, always managed to believe they could claw their way out of this dungeon. Of course it never worked, and it always drove them mad.

Zadinn put his finger on the seam, and the door swung open. He paused, observing the room's lone occupant—who, at the sight of the Dark Lord, slid to a back corner of the cell. The prisoners always did this, too, another indication of their belief that they could somehow avoid what was coming.

Zadinn stepped into the cell without a word. Kaiel Tulak moaned, raising an arm as if to defend himself. Irritated, Zadinn waved his staff, and the elion's hand snapped down to his side, locking into position with the rest of his body.

"Bring him to me," he said to Isanam. The Overlord—mask and cowl back in place—pulled the quivering elion onto his feet. Isanam dragged Kaiel across the cell and forced him to a kneeling position with face pushed toward the floor.

"You'll want to let go," Zadinn said, and Isanam released his hold on the prisoner.

Zadinn placed his hand atop Kaiel's skull. Sweat ran down the elion's skin, and the veins in his head throbbed with wild fear. Zadinn closed his eyes and reached *inside* Kaiel's mind. It was not a gentle touch. He seized the elion's thoughts with burning fingers and then clenched his fist. Kaiel jolted underneath Zadinn's grasp, screaming as his body rocked, but Zadinn ignored the prisoner and dug deeper, deeper, deeper.

After Zadinn pulled his hand back, Kaiel crumpled into a ball on the floor, whimpering as pain wracked his body. "I can feel you," Kaiel said. He placed a hand on either side of his head. "You're inside me."

"Yes," Zadinn said, "I am." He had melded Kaiel's mind to his own. This was a one-way connection, of course. Zadinn could hear Kaiel's thoughts, but Kaiel could not hear Zadinn's. "I need to know where you are at all times, because I have a job for you. I need to know where your people are."

"They'll never take me back," Kaiel said.

"Of course they won't. You must remain unseen. You will find their trail north of the Korlan Forest. Follow them wherever they go, and I will have the information I need. You shall leave upon the hour."

The elion did not protest. It would do him no good. Besides, Zadinn could use the meld to urge Kaiel in whatever direction he wanted. Should Kaiel think independently, Zadinn could always apply more force—and the urging did not have to be subtle.

"And, Kaiel," Zadinn said, "I know where you are. Always. So don't get… lost."

"Yes, my lord."

"In case you have any doubts…" Zadinn sent a spike of pain through Kaiel. The elion convulsed, seizing his skull again. "I have ways of encouraging you."

Kaiel nodded, unable to speak. Zadinn turned away and left with Isanam, not bothering to close the door. Kaiel had places to be, and Zadinn was not about to slow him down. The elion would perform his task. He knew Zadinn's capabilities. And besides, he was no doubt eager to flee the Deathlands.

Of course it did not matter. As a rule, Advocates never established melds, because even though they were wonderfully efficient, they also had fatal consequences for the recipient. The mind only had room for one consciousness at a time, and Kaiel's brain would not last long under this new stress. After a month, he would not retain a single shred of his former sanity.

"What happens next, my lord?" Isanam asked.

"We wait for Kaiel to close the distance. Once he does, I will know where the refugees are headed." He already had a hunch, but there was no need to share that information yet. "Everything in its due time."

Twenty-Three

The elion refugees began their ascent at dawn. The air bit into Tim's face, but from a certain perspective it was a comforting cold. The temperature in the other parts of the North had felt feigned, a result of unnatural weather patterns, but this was a fresh temperature brought about by the elevation of the Mountains and the promise of snow. It was a clean, living cold, not the creep of death.

The lower part of the Mountains consisted of gently rising and falling foothills. Traveling up and down this terrain proved more taxing than the flatlands of the Durin Plains, so the refugees stopped more frequently. To turn his mind away from his weariness, Tim focused his attention on the snowcapped peaks in the distance, willing them closer with every step.

In the morning light, the Mountains no longer seemed foreboding, and after the darker confines of the Korlan, the open air and daylight was quite welcoming. Tim looked back at the thick growth of trees at the base of the hills south of them. He reached out, just barely, and felt the now-familiar malevolent presence stirring within the Forest. The Korlan hung back, tentative. It still wanted Tim, badly, but now that it knew he was capable of fighting back, it kept at bay, preferring tamer prey.

Tim brushed his fingertips across the hilt of his sword, sensing the latent energy within its focusing point. After his encounter with the Hunter, holding the Lifesource was no longer difficult. In a sense, the attack had almost been a blessing. Instead of struggling with frustration for hours at a time, Tim now just relaxed his mind, reached out, and let the power flow into him. He was not successful all the time, but success often came quickly, and his failures were shorter and less frequent.

As the refugees traveled toward the Mountains, Tim practiced seizing and releasing the Lifesource, using the process to occupy his mind as he walked across the foothills. By the time the sun hung in its noon position, they took a brief rest. While the other elions occupied themselves about the camp, Tim retreated to a higher area where he could look back at the mass of the Korlan. While still close to the Forest, he'd been wary of its power and had therefore been reluctant to fully work with the Lifesource. Now that he had put some distance between himself and the shadows, he felt more secure.

Tim eased his thoughts, and the power returned easily. The process felt like moving into a gentle stream; the Lifesource pulled him along with its currents, but he only needed to assert his presence, and the waters flowed where he directed them. He probed north, toward the refugee camp. A mixture of feelings hovered around the elions, mingling through the group in a fog of human emotion. Some individuals, like Pellen Yuzhar and Jend Argul, stood out more strongly than others. In the middle of it all, Tim sensed a noticeable void, detectable by its absence. Nazgar of the Kyrlod was concealing himself, cloaking his presence to protect his mind from Zadinn Kanas.

Tim turned his thoughts toward the landscape to the south. An invisible border, unseen to the naked eye but noticeable through the Lifesource, marked the spot where the land released itself from Zadinn's blight and transformed back into the true, natural world. Right now, the refugees stood in the place of the in-between. Here in the Mountains, the land did not suffer from Zadinn's touch, but it couldn't escape the scourge entirely. Around the Korlan and other areas, the taint grew more pronounced, and to the east it was even stronger, announcing the presence of the Deathlands like a giant blister.

Tim stretched toward the source of the blight. The Lifesource in the Deathlands felt simultaneously different from and yet familiar to the power he held inside himself, like seeing a grotesque representation of oneself in the mirror. He brushed across its surface, both fascinated and repulsed by the juxtaposition of sensations this darker power stirred within him.

And then, too quickly for him to react, he realized something else: the Lifesource in the east had a *pull* to it. It grabbed him, hard, and before Tim knew it, his mind fell into a black void. The malevolence of the Korlan Forest, which he had just touched moments ago, now seemed a field of spring daisies compared to *this*, a cold vortex that dragged him forward with jarring force. Tim clamped his eyes shut, fearing that if he opened them, he would see cuts and abrasions on his body.

Tim felt a presence rising toward him, cloaked in the form of humanity but far removed from it. As he encountered this new aura, Tim could feel it was just as surprised by this turn of events as he.

You! The word was a shout inside his head as Tim tried to pull back. The voice grew softer as it came closer, trying to coax him into the shadows. *Come to me, my enemy. You may like what you find.*

Let me go, Tim thought back.

You wouldn't be the first of my victims to make such a request, Zadinn Kanas replied, *but I never oblige.*

Well, I've got something they haven't. Tim *pushed* back, uncertain of exactly what he was doing, letting the Lifesource guide his consciousness instinctively.

Tim felt Zadinn's hold falter, but then the Dark Lord reasserted his presence with a firm grasp. *You have potential,* Zadinn said, *but I have experience. You may have killed the Hunter, and you may have brought down the Kaltu Pass, but I'm on the throne.*

At the mention of the Pass, Tim twitched. *But I didn't—*

He tried to cut the thought off, but he was too late. Zadinn shifted in surprise, and there was a momentary pause before the Dark Lord spoke again. *You didn't bring down the Pass? But it wasn't the Kyrlod. I would have known.*

Tim felt Zadinn push deeper, clawing into Tim's mind, searching through the protective folds of his memory. It was the most invasive sensation he had ever experienced.

Your father? Interesting. Dead, yes, along with your mother—

The mention of his parents' death caused Tim's defenses to wane as emotion welled up within him. Zadinn forced his presence farther forward, examining Tim's life in the South—growing up with Daniel and Rosalie, building the cottage with Daniel and Rosalie, visiting Raldoon with Daniel and Rosalie, farming with Daniel and Rosalie—

Zadinn had no right, *no* one had the right to dig through those memories, but least of all *the one who had killed them.*

A conflagration of fury rose within Tim. Zadinn had probed too far, touched him in an area that was sensitive, protected—and Tim's mind defended itself. The power exploded from Tim, creating a backlash powerful enough to sunder stone, and Zadinn screamed in sudden pain. He broke away as Tim, repelling Zadinn's mental invasion, lashed back at this presumptuous intruder into his private life. The vortex that had once been so strong shattered into fragments, each shard piercing Zadinn Kanas, driving him farther away from Tim, until at last he was gone.

Tim opened his eyes and tumbled down the hill, slamming into an assortment of boulders. The air rushed out of his lungs, and it was a painful few seconds before he regained his breath. He stood up, his entire body soaked in sweat, surprised he had no broken bones. He wasn't about to do that again anytime soon. However, some good had come from it, for he had discovered a new strength.

He thought back to that night in the Pass, to right after Daniel and Rosalie had died. That moment had been the third time he'd touched the Lifesource—the first being outside the Rampart, and the second hours earlier in the cells beneath the Fort. Both times that night, Tim had touched the energy while in the grip of overpowering emotion. That power, Tim realized, was not the same as the Lifesource Nazgar had taught him to use over these last few weeks.

The magic from that night had been raw and untamed, *strong*, unlike the more passive force he now controlled from time to time. He remembered how the malichons in the dungeon disintegrated at a mere *thought* from Tim. He'd been powerful enough to destroy those two malichons with almost no effort at all, but afterward, it had taken him days to even hold the Lifesource, much less do anything with it.

"Tim?"

Tim looked up, seeing Nazgar walking toward him. Faint traces of fear crisscrossed the Kyrlod's brow.

"I'm fine," Tim said.

Irritation replaced fear on Nazgar's face. "Do not presume you are fine. I know what happened here."

"It was only an accident," Tim said.

"Not all accidents are harmless, and they do not serve as excuses," Nazgar replied. "I've been doing this for much longer than you, and so has Zadinn. You're fortunate you are protected from him in a way no other man is, and I assure you this protection saved you today. But no protection lasts forever, and even *your* defenses will crumble if you touch the Dark Lord's mind. So do not presume everything is all right just because you stand before me and breathe, and do not hear his voice in your head."

Tim swallowed, hesitating. "Will he be able to read my mind now?"

"I do not think so," the Kyrlod replied. "Not after one encounter. But do not risk a second experience. Follow me." Nazgar turned back to the camp.

As Tim stood, he glanced toward the Deathlands. "Does it make a difference when I'm closer?"

"Yes," Nazgar answered. "A large difference. Once you enter the Deathlands, Zadinn will attack your mind at every step. It's not only about his power—it's also the relationship between you and him. Each of you forms a center of strength within the Lifesource, but you cannot share that space—not just because you are enemies, but also because it is physically impossible for two opposing forces to coexist. One of you has to go."

Nazgar led him back to the camp in silence. Tim pondered the Kyrlod's words, examining them from every angle. In the end, everything boiled down to the same conclusion: he had no room for error in this fight. Had it been merely his own life in the balance, perhaps Tim could afford to lose. But it wasn't only his fate at stake—it was the fate of the entire world, and that meant he could make no mistakes. He couldn't expose himself to Zadinn again. He'd protected himself, managing to push Zadinn away, and the Dark Lord certainly hadn't expected it. Tim had surprised him, overwhelmed him, perhaps even hurt him.

He had to figure out how to seek that power again—it was his only hope. This power wasn't just the Lifesource; it was something more. He considered asking Nazgar about it but decided to hold off. This was something he had to figure out on his own.

*   *   *

That evening the elions took refuge on the sheltered side of the hills, where the winds were blessedly gentle. After everyone retired for the night, Tim left the boundaries of the camp and took out his sword under the soft orb of the moon. He held the blade in front of him, feeling the weight of the weapon in his hands, sensing the latent power thrumming within its pommel stone. He moved through the sword motions Daniel had taught him, flowing from one stance to the next. Though Nazgar's rigorous Lifesource training left him sore at the end of each day, Tim forced himself to go through the sword forms every night, regardless of how tired he was. The practice tied him to his father. When Tim pushed himself beyond his limits, he felt his mind separate from the world, and in the quiet stillness that resulted, he felt Daniel's presence standing just out of sight. *A man should hold his blade every day,* Daniel always said. *Otherwise he is not fit to wield it.*

True to this philosophy, Tim and Daniel *had* practiced nearly every day for the last six years, and Tim would not give up that link to his father. Tonight, though, Tim wanted to try something new. Zadinn's recent assault on his mind had helped him unlock a potent, deadly energy within himself, and he wanted to find it again. If he could harness this new power, make it his own, perhaps he would have a chance of defeating the Dark Lord.

Tim lowered his sword and focused his attention, drawing the Lifesource in its entirety before releasing it forth into the blade. Green light flared within the pommel stone, beginning as a weak glow that steadily built strength. Tim's palms tingled as he swung his sword, left, right, and around his head. The weapon responded more smoothly than ever, like an extension of his own hand. Tim had never felt so poised, so ready. He was already a good swordsman, but this made him feel a true master of the art.

As Tim sparred with the empty night, he tried to remember how he'd felt when Zadinn probed his mind, when the Dark Lord had gone just one layer too deep and Tim retaliated. If he could recreate this state of mind, perhaps he could unlock the power again. And, as he focused, he realized this path was about anger, plain and simple. Though his emotions had a raw, untamed age, they had also given him enough power to repel an attack from a centuries-old sorcerer. That in itself was worth noting.

He thought back further to the Kaltu Pass, probing his memories from that fateful night, bringing himself to the moment when the walls collapsed on top of his mother and father. The pain returned, a wave that threatened to crush him, but Tim opened his arms and embraced it. He wanted it to run through him, to break over him and consume him, because after the agony and grief washed through him, it left something else in its place, something cold, sharp, and *hard*. This was deeper than anger. This was hatred, and by all things that lived and died, hatred was *mighty*.

Tim drew the anger into himself, thinking of countless wrongs Zadinn Kanas had perpetrated. He thought of the dwerions in Raldoon, dragged from their homes while rain poured from the skies. He thought of the elions, betrayed by one of their own, watching the place they loved blown to rubble. He thought of the worn, weary, slaves in the Deathlands, of Zadinn's monstrous "experiments", men and women and even children tortured for hours upon end. He thought of his father and mother, slain while fighting an evil that outnumbered them on all sides.

The hatred was now deep, hot, and boiling, consuming his body in a vicious storm. As the Lifesource, formerly a gentle pool surrounding him, took a new life that was wild and potent, Tim finally began to understand. This was it. The key. When he'd used the Lifesource in anger, it had been powerful but out of control. Grief had the same effect—the Lifesource grew more potent, but also more unstable.

So what do I do? he asked himself, and the answer seemed clear. *I must shed these emotions. I must use them to gain strength but discard everything else.*

Emotion was his enemy *and* his ally. If he wanted to use this new weapon, he had to keep the parts that made him strong but discard those that made him weak. He moved through the sword forms faster and faster, the blade blazing with savage intensity, cleaving pathways through the air and leaving a faint turbulence in their wake. His mind traveled faster than the world itself, making him aware of events *before* they even happened.

Tim jumped and slashed his sword crosswise against a boulder. A hot flash of green light erupted as the blade struck the stone, passing through its center and setting off sparks of fire. The top half of the rock spun away, coasting through the air a dozen feet before crashing to the ground.

Tim stopped and released the Lifesource. The world quivered as he lost his heightened sense of perception, and everything returned to normal speed as Tim sheathed the blade, noting the steel was not even warm. The same could not be said for the boulder. Hot steam rose from its surface where the top portion had slid away, revealing a smooth, seamless face below. Tim stretched his hand toward the stone but pulled back when he felt the rising heat. He looked back to the boulder's top half, which lay two strides away. When in one piece, the boulder had stood taller than him. The portion that remained stood just above his hip.

Tim smiled. *This is something Nazgar never talked about.*

* * *

After another day of travel, the company departed from the foothills and entered the Mountains. Boblin wasn't sure how to feel about this new terrain. It was scenic, but the rising heights did not treat his stomach well. As the ground fell away behind them and their path took them higher, he felt uncomfortably queasy. The foothills had been tough, but this was worse. Where others might see beauty, he saw only an endless sequence of cliffs and crevasses, all leading to long falls and quick deaths. One might think that after Boblin took a leap from the top of the Fort's tower, he'd be accustomed to such death-defying endeavors, but to the contrary—the steep heights of the Northern Mountains only brought back bad feelings. Boblin hadn't liked being fifty or sixty paces in the air, and now he found himself a thousand paces high. *Elions were not born with wings. We belong close to good, firm ground. But focus on the positives. We're out of that horrendous forest, for one, and we don't need to return anytime soon. Besides, all we know is that nobody ever comes back from the Mountains—but that might be because they like it here, right?*

On the third morning, Boblin awakened with a frost-tipped nose. He huddled underneath his blankets, trying to wrap himself in the last vestiges of warmth, while beside him Tim and Hedro breathed deeply and easily, both still absorbed in the bliss of slumber. While Warriors of Light and egocentric superior officers could afford to catch a few extra minutes of shut-eye, Boblin figured it was high time to be up and about, much as he disliked leaving the comfort of his cot.

When he threw his covers off, the cold bit into his bare body. Boblin had never had such excellent motivation for dressing without pause. Besides, it was good for the constitution. *Nothing like a nice, crisp awakening to let me know I'm alive.*

It was still dark when Boblin stepped outside. Celia and Ana, having had the last guard watch of the night, stood by the fire and stoked the embers. The rest of the camp still slept, but they would be awake within a quarter of an hour—except for Tim, who would be out on the half hour. Nazgar kept the man out late, and the effects showed. Boblin woke up every time Tim staggered into the tent and collapsed onto his cot. Sometimes Tim did not even take off his boots before falling into a heavy sleep, and he often cried out in the middle of the night. The first time that had happened, Boblin was up and moving so fast his sword was in hand and boots tied before Tim said it was nothing to worry about. Boblin wasn't so sure about that; men didn't just cry out for no reason. Then again, most men didn't watch an entire mountain collapse on their parents.

Boblin paused to admire the rising sun as it cast light on the Northern Mountains. The blood-orange glanced off a series of peaks and mingled with the white, snow-covered slopes in a mixture of hues. The rays brushed past an occasional wisp of cloud before landing on the elion camp, bringing a trickle of warmth to Boblin's face.

He remembered how soothing it had been to watch the sunset from the walls of the Fort, but this was even better. Zadinn Kanas had not touched this place, and it didn't seem he ever would. The Mountains possessed the same primeval majesty as the Barricade. The combined might of Zadinn and his master, the Demon Lord, was powerful—but their reach did not go unchallenged, because the free folk of the North had the Maker on their side. The Maker was more subtle and more gentle, but no less powerful, and that morning, the rising sun reminded Boblin that hope lived.

For the first time, the travelers took out the fur-lined coats and boots they'd taken from the outpost in the Fertile Lands. Boblin was glad to see the gear put to use; so far all he'd gotten from the extra baggage was a very sore back.

The elions would have to climb quite a bit farther before leveling out their course and striking a northward path through the peaks, so they relied on scouts to discover safe routes across the terrain. Boblin had scout duty tomorrow—with Hedro and Wayne, of course. It never happened any other way. Maybe he could convince Tim to come along.

This morning's scouts, Faldon and Tavin, returned to the group at mid-morning and said they had discovered a corpse the size of an elephant. They weren't sure what killed it, but it had obviously been a large pack of predators. After a quiet conference with Jend, the elions decided to change course. Thirty elions were harder to kill than one elephant, but nobody wanted to go looking for a conflict—except, perhaps, Hedro, who saw such situations as opportunities to prove he was the bravest of the brave and strongest of the strong.

When night came, they made their usual camp without incident. By now they performed their evening tasks by rote, and even Tim and Boblin said little to each other as they raised one tent after another. The air felt especially cool tonight, and Boblin figured he'd wear an extra layer or two when it came time for bed. He wondered how much farther they had to travel before they reached the land on the other side of the Mountains—if it existed at all. In the North, the elions knew the landscape well and could gauge distances between landmarks, but here they had no real idea how long it would take to reach their destination. Their route was a mystery to all, even Nazgar.

At first Boblin didn't take note of Tim's silence. The refugees walked all day, every day, so in the evening nobody could muster much energy for simple conversation. But then Boblin noticed Tim went about his tasks with unusual intensity, pounding every stake into the ground with a force that approached open hostility. He watched Tim for a moment, arched an eyebrow, and then turned back to his own work. When they finished, Tim marched off. Boblin watched him go beyond the edge of camp and into the dim evening light and frowned. Either he'd managed to offend Tim in some unspeakable manner—which was entirely possible, since Boblin sometimes had the social tact of a sun-baked lizard—or the man was late for an extremely important occasion.

Boblin waited a few minutes before following Tim's tracks out of the camp and up to a small copse of trees. Tim was stripped to the waist, flowing through sword forms with immense speed. Green fire enveloped the blade, burning with savage force, leaving soft tendrils of steam as Tim shifted from stance to stance.

Boblin said nothing at first, instead just watching. Tim did not cease in his practice or even slow down. He moved faster and faster, and his face could have been chiseled from stone. Though Tim did not indicate that he saw the elion, he nonetheless spoke first.

"Hello, Boblin," Tim said, never taking attention away from the burning green blade.

"A bit cold in the Mountains?" Boblin asked. "Thinking of new ways to keep yourself warm?"

"I need the practice. It's the only way I can be ready."

"Where's Nazgar?"

"I don't know."

Boblin looked at the camp. "Don't you two usually practice together?"

Tim stopped, chest heaving as he regained his breath. The cold air had to be searing his lungs, but he did not give any indication of either noticing or caring. "Do you need something?"

Boblin raised his hands. "No, sorry. Just making sure you're all right."

"Why wouldn't I be?" Tim asked, lifting his sword again. He stood on the balls of his feet and began another iteration of forms.

Boblin watched him. "You can't keep pushing yourself like this," he said. "You stay by yourself all day and walk off alone every evening. Nazgar keeps you up until the moon is half past. At a certain point, you need to catch your breath."

Tim stopped again. His eyes had the steely color of flint. "It needs to be done, and I've only got so much time."

"You're right, but that doesn't mean you shouldn't rest."

A low, musical tone floated toward them, and both looked down the hill toward the encampment. Jend Argul was playing a fiddle of all things. Boblin hadn't any idea where the Commander had come by *that*, but Jend was well known for his talent with the instrument. Perhaps he always kept one close by, right next to his sword and collection of malichon ears—or whatever else served as the legendary elion's war trophies.

"Well, that's an end to matters," Boblin said. "If the Commander of the Frontier Patrol has time to play a fiddle, *you* certainly have no excuses."

"Maybe later," Tim said.

Boblin dropped the subject. Though Tim's demeanor bothered him, the man had watched his parents die only a fortnight ago. Maybe he just needed some time to process the situation on his own, away from others. Boblin could respect that. Yet even as he returned to the camp, part of him remained troubled. A man couldn't let himself grow cold and distant in this place. There was enough evil outside without having to fight self-manufactured demons.

Still playing the fiddle, Jend moved from a soothing tone to a fast-paced jig, and a pair of refugees stood up and started dancing. A few moments later, another couple joined them, and by the end of the song the entire camp was clapping and dancing around the campfire. At that moment, Boblin understood why Jend was doing this. Had they still been at the Fort, today would have been the Midsummer Festival, which was held every year under the stars in the Kaltu Pass. The Festival was the best time of the year, a time when the elions could dance and sing on the lawn, cherishing and protecting something Zadinn Kanas could never destroy. And why give that evening up just because the walls of the Fort were gone? It was the day of the Midsummer Festival, so the elions would dance and sing as always, momentarily forgetting the things behind them and the things before them.

The celebration continued into the night. Jend handed the fiddle to Vern, and Vern handed it to Tavin, and Tavin handed it to Ana, and so forth while the moon rose. As the music continued, Boblin found himself inevitably looking for Celia. He looked for her at the Festival every year, and he always found her—sometimes alone, other times dancing with somebody else. Tonight she was alone, standing at the edge of the firelight, watching the others dance.

Boblin's heart thudded. It was amusing, once he thought about it. *Fighting malichons in the Fort? All in an afternoon's work. Tangling with monsters in the Korlan? No sweat. Asking Celia to dance? Absolutely terrifying.* But if Boblin were to fail, at least he would do so with dignity and know he tried his best.

He stepped forward. *Easy. It's not like I'm gearing up for a one-man assault on the Deathlands.* But it sure *felt* like it.

Boblin stood beside Celia, and she turned toward him, just barely enough to let him know she knew he was there. "Hello," Boblin said.

"Hello," Celia replied.

He stood silent and counted, *one, two, three.* "Would you like to dance?" he asked.

She smiled. "Of course."

At the edge of the firelight, Ana drew her bow over the strings of the fiddle with delicate mastery. Boblin took Celia's arm and spun it around her head, bringing her in a full circle before pulling her in close and placing an arm at her waist. His heart still thumped so loud that Celia probably thought a full contingent of drums had joined the musical ensemble. "It would have been the Midsummer Festival back home," Boblin said.

"I know." Celia raised her face to meet his. "It's good that we're doing this."

Boblin looked into her hazel eyes, soft, liquid pools he could drown in. "If not for times like this, what are we fighting for?"

She tilted her head. "You're a complex elion, Boblin Kule. You're never short of a joke. You see everything through a lens of humor, even if it's only to entertain yourself and no one else. And then you turn around and wax philosophical. I find it interesting."

"I've been accused of many things," Boblin said, "but being interesting usually isn't one of them."

Celia leaned her head back and laughed, and then placed it close against his chest. *That* was unexpected, and Boblin had to do a double check to make sure his heart did not explode from his body cavity. After all, Celia wouldn't appreciate being covered in blood and gore, and Boblin wouldn't appreciate being dead.

The snow crunched underfoot as they circled in a slow, steady rhythm with the fiddle's soft music. He figured now would be a good time to kiss her, but *also* figured that he was more scared of placing his lips on hers than of taking on the entire malichon army empty-handed. Well, at least he acknowledged his limitations, even if they made him want to kick himself. "Ana is learning quickly, isn't she?" he said.

"Aye," Celia nodded, head still on his chest. "She's a fine soldier." He smelled the faint scent of soap in her hair. He had to smile. *Where in the name of Malath did she get soap in the Mountains?*

"She had to grow up fast," Boblin said.

"We all did," Celia said. "You haven't forgotten, have you? We were four years younger than Ana when those malichons captured us. *You* were the first to fight back."

"And *you* were the second," he said.

"We had to fight. Otherwise, we'd have died."

Now he *had* to kiss her. That's all there was to it. He placed a gentle hand behind her head, preparing to draw her in, and then Hedro Desh interrupted them.

"May I cut in?" Hedro asked, asserting his presence between the two of them. Caught off guard, Boblin took a half step back, and the moment between him and Celia dissipated. Had it not violated at least three different protocols of the Frontier Patrol, Boblin probably would have stabbed Hedro in the jugular with his boot knife. As it was, he courteously released Celia and bowed to her.

"Of course," Boblin said.

Ever courteous as well, Celia smiled at Hedro and grasped his hands. "It would be my pleasure," she said. She turned back to Boblin and dipped her head. "Thank you, Boblin."

"It was my honor," Boblin said. He considered taking a long jump off the nearest cliff, but melodramatics did not get an elion far in life. He moved to the side of the group and watched the two dance.

In many ways, they were his two oldest friends, having shared the same birth year and growing up side by side in these harsh lands. And yet, his relationship with Hedro had always been strained, and not just because of their mutual attraction to Celia. No one could be faulted for being attracted to *her*, the strongest, most independent elion Boblin had ever known. But Hedro Desh...

It had happened four years ago. Her name was Triste, and she loved Hedro, though Boblin wasn't sure if Hedro loved her back. Some thought Triste was as beautiful as Celia, but Boblin disagreed. Though Boblin cared for Triste as he cared for all of his comrades at the Fort, there was no contest in his mind.

They'd been fourteen, perhaps youngsters by Southern standards, but practically adults by Northern standards, and it had been the night of the Midsummer Festival, when Boblin and Hedro's relationship irrevocably changed.

* * *

"...need to stop that," Hedro said.

Boblin paused for a second. He'd been unable to ask Celia to dance, mostly because he was too karfing scared of getting turned down, and it had made him irritable. So he'd gone for a walk, heading past the mostly abandoned Patrol barracks, and stumbled upon Hedro and Triste in the shadows of the building's south corner. The two were arguing in low tones. Neither noticed him, and Boblin stepped back, unwilling to eavesdrop on a clearly private conversation.

"Why?" Triste asked.

"It's embarrassing, that's why," Hedro said. Boblin had no idea what they were talking about, and it was none of his business. "I can join the Patrol in two years. I can't afford to appear like a child anymore."

"Is that what I am—a child?" Triste shot back.

"Maybe," Hedro said coldly. "I thought you were more than that, but maybe I was wrong."

"Fine," Triste said. "Join Boblin and Celia in the Patrol. Just because I want to be a Healer instead of fight, you think less of me."

"Don't put words in my mouth," Hedro said.

"Admit it," Triste said, biting off each word.

Hedro didn't have to admit it aloud. Hedro Desh had made clear his disdain for anyone who chose to be a Healer over serving in the Patrol. Boblin disagreed—he had seen what it took to serve with Healer Prystoch and her apprentices—but it was a moot issue as far as Hedro was concerned.

"There you go again," Hedro said. "You won't leave it alone. You are a child."

Triste pushed Hedro in the chest, causing him to stumble back. "Says the one who thinks he could actually lead the Patrol one day. Fine, call me a child. Serve in the Patrol. But no matter what, you'll never be the next Jend Argul. You're just not good enough."

Hedro struck her.

Boblin, half turned away from the scene and knowing he should have left long ago, halted at the sound of the impact. He turned back to the two elions, face set in a grim line. And he knew he would never, ever have any respect for Hedro Desh again.

Triste staggered away, one hand on her cheek. Boblin heard the sob in her voice. "How could you?"

"It wasn't that hard," Hedro said.

Boblin Kule emerged from the shadows and punched Hedro in the face, slamming him against the side of the barracks. "What in the Deathlands was that, Desh?"

"None of your business, Kule," Hedro snarled, getting up.

"It's fine, Boblin," Triste said.

"Not from where I stand," Boblin said. "Are you okay, Triste?"

"Yes," she said. "Don't worry about it."

All six feet of Hedro slammed into Boblin, bearing him to the ground. Boblin held his hands in front of his face to deflect Hedro's blows. "Apologize," Boblin said through gritted teeth.

"I'll do whatever in Malath I please, Kule, and I won't have you telling me off for it."

"Quit it, both of you!" Triste said.

"Apologize," Boblin repeated. Hedro struck him in the gut, driving all the air out of him. The resulting pain that blossomed in his stomach made Boblin want to vomit. He twisted, trying to reverse their positions, but Hedro was too big.

Hedro landed several more punches before rising to his feet and bringing Boblin up with him, one hand grasped around his tunic. "Leave your nose out of where it doesn't belong," Hedro hissed.

"Just go, Boblin," Triste said.

And so Boblin left. Because Triste had asked him to, not because of Hedro. Boblin would have taken as many blows as necessary. But she had asked him to leave, so he did. And after that, he wasn't sure who he disliked more—himself or Hedro Desh.

* * *

And now Hedro stood in front of him, holding an arm about Celia's waist, ever the gentleman, ever the model soldier. Of course Hedro had indeed made it into the Patrol, and he'd served valiantly. Many in the Fort were safer because of his actions. He'd spent the better part of the subsequent four years putting his own life on the line to protect his comrades. But he'd struck a female, and Boblin would never forgive him for that.

To Boblin's knowledge, Hedro never committed such an unforgivable act a second time. A year and a half later, Triste fell sick and passed away, victim of a savage winter ailment. With her passing, Boblin and Hedro remained the only two who knew what had transpired on that night four years ago, and neither had spoken of it since.

Boblin started as Tim approached him from behind, interrupting Boblin's troubled memories. Pushing his thoughts aside, lightening his tone, Boblin clapped a hand on his friend's shoulder. "Welcome to the Midsummer Festival. It is now time for us to observe a curious ritual known as the wooing process. This is strange territory, not trod upon by those such as you or I, but interesting nonetheless."

Tim did not reply but watched the dancing in silence. "Aptly done, sir," Boblin continued. "Do not let me interrupt as you take notes."

"I'm going to kill him," Tim said.

"Who? Hedro Desh? Do tell me more. I'll offer my assistance."

"Zadinn Kanas," Tim said. "I've been watching everyone tonight. This is a good thing—this dance, this happiness—and there's no reason for something like this to end. Those like Zadinn will always threaten this way of life. Perhaps it's because he's jealous or because he doesn't understand it. I don't know what his reasons are, but I do know that something like this must be preserved. Zadinn's not just trying to destroy us—he's also trying to destroy what makes our lives worthwhile. And I'm going to kill him."

Boblin hesitated before speaking. "Zadinn has threatened us our entire lives, Tim. You're absolutely right. When our freedom is threatened, we have to take action to stop it. No one will argue with you about that, but if we sacrifice the happiness of this moment just because Zadinn may or may not come tomorrow, then he still wins. Look at the elions here. We often fight with swords and arrows, but sometimes we fight back like *this*—by enjoying our lives."

"Then I won't interrupt that," Tim said. With that, he stood up and left, leaving Boblin alone by the fireside.

Boblin swallowed hard. What had happened to his friend? He thought of the man he'd met outside of the Barricade. Boblin had liked that man, but this was no longer the Tim he'd met by the wall, or the Tim at the Fort, or even the grief-stricken Tim in the wake of his parents' death. Something had altered him, and it scared Boblin.

He looked around for Nazgar of the Kyrlod, but the prophet was nowhere in sight. Perhaps Nazgar would have an explanation for this sudden, unexplained change in the character of Tim Matthias. Or perhaps Nazgar wasn't aware of it. That thought scared Boblin even more.

Twenty-Four

A scream clove through the still night. Tim sat upright, awake in an instant, reaching for his sword with one hand and his boots with the other. Boblin and Hedro also bolted up, ready and alert, but Tim did not wait for them. Before either elion had his shirt on, Tim had raced outside.

A gaping hole ran down the side of the tent adjacent to theirs, shreds of cloth fluttering in the breeze. The sentries had begun running toward the tent as well, but Tim was closer. He leaped through the ragged opening and into the tent's interior. A single elion, Yalen, stood inside with his back against the wall, his face pale. He twitched as Tim entered, instinctively raising his hands to shield his face, but lowering them once he recognized the newcomer.

Tim looked to the side. The cot next to Yalen had belonged to Lorgels, who was nowhere to be seen. The cot was slashed to pieces, and flecks of blood covered the ground nearby. "What happened?" Tim asked.

Yalen swallowed hard. "Vrawl," he said, the word coming out in a gasp. "Vrawl."

The word made no sense. The attack must have jarred Yalen's senses. Tim looked at the ground and saw a path running through the snow, out the hole and into the night, as if a body had been dragged from the tent. A smear of red followed the trail.

Tim moved back outside, crouching down on one knee and peering at the furrows running across the snow. The markings had probably come from the heels of Lorgels' boots, leading beyond the light of the campfire and toward the snow-swept slopes beyond. A separate set of prints ran alongside the bloody path, tracks reminiscent of a cat but much larger—easily twice the size of Tim's own foot.

Tim looked at the rising peaks all around him, thinking of the enormous carcass Faldon and Tavin had seen. Only something vicious and powerful could bring down such a large creature, and no doubt this predator now stalked the edges of the elions' camp. Perhaps the Northern Mountains were about to reveal their true nature at last.

Tim grasped a hand around the hilt of his sword and followed the path down the slope and into the night, traveling alone as gentle flakes of snow swirled around him. Sparse evergreens covered the hillside, and Tim Matthias moved through the dark, the only sound the soft crunch of his footsteps and the steady rhythm of his breath. Then the trail took a sharp turn, and Tim immediately saw Lorgels' body stretched out beneath a cleft of stone that jutted from the hillside. The elion's chest had been ripped open, a frozen mask of shock and pain on his wide-eyed face and a massive pool of red staining the snow around the body.

Tim stopped, glancing in all directions. The creature that killed Lorgels had to be close by, but the falling snow had grown heavier, so it was difficult to see farther than a few feet in any direction. Tim tensed as he realized the stupidity of his actions; he'd moved without pause ever since awakening, too focused on the task at hand to speak to any of the other elions, and now he found himself alone with no one to aid him.

He heard a growl but couldn't tell from which direction it had come. He reached toward the Lifesource, filling himself with its soothing power, and his senses sharpened just enough to give him a little more visibility. He caught a flicker of motion from the corner of his eye and turned to see a sinuous, curved shape crouched on top of an outstretched rock. Tim lifted his sword as his pulse quickened, and the creature growled again. The catlike predator had a coat of white fur, camouflage that had prevented Tim from seeing it fully before now. It was *big*, easily three times larger than a gray wolf.

The creature leaped toward him, jaws wide and claws outstretched. Losing his connection with the Lifesource in a moment of panic, Tim brought his sword in front of him. He saw a flash of two long, massive canines protruding from the beast's upper jaw right before it slammed into him. Tim twisted aside and his attacker skidded past him, sliding down the hill as Tim landed on his back. The breath rushed out of him from the impact.

Tim quickly found the Lifesource again, in spite of having lost control of it, noting that his practice was of *some* use. The beast turned to face him, prepared to make another pass as Tim directed his power into the focusing point at the hilt of his sword. Green flames blazed around the blade, burning brightly against the night. The animal veered away from him, diverting its course and stopping in place with four paws on the ground, muscles coiled to spring.

The light from Tim's sword bathed the creature in an unearthly hue. It had spotless white fur, made for hunting in the snow-covered heights, and wicked claws that curled from its massive paws. Large whiskers, thick as twine, sprouted from a triangular nose on a boxy, angular head. But the beast's most distinguishing traits were the identical incisors that stretched far past either side of its mouth, at least sixteen inches in length and slightly curved. Those fangs had ripped through the tent, tearing the cloth to shreds before seizing Lorgels.

The animal stayed back, wary of the sword's fire. Tim stepped to one side. So far he believed the cat was only protecting its meal. If Tim were to move slowly and carefully, it might leave him alone long enough for him to retreat back to camp.

But the cat moved as soon as Tim did, streaking toward him in a blur, and Tim raised his sword as if it were a shield. The creature stopped yet again; apparently the move had only been a feint to test Tim's defenses. Tim took another step, and this time the beast allowed him to walk on his course. Tim took one careful step at a time, keeping his eyes on the creature.

Then Tim's boot slipped on a wet rock and he fell down. The predator pounced, and this time Tim raked his blade across its side. The cat screamed in pain as it tumbled down the slope for a second time, knocking Tim's sword from his hands. The sword's green flames winked out as the blade slid from Tim. Farther down the slope, the creature skidded to halt, its white fur swaying with the sudden stop in momentum. Before Tim had a chance to get up, the beast rose to its feet and charged toward him yet again.

A bolt flashed through the air, past Tim and toward the cat. The beast staggered in the snow, a long, black shaft protruding from its shoulder. Jend Argul materialized from the night, holding a crossbow and calmly fitting another bolt into place as he stepped forward. As Tim got to his feet, Jend squeezed the trigger again and another arrow *whizzed* through the air, burying itself in the cat's throat.

The beast writhed, but it was far from finished; two crossbow bolts did not bring down an animal of that size. It opened its mouth, baring its fangs to their full length, and let loose a vile screech before leaping toward Jend. Another arrow, this one from a different direction, slammed into the creature's ribs as Hugo also stepped into view, crossbow steady, with Ken behind him. Cornered by the three attackers, the cat screamed again as Jend released one more arrow. As Hugo and Ken fired shots of their own, the cat at last fell, shafts sprouting from its torso, its legs kicking in futile defiance. It spasmed in place for perhaps a minute, and then lay still.

"Vrawl," Jend said. He waited another minute before prodding its body with the tip of his boot.

"Vrawl?" Tim repeated. Yalen *had* been speaking sensibly, but Tim didn't recognize the word.

"They were supposed to be just stories," Hugo said.

"Nothing is just a story," Jend replied.

"What are they?" Tim asked.

"*Vrawl* means 'saber-toothed' in the old language," Jend said. "Pellen had a tapestry of one. They are the oldest cats in the world, and they're supposed to be incredibly intelligent." He paused. "I also believe they hunt in packs."

At that, another vrawl cried out in the distance, from the direction of their camp.

"Exactly," Jend said. "We need to move—fast."

With Jend in the lead, the four companions ran back to the camp. Shouts filled the air as they drew closer, and when they came into sight of the fires, they saw sentries forming a hasty line of defense against a group of vrawl that had emerged on the far side of the tents. Ana and Celia stood on sentry duty.

"Report," Jend ordered as they approached.

"They took Andre just after you left," Celia said.

"We didn't get a good look," Ana added. "One grabbed Andre and then disappeared just as fast."

"They're vrawl," Jend said.

Celia paused. "I see."

Jend called orders, directing sentries to launch a steady stream of crossbows to keep the vrawl at bay while other elions planted torches around the tents. Once the torches were in position, the cats hung back, reluctant to breach the fiery barricade. The elions formed a two-tiered line of defense, half standing behind the torches and the other half waiting in the center of camp, ready to relieve their companions at a moment's notice.

Tim counted eleven predators circling the campsite. He schooled himself to relaxation; the vrawl were certainly resilient—it took four to six arrowheads to kill one—but the elions could survive this. With a well-armed, organized defense, Tim had no reason to think any more refugees would be lost tonight.

He was very wrong.

For the first half hour, the vrawl stayed just beyond the outermost edge of the torchlight. Every so often, a cat sat back on its haunches and raised its muzzle to scream at the sky. As Tim shifted into guard duty, standing between Boblin and Hedro, he peered at the prowling beasts, wondering what this strange new behavior meant. After a few minutes, he blinked to clear his vision. The falling snow made it hard to keep the vrawl visually separated. He'd taken another tally and came up with fourteen; because the creatures were identical, it was easy to lose count.

As the night wore on, the snowfall returned with a vengeance, filling the world with thick, heavy flakes that covered the sentries in a fine fluff of white powder. Meanwhile, beyond the light of the fires, the vrawl continued circling.

"Kule," Hedro said, the first one to break the silence in a long time. "Who counted the vrawl?"

"I did," Boblin replied.

"You counted wrong," Hedro said. "There's nineteen, not eleven."

"I didn't count wrong."

"This isn't the time to bluff your way past a mistake. There's a *lot* more than eleven vrawl out there."

"I didn't count wrong," Boblin repeated, an edge creeping into his voice.

"Then why are there so many karfing vrawl, Kule?"

"There are so many karfing vrawl, Desh, because every time one screams, more arrive." Boblin left his post and strode toward the center of the camp. "Commander!"

"What is it?" Jend asked.

"More vrawl are appearing. Their numbers are growing bigger."

"How many?" Jend asked.

"Nineteen at last count."

"Make that twenty-one," Tim said as a new pair of saber-toothed beasts approached. Soon, the vrawl would number the same as their company.

Jend swore and turned to the elion at his side. "David, how much firewood do we have left?"

"Not much," the elion replied, ashen-faced.

"Answer me. How long?"

David shook his head. "Perhaps an hour. Maybe two, if we stretch it out."

Tim looked back toward the vrawl. The fire was the only thing holding back the beasts, and with wood running out of supply, time was growing short. It was only an hour past midnight, and the vrawl only had to wait it out.

At that moment, they heard a sudden snarl, and then a guard shouted out. Two new vrawl charged toward the camp, running side by side and showing no signs of slowing down.

"Formation!" Jend shouted. The sentries shifted as additional elions rushed to help, forming two synchronized lines of bowmen. The first row fired bolts and then dropped to their knees to reload while the second line fired. When the second line dropped down, the first group stood again, ready to fire.

The vrawl swerved to evade the assault as the volley of arrows descended. Black bolts slammed into the animals. One beast fell, writhing in death throes, while the other dragged itself back to the safety of the pack with a series of broken shafts protruding from its fur.

Yalen, standing near the torches on the other side of the camp, screamed and fell. The other elions turned toward him, but were too late. A white-furred vrawl materialized from the swirling snow, closing its jaws around Yalen's thigh, and Tim heard a sickening *crunch* of bone as blood sprayed everywhere. The closest sentry, Harvin, drew his sword and leaped toward the vrawl, swinging a blow toward its exposed neck.

A second vrawl appeared from the night to take Harvin, and both cats vanished into the darkness, dragging their prey with them. The screams of both elions floated on the wind, accompanied by awful ripping sounds.

It occurred to Tim that the earlier attack had merely been a ploy to distract the group, allowing the other vrawl to attack Yalen and Harvin, narrowing the sentry count by two. As the refugees threw more wood onto the fire, the flames reared higher, revealing more vrawl prowling around the perimeter, a lazy stroll in their stride, waiting for the right time to strike.

In the next hour, the cats attacked twice more, but this time the elions stood their guard and nobody died. However, tension mounted as the firelight waned. Soon the entire camp smelled of long, drawn-out terror. The elions were playing a waiting game they were bound to lose, and there was nothing anyone could do about it. As the snow fell even more heavily, the attacks occurred with more frequency. By the time the elions placed the last logs on the fire, the vrawl were performing a constant rotation of assaults, staggering their locations so the sentries had to constantly rush to defend a different spot on the perimeter.

The light grew poorer, and the refugees almost lost sight of everything, unable to see the vrawl until the beasts were on top of them. As the campfire died down, the cats grew more confident, performing fewer feints and more attacks. Two more elions fell to the vrawl, taken into the night where the pack tore them to shreds.

Tim unsheathed his sword. Soon there would be no need for crossbows. They'd have to fight these cats at close range. As he readied himself, there came a brief lull in the assault, and for a moment everything—save for the descending snowflakes—hung still. The vrawl shifted, and Tim realized they had formed a perfect line. The pack surrounded the entire encampment, a large circle of attackers encompassing a small circle of defenders. The vrawl pawed the ground restlessly but did not move.

One by one, each torch on the perimeter vanished. All that remained on the campfire were a few glowing embers. The vrawl slowly moved forward, staying just beyond range of the crossbows, waiting for the right moment.

The last embers on the fire flickered, and then died.

Twenty-Five

The darkness seemed absolute. Tim heard, rather than saw, several vrawl charging toward them. The cats screamed in unison as their pounding footsteps shook the hillside, forming a mass of fur, tooth, and claw hurtling toward the besieged refugees. Some of the elions shouted back. "For Pellen and a free North!"

Tim filled himself with the Lifesource. The falling snow reached its climax, consuming the entire camp in a frenzy of flakes that obscured all vision in a blinding mass of white, as if the weather itself were synchronized with the vrawls' wishes. And then the first wave of beasts burst from the chaos, leaping toward the elions with outstretched claws.

Flames blazed around Tim's sword. Acting on instinct, he pointed its tip toward the nearest vrawl. A beam of green light lanced forth from the blade, slamming into the enormous cat and consuming its fur in emerald fire. The vrawl flew several feet into the air before plummeting back down and landing in a charred husk of ashes, snow steaming around its blackened corpse.

Tim shifted his focus to the next vrawl, obliterating it as he had the first, and then turned to the next threat, killing the enemy one by one where he saw the greatest danger. But for every vrawl Tim killed, two more emerged from the vortex of snow. Tim was also tiring rapidly. Whatever this magic was, it drained his energy, and he knew that if he did not do something else, the cats of the night would overcome him. It wasn't enough to take them down singly. If the elions were to survive, he had to take more drastic action.

When the next vrawl appeared in front of him, leaping through the air with bared fangs, Tim dropped to his knees, two hands clasped about his sword's hilt, and drove it tip-first into the ground. At the same time, he released *everything*.

A circle of green fire shot from the blade. Though it passed harmlessly through the elions, it caught every vrawl in its turbulent wake, blasting through the entire pack in the space of a second. Dozens of cats caught fire, blasting into cinders almost instantaneously, followed by a gust of wind ripping through the entire camp. Tim screamed in agony. The spell was so potent it *burned*.

The passing ring of fire vanished a hundred paces from the edge of camp, leaving a slush of steaming, melted snow in all directions. Tim raised his eyes and looked around. Surviving elions picked themselves up, staring at the resulting scene in disbelief.

The army of vrawl lay strewn across the slope, each one a smoking corpse. Tim removed his hands, palms red and peeling, from the hilt of his weapon and fell backward into the soft snow. Flakes continued falling above him, but lighter than before. *Of course*, he supposed. The vrawl were no more, so why would nature continue to lend them assistance?

From above, Nazgar approached and offered Tim his hand. "Thank you," Tim said. Nazgar struck him across the face and Tim staggered back, face stinging as he raised a hand to his lips, feeling blood.

"What was that?" Tim asked.

"That was for your arrogance—for leaving the camp without seeking assistance first." Nazgar struck Tim again. "And that was for the atrocity you just committed."

Tim looked back at the Kyrlod, setting his jaw in a grim line. "I just *saved* us," he said.

"At what cost?" Nazgar asked. "The Lifesource is a powerful weapon, and like any weapon, the man who bears it must show discipline."

"At the expense of their lives?" Tim pointed toward the elions. "The vrawl would have killed every one of us!"

"Strike me," Nazgar said.

"What?" Tim was dumbfounded.

"Hit me! Knock me to the ground. You surely want to!"

"No," Tim said.

Nazgar slapped him a third time. "I said hit me!" He laid a fourth blow across Tim's face. "Do it!"

"If that's what you want, then fine!" Tim swung his fist through the air—but an inch from Nazgar's face, his knuckles slammed into something hard, an invisible barrier shielding the Kyrlod. He swore and cradled his hand, numb from the sudden pain.

"There are many ways to defend yourself with the Lifesource," Nazgar said, voice gentler. "You do not have to resort to outright violence. Walk with me."

Tim closed his mouth and consented, but it was hard to feel truly chastised when he knew very well that using protective "bubbles" would only have slowed the vrawl, not stopped them. The cats were persistent, and the energy to maintain such a shield would have drained Tim quickly. Still, he let the Kyrlod speak.

"I've killed many men with the Lifesource," Nazgar said. "In time, so will you, many more than you would wish. Such regret is not uncommon, after all; we are often cautioned against *enjoying* violence. But evil is a subtle force. We frequently have the mistaken notion that evil beings take pleasure from the things they do. And, without a doubt, the likes of Zadinn and Isanam most certainly enjoy causing pain and suffering. They relish in it. But darkness takes many forms. Outright corruption is the most obvious, the most transparent, but it can also take a subtler, more common form."

Nazgar led Tim outside the camp and further into the night, past the charred husks of vrawl corpses. "You might be telling yourself nothing is amiss, for you certainly did not take pleasure from killing the vrawl. But I look into your eyes, and I can tell that neither do you feel regret.

"Apathy is a road to darker things. Because if you justify this mass slaughter as a grim but necessary task, what will you do the next time you are presented with a similar choice? Will you simply do what is 'necessary'? Plenty of men commit evil, not because they enjoy it, but because they see it as the only option. There are *always* alternate paths, and our task is to acquire the strength and willpower to know the way."

"What about the elions?" Tim asked. "They certainly don't enjoy killing malichons, but they do it often. In their own words, killing malichons is necessary to survive."

"Do any of the elions know how to use the Lifesource?" Nazgar replied. "No, but you do. You have a power the elions cannot fathom. I am not teaching you the standards for surviving in the North, and I am not teaching you the standards of the Fort of Pellen. I am teaching you the standards for becoming an Advocate of the Lifesource."

"What about the Advocates of the old empire, then?" Tim pointed out. "You said yourself they used the Lifesource as a weapon in battle."

Nazgar nodded. "There is a time for everything, and I tell you with certainty that war was the first time in the history of the North the Advocates *ever* used the Lifesource as such a weapon. Let me remind you that they were the last line of defense between a falling empire and armies straight from Malath, and not one took such a task lightly. Evil is not a tangible enemy you can fight. It is an insidious idea that creeps into your soul. There are indeed times when the application of force, raw force, is the only option. You and I will both use the Lifesource to kill more before this war is over. I only emphasize that you should not employ such methods lightly, and you should not walk away from such battles without looking back and asking yourself if there could have been another way."

Nazgar gestured to the slain vrawl and continued speaking. "Every time you resort to something like this, it's easier to go forward and do the same thing another time. It is often said that the dark practices of the Lifesource are easier—and this statement is correct, but its true meaning is often misunderstood. 'Easy' does not refer to the process of using the Lifesource—casting spells and such—it refers to a mind-set. When presented with a threat, it sometimes seems the easiest and simplest solution is to kill—completely. *This* is the danger we caution against. It is harder to choose alternate routes because they require more thought, more discipline—and above all, they feel riskier. Dead vrawl pose no risk, so it's easier to kill them than to think of an alternate way to defend the camp. This is the distinction men such as you and I must make."

Two weeks ago, such a long, eloquent speech might have convinced Tim but not after tonight. There seemed no practicality in it. Tim respected the logic, but didn't see how it would have saved them. The vrawl wouldn't have stopped until the elions had killed them all, so what was the difference between Tim doing it in half a second and the elions doing it in three hours, at the bloody cost of their own lives?

Tim opened his mouth to argue but promptly closed it. When had he ever won an argument with Nazgar? The Kyrlod wouldn't back down, so perhaps it would be smarter to give the pretense of listening and save himself from a circular debate. He could progress on his own, in secret. He had to face Zadinn alone in the end anyway, and he couldn't use Nazgar as a crutch forever.

"To be honest, it's a lot to take in during one night," Tim said, trying not to overplay his agreement. He needed time to ponder this. "But I think I understand."

Nazgar smiled briefly. "Advocates at the Academy of Naxish thought these ideas were a lot to take in during a decade of training. You are an excellent learner, Tim—far quicker than the most powerful Advocates of the lost era. But neither you nor any man will ever discover a satisfactory answer to the dilemmas we now discuss. It is enough that we recognize these problems and deal with them as best we can. But come, it would behoove both of us to get back and assist the elions in repairing what remains of this camp. Such weighty issues are easier to consider when one knows he will have a cot to sleep upon."

They turned to walk back to the camp, where the elions were reassembling the tents that had been blown over and damaged during the chaos. On the way back, Tim asked, "What would you have done?"

Nazgar turned a stony face toward him. "What I might have done is inconsequential. My choices should not dictate yours. What matters is what you *have* done, and what you will do about it in the future."

That's an interesting way of avoiding the question, but I think it's because he knows he is wrong. The two did not speak to each other for the remainder of the night.

* * *

The snow abated in the early hours of the morning. The sky was cloudless, the air clear and cold. The newly fallen white covered the slopes in all directions, and the early rays of sun caused each crystal of ice to display a myriad of glittering hues.

The company proceeded across the terrain, breath steaming in the air. In spite of himself, Tim liked the cold. It spurred his blood to run thicker, imbuing him with a sense of vitality.

Though they did not expect to encounter any more vrawl soon—it was likely the entire pack was dead—they still traveled carefully. No one knew where the territory of one pack ended and another began. This spurred Tim's thoughts. He, of course, had no knowledge of vrawl, but it seemed such large predators would stay in small groups. *So what, then, caused the vrawl to attack in such numbers? And what of their territorial needs?* A creature that size no doubt had a substantial appetite, so how did one small area in the Mountains sustain forty vrawl? Again he thought of the enormous corpse Faldon and Tavin had discovered. The only way the vrawl could survive would be if they had something larger to feed upon.

"Boblin," Tim said.

"Good morning to you, too," the elion replied.

"How much do elions know about vrawl?" Tim asked.

"Nothing," Boblin replied, "except that they are very big and very dangerous. I thought they were just a legend until last night."

"How does a predator that size stay in a pack?"

Boblin arched an eyebrow. "Are you studying nature these days?"

"Think about it—it doesn't make sense for them to stay in a group. A single vrawl can easily take care of itself, so why wouldn't they separate?"

Boblin shrugged. "Malichons are a vicious bunch, and *they* stick together."

"Then what do they eat?" Tim asked.

"How should I know what a malichon eats?"

Tim thumped Boblin on the chest. "The vrawl, you three-legged goat."

"Touchy today, I see," Boblin said. "But I'd have to think it is something very big, my friend."

"Obviously, but what?"

"We could try to find out later today," Boblin said.

"How?"

"I'm going on patrol with Hedro and Wayne. Come with us. It's the only way I'll keep my sanity. If we're in the territory of a new pack—not saying we are—we'll find carrion just like Faldon and Tavin did. We'll bring along some firewood and roast our dinner in the middle of the vrawls' feeding grounds. What do you say?"

"I felt like going for a walk anyway," Tim said. "I don't walk enough these days."

The four left in early afternoon to scout. It was nice to get some distance from the bustle and noise of over thirty elions hiking through the mountains. Unburdened by the larger group, the four scouts moved lightly through the peaks, gliding across terrain that had been untouched by man for centuries. Peaks surrounded them on all sides, closing them off from the outer world and sealing them in a mystical place where time had no meaning.

They found themselves in a valley of sorts, enclosed by a ring of snow-capped mountaintops and full of deep drifts. Each scout was equipped with a pair of snowshoes, which allowed him to move quickly—except for Tim, who'd never worn snowshoes before, so it took him some time to get used to the more awkward, deliberate way of walking. More than once he found himself on his back as a result of not lifting his foot properly. Every time the rear prong of a snowshoe snagged on a drift, down Tim went, and getting up was even harder. Boblin had a good laugh whenever that happened.

Tim realized that, notwithstanding their expertise on snowshoes, the elions were *lighter* than he was. As a rule, elions were tall and lean, but their physical differences weren't all that aided them. They carried themselves differently; their snowshoes did not sink as deeply into the snow, and on the rare occasion an elion fell, he sprung back up with no problem. Tim thought of ailar and realized such talents came naturally to these folk. They were a nimble, agile breed.

"There's a split between the peaks ahead," Hedro said, pointing due north. "We should travel there. It will give us the best view over what lies ahead. Try not to fall behind, Matthias."

It took half an hour to cross the valley and climb the slope. The valley fell away, and in spite of the chill air, sweat streamed down Tim's back by the time they neared the fissure. He placed a hand on the rising rock to steady himself and peered forward. Another valley dipped down, but this basin was the size of a lake compared to the pond behind them. The valley's berth, however, was not the first thing that caught their attention. On the other side of the formation, a massive skeleton rested, its ribs forming an enormous barrel of bones curving up from the spine to the sky. Shreds of brown fur fluttered from the bones, along with chunks of red meat.

"It's another one," Boblin said, "just like Faldon and Tavin found."

"How do you know what your cousins found?" Hedro said. "You weren't with them. You make too many assumptions. We should investigate." He pushed through the crevice and made his way down the other side. Wayne dutifully followed.

"This is important, you see," Boblin said to Tim. "Hedro needs to prove he's not afraid of the skeleton, so we'll walk down there, learn nothing of use, and then turn back. It's already clear we can't take this route, because vrawl will be here. But what do I know? I'm not in charge." Boblin bounded over the fissure, a feat Tim could not accomplish in snowshoes. After Boblin passed through, Tim inelegantly struggled past the obstacle, counting himself lucky he didn't stumble and roll down the opposite side.

In spite of Hedro's objections, the corpse was clearly similar to the one Faldon and Tavin had found. Tim had seen elephants in traveling menageries, and this skeleton had the same shape, but was still much larger than the average elephant.

Though Boblin grumbled about the ordeal—mostly because it was Hedro's idea—Tim also wanted to get closer. He didn't expect answers, but he wanted to examine this thing. He ran his hands up and down the bones. The remaining meat was ragged and dry.

"This wasn't killed recently," Tim said. "Even so, it's best we avoid this valley."

The rib cage stood easily three times as high as Tim. It took him twenty-six paces to walk the length of the corpse. When this creature still walked, the ground surely shook. "You were right," he said to Boblin. "*This* is what feeds two dozen vrawl."

* * *

It took another hour to find a suitable course around the valley. By the time they returned to the company, evening was upon them. The refugees found another gentle hillside to make camp with double the usual nighttime guard. They were not about to grow lax in the wake of the previous night's events.

Tim knew he needed to think of a way to keep the camp safe. He wasn't truly concerned about the vrawl. If it came down to it, he'd eliminate them like he had before. But he knew Nazgar wouldn't like this, and he decided he would prefer to avoid spending energy on an ultimately fruitless argument. Better to accede to Nazgar's wishes so Tim could focus on his real goal: Zadinn Kanas. He needed to prepare himself for that battle, to walk into the citadel and end the dark sorcerer's life. Tim didn't care if he had Nazgar's—or anyone's—respect afterward. It was his job, and he was going to do it in whatever manner he deemed best. But *before* he did that, it was better to avoid undue confrontations with the Kyrlod. So he sought out Nazgar, and found him sitting by the fire in deep conversation with Pellen.

"Tim," the white-haired elion said, "sit with us."

"By all means." Tim complied with Pellen's wishes and took a seat beside the fire. In front of him, the flames danced and logs popped, sending sparks floating up into the night air. "I was hoping for a word with Nazgar."

"Of course," Pellen replied. "First, though, I ask you to entertain an old elion's wishes."

"Certainly," Tim acquiesced.

"Look into the fire, my son," Pellen said.

Tim gazed at the flames, which were orange at the edges, blue at the center. A thin film of white ash, red embers glowing within, covered the logs as the flames consumed their fuel.

"What do you see?" Pellen asked.

Tim peered closer. He did not notice anything of import about the camp-fire, and uncertain as to the nature of Pellen's wishes, he turned back to the Fort's leader. "I don't follow."

"What do you see?" Pellen repeated.

"I see…fire." Tim looked again at the flames. "Logs. Ashes. Embers."

"Anything else?" Pellen said.

Tim paused. "No."

"Is it possible you are not searching hard enough?"

Tim paused again. "Yes."

Pellen leaned forward. "Is also it possible you are searching *too* hard?"

Tim felt tense. The dangers of the night were very real. The vrawl could attack again, or a newer, unknown threat could strike from the shadows. He wasn't sure if this was the time or place for riddles. *Patience*, he cautioned him-self. *Remember, the objective is to defeat Zadinn Kanas. Everything else is secondary. Humor the elion.*

"Yes?" Tim replied, more of a question than an answer to Pellen's probing.

"Hence the lesson," Pellen said. "Because I told you to look into the fire, you presumed my request to be one of significance. You are looking for something, digging to find a deeper meaning, when there is simply nothing else there. It is only a campfire. Being the Warrior is a great task and a ter-rifying one, but don't lose yourself in the process. Remember what it means to sit by a fireside, take in the night air, and simply enjoy what you have before you."

Tim wanted to pound the ground in frustration. The message was the same…from Boblin, from Nazgar, from Pellen. *Relax. Don't push yourself.* But the truth was transparent. The elions had let their guard down the previous night. They'd relaxed, grown complacent, and vrawl had attacked. Then they lost comrades in the face of terrible danger. They couldn't afford the same mistakes. Something had changed within these refugees. Perhaps it was because they were now in the Mountains, away from the true North, and had lulled themselves into a false sense of security. Or perhaps it was because they had given up. Tim did not know what had changed the elions, but he was not going to sit by when danger waited on the doorstep. He *had* to push forward, even if they could not.

All the same, Tim let things be for the moment. He could either use his energy to argue with Pellen and Nazgar tonight, or save it for the citadel of Zadinn Kanas. So he nodded in agreement, leaned back, and let the warmth of the flames soak his face. In time, Pellen left, leaving Tim with Nazgar.

"What do you think of him?" Tim asked the Kyrlod.

"He has helped many an elion keep his or her sanity in the North," Nazgar said. "It is not an easy task and not often rewarding. He has been their greatest leader."

He was also their only *leader.* Tim did not voice that thought, either. Best to get on with the task at hand. "The vrawl will be back," Tim said. "We know fire keeps them away, but the wood won't last all night. Likewise, I can make fire with the Lifesource, but I can't hold the spell in place all night. Is there a way to let the spell stand on its own, without requiring my constant focus?"

"Standing spells are not unheard of," Nazgar said, "yet they are difficult and dangerous. When you hold the Lifesource, you guide its course. On the other hand, if you leave a spell to stand on its own, it can grow outside your control and threaten those around it. That being said, I feel the vrawl present a greater danger than that of leaving the spell unattended. So let us begin work."

With Nazgar's guidance, Tim practiced with a tiny flame near the campfire. It took some effort to get it right, and Tim realized this whole situation was brutally ironic. Standing spells were apparently a matter of convenience rather than energy. By the time he completed this work, he was just as exhausted as if he'd held the spell in place all night.

Eventually, though, he built a low wall of green flames around the camp. By the end of it, he could barely stand, and a pair of vrawl had begun patrolling at the edge of camp. As time passed, more vrawl joined the pack, but they were unwilling to cross the fire border, so the elions passed the night in peace. Tim Matthias, however, did not sleep so peacefully. He dreamed again of the black cloud with the red eyes. It waited for him and consumed him, and all was dark.

Twenty-Six

Quentiin Harggra dropped a massive slab of stone into the back of the cart and paused to catch his breath, chest rising and falling with each gasp. His body ached all over. He wore no shirt, and his skin glistened with a mixture of dirt and sweat. Twigs and soil filled his tattered beard, sticking out in all directions. His muscles were hard and chiseled after two weeks of slavery. Lashes crisscrossed his back, where older scars had already been replaced by new, red streaks, the pain ranging from fiery agony in some places to a dull throb in others.

Quentiin could not stop for long. The malichons were always watching, eager to discipline those who moved too slowly. He walked back to the Pit, noting that the sharp stone path no longer affected the hardened, scabbed soles of his feet. Upon reaching the quarry, he wrapped both arms around the next chunk of stone, lifting it and turning around once more.

He walked the path by rote, a spoke in a wheel, doing his task without emotion or thought. At least, that was how Quentiin wanted to appear, and it was working. Some of it was genuine. Quentiin's mind often grew numb in the repetitive rhythm of the day. But he never lost sight of the greater goal—to always look for an avenue out, a crack in the system, a flaw he could exploit to win freedom.

He had not found one yet. This lack of possibilities worried him at first, but he soon set those thoughts aright. The malichons intended to keep him captive for the rest of his life, so in a sense time was irrelevant. If he were to escape, then he had to do it right.

The blast of a horn announced the noon break, so Quentiin carried his load the rest of the way and dropped it into the back of the cart before joining the line of slaves shuffling through the quarry. They looked miserable, faces full of weariness and strife as they walked across the ground with hunched backs and stooped shoulders. It was easy to spot those who had been here the longest. Some, like Quentiin, remained fresh and healthy—as healthy as one could be in this dismal environment—while others were mere skeletons with nothing left but the frames of their bodies and taut skin covering their bones. Slaves died every day, and Quentiin could pick out which ones had little time left. He could even say with relative certainty that a slave in this very line would be dead by nightfall. What had been shocking at first was now routine.

Lunch was no different than breakfast, which was no different than the previous night's dinner, each one a steady line of meals trickling back to that very first day. The only variable in the gruel, as thick and gray as ever, was how hot or cold it might be. On a good day, it steamed and filled the body. If nothing else, the food stuck to one's ribs, providing a bellyful of energy. On most days, though, the slaves received cold bowls of mush that coagulated into clumps.

Quentiin took his noon repast with the dwerions from Raldoon. His companions barely spoke, if it all, and today they ate in total silence, each lost in his or her own thoughts. Some did not even raise their eyes from the meal, fixated on their bowls, as if another prisoner's gaze might reflect the loss of one's own humanity. As he ate, Quentiin surveyed his comrades from the corner of his eye. He had not yet decided whether or not to include them in his escape plan. He'd originally assumed they would plan it together, but now he knew that could never work. It would have been a good idea, for the dwerions of Raldoon were a formidable force when united. But that was before he'd realized what this place had done to them. It had robbed them of their spirits.

Even Jolldo, his oldest friend, forbade him to speak of escape again—and that was the crux of Quentiin's dilemma. If he mentioned an escape plan, even a viable one, would they go through with it? He feared they wouldn't. Another, darker possibility gnawed at him. He did not know if he could trust any of the dwerions, except for Jolldo. Jolldo would die before betraying him, but as for the others…well, Zadinn's evil did funny things to folk. The Tulak family had given up the elions' Fort to curry favor with the Dark Lord.

If Quentiin mentioned an escape plan, would someone tell the malichons? Such an act would gain much favor with the slave drivers. The informant might get good work detail, better food, and more comfortable sleeping accommodations—a whole mockery of privileges in a place that offered nothing.

The other option, then, was to escape alone. Once he made it out, he could seek out the elions who'd escaped the Fort—he knew some had survived, regardless of what the malichons might say—and aid them in their struggle against Zadinn. After all, if he was good enough to escape, he was also good enough to get back in, this time with a team of elions. Then, in a fitting reversal of the events at the Fort, they could open the front doors for their comrades.

Logic made Quentiin favor the second decision, but the thought of leaving his fellow dwerions behind all over again bothered him. He'd crossed the Rampart to find his friends, and now that he'd found them, he could not let them languish forever in this place. He could justify it by saying he was leaving to save them—and that was the absolute truth—but it *felt* like saving only himself.

After the noon period ended, Quentiin and Jolldo returned to the Pit for the rest of the day. They were often paired together, and Quentiin did not think this was mere happenstance. The malichons knew these two shared history, and they also knew Jolldo was thoroughly broken. They hoped his example would help "condition" Quentiin. However, of all the areas he could go, he liked the Pit the least. Though the work was not as arduous as filling carts at the pens or dragging the carts back and forth, it was still the worst. This quarry, located thousands of feet above a fiery chasm, was a tangible representation of the evil that pervaded every corner of this fortress.

By now, crossing the rickety bridge no longer weakened Quentiin's stomach. The structure might rattle and sway, but it had not broken yet. The heat blasted him as he moved, singeing the hairs on his beard and head. By the end of every day, Quentiin always found himself covered in a thin layer of ash from the constant barrage of fiery air.

The two dwerions stepped off at the far side of the bridge and hammered chisels against the stone. Some pieces came free more easily than others, but this current section did not. They worked long and hard before pulling a reasonable chunk from the wall. They then passed it to a pair of men, whose job was to transport stones across the bridge to waiting carts.

Quentiin and Jolldo moved down the wall, where another pair of slaves, a man and girl, wrestled a piece of stone from the wall. The man was aging, well into his later years, and the girl much younger, no more than twenty. A malichon stood by, watching them work.

The man did not appear to be doing well. His face had grown gray and his breathing came in gasps, each gulp of air seeming to take more effort than the last. His body trembled as he tried to extricate a piece of stone from the quarry wall. The narrow ledge on which they worked only served to make things more difficult—and more dangerous. The girl aided him as best as she could, but she kept glancing nervously toward their malichon overseers. Her companion's age and poor health would not serve as excuses for failing to work quickly.

When the piece of rock broke free, the burden of its weight shifted to the old man, and he stumbled. Quentiin saw exactly what was about to happen. It was like that game they played in Raldoon, in which they arranged tiny slabs of stone upright in rows to create intricate formations and then tipped the very first stone. Each little stone slab struck the next, propelling forward into a predictable pattern and an inevitable conclusion. Quentiin stepped away from the wall. He had to warn them.

"What are ye doin'?" Jolldo asked in an urgent hiss.

But Quentiin was too late. The old man fell backward, trying unsuccessfully to combat the weight of the boulder, and his heel slipped over the edge of the precipice. For a moment, everything hung still, and then the stone fell from his shaking hands, crashing onto the planks as he tilted back, one hand windmilling against the air in useless resistance. His other hand, chained to the girl's wrist, pulled her with him. Both man and girl fell from the edge of the wall, tumbling toward the fire below. At the last second, the girl caught the ledge with her free hand. She hung over the Pit, clinging to salvation while her companion dangled below her.

"Hurry!" Quentiin said to Jolldo, pulling his friend with him as he ran toward the stranded pair.

"Down!" a nearby malichon snarled as it stepped in front of them, uncoiling its whip and lashing both dwerions across the front. The blow knocked them over. Quentiin would have risen, regardless of the malichon, but the creature stepped forward and slammed its boot into Quentiin's back, pushing the dwerion down and holding him there. "This should prove amusing," the malichon said, watching the two helpless slaves at the edge of the Pit.

"Kendall," the old man said. "Kendall, listen to me."

"Hold on!" she said. "We can make it back up. I've almost got it." But she had only a feeble grip, her fingers slipping. A nearby malichon merely watched in silence, making no move to aid the prisoners.

"Kendall!" the older man said. "Kendall, pay attention. I need a promise from you."

"What?" she asked. Her hand slid further. Again, like in the game of stones from Raldoon, the pieces were falling toward one conclusion, and Quentiin could only watch.

The man still held his chisel in one hand. "Swear to me that when the time comes, when you are old, you will do for someone else that which I now do for you." He lifted his chisel, and for a brief moment, appeared to regain the strength of his youth. Eyes fierce and burning, he struck the link of chain holding him to Kendall. The chain broke apart quite easily, and the man fell soundlessly into the chasm of fire below.

Kendall screamed as she swung her freed hand up, gaining a better handhold on the stony ledge. With slow, steady determination, she pulled herself to safety. Then, after all that had happened, the malichon nearest them stepped forward and grabbed Kendall's wrists in its hands.

"What are you doing?" it asked.

Her eyes flickered. "I must…return to work."

"We have rules here," the malichon said. "Your partner has failed us, but he is now dead, so you must bear the responsibility for his failure."

The malichon wrested Kendall's grip from the edge, held her out from the ledge, and then released her without a word. Kendall cried out, falling downward into the Pit, becoming a mere speck as she descended into the fire. In moments she was gone.

Quentiin had seen many atrocities here, and he had long kept himself in check. But not so now, not after witnessing this, and there was nothing greater than a dwerion's wrath.

The malichon holding its boot against Quentiin's back expected no reaction, and Quentiin caught it off guard as he surged up and pushed his captor off balance. Quentiin pulled Jolldo with him, swinging his friend around like a bludgeon into the malichon. All three went down in a heap, Quentiin on top, and as they struck the ground, Quentiin slammed his chisel against the link of chain connecting him to Jolldo. It had worked for the old man, and it now worked for Quentiin. The chain broke, and Quentiin was free.

All of this happened in under a second. Quentiin's unbridled fury lent him an excess of speed and force. The malichon who had murdered Kendall was still rising from the edge when Quentiin reached it. The dwerion slammed into the slave driver, a roar exploding from his lungs. The malichon did not even have time to react. Quentiin knocked it away, and the whip fell from its grip, rolling off the ledge—a third victim for the flames of the Pit.

"You karfing son of a three-legged goat!" Quentiin screamed, raising a fist and punching the malichon in the face. The back of the creature's head slammed into the stone. The malichon lifted its arms to fight back, but blood-wrath flowed through Quentiin's veins. He put another fist in the malichon's face, and the slave driver's nose exploded in a spray of blood. When Quentiin punched it a third time, the malichon's pointed teeth shattered beneath his knuckles. He then grabbed the slave driver by the tunic and hauled it to its feet.

"Ye're goin' into the Pit, too, mate," Quentiin said, stepping forward to the ledge.

"No...please..." the malichon said.

"Now why in Malath would I listen to that?" Quentiin replied.

And then three other malichons grabbed Quentiin from behind, ripping his prisoner from him. Quentiin fought back, but they surrounded him and lashed him with their whips. He was forced to retreat from the ferocious assault. They cornered him against the wall, striking him with blows so hard his vision sparked. His defenses slowly failed as he slumped over, barely clinging to consciousness.

The malichon he had attacked stepped forward, standing over Quentiin's crumpled form. The guard was more composed now, no longer a sniveling wretch pleading for its life, and deep grooves of hatred etched into its face. The malichon kicked Quentiin in the ribs so hard it lifted him into the air and slammed him against the stone wall. Quentiin slid to the ground, blood trickling from his lip. The malichon took a whip from a comrade and struck Quentiin with it, the blow landing nearly hard enough to shatter his ribs.

Quentiin did not exaggerate the circumstances of any situation. He assessed events truthfully, never under- or overestimating outcomes. This was the real thing now. He saw it in the malichon's eyes—the slave driver was going to kill him. None of its comrades would stop it, and none of the slaves would save Quentiin. But someone else *did*.

"Stop!" a voice cried. The malichon halted, its whip raised for another blow.

The slave drivers immediately stood at attention, moving into impeccable lines to make way for Veldor the Slavemaster. Veldor approached Quentiin, striding purposefully down the makeshift aisle, his black cape billowing behind him.

Quentiin's former victim turned toward its master. "My lord, the dwerion—"

"I know what he did," Veldor interrupted. "I saw it, and I also saw your pathetic excuse for resistance. And *then* you pleaded for your life like one of them! I would kill you myself, but your offense grows light in view of a greater offense—*this*." He turned to Quentiin, who forced himself to rise, though it took all of his effort, every fiber of his body screaming in agony. Whatever Veldor had planned for him, he would meet it on both feet.

"You shall have your revenge, Gald," Veldor said to the malichon, "but not yet."

The Slavemaster looked at Quentiin. "You expect me to strike you. I would, but from the looks of things you are well acquainted with physical punishment. Yet you still stand with each foot on the ground, as if that wins you a battle of sorts. It does not. On the contrary—it makes you a more pleasing specimen. What is your name?"

"Quentiin Harggra," Quentiin replied. He did not address the Slavemaster with a title. Veldor had not earned it.

"Isanaiu mentioned you were a dwerion of interest, Quentiin Harggra. You are a woodsman, no? What gives you greater pleasure—felling a sapling or bringing down an oak? The sapling is young and supple. It bends easily and does not resist. When you find an oak, though, it is a challenge! It stands stiffer and mightier than all the rest, but when you have finally hewn its trunk from its roots, the oak *will* fall—and when it falls, it *crashes*. When an oak is down, it will not get back up no matter what. It is done, spent, and you know that you have won.

"We can administer physical punishment to you—and so we shall—but we must do more." The Slavemaster reached forward and seized Quentiin's head between his hands. "*This* is our enemy, my comrades. And this, Gald, is what we must destroy. Somewhere in this fragile skull, a mind exists, and it still believes it will outlast us. We will prove it wrong." He released Quentiin, wiping his hands on his shirt as if they were grimy.

"Gald," Veldor continued. "You wanted this dwerion to beg for his life, but I promise you this will be more enjoyable. Because when I am done, Quentiin will beg us to *take* his life—a request we *will* grant, but not as soon as he will like."

Veldor ordered Gald and two other malichons to bring Quentiin across the bridge. Quentiin did not resist. The game was on, and now it would play out. He'd need all his strength to win, so instead of wasting it on useless struggles, he stored it for the future. That said, his body could barely withstand physical stress of any kind, even walking.

Veldor allowed the malichons to beat him further, and Quentiin nearly slipped into unconsciousness. Though he'd regained some strength by the time they started walking again, he knew it was a charade he could not keep up for long. Veldor said there was something the malichons wanted to show him, and Quentiin was sure he wouldn't like it. *Well, I've gotten m'self into this mess. There's nothin' for it but to keep my back straight through it all.*

They walked across the bridge, through the slave pen, and past the shaping area. For a moment Quentiin thought they meant to show him the graves of those who had attempted to escape. However, they instead took Quentiin toward a stone wall at the west end of the pen. Quentiin had never come this far before, as there was no work to be done over here. As they neared the structure, he realized the mouth of a tunnel stood out from underneath a cleft in the rock. *There is a tunnel out here? Escape is goin' to be easier than I imagined, laddie. Better yet, they're showin' the karfin' place to me.*

Then he noticed the smiles on the faces of each and every malichon. They liked this place, and things malichons liked did not bode well for others. Veldor led the way into the tunnels, and the other malichons pushed Quentiin in from behind. The roughly hewn walls enclosed them on all sides, cutting off daylight, cloaking the group in darkness. Veldor lit a lantern, and they walked forward. The stony ground scraped against Quentiin's feet.

They traveled about five hundred paces before the passage opened to a much larger cavern, where the path sloped down before flattening out to a smooth landing. The center of the room had been dug out, leaving behind a square hollow about fifteen feet deep.

"Come," Veldor said, his tone almost cordial. "Walk a bit further, Quentiin." The Slavemaster stepped toward the center of the cavern.

Quentiin noticed the area was mostly empty, save for a few vacant shelves caked in dust and leaning against one wall. The hole, however, was a different matter. A leather harness, meant to fit around a torso, hung from a winch in the ceiling. A rope led from the winch across the ceiling and down to a lever on the ground, the harness dangling above the hole like a malicious fishing hook.

Veldor stopped Quentiin at the edge of the hole. The pale light from his lantern filtered down through the shaft, hitting the bottom in murky pools. Quentiin could vaguely see gray blocks scattered across the floor below, each structure about six handspans across and standing taller than the average man. Smaller, bleached rocks rested on the surface of each larger block.

"What do you think, dwerion?" Veldor asked.

"Yer artwork is lousy," Quentiin replied. "No sense of imagery."

Veldor chuckled. "I'd never thought of this as 'art' before, but I believe the dwerion is right. Look more closely, Quentiin. You are missing something."

Veldor pointed at the nearest block, and Quentiin then realized the white "rocks" were not stones but skulls.

"Do you see any bodies?" Veldor asked.

Quentiin did not reply. He still hadn't figured out the purpose of this bizarre scenario. Perhaps the malichons beheaded prisoners and threw the heads down into this hole—but why show it to him? It was disgusting, to be sure, but he'd heard of worse things in the slave pens by now. He'd *seen* worse things. They could not expect a pit of bodies to dishearten him much, and the whole point of this midafternoon stroll clearly was to disturb him. They hadn't come here to share a pint and play chess.

Veldor continued. "The heads stick above the stone, but the bodies are *inside* the stone. We mixed that stone ourselves, you see. If you blend water and rock in the right amounts, it creates a thick liquid that hardens over time. The mixture was still moist when we lowered the prisoners in. We left them while it solidified—but not for long. We soon came back."

Veldor pointed toward the shelves on the wall. "There, we kept boxes filled with scorpions, and that's where the true fun came in. We played a game in which we drew straws, and whoever won the draw got to throw the box into the pit while the rest took bets. No one knew where the box would land, but when it did, it *shattered*. We placed bets on which prisoner the scorpions would attack first, which would survive longest, which would lose his eyes, and so forth. What do you think of that, Quentiin Harggra?"

Quentiin remained silent.

"I thought as much," Veldor said. "You might want to know why I am showing you this. You have seen us do much, and you will see us do more." Veldor grabbed Quentiin by the hair, pulling hard enough to make Quentiin wince, and planted his other hand on the small of Quentiin's back. He pushed the dwerion forward so Quentiin's toes teetered on the edge of the abyss. Veldor leaned forward and whispered in his ear. "I wanted you to see this place so you'll know how you will die."

They sent Quentiin back to the Pit, but he could barely move. His body could not sustain work for long, and sometime in the afternoon he lost all consciousness. He woke up chained to the walls of his cage, left there all night without food or drink.

Matters had changed. He'd previously thought he could hold out as long as need be, but now that the malichons had turned their attention to him, he knew he didn't have long to survive. The guards' brutality was too intense. He'd need to escape within the week, now.

* * *

Kaiel Tulak fell onto the ground outside the Korlan Forest. He'd traveled almost ceaselessly, only stopping for brief naps and meager meals. Though it normally took five days to walk from Zadinn's citadel to the Korlan, he'd done it in three. Kaiel looked up at the trees, which swayed in the breeze like a conscious thing. He did not know much of this place, only vague things mentioned by Pellen Yuzhar.

But Kaiel was no longer the elion who'd heard those stories. He was now a different elion in a different lifetime. He followed a distant master, one embedded deep within his mind. Kaiel could feel *him* back there, a black presence always watching and waiting. If he moved too slowly or in the wrong direction...

He'd done just that the first day. The Master, not pleased with Kaiel's progress, had *nudged* him onward. Oh, how that had burned. Sitting at the edge of the Korlan on the brink of nightfall, Kaiel whimpered aloud at the memory.

In any case, Zadinn was not upset with Kaiel anymore. He was, however, clearly warning him against going into the forest. *Even I cannot protect you in there,* the voice whispered. *If you decide to go inside, I will kill you myself. Either way, you will not leave those woods alive.*

"I won't disobey," Kaiel said aloud.

I know, but rest now. You need to follow their trail soon. Get close to the Warrior, and I will reward you upon your return.

Kaiel Tulak remembered his last reward all too well, and tears leaked down his cheeks. The reward would be bad enough, but a punishment would be worse.

Twenty-Seven

Boblin stood at the edge of camp with the morning sun glowing faintly over the snow-encrusted landscape. He always liked this time of day, when the rays of light pushed back the frigid chill of night and the resulting warmth seeped into his bones with a tingling sensation. He shook himself as newfound vitality coursed through his veins.

The evening watch was over, and morning was here. Celia Alcion stood beside him, facing east. Ana had taken ill the previous night—nothing serious, only a fever brought on by the rigors of travel—so Boblin had taken her place.

"What do you think?" Celia asked him, breath misting in front of her face. They had passed most of the watch in silence, as expected during sentry duty.

"I prefer to think as little as possible," Boblin replied. The musty scent of smoke from the campfire wafted toward them, coupled with the tang of early dawn. "But despite my best efforts, I manage to have a thought or two. It's not a pleasant experience, let me assure you."

She smiled in the faint light. By the Maker, how he loved that smile. It was probably the single best thing about her, bar none. "I find that hard to believe."

Boblin smiled back. "I think things are balanced on a knife's edge right now," he said softly. "That's what I think." He didn't wish to put it all into words, but the odds were against them. They had lost six during the vrawl attack, Tim had grown cold and distant, and Nazgar remained as enigmatic as ever.

"Do you think there's hope?" Celia asked.

"I don't know," Boblin said. "But while there's breath in me, I'll push on." She acknowledged him with a nod, but said nothing. He turned to face her, just as the sun crept past the horizon and glinted off the armor of her chain mail vest. "Do *you* think there's hope?" he asked.

"Yes. I do."

And that is why I will keep pushing on, Boblin thought to himself, but he did not say it.

"Good morning," Ana's voice said, and the two sentries turned to look at the younger soldier. The girl stood in the morning light, fully dressed, appearing slightly fatigued but none the worse for the wear.

"Feeling better?" Celia asked her friend.

"Yes, the worst of the fever passed," Ana said, "though it wasn't fun."

"Ready to march?" Boblin asked her.

"Always," Ana said.

The camp stirred to life as the elions readied to leave. Supplies had thinned, leading to a concerned discussion about rationing. The adventure stories Boblin heard as a child always skipped the parts about rationing and sleepless nights. Those elements didn't make for great entertainment by the fireside. Still, the group would find a way to make it work. Maybe they could eat the vrawl. Tim certainly knew how to roast the beasts—thirty at a time—but at that stage, they were too well-done for Boblin's tastes. He liked his meat with some red in it.

None of the predators had appeared the previous night, and Boblin suspected their troubles with the vrawl might be over. That didn't mean the elions would cease to be vigilant. Boblin's conversation with Celia this morning reflected the mood of the rest of the camp, and it was clear this journey was taking a toll on the refugees. At the start of their quest, it was enough to just keep moving—they were alive and free. But the days since the Fort's fall had blended into weeks, and now they'd lost companions and had nothing to show for it. Though nobody said it, Boblin knew many were asking themselves if there really was a reason to be chasing ghosts from two centuries past in this forsaken place.

Every elion of the Fort trusted Pellen Yuzhar and would willingly follow him even into Malath. But Nazgar, not Pellen, had sent them into the Mountains. The Kyrlod clearly knew more than he let on, and that always irked some. Boblin was willing to follow Nazgar—the Kyrlod had, after all, chosen him of all the elions to find the Southerners, and also had helped the refugees in their escape—but the other elions might not be as patient, especially if another disaster came.

They began this day's journey by following a route between two peaks, a path between a pair of sheer, flawless walls rising on either side of them. The snow was light and shallow underfoot, allowing them to travel with ease as they followed the slope gradually upward. In a way, this place felt like a strange imitation of the Kaltu Pass.

As the ground took them up and out of the pass, Boblin saw rows of eagles' nests dotting the upper reaches of the highest walls. Boblin looked to the sky in hope of spotting a few of the majestic birds in flight. He caught a few glimpses of shapes taking off at the very tops of the cliffs, but the small dots vanished quickly.

After the path leveled out and the walls widened, the refugees made it to the top of a large, circular plateau coated in a flawless expanse of white snow. A ring of peaks enclosed the tabletop surface, and the only object marring the empty landscape was a rocky formation near its center. An opening in the peaks led to the other side of the pass, where the landscape sloped back down at a much steeper angle.

The elions crossed the plateau in earnest and came upon the rocky mound. As they neared the pile of stones, Boblin knitted his brow in confusion. "Ken," he said to the scout beside him, "that mound of stones isn't natural. The formation is too deliberate."

Ken faltered a step. "You're absolutely right, Kule. We should have noticed."

The two elions broke forward from the group to get a closer look. Something atop the pile glinted in the sun—chain mail—and Boblin called out, alerting the others. The rest of the elions hurried to the odd structure. Boblin soon discerned shapes within the rubble. The glittering mail came from an old chest-piece, caked in rust, and several aged helms lay scattered across the ground. In the very center, crumbling remnants of skeletons, bones still inside armor, laid with shattered swords across their chests. The splintered mast of a broken standard stood upright in the snow, strips of cloth fluttering in the breeze.

This place was the site of someone's last stand. Had these victims been fighting vrawl? The cats could have easily trapped their victims on this plateau, gradually wearing the defenders down. Though there was likely no immediate risk for the elions—vrawl only seemed to come out at night, and there was plenty of daylight—Boblin still felt a rising sensation of dread. The sight of dead bodies did that.

The sharply defined corner of a rectangular block stuck from beneath the stones, a desiccated skeleton stretched across its surface. The block was made of a semitranslucent material, and the sunlight reflected off it in a scattered array of rainbow hues. *Crystal. That's a huge chunk of crystal.*

The human lying across the stone had clearly died protecting it. Perhaps the group of travelers had discovered a crystal lode within the Northern Mountains and prepared to make off with the prize, but on the way back, came under assault from…what? Not animals. Only men warred and killed over senseless commodities. Could it be local tribes, perhaps other residents of the Mountains?

"Stand back!" Nazgar called out with unusual sharpness. Boblin stepped away from the pile as the Kyrlod strode over. Boblin had rarely, if ever, seen the prophet this tense. He almost expected a monster to explode from beneath the pile, but the rubble remained decidedly still. As Nazgar approached the buried object, face set in a grim line, he pushed the skeleton aside and brushed the snow off the crystal with his bare hands, heedless of the cold. Boblin watched Nazgar, who focused on the crystal with gaze unbroken and eyes unblinking.

"What is this?" Boblin asked Tim.

"I'm not sure," Tim replied, "but Nazgar knows, and I think this is why he brought us into the Mountains."

"Other than the Army, you mean? And, I suppose, the local wildlife. The scenery is *so* nice, after all."

"Yes," Tim said, ignoring the sarcasm, "other than the Army."

Boblin looked back at the armaments on the ground. For the first time, he noticed a shield with the brown outline of a soaring eagle emblazoned on its front. Bars of blue ran across its background. "By the Maker, that's the symbol of the Jovun dynasty."

Nazgar fully uncovered the piece of crystal. It was perfectly rectangular, shaped at exact right angles, certainly an oddity. But Boblin was more focused on the oddity *within* the crystal. A man lay inside the block, arms at his sides and eyes closed. He wore drab brown military clothes, gold links adorning his cuffs and collar. The Jovun eagle was embroidered upon his left breast, and a velvet cape draped over his shoulders, held around his neck by an emerald clasp. Boblin recognized this man from a portrait in the Fort's Hall of History. This was Ladu Jovun IV, son of the Emperor.

Boblin certainly hadn't expected him to be sealed inside a chunk of solid crystal. Tim, on the other hand, seemed utterly unsurprised by this discovery. He studied the scene with uncanny intensity, face flat and expressionless. Like

as the Patrol fired arrows at them. Then, at the last moment, a sarchon dipped back down in a flash of movement and grabbed Tim Matthias by his shoulders, digging in deep with its claws. Tim never had any time to react; the sarchon rose back into the air as quickly as it had descended. Boblin fired his bow, but his shot went wide, and by the time he'd notched another shaft, Tim was beyond reach. He could only watch as the Warrior of Light was taken into the blue sky. "Karf!" Boblin screamed.

"Fall back!" Jend called out. "Full retreat!"

"Full retreat?" Boblin shouted at the Commander. "They just took Matthias!"

"I have eyes, Kule!" Jend shouted back. "I know full well they took him, but we cannot withstand a third strike! Now move!"

Boblin knew Jend was right. Fighting against winged attackers was too taxing for a prolonged battle, and the sarchons seemed infinitely numerous. The birds would not stop until all the elions were dead, and with the other refugees now safely away from the plateau, they had nothing to gain from staying here. The Warrior was on his own.

That did not make it any easier for Boblin to turn his back. Nonetheless, he followed Jend's orders and joined in the retreat, while behind him the sarchons prepared their third descent.

Boblin felt a hand on his shoulder and turned to see Nazgar beside him. "I need your help," the Kyrlod said.

"What in Malath are you still doing here?" Boblin yelled. "Why didn't you leave with the others?"

Nazgar pointed at the pile of rocks in the center of the plateau, a hundred yards away by now. "We cannot leave him behind."

"You're talking to the wrong person," Boblin replied. "It's the Commander's call!"

"Not Tim," Nazgar said. "The Prince."

"The Prince? What do you mean?"

"Ladu Jovun IV is every bit as crucial to our victory as the Warrior of Light. We must rescue his body!"

The boiling flock of sarchons had reached its peak, and as Nazgar spoke, a new wave of attackers swooped down. Running to the crystal would only put Boblin closer to the danger, and he would much prefer to get *away* from it. "How?" he asked.

"I will protect you," Nazgar replied.

Boblin growled in frustration, but he stopped and turned back. He looked over at the crystal and then up at the rapidly flapping predators. Nazgar was a man of secrets, but he did not lie. If he said that the elions needed the Prince, then the elions needed the Prince.

Karfing Kyrlod and their karfing prophecies. "Okay," Boblin said, running toward the rocks. Nazgar ran, too, easily keeping pace with Boblin. Impressive for a man who was literally centuries old, but Boblin expected nothing less. Nazgar was just *full* of surprises. *He probably takes a three-hour jog before breakfast every morning, too, after finishing fifty one-handed pushups.*

The sarchons moved more slowly this time, cautious of the elions but still determined to drive them away. Or maybe this was just entertainment for them. *If I were as ugly as they are, I'd bite off heads for a pastime, too.*

When Boblin reached the rectangular block, he examined it closely. Two ropes were attached to the front end, almost like a harness. Apparently the guards had been transporting the Prince like this for some time. Well, at least Boblin wouldn't have to push and drag this whole bloody mess across half the plateau. *That* would have been too much.

Nazgar stepped forward, putting himself between Boblin and the sarchons. The creatures were only seconds away. "I can hold them off," the Kyrlod said.

Of course, one old man against a flock of birds from Malath. That sort of thing happens all the time. But Nazgar hadn't steered him wrong yet. Boblin reached forward and grasped a length of rope in each hand. He didn't know how heavy this block would be, so he pulled with a hefty effort—and the rope, old and rotten, snapped free of the crystal, leaving Boblin with a strand in each fist.

"Why does everything have to be such a karfing bother?" Boblin said in frustration. He kicked the crystal, belatedly realizing this was not a very respectful thing to do.

"One day, I will discuss your language with you," Nazgar said in a mild tone.

"This isn't a conversation I'm going to have right before a flock of oversize bats rips us to shreds," Boblin shot back. Just as he finished his sentence, the sarchons engulfed them in a swarm. Boblin steeled himself, preparing to feel claws digging into his back. Instead, he heard a noise like thunder and the entire ground shook, causing him to fall onto his back. He looked at Nazgar and beheld an awesome sight.

The Kyrlod stood with feet planted, arms stretched out on both sides, a ball of purple flame dancing in the palm of each hand. Nazgar closed his fists and made a twisting motion. A bubble of air exploded from his hands, shimmering as it moved, and knocked the sarchons back a dozen paces. The wave held the birds at bay, clearing the air around them. It was as if Boblin and Nazgar stood in a domed building, but instead of stone, the ceiling and walls were made of writhing, angry sarchons.

The creatures milled about and then struck again. This time, Nazgar threw one of his fiery balls into the horde. Purple flames slammed into the first sarchon, consuming its body. Nazgar immediately threw two more fireballs at the birds, burning through their ranks like they were dry tinder. He followed this with another huge bubble of air, forcing the sarchons to scatter back into the sky.

Why didn't he do this before? Boblin wondered, but now was not the time to ponder questions of deep logic. Boblin reached forward and pushed the crystal, just to see how heavy it was, and found it quite light. It slid at only a gentle touch. *Now to get out of here.* He looked around, and an idea came to him. It was mildly disrespectful—both to Nazgar and the Prince—but maybe that was why Boblin liked his plan so much.

"Let's go," he said to the Kyrlod. He grabbed Nazgar by the tunic and leaped onto the crystal, landing on his belly as if sledding—and that was the point. His momentum launched the crystal forward across the icy snow. The surface of the plateau formed a gentle slope toward the pass at the north end of the peaks, and Boblin fully planned to use that slope to his advantage.

The crystal sped across the snow, elion and prophet atop it, rapidly gaining speed as it hurled past the sarchons. The winged creatures took flight, and the two companions soon were at a safe distance from them. Boblin saw that Nazgar was laughing. *I always knew the Kyrlod were a bunch of sun-baked lunatics.*

As the projectile sped down the slope, Boblin realized he would soon need to apply direction to his course in order to reach the pass ahead. The gap in the stone walls was wide, but if he steered wrong they would end up splattered against the peaks. As the oncoming walls neared with ever-increasing speed, Boblin pushed with his hand against the snow to align the sled with the pass. Faldon and Tavin, still guarding the retreat, gaped at the approaching pair. *Yes, cousins, Kule came back with the bloody circus.*

After they shot through the gap in the walls, Boblin noticed something very unfortunate. The trail took a sharp turn to the west, leading them toward a stone wall, beyond which stretched a brief expanse of ice, ending in a sheer cliff. There was no avoiding it. He reacted instantly by shoving Nazgar off the sled—more disrespect—and using both hands to try and curb his speed. He was only marginally successful. The crystal slammed into the wall of stone, halting it. That was good for the crystal and its internal resident, but not for Boblin. His momentum threw him up into the air, over the wall, and onto the icy expanse, where he found himself sliding again, this time alone, toward the edge.

Boblin reached forward with his hands, but there was nothing to grab. The surface of the ice was too slick. Someone shouted out, and Boblin looked up as Jend Argul threw a climbing pick toward him. Boblin grabbed the pick, raised it high, and slammed the sharp end into the ice, causing frosty fragments to spray in all directions. However, the pick did not hold. Boblin struck the surface again and again, to no avail, as icy sparks showered all around him.

Boblin's feet shot out over the edge of the cliff. He raised the pick one last time, swinging with as much might as he could muster. The tip of the ax left a jagged crevasse of ice chunks in its wake—and then finally grabbed hold at the edge of the cliff. Boblin jerked to a halt, clinging to the ax with one hand as he dangled helplessly over the depths of the abyss.

Twenty-Eight

Tim screamed in pain as the sarchon's talons bit into his skin. Below him, the figures on the ground shrank to specks. His stomach lurched as the creature took him higher and higher until he could see the entire expanse of the mountains beneath him. Other sarchons flew around him, spinning in circles as they formed up for a third assault on the forces below. *The elions should retreat. They're fighting a losing battle down there.*

Tim filled himself with the Lifesource, the power thrumming and vibrating within him. He expected the sarchon's jaws to crush his skull at any moment, but nothing happened.

Comforting though the Lifesource might be, it had no immediate use. As much as Tim wanted to incinerate this monster, the bird was his link to life. If he were to kill the sarchon, he would plummet to the ground and end up quite dead. Though he knew how to make shields with the Lifesource, he didn't trust his skills enough to feel certain he would survive the impact.

The sarchon banked to the left toward the nests on the peaks, aiming for an aerie resting on a stone outcrop that jutted from the mouth of a cave. The nest was as wide as Tim was tall, comprised of an assortment of twigs and white fur. Tim recognized the fur as that of a vrawl. Though the saber-toothed beasts might be ferocious, they were tame kittens compared to these winged monsters. The sarchons, with their gray skin, sharp teeth, and burning red eyes, reminded him of the malichon army, every bit as savage and intelligent as Zadinn's troops.

Upon seeing the nest, Tim knew why he had been spared thus far—a dozen infants eagerly awaited the arrival of a new meal. As the adult carrying Tim soared toward the nest, the tiny birds clambered to their feet, flapping their feeble wings in excitement and rearing their triple heads back, mouths open wide for the incoming morsel. Tim braced himself as the sarchon carried him over the nest, his feet hanging just above the gaping mouths of the babies. The young birds scrambled below him, screeching in anticipation.

Tim reached toward his belt and unsheathed his sword as the adult released him into the nest. When he landed, Tim unleashed his powers, and his sword blazed with its familiar green fire. Surprised, the infants scattered away from him. One youngster, not as wary as its siblings, hopped forward with jaws snapping. Tim directed his sword toward the threat, fire lancing from the tip, and the tiny monster exploded in a ball of flame.

From the edge of the nest, the mother screamed, causing Tim to stumble in momentary disorientation as she launched toward him. Tim rolled toward the very back of the nest, tumbling over the edge and onto the stone perch that led into the cave. He flipped back onto his feet, sword in both hands, and the sarchon curbed her flight at the lip of the nest, hissing at him with her central head. Her other two heads swiveled, waiting for an opening to strike. Tim suspected that if not for her children, she might abandon the attack and fly away, but she would die before leaving her nest exposed.

Fine with me. They struck at the same time. Tim unleashed a wave of fire from his sword, engulfing the twigs and fur of the nest in a blazing conflagration. The sarchon launched at him, claws outstretched and jaws wide. Tim pulled his sword back, attempting to hold it crosswise in front of him in a defensive posture, but he was a fraction too slow. The sarchon's talons raked across his chest, and he fell onto his back into the cave. In the nest, the infants screeched in agony as green fire consumed them.

The sarchon breathed hot air onto his face. Her breath carried the rancid, foul smell of decay. She twisted her right-most head toward him, drooling a fountain of saliva, but Tim pulled away just in time. The oozing droplets struck the floor of the cave, immediately creating deep pockmarks in the stone. She pinned his right arm to the ground, his sword pointing away from her. While keeping this hand around the leather-bound hilt, Tim managed to raise his left hand and release a wave of pressurized air with the Lifesource, knocking the sarchon back. Tim rose to his feet, and a blast of flame shot from the blade, plowing into the wall of the cave. Chunks of stone exploded forth from the impact, leaving a trench in the wall.

The sarchon leaped forward again, and Tim continued the arc of the sword, taking her left head off in a clean sweep. Flecks of black blood burned his forearm and Tim gritted his teeth. She had two heads left and showed no signs of slowing. When the sarchon struck again, he drove his blade deep into her chest, and fiery green flames enveloped her body.

The momentum of the attack pushed him backward. His heel slipped on a ledge and he stumbled, balance wavering. Too late, he realized he had backed into an enormous hole in the floor. As he yanked his blade from the sarchon's burning body, he lost footing. Arms pumping uselessly against the empty air, Tim fell into the shaft.

In his shock, he lost hold of the Lifesource. His sword's green light winked out as it fell, and the inky darkness closed all around him as he went down, down, *down* into unknown depths to an unknown fate. Tim felt several long seconds pass. His mind did not think, did not react. He was completely *numb*. He couldn't seize the Lifesource, as he was conscious only of his complete and utter free-fall, expecting at any moment to land against a stone surface with crushing, bone-breaking force.

Instead he landed on his back in a pool of frigid water, which only made the impact *slightly* less jarring. Tim's breath rushed out of him as he plowed into the icy depths. Survival instincts taking over, Tim kicked with his legs and pulled with his arms, bringing himself back to the surface in a spray of water. For a moment he couldn't breathe, still winded from his landing. He briefly went under a second time but then surged back up as he successfully treaded water, keeping himself afloat while his lungs opened. He sucked in gulps of fresh air, and his thoughts locked back into focus. *I'm alive. I'm alive. Now swim!*

As his breath regulated to a more even pace, Tim stroked more smoothly. Absolute darkness surrounded him. He had no bearing in any direction and no way of knowing if there was a shoreline to this pool. For all he knew, he was at the bottom of a single deep shaft with walls enclosing him on all sides. There would be no return to the day for him, and he'd tread water until his muscles gave out and he went under.

He had to focus, and his first thought was, *Gain some light.* He bumped into a hard surface, and his heart lurched in temporary panic before he realized it was only a rock, a big boulder jutting up in the middle of the pool. He was lucky he hadn't landed on *that*. He grasped the surface of the stone, grateful for the respite from treading water. *Now, light.* He could have used his sword for light, but it was beyond his reach in the depths below. Then he had another idea; Nazgar had said focusing points were *anything natural*. Anything untouched by men could be a focusing point, and Tim would bet no man had ever scarred the surface of the rock to which he now clung.

Tim closed his eyes and summoned the power. He'd never before realized how warm the Lifesource was, but now he felt it running through his veins like hot blood, restoring vitality to his limbs. Tim transferred the energy to the stone beneath his hands, and it glowed with a dim light. For a second Tim lost his hold on the Lifesource and blackness returned to the cavern, but he seized the power again and performed his actions with more assertion. The light flared back into existence, emanating from deep within the boulder. Tim squeezed his eyes shut against the sudden radiance but slowly opened them again, adjusting to the illumination.

He climbed from the water and onto the surface of the boulder, maneuvering into a sitting position. He looked around, fearing he would see no shore, but his worries proved groundless. The shaft above him was merely a hole in the center of a larger dome. Stalactites covered the ceiling, glistening in shades of white, red, and orange, all sparkling in the light from the rock. But even with the light, the waters in the cavern remained black and impenetrable. They stretched about sixty paces in either direction before coming to a shoreline, which stretched back into the recesses of the cavern.

Tim didn't know what he might find on that shoreline, but he had no choice. He slid off the rock and back into the frigid pool, striking out for the shore. The cold leeched all the strength from his muscles and made his bones ache. He gasped for breath the whole way, and by the time he reached the far side he had no energy left. He dragged himself onto the rocky bank and lay on his side. The long gashes the sarchon's talons had left in his shoulders throbbed anew, pain pulsing in cadence with his heartbeat. The bleeding had slowed to a mere trickle, but it did not lessen his discomfort.

The situation was grim. He was stuck in a deep cavern with little hope of a way back to the surface, and to make things worse, he had lost his sword. Though maybe he *hadn't* lost it. Nazgar had told him that, over time, most Advocates developed links to their focusing points. Tim reached out with his mind, probing the waters in an attempt to locate the sword. For a long time he felt nothing, but then a faint sensation nudged the recesses of his mind. He sought out the bond, focusing his mind firmly upon it. Once he had a solid grasp, he pulled with the Lifesource, feeling a thrill of success as the blade rose through the waters toward him. The connection between him and the stone grew stronger the closer it came, until he saw the sword beneath the water's surface, glowing with green fire and speeding toward him. As it breached the waters at his feet, Tim pulled it from the pool.

Tim released the Lifesource, weakened by these efforts, and staggered away from the edge of the pool. Once he made it farther onto the shore, weariness crashed upon him and he fell. Shivering from the cold, tired from battle, and wracked with pain from his injuries, Tim Matthias clung to the edge of consciousness. He did not fight it. The boulder in the center of the pool lost its light, and Tim fell into a fitful slumber, while the absolute darkness of the deep earth swallowed him.

* * *

Don't look down.

Boblin clung to the pickax with one hand. His other arm hung uselessly at his side.

Don't look down. You were never supposed to look down, not when you were high up. Everybody said it just made things worse.

Boblin looked down.

He instantly regretted it. The distance was too far to guess at. It could have been two thousand paces, or ten thousand. He was terrible at estimating such things, and besides, it didn't matter. From this height, dead was dead. The only difference was how long Boblin would have to think about it before he landed. Tiny tops of evergreen trees flecked the ground, and between them a winding river ran north to south in a thin blue ribbon. Sporadic patches of snow covered the landscape. Viewed from a different situation, the sight would have been peaceful, idyllic.

Not so for Boblin. His heart was beating so fast he was surprised it didn't erupt from his chest. *That* might have been a mercy, since it would be a much faster death than falling from here to…there. The muscles in Boblin's right arm screamed in agony, but he would hold on to this pick, regardless of the pain. The pick was *life*, and that offered quite an incentive to take his mind away from the physical pain. The problem was that sooner or later the tip of the ax would break free from the ice, and then Boblin would have to see how well he fared at turning into an eagle.

"Kule!" Commander Jend called.

Since Boblin was hanging below the edge of the cliff, he could not see anything on the surface above him, but he surely hoped that, selfish as the notion might be, someone was braving the icy expanse to come to him.

"I'm here!" he called back, voice wavering. He wished he could have shown a little more bravery, something more befitting a soldier of the Frontier Patrol, but this was a clincher and no mistake.

"I'm throwing a rope to you!" the Commander shouted.

Thank the Maker. Boblin was grateful Jend asked no further questions, no "Are you all right?" or "How long can you hold on?" In times of crisis, folk often wasted time bandying about such idiotic formalities without stopping to think of how useless such inquires were. *Of course* Boblin wasn't all right, he was hanging from the edge of a karfing cliff, and *who knew* how long he could hold on, because it wasn't as if the rescuers were going to stop for afternoon tea. Jend Argul, solid as ever, only communicated what was necessary.

A length of rope slid over the edge of the ice, a blessed sight...and quite out of reach. "Move it to the right!" Boblin called back. The rope moved *away* from him, and he cursed. "Karf! My right, your left!"

The rope reversed course, swinging back over the emptiness, but Jend could only maneuver it so much from his position. A crystal of ice near the surface of the pick broke free and tumbled past Boblin's face. Still too far to reach, the rope snagged on a jagged edge of the cliff. Boblin saw it twitch and knew Jend was doing his best to maneuver. The small cleft holding the rope back was so small, so *minor*, but in the way.

"I'm going to pull it back and try again!" Jend said.

"No!" Boblin said. "There isn't enough time!" There was a slim possibility he could stretch just far enough to grasp the rope, but any such movement would surely pull the pick free. It was a gamble, and Boblin hated gambling. He never won. He preferred games like chess, in which he could control his side of the board through logic and strategy.

It didn't matter, though. It was time to pull a card from the karfing deck of fate. Boblin threw himself toward the dangling rope, hedging everything on an all-or-nothing move. Had he stopped to think about it, he probably wouldn't have mustered the courage quickly enough, but he just went for it, no thought involved.

It saved his life. The pick came free, accompanied by a substantial shower of crystal fragments, just as Boblin's hand closed on the rope. His stomach lurched as the line slid with his added weight, but then it stopped as Jend and the elions on the other end put their strength into holding it back. Boblin released the ax so he could grab the rope with both hands. It tumbled away, swallowed up by the maw of the wilderness.

"I've got it!" he shouted, voice now rattled beyond all recognition. He was surprised he could speak at all. As the rope tugged him upward, Boblin tried to assist by grabbing the edge of the cliff, but sweaty hands against slick ice were no good, so he merely clung to the rope as the others dragged him across the expanse. The surface was painfully cold, but he did not care. He welcomed it.

Jend and the other elions pulled steadily and gradually as they brought Boblin back over the ledge from which he had been propelled. The wall stood at about waist height, but once over and onto the path, Boblin wished it was a league high. He wanted anything and everything between him and that karfing cliff.

Boblin slid over the edge and landed with two feet. He *wanted* to collapse and let the shakes consume him, but now was not the time for that. This was the North. If he could not recover quickly, even from a harrowing, near-death experience, he would not last long in this place. The sarchons could come back, the vrawl could attack, or Zadinn karfing Kanas could appear from out of the air, unleashing fire and lightning upon them. If one couldn't take it in stride, one didn't survive.

Boblin handed the rope back to Jend. The Commander took it, nodding at Boblin. Again, he voiced no questions, but Boblin answered anyway. He let out a rattled sigh and said, "I'll be fine, sir. A minute to catch my breath is all. Thank you."

The Commander smiled. "You kept your head, Kule. Well done."

A compliment from Jend was almost as good as a compliment from Pellen Yuzhar. At that moment, Boblin knew he *would* be all right, no matter what.

*　*　*

Now that Boblin was safe, the company's attention turned to the man in the block of crystal Boblin had so unceremoniously brought into their camp. "What is this?" Hedro Desh asked as the elions formed a semicircle around the strange sight.

"He is Ladu Jovun IV, son of the emperor," said Pellen Yuzhar. The group parted to allow room for their leader as the old elion walked to the block and placed his palm on its surface. It was a lonely sight, the ancient elion standing near the body of a young warrior. "He and I were friends on the battlefield, but we became separated before the final conflict. This crystal is what we came here to find."

"Does he live?" asked Ken.

"That I do not know." Pellen lifted his head and looked toward Nazgar. "What now, old friend?"

"The Prince is alive," the Kyrlod said, stepping next to Pellen. He faced the group. "Those who try to cross the Mountains will die. It is inevitable."

"Then why did you bring us here?" Hedro asked, face tight. An angry murmur followed his question.

Nazgar remained unperturbed by this dissent. Pellen, however, raised his voice in response. "I would have you show more respect to one of the Kyrlod," he said, "and if you will not do so for his sake, then do so for mine."

"But *he* brought us here!" Hedro said.

"My son, one day you will wish you had spoken less and listened more," Pellen replied. "Nazgar did not bring us here to die. If you would be silent, he will finish sharing his thoughts. One must be patient when dealing with Kyrlod. A puzzle is constructed only one piece at a time."

Uneasy silence settled over the group as Nazgar cleared his throat. "I did not mean for you to think I deceived you," he said to them. "I've told you we need a talisman of protection to survive the Mountains. The Mountains and the Barricade keep Zadinn confined between them, a wall to his south and peaks to his north. But that which would hold back the Dark Lord will also hold us back.

"In the last battle of the Invasion, the remaining Advocates sealed Prince Ladu inside this crystal to protect his life. The men who fled the battlefield took him with them. I found the soldiers on the borders of the Korlan Forest, and from there I sent them into the Mountains. I thought Ladu would be *their* talisman, like the Warrior is ours. He is an emblem of the golden times, and I believed that would be enough. I'd hoped they would make it through and find the Army of Kah'lash, but it is clear they fell to the sarchons."

"We don't have our talisman anymore," Hedro said. "Matthias is gone."

"A talisman is symbolic as well as literal," Nazgar said, looking back toward the plateau. "A man does not find Those Who Wait unless he champions a cause great enough to call them forth, but the Warrior of Light is the greatest champion ever born. Whether or not we will live remains to be seen, for we are now separated from the Warrior. It may be our fate is to be sacrificed to the Mountains, while the Warrior endures to find Kah'lash."

Nazgar turned back to the block of crystal. "But I do not think so," he said in a low tone. "We have found the Prince. He did not find the Army of Kah'lash, but we have found him." He looked at the elions again. "I ask you to stand back. This will not be easy on this man."

"I will stay here," Pellen countered. "I am one he will recognize. That may be of some help."

"Agreed," Nazgar said, kneeling in front of the block. He closed his eyes, placing his palms on the surface of the crystal, and took a deep breath. Glowing yellow dots appeared beneath Nazgar's fingers, spreading outward in concentric circles. As the waves rippled across the face of the crystal, they took on many colors—blue, red, green, and purple—starting slowly but steadily becoming more frantic.

Boblin gave himself a good shake. The Lifesource was beyond his comprehension. Tim might be all well and good with learning to create fire at the snap of a finger, but Boblin preferred the usual flint and tinder. Some things were best left unexplored, and Boblin believed magic was one of them. *Besides, isn't it dangerous for him to do this?* Nazgar had countlessly repeated that he dared not use his powers, since doing so would open his mind to Zadinn Kanas. And yet he had used the Lifesource twice in the span of an hour, once against the sarchons—though Boblin wasn't objecting—and now on this crystal.

Incandescent ripples enveloped the crystal in a storm of rainbows. Boblin shielded his eyes from the chaos. *When Ladu wakes up, all of his hair is going to be singed clean off. I wonder if the Prince is okay with being bald, as well as two hundred years older.*

Without preamble, the crystal vanished. Prince Ladu lay in the snow, motionless for a handful of seconds before he stirred. His eyelids fluttered open and then closed again. Suddenly he bolted upright, eyes opening and—quite literally, Boblin had to say—widening to the size of small moons. His face had a wild, frantic look.

"Wha—?" He coughed, but made no other sounds. His jaw opened silently at the air, trying to form words but unable to.

"Easy, my friend," Pellen said. He put a hand on Ladu's shoulder, but the Prince scuttled away from him, bumping against a ledge at his back.

Ladu looked at Pellen and then Nazgar. "Whuereyuuu?" he managed, jaw still working in a circle.

"You need to rest," Nazgar said, touching Ladu's shoulder. This time, the Prince did not resist. "You are safe. We are friends of your father, but you need to relax. You have been in the crystal for some time."

At the mention of his father, Ladu slumped down like a marionette with its strings cut. Boblin did not doubt the Prince was a strong man, but a two-hundred-year nap was bound to have adverse effects.

"Water," Pellen said. Hugo handed him a flask, and Pellen placed the tip near Ladu's lips. The Prince tried to take the skin but could not even close his hands around it, so Pellen poured the water into Ladu's mouth. Pellen gave him only a small trickle before taking it back. "I warn against having too much, my friend," he said gently.

Ladu nodded. After swallowing, he managed to speak, though it took a visible effort. "Who...are...you?" he asked.

"It is I, my friend. Pellen Yuzhar."

"Pellen?" Ladu whispered, features creasing in confusion. He raised a hand to his forehead, but his arm flopped uselessly back down to his side. "You...are so old." He coughed. "How long is it? How long...since the battle?"

Nazgar and Pellen looked at each other. Nazgar lifted one eye, giving a barely perceptible twitch of his head that said, *Don't tell, not yet.*

"I disagree," Pellen said, looking into the Kyrlod's eyes. "The truth is best." He turned back to Ladu. "It has been two hundred years, my friend."

Ladu's eyes rolled back, and he fainted against the wall.

"That is not how I would have done it," Nazgar said. "But he had to find out, and I suppose sooner is better."

All things considered, Boblin thought, *the Prince took the news fairly well.*

Twenty-Nine

Tim awakened in a fit of shivering, surrounded in absolute darkness. At first, he could not remember where he was, and for a brief instant he wondered if this was death. He sat up, feeling around with his palms to get his bearing. The stone floor was cold and hard. *Am I in Malath?*

Twin flares of pain blazed across his shoulder blades, and in a flash he remembered the sarchon's talons biting into his skin as it carried him high into the sky. His initial panic subsided as he recalled the events of the past few hours, but the underlying sense of fear remained. He was, after all, lost in the bowels of the Mountains without any real hope of escape.

His knuckles brushed the hilt of his sword, and he breathed a deep sigh of relief. He summoned the Lifesource, infusing the focusing point with its power, and the blade slowly glowed to life.

Tim stood, his tired, sore limbs aching in protest. The wetness from his damp clothes had seeped deep into his skin, penetrating him to the core with coldness, and the wounds in his back continued their dull throb. He reached over his shoulder, touching a gash with the tip of his finger, and jerked back as it flared in pain.

He turned in a circle, inspecting the walls of the cavern. Numerous small tunnels, set in the wall a little higher than his waist, led out of the cavern and into the recesses beyond. Tim approached the nearest of these passages, peering into the shaft and lifting his sword to provide more light, but it ended in a solid wall less than a dozen paces in. No good. He walked over to inspect the next shaft, which stretched away farther than he could see. He forced his sword to shine even brighter, and though it couldn't entirely illuminate the shadowy depths, he could see that the path sloped upward.

He swallowed. He would have preferred to see daylight at the far end. He could see himself clambering up the tunnel on his stomach, dragging his body forward using his hands and elbows. Perhaps it would lead him to the surface, but what if it didn't? The unknown ate away at him. The tunnel might close off two hundred paces away, forcing him to retreat. Or maybe by that point he'd get stuck and wouldn't be able to go back. Or he might come to a sarchon hive filled with the bloodthirsty birds.

Tim had thought about the Mountains a lot these last few days. Though Nazgar had said they were meant to prevent Zadinn from moving farther north, Tim wasn't sure this was the whole truth. He felt certain these peaks wanted *him*, just like the Korlan had wanted him—to absorb the Warrior of Light and drain away his powers for more malevolent purposes. Tim wouldn't take the tunnel without first exploring other options. It could be a trick, and Tim Matthias would not be tricked.

He examined the rest of the holes around the cavern. Most, like the first, stretched only a few paces before ending. Two others appeared to go much further, but both led down rather than up. That left Tim three choices: two deeper, one higher. Well, that was as much information as he was going to get, and if he had to take a gamble, then he might as well gamble on the path that led up.

Tim hoisted himself face-first into the tunnel, sword strapped across his back. He kept the blade illuminated, its light shooting out over his head and into the passage, but the flames did not burn him. In fact, he could not feel them at all. He lay on his stomach, two arms reaching forward, and grasped a handhold to pull himself up.

The fact that he could not turn his head around bothered him, and as he moved forward, the soles of his feet prickled as if something were coming from behind. The walls of the passage scraped at his sides and stomach, and his numb muscles tied up in knots, but he did not stop. He soon lost all track of time as the passage continued its gradual incline, and he measured the tunnel by counting the lengths of his body. After fifty lengths he stopped to rest, throat choked with dirt. His thoughts turned to food and water. He wanted to close his eyes and sleep, but letting his guard down could prove to be a fatal move. He needed to press onward, painful as it was.

He counted to two hundred before proceeding again. And that was how it went—fifty lengths of his body, followed by a count of two hundred for rest. It did not take long before he lost track of how many repetitions he had gone through. It felt like he was outside his body, an observer of a journey both arduous and painful, and all the while the moving became harder and the rests felt shorter. After a lifetime and a half, the passage widened, and Tim's heart swelled. Though he saw no sign of daylight, it did not matter. It was an end to the tunnel, and that was enough for now.

At last Tim pulled himself free from the narrow space, only to find himself in another tunnel. This was much different—tall enough to stand in and wide enough for five men to walk abreast. Tim stood to his full height and smiled. *Much better.*

Something cold dripped onto his head. Tim looked up and saw hundreds of tiny stalactites covering the ceiling, glittering in the light of his blade. Drops of water plopped from jagged spikes, landing near his feet, and trickles of moisture also ran down the halls of the passage, flowing over the multicolor veins that streaked the tunnel walls. Tim stepped near the closest source of water and peered at the liquid. It looked much clearer and fresher than the waters from the large pool in the first cavern. It might not be safe, but his throat was parched and his body needed *something*. It was a risk he'd have to take. He pressed himself against the wall and opened his mouth wide. The droplets of water landing on his tongue were the purest bliss imaginable.

Tim stepped back and wiped his lips. No need to linger longer than necessary. It was time to move on, so he continued down the new passage, counting in paces this time, and after five hundred steps he stopped near more water. He had to get some rest. He'd been unwilling to stop in the other tunnel because it was unsafe. It would have been akin to giving up, but this time it was true fatigue that tired him, not the weariness of despair.

He slumped against the wall, eyelids fluttering and the light of his sword wavering. Here in the cave, alone in the darkness and on the verge of sleep, Tim realized how much his life had changed. Barely a month had passed since he'd practiced sword work behind the cottage with his father, only four weeks since he traveled into the woods to check the traplines and returned to find everything was different.

All things changed with time. Men barely noticed it because the biggest changes always happened in increments. A man only realized how far he'd come when, at the end of a long road, he stopped and looked back. Then the man also realized the road did not end here, but took a sharp turn into shadows and mists. He had no choice but to step forward, because there was no going back.

* * *

Tim did not know how long he'd slept. When he woke up, he was shivering again, and the scars on his back burned with feverish intensity. He reached back to touch one and jerked from the pain upon contact. His finger came back coated in pus. The wound was infected. Tim stood up, one hand on the wall for support. A bout of dizziness overtook him, and he leaned against the wall until the vertigo passed. When he swallowed, his throat felt thick and swollen, and another fit of chills rushed through his body.

He splashed water on his face, drinking some to quench his thirst. He didn't have time to sit and let the fever run its course. He *had* to walk. At best, the sickness would leave him ravaged and weak, and at worst, it might kill him. Either way, he needed to get as far as he could before his strength gave out, so he lifted his sword and filled it with light.

As the hours passed and his sickness grew worse, Tim found he had to stop frequently. The tendons of his aching muscles felt like they were dripping liquid agony. The path he took traveled up and down, back and forth, in an endless maze. He soon forgot about what was behind him or in front of him; all that mattered was putting one foot after the next.

After a time, the path led through a new cavern, a glittering beauty filled with brilliant gems—a treasure hunter's fortune, containing wealth beyond imagining—but Tim barely noticed. Too much pain clouded his mind, too much suffering wracked his body, for him to appreciate the scenery. He stumbled across the expanse of uncut stones, his sword illuminating a sparkling path through the cavern, until he found an opening up and out.

This was how it went, from tunnel to cavern to tunnel again, through passages and chambers too numerous to count. He did not necessarily stay on one continuous path, but always followed routes that traveled upward. He came upon underground lakes, some dwarfing the large one he'd fallen into, others little more than small pools. He crawled through passages both narrow and wide, on occasion facing a dead end and forced to turn around, losing both time and energy.

No longer following a pattern between traveling and resting, he walked when he could and stopped when he had to, stumbling into corners of caverns to slip into brief fitful slumbers. As the fever grew worse, the light from his sword weakened, losing its strong radiance and becoming only a dim lantern in a dark cavern. *How did I come to this place?* Tim asked himself, and the answer came to him. *Nazgar of the Kyrlod.*

Tim did not *blame* the old man for bringing him here. It was only a misunderstanding—a difference in philosophies, to be exact. Nazgar saw things one way, but Tim saw things the *right* way. It was surprisingly clear, now that he thought about it.

Tim knew Nazgar did not mean him ill. On the contrary, he felt certain the Kyrlod meant well but had grown complacent in his old age. Tim had discovered the truth here in the Mountains, when facing Zadinn's presence in the foothills, when unleashing the might of his power upon the vrawl, but Nazgar did not want him to fully live it. In reality, Tim discovered the truth even *before* entering the Mountains. He'd known it since he was in the cells below the Fort of Pellen, where mighty anger had served as a powerful weapon.

But the subsequent tragedy of his parents' death had weakened his mind, and if Nazgar hadn't distracted Tim with ineffective methods, then perhaps Tim would be much farther along in his training. He'd spent weeks struggling to attain a power he could already use with devastating force. He'd almost died in the Korlan while trying to seize the Lifesource as the Hunter descended upon him, when a week earlier he'd had no problem incinerating two malichons with hardly a thought. *But,* he reflected, *perhaps it isn't such a bad thing. If I hadn't submitted to Nazgar's fallacies, I might have never understood the flawed nature of the Kyrlod's principles.*

Tim trusted Nazgar because the old man was timeless, and such a long life accrued wisdom. But that, he now decided, was the problem. Nazgar was not subject to time—he stood outside of it. He had lived for centuries and would live centuries more. Tim and the elions remained subject to the *now,* the *present,* and while Nazgar could bide his time, they could not. If their endeavor failed and the North remained under Zadinn's sway, what did Nazgar care? Perhaps in a thousand years, a new Advocate would be born, one who could attempt once more to shift the balance between Harmea and Malath. Different rules, however, governed Tim's actions. He had a duty to see the elions and the others of the North to freedom *now.*

Tim steeled himself and gathered his energy—not the ineffective meditation Nazgar had taught him, but the raw power he *knew* existed inside him,
the potent force he'd used first in the Fort and most recently in the Mountains.
Well, the Kyrlod was not here anymore. Tim had acquiesced to Nazgar's wishes
only so he could use his strength to survive at a time like this. This was his hour,
the time to cast aside Tim Matthias and become the Warrior.

Tim continued onward, a grim destination in mind. The light from his
sword, faint and almost gone entirely, returned with savage radiance. This time,
tendrils of shadow tinged the edges of the green flame. Tim noticed the change
in color and approved. It made him feel stronger, more dangerous. He staggered
into a new passage, where trickling water ran down the walls. This tunnel wasn't
as wide and accommodating as the previous path, and a hundred paces in, the
wall became dangerously narrow. He saw a crack ahead of him, thin enough
that he would have to take it sideways. One careful step at a time, Tim scraped
into the treacherous confines.

On the other side of the crevice, he saw the next passage was far more
traversable. He sucked his stomach in, dragging himself through the rest of the
way, and as he broke free, he slipped and landed on hands and knees among a
scattering of jagged rocks. The brutal impact jarred a kneecap, and blood ran
from his left leg. The unexpected pain pushed all thoughts from his mind. Tim
felt an immediate, irrational anger toward all inanimate objects around him.
The Mountains will never let me out! He climbed and climbed, but felt he made
no progress. He hurdled obstacle upon obstacle…but now *this*. When he stood
up, he struck his head on the low roof, and that did it.

Tim screamed in rage. Blazing green fire erupted from his sword. The shadows
within the light rippled as Tim surrounded himself with the inferno. He pushed
the flames forward, blasting a path through the tunnel, and the stones evaporated
under his wrath.

However, matters only grew worse. In the wake of the fiery conflagration,
the stones beneath his feet turned so hot they smoked. Tim felt the heat through
the soles of his boots, and he jerked in surprise. At the same time, a reservoir of
water held behind the wall burst forth in a frothing wave, and the surging river
carried him forward down the passage, gaining speed as the floor opened up
beneath him and he plummeted.

Shooting out on the other side of the waterfall, he fell into a very small
pool. In a few short strokes, he was out of the water and onto the bank.

Tim screamed again. The tunnels were mocking him. He was no better off now than when he had started out, still at the edge of a pool within an empty room and no sign of daylight from any direction. He slammed his sword against the cavern's walls. If he could not climb out, he would hack his way free, slashing until the walls yielded to his might. He would not die down here. No, he would emerge more powerful than ever, and when he did, Zadinn Kanas would know that his enemy was strong.

Tim's sword scored deep, burning open gashes into the wall, but revealed nothing on the other side. He cut in as far as he could, but eventually feverish exhaustion overtook him. He fell onto his back, and once again the lights went out, leaving him in darkness. The pain from his sickness, along with a multitude of scrapes and bruises, consumed his body. He thought he might be dying, except no man deserved a death this painful. Tears sprang to his eyes as he curled into a ball.

Tim wanted only to hear Daniel's voice once more. He wanted Rosalie to envelop him in her arms and hold him in a mother's warm embrace. But his parents were not here. They were dead and gone, and he was left behind. Grief overtook him, and he sobbed aloud, weeping in the caverns, witnessed only by the shadows that covered him with their blanket.

Thirty

Boblin watched Nazgar from across the campfire. It had been two days since they'd revived Prince Ladu Jovun IV from the crystal. Nazgar sat with a bowl in his lap, eating one slow spoonful at a time, eyeing the flames in front of him. His face remained as mysterious as ever; Boblin could never tell what was going on behind those eyes.

Other elions sat near the fire, but the crowd gradually dispersed as the evening wore on. Boblin bided his time, pretending to occupy himself with sharpening his boot knife, and when everyone else finally left, he walked over to the prophet.

"Hello, Boblin," Nazgar said.

"Good evening, sir," Boblin replied.

"You have some questions for me," Nazgar said.

Boblin wrestled with what to say, but decided a direct approach was best. Nazgar might speak in riddles, but that didn't mean he would be patient if someone else did the same to *him*. Nazgar was not Pellen Yuzhar; in some ways the two were alike, while in others they were not. Both carried the wisdom of long years, and both placed high value on moral integrity, but Nazgar was far more enigmatic and, at times, colder.

"Why are we still safe?" Boblin asked.

Nazgar arched an eyebrow.

"You used the Lifesource," Boblin said. "You used it against the sarchons, and you used it to free Ladu from the enchantment. But you've said the Lifesource will open your mind to Zadinn, so how is it that we're still safe?"

Nazgar held his hands out, palms open. "I used my powers to help you escape from the Fort, did I not?" he said.

"I won't object to that," Boblin replied. "But it's still risky, isn't it?"

"Your observations are correct. Matters, however, have changed."

This time, Boblin arched *his* eyebrow. "I assume you're not talking about the snow, though it is strange, during summer of all times. I wouldn't have expected it, would you?"

Nazgar smiled briefly at the rebuttal and then tightened his face again. "Something happened several nights ago, a terrible thing, but I won't deny that some good did come from it. This…incident…shifted a certain balance within the Lifesource."

Boblin sighed. "I don't wish to be disrespectful," he said, trying not to grit his teeth in frustration, "but I've always done all you wished, sir, without question. So could we cut to the proverbial chase? *Please*, for once, stop with the riddles and give me a direct answer."

Nazgar looked at him, and Boblin felt himself wither underneath that stern gaze. He pulled back, wondering if he'd pushed too far. After all, Nazgar, if now willing to use the Lifesource, could very well incinerate Boblin on the spot.

Then the Kyrlod's face broke into a wide grin, and he laughed heartily. He squeezed Boblin on the shoulder. "It's no wonder Pellen speaks so highly of you, my friend. You have a practical mind, and sometimes I forget that others do not appreciate my lengthy digressions. When the vrawl first attacked, Tim Matthias used the Lifesource against them. This shifted the balance I speak of. The Warrior isn't just a talisman of safety in the Mountains. He also provides us with another kind of protection. As his presence in the Lifesource grows stronger with each day, it also becomes more difficult for Zadinn to track me.

"The more a man uses the Lifesource, the stronger his powers become. Tim unleashed a horrific amount of power on that night. Most Advocates take years to realize their full strength, but Tim has almost reached his potential, though he does not yet know how to harness it. In short, his presence has become so great that the Dark Lord can no longer sense me. Therefore, I am free to do as I wish." He snapped his fingers, and a purple flame danced above his hand.

"What do the colors mean?" Boblin asked. "Your fire is always purple and Tim's is always green. When I start a fire, it's red, yellow, and orange, but we can ignore that."

"The Lifesource is the essence of light," Nazgar said. "Pick any color of the rainbow, and you'll find an Advocate whose magic displays that color most prevalently. But beware the black shadow, a shade different than all the others." He waved his hands, and the flame disappeared.

"I'm worried about him," Boblin said.

"Your friend is alive," Nazgar replied softly.

"That's not what I meant," Boblin said just as softly.

Nazgar turned from Boblin. Flickering firelight flitted across his face, which could have been chiseled from stone. "A double-edged sword cuts both ways. Tim has learned his powers almost *too* fast; he's gained strength but hasn't learned the discipline that must go with it. To make matters worse, he's acquired his powers while still suffering the heartache of loss."

"That's what I mean," Boblin said. "Since we entered the Mountains, I felt him grow more distant. He laughs less and broods more."

"The Warrior is in a dark place," Nazgar replied. "I tried to help him, but I do not know if I did enough."

"Is there anything *I* can do to help?"

"He is beyond our reach," Nazgar said. "If he returns, however, you might be the only man in this camp he trusts. You can forestall him while he stands at the brink of the abyss, but he must be the one who steps away."

Boblin remained silent for a time. "I liked talking to Pellen better. He has a way of making everyone think all will turn out for the best."

"In many ways, Pellen is a better individual than I," Nazgar replied. "No other elion could have held a shattered people together while the world crumbled around them. But being a leader is not my business."

"What *is* your business?" Boblin asked.

"To be here."

It was back to riddles again, but Boblin decided to press his luck. "I have one more question. The sarchons—you recognized them."

Nazgar nodded. "You observe a lot, my friend."

"This place will kill you if you don't pay attention to the details."

"I know what the sarchons are," Nazgar admitted. "I did not expect them to be here, but it makes sense. They were once a part of Zadinn's army."

"From the Invasion?"

"Yes," Nazgar said, "but after the battle, they became a problem. The sarchons are not of this world, and they suffer from an insatiable hunger. Even when they've gorged themselves beyond all recognition, they desire to kill more. After the war ended, the sarchons had nothing to satisfy their bloodlust and became impossible to control. So Zadinn banished them, and now we know where he sent them."

"I see," Boblin said. *Yes, he does not have Pellen's touch. But as he said, his business is to be here—not to make me comfortable.* He stood up to leave. "I appreciate your time, sir."

"Wait," Nazgar said. "There is one more topic we must discuss."

Boblin turned back to the Kyrlod. "Of course, sir."

"It is time to begin your training," Nazgar said.

"*My* training?" Boblin asked. "I have no aptitude with the Lifesource, I'm quite proud to say."

"Just because you cannot fight with the Lifesource, does not mean you will not fight against those wielding it," Nazgar said. "You, of course, are familiar with the emphasis your Commander Jend places on ailar. The art of hand fighting has roots in ancient history. In times of old, it is said, the most proficient students of ailar could train themselves to anticipate and evade an Advocate's attacks."

"I see," Boblin said. "Not a bad skill to have, I suppose."

"No, not bad to have at all," Nazgar, said standing up. "Let us begin."

* * *

"Wake up, Kule," Hedro said. "Jend called a meeting."

Boblin pulled himself out of sleep. He had a newfound appreciation for what Tim went through when Nazgar trained him. He was battered and bruised from the previous night, but it had been time well spent.

Hedro threw open the tent flap. "Come on. We don't have much time."

Boblin pulled his boots on and threw a cloak over his shoulders. It was early morning, but no trace of dawn had yet appeared. The wind swept across his face as he walked toward the group of elions standing near the campfire. He shook himself into a more alert state. Hugo and Ken were there, along with Celia, Ana, Faldon, Tavin, and Hedro. Jend did not call such meetings lightly, and Boblin felt a twinge of unease upon seeing the gathering of soldiers.

"Our situation is grave," the Commander said without preamble. "These last few days, the sarchons have flanked us in a fashion that appears to be quite coordinated. They forced us down a specific route, herding us as they wish. Now matters have reached a crux." He turned to the Rindar brothers. "Report."

"Good news," Hugo said. "We are one day's travel from exiting the Mountains."

"Bad news," Ken followed. "The sarchons have us boxed in. Our only way across is a passage that leads directly through the last mountain's peak."

"That's where our problems begin," Hugo continued. "The tunnel is infested with sarchon nests."

Faldon spoke for the rest of the group. "You are suggesting we take this course?"

"It is the only course," Ken said. "The sarchons surround us on all sides, and the only reason they have not attacked is that they are deliberately waiting for this opportunity."

"They display an uncanny level of intelligence for wild creatures," Hugo said. "Their every move up to this point seems quite calculated."

"So what's our move?" Hedro asked.

"We take the tunnel," Boblin said. "Nazgar told me about the sarchons. Zadinn summoned them from Malath during the Invasion. They are the sole reason nobody has ever returned alive from the Mountains. If we want to get out, it has to be on their terms."

"Kule is correct," Jend agreed. "To avoid death, we must charge into its face."

"Just another day in the Patrol," Celia said. In spite of the grim situation, everyone in the group chuckled at that.

"We came up with a name for the passage," Ken added.

"Is that so?" Commander Jend asked.

Ken nodded. "We call it Malath's Teeth."

* * *

Kaiel quivered, hunkered down on the other side of a boulder, his once-strong body now no more than a ragged, withered shell. He clutched the steady rock with both hands and peered over its side. The refugee camp sat on the slope below him, lit by a single fire in the center.

Kaiel's master had chosen well. Only an elion well versed in the manner of the Frontier Patrol would know how to avoid detection from other elion scouts. That, at least, should make Zadinn happy. He had finally found his "people," as the Dark Lord sometimes termed the refugees. Kaiel did not liken himself to one of them, though. They were too weak to consider the decisions he had made.

The journey had not been easy. Kaiel had survived thus far by traveling in the wake of the elion party. They encountered each danger first, thereby paving the way for him. By the time Kaiel reached vrawl territory, Matthias had already slain all of the saber-toothed beasts, and when he got to sarchon territory, the birds were fully occupied with the refugees. And now the elions faced a decision between certain death and *almost* certain death—barely a choice at all. Kaiel wondered how it would play out.

A jolt of pain pierced his mind as a set of cold fingers wrapped around his brain. Kaiel jerked, but it was no use fighting; the struggle would only make matters worse. So he clung to the edge of the rock, trying to embrace the agony rather than letting it overcome him. He only partially succeeded. He bit his lip to keep from crying out. The Dark Lord would not be pleased if Kaiel gave away his position. He soon felt the warmth of blood drip from the corner of his mouth, and squeezed his eyes shut.

No, the voice said. *I need to see!* Kaiel's eyes opened of their own accord, and an invisible force pushed him up from behind the rock. Zadinn had taken command, and it made a *burning* sensation in Kaiel's body. It was not Kaiel Tulak who looked upon the refugees. It was the Dark Lord, seeing through the eyes of his servant. *Where is he?* the Dark Lord's voice rumbled through Kaiel's head. *Where has he gone?*

"I don't know," Kaiel whispered. "I don't know what you want." His muscles slackened, and Kaiel slumped into a snowdrift behind the boulder. He lifted his arms, just to verify that his limbs were back in his control.

You must continue to follow, the Dark Lord urged Kaiel. *You have not earned the reward, not yet.*

The reward. Kaiel trembled. He didn't even want to think of it.

Thirty-One

Quentiin slumped to the floor of his cell, hands chained together. Apparently spitting on Gald was considered offensive. The malichons had beat him over the dinner hour before locking him in his cage. Quentiin leaned over, moaning as the pain washed over him.

Outside the cell, a malichon strode toward him, making its rounds past the prisoners' cages. "Silence," the malichon said, turning toward Quentiin.

"I'm sorry," Quentiin said. "It's just…it hurts, sir."

"I did not ask you to speak," the guard replied. "Do not give me cause to deliver further punishment."

As the guard resumed its rounds, Quentiin shuffled forward on his knees, pressing up against the bars of the cell. "Water," he said weakly. "Could I please have some water?"

The malichon placed a hand on the coiled whip at its belt. "I said *silence*!"

Quentiin began to weep. The malichon snarled, striding toward the cage. "If you want a reason to weep, I will give you one!" It shoved the door open and stepped inside, hand raised to strike.

Quentiin moved in the blink of an eye. As soon as the malichon crossed the threshold, Quentiin surged to his feet and slammed his left shoulder into the guard. As the malichon stumbled, Quentiin wrapped his chains around the guard's throat and pulled tight. The malichon struggled, but Quentiin refused to let go, clinging to his opponent with grim determination.

"If I don't make it out o' here, I will see ye in Malath," Quentiin growled. "An' then we'll see which of us makes the other weep, d'ye ken?"

The malichon raised a hand and clawed at Quentiin's face. Its nails scraped the dwerion's skin, drawing blood, but Quentiin was used to that by now. It didn't hurt any more than being whipped, and it was certainly more gratifying.

As the malichon's struggles subsided, its body gradually slackened. Fearing a trick, Quentiin held for a count of fifty before releasing the malichon's limp form. "Good riddance," he said.

Quentiin removed the guard's cloak and pulled the body over to the cell's corner, where he covered it with a brown blanket. He took the malichon's keys and unlocked his chains before donning the hooded cloak. It was an imperfect disguise, but it would have to work. He also took the malichon's sword; though he hated touching such a vile weapon, it could keep him alive tonight.

When Quentiin spit on Gald, he'd hoped for a punishment of this very nature. By chaining Quentiin's wrists together, the malichons had inadvertently provided him the shackles to use as a crude weapon—and now, the escape was on. Quentiin stepped out of his cell and pulled the hood tight over his head, shrouding himself in its darkness. It was only a short distance to the edge of the slave pens, but Quentiin was not taking any chances.

It was difficult to walk at an even pace. He wanted to break into a run, but that would be akin to suicide. He counted as he walked, ensuring his foot landed on every other number and not before. Every cage he passed without incident, he counted a victory. He glanced at each slave within, burning his or her face into his mind, claiming responsibility for every single one. He *would* return with an army at his back, and in the meantime, his escape would give them hope. The fact that it *could be done* would lift their spirits. Perhaps someone else would try and also succeed—and the spell would break, and the prisoners would be free.

Another shape materialized from the night and walked toward him. While the cloak would help Quentiin blend into the night, he knew that because of his height, there was no way another malichon would mistake him for a guard. He turned to the side, stepping into the shadows between a pair of cages, crouching low in the dark and remaining still. He placed one hand under the folds of his robes and gripped his sword. The malichon guard walked past Quentiin's hiding spot without so much as a glance toward the dwerion. When the moment passed, Quentiin relaxed his grip and stepped forth again.

Now he came to an open stretch of the slave pen, walking across the field of obsidian stones where he had labored many days in the sun's searing heat. With nowhere to hide, he took his steps carefully, first one, then another…and another. He crossed the opening and veered to a section of the wall running parallel to the gate, keeping his distance so that the malichons stationed near the entrance would not see him. He made his way forward, pressed against the wall the entire time, until he came within sight of the gate. Two malichons stood at guard, so Quentiin remained in concealment, absolutely still. And then he waited.

The change in shift came, as he knew it would. The two malichons departed down the path, heading toward their quarters at the opposite end of the Pit from the slave cages, leaving the gate unmanned for the briefest window of time.

Quentiin allowed himself a smile. At the end of the day, the malichons were the same as any other troop: some lazier than others, and just like in the Alcatune Army, leaving one's post a minute or two early was by no means unheard of.

Quentiin hurried to the gate, pulling the ring of keys from his belt and placing it in the lock with a clean *snick*. He pushed the door open and stepped outside. Before tonight, no escape attempt had ever breached the walls of the slave pen. *So even if I don't make it all the way out, at least I'll have a spot in history.* He stepped into the streets of Zadinn's city. He was not free, not yet, but he was much closer. Now it was time for a guessing game. Quentiin didn't exactly know his way around this city, so he would have to learn fast. Heading for the main gate was a gamble in itself, as it was likely to be more heavily guarded than the slave pen, but Quentiin knew of no other route to take.

Quentiin did not like games of chance. He played chess, for the Maker's sake. He liked to know what pieces were against him and how he was capable of fighting. But this was a karfing game of dice, and Quentiin absolutely *loathed* dice.

Zadinn's citadel, which dwarfed all other buildings, was easy to spot. Quentiin used the domed palace as his guide, keeping it within sight but also careful to stay at least two blocks away. The citadel was well and good for providing directions, but Quentiin wasn't about to walk up to it and dance a jig on its steps.

The moon in the sky was only a quarter full. Quentiin would have preferred more light, but he wasn't about to be picky. Upon reaching the center of the city, he assessed his situation once more, looking for the safest path to the gates.

That was when the cry of alarm sounded behind him. A clamor rose from the Pit, and Quentiin knew his time was up. His first instinct was to run, but he suppressed it. Running would make him more visible, when he might otherwise blend into the background. So he continued walking with slow, deliberate steps. Seconds after the alarm, three malichons raced from a nearby barracks and Quentiin stepped into a side street. He waited until the malichons rushed past him, and then counted to an even twenty before stepping back into the main street. He continued on his way, walking much more briskly this time.

"Halt!"

Quentiin stopped and turned around, cursing to himself. One of the malichons had apparently seen him move. The guard stood a way down the street behind Quentiin. Only two things kept the game from being completely up at that point. One, the malichon stood far enough away that the difference in height was not immediately apparent, and two, the mind had a way of playing to its own biases. No slave had ever walked free in the streets of Zadinn's citadel before, and as such the malichon's thought process would take a few precious moments before it caught on to the reality of the situation.

But Quentiin had to take every advantage of his rapidly shrinking sliver of opportunity. The malichon walked toward him, and there was no way the dwerion's disguise would hold more than a handful of seconds. Quentiin bolted, tearing his robe off so that it would not hinder his movements, and ran for all he was worth. The malichon cried out and took up pursuit, shouting another alarm as it did so. Quentiin uttered every curse he knew—and even invented a few right on the spot—as he raced through the city, heading straight for the main gate. The battlements beyond rows of buildings drew nearer with every stride.

He came free of the last set of buildings, face-to-face with the outer battlements, where in front of him the drawbridge lay open to the plateau beyond. Quentiin's feet landed on the cobblestone path, and he began to think that he might make it. He put every ounce of his being into reaching the drawbridge. Once in the open, beyond the plateau, he could hide among the rocks and valleys of the Deathlands. He just needed to *get* there. Quentiin closed the distance to the arched gateway, scarcely believing it. *I've done it. I showed those sons of goats!*

Then a cloaked, hunchbacked figure slammed into him. Quentiin recognized the creature from the day of their arrival. *The Gatekeeper.* The hunchback grasped Quentiin's forearm with bone-white, skeletal fingers. Its claws dug into his skin as the Gatekeeper lifted Quentiin off his feet and swung him sideways. Quentiin's body struck the battlements with jarring force. The blow should have rendered him senseless, but his willpower did not allow it—not when he was this close.

Quentiin got to his feet, unsheathed his sword with a growl, and swung the weapon at the Gatekeeper. The creature hissed from within the depths of its hood, stopping the blade in the firm grip of its palm. The sword vibrated from the impact, but the Gatekeeper didn't flinch. It wrested the blade from Quentiin's grip and threw the sword to the side.

Quentiin slammed into the Gatekeeper with enough force to knock a man flat, but the hunchback barely stumbled. Roaring with anger, Quentiin delivered a solid uppercut against the side of its hooded face, and again the creature showed no reaction. It merely stepped forward and threw Quentiin against the wall for a second time.

By then, the pursuing malichon had caught up with him, along with several others who had joined the pursuit. They surrounded Quentiin's sprawling figure, leveling their sword tips at his body. Quentiin heard a *clacking* sound from above and realized the Gatekeeper was laughing at him. It became apparent to Quentiin that the lowered drawbridge had been a taunt, the Gatekeeper's cruel trick for its own amusement.

Quentiin wanted to scream in rage, to pound the ground with his fists and spew a multitude of obscenities. He'd been so close, *so karfing close*, and it was all for nothing, but he did not give his captors the satisfaction of seeing his frustration. Besides, Quentiin now had a brutal punishment in store, regardless of any apology *or* any further transgression on his part, so he now had an odd sort of liberty to do as he wished. Therefore, when a malichon tried to bind him, Quentiin punched the creature in the face.

Two other malichons seized Quentiin, jerking his hands behind his back and clamping shackles on him. The first malichon, a snarl on its lips, backhanded Quentiin across the face. Quentiin's head snapped back, and when he righted himself, he leaned forward to spit out a tooth. The malichon seized Quentiin's jaw in its hands, bringing the dwerion's face close. "Think of the most painful experience you've ever had," the malichon said.

Quentiin did not reply. He just glared back.

The malichon smiled. "It won't *begin* to compare to what you'll feel in an hour."

* * *

They dragged him back through the city, toward the awful, evil walls surrounding the Pit. Upon seeing that terrible place once more, Quentiin's legs weakened. For the first time, he wondered if he'd be able to hold out against whatever they had in store for him. He'd fought long and hard, but now he'd breached the walls and killed a guard. Veldor had promised to break him, and now Quentiin felt a new kind of fear, one he hadn't thought possible—he feared Veldor might succeed.

When they entered the pen, the Slavemaster was waiting with a group of malichons at his back. The guards threw Quentiin facedown at Veldor's feet, and the Slavemaster turned Quentiin over with the tip of his boot. "Get up," Veldor said. Quentiin struggled to his feet, difficult as it was with his hands bound behind his back.

"Bring him," Veldor said to Gald and another malichon. The two grasped Quentiin's arm, Gald's fingernails digging so tight they drew drops of blood.

At first, Quentiin thought that they would take him to the caverns, where they'd bury him in rock and cover him with scorpions, but the malichons dragged him downhill toward the Pit. Quentiin saw the entire body of slaves standing at the edge of the fiery chasm, and he thought he understood their plan. *They are about to make an example of me. Just like they did with the last ones who escaped. Well, it's goin' to be my job to take it on two feet.*

Quentiin pushed aside his fear, hardening his resolve. *I ain't goin' to scream, no matter how bad it gets. I got to keep my mouth shut an' make a dwerion of m'self.* It would be hard, but Quentiin had never asked for the world on a golden plate. No sir, he handled life like everybody else, one day at a time. If yesterday was bad, tomorrow had to be better.

Gald and the other malichon took Quentiin to the edge of the gaping maw and held him between them. Quentiin supposed they *might* drop him into the flames, but he didn't think things would be that simple. A death like that would be too fast, and these creatures wanted to savor his pain. Veldor, following behind the rest, approached Quentiin. Behind him was the guard from the cages, alive and well, albeit with a large, purple welt around his throat. Apparently Quentiin hadn't killed him. *Pity.*

"You forget, slave, that I swore I'd win this battle," Veldor said. "You must know I'm quite grateful you didn't kill Hoteb, because if you had, law would require me to execute you. Since you did not commit the unforgivable crime, I am allowed to be a little more…creative in my punishment. But first, I will let Hoteb exact some retribution."

The guard approached Quentiin. "Insolent scum," it said. It delivered a punch so forceful that Quentiin rocked back against the malichons holding his arms. Hoteb continued to strike blow after blow, each more savage than the last. Quentiin spat out a good quantity of blood before Veldor ordered Hoteb to step aside.

"Before we continue, I must settle another matter," Veldor said, clapping a hand on Hoteb's shoulder. Moving hideously fast, Veldor unsheathed his sword and plunged it into Hoteb's stomach. Caught by surprise, the malichon opened its mouth wide, but no sound came out.

"Your incompetence disgusts me," Veldor said, jerking his blade from Hoteb's stomach. Hoteb stumbled, teetering on the edge of the Pit before falling backward into the flames.

"Now," Veldor said, completely at ease. He could have been discussing plans for dinner. "I would like your assistance, Quentiin Harggra. I need help making a choice." He leveled a finger at two prisoners, and a pair of guards seized the pair. The malichons dragged the two up to the very edge of the Pit and turned them around so they faced the group. Both prisoners were young men, barely past their teenage years.

"Punishing *you* appears to have no effect, my friend," Veldor said. "So instead, I will grant you the right to make a choice. Which one shall I kill?"

The two prisoners looked up, and Quentiin felt like Veldor had plunged an ax into his stomach. The fear in the slaves' eyes was as evident as the midday sun. Quentiin clenched his teeth and issued a low growl. "That ain't a choice," he said.

"But it is, my friend," Veldor said. "If you do not pick one, I will kill them both. Please do not make them wait to see who will live and who will not. Such cruelty is rather unbecoming."

So this was how they meant to do it, at the very last. Of all the punishments they could devise, Quentiin had expected to bear the suffering himself. That made it easy, but this was something else entirely. Quentiin wasn't going to condemn *either* man. That was what the malichons wanted—to make him into one of them.

"No," Quentiin said.

"That is not an answer," Veldor said.

"I ain't yer puppet," Quentiin replied.

"If you do not choose, you're killing them both. Can you really stand that?"

"I ain't killin' anybody!" Quentiin shouted.

Veldor lost his temper. "Pick!" he shrieked, spittle flying from his lips. He seized the two prisoners by their necks, one in each hand. The men choked and thrashed against his crushing grip. "Pick the one who will die!"

"I pick me!"

Veldor suddenly stopped, looking Quentiin in the eye as he spoke, his voice calm and even "That isn't a choice," he said—and pushed one of the men into the Pit.

"I said pick me!" Quentiin screamed. "I'm the one ye want! Ye're supposed to kill me!"

"Do you really want me to kill you," Veldor snarled, "instead of them?"

"Yes! I want ye to kill me, ye karfin' son of a three-legged goat!"

"Well," Veldor said, smiling and straightening himself. He relaxed his grip on the other slave and turned to look at Gald. "Did I not tell you Quentiin would beg us to take his own life before the end? As you can see, we have succeeded."

Veldor shoved the second prisoner over the ledge. The man screamed as he fell into the depths of the Pit. "I always win, slave. No matter how hardened you think you might be, no matter how valiantly you fight back, I will outlast you, I will wear you down, and when you die, you will know *I am the master.*"

He struck Quentiin. "If you speak one more word during the rest of your time here, I will kill a slave. If you are not the first one at work in the morning, I will kill a slave. If I suspect you are even thinking the word 'escape,' I will kill a slave. Understood?"

They had him at last. They'd cornered him and taken his claws. He had nothing left.

"Do you understand?" Veldor repeated.

Quentiin met the Slavemaster's eyes. "Yes," he said. The word tasted like broken glass in his mouth. "I understand."

"You spoke," Veldor said curtly. "Kill one more." He turned back to Quentiin. "You should have *nodded,* my friend. That's how it is done."

* * *

Zadinn Kanas sat alone with his thoughts. Kaiel's information was proving most useful. As Zadinn suspected, the elions were seeking the Army of Kah'lash—and crossing the Mountains in order to do so. He had to admit, he was impressed. Most travelers to the Mountains did not make it past the vrawl, and those who did fell quickly to the sarchons. The refugees, however, had so far survived the vrawl *and* the sarchons. That was a fine achievement.

Zadinn had been warned against going into the Mountains himself. He neither possessed a "talisman," nor thought he would ever obtain one. Some things were beyond even his control. But not forever—and that was the beauty of it. The Barricade had stood in his way for years, but after all this time it had yielded to him, if only temporarily.

And this *new* turn of events was excellent. Zadinn knew of the Army of Kah'lash, an unseen force that waited behind his back. He had sent several forays into the heights of the mountains, looking for a way across, but his scouts never returned. Now, however, someone was *finally* about to break the impasse. Better yet, the Warrior would do all the work, and the elions would do all the dying.

Zadinn could see the end game clearly. Sooner or later the Warrior would find Those Who Wait and return to assault the Deathlands. When they arrived, Zadinn would be ready. He couldn't ask for a better opportunity: Warrior, Kyrlod, and Kah'lash, all at the same time.

The room trembled as the Guardian announced Isanam's arrival. Zadinn settled into the bones of his chair. He smiled, breathing in the chamber's green vapors. Nearby, the Cauldron of Souls stirred. When Isanam entered the room, he removed his skull-mask and knelt at the base of the dais. "My lord," he said, keeping his eyes focused on the floor.

"Rise," Zadinn ordered, and the Overlord obliged. "The Tulak prisoner has found the refugees. They are in the Northern Mountains."

"Shall I send my troops after them?" Isanam asked.

"Of course not. You know as well as I that they would not make it past the vrawls' first assault."

"Then what do you wish of me?" Isanam asked.

"The refugees are seeking the Army of Kah'lash. We must turn this to our advantage. It is an opportunity for victory. We must prepare for the Army's arrival; you have one fortnight to make our army as fit as it was when we came out of the Desert."

"As you command, my lord," Isanam said.

"One other matter," Zadinn said. "The Kyrlod and the Warrior will have a plan for getting behind your lines and into my city. Do not hinder their efforts."

Isanam hesitated. "Sir?"

"I expect to be obeyed," Zadinn said, narrowing his eyes.

Isanam composed himself. "Yes, my lord."

"Dismissed," Zadinn ordered. Isanam bowed, replaced his mask, and departed.

Zadinn felt the Warrior's presence growing stronger each day, and of late, also sensed a faint darkness blooming inside the young man's heart. He liked this, as it might give him the opportunity to bring the Warrior under his sway. If not, at the very least the Warrior would be weakened and easier to kill.

Kaiel's discovery of the camp had allowed Zadinn to discern his enemy's precise location within the Mountains. From here on out, Zadinn could follow the Warrior's journey every step of the way. He would know exactly *when* and *where* the attack was coming from. Kaiel Tulak had lost his usefulness, but that was of no consequence. The elions were about to enter into a battle for their lives against the sarchons, and Tulak would be caught in the feeding frenzy. After all, it was only fitting that the prisoner should die with his former friends.

Thirty-Two

B oblin finished tying the bundles on his knapsack. The entire camp moved quickly but silently, shrouded in darkness. After some debate, they decided to try their escape by night, so with daylight still many hours away, they prepared to set out. Boblin wondered how many elions would see the sunrise. It was risky, but it gave them a chance to sneak through the cavern while the sarchons slept. Boblin wasn't optimistic about the plan, but they had nothing to lose—other than their lives, he supposed.

Boblin surveyed his comrades, twenty-eight in total. Of those who had set out from the Fort for what now seemed a lifetime ago, only these names, these faces, survived. And not all would see the other side of the cavern.

Boblin placed himself near the group's western flank. Jend had handpicked these positions, and perhaps that was why Boblin felt so somber. As a member of the Patrol, he'd always assumed responsibility for safety of the Fort, but he'd never felt the burden as fully as he did now. It was one thing to fight in a pitched battle— to react to circumstances and do what needed to be done—but this was different. The elions were walking into the jaws of a trap, and it was Boblin's job to ensure the aforementioned jaws did not crush his comrades.

The group traveled in a tight pack up the slope and toward the cavern, silent save for the crunch of footsteps on the snow's crust. Boblin looked up at the starstudded night, nearly expecting to see a swarm of sarchons rise up to blot out the moon, but nothing disturbed the air. Moonlight glanced off the surrounding landscape, casting the snow in a faint glow and bathing the refugees in a ghostly hue. Boblin's breath misted on the cold air in front of him, and he flexed his numb fingers to keep the circulation flowing. He would have need of his swordarm before the night was over.

So it was that the last remnants of the Fort of Pellen traveled under cover of night toward Malath's Teeth.

* * *

Tim opened his eyes, a haze of confusion clouding his mind. For a brief moment, he thought he heard a chorus of whispering voices just out of earshot. He turned to catch the source of the noise, and saw a wisp of black smoke flutter across his field of vision. He blinked once, and the cloud cleared and the voices went silent. He blinked one more time, and the world around him sprang into clarity. *Just the remnants of a fever dream.*

Things had been going well yesterday. He'd slowly regained strength as he made progress through the caves. Then, after his accident, he lost control—his anger flared, his powers burst, and his grief wore him out.

Emotion—he'd made *that* mistake again. He should have known better; he'd come to the realization that, even though grief and anger provided him access to the power he needed, such emotions overwhelmed him. They weakened him and distracted his focus. The only way he could survive, now and when he finally faced Zadinn, was to purge himself of those weaknesses. He'd been trying to do this ever since that first night in the Mountains, but he'd been lax in his discipline, and in the end he'd paid for it.

He didn't dwell on his mistake, but instead allowed it to serve as a lesson. He would deal with it and move forward. Seen in that light, his time in these caverns was not ill spent at all. He'd been on the cusp of true understanding, true transformation, when he entered the Mountains, but it was down here, alone and free of Nazgar's influence, that he finally thought he understood.

Tim sat up and immediately realized something was different. While he slept his body had expelled the fever, and the sickness was gone. He no longer shivered, and only a faint sheen of sweat covered his brow. The scars in his back still throbbed, but the pain felt ordinary—healthy, even. Though his body remained ravaged and weakened, something inside of him said the worst was over. *Good. There's no time to lose.*

Zadinn Kanas remained in power because men feared to take the necessary steps to destroy him. He reigned like a raging fire, and it was useless to sprinkle a few drops of water on the blaze. If the refugees wanted to stop Zadinn from burning their homes, they had to take the fire to the Deathlands and burn *his* home.

Tim would slay the Dark Lord, and afterward he could take up the crown of the kingdom. Who would object? Kingship would be his right, and with it he would methodically expel all evil from the land. He would torch the malichon empire with fire and sword, so never again would anyone think to rise up and enslave his fellows.

Tim stood, sword in hand, and gathered his energy to illuminate the focusing point. That was when he realized something *else* was also different—because when he reached out to summon the Lifesource, he found nothing but a vacant hole. The power was gone.

The sickness has left me in a worse state than I realized. I need to gather my thoughts and relax. He hadn't needed to do this in a long time. Ever since the vrawl attack, seizing the Lifesource had become an instantaneous reflex. Tim was no longer accustomed to the more meditative process, but he schooled himself to patience and began again.

His efforts proved fruitless. Shock faded to frustration, which in turn gave way to panic. Tim had experienced difficulties grasping the power before, but not like this. Even in failing to seize the Lifesource, he had always been aware of it, but this time the ability to lock in to the power was simply *gone*. His heartbeat quickened. Without the promise of light to come, the darkness around him seemed darker. *What is wrong with me? Where did it all go?* He heard a rustling sound and jumped. An attack could come from anywhere, at any time, and he would not know it until too late.

Stop! He was doing it again, letting matters of the flesh rule his mind. He wrapped his hands around his sword and forced himself to breathe deeply in…and out…and in…and out. He imagined a mountain of ice, and then he *became* that mountain, fortifying mind and body in sheets of ice. He needed to be this mountain at all times, frozen on the outside and empty on the inside. Anger and grief, hope and fear, love and despair—the Warrior had no business with those things.

Now he noticed a very faint glow in the distance and walked toward it, one hand on the smooth rock of the cavern, keeping his course steady and true. The light came from an open shaft in the wall—a tunnel that went up and could only lead to the outer world. A flash of hope surged in him, but he immediately swept it away. Hope might feel good, but he worried it would turn on him later. He had to reserve his energy for the task ahead.

Tim sheathed his sword and clambered into the tunnel. It was no wonder he hadn't seen this light before; it was so incredibly dim that any illumination from his sword would have drowned it out. In the face of salvation, Tim summoned every drop of strength from his weakened muscles and climbed upward.

The shaft was much longer than many others he'd traveled through, but for once Tim didn't notice its length. He focused all his attention on the gray light above him. It was night in the world above, but it did not matter. The Warrior of Light was alive, and he was returning to the surface.

*   *   *

The refugees stood before the entrance to Malath's Teeth as they waited for Hugo and Ken, who had entered the cavern to see if the sarchons were truly asleep. Boblin clenched his jaw to keep his teeth from chattering. *Why does it have to be so karfing cold?* It was hard enough fighting sarchons, and now he'd have to do it with icicles for fingers.

After a short wait, Hugo and Ken materialized at the front of the cave. "They're roosting like chickens," Ken said to the refugees. "Asleep, every one of them."

"Let us set forth then," Pellen said, "and may the Maker preserve us."

Here we go, Boblin thought. *May the Maker preserve us indeed.* Upon entering the cavern, Boblin realized Hugo and Ken had aptly named it. Rows of stalactites and stalagmites filled the wide, long space, appropriately invoking the vision of long, sharp teeth—incisors that could rend flesh and choke their victims to death. The refugees had to meander through a maze of twists and turns that wound between the stalagmites on the floor. With the opposite end of the tunnel far out of sight, Boblin realized it would be quite easy to get lost inside this labyrinth.

A ring of ledges surrounded the cavern, filled with over a hundred sarchon nests of all shapes and sizes. If even half the creatures awoke, the elions stood no chance of reaching the far side. Boblin kept a hand on his sword, though he knew full well the blade would do him no good if the flying hordes descended upon them. Acutely aware of every step, he cringed every time his boot ground upon a pebble, and took pains to muffle even the sound of his own breathing.

The slightest noise could wake the winged menaces slumbering less than a dozen feet above their heads.

Soon the southern entrance disappeared from sight, the "teeth" obstructing the view both forward and back. Though enough light remained to see forward a few paces, it grew way too dark for his comfort. *Can this get any worse? Here we are, walking right through the jaws of death while cold, half blind, hungry, and tired.* Sometimes Boblin suspected the Maker was doing nothing more than having a good, hearty laugh at his expense.

After an hour the refugees arrived at a small ledge where a pair of sarchons slumbered. The elions moved around the edge of the shelf, doing their absolute best to not disturb the two creatures, and Boblin kept one eye on the sleeping birds. He thought one stirred and immediately held his breath, but the sarchon soon settled back into its sleeping position. *Just my imagination. Good work, mate. The Frontier Patrol needs an elion who jumps at shadows.*

Boblin released his sword. The rest of the group continued moving forward, unaware of the brief, but false, alarm. *See? Everything's fine.* The sarchon moved again, but this time Boblin purposefully ignored it.

And then one of its eyes opened wide, a burning red orb that took all of them in.

*   *   *

Tim reached a point where he could pull himself free from the more constricting passage and into another tunnel, this one big enough for him to stand upright in. The end of the passage was still several hundred paces away, but Tim did not care. He was on his feet and whole, and the surface was within his grasp.

An angry screech wailed behind Tim, and he reacted without thinking, ducking as a sarchon appeared. The creature flew above his head, hissing as it passed. Tim reached for the Lifesource and still found nothing. He awkwardly pulled his sword free of its sheath; it had been too long since he'd practiced without the aid of magic, and now he realized how much this handicapped him. He had grown too dependent on the Lifesource, and now he felt like he was fighting blind.

Tim was a good swordsman, able to recite the forms in his sleep. He dropped into a defensive stance, every move an ingrained reflex, and nicked the bird's wing as it flew by a second time. The sarchon retreated, but not before a drop of its burning blood landed on Tim's forearm. The scars on his back instantly throbbed with the effects of the poison that had caused them. A chorus of angry cries echoed down the tunnel as a flock of sarchons, excited by the presence of fresh prey, turned around the corner into view, streaming down the passage toward him.

* * *

Boblin swore. The sarchon reared back, letting out a piercing shriek and flapping its wings at the refugees. Six arrows flashed through the air, and the bird fell dead, but it was too late to stop the inevitable. All around them, the inhabitants of Malath's Teeth awoke, rising into the air and filling the cavern with a chorus of screams.

"Move!" Jend yelled. There was no use standing their ground against this many. The group fled, doing their best to stay in formation—their most valuable survival tactic—but the terrain soon turned against them as the stalactites and stalagmites forced them apart. In a short time, their rudimentary defense formation crumbled, torn apart by necessity and by the Teeth, and the refugees scattered as the first wave of sarchons *swooshed* down on them.

Boblin faced two of the birds alone. Fighting two opponents at once was already bad enough, even when the opponents had a single head apiece, but each sarchon had *three* heads. This meant that even if Boblin took two heads off in two swings, he still had four more to contend with. Here at last, Boblin Kule finally had proof that life was indeed unfair.

As the sarchons flew at him in tandem, Boblin ducked and rolled, moving his sword in a blur. He stabbed the first sarchon in the chest, barely leaving enough time to deal with the second. When the creature landed atop him, pushing him down, Boblin forced his knee upward and knocked the bird away from him, even as its teeth snapped inches away from his neck. Boblin flipped back onto his feet, swinging his sword once, twice, thrice, and the sarchon's now headless body fell to the stone floor.

Chaos reigned as the birds attacked the elions from all sides. Ironically, the towering stalactites and narrow passages that separated them now served as the best shelters available. Within the tiny corridors, the sarchons could attack only in small groups.

A hundred paces away from Boblin, six creatures swarmed over Kintel, ripping and tearing. Boblin heard the elion scream, but the cry ended in a mercifully quick fashion. The same could not be said for all of the sarchons' victims. One bird pulled Gerard right off his feet, raising him into the air before flinging him into a nest of infants. Boblin ran toward his comrade, but not before a dozen tiny sarchons latched onto every inch of Gerard's body. He shrieked as they devoured him one tiny bite at a time. As Boblin leaped toward the ledge, a sarchon grabbed him from behind and pulled him off his feet. *Karf, now it's my turn.*

Boblin thrust his sword upward, and it slid into the notch of the sarchon's breastbone with a satisfying *crunch*. The bird screeched, striking at him with one of its heads, but Boblin had his other hand ready, a blade in his palm. He stabbed the sarchon in the eye, and the creature thrashed in pain, losing its sense of direction and slamming against a wall of the cavern. Elion and sarchon tumbled onto the nearest ledge, landing on the floor in a clatter of pebbles. As Boblin extricated himself from its clutches and pulled his sword from the sarchon's chest, the creature attempted one more feeble attack, but Boblin ended its life with a final thrust.

Boblin rolled off the ledge, landing lightly on his feet. His arrival did not go unnoticed, however. Nearby, several more sarchons saw him and took flight, hot on his heels.

Boblin fled toward the nearest grouping of stalagmites, diving into the shadowy corridors of the conical structures. The raised mineral deposits would slow the sarchons, but not stop them completely. In moments, Boblin was entirely separated from the rest of the group. It was just him and the sarchon; he couldn't see the birds, but he knew they were there, following his trail. It reminded him of hide-and-discover, a childhood game he'd played. One person, the searcher, gave the other children a chance to run about the Fort and find an appropriate place to hide. Then the searcher looked, rounding up the others one at a time until her or she found them all. Well, the child's game was now a deadly reality, a brutal game of hide-and-discover amid the labyrinth of Malath's Teeth.

* * *

Celia steeled herself. From the moment they entered the cavern, the elions had played right into the sarchons' hands. Now the refugees were separated, scattered to all sections of the cave, and the battle was on the sarchons' terms, in the heart of their territory.

"What are our options?" Ana asked Celia, crouching by her side. Though ashen-faced and trembling, the younger soldier's mouth was set in a forceful line.

"Bad and worse," Celia replied. "We can stay here and let the sarchons find us, or we can run into the open and save the birds the trouble of looking."

"Very well, then," Ana said, "I don't see how staying here does us any good. I say we keep moving."

"I agree." Celia placed a hand on her friend's shoulder. "Are you ready?"

Ana exhaled, forcing the fear out. "As ready as I'll ever be."

"Then let's go." Celia stood first. A long expanse of empty, unprotected floor stretched in front of them. The next shelter was thirty paces away. They could make it in seconds if they ran. So they ran.

They had almost reached safety when a pair of sarchons appeared ahead of them, and Celia cursed. The birds had been *waiting* for them. Celia pulled at her sword, ducking into a roll to dodge the first attack. The sarchon *whisked* through the air over her head, claws brushing the tiny hairs on her skin. Celia came back up and slashed her blade horizontally across the sarchon's wing, shredding its taut skin. The crippled bird fell to the ground, hissing at Celia. "Ana!" Celia yelled. "Take out their wings!"

She risked a glance toward her comrade. Ana had dropped two of the birds and pirouetted to face a third head-on. *Good girl.*

Before Celia could leap to Ana's aid, though, the sarchon she had injured leaped toward her in a hopping maneuver across the ground. Though it could not fly anymore, it still had three hungry, lively heads. The sarchon jumped on her, and Celia raised her sword to skewer it as they tumbled. Burning blood rained all over her. After hitting the floor, the sarchon thrashed a few seconds before dying. Celia tried to pull her sword free, but it was lodged in the dead creature's ribs. She placed a boot on its carcass and pulled. No luck.

She heard a tearing sound and turned in time to see Ana's lifeless body tumble to the ground. A sarchon stood over the fallen elion, blood dripping from its jaws. *No!* A flash of pain and rage consumed Celia. She ripped her sword from the sarchon's body in front of her and faced Ana's attacker with a cry of anger.

She was so karfing brave, and look where it got her. Ana had been her charge, a stellar soldier in the making, and Celia had failed her. A tear stung her eye as she attacked. The sarchon rose into the air, coming at her with wings outstretched. Celia did a full circle, staying out of the grasp of its talons, and struck its left-most head from its shoulders. The sarchon pulled back, screeching in pain and flapping awkwardly to rise back into the air. It spit a stream of steaming saliva from its right-most head and Celia dodged to the side, the jet of saliva steaming where it hit the ground.

The sarchon struck again, and this time Celia was not fast enough. It knocked her sword out of her grip, and Celia covered her vitals with her forearms. When she landed on her back, she slipped her knife free from her belt, plunging the blade deep into an eye on one of the sarchon's heads. She had no interest in encountering that burning saliva anytime soon.

She brought her knee up, striking the sarchon in the chest and maneuvering herself free of its clutches. As she rolled to a standing position, she delivered a punishing kick directly to the sarchon's body. The creature slammed into the nearest wall, momentarily stunned as it slid to the floor. Celia faced the sarchon, completely weaponless save for her own two hands. But, as Commander Jend had taught them, that didn't make her defenseless in the slightest. The sarchon came back to its feet, staring grimly at her with its one remaining head, eyes burning.

Celia glared right back. "Come on," she said. "Show me what else you've got, you karfing piece of hisht." The sarchon enveloped her in its wings. Celia lifted her left forearm, holding the sarchon's jaws at bay, and punched it in the side of the head. Its claws raked across her chain mail vest, leaving score marks. The combatants slammed against the wall, each vying against the other's grip for supremacy.

The sarchon leaned forward, opening its jaws wide, and Celia felt its hot breath on her face. She shifted her grip just slightly, purposefully giving the sarchon an opening to strike. It lunged forward with its head, teeth snapping, but she stopped it by wrapping her hands firmly around its neck.

"This is for Ana," she said, and then snapped its neck. The sarchon's dead body crumpled forward, and all would have been fine, had its momentum not carried Celia to the ground. As Celia hit the floor yet one more time, the back of her skull struck a rock, and she lost all consciousness.

* * *

Tim planted his feet as the attack came. As the sarchons swooped down the narrow passage, he tried, again in vain, to seize the Lifesource. A tiny flame of fear flickered inside him, but he stamped it out. *It's time to do this the old-fashioned way.*

When the birds reached him, Tim pirouetted, blade flashing. He kept his movements light and quick, just like practicing the sword forms atop a stump. As he fought, Tim made his way toward the end of the tunnel. It was imperative that he get free from this constricting passage and into the open space. If he stayed in here, sooner or later the birds would overwhelm him.

The narrow boundaries of the tunnel worked to his advantage by preventing the sarchons from completely surrounding him. This allowed him to keep his opponents at bay—though not without suffering several injuries. Blood ran profusely from several gashes on his arms, chest, and back. However, for every wound he bore, two sarchons lay dead. He learned to take out their wings first, crippling them and making them easier victims. His arms soon grew tired from fending off attacks, and before he knew it, he stumbled and dropped his sword. A sarchon struck instantly, grabbing Tim's boot in its jaws, piercing the leather with its teeth. As the creature dragged him across the ground, the other sarchons surged forward to follow.

Tim tried to free himself, but it was no use. Then, without warning, the creature let go. Tim pulled back, wondering what this sudden turn of events meant. The sarchons closed around him in a ring, but did not attack. After several moments passed and nothing happened, Tim carefully stood back up. At that moment, the sarchons at the far end of the cavern parted and Tim heard a soft scratching sound at the back of the cave. A new set of red eyes appeared in the blackness, growing larger as they approached.

It was an enormous sarchon, the queen of the hive. She emerged from the shadows, her two lateral heads swiveling to survey the scene and her central head focused on Tim. An enormous, bloated sac hung underneath her belly, wobbling as she moved. Tim had no weapons with which to defend himself. He could only watch as the queen advanced, intent on her new prey.

* * *

Boblin came to a fork in the path, and he hesitated before selecting the route to the right. His pursuers were still behind him, so he couldn't stop for long. Every now and then, an elion's final cry pierced the air. Boblin hadn't encountered any of his comrades yet, unless Luc's dismembered body counted. *I expected things to be bad here, but this is worse.*

He heard a sniffing sound behind him. Apparently these creatures also possessed a keen sense of smell, as if they weren't dangerous enough already. Boblin was glad Zadinn hadn't been able to tame these birds; fighting malichons and sarchons *together* would have been a complete nightmare.

As Boblin rounded yet another curve, he stumbled upon another sarchon. It stood facing the other direction, crouched forward on two feet with wings folded and nose to the ground. Boblin halted, tensing himself. The creature didn't notice him, but Boblin was not about to try his luck. He stepped back, taking each move with agonizing slowness, never taking his eyes off the bird. After he rounded the corner, he ran, keeping his footfalls light to avoid making noise.

When Boblin returned to the fork, he heard his original pursuers, who were much closer now. As he neared the Y-shaped intersection, he immediately took the opposite path, hoping there wasn't yet another bird down this route.

Unfortunately, there was. This one saw him and snapped its jaws, hopping toward him. Boblin turned the other way, and immediately saw the first sarchon making its way toward him, steaming drool dripping from its jaws. "Come on," he groaned. *I never, ever get a break.*

Boblin drew his sword, but it wouldn't do him any good. If he turned to fight one sarchon, the other would strike. The birds steadily closed the distance, in no particular hurry. They knew this tasty morsel wasn't going anywhere.

Boblin wondered which would attack first, but in the true manner of his luck, they *both* attacked, rising into the air simultaneously. Neither wanted the other to get the first bite.

Boblin jumped. There was a small shelf in the stone above him, and he grasped the ledge with his fingertips, barely pulling himself out of the sarchons' reach. In the air below him, the two sarchons collided into each other and tumbled down. Upon hitting the floor, the birds reared back, hissing and fighting each other in earnest. *Excellent. Enjoy yourselves, my friends.*

Boblin finished climbing onto the shelf and ran thirty paces to its end, where he leaped from the edge back onto the ground. The two birds stayed locked in combat behind him, leaving him free to escape. The route in front of him dipped up and down several times before reaching a wide-open space. Boblin approached this new location hesitantly; it was too exposed for his liking. But then he saw the bodies at the end of the space. One was Ana, the other was Celia, and a lone sarchon approached both of them. *No!*

Boblin raced across the open expanse. The creature heard him approach and turned to face its attacker. The combatants clashed near a thick set of stalactites, sword against tooth. Boblin parried the sarchon's attacks with desperate urgency. He *had* to get to the two elions, even if they were both dead.

He killed the sarchon with no time to spare. If nothing else, he was learning how to fight these creatures. Boblin turned back toward his companions. His stomach lurched when he saw Ana's body, blood pooling beneath a gaping hole in her neck. *No. Not when she was so young. Not when she was so good.*

He fell to his knees beside Celia's unconscious form, placing his ear against her chest, and breathed a sigh of relief once he heard her faint heartbeat. Several sarchons lay strewn about the floor. So the two had made a stand here, and Celia lived, but Ana had paid the final price. The Mountains demanded a hefty sum from those who would cross them. *It had better well be karfing worth it before this all is over.*

Boblin could not linger here long. It was too exposed, and more sarchons were likely to return. Boblin scooped Celia up in his arms, turning her so she rested over his left shoulder and leaving his right hand free to fight with his sword if he needed. He glanced at Ana's body. It wasn't right to leave her here, but he could not carry both elions, and he had to keep Celia safe.

"You were among the best of us," he said to the fallen soldier. He turned back toward the shadows of Malath's Teeth, carrying Celia as he forged onward into the darkness.

Thirty-Three

Tim felt an unexpected spark flare at the back of his mind. *The Lifesource!* As the giant sarchon loomed over him, he seized the power without hesitation, raising his hands to unleash a buffet of air that knocked the queen back a dozen feet. The turbulent force also caught the smaller birds, throwing them against the cavern walls like pebbles in a windstorm. Many did not rise.

The queen, for all her size, was fast. She screeched and swiveled to face Tim again. The sound of her cry hurt his ears. Tim flinched, and the Lifesource fled. He grasped it again, but it felt like trying to hold water in cupped hands—there for a second, then gone. He reached a third time, but by then, he could not even sense the power anymore. *What in Malath is happening?*

The sarchon stepped forward, dipping down with her left head and opening her mouth. She let forth a stream of foaming saliva that landed just a few paces in front of Tim. When the liquid landed, it began hardening to rock right before him, and Tim realized she was building a wall of stone from her very own spittle. The other sarchons gathered *behind* him, adding to the wall with their saliva so that Tim found himself boxed in by four rising barricades.

He was more confused than scared by this new development. True, he would be unable to escape the saliva-stone prison, but neither would the birds be able to reach him. *How is this to their advantage?* The walls soon passed his head, sloping to form a central peak as the roof closed over him. Tim steeled himself. This turn of events could give him time to reclaim his powers, and once he had regained the Lifesource, neither walls nor sarchons could stop him.

The last beam of light faded as the stone sealed up, leaving him in absolute darkness. Tim settled down in the corner of his cell, still unsure as to the sarchons' next move but unwilling to waste time thinking about it. Then something slammed against the wall to his rear. Were the birds throwing themselves against the stone cage? No, that did not make sense. They would not trap him just to pound on the encasement.

When the wall *thumped* again, something sizzled, and Tim stretched his hand out to touch the rock. He pulled back quickly as a burning heat scalded his palm. The surface of the stone felt moist, almost like…*like getting burned by sarchon blood.*

Then he noticed patches of pockmarked gray light filtering through the wall as a handspan-size section of rock eroded. Silvery liquid dripped from the hole's retreating edges, and Tim glanced through the opening to catch a glimpse of the queen sarchon extending her right head toward him. As she opened her jaws, a stream of fluid shot from her mouth and struck the opening near his face, sizzling on contact. Tim instantly realized the saliva itself was causing the erosion.

Smaller projectiles hit all sides of his prison as sarchons followed their queen's example, dousing the rock with venom. Before, Tim wondered why the sarchons had three heads, and now he understood. It was a hunting mechanism. One head trapped the prey in a stone prison, and the second head produced entry points to reach the ensnared victim.

The third head did the eating.

* * *

Boblin held Celia over his shoulder with one arm, sword in his free hand as he hiked up a steady slope. The rising elevation likely meant they were nearing the far side of the cavern, but the incline tired him. The sarchons had not left him alone, either. The body of one rested a hundred paces back, where he'd been forced to fight one-handed while still clinging to Celia. He hoped he didn't have to carve his way through many more of the creatures.

The path soon grew so narrow it could fit only two people abreast. On either side of him, the walls stretched high, reminding him of one of the North's dried-out gullies. Meanwhile, the slope before him grew so steep it became nearly—but not quite—impossible to climb.

Boblin did not like this. He had walked into an easy chokepoint, and if things got bad in here, he might not have a way out. However, he no longer had the luxury of choosing his route. He could take risks if traveling alone, but with Celia to look out for, he had to get to the other side of the cavern as quickly as possible. This was the most direct path, so it was the path he'd take.

Boblin mounted the rising trail, sheathing his sword so he'd have one free hand to keep purchase on the vertical path in front of him. His muscles ached from the strain of the climb, and his breathing grew heavy and labored. When he reached the trail's summit, he looked down the slope behind him and stopped. Three sarchons, crawling side by side, approached the base of the small rise, noses to the ground. One leaned forward, stretching out its necks, and looked up.

Boblin stepped out of sight before the creature could see him. He was safe for now, but his scent would lead the pack up here eventually. It was time to move faster. The path continued much as it had below, with tall walls blocking any escape to either side. *Well, I'll just have to be quick about it. The far side has to be close.* However, the trail led only a short distance before dead-ending against a flat stone wall. *So much for thinking this was the way out.*

Boblin retraced his steps to the ledge and risked a quick glance over the side. Three more birds had joined the first group of sarchons, and all six now traveled up the path toward him. Boblin was completely trapped without any chance of getting back down, and the only way to the bottom of the hill was *through* the sarchons. Fighting against three would have been difficult and dangerous—but fighting through six was suicide.

Boblin returned to the dead end and considered his options. A narrow cleft rested in the wall, just above his head, so he set Celia down and pulled himself up for a cursory glance. The niche was narrow, but deep enough for two people to lie in side by side. It would serve for a rudimentary shelter, and though Boblin didn't like cornering himself, he could not fight the entire sarchon pack. His only chance was to remain hidden and hope the creatures abandoned their pursuit. *Not a great gamble, but I'm out of options.*

Boblin lowered himself back down and picked up Celia, rolling her body into the crevice before climbing up next to her. He pushed her deep into the shadows and lay on his side in front of her, able to tip his head just far enough to keep an eye on the narrow space outside. His thudding heartbeat filled the tiny space in the confines of the cleft. With his luck, the sarchons probably had the ability to hear such sounds a mile away.

The first sarchon came into view, crawling on its feet and the elbows of its wingtips, the very image of a creature on the hunt. When it reached the open area and saw no prey, it paused and perked its head, nose sniffing the air. It moved again, slowly and warily, as its comrades approached. The sarchons spread out across the narrow space, searching for the vanished prey.

Boblin's pulse pounded with a rhythmic drumbeat. He held his sword in front of him, clutching the hilt with sweaty hands, fearing even the noise of his breathing would give him away. The creatures milled around the narrow space, thoroughly confused. Every now and then one snapped at its comrades, but unfortunately none of these turned into all-out fights. If they were to kill one another, fewer would be left for Boblin to deal with.

It went this way for several minutes before the creatures, moving reluctantly, retreated to the ledge. The sarchons knew they'd been tricked, and they did not like it. They continued smelling the ground, attempting to discover how the elion had disappeared.

The leader eventually left the summit and began its descent. The others followed, stepping out of sight one at a time, but just before the last bird shuffled toward the edge of the hill, Celia stirred and mumbled. The sarchon hesitated, head cocked at such an angle that Boblin thought of a demonic chicken. Had the situation not been so grave, he would have laughed at the image. The bird turned back to the crevice, eyes settling directly on their hiding spot, and it hissed.

Boblin made his next choice very swiftly. Fighting through six sarchons *would* be suicide. But if he could buy Celia's safety, it was an okay trade for him. So he didn't hesitate. He rolled forward, dropped from the ledge, and raised his sword above his head. Then he ran straight toward the sarchon pack.

* * *

Tim pulled back as a fist-size chunk of rock fell from the ceiling and landed in front of him. The edges of the newly formed hole in his saliva-constructed encasement steamed. A sarchon thrust its face against the opening, but the hole was not big enough for it to fit through—not yet, at least. A multitude of these openings now surrounded Tim, and though no sarchon could get inside at the moment, Tim saw the inevitable conclusion in front of him. Within a few minutes, the sarchons *could* stick their heads into the holes, and he did not have enough room to elude all of them. He essentially sat inside a giant feeding trough, and once his captors had made enough progress, they would reach inside with their hungry mouths—biting, chomping, and feasting—to pick him apart from a dozen different angles.

He felt fear rising again. This time he didn't crush it but allowed it to come forward, just long enough for him to grasp it and separate those parts that made him strong—awareness, heightened sensation, focus—from those that made him weak. He gleaned what he could from it, and discarded the rest.

Yes, this is the way. He only needed to retain his resources, retrace his steps, and the Lifesource would be his. The sarchons could not stand against the Warrior of Light.

One of the holes in his stone cage had gotten considerably larger. A sarchon threw itself against the opening, splayed on the outside with outstretched wings, and shoved its central head through the hole. Tim bumped against the rear of his prison as the sarchon snapped its jaws in his face. Saliva fell, smoking near his feet, and the sarchon retreated. It could not reach him from this angle. Tim backed up again, but the holes were all around him. Soon there would be too many directions of attack, and he could not evade them all at once.

Tim laughed in cold amusement. This would be hopeless for any other man. He was almost excited for the upcoming climax, the chance to test himself against these creatures of the underworld. Once he seized the Lifesource, perhaps he would draw it out for as long as possible, toying with the sarchons as they had toyed with him.

The queen sarchon bellowed, her saliva splashing against the opening, and the erosion continued. There was no escape, but that was okay. Tim did not *want* to escape, not from an opportunity like this.

* * *

Boblin slammed into the first two birds, catching them completely off guard. As they twisted to either side, the remaining four sarchons turned back toward him. Boblin dove headfirst down the slope, breaking through the cluster of winged demons. The sarchons had not anticipated outright aggression, and Boblin used this element of surprise to get ahead of the pack.

He landed on the slope and tumbled down the far side, bumping and rolling over the rocks with jarring force. It was painful, but pain was better than death, and he now had a head start. The six sarchons rose into the air and flapped their wings. Excellent, everything was going to plan. Boblin's worst fear had been that one or two sarchons would stay behind and find Celia, but these worries were unfounded. All six stayed on his trail, and Celia was safe. That was all that mattered to him.

Of course, Boblin now had to face *his* predicament—a secondary problem, but a problem nonetheless. Boblin needed to think fast and on his feet to pull through in one piece. He hit the base of the trail and rose to his feet, the sarchons gaining fast behind him. He hesitated for a moment, wondering if he should confront them now and get it over with, but he decided against it. If he kept running, he might find a better place to make a stand. Plus, the farther they were from Celia, the better. It would not do to have the sarchons return to her. So he ran, drawing his pursuers through a forest rich with rock formations.

Without warning, Boblin slammed into another elion, and the two stumbled to the side. When Boblin pulled back, he got a good look at the newcomer and blinked in surprise. The other elion swung a sword at Boblin's head, but Boblin ducked and rolled, narrowly escaping as his attacker struck again. The blade missed his prone body, *clanging* against the stone floor of the cavern, and Boblin moved to a standing position, drawing his sword to face his opponent.

"Hello, Boblin," Kaiel Tulak said.

* * *

Celia stirred into wakefulness, taken aback by the darkness. True, the caves weren't bright to begin with, but the blackness now surrounding her seemed even more complete. Confusion clouded her mind; she obviously wasn't in the same place where she had lost consciousness.

She tried to sit up, but almost immediately struck her head against a low ceiling. She lay back down, pulse quickening as she reached out her hands to touch the walls surrounding her. She lay in a narrow, confined space, like an oubliette at the bottom of a dungeon. *What in Malath?*

She reached for her sword, but it was not there. *Of course not.* She had lost it in the last fight, in which she and Ana had tempted fate, and only one had survived. But Celia had no time to mourn—that would come later. First, she had to find out how she'd been moved to this new place. Celia considered the possibilities. Perhaps she was in a sarchon nest, meant as food for their young.

She prayed to the Maker this was not the case, for she had precious little with which to defend herself.

Celia crawled to the edge of her prison. She didn't know if she would like what she was about to find, but that was of no consequence, because going forward was her only option. That was the problem with some people, she decided. They focused too much on *what they couldn't control*, and that was no way to go about solving matters.

She arrived at the edge, prepared to face whatever came next, but was pleasantly surprised—though significantly more confused—to discover she had been resting in a niche within an empty cavern. She saw no sign of sarchons. *Where am I?*

She heard a clatter of pebbles and tensed, hand going for her sword a second time. *No sword, Alcion. I'll to have to do it by hand again.* She didn't know if it was better to jump into the open or stay hidden. Leaping out gave her a better chance at fighting, but would also expose her. Hiding gave her a chance of remaining unseen, but if she were found, she had no way to defend herself in this narrow cleft.

"Celia!" Hedro Desh said as he appeared over the lip of the rise. "I've found you."

Celia let out a breath. "Where are we?" she asked, extricating herself from the tight confines.

"No need for that," Hedro said, offering her his hand. She accepted his help down from the ledge and slid into a sitting position, needing a minute to gain her bearings.

"How did you find me?" she asked.

"Sarchons," Hedro said. "I saw them gathering here, and I thought somebody might be in trouble."

"I was with Ana," Celia said. She swallowed. "She didn't make it."

Hedro's face fell. "Oh, no." He sat and placed his arm over her shoulders. "I'm so sorry, Celia."

"It was the risk we all took," Celia said. "It sure doesn't make it easier, though."

"No," Hedro said. "I don't suppose it does."

She let herself sit, allowing the grief and sorrow to wash through her as much as she could for the moment, and then took a breath. "We need to keep moving."

"Yes," Hedro replied, "We do. Follow me."

"Hedro," she sad.

He turned to her. "Yes?"

"Thank you for coming back for me."

He leaned forward, gently brushing his lips against her cheek. "Of course."

* * *

Boblin's mind tried to wrap itself around this turn of events. "It wouldn't do any good to ask how you got here, would it?" he asked Kaiel.

"I followed," Kaiel replied. "I was one of you. I know how your scouts operate."

"Did you have a nice time in the Deathlands?" Boblin asked. "How's Zadinn? Doing well, I trust?"

Kaiel spat. "You know nothing of the Dark Lord. You will all grovel at my feet before the end. He promised me."

A sarchon swooped overhead, and Boblin ducked. The creature's feet passed so close he felt a rush of air over his shoulders. In front of him, Kaiel swung his blade at the bird, and the sarchon pulled back into the sky. So the pursuers had arrived, but Boblin had Kaiel to contend with.

The traitor elion rushed at him. Boblin dodged the attack, and by the time Kaiel came back around, Boblin's sword was up in defense. The steel of their blades rang in the stillness of Malath's Teeth. "Those birds will kill us both," Boblin said.

"No, they won't," Kaiel replied. "I'll feed you to them." He resumed his attack, and Boblin pulled away. The two combatants whirled, moving across the floor in a deadly dance. They had received training in the same techniques; Boblin knew every move Kaiel could make, and Kaiel knew every move Boblin could make. It was an even match. The sarchons curbed their attack, satisfied to be malevolent spectators. It was as if watching their prey fight each other was as enjoyable as the hunting.

In a bizarre way, Boblin found this new battle refreshing. He only now realized how long it was since he and the other elions had fought something other than monsters. Kaiel was not a creature from the Korlan, a fanged vrawl, or a winged sarchon. He stood on two legs and wielded a sword. This was good, old-fashioned combat, where Boblin didn't have to worry about venom or getting bitten in half.

As the two elions dueled, the six sarchons moved closer to the battle, toying with the combatants by rising into the air and launching quick attacks. One or another would dive, sometimes at Boblin, sometimes at Kaiel, and sometimes at both. As each elion defended himself from the flying creatures, the birds then pulled back, leaving the elion to recover and return to the duel. The sarchons weren't doing this for the sake of the hunt—they could likely kill both elions—but merely because it provided good sport.

Boblin had to end the fight. Soon the birds would tire of their fun, and take him and Kaiel for good. Perhaps, though, he could turn the sarchons' playact to his advantage. The next time a pair of sarchons struck, Boblin did not turn away from the fight, knowing the sarchons weren't going to complete their attack. It was just another feint, and he wasn't buying it.

Kaiel, however, did. He turned around to defend himself. Boblin ignored the sarchon and drove his sword into Kaiel's shoulder. The elion spun around, screaming in pain and rage. Boblin moved quickly, slamming his right hand against Kaiel's wrist. Kaiel's fingers shot open, the nerves stunned, and he dropped his sword.

Boblin pulled his blade free as all six sarchons rose up in the air behind Kaiel. Boblin kicked the elion in the chest, and Kaiel fell into the clutches of the birds, screaming as they swarmed over him. Boblin watched as the sarchons pulled Kaiel into the air and flew away, carrying their prize with them.

"I told you I'd kill you, Kaiel," he said.

Boblin was finally able to stop and look around. He was at the end of Malath's Teeth, where an open cavern loomed into view less than a hundred paces away. Beyond, the white snow beckoned, glowing in the moonlight. He'd survived, but there was one problem: Celia was still in there, and he sure as Malath was not leaving her behind.

Boblin turned around and ran back into the darkness.

* * *

The sarchons clambered up the sides of Tim's stone prison. Tim could almost feel the seconds sliding as the birds neared him. He slumped, feigning defeat, and closed his eyes. *It's now or never.* The Lifesource would be his, or the sarchons would have their feast. As he let his mind float away, he almost casually bumped into the magic. He could not help but smile as he allowed it to enter his veins.

This was not the weak, impotent Lifesource Nazgar had showed him how to command. It was complete, total power—a tidal wave of shadow, untainted by the Kyrlod's feeble influence. Tim let the birds come so close he could almost feel their talons scraping his skin, and then he directed the magic toward them. The sarchons stood no chance. Black flames spurted from Tim's fingertips, slamming into the birds, and the sarchons shrieked in agony as oily fire devoured their bodies.

Tim *pushed* against the prison walls. The stones erupted and he stepped out into the open, a nimbus of shadow surrounding his body. The sarchons milled back, terrified by this dark angel rising from its grave. He concentrated his energies in their direction, and their bodies flared red-hot until Tim saw the outlines of their skeletons. The birds' skin melted away in seconds, and then their bones vaporized, leaving only dust.

The queen sarchon hesitated, and Tim smiled at her. Her kind had stalked and devoured his companions without mercy, but now it was his turn. He threw a ball of black fire at her. She shrieked as it slammed into her body, writhing beneath the flaming onslaught, but Tim wrapped cords of air around her to hold her in place. She was helpless to resist as the inferno devoured her body, and in moments she was a charred, smoking corpse.

She had dared to threaten the Warrior of Light and paid the price—as would anyone else who stood in his path. Tim filled the tunnel with a maelstrom of fire, eradicating every sarchon that had attacked him. He stood at the center of the swirling vortex, hands raised above his head, ending the blaze by clenching his fists tight.

The silence felt so pure, so right. Steam lifted from the floors and walls of the passageway. Remembering his earlier mistake, Tim created a pathway made of air so he could walk above the ground and avoid the hot stone underfoot, traveling the last hundred paces of the tunnel in total silence. His time here had been painful, but he was a mightier man because of it.

* * *

Boblin hesitated. He couldn't remember which way to go. He'd retreated from the opening, heading back the way he'd come after leading the sarchons away from Celia, but now he wasn't sure he'd taken the right path. The first time he led the sarchons this way, he'd been rather preoccupied, and he hadn't had time to sit and place brightly colored markers at every turn. So here he was, standing at a crossroads of stalactites, trying to gain his bearings.

He'd led the sarchons *down* a slope on his way over here. Consequently, he needed a path that led him back uphill. But three of his options led across flat ground for an indefinite direction, and the fourth path led *down* toward a dark passageway. Boblin peered toward the tunnel at the bottom of the slope. He must have taken a wrong turn, for he had no memory of this route. It frustrated him to no end. For every second he wasted playing "Find the Karfing Treasure at the End of the Maze," Celia came closer to danger. *An entire sarchon hive could be surrounding her right now.*

Boblin turned back. He needed to go to where he'd fought Kaiel and retrace his steps again. He would lose precious time, but it was better than standing here like a sun-baked lizard. But then he paused; he was almost certain he heard footfalls echoing from within the long tunnel behind him. He looked down the slope toward the corridor. What sort of person—*or thing*—was walking down there?

Boblin almost convinced himself it was an illusion, until he heard footsteps again. No way were those sarchon footsteps. They sounded entirely human.

Then Boblin felt something very odd indeed, like a cold wave of air had surged from the mouth of the tunnel and washed over him. In its wake, he knew down to his bones that something extremely dangerous and evil was coming toward him. Boblin unsheathed his sword and settled into a defensive stance. He briefly wondered if he should run, but decided this was not something he wanted at his back. *Better to face it here than let it run amok in the shadows of Malath's Teeth.*

The footsteps grew louder, and Boblin again felt the cold wave of air. Whatever was approaching radiated a frigid presence the same way the sun radiated heat. He reconsidered his decision not to flee, but then a man stepped into view.

Though the person who came from the passage wore the face of Tim Matthias, it was not Tim anymore. Boblin barely recognized him. Tim's shirt and trousers hung in shreds, and his body bore countless cuts and scrapes. Streaks of dirt and ash covered his skin, as if he had walked through a hurricane of sharp blades and then doused himself with a bucket of fire. His face seemed chiseled from stone, and his eyes no longer had a healthy, blue color but were gray and hard.

Tim did not react at all upon seeing his old friend. He simply brushed a lock of hair away from his face and said, "Hello, Boblin," his tone as unforgiving as his eyes.

"Hello," Boblin replied. He felt as wary as a mouse in the gaze of a hawk. Only they were not mouse and hawk—they were Tim Matthias and Boblin Kule, two strangers who had become the best of friends.

Everything Boblin and Nazgar feared appeared to have come true.

* * *

Tim didn't allow himself to feel happiness at seeing Boblin. He wanted to shout with joy, *ached* to, but he could not allow it. The Warrior had no time for such things.

"Where are we?" Tim asked.

"Malath's Teeth," Boblin replied. The elion held his sword in one hand, a sensation of wariness emanating from him as he stood framed in the outline of the tunnel. It gave Tim pause; Boblin looked at him as if he expected a monster to appear and swallow them both whole.

"Malath's what?" Tim asked.

"That's what the Rindar brothers named it," Boblin replied, shifting his stance, poised on the balls of his toes as if ready to strike. "It's a sarchon hive, our only way out of these caves."

Tim narrowed his eyes. Something else was going on here, and he didn't like how it felt. "The sarchons won't be a problem. I've killed them all."

A dim voice at the back of his mind told him that this new turn of events, coming across Boblin in the tunnel like this, should surprise him. After all, he'd been separated from the elions days ago, taken to an entirely different part of the Mountains, and it just so happened that he now bumped into Boblin? But Tim ignored it. It was certainly an odd coincidence, but entirely within the realm of plausibility. He was here, and Boblin was here, but the goal was to get out of the cave.

Tim stepped toward Boblin, but the elion did not turn to leave. He, too, took a step forward, as if he meant to stop Tim. Tim noticed Boblin had not yet sheathed his sword.

"There aren't any sarchons behind me," Tim said. "Let's go."

"Tim," Boblin said, "what *happened* to you down there?"

"Nothing." Nothing Boblin would understand, at least.

"Goat *hisht*," Boblin said.

Tim narrowed his eyes even more. "Put away your sword."

Boblin's jaw tightened. "What was the first thing I ever said to you?" he asked.

"Welcome to the North," Tim replied. "Why?"

Boblin stepped forward again. "I just want to be sure you are yourself."

That made Tim smile. "I've never felt more whole in my life," he said. He was sure of it now—Boblin was visibly frightened of him. Well, Tim had a grisly task before him, so Boblin *should* be frightened. It couldn't be helped.

"We need to find Celia," Boblin said.

"Is she down here?" Tim asked.

"I'm afraid so."

"Then she's probably already dead," Tim said.

Boblin looked at him like Tim had just planted a sword in his back. Well, Tim hadn't betrayed the elion; he'd just told him the truth. Boblin needed to rid himself of this attachment, anyway. It would be his undoing.

"Go along if you like," Tim said. "But we need your skills for this war. If you ask me, you're only going to get yourself killed, too."

"What have you become?" Boblin asked.

"Only what is necessary," Tim answered. "Either come with me, or go into the caves and die. It's your decision."

Something strange happened in Boblin's eyes, a strange resolve coming over him, a transformation that completely mystified Tim. Four weeks ago, he would have understood completely, but since entering the Mountains, he'd slowly lost his ability to comprehend the depths of human morality.

He stepped past Boblin. He didn't need the elion to tell him how to get out of here; he could feel the fresh air wafting down the path to the left. He wondered how many elions would be waiting for him when he arrived—how many had survived and how many had thrown their lives away like Boblin was now about to do. He needed as many as possible for this battle.

Then again, perhaps the elions wouldn't matter once he'd found the Army of Kah'lash. The Mountains demanded sacrifices, after all. Nazgar claimed Tim was their talisman of protection, but now Tim suspected the Kyrlod was wrong in this, just as he'd been wrong in so many other things. Perhaps the refugees were the talismans, meant to protect Tim by buying him passage with their blood.

Boblin spoke softly. "Daniel would be disappointed."

Tim snarled, striking a savage blow with the Lifesource and knocking Boblin across the tunnel. The elion's body smashed against a rock wall, and Tim pinned him in place with the Lifesource, Boblin's feet dangling above the ground.

"Would you like me to do the sarchons' work for them?" Tim said, his voice a hiss. "Because I can."

He expected to see fear return to Boblin's eyes, but instead he only saw sadness. "I had hoped I was wrong," Boblin said. Tim released him, and Boblin slid to the ground.

"About what?" Tim asked.

Boblin stood up, reasserting his grip on his sword. "You've changed," he said.

"Only for the better."

"No, not at all." Boblin swallowed hard. "I don't think I can let you go back to them—not like this."

"You think you can stop me?" Tim asked.

"I think I have to try," Boblin said.

Suddenly everything made perfect sense, snapping into place with perfect clarity. The realization rocked Tim's mind. He'd known the Dark Lord was treacherous, insidious…but only now did he realize how far Zadinn's wickedness stretched. Boblin was working for *him*. Working for Zadinn.

Tim had met Boblin almost immediately after entering the North, *right when the malichons first attacked*. It was far too fortuitous to be coincidence. Boblin must have led the malichons to the Southerners and then ordered them into battle so he could later step in and save the Matthias family. Then Boblin led them to the Fort, where Nazgar—perhaps also in league with the Dark Lord—waited. There, the two worked together to bring about Daniel and Rosalie's demise, allowing the two traitors to apply leverage against the Warrior of Light from two angles, one posing as friend and one posing as mentor, using Tim's weakness to back him into a corner, pushing him further from the path of true strength.

—this is preposterous—

But something happened that neither anticipated—Tim realized the truth. He'd been wise enough to suppress it, to hide his discovery from them, but they suspected he was straying from their influence. Then they were separated, and

Tim realized his true strength. So Boblin came into the caves to hunt Tim down and had at last found him. But he realized now Tim knew too much, that Tim had grown too powerful, and now Boblin planned to end Tim's life before the Warrior could break free to wreak havoc upon the Dark Lord.

—*he is my best friend*—

"Traitor," Tim said, striking again, but Boblin was ready this time. Tim had forgotten how blindingly fast the elion could move. Boblin ducked low and rolled, while Tim's attack shattered the stalactite where he had stood moments before. Fragments of stone came down in all directions.

Tim unleashed a wave of fire a mere second after Boblin reversed course and took cover behind a screen of rocks. The flames washed across the empty space, leaving vapors of smoke. Tim summoning the inferno he had used to destroy the sarchon queen, wreathing his body in dark fire, but Boblin had moved *again*. Each time Boblin dodged an attack, he moved a little bit closer to Tim.

Tim had always respected Boblin's fighting ability, but he hadn't quite realized the true extent of the elion's skills until now. Boblin Kule was quite possibly the deadliest opponent he had ever faced. No other elion would have survived these attacks. Tim held nothing back; he'd used his power to kill an entire hive of sarchons and a whole army of vrawl. Even Nazgar would be sweating buckets just trying to stay alive right now.

Boblin was now almost atop Tim. He slipped in, moving *between* a pair of deadly spells that could have sliced him in half. Tim saw the elion's face, and where he expected to see hatred and violence, he saw only mind-numbing sorrow.

—*that's because he's trying to stop me from becoming a monster*—

"Please," Boblin said, "don't do this."

"How long have you been working for him?" Tim said. This time he attacked with his sword, a personal attack for a personal offense, but even in a haze of sadness, Boblin moved and blocked the blow. "How long have you been Zadinn's servant?"

Boblin jerked in sudden surprise—

—*he doesn't work for Zadinn, not Boblin*—

—"By the Maker, Tim, I'm not your enemy!"—

—and Tim seized him by the neck. Boblin couldn't move. Tim wrapped the Lifesource around the elion, immobilizing him, pinning Boblin against the ground and choking him. Boblin could not get any air, and could only move his eyes. He shifted his gaze to meet Tim's, and Tim Matthias at last saw his own reflection in Boblin's pupils.

What have I become?

His image scared him. He did not see the man he *thought* he had become. Instead he saw his hard features; he saw the absence of light in his eyes; he saw the terrible evil that had spawned within him while he had looked the other way.

He saw a man killing his friend.

Tim's sense of determination faltered, and his grip lessened enough for Boblin to speak.

"Maybe you'll kill Zadinn," Boblin said. "Maybe he'll kill you. Either way, the rest of us lose."

Tim hesitated.

Why save a world if I must destroy everything good in order to do so?

He felt himself come unhinged, everything he thought he'd learned these last few weeks turning in on itself and collapsing. He released Boblin and fell to his knees. *What am I doing down here? What made me think any of these things were good, decent, justifiable?*

"May the Maker forgive me," Tim said, his breath coming in a sob. Shaking, he turned from Boblin. He felt sick, lost. He heard the elion regaining his wind, breath coming in rasping hacks as he cleared his throat and sucked in air. *Will he still call me friend, after this? I have lost the right.*

"It's okay," Boblin croaked. "You're not alone."

Tim could not look at him. "No. I *have* to be alone."

"No one has to stand alone," Boblin replied. "Not even the Warrior of Light."

"You don't understand," Tim said. "I can't go back like this. You need to leave this cave. Leave the Mountains and find the Army. I must stay here."

The silence between them stretched for nearly a minute before Boblin spoke again. "I will leave for now, if you wish. Take the time you need, but when you are ready to come back, I'll be right outside the cave. Even if no one else waits for you, I will." Boblin stood and walked away.

Tim turned and crawled back down the passage, toward the tunnel where he had fought the sarchons. He collapsed, an all-too-familiar sense of despair creeping over him. He had no idea what to do anymore.

Thirty-Four

Boblin's heart pounded as he ran through Malath's Teeth. Bruises covered the sides of his neck, where Tim had nearly choked him to death. Even breathing hurt. Boblin was all too aware that things teetered on the brink of destruction; the future balanced on a razor-thin ridge.

It was as Nazgar had predicted. Tim strayed close to the path of corruption and darkness—and if not for this chance meeting, perhaps all would have been lost. For now, hope remained, but only a sliver.

Nothing is certain, Nazgar had said. *You can forestall him while he stands at the brink of the abyss, but he must be the one who steps away.*

Before this hour, Tim had not known he was even near the abyss. He'd finally realized the truth of it, during their fight—Boblin had seen it in his eyes—but Tim still had to choose whether or not to step away. Boblin wasn't sure if he should have left Tim alone, but it seemed the only option. Tim had to make the last stage of this journey by himself, and Boblin couldn't risk doing or saying the wrong thing at a crucial moment. Either Tim turned back, or he didn't; it was in the Maker's hands now. So Boblin simply prayed.

As Boblin reached another junction of pathways, he found himself standing right in front of the hill where he had left Celia. *Of all the karfing things.* He'd run past this spot earlier, during his first frantic search, and completely missed it. True, this mistake allowed him to find Tim, but Boblin really needed to grow a pair of eyes. He couldn't be losing his bearings like this; it didn't bode well for his continued survival.

He ran up the hill, knots in his stomach. Anything could have happened to Celia in the time since he'd left her up here. Making it to the top in seconds, he ran into the open plateau, half expecting a flock of sarchons to swarm him. Instead he collided into Hedro Desh. On the defensive, the two elions simultaneously struck, their swords clashing before they recognized each other.

"*Karf!*" Hedro swore, backing off and lowering his weapon. "What was that about, Kule?"

"I didn't know who was up here," Boblin said.

"Well, *we* are," Hedro said, pointing a thumb over his shoulder toward Celia Alcion, who stood alive and well behind him. Relief flooded through Boblin, but he couldn't prevent feeling a faint nugget of disappointment. *Of course Hedro would be the one to find her. Forget anything I did to help her. She was unconscious so she doesn't know about it.*

The selfishness of this sentiment only soured Boblin's stomach further. He pushed it away, feeling guilty the thought had even crossed his mind. *I have to be better than that. The important thing is she is alive and safe. I'm not owed anything for saving her, so I can't dishonor both myself and her by thinking such things.*

"Where did you come from?" Celia asked him.

"I was…I was at the end of the Teeth, but nobody one else was there," Boblin said. "I turned back because I thought…well, others had to be back here."

"Too late for that," Hedro said. "I've covered this spot. Nobody is here."

"How did you two come across each other?" Boblin asked.

"I hit my head on a rock when I was fighting a sarchon," Celia said. "I don't remember anything else, but I woke up in a hole in the wall. I think they took me there."

"The sarchons?" Boblin said.

"Yes, the birds," Hedro interrupted. "You might have noticed them by now."

"As a matter of fact, I did."

"Anyway, I woke up here, and that's when Hedro came by," Celia said. "But we should get moving."

The three companions ran back down the hill. Boblin turned to lead them north toward the cave's mouth. The passage remained blissfully clear of sarchons, but no one took the reprieve for granted. Less sarchons here only meant more sarchons elsewhere.

Sure enough, as soon as the trio came within sight of the exit, a swarm of the birds rose into view behind them, filling the air with their shrieking cries. Boblin swore, pushing on harder, as the creatures began their final attack. On either side, other elions also emerged from the maze of stalactites and stalagmites, running for freedom in clusters of two and three.

At the mouth of the cave, Jend Argul stood next to Hugo and Ken, holding bows with arrows nocked. As the sarchons came within shooting range, the elions unleashed a volley of arrows and several birds crashed down. More soon took their place, one making a pass at Boblin and nearly snatching him, but he jerked to the left and it barely brushed by. Others were not so lucky. A hundred paces away, a group of sarchons engulfed Vern and Quera with a flurry of wingbeats. At the last second, Vern shoved Quera to safety before diving into the cloud of birds to distract them. The sarchons swarmed over him as Quera ran from the massacre, face numb.

We can't keep this up much longer, Boblin thought. There were too many sarchons, and the mouth of the cave was too far away. Even with Jend and the Rindar twins firing volley after volley, it was not enough. Boblin felt cold inside. *So close, only to die within sight of the finish.*

And then Nazgar of the Kyrlod appeared out of the shadows, stepping forth to stand by Jend Argul. As the wizened old man raised his hands into the sky, balls of purple fire flew from his outstretched palms. The blessed purple flames passed through the air above their heads, providing a final screen of protection. Dozens of sarchons fell, their burning husks landing in smoking piles.

Boblin, Celia, and Hedro reached the exit in the midst of the ensuing pandemonium. Jend ordered everyone outside the cave. The elion refugees, now more a rabble than a unit, raced from the awful cavern without so much as looking back. Outside, the snowcapped slopes sparkled in the moonlight. By the Maker, it was the most beautiful thing Boblin had ever seen. He staggered onto the white expanse, sinking to his knees and gazing up at the stars burning bright and fierce. He closed his eyes. They'd survived, and though this nightmare was far from finished, they now had a temporary reprieve. He raised his arms and sucked in a long, deep breath of clean air.

Boblin counted the survivors. *Twenty-two.* He could name those who had not returned. He'd just seen Vern die, watched Gerard and Kintel fall earlier this night, and found Luc's and Ana's bodies in the caves. Vera was the final missing one. Six elions in total, taken by Malath's Teeth and never to return.

Mandar Kule stood by him, placing a hand on his son's shoulder. "We live to see yet another dawn," Mandar said. "It is a blessing."

"Not everyone," Boblin said. "I knew some wouldn't survive."

"We all knew it," Mandar agreed, and Boblin thought back to Tim. *Welcome to the North.* That said it all.

Boblin stood. "I need to talk to Nazgar." He made his way through the survivors to the Kyrlod, who stood apart from the rest, watching the caves to see if the sarchons would pursue. Boblin did not think the creatures would appear. Though the birds were not shy of attacking elions, they apparently adhered to strict territorial boundaries.

"We need to speak," Boblin said. "I saw Tim."

Nazgar turned to him, his gaze sharp. Elions nearby fell silent, and Boblin swallowed hard. He didn't mean to have an audience, but it was too late for that now. "In the caves?" the Kyrlod asked.

"Yes," Boblin said, unconsciously touching the bruises on his neck.

"Where is he now?"

"Still down there," Boblin replied. "He wanted to stay."

Nazgar's eyes drilled into Boblin, and his face tightened with suspicion and apprehension. Such intense scrutiny made Boblin want to shrink to the size of a pebble. Nazgar was obviously scared, and this made Boblin more frightened.

Nazgar's tone was so hard Boblin almost expected to hear the icy landscape fracture around them. "Why?"

Boblin dreaded the consequences of what he had to say next. "He's changed."

"As we feared."

Boblin nodded, and an uneasy murmur rippled through the elions. He had no way of knowing if they were fully aware of the danger Tim was in, or what this meant for them if the Warrior changed his path, but Boblin had to finish his story. They had to know Tim could still be saved. He hastily cut over their rising voices. "I think there's still hope."

"Tell me everything," Nazgar said.

Boblin spilled out the story in a rush, telling enough of the truth so the Kyrlod and the elions would understand but not so much that they would abandon Tim. He wasn't so sure the elions would wait if they knew how close Tim came to killing Boblin. But they *had* to wait. If Tim were to choose to come back, it was imperative he have friends outside the cave. He had to know others believed him capable of salvation. Otherwise, he might not believe it himself.

Boblin explained how Tim had become aware of his own darkness, how the man faltered when he came face to face with his reflection, but when Nazgar heard this, he only looked more worried. "His course is still unknown, then," the Kyrlod said softly.

"Better unknown than the wrong one!" Boblin protested.

Nazgar shook his head. "If I knew him to be an enemy, I would go into the caves and face him, and if he has redeemed himself, we could continue our quest. In either case, I would know what must be done next. Instead, I must deal with the unknowable." He turned toward Pellen Yuzhar. "What say you, old friend?"

Pellen glanced at the caves and gave a deep sigh. "Therein lies our best hope and our worst enemy," he said. "If we stay and he returns an enemy, we die. If we leave and he comes out as the Warrior, we forfeit his aid."

Boblin searched his mind for something, anything, to convince them to stay. He had to give the right explanation. Too much was at stake. Many refugees—Jend, Hugo, and Ken among them—looked north toward the pass exiting the Mountains. They had good cause for being afraid, because if Tim had embraced the darkness, he would kill them all when he returned. Seen in that light, it was better to find the Army of Kah'lash as soon as possible. They would need all the help they could get, to fight Zadinn Kanas *and* Tim Matthias.

But Boblin's gut told him to stay, and more important, he had *promised* to stay. He tried to think of something more to add to this, because he had nothing but a faint sense of honor and a glimmer of faith, and he didn't know if that was enough. "We need to stay," Boblin insisted.

"What makes you say this?" Nazgar asked.

Boblin looked at the Kyrlod. "Because he's my friend."

Of course it had to be Hedro Desh that spoke up. "That's not just cause," the elion said. "It isn't worth risking our lives."

The tension in the air snapped. Boblin rounded on Hedro, only barely restraining himself from taking out his sword. "I gave my word!" he said. "Does your life matter more to you than keeping an oath, Desh? You can leave the Mountains and mate with a three-legged goat for all I care, but I am waiting because I swore I would!"

"Kule!" Jend barked.

Boblin snapped to attention. *That was a fine display. Conduct very befitting a soldier. I'm an imbecile.*

"Learn your place!" the Commander said. The rebuke stung, but Boblin knew it was true. "This decision belongs to Pellen Yuzhar and the Kyrlod. Show some respect to your fellow soldier."

"I apologize," Boblin said, lowering his face. "I spoke without thinking." He still frothed on the inside, though. He wanted to pound Hedro's skull, but the fact that Jend was right only made the sentiment burn more.

"Nonetheless," Commander Jend finished, "an oath matters indeed. I appreciate and understand your sense of duty. If you must wait here to keep your word, I will stand by your side and help you to do so."

Nazgar nodded. "I still do not know what our best choice is. But if you are bound to stay, then I too will stay. Matthias will emerge as either our friend, or Uklith's newest advocate. If he comes out as the former, he will need us, and if he emerges as the latter, I will match my skills against his, to the death. But it might be best for the others to leave, to ensure their safety."

There was a long silence. Pellen sat, hands clasped and eyes closed. At last he looked up and met Nazgar's gaze. "No," the white-haired elion said. "If this is our fate, we will meet it as we always have. The Fort always stands behind its people. We stay."

"Aye," Hugo and Ken Rindar concurred.

Prince Ladu stepped forward. "I don't know this man," he said, "but there is good in all men. If there is a chance he can redeem himself, we cannot abandon him."

That was all it took. Not even Hedro would speak up—not when Pellen, Jend, and the Rindar twins agreed on this course of action. They were the Fort's most respected leaders, and the other elions would follow them to Malath if asked.

"Thank you," Boblin said softly. He turned to the mouth of the cave, which formed a hole against the backdrop of night. Somewhere inside that cavern, the future teetered on the point of a sword. It was out of their hands. And so the waiting began.

*   *   *

Tim Matthias sat alone. He could use the Lifesource to light his sword and illuminate his surroundings, but he was too afraid to touch the power. He wasn't sure he could trust himself with it. He still felt his fingers around Boblin's throat, squeezing the life out of his friend. In his mind, he again saw his reflection in Boblin's eyes. He had looked more like Zadinn Kanas than Tim Matthias. *How did I lose myself like that?* In the Mountains he thought he'd discovered the truth. It had seemed so simple. So *right.*

And yet, now that he thought about it, these past few days in the caves seemed a blurry haze, like he'd been in a stranger's body, walking through a fog that muffled his perception. There were periods of time he barely recalled, bits and fragments of the fever that wracked his body—mind delirious, all thoughts erased save for the single-minded drive to murder Zadinn Kanas.

Tim leaned against the wall and closed his eyes. The Lifesource waited inside of him, ready to spring forth its violent power. *The Lifesource is like a lake fed by two rivers,* Nazgar had said. *The first river flows from the Maker...but the second stems from the Demon Lord.*

Tim harbored no doubts as to which power lurked just around the corner, begging for him to take hold. He recalled the brief period of time, mere hours ago, when he could not even sense the magic, and wondered what it all meant. At the time, the perceived lack of the Lifesource's presence scared him, but now he thought such unawareness might feel like bliss. Today, perhaps, he feared the power and would not touch it, but how long would that sense of caution last? What if he returned to his previous state of mind, seized the Lifesource and went on a destructive rampage? He didn't think himself capable of such an atrocity, but *that* was the crux of the matter. The change had been slow and insidious. It wasn't like he was Tim Matthias one day and a servant of darkness the next—no, it didn't happen like that, because resisting such blatant impulses was easy.

The change had occurred subtly, one small step at a time, one slip in the wrong direction, as he descended into corruption. Tim didn't know if he could ever fully redeem himself, because the danger of corruption would always remain.

He had a few options. The first was the most drastic but perhaps the safest. He could take his sword and drive it into his own chest. He couldn't ever trust himself again, and by killing himself he could at least protect the world from the threat of what he *might* become. In a sense, though, that would be embracing the evil instead of rejecting it.

Another option was to stay in the caves, but that presented too many unknowns. *What if I turn back to the darkness? And what good am I to anyone—to the elions and to the North—if I hide away in the Mountains forever?*

Or he could leave and return to the elions, but what then? Would they take him back, knowing he'd assaulted Boblin? Would Nazgar still teach him? Would he ever be fit to face Zadinn Kanas? Would he *become* the next Zadinn Kanas? There were so many potential disasters, so many ways to lose everything.

Perhaps, though…perhaps…

Tim raised his head. The voice that spoke was from within, but it was not his own. It was that of his mother, Rosalie Matthias.

Emotion stirred within him. He hurried to stamp it out, as he'd taught himself to do, but then stopped and hesitated.

Perhaps what? he asked.

It wasn't really her. Rosalie was dead, and nothing would ever change that. But it *was* her essence, that which she had left behind, and she still guided him, as all mothers do. *Perhaps you aren't thinking about this the right way. Wherever you look, you see pitfalls. Whenever you have a choice to make, you see dangers. But how is that different from any other day? The attack at the Fort could have ended in disaster. When you faced the Hunter in the Korlan, it could have ended in disaster. But did you surrender at the Fort? No—you faced the enemy. Did you flee from the Hunter? No—you stood your ground.*

Could it be as simple as that? Tim didn't know. *I can kill myself and save Zadinn the trouble. I can stay here and let the elions march to their deaths unaided. Or I can leave this place and find my friends.*

Hope swelled within his chest. He felt something heavy and oppressive lift from him and pull back, a malevolent cloud that had hung about his mind— one he had welcomed in at first but now turned away. *I can face the evil inside, just as I faced the evil from without. Will I win? That cannot be said.*

But better than rotting away in this cursed place.

Tim stood up, letting a sensation of light and happiness flow through him uninhibited, refusing to suppress it. He allowed himself to *hope*, to *feel*. Such gifts made him human, and yes, he had his flaws, but flaws were not to be turned away. They were to be embraced, because they were *life*.

Tim walked forward, passing through the tunnel toward the surface, and opened his mouth to breathe in the fresh air, welcoming it as a part of the world. It might take time. The road might get harder. But if greater terrors lay in front of him—and surely some did—he would simply take them as they came.

When he first began making this journey upward, only a few hours ago, he'd declared himself a different man, and this still held true—a changed Tim

Matthias was indeed returning to the surface, but not the Tim of the dark caverns. This change was for the better. The man now returning was one who had seen the worst and made the best choice—to leave it behind.

* * *

Tim approached the end of Malath's Teeth in silence. He had carefully followed Boblin's trail through the maze of stalactites and stalagmites, and now only a short expanse of empty floor remained between him and the cave's opening. He could see the nighttime sky outside the cavern and felt the welcome bite of the cold snow. As he walked, he saw none of the still-living sarchons that had assaulted Boblin and the others. The creatures were there, watching from the dark, but they recognized the one who had slain their queen and chose to keep their distance.

Tim remained apprehensive about returning to the elion camp. He did not know what sort of welcome, if any, waited for him there. But he'd made his choice to move forward, and he wasn't turning back now. Besides, this last stage of his journey refreshed him; with every step toward the outer world, he shed a bit more of the shadow that had tainted him, leaving it in the very caves where it had spawned.

Except that his corruption *hadn't* started in the caves, had it? It had started long before that, when Timothy Matthias watched his mother and father die in the Kaltu Pass. The Mountains had merely nurtured the evil, bringing it to fruition. Every person had the capacity for evil, Tim supposed. The only difference was whether or not it had cause to rise—and, more significant, if the person was strong enough to resist the temptation. Because everybody also possessed an equal capacity for good.

The darkness would never fully leave. Not all scars healed, but that was not a bad thing, either. It served as a reminder, a warning. When Tim took his first step outside, from stone cavern to snow-swept slope, gladness overwhelmed him. He knelt on the snow's icy crust and looked up at the sky. He took a deep breath, letting the free air sear his lungs with its cold touch. The night air had a jagged edge, the bite of life, of reality. He looked around but did not see any comrades. What had he truly expected, though? He'd almost killed Boblin Kule; he had only gotten what he'd deserved. It was okay. He'd bear this burden alone.

He'd do his best to defeat Zadinn and return the land to its people. When this was finished, he would find the elions from the Fort and let them know of his remorse. They need not welcome him back, but it was his duty to admit his fault. He tried to ascertain which direction was north. He had the Army of Kah'lash to find, and he might as well get on with it.

Then he saw a group of shapes on the snow. His breath caught in his chest, and he looked closer. The elion refugees stood on the slope in front of a steep peak, a ring of tents surrounding the camp's perimeter. Tim smiled. Perhaps, if the Maker was kind, he would *not* have to do this alone. Perhaps he would have good friends to stand by his side.

A lone elion stood away from the edge of the group, closer to Tim than the rest. As Tim approached, the guard looked up and their eyes met. Boblin Kule's body visibly stiffened. It was on Tim now. He raised his hand in greeting, and after a moment, Boblin raised his in response.

"I was wrong," Tim said.

Boblin reached out his hand. "All that matters is that you are here," he replied. "The past stays in the past." Tim clasped Boblin's hand, and they embraced.

"You missed most of the fun," Boblin said. "All the hard work is done."

"I *let* you do the hard work," Tim joked. "I wouldn't want you to feel inadequate."

The other elions caught sight of Tim, and few bothered to conceal their shock. Many hadn't expected him to return. He and Boblin walked to the campfire in the center of the ring of tents, where Nazgar of the Kyrlod stood. The orange flames outlined his cloaked figure as he looked at Tim with an expressionless face. Nazgar gave him a slow nod, and when Tim came closer, the muscles in Nazgar's jaw pulled tight.

"I need your help," Tim said to his mentor.

Nazgar's face still betrayed little expression, but the muscles relaxed visibly. The apprehension had faded, vaporized on the night air. "I'm glad you have returned to us, my friend."

"I'm glad, too." Tim felt even better than he had when leaving the caves. Tonight, all would be well. Tonight, he was among friends.

Thirty-Five

The next morning, the survivors prepared to depart from the Mountains. They broke camp without speaking, the horrors of Malath's Teeth still fresh in their minds. By now, they were down to half their initial number that had fled from the Fort mere weeks ago. Nazgar had spoken the truth—few survived these heights. Early in the day, Hugo and Ken reported that they found a place to begin their eventual descent. Today's journey would be easy, and there was no doubt they had earned it.

The refugees rounded a curve in the peaks and saw the vast expanse of uncharted northern wilderness stretching across the horizon. A thick mass of evergreen treetops covered the land as far as the eye could see. Occasional breaks in the tree line revealed groups of lakes dotting the landscape. These lakes varied in size from very small to enormous, and when the sunlight struck the waters of each surface, the aqua hues glittered with myriad colors. Stone boulders and rolling foothills covered the wilderness.

The scenery had an untouched, pristine feel, similar to but different from that of the Fertile Lands. The Lands were majestic in their own right, but did not compare to this untamed, primeval wilderness. In many ways the Fertile Lands reminded Tim of the South—warm, thriving, even humid at times—but this was the true North, the North as it should have been. The air was crisp and scathing, but not in the manner of Zadinn's wastelands. Here, the breeze's cutting edge felt good. Here, a man could pit himself against the deep snows of winter and relax in the cool afternoons of summer.

Tim was not the only one struck by the serenity of this uncharted wild. All the elions looked in awe at the sight, every one secretly wondering what it would be like to stay here, to drop his or her duties and build a new home. The Mountains would stand between them and the Dark Lord. But too much rested on their shoulders. Behind them, their loved ones lay dead within Malath's Teeth. Farther back, friends and family languished in the Pit. And farthest back yet, their comrade's bodies lay in the ruins of the Fort of Pellen, the only home they had known during these long years of oppression.

The peace and solitude here could only be temporary. They could not have their friends die in vain, and they could not abandon the captured ones to a life of torment and slavery. Their descent took the rest of the morning as their path wound among the peaks. By early afternoon their trail gradually thinned to a narrow ledge of perhaps twenty feet, taking a more direct course toward the ground.

"I hate this," Boblin said to Tim as they walked. "The last time I was this close to the edge, I was a mile in the air, hanging by one hand."

"A mile?" Tim asked.

"Maybe more," Boblin said.

"Why are you complaining, then?" Tim asked. He smiled. "We aren't even *half* that height right now."

"You're a sarcastic piece, do you know that?"

"My pleasure," Tim grinned. It felt good to joke again.

The ground evened out so gradually and imperceptibly that they barely noticed it by the time they reached the wilderness floor. Down here, the pine trees that had seemed so small from above filled the air with the scent of their needles. In the sky, the sun had moved into late afternoon. Now, at last, Tim felt comfortable. This place did not have the humidity of the Fertile Lands or the North's harsh winds or the cold snow of the Mountains. This was simply a summer afternoon—nothing more and nothing less.

When they finally reached the base of the Mountains, Tim and the rest quickly realized nobody had any idea where to go next. They'd given so much thought to crossing the Mountains that they barely thought about what to do when they reached the far side. It wasn't like the Army of Kah'lash was sitting right in front of them, lined up and waiting to march.

"Do you know where the Army is?" Tim asked Nazgar.

"No," the Kyrlod answered. "I suggest we travel toward water. The Army numbers over ten thousand, and they may depend on lakes to survive."

"How much do you know about the Army?" Tim asked.

"I only know that they wait," Nazgar said. "Nothing more."

The company headed due north toward a large lake they had spotted from above. As always, scouts traveled ahead to gain bearings and find new routes. No one complained as the day passed without incident. After their experiences with the Korlan, the vrawl, and the sarchons, the elions had little desire for any more excitement. Even more fortuitously, fresh game lived in these woods, and the refugees were able to enjoy their first satisfying meal in a long while.

After dinner Tim knew he could not put off the inevitable. It was time to speak with Nazgar. He hadn't touched the Lifesource all day; until he understood what had happened in the caves and knew he could trust himself, he was not using the power. He found the Kyrlod standing beside his tent, facing south toward the Mountains. Tim realized how profound this change in direction was. Few had ever looked *south* to the Mountains. Before today, the peaks had always waited to the north, but now they stood to the south—not a trial to overcome, but a thing of the past.

Tim stood next to the old man. Nazgar glanced at him, but said nothing and turned back to look at the range. Tim felt an urge to speak, but quelled it and let the silence stretch. Tonight he was going to turn things upside down by letting Nazgar be the first to break the endless silence. It went on for some time, and on several occasions Tim almost opened his mouth, but always schooled himself back to discipline. As the minutes slid by, he relaxed. *We have all the time in the world. Why rush things now?*

The silence lasted for nearly half an hour before Nazgar spoke. "I did not know what to expect on this side of the range."

"This place has a distinct feel," Tim replied, "but I like it even more so than the Fertile Lands. In a way the Fertile Lands were as unnatural as the rest of the Northern wastes. But this place—it's real."

Nazgar did not reply and again the time passed. After a while, Nazgar gave Tim a sidelong glance, but Tim returned the look without breaking composure. Nazgar made an appreciative noise. "You *have* changed."

"For better or for worse?" Tim asked.

"What do you know of change?" Nazgar asked in response.

Tim shrugged. "It happens."

"Some change is good," Nazgar prompted.

"But other kinds of change can be bad."

"Sometimes, it is neither good nor bad," Nazgar said. "It is just different."

"Sometimes," Tim said, "all three kinds of change happen at once."

Nazgar nodded. "One does not watch his parents die without suffering."

"Do you suppose Zadinn watched his parents die?" Tim asked.

"Actually, he killed them," Nazgar said.

"Why did he do those things?"

Nazgar turned to look at him. "I think you know."

"That's what scares me." Tim looked away. Zadinn didn't bother himself with questions of morality. He did as he pleased.

"You *should* be scared."

"What's the difference between right and wrong?" Tim asked.

Nazgar gave him yet another one of his stares. "Every man knows the difference between right and wrong."

"Zadinn believes his ways are right," Tim said.

"Does that *make* him right?" Nazgar asked.

"No," Tim said.

"Still scared?" Nazgar asked.

"Yes."

Nazgar turned to the woods. "Then walk with me, friend." The two left the encampment. In the Mountains or wastes, they would have been afraid to leave the firelight behind, but it was no problem in these woods. This land might be untamed, but that was what made it safe.

"Why are you scared, Tim?" Nazgar asked.

"I don't want to become the next Zadinn Kanas. You warned me about this after the vrawl attacked. You didn't use those exact words, but you told me I shouldn't always resort to force to ensure victory. Boblin mentioned it too—about keeping my humanity and how it's a way of fighting back. I pretended to listen, but I didn't. I was too focused on the enemy, on Zadinn. I thought I was only doing what was necessary—surviving."

Nazgar looked at him. "What do you think of this?"

"I can't lose who I am," Tim said. "That's what I think. I became someone else in those caves. I thought emotions were a sign of weakness, and I didn't think I could afford to be weak. But they aren't a weakness. They make me human. I lost who I was, but that's not what really scares me. What scares me is that I didn't realize it, not for some time. But then I met Boblin in Malath's Teeth—"

"I know," Nazgar said.

Tim swallowed. "Did he tell you what happened?"

"I did not ask him."

"I almost killed him," Tim said. "I had convinced myself he was Zadinn's servant. And the way I used the Lifesource—it was different."

"Did you enjoy it?" Nazgar asked. "The Lifesource? The violence?"

Tim paused before answering. "I didn't enjoy it *or* hate it. That's my point— I'd cut off all means of caring. After the fight with the vrawl, you warned me about apathy, but that is exactly what I embraced in the caves. If I had looked back and said, 'regrettable but necessary,' maybe I'm not Zadinn, but I'm still headed in the same direction."

"So we return to the same place we were after the vrawl attack," Nazgar said. "Of course, there remains room for confusion. Zadinn does things he believes are regrettable but necessary, and yet I've also done things I believe were regrettable but necessary. But I'm not Zadinn, and I don't foresee becoming him."

Tim allowed himself a wry smile. "I made the mistake of thinking you could make things clearer."

"My friend, you will never have a clear answer to these questions—no man will. While there is an established difference between right and wrong, good and evil, there is no set of rules for choosing between the two. You cannot consult a rule book every time a choice must be made. Every decision is based on many combinations of circumstances neither you nor I can foresee. You must choose and accept the consequences. That is the only guidance I can provide."

Tim swallowed. It was far from comforting, but it also made an odd sort of sense. "I wish it was easier."

"If it was easy, life wouldn't be so much fun," Nazgar said.

"The Lifesource left me, you know," Tim said. "Then it came back, but it felt different. You once told me it was a lake fed by two rivers—one from Harmea, and the other from Malath. I think I used the other river."

"I don't wish to confuse you more," Nazgar said, "but I *did* oversimplify when I compared the Lifesource to two rivers. In the end, the Lifesource is a *tool,* used to serve many ends, and from today until the end of time, men will blame their actions on their tools. The rivers I spoke of do not exist within the Lifesource." Nazgar tapped Tim's chest. "They exist in *here.*"

"This power felt different, though," Tim said. "It felt...wrong."

"What color were the flames?" Nazgar asked.

"Black."

"It was a warning. The Lifesource was telling you that you had changed."

"Am I still changed?" Tim asked.

Nazgar shook his head. "Don't you see, Tim? It is *your* choice. Do you want to be the man you were in the caves?"

"No," Tim said.

"Then don't be! Be with friends. Smile when the sun rises. Stay true. When you are not sure what is right and what is wrong—choose, and accept what comes afterward." Nazgar paused. "You will not always make the best decision. Mistakes are, after all, *also* part of what it means to be human. That is okay, too."

Tim felt something loosen in his chest. It was not just devastatingly complex—it was also incredibly simple. "The Lifesource?"

"Merely a tool, my friend," Nazgar said softly, "nothing more."

Tim breathed in the night air, lifted his hands, tilted his head back, and let the power flow into him. It felt as beautiful as ever. The darkness was not there. It had *never* been there. It was only a mirror reflecting his own heart.

Tim laughed. For a moment he felt as free as when he'd lived in the South. Of course, he was *not* the same man he'd been there. He was not a better man or a worse man…he was just a different man, and that was the way of things.

* * *

Boblin entered his tent, tired and ready for sleep. As he arranged his bedroll on his cot, Hedro stepped into the tent beside him. "We need to talk," Hedro said, making his superior size quite apparent, arms flexed ever so slightly in an intimidating posture. "You seem to be mistaken about something, Kule, and her name is Celia Alcion."

Boblin drew himself up to his full height. "About what am I mistaken?" he asked, voice low.

"I saw you in the caves," Hedro said. "I saw you in the Korlan, and I see the way you look at her. So let's be clear about something. She doesn't belong to you, and I suggest you leave it at that."

Boblin narrowed his eyes. "That's not how it works, Desh. She doesn't *belong* to anyone, you included."

Hedro moved incredibly fast, sweeping Boblin's leg out from under him and dropping him. As Boblin felt the wind rush out of him, Hedro pinned his arms so he could not fight back. "Yes, she does," Hedro said. He twisted Boblin's wrist counterclockwise. "Understand?"

"Go to Malath," Boblin shot back, grimacing to prevent tears. Hedro twisted harder, and Boblin bucked his hips upward to knock the bigger elion off balance. Boblin turned to the side, rolling away from Hedro, and rose to his feet with arms held in a defensive stance.

The tent's cramped interior left neither elion much room for maneuvering. Hedro feinted right, then jerked left and tackled Boblin around his midsection, bringing them both crashing down once more. Hedro leaned into Boblin's windpipe with his forearm, so Boblin was able to breathe in only the barest gasp of air. "Give it up," Hedro said.

"No," Boblin replied.

"Why are you so karfing stubborn, Kule?"

"Why did you hit Triste?"

Hedro froze, anger flaring in his eyes. He grasped Boblin's tunic with both hands, rising back into a standing position and raising Boblin into the air. He slammed Boblin down onto his cot and Boblin's head struck the iron side of the frame, vision flashing. "None of your karfing business. We're done here." He released Boblin and backed away. "Watch yourself, Kule."

Boblin said nothing. Hedro ducked out of the tent and let the flap fall shut behind him. Boblin raised a hand to his neck and winced at the resulting sensation.

So this was it, then. What had gone unsaid for so long was finally out in the open. Celia and Triste—one he loved, one he had let down—and Hedro Desh. Boblin arranged his bedroll in silence, climbing beneath the covers and lying on his back. He stared at the ceiling, mind a whirlwind. Thoughts of frustration, of regret, of things left undone, of matters unsettled, of sentiments unvoiced, all jumbled through his mind.

He told himself to get over it, that it had just been a scuffle. *Hedro was itching for a fight, so I gave him one. Leave it at that and move on—we have a war to fight.* The sounds of night washed over him, and he fell asleep, troubled by the past, frustrated by the present, and uncertain of the future.

Thirty-Six

At noon the following day, the scouts reported that the group should reach the lake by nightfall. They also reported smoke on the western edge of the water. This news created visible excitement within the company. Smoke meant other people. *The Army of Kah'lash.*

The elions proceeded with caution. Strangers in this land were obviously uncommon, and not even Nazgar knew how the Army would react to their arrival. Jend sent Boblin with Hugo, Ken, and Hedro to continue scouting, ordering them to get as close to the smoke as possible.

Unburdened by the rest of the group, the four elions moved quickly and silently through the forest. Not even the animals noted their passing. This, Boblin knew, was what it meant to be in the Frontier Patrol—to be unseen and unheard. It was the way of the Fort, and they knew it well. Ken took them through a stand of thick trees inside a deep gully before traveling to the top of a ridge, where they had a view down to the nearest lake. The waters stood less than a mile away, and a blank stretch of sandy shoreline covered its western edge. Canvas tents covered the beach, and smoke from several campfires wisped into the air.

The scene mystified Boblin. Why would any civilization on this side of the mountains resort to tenting as a way of life? *Well, what did I expect? A gilded city in the clouds? A general astride a dragon?* Of course, maybe the people on the shoreline weren't the Army of Kah'lash. They could be anybody. Perhaps it was a vacation home for the malichons—after all, what did Zadinn's malichons do all year in the Deathlands? Sit and brood? It had to get awful tiresome. *If I were a malichon, I'd want a nice place to stay in the summertime, and it might as well be near a lake, given the fact that I would always smell like a rotting ju-fish.*

With Ken in the lead, the group took a path down the ridge, using a line of trees to conceal their approach. After reaching the forest floor, they continued north. Looking around, Boblin noticed something. On the south side of the ridge, they'd seen a regular assortment of wildlife, but here on the north side, animals were conspicuously absent. Boblin hesitated uncomfortably. He'd feel much better if there were even a small sign of life, but the woods remained still and silent. This wasn't necessarily a sign of danger, but it *did* mean they were no longer alone.

Without speaking, Boblin touched Hugo's shoulder and raised a finger to his lips. The other two scouts also halted. "What is it?" Ken asked.

"There's somebody else out here," Boblin replied. "The animals are all gone."

Ken looked around and nodded. Hedro put a hand on his sword.

"Please remain still," a new voice said. A big man stepped out from behind a blueleaf tree. He wore two swords crossed behind his back and a large knife in his belt. Hedro tightened his hand around his sword, but when Ken gave him a sharp look, he lessened his hold.

"Greetings," Hugo replied.

The big man laughed. "You're a bold sort, aren't you? You come clear down the other side of the Mountains and then march straight through the woods without even looking around first. I'd think the vrawl and sarchons might have taught you more caution."

"After a sarchon pack, one man in the woods isn't something we're all that concerned about," Hedro said.

"Easy, Desh," Ken said. "There's no need for bravado."

"Are you the leader here?" the man asked Ken.

"That would be me," Hugo said, stepping forward.

The man sharpened his eyes. Differentiating between twins was not easy. Boblin could almost see him wondering if this was a trick—one officer posing as another. "Very well," the stranger finally said. "Might I ask your names?"

Hugo nodded. "I am Hugo Rindar, and this is my brother Ken, along with our comrades, Boblin Kule and Hedro Desh. May I ask who you are?"

"I am Gendar Halion," the man said. "Forgive me, but I must ask you to relinquish your weapons."

"To whom are we relinquishing them?" Hugo insisted.

The stranger lifted his arms, and the forest stirred as a dozen other men materialized from the trees. Each wore light clothing, but all were well armed. The twelve men encircled the small company. They did not make any threatening gestures, but there was no need; this was a sheer display of both force and skill. The members of the Frontier Patrol might be excellent scouts, but even so, a party three times their number had caught them completely unaware.

"I am Captain Halion of Division Five in the Army of Kah'lash," Gendar said. "These are my men. We wish you no harm, only to know who you are and what business you have in these lands."

"We will surrender our weapons," Hugo said. "We too mean no harm, but I do not have the authority to tell you our business. If you allow me, I will gladly bring you back to our company. Our leader would be more than willing to speak with you."

"Take me to him," Gendar replied. The elions handed their weapons to the men of Division Five and turned back south. Two men stayed up front with Gendar, and the rest vanished into the trees. Every so often, Boblin caught a glimpse of one moving through the surrounding undergrowth, but shadows were easier to follow than these men.

They had found the Army of Kah'lash, but Boblin hoped they numbered more than twelve.

* * *

The company stopped to rest in a clearing. Tim lay down atop a rock, letting the warm sun play over his face. Within minutes, a comforting drowsiness stole over him, and he hung on the cusp of what was probably his first relaxed sleep in weeks.

The returning scouts, however, broke the silence as they stepped into the clearing. Tim opened his eyes and sat up. A stranger had returned with the elions. The newcomer was uncharacteristically large; he wore two swords across his back, and Tim didn't doubt he could wield one in each hand.

Hugo saluted Jend. "Sir, this man came upon us in the woods. This is Captain Gendar Halion of the Army of Kah'lash." A silence settled over the company, and Tim looked toward Nazgar, but the Kyrlod's face betrayed no emotion. This turn of events didn't necessarily surprise Tim either; the lands north of the Mountains belonged to the Army, and it was doubtful any *but* the Army lived here. However, it did feel unnaturally sudden.

"Well met, Captain Halion," Jend said. "I am Commander Jend Argul of the Frontier Patrol."

"Do you lead these elions?" Captain Halion asked.

"I command the Patrol," Jend replied, "but I am not our leader."

"I must speak with him," Gendar said. "I don't wish for bloodshed, but you are trespassing on our lands. I would like to know how you came to be here and what your business is."

A cluster of more well armed men appeared from the woods. Several elions tensed, putting hands on their weapons.

"Enough," Pellen said sternly, raising a hand. "This is blatant foolishness. We have nothing to fear from one another. Captain Halion, we come seeking the Army's aid. I am Pellen Yuzhar, leader of the Fort of Pellen. We come from the southern side of the Mountains. We've crossed many leagues in search of Those Who Wait, and I wish to present our case before your leader."

Gendar and his men relaxed, and the refugees followed suit. "I will escort you to our camp, then," Gendar said. "You should know, however, that we do not lightly grant requests for assistance. You must first prove your case is worthy."

"I understand," Pellen replied. "Observe, though, that we have crossed the Mountains and lived. Is that not evidence of our worthiness?"

"Crossing the Mountains was the easy part, my friend," Gendar replied. "Others have done it before you. All things change with time."

Nazgar stroked his beard but said nothing. An uncomfortable silence hung over the company as the elions prepared to depart. Neither group felt threatened by the other, but they were different folk from different worlds. The Army did not know who these outsiders were, and the elions did not know what to expect from Those Who Wait. Nazgar had ascertained the Army's sole purpose was to serve those in need, but apparently the Army had the liberty to determine what constituted worthiness. The people of Kah'lash knew nothing about Zadinn Kanas. Like Nazgar, they existed outside of time, and the refugees' two-hundred-year struggle might be nothing to them.

Tim brushed the hilt of his sword with one hand. He'd forced himself to begin practicing again. He couldn't fear the Lifesource, and he couldn't fear himself. As Nazgar said, men were bound to make mistakes. All he could do was learn from them and refuse to repeat them. In some ways, fighting the corruption in his heart was easy. He just had to deny it. When he felt it begin to grow—and it still did—he turned it aside. Sometimes, he burned through his rage by exercising vigorously. Other times, he deflected it by joining friends and giving in to laughter. He kept a little bit inside, just a sliver, a sharp edge to give him focus and determination.

The power no longer felt corrupted, though. The Lifesource was a reflection of his soul, and for the first time in a while Tim didn't mind what it showed him. *All it took was a smile and a laugh.*

He hoped Daniel would be proud. Regardless of his inner peace, the pain of loss still hurt. Everything tied back to that one night in the Kaltu Pass. If Daniel and Rosalie hadn't died in front of him, the darkness might have never surfaced. It was strange to think such things could be born from love, but in the end, love also quenched those same dark thoughts all over again.

Tim wished his parents were here. The world north of the Mountains was the kind of place Daniel and Rosalie had looked for all their life. The Matthias family could have built a home here, in an isolated corner of the world, while time passed by around them. At the same time, though, abandoning their duties would have subjected the people of the North to lives of pain, and a man couldn't turn the other way when another was in need.

As the day wore on, the mood lightened, and the icy atmosphere hanging over the other soldiers broke away. "When did you learn of our presence?" Jend asked Captain Halion.

Gendar shrugged his shoulders. "We've been following you for the last few days. We found your trail a league north of the Mountains."

Jend faltered. "You've been tracking us ever since we've arrived." He shook his head. "I need to have words with my scouts."

"You're noisy," Gendar replied.

Tim missed a step. *Noisy?* An elion could be quieter than a ghost, from what he'd seen.

"It is not enough to blend into the background," Gendar continued. "You must become a part of it."

"I appreciate your courtesy in speaking to us first rather than resorting to force," Jend said.

"If you don't know a stranger's intentions, there is no need to use force," Gendar said, "not right away."

"You allowed my scouts to bring you into our camp," Jend said. "It could have been a trap."

Gendar laughed. "I saw no cause for concern."

"We do outnumber you by a fair margin," Jend pointed out.

Gendar shrugged. "I still wasn't worried."

Tim looked at the men from Division Five. Without a doubt, every last elion in the Fort of Pellen was a fierce fighter, but the Army of Kah'lash was another breed entirely. If it had come to an open skirmish between the groups, Gendar's men would have slaughtered the elions. Tim was sure of it. *If these men join our side, we might have a chance against the malichon hordes.*

Late in the afternoon, they arrived at the Army's camp. It was an unusual sight. The Army's accommodations were sparse, to say the least. Rows of tents lined the shore for miles, creating thousands of triangular mounds, all arranged in neat, tight formations. Smoke rose from hundreds of fires. Tim wasn't sure if he'd expected a city or a fortress, but he definitely didn't think to find a *camp*.

A troop of sentinels stood guard on the encampment's southern border. Like the men of Division Five, the sentinels' appearance spoke more of skill than of brute force. The Army was not built of heavily armored knights on horseback. They were men in leather jerkins, carrying sturdy swords. This, though, gave Tim more confidence in their skills. Gilded knights would have been too extravagant, all show and nothing else. Besides, throwing a mighty force against the Dark Lord was not a path to victory. They had to win by being smarter and deadlier, not bigger and heavier.

Upon reaching the sentries, Gendar ordered them to stand down, and the guards parted so that the company could pass unhindered. They even allowed the elions to keep their weapons, and a small detachment of sentinels remained with the refugees, escorting them into the heart of the camp. They walked past rows of tents with soldiers clustered around fires, some cooking, others conversing, and several playing chess.

Many stopped to watch as the elions passed. Though the presence of newcomers in the camp was doubtless a surprising occurrence, the Army did a good job of suppressing emotion. Strangers might be unusual, true, but these men didn't let an unannounced visit throw them off balance. Tim could see it in their eyes—they hadn't expected this, but that was no reason to get excited. They were trained to take change in stride, adapt to it, and deliberately decide upon a response.

"You will have lodging for the evening," Gendar said. "The Council will wait until tomorrow morning to hear from you."

"We appreciate your hospitality," Pellen replied. "I know you aren't accustomed to outsiders, but you show us great respect."

"You've shown us the same," Gendar said. "It's only right to return the favor."

The Captain led them to a cluster of tents. The fires were lit, and each man had a ready-made bedroll. Tim smiled. He'd been setting up and breaking camp every morning and evening for the last month. It was pleasing to have the work done for him.

"Have you and your people always lived here?" Pellen asked.

"We've only been here for a short time," Gendar said. "A fortnight ago, the Council ordered us to leave our city and make camp on this shore."

"Do you know why?" Pellen asked.

Gendar shook his head. "No."

"Where is your city?" Jend asked.

"I can't tell you that."

"Forgive me," Jend said. "I didn't mean to intrude."

"You didn't," Gendar replied.

Tim looked at Nazgar. The Kyrlod was looking at Gendar the way a scholar might look at an ancient book written in an unfamiliar language. The Kyrlod had at last found something he didn't fully understand, and it intrigued him. *He should feel right at home here, trapped in a sea of ambiguous answers and mannerisms.*

Gendar left them, and soon a group of soldiers brought food to the refugees. It was a healthy meal of meat and potatoes, and though Tim didn't know what sort of animal the roast came from, it tasted fresh and well-seasoned. The company gratefully accepted the food; after everything else, it was nice to spend an evening setting their cares aside. The Army established sentries around their camp—as much for the elions' protection as to keep an eye on them—but even that was not bothersome. The Army's caution was understandable, and the elions had no intention of provoking them.

After dinner, Nazgar and Pellen approached Tim. "Gendar has asked us who will go before the Council tomorrow morning," Pellen said. "Nazgar will come with me. Are you willing to join us?"

"Of course," Tim replied.

"We don't know what we're dealing with," Nazgar said. "Even I do not know what rules govern these people. Your presence is a gamble. It might sway them to our cause, but it could also turn them against as."

"The Army is dangerous," Pellen said. "We already know that. They've shown us hospitality, but they don't know who we are. When they *do* learn, it might change things."

"I considered hiding you," Nazgar said, "but they will find out who you are, one way or another. It's better to remain honest."

"I don't think the Army is going to hurt us," Tim said.

"Neither do I," Nazgar replied, "but remember we're at a point where the rules are unclear. It was simple in the North—us against Zadinn. The Army, though, has no claim to either side. We can't predict their behavior."

"Do you see any shadows? Fragments of the Army's future?" Tim asked.

Nazgar shook his head. "No, and that is the single most unusual thing I've encountered in this camp. Strong-willed people possess hazier futures than others, but even with such men, I still see something, if just a mist. With the Army, though, I see *nothing*. I've never experienced this before."

"Well, at least things will be interesting," Tim noted.

Pellen chuckled and patted Tim on the shoulder. "You'd have done a fine job leading the Fort through two centuries, my son. You already know how to take things as they come. All we can do is act on the information we have."

"Two centuries is a long time, sir," Tim said dryly.

"I won't argue that." Pellen said, touching his snowy beard. "But it does give a man most excellent facial hair."

Behind him, Gendar approached the fire. "Captain Halion," Pellen said. "I've decided who will come before the Council tomorrow. I would like you to meet Nazgar of the Kyrlod and Tim Matthias."

For once, Gendar *was* visibly ruffled. His eyes widened, and his mouth worked open and shut. After a moment, he gave over to a hearty laugh. "A Kyrlod? By the Maker, you *are* an interesting company." He turned on his heel and walked away, shaking his head, and Nazgar and Pellen exchanged a look.

"That was well done," Nazgar said.

"You have my thanks," Pellen said. "After all, if we have one of the Kyrlod with us, who knows what else we have?"

"Aye," Gendar called back to them. "Who are you going to throw at us next—the Warrior of Light?" He boomed in laughter again.

"Anything's possible," Tim said quietly. *Tomorrow will be interesting.*

* * *

Tim rose before dawn. The morning air felt surprisingly refreshing. When he stepped outside, he saw a faint mist hanging over the shores of the lake. Summer was drawing to a close, and autumn was on the way. He walked to the fire, where Jend stoked embers. The Commander saluted, and Tim returned the gesture.

"This is it, friend," Jend said. "We made it across the Mountains. Now it's time to make it mean something."

"What do you think of these people?" Tim asked. "Can they do it?"

"The Army?" Jend said. "Aye, they'll do the trick. These men are deadly. They don't show it off—they carry themselves lightly—but they're a force to be reckoned with. We outnumbered Gendar's men by three to one, but if it had come to a fight in the woods, all of us would have died…except for you, maybe."

Jend didn't mean anything by his last sentence, but it turned Tim's heart cold. Every elion here knew what he'd done to the vrawl. Did they still expect him to behave like that? *Well, why wouldn't they? I haven't given them any reason to believe otherwise.* They probably didn't understand what it meant. They couldn't. They hadn't struggled with the darkness. Tim breathed in deeply. *Remember what Nazgar said. All men make mistakes. Just don't repeat them. I don't have to be that person. It's my choice.*

"You're a fine leader, Tim," Jend said, cutting into his thoughts.

"I don't recall leading anybody," Tim replied.

Jend laughed. "Why do you think we're here? *You* brought us to this place."

"This was Nazgar's idea," Tim pointed out.

"He said we should cross the Mountains, but we followed you," Jend said. "We had lost everything, and you gave us something to hold onto. Without that, we'd still be in the Fertile Lands."

"What about you?" Tim asked. "I think they followed you as well."

"I'd deny that, just like you did, but that's what makes the difference." Jend pointed south. "Zadinn Kanas proclaims himself a leader, and he is one—he's ruled for over two centuries. So what is the difference between us? Zadinn thrust himself into the position, took it as if it were his right. You, me, Pellen Yuzhar—we didn't ask for it, we didn't place ourselves over others. No, *they* decided to follow *us*, and we just accepted the responsibility."

"So what do you do when the choices get hard?" Tim asked.

"I choose, and see what happens. Sometimes your only choices seem like bad ones, but that doesn't take the responsibility away. When the consequences of my decisions arrive, good or bad, I accept them. It's the only way to keep my sanity."

It was the same thing Nazgar had said. *There's something to all of this, after all,* Tim decided.

Eventually Nazgar and Pellen arrived, and the four ate a morning meal by the fire. At daybreak, Gendar showed with the summons, leading them away from the camp into the woods. Tim stayed in the back, letting the older two lead, but they did not travel far before coming to a cottage. Two sentinels stood guard at the front door, each holding a spear. As Gendar approached, they stepped away from the entrance.

Gender entered first. "The visitors from the North have arrived," he said.

"You are dismissed, Captain Halion," a voice replied. Gendar ducked away, allowing the other three to pass into the cottage. He shut the door behind them.

The interior of the cottage was long and narrow, with a wide platform at the far end of the hall. A man in a white robe sat in a tall chair atop the platform, four women in chairs to his right and four men to his left. When Pellen, Nazgar, and Tim entered, all members of the Council stood up. Pellen bowed, and Tim and Nazgar did the same.

The man in the center spoke. "I am Falverion, First Speaker of the Council for the Army of Kah'lash. Tell us how you came to be in these lands."

"I am Pellen Yuzhar. We come from the Northland, where we have long suffered under Zadinn Kanas. We crossed the Mountains hoping to gain your aid."

"You did not answer the question," Falverion said. "The Mountains kill nearly all who try to cross them, and while the fact that they did not kill you is worthy of note, it is not enough to gain our assistance. Our mandate is to wait, not to serve."

"Nazgar of the Kyrlod guided us," Pellen said, gesturing to the prophet. "He stands here with me. We do not know your customs or rules, but as we speak, the Dark Lord persecutes those we left behind. What must we do to earn your assistance?"

"You may not like the cost," Falverion replied. "The Kyrlod made us who we are today. Not this Kyrlod here, but one of his brothers. Nazgar knows, as I know, that no Kyrlod is allowed to serve as a talisman. I know the Mountains, Pellen Yuzhar, and I know their rules. So I repeat, how did you cross the Mountains? Where is your talisman?"

A sudden impulse seized Tim. He briefly felt like he'd moved outside his body. Rather than partaking in what followed, he was just an observer. He stepped forward and pulled his sword from its sheath in a rasp of metal. Green fire consumed the blade as Tim pointed it toward the First Speaker.

"I am the Warrior of Light," he said. "I am the talisman, and I kept these people safe when they crossed the Northern Mountains. It is my duty to face Zadinn Kanas. You knew this day would come, as I have also known. It is time to stop waiting and time to perform your duty."

Falverion looked at him, face expressionless. Then he turned and looked at his comrades.

"It is him," one of the women said. "He is right, Speaker."

"The time is here, Speaker," one of the men said.

"It is him," Falverion concurred. In one smooth movement, all nine Council members knelt. "I speak for the Council," Falverion said. "We will aid you."

Tim felt awkward. He didn't know what had driven him to say those things or act that way, but it had worked. Pellen and Nazgar both looked at him with new respect. "Well done, my friend," Nazgar said. "Did you know all along?"

"Know what?" Tim asked.

"The Army is sworn to follow the Warrior. He is given leave to call them forth, and they will do as he says."

"No," Tim said, "you told me you didn't know how the Army would respond."

"I didn't at the time," Nazgar said, "but I know now." He pointed toward the wall behind Tim. "One of your shadows just told me is all."

Try as he might, Tim felt sure he would never, *ever* understand the Kyrlod.

Thirty-Seven

Even though preparations to leave began almost immediately, the process took three days. There was much work to be done. Five divisions comprised the Army of Kah'lash, each numbering two thousand troops. During the three days of preparation, Commander Jend and the elion soldiers held long councils with the Army's leader, General Algar. Boblin frequently attended these meetings, as well as Prince Ladu, to discuss the strategy for assaulting the Deathlands. The plan would have to be a good one, because even ten thousand was a small force compared to Zadinn's army.

Tim spent his time with Nazgar, who increased his training at a frantic pace. The Kyrlod taught him countless spells to the point where Tim wasn't sure he would remember them all. "I hope for your sake you do," had been Nazgar's response. And these weren't just theoretical lessons; Nazgar often took him into the woods, where they dueled sorcerer to sorcerer. Tim thought he knew how dangerous Nazgar was, but it turned out he didn't. The Kyrlod was fast and good, maintaining the same mentality about training with magic that Tim's father had held about swords: it was a disservice if the training didn't hurt as much as the real thing. After some of those fights, Tim found himself surprised to even be alive.

One evening, Falverion and the Council asked Tim to join them alone. Tim honored their request, though somewhat hesitantly. He wasn't sure what the Council expected from him. The Warrior of Light obviously held some significance to these people, but Tim didn't know anything more than that. On this subject, Nazgar was of no use. When Tim asked him about the relationship between Warrior and Kah'lash, Nazgar resorted to his usual ambiguity. "When you spoke before the Council," Nazgar had said, "it became apparent that Those Who Wait were merely waiting for the Warrior. I know nothing else." If the Council had specific expectations of him, Tim didn't know what they were.

As it turned out, all they wanted was to share a meal with him in the dining hall. "I've decided to spare you some discomfort," Falverion said. "It's clear you wish to know more about the Army. However, you are hesitant to ask, for fear it might dislodge our trust in you."

"If you're going to be that frank," Tim replied, "I should be honest, too, and admit you are correct."

"Do not be disturbed," Falverion replied. "Any man worthy of being the Warrior is also a man of humility, and as such, does not presume to know much about a people he's never met. My friend, we'd worry more about a Warrior who claimed to know everything than a Warrior who claims to know nothing. You are the latter, and that is a great consolation to us."

"I have to go back to a very dangerous place," Tim said. "I don't want people following me there, thinking I know how to keep them safe. I don't. As a matter of fact, I hoped the Army would know what to do."

"We return to what I first said," Falverion admonished. "If we, the Council, were to claim to know best, *you* should be worried. We've never seen your North. We don't know Zadinn Kanas."

The First Speaker pointed to the window. "Out there, your Commander is meeting with our General. Right now, Jend Argul is our best chance to prepare for battle. He knows the Deathlands more intimately than anyone here. General Algar commands the troops, but he cannot fight an enemy he does not understand. That's why they meet every day, to formulate a plan. However, I digress. You wish to know more of us? I can tell you some, but not all. We've lived in this world for the same length of time as the Kyrlod. While the prophets roamed the lands, we stayed here, for the Kyrlod were meant to take part in events, while we were meant to stand aside.

"Our city is a week's journey from here. A fortnight ago, we received a sign and consulted the stars. They told us to leave our city and make camp on the edge of this shore. We knew nothing else, but we do not ignore the stars. Shortly after arriving, our patrols reported movement from the Mountains, so the General sent Captain Halion to investigate. When the Captain returned, you were with him. Men who ask us for help must pass a test. First, we ask outsiders for their talisman. Then, we send them to an island in the middle of this lake, where they are left without food or water for one week. Many die, but a few survive."

"What's the point of the island?" Tim asked. "Does it determine worthiness?"

"No," Falverion said, "we decide when we meet the people. The island serves no purpose, except in the minds of those who must wait there. To them, it is everything—a test, a trial, and a judgment. In reality, it is nothing."

"You let people die there?" Tim asked.

"Yes. Sometimes a small mound of earth accomplishes what the Mountains cannot."

"Even people you would have served? You let them die?" Tim wondered if the elions would have survived the week, but of course they would have. They'd survived two centuries, so they could survive seven more days.

"None that we chose to serve have ever died there. Of those we would not serve, some have died and others lived. Those who live are sent back. I don't know if they return to their homelands or die in the Mountains. It's been over a thousand years since we last saw outsiders. I doubt any here would know of their tales or their causes."

"You didn't send us to the island, though," Tim said. "Why not?"

"You are the Warrior of Light," Falverion replied. "Most talismans are objects; very few are people. You are a rare exception, Timothy Matthias. A Kyrlod named Azrindar once dwelled with us. We've served other causes, but we are named Those Who Wait because we, like all men, wait for our final hour. Azrindar said that when the Warrior of Light arrived, our time of waiting would be over. You're given leave to enter this land and call us forth. There is no need for casting you to the island."

"I appreciate your consideration," Tim said dryly. "One week is a long time to go without food."

"One other thing," Falverion said. "You are permitted to come here, but only once. After you leave, you cannot return."

Tim faltered, spoon halfway to his mouth, and then steadied himself and continued eating. He'd been holding onto faint hope that when everything was done with Zadinn—if Tim won—he could come here and quietly disappear. These lands had captured his heart in a way he could not describe; the rugged wilderness beckoned to him. Nothing waited for him in the South but memories and a burned cottage. This was a place where he could let his wounds heal and live out his days in content.

Well, it had only been a faint hope anyway. He didn't see himself winning this battle, and besides, fair was fair. Few men crossed the Mountains and lived, but Tim had survived. On top of that, he could ask anything he wanted from the Army. He supposed this kind of honor could only be granted once. "This is a beautiful place," Tim said. "I wish I could return, but I understand."

Falverion smiled, but the curves on his face looked old and sad. "It is not the way of things for people to return. No man fully understands the ways of the Maker. I hope, at the very least, that we can bring you victory. I hope we can bring you that much."

I hope so, too.

* * *

The following morning, the Army of Kah'lash departed. They would travel by water, following a river that ran from the southern end of the lake and back into the Mountains. As such, the return journey would be much faster than if on foot. Tim was in a canoe with Boblin and an Army soldier named Trigger, of all things. Tim had never heard such an odd name before.

In the early morning light, the three companions carried their canoe to the lake's rocky shore. Trigger stood at the rear of the canoe and pushed its nose into the water. The lake had a bluish sheen, but Tim could see all the way to its bottom. White and brown pebbles covered the sandy floor, which took a sharp drop downward until all Tim could see were turquoise depths.

A thin mist hung over the lake's placid waters. As they pushed off, Tim felt like they were crossing a barrier into another world—which was true, in a way. They were crossing the barrier back into the world of the North—Zadinn's world. *It's like crossing the Rampart all over again, but so much has changed since then.*

Tim wrapped himself in the peaceful calm of the morning, trying to linger in this place as long as possible, because he was never coming back. As the shoreline fell away behind them, he turned to look at it one last time, locking the scene of evergreen trees and rocky foothills forever in his mind. This wasn't his home, though, and neither was the South anymore. If Tim defeated Zadinn, he'd make a new home in the North. The elions were his people now.

Beside them, countless other canoes pushed off from the shore, and the morning fog consumed them all. The soldiers left in stages, five hundred men at a time; Tim and the elions were just the first wave of many. Upon reaching the North, they would set up camp and wait for the remainder of the Army to arrive. They'd march around the Deathlands before turning back to strike from a southern direction, assaulting Zadinn's fortress at its front gates.

When Tim asked Boblin what the strategy was, the elion just gave a noncommittal grunt. "We're working it out," he said.

"That gives me great confidence," Tim responded.

"Good," Boblin answered in the same tone. "It's better that way, because if I told you what we've come up with so far, you'd lose all hope."

Trigger, it turned out, had a healthy sense of humor. As they rode throughout the day, they came to enjoy his hearty laughter and face-splitting smile. He told them about living in this land—what it was like as the seasons turned and the passing of long years. He did not, however, speak of his city, nor did he tell them anything regarding other outsiders who had come before the elions. Such topics, it seemed, were not spoken of. Tim liked listening to the soldier talk. Trigger wasn't like Boblin or him. None of the Army soldiers were, for that matter. They stood separate, apart from other men—but they could still be friends.

Prince Ladu rode in a canoe near Tim's. Tim hadn't had a chance to become fully acquainted with the man. They'd shared a few sparse conversations, but Tim was so consumed with training that he scarcely had a moment for anything else. He wondered how the Prince was coping with this new life, but Ladu seemed to be handling it well. *It has to be strange for him. The last battle against Zadinn must be as clear as yesterday in his mind.*

Pellen's presence certainly comforted the Prince. They'd been friends on the battlefield, and Pellen was a link back to Ladu's old life. Like Tim, though, Ladu appeared to accept change whether he wanted it or not.

At midday they passed from the lake onto the river and soon sped into the Mountains. Swift, snowcapped peaks rose on either side of them, jutting high into the air. From down here, it was a breathtaking sight, though not enough to eradicate the refugees' memories. They knew the evil that lurked within those stone heights. Tim thought back to his first impression of the Mountains. They were like sentinels standing at the gateway to another realm, and they showed no mercy.

When night fell, they pulled over to the nearest shore. The Army made camp efficiently, and in no time at all, a multitude of cooking fires speckled the riverbank. Summer was drawing to a close, and though the days were still warm, the night air carried a slight chill. It wasn't as cold as the snows of the Mountains, but Tim put on extra layers of clothing. He huddled by the fireside with Boblin and Trigger as they ate their evening meal. "Something confuses me," Tim said to Trigger.

"A *lot* confuses him," Boblin interjected.

"Assuredly," Tim agreed without missing a beat, "but humor me. How far does the river take us?"

"Right through the Mountains, to the border of the Deathlands," Trigger replied. "You'll find it much easier than climbing up and down those peaks night and day."

Tim furrowed his brow. "If the river travels all the way, why didn't we take it through the Mountains when we were traveling north?"

"It would have saved a lot of time," Boblin concurred. "Not to mention several encounters with vrawl and sarchons."

Trigger squared his shoulders. "The way is not open to those who have not proved their worth. A talisman must unlock the passage first." He paused, as if for enigmatic effect.

"Un-bloody-believable," Boblin said. "I'm going to find this talisman and give him a piece of my mind."

Trigger abruptly broke out in laughter, slapping his knee as he shook with mirth. "And they say those who dwell beyond have no sense of humor. I'm joking, my friends! Come, take a look." Tim and Boblin exchanged a glance. Apparently, the Army's brand of humor was as strange as everything else about them.

Trigger picked up a stick and drew a map in the sand with two lines, the first significantly above the second. "It's much simpler than that. You see, here is the river, and *here* is where you would have entered the Mountains. Elevation, my boy. You can't reach this river when you are traveling to our lands. It's above your heads!"

He slapped his knee and laughed once more, as if this were the most priceless joke in the world. Tim could almost hear Boblin saying that this was what passed for entertainment when you were separated from the rest of civilization, but the elion wisely refrained.

"How do we get down?" Boblin asked. "Don't tell me I have to jump. I already tried that once."

"Waterfall," Trigger said. "Fear not. We'll pull over before we make it that far, but it will be an easy descent after that."

When dinner ended, Tim reluctantly sought out Nazgar. He was more tired than ever, but he couldn't slow his training now. He expected another walk in the woods and perhaps a duel to follow. His body still ached from sparring last night. Nazgar had trapped him in the air, upside down and unable to move, and had somehow *tightened* the air around Tim, causing excruciating pain, before just walking away, telling Tim he'd have to use the Lifesource to cut through the spell. It was a painful hour before Tim figured out a way to free himself.

Instead of taking their usual walk, though, Nazgar brought Tim into his tent. The two sat on either side of a table, a lantern between them. "I only have one thing left to teach you," Nazgar said. "Then, your training is done."

"Done?" Tim asked. He hadn't thought it would ever end.

"For now, at least. If we had more time, I'd tell you more, but this is no longer practical. The days are against us, and you need to rest for the trials ahead. Zadinn will attack both your mind and your body, so tonight, I will give you one last weapon.

"The Lifesource needs no actions, no words, to work. Advocates frequently accompany their efforts with words and gestures, but that is merely dramatic effect."

Tim understood this. The Lifesource was a function of the mind, a function of willpower. He sometimes used his hands to guide his thoughts, but it wasn't necessary. At first, he'd found this odd; one usually imagined a magician uttering obscure phrases and incantations, maybe even waving a magical wand around. Real life, however, was different than the stories.

"There is an ancient magic called the tongue of Homdee," Nazgar said. "This magic derives from the Lifesource, but it is raw and untamed. Advocates learned the tongue of Homdee, but most never employed it. *Every single spell* of Homdee requires balance, and the magic has a steep price: the caster must always suffer what he inflicts."

Nazgar reached into his pouch and put his focusing point on the table, where it glowed blue. The light flashed outward, ensconcing them in a shimmering dome. "Right now, we are protected. The focusing point creates a barrier around the magic. This is the only safe way to teach the language of Homdee. I encourage you to touch the focusing point. Otherwise the spells *will* be cast, and we would not want that."

Tim touched the stone, and a tingle ran through his body. He didn't like the sound of Homdee. It sounded very unstable—maybe even suicidal.

"The last spell of Homdee was cast on Uklith, Demon Lord of Malath," Nazgar said. "Uklith had created a portal between Malath and this world, preparing to make it his domain. A single man casting Homdee is unspeakably dangerous, but it took three Advocates to stop Uklith."

"What was the consequence?" Tim asked.

"You do not want to know," Nazgar replied. "The spell killed every living being in Agrazab, and the Advocates suffered worse than death. They were not rewarded for saving the world, but punished instead. Sometimes that is the way of such things."

Tim felt cold inside. All this time, he'd been wondering how he could defeat Zadinn. It sounded like Homdee would do it, but at what cost? He no longer wanted to hear what Nazgar had to say.

The Kyrlod watched him from across the table. "I don't know who is stronger—you or the Dark Lord. The power I am giving you is not used lightly. There are many spells of Homdee, but tonight I give you only one, the Banishing Spell." Nazgar folded his hands and leaned forward. "*Laiscete oin sperenze. Vu chentre.*"

The blue dome of light wavered, and the lamp in front of them dimmed. The air grew chill, and the tabletop in front of him felt like ice.

"Repeat it," Nazgar said.

Tim said nothing. He didn't want to.

"Say it!" the Kyrlod said, his eyes burning.

"*Laiscete oin sperenze, vu chentre,*" Tim said. His voice trembled. The moment he spoke the words, they seared into his memory forever.

Nazgar bowed his head. "The Banishing Spell will rid you of any enemy, no matter how powerful—*any* enemy. It removes your nemesis from this world, from reality itself, and sends him to an eternal void, an empty place of darkness…forever."

Tim didn't think he could wrap his mind around this. It was not a banishing spell; it was *the* Banishing Spell. His heart thudded. "What's the price?" he asked.

"It will happen to you too," Nazgar said. "You are also sent to an empty void, and you can never come back."

Tim felt like he was going to be sick. No sane man would ever use that spell. No *insane* man would ever use that spell. An evil, corrupted mind might be willing to subject someone else to that torment, but no man would do that to *himself*. Slit his wrists, yes. Hang himself, yes. But a never-ending limbo? No.

"It would work on Zadinn?" Tim asked.

"It would work on anybody," Nazgar replied. "I am compelled to give you this knowledge, because it is your right to know. As I said, we aren't always rewarded for saving the world. Sometimes we are punished."

Tim looked away for a moment. "I don't think I could do it," he said.

"I want you to have the knowledge, nothing more," Nazgar said. "There are always other ways."

"What do the shadows tell you?" Tim asked.

"Nothing," the Kyrlod said. He gave Tim a long, sad look. "Your training is complete, my friend."

Tim was wordless. Nazgar touched the focusing point, and the dome disappeared. Tim left the tent and staggered beyond the firelight to the edge of the campsite. There, he leaned over and vomited.

Laiscete oin sperenze, vu chentre. The words whispered at the edge of his thoughts.

* * *

Zadinn stared at the Cauldron of Souls. The feeling had faded, but the memory remained. A moment ago, he'd thought he felt a cold touch on his mind, almost reminiscent of his former Master's touch. Uklith's presence had been both pain and ecstasy, and as much as he feared it, Zadinn knew it had guided him.

But Uklith had been decidedly silent for the last two centuries, and anyway, this feeling was different. It was not a guiding touch, it was an unsettling feeling, and Zadinn did not like it.

Whatever it was, it couldn't be the Warrior. Perhaps it was the Kyrlod, meddling in the old magic, but not even the prophets were fool enough to use it for its deadliest purposes. Zadinn didn't like the old magic, because a sword that cut the man holding it was of no use. Zadinn pushed the thoughts aside. He would worry about it later.

A new presence interrupted his musing. Isanam stood outside the door. Zadinn straightened in his chair and bade his servant to enter. The Overlord walked into the throne room and knelt before the dais. "The malichons are ready," Isanam said.

"Good," Zadinn replied. He walked down from the steps of his dais and left the throne room. Isanam followed Zadinn as he strode down the hallway. When they reached the entrance to the citadel, Zadinn waved his hand and extinguished the flames covering the doorway. They left the palace and walked to the top of the battlements. The afternoon sun shone down on the Deathlands, bathing the scene in a bloodred hue.

The malichon army assembled on the slopes of the Deathlands, arranged in perfect lines, row upon row, thousands upon thousands, line and rank covering the base of the plateau. The troops stretched all the way to the horizon, looking like a sea of black-armored insects ready to stream forth and do their leader's bidding. The dying light glinted off their armored bodies.

"About face!" Isanam yelled, his voice booming across the endless ranks. As one, the malichons turned. The motion was swift and uniform. Not a single man faltered. "Forward march!"

The malichons moved forward, marching forth across the Deathlands. The sea of black was on the move. Zadinn watched the scene and laughed. It was so perfect, so fitting, so *right*. His laughter rolled over the marching troops, cold and utterly mad, while the malichons continued marching. The Army of Kah'lash was coming, but when it arrived, the malichons would be ready.

Thirty-Eight

Celia sat alone by the fire, gazing into the flickering flames. Every so often a log made a popping sound followed by a light shower of floating embers. Ordinarily, Ana Teldin would have occupied the overturned stump next to Celia, but that space was vacant. Celia had lost her traveling companion, her protégé, and most important, her friend.

It had been Celia's duty to lead Ana, to show her the ways of the Frontier Patrol and teach her how to survive in the harsh lands of the North. Celia felt she'd failed. Many elions had lost their lives on this journey, but none of the others were in Celia's charge. It made Celia want to hang up her sword and leave the Patrol, but Ana would not have wanted that, so Celia would have to fight in Ana's name and make the loss worthwhile. That's all there was to it.

She glanced away from her fire, surveying the rest of the camp. The Army of Kah'lash was something else, no doubt about that. Every last one of these men and women were capable fighters—warriors of the finest caliber. Ana would have liked them and would have learned much from them.

Celia would miss this place on the far side of the mountains. It had a certain mystical quality to it. She loved the sights of lakes and trees, the sounds of natural wildlife, the smells of evergreens and fresh loam of the earth—and the clean quality of the air. But as much as she found these uncharted lands romantic and appealing, she felt a rightness about their journey south. She was returning home, where she belonged. The wastelands of Zadinn's domain might be harsh and inhospitable, but it was all she had ever known, and it was where she belonged.

She wondered if Hedro Desh would visit her tonight. He'd done so on several recent occasions, and the visits always left her feeling conflicted. She would not deny she felt a degree of attraction to him—even more so after he had come for her in the caverns of Malath's Teeth and rescued her from the quicksand in the Korlan—but something always nagged at her. She couldn't quite put a finger on it, but knew it had something to do with the way he held her hand. She let the issue nibble at the corner of her mind; when he held her hand, his touch was gentle but firm, and his skin soft but strong. By all observable accounts, she noted, it could be considered a perfect hand. Truly, but still...

He had kissed her the previous night. More importantly, she had kissed him back, but she hadn't decided if she would let him kiss her a second time. She had to figure out what was wrong with that hand.

Almost right on cue, footsteps approached from beyond her tent. So he had returned after all. Maybe tonight, she could put this issue to rest once and for all. But when she turned around, it was Boblin Kule, not Hedro Desh, who stood by the fire.

"Hi, Celia," Boblin said.

"Hi."

He stepped forward, gesturing to the empty spot. "Care if I join you?"

"Please, do."

Boblin sat by the fire, and for a few long moments, they remained silent. That was fine by Celia; there wasn't much that needed to be said. They had known each other their entire lives, and with such friendships words weren't always necessary. It was enough to just be there. Come to think of it, though, she and Boblin had not spoken much since the Mountains. He had kept his distance from her, though whether intentionally or by circumstance, she could not say.

Quit lying to yourself, she chided. She knew *exactly* what this was about. She just hadn't allowed herself to openly admit it. More than anything else, she should reprimand herself for avoiding the issue when she should not have, not for so long. Life was too short to disregard such matters. She knew it had everything to do with Celia, everything to do with Hedro, and everything to do with Boblin.

Boblin and Hedro's relationship had always been strained, more so in recent years, but it had been that way for as long as she could remember. Their personalities were just different enough; both meant well, but Hedro approached the world with machismo and bluster, while Boblin approached it with wryness and nonchalance—not a recipe for a great friendship.

She knew how Boblin felt about her. She saw it in the way he blushed when he spoke to her, the way he averted his eyes when she gazed at him too closely, the way he held her when he asked her to dance. But the more important question was, how did she feel about Boblin?

It was a hard question, considering he was a childhood friend who had been a part of her life as long as she could remember. For that relationship to change in a way she could not anticipate or control was something she preferred to avoid rather than approach head-on. She had her hands full with serving on the Patrol and defending the North; the Patrol was straightforward and concrete, but matters of the heart were much more complex.

Boblin broke the silence, cutting through her thoughts as he spoke. "How are you, Celia?"

"It's been tough."

"I never had a chance to tell you I'm sorry. Ana was a great soldier."

"It should have been me," Celia said.

"No," Boblin replied. "It shouldn't have been either of you."

"But if I had to choose," Celia said, "I would have chosen me."

"And Ana would have chosen herself," Boblin said. "As I'd have chosen myself. It's a truth we accept when we join the Patrol."

They both lapsed into silence once more, and the faint rustle of the night breeze brushed over them. Boblin leaned back from the fire and gazed into the sky. Celia followed his gaze, looking into the inky darkness spotted with countless stars. Smoke from the fire wafted over their heads.

"Hmm…" Boblin pointed toward a cliff above them. "I think I recognize that one. It's hard to forget a peak when you're hanging from it by one hand. It isn't really a pleasant experience."

"I couldn't imagine," Celia replied.

"It looks much different from down here," Boblin said. "I'm still not keen on it, though. I tell you what, at the time I'd have given my right arm for the ability to fly."

"I do believe your right hand was the one you were holding on with," Celia said, "so I wouldn't be so quick to give it up."

Boblin burst into laughter. "My life is a success. I got Celia Alcion to make a joke."

"Don't set your goals so high." Celia purposefully kept her voice flat. "You're bound to be disappointed."

Boblin laughed harder. "You never told me you were funny. I feel like I've been missing out."

"Perhaps you have."

Boblin cut his laughter short, leaning toward her. There it was—the telltale blush creeping into his cheeks. Celia tried very hard to keep her features smooth and even, but it *was* tempting to smile.

"Thank you, Celia," he said. "I needed a laugh. I really did."

She allowed herself to smile. "I needed it as much as you did. There's a tough road in front of us. We can't go into it with a heavy heart, else we're bound to lose."

A flicker of hesitation passed across Boblin's face, but he stamped it out. He opened his mouth, closed it, and then opened it again. "Would you like to go for a walk?"

She smiled again. "I would." Boblin offered her his palm, and when she placed her hand in his, she felt something in her mind *click*.

She'd figured it out. When she held Hedro's hand, his touch was flawless and perfect. Boblin's, however, was not. His hand was calloused, rough around the edges. In short, it was *real*—and that made all the difference.

It had been a long time since she and Boblin had truly conversed. But that was okay, because tonight she was spending time with her friend, and that was all that mattered.

* * *

The company traveled south, speeding along the waterway. By the end of the fourth day, they left the river and prepared to make their descent. As they paused at the edge of the Mountains, Tim looked across the land to which they were returning. The desolate landscape had become disturbingly familiar, and it almost felt like returning home. Their time in the Mountains felt surreal, separate, and like it or not, this barren wasteland of gray stone was where he now belonged.

One particular area of the landscape appeared markedly different than the rest—the orange stone of the Deathlands, which created a massive blemish on the horizon. When Tim looked at it, a tremor ran through his body. He didn't want to go there; he wanted to do *anything* but march to that plateau and approach that city. He'd felt Zadinn Kanas from a distance, and that was bad enough. In person, Tim would be face to face with a man who wanted to break him, make him scream, and then kill him. But Tim had to do this. If he didn't, Zadinn would pursue him until the end. *Better to meet it on my own terms.*

The descent from the Mountains took all day, and by nightfall the group camped at the foot of the range. The barrier of the Korlan Forest stood to the west. There was no need to stray back there again. Tim was done with that place, just as he was done with the Mountains. He was no longer a talisman, but he wished he could roam the rugged northern wilderness one last time.

The dawn brought a familiar wind, which cut across their faces as Commander Jend led the group south. Jend stayed as far west as possible, avoiding even the outermost edges of the Deathlands. Although five hundred men of Kah'lash were more than enough to take on a malichon patrol, there was no point in attracting unnecessary attention.

Tim still knew nothing about the battle plan. He'd never seen Zadinn's fortress, but he didn't think throwing even ten thousand men at it would do much good. Furthermore, there was the matter of getting inside. The Army might be fine sparring on the slopes of the Deathlands, but Tim had different ideas. It was quite clear to him that he, if nobody else, had to make it *inside* the walls of the city. At the very least, he could occupy Zadinn while the others fought the malichons. If Zadinn partook in the actual battle, not even the Army of Kah'lash could withstand him. Tim needed to keep the Dark Lord busy, but he didn't expect to just knock on the front door and be invited inside.

As days passed, Tim became aware of his own strength, both in body and in the Lifesource. His former nightly training usually left him drained, but now that Nazgar had ended his lessons, Tim felt his body slowly recuperating. His latent powers waited beneath the surface—a small comfort, but a comfort nonetheless.

One month and four days after Tim and his family first entered the North, the Army of Kah'lash gathered south of the Deathlands. All was quiet on the Durin Plains; time hung suspended, caught in the grip of the oft-mentioned calm before the storm. At night, Tim frequently dreamed about walking atop a razor-thin ridge, with a canyon of light on his right and a chasm of darkness to his left. He always woke from these dreams bathed in sweat.

The other contingents arrived one at a time, and the groups of soldiers spread across the plains. Tim realized the campfires would betray them to the malichon sentinels, but when he mentioned this to Boblin, the elion said, "We can't stay hidden forever."

"What's the plan, Boblin?" Tim asked. "Nobody's telling me anything. I need to know how to get into the citadel."

"The plan," Boblin said, "is to get you into the citadel."

Boblin wouldn't say more, and Tim left the issue alone. Ever since the Mountains, he'd been careful to control his temper. Everything hinged upon his battle with Zadinn. Tim was so karfing scared that he woke up screaming in the middle of the night, and the least he expected was a plan, even a fragment of one, so he wasn't sinking into the unknown. No matter how dangerous the plan might be, at least he would *know*.

He pulled his sword from its sheath as his rage trembled on the verge of reawakening. The anger climbed, trying to pull Tim into another vortex of cynicism and self-pity. He breathed deeply—in, out, in, out—and *denied* it. Then he seized the Lifesource, funneling it into the blade, and the sword glowed a pure, wholesome green. Holding it in front of him, he faced the Kaltu Pass. *Mother, Father, give me strength. These people want something from me, and I don't know how to give it to them. I don't care what happens to me, only what happens to them. I care that you are proud of me.*

"Tim," Boblin said from behind him.

Tim released the Lifesource and his weapon went dark. "I'm sorry," Tim said. "It's just…if I don't know what's going to happen, I don't know how to be ready."

"We have a plan," Boblin said, "but some things still need to fall into place. When we're ready to march on the Deathlands, we will let you know. It's Nazgar, Tim. He said you couldn't know until then."

"Then I have to trust him," Tim said. He sheathed his sword.

"Scared?" Boblin asked.

"What do you think?"

"Me, too."

"You're too ugly to be worth a malichon's time," Tim said. "Get over it."

"Go mate with a three-legged goat," Boblin said. "Besides, are you even any good with the Lifesource these days? I hear you'll need it." He crossed his arms and looked at Tim quizzically.

"Very well," Tim said, winking at his friend before brushing past him toward camp. He summoned the Lifesource and waved his hand toward Boblin, causing his friend to rise into the air and rotate upside down.

"Is that all you can do?" Boblin retorted, face turning red as blood rushed to his head. "Unoriginal. My grandmother could do better!"

"Be thankful I'm letting you keep your clothes on," Tim said. He patted Boblin on the cheek before marching away.

"That's very nice," Boblin said. "Let me down, and we'll settle this like real soldiers—no tricks, no weapons—me against you. Come on. Afraid?"

Tim kept walking and smiling. "Tim?" The color in Boblin's face now resembled a garden beet. "Let me down! Karf!"

* * *

Boblin wondered how long this was going to take. He already had a headache from hanging upside down. *What a sneaky son of a three-legged goat. Then again, I asked for it. Why did I start an argument with an Advocate? They never play fair. Push them far enough, and they show off by throwing fireballs around.* Abruptly, Boblin shifted right side up and dropped to the ground.

The one good thing about all this was that Tim's genuine personality was back. He was neither the Tim from the Mountains nor the Tim from the other side of the Barricade, but a new man altogether. He was wiser, calmer, happier, and at the same time, more solemn. Tim had entered the Mountains an angry man who could use the Lifesource, but returned as the Warrior of Light.

Ironically, this was why they couldn't let Tim know about the plan. The stranger Tim—the one Boblin had feared— would have been perfectly willing to go along with it. This Tim, the transformed Tim, would not allow it, and that was why it had to stay secret.

A shadow moved at the corner of Boblin's vision, but it was only Hedro. As the big elion stepped forward, Boblin felt tension crackle in the air and stiffened.

"You didn't listen to me, Kule," Hedro said. "I don't want to do this, but lessons have to be taught."

Boblin moved in a blur, faster than Hedro expected, and slammed his fist into Hedro's jaw. The soldier staggered back a few paces, the shock on his face giving Boblin extreme pleasure. It didn't last long. Hedro came in low under Boblin's arm, striking the rib cage with his elbow. Boblin stumbled, losing balance, as Hedro completed a spin and kicked toward his midsection. Boblin blocked the kick at the very last second, dropping his arms crosswise to divert the blow, but it still caused a jarring impact on his forearms.

Hedro came in and delivered a knife-edge blow to Boblin's clavicle. Boblin crumpled, but not before sweeping Hedro's feet out from under him. Both elions fell away from each other, rolling back into a standing position to come face to face, trading blows in earnest. Soon both elions were bloodied and bruised.

"What in Malath is this?" Commander Jend's voice rang loud and hard, but soft in comparison to the expression on his face. Both elions stopped midbrawl as the Commander glared at the two and crossed his arms.

"It was a disagreement, sir," Boblin said. He was surprised to see a hint of shame on Hedro's face. He thought Hedro hadn't a drop of humility in him. Of course, Boblin surely felt some shame of his own.

"A karfing *disagreement*?" The words stung. Jend strode forward and backhanded each of them across the face, first Boblin, then Hedro. Neither elion flinched as Jend spoke through clenched teeth. "We have a disagreement with *them*!" He pointed north, toward the Deathlands. "I don't care what caused this sorry excuse for a fistfight. You're in the Frontier Patrol. If you have a problem with each other, bite your karfing tongues until they bleed!"

Jend took a deep breath. "Do you see that hill to the south?"

The landmark stood perhaps an hour's walk away. "Yes, sir," Boblin said.

"Do you see it, Desh," Jend asked, "or have your karfing eyes fallen out?"

"Yes, sir," Hedro replied, "I see it."

"Good," Jend said. "Kule, walk to that hill. Carry Desh on your back every step of the way. When you reach it, turn around and walk back. Desh, you will carry Kule as he carried you. When you get back, you are going to dig a hole together *here*." Jend pointed to the ground. "Dig it deep enough to stand in up to your full height, and when that is done, fill the whole thing back up again. Provided each of you still has a brain between his ears, which I highly doubt, spend some time thinking about your actions tonight. Understood?"

"Yes, sir," they replied. Jend pivoted on his heel and walked away. Boblin and Hedro exchanged a look. This was going to be a long night.

* * *

At the end of the week, the Army of Kah'lash stood gathered in full strength. The assault was to begin the following morning, and as evening arrived, Nazgar told Tim they were holding a council of war. Tim followed Nazgar to General Algar's tent. The General sat at the head of a large oak table. The Army's five captains sat along one side, and Jend's council sat along the other: Hugo, Ken, Faldon, Tavin, Hedro, Boblin, and Celia. Pellen Yuzhar and Prince Ladu Jovun IV also sat at the table.

"This will be quick," General Algar said. He looked up and down the table, meeting each soldier's gaze before moving on. "All of us, save for the Warrior, know the plan. This is merely an opportunity to discuss final matters."

He turned to Gendar. "Captain Halion, is Division Five ready?"

"Yes, sir. We're honored to perform our duty."

The General nodded. "For the Warrior's benefit, I will outline our plan. Zadinn has at least forty thousand troops behind his walls, but the true number may be twice that. Three to one is fair odds for my men, but we are outnumbered, regardless. We have one advantage against Zadinn: he does not know our number. At first light tomorrow, Division Five will march on the Dark Lord's fortress and assault the gates. This will draw the malichon forces out onto the field."

"What about the other four Divisions?" Tim asked. Throwing two thousand men at that plateau was senseless. They'd need every man available to have any hope at all.

"They will not be marching," Algar said.

Tim looked around the table. The soldiers' faces were impassive. "I don't understand," he said.

"It is our best hope," the General replied. "Two thousand men or ten thousand men—it makes no difference. We cannot breach Zadinn's walls, but we can bait his forces into the open. Zadinn will think the Army of Kah'lash has come to destroy him, and he'll unleash the full might of his army. The Kyrlod and the Warrior will go to the city's edge and wait for the malichons to leave. After the battle has started, they can enter the city without hindrance. From there, I fear the pair will be beyond our aid."

"But what of Division Five?" Tim asked. "You can't expect them to stand against eighty thousand men!"

"We must employ a strategic advantage," the General replied. "The rest of the Army will wait while Division Five withstands the first blow. Then, only after the trap is set, they will march in and attack from both sides. We'll strike Zadinn in a pincer movement, four thousand men hitting the malichons on either flank. This element of surprise is our best asset."

"That's suicide," Tim said.

"No matter how we go about it, it is suicide," Algar said. "We must play to our strengths, nothing more and nothing less."

Tim sat back. Now he knew why they hadn't told him the plan. Two thousand fighters were going to sacrifice themselves so he could sneak in the front door. Then eight thousand more would sacrifice themselves just to buy him a sliver of time. It was unthinkable. "This is wrong," he said.

"It is necessary," Jend replied.

Tim turned to Nazgar. "Tell them what you know of necessity," he said. *If anybody can talk them out of this, Nazgar can.*

Nazgar shook his head. "I was teaching you a lesson for the times, Tim," he said. "And you learned it well, I am pleased to say. However, necessity always rules in the end—tomorrow, of all days."

Tim was on the precipice of an outburst, but he calmed down. He forced himself to see the twisted logic of the situation. As Algar said, no matter how they went about this, these men and elions were marching to their death. They'd known that since they left the Mountains over a week ago. As far as strategies went, this was the best possible tactic. "You were wise to keep this from me," he said.

"No good man likes seeing others suffer for his cause," Pellen said, "but a strong man continues to carry his torch nonetheless."

"What about the elions?" Tim asked.

Jend returned his gaze. "If we want to draw Zadinn out, he must know the Fort of Pellen is here. The elions must march with Division Five."

No.

Jend continued. "He must know it is *all* of us. We will have to stand at the front, the bait's golden lining."

"You'll all die!" Tim said. "I didn't bring you across the Mountains so you could throw yourselves against a wall of malichons!"

"There is no better way to die," Jend said.

The worst part was that it all made sense. Tim expelled a long, weak breath. "I see," he said. "May the Maker light your path." It was the only thing he could think to say, but the words sounded feeble and weak.

"If there is anyone the Maker needs to stand beside, it is you," Pellen said. "You have our gratitude, Tim Matthias. The courage it takes to stand against an army of malichons is nothing compared to what it will take to walk into the Dark Lord's citadel."

Tim was suddenly very tired. He just wanted to sleep. Morning would come much quicker than he wanted. The council continued for another hour, but he barely remembered any of it. When the meeting ended, Tim walked back to his tent and looked toward the Deathlands. Dusk had fallen, but he could still see clouds on the horizon, blacker than the surrounding night, alternating blue and silver streaks running across their undersides. In the west, the dying sun tinged the horizon with blood.

Tim felt like he was strapped to a rolling boulder tumbling down a hill. The boulder was moving faster and faster, traveling toward a wall of sheer rock, and he could do nothing to stop its course. It was all beyond his control.

He touched his sword. It glowed to life, but the light was now less than reassuring. He felt he should do something momentous, something to prepare, but he only wanted to rest. He collapsed onto his cot and stared wide-eyed at the ceiling. Even in exhaustion, rest did not come easily. At last he slipped into fitful slumber.

On the eve of the final battle, night hung still over the camp.

Thirty-Nine

Something was different today. Most of the malichons had disappeared from the Pit. As usual, Quentiin began work in the morning before any of the other slaves. If he didn't start first, the price was too steep. The malichons had already killed two prisoners, both children, on Quentiin's "behalf" this week. Veldor understood quite well that killing women and children affected Quentiin more than killing men.

The guards now played games with him. Knowing he was forbidden to speak, they periodically approached him and asked questions, telling him that if he didn't answer, they would kill a prisoner. But per Veldor's decree, if he spoke at all, they also killed a prisoner, so either way, somebody died. The malichons always made sure the two potential victims differed: old or young, male or female, boy or girl.

Quentiin didn't know how long he could endure this new torment and had begun thinking of ways to kill himself. When he first arrived, he'd vowed not to let the malichons break him, so he had separated a portion of himself and locked it away deep inside his soul. But now, in spite of everything, they had gotten past his defenses and placed him in a corner from which he saw no escape.

He knew that by killing himself, it would mean Veldor had won, and though Quentiin didn't want to grant the Slavemaster this satisfaction, it was more than just his dignity at stake. The other slaves suffered because of his existence, and if Quentiin were to commit suicide, he could spare them further torment on his account. Put in this light, the decision was simple. Quentiin could not allow others to continue dying for the sake of his pride. Now he just had to find a way to do it. The malichons no longer allowed him to work in the Pit, where it would be easy enough for Quentiin to toss himself into the flames, because even though Veldor wanted Quentiin to kill himself, he didn't want it to be easy. And so with one hand Veldor drove Quentiin toward suicide, and with the other hand he deprived the dwerion of all means to do so. This was the closest place on earth to Malath, and only madness reigned.

Today, however, the slave pen was nearly empty. The malichons had left for the Deathlands without any explanation, leaving behind only a skeleton detachment to guard the prisoners. From a rough count, they had left approximately one guard for every four slaves, and Quentiin would play those odds any day.

As the bell for the morning meal sounded, Quentiin turned from his work and walked toward the stone building. He had only a vague plan in mind, but that did not worry him. He could flesh out the details as he went. He saw only two possible outcomes, one slightly grimmer than the other, but either was acceptable. If he could rouse the others with his example, the slaves might rise up, and things would take a turn for the better. And if he failed to rouse his comrades' spirits, the malichons would kill him, because today Quentiin was going to break the unbreakable rule. Either way, dead or alive, Quentiin's time as a slave was at an end, and that was enough to put a smile on his face. He found it beautiful, even liberating. Things could get no worse, so Quentiin now found himself free to do...*anything*.

Quentiin took his place in the breakfast line behind a row of elions and waited in silence for his gruel. These days he ate by himself, and his fellow slaves didn't mind because close proximity to Quentiin meant greater risk of being caught in a malichon game. Quentiin had a contagious disease, after all—the disease of independence, and the guards were doing their best to make sure no one else became sick.

Today, however, he sat with his people from Raldoon. He trusted them the most, and if anybody remembered their true selves today, it would be them. As Quentiin sat across from Jolldo, he looked his old friend in the eye, cleared his throat, and spoke.

"We can kill 'em today," he said. "All of 'em."

Jolldo choked, dropping his spoon.

"Quentiin!" Yagglem said. "Be silent, d'ye ken? They'll hear ye!"

"Have ye counted 'em?" Quentiin said. "Most are gone. We ain't goin' to get a better chance than this!"

"Quentiin," Jolldo said, "ye need to be quiet *now*."

"Listen, laddie! There's far more of us than them. This is our chance!"

"An' even supposin' we get past 'em, what then?" Jolldo hissed. "Ye don't think the others have disappeared, do ye? There's a whole city out there!"

Quentiin pounded his fist on the table, and a nearby guard turned toward them. *Good.* Quentiin *wanted* them to notice. "Then we all die today. Is it any different than what's already goin' on? They've taken everythin' from us, mate. At least we can die the way it should be, with a bit of honor an' backbone!"

Jolldo shook his head, face hollow and eyes dead. "I'm sorry, laddie. I really am. Please don't say anythin' more. It ain't no use."

Quentiin should have known. They'd lost it, long ago. The villagers' spirits had died the night Raldoon burned, their bodies now empty shells.

"I pray I've misunderstood something," a voice said from behind, and Quentiin turned to see a malichon standing over them. The slaves grew deathly silent.

"I thought I heard *this* one speaking," the malichon said, looking at Quentiin. "Were you?"

Quentiin returned the malichon's gaze, but said nothing.

"A yes or no will suffice," the malichon said. "If you don't tell me, I will kill this one." It pointed at Jolldo, and Quentiin stood.

"I told 'em," he said to the guard, "that I slept with yer mother last night."

The malichon hissed, raising a hand to strike, but Quentiin was faster. As soon as the malichon moved, Quentiin picked up his steaming bowl of porridge and threw it into the guard's face. As the malichon shrieked, Quentiin leaped forward and drove it to the ground with one shoulder. He then turned and ran to the kitchen, leaping onto the countertop and sliding across to the cooking area.

The kitchen slaves scattered as Quentiin landed among them. The door burst open and the malichon guard staggered inside, teeth bared in a snarl, red streaks on its face from where the burning porridge had struck. It uncoiled the whip and struck, but Quentiin turned and caught the whip around his forearm, absorbing the impact while still standing. He'd had a lot of practice underneath these whips, after all. Quentiin used his leverage to pull the malichon forward, kick it in the stomach, and pull himself free.

Quentiin looked for something to serve as a weapon and saw a flash of metal. He seized the object before leaping back onto the counter, once more sliding across and back into the dining area. The others had to see what Quentiin prepared to do next; otherwise, they might not believe. Quentiin rolled into a fighting stance to face the guard. While the slaves in the hall watched, the two combatants faced each other. From the far end of the room, more guards rushed toward the conflict, but they were too far away to make a difference.

The malichon swung its whip at Quentiin once more, and this time, Quentiin ducked underneath the lash, head-butting the malichon in the gut. The guard fell against the countertop, landing on its back and dropping the whip.

Quentiin had the opening he needed. He lifted the butcher's knife he'd taken from the kitchen cutlery moments before and drove the blade straight into the malichon's face, destroying the slave driver's visage in a spray of flesh, blood, and bone. As the malichon's body slumped over, Quentiin placed a foot atop it and raised the gore-covered knife above his head.

"There are more of us than them," he said to the slaves. "Today, we can kill them—all of them."

Behind him, the kitchen door opened and four more malichons swarmed into the room. They attacked Quentiin with brute force, wresting the butcher's knife from his grip and throwing him down. Quentiin hoped, prayed, to hear the others rising up above him. A roomful of slaves could kill four malichons. This was their hour of freedom—but the slaves remained motionless. The guards kicked Quentiin, landing punishing blows on his body, and Quentiin felt his spirits fall, but only a little. He'd known this might happen. He was sad but not entirely surprised. *It was worth a go, I suppose. It would have been nice if it turned out the other way, but this is what I expected. At least it's over.*

Veldor the Slavemaster strode into the room, cape behind him. Upon seeing the dead malichon, he turned toward Quentiin, his face hard. "What have you to say?" he asked.

"Eat hisht and die," Quentiin replied.

Veldor sighed. "We both knew it would end this way, my friend. I'd like to keep you around longer, because you entertain me, but I must adhere to the rules. You have committed the unforgivable crime and slain one of the higher blood. For this you will die."

Veldor waved a hand, and Gald stepped forward. "Take the dwerion to the caves," Veldor said. "Ensure that his death is slow."

"Of course," Gald concurred, a sickening smile on his face.

Veldor looked at Quentiin. "Your suffering has only begun. You will scream many hours before this day is done. Still, I fear you will not see tomorrow's sunrise."

* * *

Tim opened his eyes. *Morning.* He had wondered if the sun would rise today. Now that it had risen, he wondered if he would see it set.

The dim, early light illuminated the campsite as he and Nazgar prepared to depart. Tim did not bother putting on any armor; chain mail would do him no good where he was going. He buckled his sword around his waist, put on a leather shirt, and laced his boots. After that, he met Nazgar by the fireside, and without another word, Kyrlod and Warrior walked toward the Deathlands.

Tim was glad no one saw them leave. He didn't feel like speaking right now. When they passed the edge of the camp his legs trembled and he took several deep breaths, trying to calm himself. He should have been able to make it this far without losing heart. *I hadn't realized I was a coward.*

And yet, coward or not, he had a job to do. Two thousand men were about to throw themselves into the jaws of Malath for him, and if they could do that, he could walk into a city. As he and Nazgar approached the Deathlands, the landscape changed. The wind grew silent, falling so eerily still that time itself felt suspended, while the rock beneath their feet changed color from gray to reddish orange, growing rougher and more abrasive. The sun rose into the sky, causing waves of steadily increasing heat to roll over them.

Boblin had told Tim the climate of the Deathlands was very different than the rest of the North. He claimed Zadinn's very presence acted like a whirlpool, pulling all heat in the North toward him, leaving the plains barren and cold while the Deathlands sweltered. *Perhaps,* Tim thought, *Boblin had it backward.* Maybe Zadinn's presence wasn't *pulling* everything into the Deathlands. Instead perhaps it was killing the land, starting at the city and radiating outward. It might be only a matter of time before the rest of the North mirrored these lands. After all, Zadinn served Malath, and what else was this place but a reflection of the underworld?

The dark citadel loomed closer as the two traveled north. Even from this distance, Tim could see a mass of malichons at the base of the plateau. Zadinn definitely knew the Army of Kah'lash was here. The elions would arrive in several hours, tired and footsore, while the malichons were fresh and ready for war. Tim hated it. His friends were marching forward to fight this endless horde alone, and he could do nothing to change their minds.

He and Nazgar turned west, giving the malichons a wide berth, and after they had enough distance from the enemy troops, Nazgar stopped. "This is as far as we go for now," the Kyrlod said. "We must wait for the battle to begin, and then we will enter the city behind the malichons."

And so the waiting began. Tim realized standing still was worse than moving. Now that the end had begun, he didn't want to slow down. He pulled the Lifesource around him for comfort, and the focusing point on his sword glowed.

Then his mind bumped against the presence within the citadel. *Zadinn.* He felt the Dark Lord waiting, his power surrounding him, and Tim trembled all over again. *Why am I here? What do I hope to accomplish? Do I really think I can win?* He felt cold as a leaden weight descended on his body, rooting him in place while the sensation of darkness to the north grew stronger. Zadinn was going to destroy Tim, consume him, and bleed him out on the stones of the citadel.

"He's too strong," Tim said to Nazgar. "He's going to win." The weight crushed him, and he fell over. The world went black and time ceased.

When Tim opened his eyes and sat up, Nazgar was gone and the Deathlands had changed. The land had become a bloodred mass of rock and stone, with thorny vines snaking across the ground. Twisting canyons and steep gorges crisscrossed the landscape, wisps of smoke rising from the depths of each crevasse and into the sky.

And the plateau overshadowed everything. The fortress had grown to a behemoth of unimaginable size, obsidian walls rising hundreds of feet into the air, towers at the corners of the parapets soaring high. Yellow windows marked the face of each tower, staring across the forsaken land like unblinking eyes. The fortress had a shape both jagged and sinuous, a macabre blend of art and violence that sent waves of pure evil rolling across the Deathlands, lashing at Tim's mind with terrible strength.

Tim fell onto his knees and lowered his head. *This is what Zadinn Kanas will become.*

Abruptly, the vision ended. Darkness washed over Tim again, but this time when he opened his eyes, the world had returned to normal, if he could call it that. The fortress was not as large, but the evil, the real danger, remained. Nazgar sat nearby, watching Tim shake and perspire.

"No one will force you to continue," Nazgar said. "You can choose to leave and never look back. Or you can choose to walk into his palace and face him. Choose, and accept what follows."

Either way, Tim figured he would die. But as Nazgar had said, *it was his choice.* He did not know what would happen if he went to the citadel, and he did not know what would happen if he fled the Deathlands. The roads of the future were too complex and multilayered for a simple man to understand. That was the Maker's business alone, and Tim's business was here, today, to make this choice at this moment…and accept what came after.

Tim rose to his feet, brushing the dirt from his clothes and looking at Nazgar. "Let's go," he said.

* * *

Boblin stared at the horizon. He wore a sword at his waist, a chain mail shirt over his chest, and a crossbow across his back. The overhead sun beat down on his group as it climbed into the sky, casting the orange and red glow of the Deathlands in a bloody hue.

He marched with the other elions and the men of Division Five, moving forth across the stunted landscape, facing the yet-unseen plateau of Zadinn's citadel to the north. A light breeze picked up, but it brought no respite from the heat, only a swirl of dust and a faint scent of fear, the kind that came from those marching toward inevitable doom. There was nothing wrong with fear, though—in the North, it was part of everyday life. One simply accepted it and moved on.

Soon they would come within sight of the plateau, where Isanam and the malichon army waited for them. All that remained was the slow crawl as the two forces moved toward one another. The Army of Kah'lash resembled a length of melted steel, soft and pliable, stretched across the surface of an anvil, and the malichons were the hammer poised above, ready to fall. The hammer hadn't descended yet, but it would soon, and it was Division Five's job to survive that blow, absorb the shock, and not break.

The sun continued climbing, but the hour was irrelevant. Boblin wondered where Tim and Nazgar were right now. *Probably sunning on a rock, enjoying ale and cheese until the battle is over.* Maybe if Boblin was lucky, he'd find out where they were and join them for a brief spell. Something told him lunch was not on today's agenda.

Boblin unconsciously touched a leather pouch hanging on a string around his belt. The Army was privy to a unique weapon similar to that which had destroyed the walls of the Fort, but more potent, and they had helped the elions build a sizable arsenal of the pouches before setting out. Boblin had practiced last night, just to get a feel for it. The weapon should help even the odds. It wouldn't save them, not by a long stretch, but it would allow them to bloody Zadinn's nose a little.

Hedro marched next to him. The two had formed an uneasy, unspoken truce. Today, only their homeland mattered; today, all other disagreements had become absurdly petty. Their lives depended on unity and watching each other's backs. Farther down the line, Celia marched, ready as ever to take on the grim task in front of them.

The soldiers took a brief respite, a mere quarter of an hour, to conserve energy. Boblin sat on a nearby rock and drank from a flask of water. Nobody spoke, for there was nothing to be said. As Hedro found a spot next to him, Boblin silently offered him the flask. Hedro nodded in appreciation, taking the skin and drinking deeply from it.

"What do you think of this?" Hedro asked, lifting one of the pouches from his belt.

"We'll see," Boblin said. "The malichons won't expect it. It won't hold them off forever, but it will stretch things out."

"That's what makes it fun, right?" said Hedro.

"Right." Something pricked Boblin in the side, and he turned around. A rose of all things, withered and tiny, jutted up from a crack in the stone slab. It had no place in this land, but here it was, a lone blossom of life amid a landscape of death. Boblin pulled the flower from the crevice, placing it in the front pocket of his shirt. *For luck.*

Soon after, they resumed their march, and within an hour came in sight of Zadinn's fortress, a silent, watchful stronghold hunkered atop the plateau on the horizon. Behind the battlements, plumes of fire and smoke leaped into the sky. The prisoners from the Fort—and the dwerions from the South—were no doubt behind those walls right now, cringing under the whip.

And in front of the plateau, on the slopes of the Deathlands, the malichon army waited. Boblin had already known Zadinn's force was big, but he still gasped upon seeing the massive, never-ending sea of dark-armored troops. There had to be at least fifty thousand malichons out there. The proverbial hammer now hung poised above the anvil, ready to strike.

Upon seeing the other army, Zadinn's forces chanted in unison, stomping on the ground in anticipation. He couldn't make out any of the words, but they couldn't be good. *Well, this is what we came for. Time to tip the scale and see how the weights hold out.*

The malichons started forward, moving slowly at first but steadily gaining speed. Captain Halion shouted orders as the Army of Kah'lash moved into uniform, blocked positions, while Commander Jend took charge of the elions. Boblin planted his feet. He felt like he should grow roots, so he could entrench himself in the stone to withhold the coming clash. The hammer was falling, and he needed to brace for it with everything he had. He loosened his sword in its belt, grasping the hilt with sweaty palms. *How in the name of Malath did we end up on the front line? We'll be cut to shreds.*

Now the malichons were charging in full force. They had their mortal enemies, the Fort of Pellen, in sight, and they had every intent of grinding the elions into fine powder. The earth didn't just shake, it *thundered.* Jend Argul stood in front of the elion refugees as Hugo and Ken raised the battle standard of the Fort of Pellen into the sky, where it unfurled to reveal the sigil of a yellow sun against a black background. This was their signet, their motto, their existence—a single light in a field of darkness.

"Comrades!" Jend called, voice carrying across the ranks. "I ask you, when we were assaulted in our homes and our comrades died, was it for naught? When the vrawl surrounded us in the Mountains and our friends fell, was it for naught? When we marched into the very teeth of Malath and still more were lost, *was it for naught?*"

Jend raised his sword above his head. "Pray to the Maker that you stand firm, that you do not falter, and that your blade sings true! Death comes for us, and we will meet it by spitting in Zadinn's unholy face!"

In tandem with Captain Halion, Jend yelled a final command: "*Charge!*"

In that moment, Boblin shed all his fears. He'd never expected anything but death in these lands, yet he had lived and persevered. He felt no more fear, no more regret, knowing this was the hour the elions had waited for. Knowing that, he was content. And should he die here today…well, he was content with that, too.

Boblin unsheathed his sword, raising his voice in a war cry. The others joined in—Hedro and Celia and Wayne and all the rest. The banner of the Fort fluttered above their heads. The day was here; the time was now. Boblin charged with his comrades into the face of death, never looking back.

The rose slipped free from his tunic and fell, tumbling end over end before landing to the earth in a shower of petals.

Forty

Tim and Nazgar were behind the rear of Zadinn's army when the malichons began their charge. The ground rumbled beneath Tim's feet as the two armies converged. Tim knew he wouldn't like what he saw, so he forced himself to look away from the ensuing conflict. The Army of Kah'lash was a pebble setting itself against a boulder, and many of his friends were about to die.

All the more reason to do my job quickly. He would be more help to his comrades by fighting Zadinn than by watching the Army's hopeless stand, so without a word he turned and directed his attention toward the city ahead of him.

It felt like they covered the distance in no time, but when they reached the base of the plateau, Tim saw the sun had long passed its noon peak. As the two men began the arduous climb, clambering between sharp rocks and thorny vines, the heat grew more intense and the slope steeper. After a half hour they reached the summit, where Tim paused to catch his breath as large trickles of sweat rolled down his back and face. *I haven't even reached Zadinn's palace, and I'm already worn out.*

On the fields and plains of the Deathlands the two armies, now locked in full combat, raged across the landscape in a sea of bodies. Tim watched only long enough to gather his strength again.

The city walls stood before him, reminding Tim of the Rampart—except that the Rampart exuded mystery, and these walls exuded evil. Tim looked up, thinking he'd see sentinels atop the walls, but the parapets were surprisingly empty. He and Nazgar stood facing a closed drawbridge, which had been pulled vertically against the walls with a portcullis covering its oak planks. A light breeze ruffled past the two men, disturbing the bizarre serenity of the scene.

"What now?" Tim asked.

"I am not sure," Nazgar replied.

The city felt dead, unnatural. Tim expected to at least see *some* activity, but nothing moved at all. Behind them, the sounds of battle floated on the breeze as a gust of hot air blew dust in front of them. After a few long moments, the steel bars of the portcullis creaked and then lurched upward, rising with a metallic grinding. Tim looked back to the tops of the battlements, thinking he would see sentries now, but the parapets still remained empty.

After the portcullis had risen to its apex, the planks of the drawbridge moved, descending to present an eerie invitation to enter Zadinn's domain. As the opening widened, Tim caught a glimpse of the city within, which stood as silent and devoid of activity as its outer walls. Rows of empty stone buildings lined empty streets, windows boarded and doors closed.

"It seems we are invited," Nazgar said.

Tim put a hand on his sword as they walked across the drawbridge. He kept expecting hidden guards to attack them, but nothing happened. The longer the silence stretched, the more his unease heightened. As he passed under the teeth of the portcullis, he again thought of the Rampart and realized this moment was a bizarre, even macabre, repetition of his first passage into the North, when he had crossed through the tunnel in the wall along with Rosalie, Daniel, and Quentiin.

As they entered the city, Tim saw a hooded figure standing near the doorway, cloaked in a flowing brown fabric. The creature's face remained shrouded in darkness within the hood, but fleshless, bony fingers protruded from the arms of the robes, grasping the winch that controlled the portcullis. The creature turned its cowled head to watch their progress but remained silent.

"The Gatekeeper," Nazgar said. "More than a legend, I see."

After Tim and Nazgar crossed into the streets, the Gatekeeper cranked the winch to bring the drawbridge back up behind them. As the door creaked shut, locking into place with a sense of inevitable finality, the creature emitted a rasping laugh.

There was nothing to do but go forward, onward and deeper into the deserted city.

The buildings lining the streets did not vary in size, shape, or color. Every structure formed a precise, gray rectangle with bare windows at exact intervals on every side. The empty windowpanes, soulless spectators observing the opening stages of the final conflict, served as the only witnesses to Warrior and Kyrlod's silent journey down the street.

The first sign of other activity came when a plume of flame shot into the sky from the northwest corner of the city. Tim looked in the direction of the flame and saw an enclosure surrounded with drab wooden walls.

"The slave pen," Nazgar said, following Tim's gaze. Tim briefly thought of Quentiin Harggra and the dwerions from Raldoon, but he couldn't delay. If he succeeded in the citadel, the slaves would have their freedom, and if he failed, nothing changed.

They left the empty buildings behind and approached the citadel of black stone, gazing upon its opaque windows and the gargoyles at the head of the steps. They mounted the steps together, flames raging at the entrance to the citadel, the heat lashing against Tim's face while the gargoyles continued watching in silence. When he and Nazgar reached the top of the steps, the flames died, revealing a black void in their absence.

Tim looked at Nazgar. "Is this what you expected?" he asked.

"I did not create a list of expectations," Nazgar replied.

Tim did not ask any other questions. This game was becoming disturbingly simple. They only had one task: go forward. Zadinn controlled the situation; Tim and Nazgar merely followed the current for now.

In front of them, the hallway beckoned. The two stepped into the passage, pausing to let their eyes adjust to the reduced lighting. They stood in a roughly circular room, which narrowed into the continuing hallway. After waiting long enough to acclimate to their surroundings, they stepped forward again, Nazgar in the lead, but they did not make it far. Around them, the walls rotated of their own accord as panes of obsidian stone sealed the exit behind them and the hallway in front of them. Before the two men lost what little light they had to begin with, Tim saw a new, much smaller doorway opening near the base of the wall to the left, rising in a semicircular fashion until it stood three feet in height.

"Tim—" Nazgar began, but he cut off as the room plunged into complete blackness. Something slithered.

"*Who disturbs the master?*" a voice said, echoing off the walls.

Tim immediately unsheathed his sword, and the weapon flared into life. In the faint light, he saw flailing tentacles writhing from the hole in the wall, waving as if testing the air. As he watched, an enormous *thing*, an amorphous being connected to the gyrating limbs, struggled through the opening and into the room. One tentacle lashed at Tim's wrist, striking the sword from his grasp and returning the room to darkness.

"*The Lifesource will not serve you here,*" the voice boomed. "*I am the Guardian.*"

Tim reached for the Lifesource, but he could not grasp the power. He felt another tentacle wrap around his waist and tried to pull away, but it did him no good. The tentacle jerked him off the ground and flung him into the air, where another caught him. In the dark he caught flashes of a pair of twin red eyes, an open mouth, and serrated teeth.

"Nazgar!" he shouted, but silence greeted his cry. Tim pulled a knife from his belt, slamming it into the tentacle around his waist, and the creature hissed in pain. Its limb shuddered, relenting just enough for Tim to push through and tumble free. He felt his sword through his mind, sensing exactly where it was, and ran for the weapon.

Another tentacle snaked forward, wrapping around Tim's ankle and pulling him back. Tim fell onto his face, scrabbling against the concrete floor, and the Guardian's limb dragged him toward its open maw.

* * *

When Tim's sword revealed the creature, Nazgar cursed. He should have guessed Zadinn would have a Horror guarding his doorstep. The room fell into blackness as the creature knocked the sword from Tim's grasp.

Tim wouldn't know its secret, and Nazgar didn't have any time to communicate. He reached inside his belt pouch, grasping for his focusing point, but the Guardian was one step ahead of him. One of its countless limbs yanked Nazgar into the sky, as it had done with Tim, and the pouch fell from Nazgar's hands. He instantly sought the Lifesource, feeling the barrier the Guardian had created between him and the power, but brushed it aside as easily as a cobweb.

Of course, he immediately gave himself away, and now the Guardian would be desperate to silence Nazgar before the Kyrlod could warn Tim. The creature flung Nazgar across the room, slamming his body against the wall, dazing him so much he lost hold of the Lifesource. The Guardian slammed him against the wall one more time before releasing him. Nazgar slid to the floor, white sparks flashing across his vision.

* * *

The Guardian threw Tim into the sky before catching him yet again, tossing him between its many limbs, toying with its helpless prey. "*I am a Horror, boy! Do you like me?*" the creature taunted.

A Horror. Tim had heard of them before. At the school in Vonku, he'd been instructed in many subjects, including myth-tales. Myth-tales contained many creatures, some real and some imaginary. One Horror supposedly lived in the Odtune Mountains, but nobody Tim knew had been curious enough—or crazy enough—to find out for themselves. The creatures came from ancient times, where it was said they could delve into minds to learn a victim's greatest strength and take it away. Thus a man with awesome strength would be feeble as an infant in a Horror's grasp, a master swordsman would not be able to hold his blade straight—and an Advocate would not be able to use the Lifesource. Men had no defense against a Horror.

A tentacle wrapped around Tim's upper arms, holding him in the air as the Horror's mouth opened underneath his dangling feet. Tim could almost see a light of amusement in the creature's red eyes. Its teeth glistened. The limb held Tim suspended for a moment and then lowered him toward its gaping jaws.

* * *

Nazgar wiped a trickle of blood from his eye. He had to move slowly so as to not attract attention. As he inched across the floor, he reached out with one hand ahead of him until he felt the soft leather of his pouch beneath his fingertips. Nazgar upended the pouch, and the smooth, perfect marble tumbled into his trembling palm.

The Horror noticed. It moved in a blur, striking at Nazgar with a tentacle. This time, Nazgar was ready. As the limb came within a hairsbreadth of his face, Nazgar lifted the focusing point high, and the stone flared a brilliant, blinding blue.

* * *

Tim struggled against the creature's hold, but it did him no good. His boots hung a handspan above the Horror's teeth, and he felt the heat of its breath on his soles. Nonetheless he continued to seek the Lifesource, hoping to find a way, a crack to slip through, but the barrier between him and the power was seamless.

Then a blue light cut through the air, and Tim noticed Nazgar standing in the far corner of the room, wreathed in a blue aura. The Horror hissed, lashing at the Kyrlod with tentacles in every direction, but Nazgar had surrounded himself with an invisible wall of protection, and the creature's limbs slammed ineffectually against the Kyrlod's blockade.

The light of Nazgar's shield hit Tim's eyes so forcefully it pushed all thoughts from his mind, except a single memory from a class in myth-tales. As if in a dream, Tim saw a companion at the school in Vonku, an older man named Jalen, raise his hand from the back of the classroom:

"Horrors ain't dangerous at all," Jalen said. *The entire class turned to look at him. Jalen was known for being a little strange.*

"Do you care to clarify?" the instructor asked.

"It's all in yer mind," Jalen said, *tapping the side of his head. "It's fear that makes 'em dangerous, nothin' else."*

"Well," the instructor said, "you are more than welcome to go to the Odtune Mountains and prove what you say is true. Until then, let me conduct this lesson."

Jalen didn't say much after that.

Tim sought the Lifesource again. The barrier the Horror held in front of the power felt as real as ever, and so did the hot breath at his feet. No, Jalen would have been quite dead in the Odtune Mountains. Except…Tim *had* used the Lifesource when the Guardian came into the room. The Horror should know his strength, already have cut him off, but it was only *later*, after the Guardian said Tim could not use the Lifesource, that Tim felt the barrier form.

Tim tried to reach the power again. The blockade was in place, but he thought maybe it felt a little weaker. Then he looked over and saw Nazgar holding the focusing point, having no trouble at all using the Lifesource. Nazgar knew the creature's secret, and as such, its powers proved useless against him.

Renewed with certainty, Tim pushed against the barrier with a more assertive force, and as the wall between him and the Lifesource shattered, the magic flooded into him once more with its soothing yet powerful presence. The Guardian shook Tim violently, trying to rattle him into submission, but it was too late. The Lifesource surged through Tim's veins, pulsing with barely controlled energy.

The Guardian released Tim, dropping him straight toward its open mouth. Tim reacted instantly, throwing a protective shield between him and the Horror's teeth, simultaneously rolling away from the creature and back to the ground. A dozen tentacles reached for him, but Tim fenced himself in with a ring of green fire. The Guardian pulled its limbs back, but not quickly enough. The fires burned its skin, and a tentacle shriveled. The Guardian screamed—a high, keening sound—and for a moment, Tim's control over the Lifesource wavered.

Then a blue lance of light shot from Nazgar's focusing point, striking the Guardian and slamming it against the wall. The Horror shrieked and struggled, but the spear of light held it pinned against the wall.

"Tim!" Nazgar shouted. "I cannot hold it by myself!"

Tim realized the Horror was slowly pushing free from the Kyrlod's grip. Nazgar held the focusing point high, but beads of sweat had formed on his forehead and his arms trembled from the strain.

Tim raised his hand. A bar of green fire shot from his palm, striking the Guardian from the opposite direction, combining with Nazgar's beam to form a blue-and-green V holding the Horror in place. The Guardian writhed in pain as light consumed its body, dissipating into vapors that dispersed into the air, leaving behind a few faint tendrils of smoke.

Tim lowered his hands. Light returned to the room, and the two companions could see each other clearly once more. Nazgar put the focusing point back in his pouch, his face gray. The battle had clearly weakened him.

Tim picked up his sword. "Did you give me that memory?" he asked.

"I cannot fabricate a memory," Nazgar said. "The knowledge existed in your mind. I just unlocked it."

"So that's where a Guardian gets its power," Tim said. "It drains your mind."

"Yes," Nazgar added, "it is a deadly weapon. Be wary for further deceit, for in this place, Zadinn will assault your mind as well as your body."

Tim wondered what to expect next, but he didn't have to wait long. The walls shifted again, and the hallway returned, revealing a long, dark path leading deeper into the citadel. Tim took only a handful of steps before a light mist rose and spiraled around his ankles with a cold, wet touch. The mist slowly filled the entire corridor, consuming the path with an ebbing, fluctuating fog, and Tim looked back at Nazgar. The Kyrlod's face was thin.

"We'll go in together," Nazgar said, "but I don't believe it will matter."

"Do you know what it is?" Tim asked.

"I believe so," Nazgar said. "This passage touches the veil between our world and Malath. The moment you and I step into the mist, it will separate us. We'll have to make the journey alone."

He gripped Tim's shoulder. "There will be things in there. Some might be real, others imaginary. The only way to survive is to reach the end. Fight if you have to, run if you must, but above all else, *do not leave the path*."

Tim looked at the fog-filled corridor. "Stay on the path? That's all?"

"I hope so."

"I miss the days when you knew everything," Tim said. He turned to the hallway and gripped his sword. The blade glowed green, filling him with a comforting tingle.

"Stay on the path," Nazgar repeated.

"Right," Tim replied. He lowered his sword and stepped into the writhing mists.

*　*　*

In midcharge, the Army of Kah'lash came to an immediate halt. Boblin had to commend Captain Halion; the man had trained his soldiers well. It was all part of the plan, and it worked wonderfully. The malichons had been bracing for an impact with the Army, but when the Army unexpectedly stopped, the malichons were forced to rush farther forward than they had anticipated, and their well-constructed charge turned to a disorganized stumble.

That was when the Army of Kah'lash unleashed its second surprise. In a single uniform motion, every soldier threw his or her explosives into the sky. Thousands of small leather sacks sailed into the air, each performing a graceful arch before landing inside the malichons' front lines. The effect was instantaneous. The pouches exploded on impact, and a sequence of massive detonations shook the forefront of Zadinn's army. Fountains of earth and stone shot skyward. Hundreds of malichons exploded, and the deadly shrapnel raining back down killed even more enemy troops.

The powder inside the pouches was similar to the Fort's explosives, only more potent. Furthermore, the weapons did not require flame to start. They used juice extracted from oaktree root, and every man carried a flask of the juice with him.

None of the elions hesitated in preparing the second assault. Boblin pulled another pouch from his belt and squeezed a few drops of juice inside it. He paused, waiting for Jend's signal, and then threw the explosive at the malichons. As soon as the explosions sounded, Boblin immediately pulled out his third pouch. This was the Army's sole advantage, and they made full use of it. The front lines of the malichon army detonated once, twice, thrice. Boblin's ears rang as the repeated concussions rocked the battlefield, throwing hundreds of enemy troops backward.

As the growing ranks of dead malichons littered the ground, the enemy formation momentarily broke under the unexpected barrage, but not for long. The malichons soon reformed their ranks into interlocking segments and marched forward, pushing past their slain comrades.

Boblin joined in with two more desperate volleys as the Army pushed its advantage to the limit, but this time the enemy troops did not falter. Instead they continued moving even as death rained upon them, marching through the explosions. The Army abandoned the pouches and surged forward. Boblin saw the massive horde of black-armored malichons bear down upon them and gave a shout of defiance, knowing it was useless. They were water breaking against stone.

The Army picked up speed and force as it closed the remaining distance. Boblin had thrown away all fear during his first charge, and now a seemingly endless rush of energy flowed through him. Every fiber in his body seemed to know death or salvation could come at any instant—and the closer he was to death, the more alive he felt.

The two armies slammed into each other, the impact rattling Boblin to his very core. The sheer force of the collision caused some to sail into the sky, somersaulting over their opponents and landing in a jumble of broken bones. Boblin leveled his sword and struck his first malichon while still running full tilt. The creature didn't have time to deflect Boblin's thrust. Boblin drove his sword into the malichon's chest, killing it instantly, and then pulled his blade free as madness reigned all around.

Boblin knew he wouldn't survive unless he reunited with his allies, but he couldn't plan that far ahead. There were too many malichons around him, and he was constantly spinning to fend off attacks. He moved his blade as quickly as possible, ignoring the rising ache in his arms as black blood sprayed everywhere. Nearby, he caught a glimpse of Gendar Halion pulling his twin swords from his back and leaping forward with a blade in each hand, cutting enemies down like grain at harvest time. Farther down, Jend, Hugo, and Ken formed a defensive triangle, holding their ground as the banner of the Fort of Pellen fluttered above their heads.

The bloodred sun beat down upon the Deathlands as the two armies vied back and forth. Meanwhile, in the skies above, the crows and vultures began to circle.

Forty-One

Quentiin did not struggle as Gald bound his hands. He would not have chosen for things to end this way, but he had done what he could. His days as a slave were over, and no more prisoners would die on his account. He knew this might happen—he *expected* it—and he would meet it with head held high. Besides, his refusal to struggle disappointed his captors. Veldor and the others wanted him to break down, beg, plead, and cry out, and he sure as Malath didn't plan on giving them *that* satisfaction.

They didn't even have to drag him to the caves, where death awaited him. No, he walked of his own accord, alone and unaided, back straight. Inside, however, he felt numb. Everything around him, slaves and slave drivers, the sound of his own footfalls, the brush of hot air from the flames of the Pit, came across as dim and muted.

As Quentiin passed Jolldo, he looked into his friend's eyes. He felt no anger toward Jolldo, only pity. Once, Jolldo would have stood by him to the very end. That time was no more. Quentiin turned back to the path ahead, rocks crunching under his feet as he set forth on his last march, a condemned dwerion walking to the gallows. But here in this place, his crime had been neither thievery nor murder. No, he had committed no more than the crime of having a free spirit, for in this place, the cherished liberties that served as every being's birthright instead became death sentences.

Quentiin looked southeast, where the dome of Zadinn's citadel stood beyond the outer walls of the slave pen. Tim and Boblin were probably out there right now, launching an assault on the Dark Lord's fortress. Quentiin didn't expect a victory to come from it—the enemy was too large—but he still hoped the elions could deal a vicious blow to Zadinn before the day was done.

As they reached the caves, Gald stepped ahead of Quentiin and took him by the tunic, dragging him into the tunnel. The gesture was completely unnecessary, merely a way for Gald to demonstrate that he was in control. Quentiin just laughed. The slave drivers looked at him as if he had gone mad, and that made Quentiin laugh harder. They should have known. He'd gone mad weeks ago.

His captors, three malichons in addition to Gald, lit torches in the hallway before continuing deeper into the passage. Gald held onto Quentiin, just as he held onto his illusion of control, and behind them, a fifth malichon stepped into the tunnel with a wooden box cradled in its arms.

The tunnel opened into the cavern Quentiin remembered from his last visit. Nothing had been disturbed in the time since Veldor had taken him here, and Quentiin saw his same footprints etched in the dirt. The rectangular pit, with its empty harness dangling in the air above their heads, beckoned to him. Quentiin almost found it to be a welcome sight, a glass of water at the end of a long road. The malichons set fire to the torches around the room, and light and shadow flickered across the walls, creating a rhythm for the grisly dance about to commence. At the far wall, Gald turned the winch, which held the harness in place, and lowered the leather device until it hung level with the floor.

"Bring him," Gald said, and a malichon pushed Quentiin forward toward the harness. Gald lashed the straps around Quentiin's waist and shoulders, pulling them much tighter than necessary, while the malichon with the box stepped forward, offering a toothy smile.

"I believe you know of this," Gald said, opening the lid to the box just a crack. Quentiin heard a buzzing, clacking sound from inside, and remembered Veldor telling him about the scorpions. Gald reached inside and prodded one of the insects free, flicking it with his forefinger and into the hole below. "Now, it is waiting for you to arrive. It will make things more interesting." Gald stepped back and placed a hand on the winch.

Quentiin spoke for the first time. "I ain't goin' to survive this."

"An astute observation," Gald replied.

Quentiin cocked his head. "D'ye believe in ghosts, Gald?"

Gald's response was everything Quentiin could ask for. The malichon's features whitened with fear before he managed to smooth his face over again. Quentiin smiled. He should have known malichons were superstitious sons of goats, and if Gald now jumped at shadows for the rest of his life, Quentiin could rest much easier.

Gald cranked the winch, and Quentiin rose into the air until he hung above the pit. Gald stopped momentarily as the other malichons prepared a vat of liquid rock below the hanging dwerion. The process went slowly, but Quentiin didn't expected this to be quick; the malichons wanted to heighten his fear by drawing things out.

At last the malichons drew back, their task complete. *About time*, Quentiin thought. His arms and legs ached from the strain of the harness, and he was ready to return to solid ground. As the malichons lined the edges of the pit in anticipation, Gald grasped the winch's handle again.

"Shall we cast bets?" he asked.

"Not until he's in the vat," another malichon replied. "That's when we find out how much of his backbone truly remains."

"Aye," a third concurred. "He might appear brave now, but that will end soon."

Gald looked up at Quentiin. "This is your last chance to make amends. After this, we cannot turn back."

Quentiin sincerely doubted any "amends" would save him now. Gald was only trying to elicit a response, and when Quentiin did not reply, the malichon lowered the harness. Below Quentiin, the liquid rock waited, ready for a new victim, while above, the scorpions buzzed in their box. Try as he might, Quentiin couldn't fully suppress his fear. The malichons, especially Gald, held much animosity toward him, and Quentiin did not expect them to hold anything back. Then again, if their positions were reversed, Quentiin wouldn't have held back either.

As Quentiin passed the malichons on his way down, one spat on him, but he ignored it. On the floor of the pit, the skulls and bones of other slaves who'd met their demise waited for him to join them. Quentiin guessed he was about two body lengths away from the liquid rock. Several long seconds followed, and the soles of his feet almost touched the wet cement when a new voice spoke.

"Now see here, laddies, I don't think I can allow this."

Quentiin looked up. He couldn't see beyond the malichons, but he recognized Jolldo Graff's voice.

"Return to your work, slave," Gald said.

"Go to Malath," Jolldo replied, and Quentiin heard a clamor of voices as a group of dwerions surged into the chamber above. Wood crashed and splintered. Yagglem materialized above him, sword in hand, and sliced a malichon guard open from waist to neck before pushing the body into the pit, where it tumbled past Quentiin before landing in a broken heap on the liquid rock.

Meanwhile, the winch holding Quentiin in place began rising. When he came level with the rest of the chamber, he saw three malichons fighting against six dwerions. Vellgo stood at the winch, raising Quentiin to safety, and Gald lay nearby, crumpled against a row of shattered wooden shelves. As Quentiin rose into view, Gald climbed back onto his feet and swung his sword toward Vellgo's head. Vellgo turned, countering the blow with his ax, and, in doing so, released the winch.

Quentiin plummeted back down, but before he struck the liquid rock, he jerked to a halt and rose again just in time to see a malichon plunge a sword into Arrlin's chest. The dwerion staggered back, blood spraying from the wound, as the malichon pulled his blade free. Arrlin collapsed, the life gone from his eyes.

Jolldo reacted viciously, attacking the malichon from the side and disarming him. He seized the guard and threw him into the pit. The malichon fell past Quentiin, screaming as it landed in the mixture with a soft *plop*.

Briiga now stood at the winch, raising Quentiin to safety. Behind Briiga, Gald and Vellgo still fought in the corner of the room. The last malichon tried to attack Briiga, but Yagglem intervened and stopped the guard with a sword through its shoulder blades. The guard went rigid, collapsing onto its knees as Briiga pulled Quentiin to safety.

In the corner, Gald disarmed Vellgo, swinging his sword in an arc and bringing it down toward Vellgo's head, but he was not quick enough. Quentiin tore free from the harness and crossed the distance in a blink, slamming Gald to the ground. Gald drove his knee into Quentiin's chest, pushing Quentiin away and getting to his feet. Quentiin rolled to the side, weaponless, and stood up next to the wall as Gald reclaimed his sword.

Gald lunged toward him, but Quentiin sidestepped the thrust and then pulled a torch from a nearby sconce, just in time to duck another blow. He drove the flaming brand into Gald's face, and the malichon shrieked in agony as Quentiin pulled Gald's sword away. For anybody else, he would have willingly used the blade, but not for Gald. He threw the malichon down, wrapping one hand around Gald's neck while continuing to push the burning torch against the skin of the malichon's face. Gald screamed, writhing as his skin melted. The sickening smell of burning flesh wafted to Quentiin's nostrils, but he held on for as long as it took, and when Gald's struggles finally ceased, Quentiin discarded the torch. Gald's face was charred beyond recognition. Quentiin kicked the body into the pit, not even bothering to watch it fall.

He turned to face his comrades. "How did ye do it?" he asked.

"We were in the shapin' area," Jolldo said. "There weren't many malichons there, an' they were easy to overcome."

"Ye saved me, brothers," Quentiin said. "I don't know that I can ever thank ye."

"No, Quentiin," Jolldo replied, "you saved *us*." The others nodded.

"We wouldn't o' had the stomach to free ourselves if'n you hadn't fought first," Yagglem said. "I'm afraid we're in yer debt."

"Then let's pay our debts off together," Quentiin said, gesturing toward the tunnel. "Let's go to the Pit and end this."

*   *   *

Boblin was surrounded on all sides. In the beginning, he was able to see his other comrades, but now he could only see malichons. Ironically, this was probably the reason he still lived. Focused on fighting the main group, the malichons did not perceive a lone elion in their midst to be a threat. Still, Boblin knew he didn't have much time. He needed to find his way back to friendly territory before he caught a stray ax in the skull.

He turned south, hacking and slashing his way through enemy ranks as the malichon army continued surging forward. A shove from an enemy troop sent Boblin to his knees—which, in fact, saved him, because Boblin fell just as another malichon swung a sword through the space where his head had been.

Boblin reacted fast. Still on his knees, he drove his sword into the malichon's stomach. The malichon fell backward, and Boblin pulled his weapon free. The other malichons marched on, trampling their comrade's body underfoot, as Boblin stood up to counter another blow. He cut this newest malichon's head from its shoulders and saw a hole to freedom beyond, an open space unoccupied by any fighting. If he could make it just twenty paces, he would be free from this nightmarish horde. He needed to move fast; his chances of surviving, with enemies and swords everywhere, decreased by the second.

It proved too good to be true. As Boblin stumbled toward the hole, something knocked him facedown, and a crushing pain exploded at the base of his spine. This time his training saved him. Overcoming the instinct to writhe ineffectually, Boblin commanded his muscles to move and rolled onto his back, in time to avoid a mace that crashed down beside him.

Above him, the malichon swung the mace around, winding up for another blow, but then a crossbow bolt slammed into the malichon from behind, punching through its armor as the arrowhead sprouted from its chest. The malichon lost its momentum, and a second bolt struck it in the throat to end its life.

Hedro Desh stepped from out of the fray, lowering his crossbow and offering Boblin a hand. Boblin took his grip, climbing to his feet and retrieving his sword.

"Easy there, Kule," Hedro said. "I can't always look out for you." For once, Boblin welcomed the elion's self-assured grin.

In that instant, another malichon struck from the side, swinging an ax at Hedro's exposed flank, but Boblin placed himself in front of the blow, raising his sword to deflect the malichon's weapon. The jarring impact disarmed both Boblin and the malichon, but Commander Jend didn't teach *ailar* for nothing. Boblin lunged forward, coming in low and fast, and delivered a knife-edge blow to the malichon's throat. As the creature fell to its knees, Boblin followed up with a kick that laid the malichon on its back. In the same smooth move, Boblin retrieved his sword and drove the blade into the malichon's chest.

"You were saying?" Boblin said to Hedro, showing a slightly cocky grin of his own.

"Point made," Hedro replied. "Are you hurt badly? I saw that malichon hit you in the back."

"I'm fine." Boblin doubted he had more than a bruise; the armor had taken the brunt of the attack and protected him from serious injury. "We need to get out of here."

"Agreed."

In a few short strides, the two elions stepped away from the edge of the battle and took shelter in a small copse of stunted trees. As the air rang with the sounds of steel and death, they crouched behind the stunted tree trunks to catch their breath and assess the situation.

"Do you know where the main body of Division Five is?" Hedro asked Boblin.

"No," Boblin answered. "I got separated during the first wave of the charge."

"Me, too. I'd hoped you might know more."

"Sorry to disappoint."

Lacking any better options, they began moved along the sheltered length of trees, skirting the enemy while seeking out the rest of the Army to lend aid where it was needed most. The other four divisions were an hour off, if not more, so it would be a long time before they could count on reinforcements. If the two elions wanted to survive, they had to play this game carefully. As the tree line curved southeast, Boblin saw a short ridge of stone running directly east, and beyond it, the standard of the Fort of Pellen, fluttering next to the banner of the Army of Kah'lash. However, a sea of malichons surrounded the two banners, converging ever inward to crush the freedom fighters.

Boblin exchanged a glance with Hedro. Their fellow elions were deep in the middle of enemy troops, and the two of them alone couldn't make a dent in the malichon forces. *This is bleak.* Boblin laughed abruptly. *Bleak? That's a karfing streak of optimism.* Rainy afternoons were bleak. This was a hurricane.

Hedro looked at him. "You laugh at the oddest things, Kule."

For some reason that made Boblin want to laugh even harder. He surveyed the territory. The eastern ridge, which rose to a height of about four feet, stood on the malichons' western flank, running north to south. Boblin removed his crossbow, and Hedro raised an eyebrow.

"We can put that ridge between ourselves and the malichons," Boblin said. "We've got our crossbows. We can start a flank attack from there. The wall will protect us for a little while."

"I like it," Hedro concurred.

The two elions raced across the short stretch of open terrain. When they reached the ridge, they lowered themselves beneath the wall and prepared their weapons. Hedro pulled a pouch from his belt and unscrewed his flask of juice. He looked at Boblin. "Let's use these first. It'll get their attention."

And kill a fair number in the process. "Splendid," Boblin said, doing likewise. Synchronizing their movements, both elions squeezed a few precious drops onto the powder and then threw the explosives over the lip of the stone wall. The pouches landed in the middle of a pocket of malichons, detonating on impact. A plume shot skyward, throwing a dozen malichons in several directions. Those that landed—whether in one piece or several—did not rise again. A brief gap opened in the enemy force, and the two elions unleashed another pair of explosives, the resultant concussions rocking the mass of enemy troops.

Without pausing, Boblin fitted an arrow to his crossbow and fired, taking a malichon between the shoulder blades. Hedro followed suit, and the enemy flank scattered.

Boblin ducked as a long, feathered shaft shot toward them, striking the ground between him and Hedro, followed by an entire volley of arrows as the malichons reorganized to face this new threat. Over twenty bolts clattered around the two elions, one passing so close to Boblin he felt air rush past his cheek. *This is about to get interesting.*

* * *

Tim could not see through the mist. As the fog rose around him, obscuring his vision, his sword illuminated the stone floor in a pool of green light. He took a few tentative steps, the vapors dissipating as he moved through them. He listened for sounds, but the surrounding air felt heavy and oppressive, and the hallway was uncomfortably quiet. At first he couldn't pinpoint the exact source of his unease, and then after he took several more steps forward, he realized he could not hear even his own footfalls.

Behind him the fog closed as quickly as it had parted, the vapors forming a curtain to conceal his exit. After he'd spent several minutes in the deep mists, the fog lifted, separating enough for him to see perhaps ten paces ahead but no more. Entrails of fog clung to the edges of the walls, but at least he now had a clearer view, and as he stepped into the opening, he heard the comforting sound of his boots striking the floor.

He turned to see if Nazgar was behind him, but the Kyrlod was nowhere to be seen. Then a roar shattered the silence, and a large shape hurtled through the vapors. As the creature neared, Tim glimpsed a long muzzle with white teeth flashing in the dark. The beast emerged from the mist, standing twice Tim's height. Crooked arms jutted from its torso, ending in tipped claws, and saliva dripped from its jaws as it lunged toward him. Tim raised his sword and a spear of light lanced from the tip of his blade, striking the beast in the chest. The monster instantly vaporized, proving it had been no more than an illusion.

In this place, Zadinn will assault your mind as well as your body.

The unexpected attack left Tim on edge, and not being able to see more than a few paces in any direction only exacerbated the situation. He wiped his face clean of sweat and turned back to the main corridor, coming face to face with Quentiin Harggra, who was draped in chains and had blood running down his temples.

"Tim," Quentiin said, "thank the Maker I found ye."

Tim hesitated. Nazgar had said Quentiin was in the Pit, not *here*. The dwerion walked toward Tim, a worn length of chain dangling between the shackles that held his wrists together. "Take 'em off, laddie," Quentiin pleaded. "Please take 'em off."

Tim stepped forward and noted that his footfalls had gone silent again. He narrowed his eyes. "How do I know you're real?"

"What d'ye mean, laddie?" Quentiin asked. Tim walked past the dwerion, careful not to touch him. He didn't know if the illusion was dangerous or not, but he had no reason to take unnecessary risks.

"Please, laddie," Quentiin said. "Please!"

Tim turned and ran. He couldn't stand the image of a broken, weeping Quentiin. It was just another illusion. It *had* to be.

And what if I'm wrong?

Then I just left my friend behind with the monsters in the mist.

What disturbed Tim the most was how Zadinn knew Quentiin, or at least the illusion of him, would affect him. The Dark Lord knew Tim's weaknesses. But how?

As the thick fog closed in again, a chorus of voices surrounded Tim. A teeming mass of black shadows shaped like men appeared in the corridor. The wraiths grasped and clutched with open palms, but Tim did not turn to them or leave the path. As he passed, the silhouettes faded away, replaced next by a horde of reptilian monsters that stood on two legs, cloaked in armor.

One of the lizard-like creatures leaped toward Tim with a high-pitched screech. Tim caught it on his sword, expecting it to vanish like everything else, and was surprised when his blade instead struck flesh. The impact carried Tim and the creature onto the ground, and he drove his weapon further into the lizard's chest. The creature lashed at him with clawed hands, scoring three deep gashes across Tim's side. Tim pulled away, tearing his sword free.

Next, a sarchon launched itself from the ceiling. Tim faced this latest attack, swinging his sword in an arc and taking all three of the bird's heads. Tim turned back, prepared to fend off another attack from the lizard-creature, but it had vanished. *Real or imaginary?* He had no way of knowing. The passage had fallen silent once more, and Tim stood still, regaining control of his breath. He swallowed hard, wondering how much more of this he could take.

After Tim walked another dozen paces, Boblin stumbled from the shadows and fell onto his knees in the corridor, cradling Celia Alcion's head in his lap. "It's all lost," he said to Tim. "All lost!"

Tim continued walking, refusing to meet Boblin's eyes, even when his friend let out an anguished howl. Other people he knew came forth from the mists—elions from the Fort, old friends from Vonku, family members from long gone. He ignored them all, but could not shut out their pleas, and as he walked, tears formed in his eyes. He knew it was all false, all lies, but it didn't matter; he was still turning them away, still rejecting them, still leaving them in the darkness.

Suddenly all forms but two vanished, and when Tim saw them, he stopped. Rosalie Matthias came forward first, touching her son's trembling arm as she looked up at him. "Your father and I need you," she said. "Please, my son. Don't leave us here."

Behind her, off the path and in the mists, Daniel Matthias hung by his wrists from the wall. Tim's father raised his head and met Tim's gaze, his eyes empty and devoid of hope. "Save your mother, Tim," he said. "If you cannot save me, at least save her. Turn and go from this place."

Tim shook with grief. "No," he said.

Rosalie fell, clutching the leg of his pants and sobbing. "Please, Timothy. Please!"

"Son," Daniel said. "You don't know this place. You don't know what it has done to us. Don't leave your mother. Don't abandon us!"

"No!" Tim said, pulling away from Rosalie. He could barely see through the tears blurring his vision. Agony tore through his body; the sight of his mother and father, alive but shackled in torment, was too much. Nonetheless, he forced himself to take a step forward. Their cries rose all around him, but he continued walking. Nobody else was there—just Tim and his mother and father. They needed his help, and he couldn't give it to them. He took another step. *How long can this go on?* He took another step...

And all stopped, except for the mists that never seemed to end. Tim sank to the floor, dropping the sword and allowing its light to wink out. He needed to rest, just for a few seconds. As he fought against a despair that threatened to overwhelm him, the fog parted, revealing the outline of a door in the distance. *It's almost over.* The end was in sight.

Tim stood up, reaching for his sword, and one more roar shook the passageway. Yet another pool of mist rose behind him, and a familiar blue light exploded from within the fog as the floor vibrated. Nazgar flew from the mists, landing at Tim's feet in a heap of torn clothing, cradling a broken arm against his chest. Tim placed the Kyrlod's good arm around his shoulder and hoisted him onto his feet. Fear was etched in Nazgar's face. "We need to move fast," the Kyrlod said, his voice hoarse.

Footsteps thundered, and Nazgar pushed Tim to the side, where mist still covered the walls. "Hide!" he said. "It can't see very well in the fog!"

Tim abruptly stopped him, placing a hand on the Kyrlod's chest. "What about Boblin?" he asked. "He hasn't come out yet."

"Tim," Nazgar said, face despairing, "Boblin is dead."

Tim had had enough of these karfing illusions. He raised his sword and ran it through Nazgar. The Kyrlod disintegrated like all the others before him. The shadow of the approaching beast also melted away.

"Boblin didn't come in with us," Tim said bitterly. "I would have expected you to know that." The fog lifted once more—perhaps for real this time—and as the passageway cleared, Tim again stood with Nazgar. The Kyrlod looked in much better shape than his illusion had, though he bore cuts and scrapes from their struggle with the Guardian.

"Are you real?" Tim asked him.

"Are *you*?" Nazgar replied.

The answer would have to do. Tim approached the massive door at the end of the hallway. Iron straps bound its oak frame, and a large brass knocker was mounted on its surface. Tim reached out with the Lifesource and felt a cold presence on the other side of the door. Merely touching it made him want to shrink away. Well, this was what he'd come for. This only had one ending, and there wasn't anything to do but continue. That being said, Tim wasn't sure anybody—even the Maker—knew what that ending would be.

"What do you suppose?" Nazgar asked.

Tim raised an eyebrow. "I thought I was the one who asked the questions."

"I like surprising my students," Nazgar said.

Tim turned back to the door. "I believe in being a polite guest. I suppose that means I should knock." He seized the brass ring and pounded it against the door three times. *Boom, boom, boom.* The sound echoed in the hallway, and Tim stepped back from the door. Nothing happened for the first few moments, and then the door swung open of its own accord. Tim placed a hand, clammy with sweat, on the pommel of his sword. *Every man makes a choice. Choose, and accept the consequences. And this is my choice—to face him.*

Tim stepped into a circular room. A dim glow hung over everything, filling the chamber with shadowy light. A long carpet ran down the middle, with vents running along the floor on either side of the path, emitting green light and noxious fumes. Mists covered the surface of the floor, and rows of skulls rested on ledges. In the center of the chamber, a chair forged from human bones sat atop a raised dais. A man lounged in the chair, drumming his fingers on the armrest with a wistful smile on his face as he cradled a staff in his lap. Flowing robes covered his body.

As Tim entered the chamber, Zadinn Kanas lifted a hand to brush a lock of black hair away from his forehead, and the eyes of the two men met for the first time.

Zadinn showed his teeth when he smiled. "Welcome, my friend."

Forty-Two

The Warrior of Light and the Dark Lord faced each other from across the room, an eternal span of seconds stretching between them. For a moment Tim felt removed from the world, as if he stood on the edge of a great canyon looking down into a chasm. This was about more than just him and Zadinn. It was something much bigger, colossal.

Tim stepped forward and Nazgar followed behind him. The air in the chamber grew deathly still as Zadinn stirred in his chair, sitting up straighter and putting a hand around the base of his staff, his smile never leaving his face.

Tim heard water boiling and looked to his right, where a massive black cauldron sat atop another dais in the room's far corner. Green lights played above the surface of the water, and the faint shapes of ghostly wraiths rose and fell in the light.

"Zadinn Kanas," Tim pronounced. "I am here to remove you from these lands."

Zadinn waved a hand. "My friend, I am shocked and appalled at your lack of courtesy. I give you free entry into my palace, my home, and you have only thoughts of battle."

"My friends are dying on your doorstep," Tim said. "With all due respect, I'd like to get on with this."

"Get on with what?" Zadinn asked, looking around in a casual, nonchalant manner, acting as though he and Tim were merely having afternoon tea together.

Tim prepared to draw his sword, but stopped when he felt a bolt of air rush past him. Behind him, Nazgar rose into the air, unbidden, and slammed against the closest wall with a jarring impact, where he hung locked in place with arms at his sides and feet dangling above a ledge of skulls. Tim turned back to Zadinn. The Dark Lord's false smile had disappeared, replaced with a cold, narrow visage, his eyes burning with a faint yellow light.

"Please do not touch your weapon," Zadinn said softly. "I did my best to start on a positive footing. If you persist in your need for violence, I will kill the Kyrlod."

Tim hesitated and then let his hand fall away from his sword. Nazgar spoke to Zadinn. "Your arrogance will be your undoing."

Zadinn's smile returned. "The prophet speaks. Did you know I killed your brother of the Kyrlod in the very same spot I now hold you? Then again, your kind always did like things that come full circle."

"Ragzan was not a Kyrlod," Nazgar said.

Zadinn nodded. "Perhaps not. But he *was* your brother."

At this, Nazgar fell silent, and Zadinn turned to Tim. "You never had the pleasure of meeting Ragzan, young Matthias. If you had, you might have noticed he bore a striking resemblance to our friend here. There's nothing quite like identical twins."

Tim tried unsuccessfully to mask his shock. Nazgar had told him of Ragzan, the renegade Kyrlod, but he'd never mentioned anything about the prophet being family, much less his *twin*.

"The Maker made this place a world of balance," Nazgar replied. "Ragzan and I served as counterpoints to each other, and though you might think you know what that means, Zadinn Kanas, you do not."

"I imagine both of you kept many secrets," Zadinn said. "Thankfully your brother is dead, and only you remain. But I did not open my doors to bandy words with you. No, I wish to speak with young Matthias."

Nazgar did not reply, so Zadinn turned back to Tim. "I mention the Kyrlod's late brother to make a point. I'm sure you're aware your instructor has a tendency to conceal things."

Tim tried to relax, relieving his body of tension. "Everyone is entitled to secrets." Zadinn's ploy was obvious; he wanted to drive a wedge between Tim and Nazgar by planting seeds of distrust, but Tim wasn't about to play that game.

"True," Zadinn agreed. "However, you might want to know *certain* secrets, especially when they govern the course of your life and death."

"I prefer not to know. It keeps things more exciting."

Zadinn leaned in his chair, rolling his eyes skyward. "Nazgar told you about the 'shadows,' didn't he? I didn't think he'd still be using *that* lie."

"It is not a lie," Nazgar said.

Zadinn tilted his head toward Tim. "Did the Kyrlod ever tell you about the war?"

"You mean the one taking place on your front lawn?"

"No, the Ancient War."

Tim fell silent. He didn't want to give Zadinn a response, didn't want to admit he'd never heard of any Ancient War, but Zadinn said no more. The Dark Lord arched an eyebrow, waiting for Tim to speak as the seconds dragged.

"No," Tim finally admitted. He looked to Nazgar, but the Kyrlod said nothing.

Zadinn pointed at himself, and then at Tim. "Both you and I have been manipulated, do you know that? Earlier the Kyrlod spoke of balance. Well, in order to achieve this purported balance, the supposedly omnipotent Maker and his nemesis, the Demon Lord of the underworld, made a pact. Had they fought for control of this world, the battle would have ripped the universe apart. So instead they created a fiction with two halves, one half called 'good' and the other called 'evil.' In doing so, the Maker and the Demon Lord allowed themselves to wage their war with human surrogates. And this, my friend, is the part of the tale where you and I come in. Thanks to me, Malath has held sway in the North for some time, and so our masters deemed that I be challenged.

"You were born, imbued with powers you barely understand, and then granted the mantle of the Warrior. But this is a joke and a lie, a crown of false gold. If you and I battle today, the scales will ultimately tip, either toward Harmea or Malath, in one direction or another." He paused. "I do not think you will win, but even if you do, it will bring you no peace. It will only be the beginning of a long and arduous task with neither thanks nor reward, because the balance is meant to be tested. Before long, a new threat will rise, and you will need to overcome it or die. And if you win that battle, still another danger will arrive, and another after that, on and on without end, as you fight wars for an omnipotent being with little sense of mercy or gratitude, on your way down a long road with little comfort at its finish."

Tim met Zadinn's gaze. "You seem to be handling your road well. And if I wear one mantle, then you wear the other. I don't see you hesitating to play your part, if that's what it is."

Zadinn pounded his fist on the throne. The light in his eyes took on a keen, sharp glow. "My master deceived me, just as the Kyrlod deceived you! I did not know this would happen, for I did not learn of the war until too late. Now that I know of it, I wish to bring it to an end."

"How do you propose to do that?" Tim asked.

Zadinn spread his arms. "Together. Should we fight, one of us will fall, and he who remains standing will surely face a new challenge on the morrow, so on and so forth until time ends. But that is only if we, the surrogates, choose opposite sides of the board. However, if we unite, neither Harmea nor Malath could withstand us. We could break our chains and forge a new world, this one beyond the eye of the immortals. The Kyrlod kept this truth from you because he serves the Maker, and his sole goal is to make sure you remain enslaved. I, on the other hand, wish to set you—to set *us*—free."

Tim let his hand inch toward the hilt of his sword again, carefully watching Zadinn for a reaction. "For some reason, I don't believe you."

"You are a pawn, Warrior, a pawn on a chessboard of the cosmos, white pitted against black. I say we break that board and scatter the pieces! What do *you* say?"

"This requires both of us?" Tim asked.

"Yes," Zadinn answered, "it is the only way."

"And when it is finished? What then?"

"We rule this world, side by side."

Tim shook his head. "I don't think you'd be content with that. You might need me to help you remake the world, but once that is done, what then? You wouldn't share your kingdom with me. No, you'd find a way to kill me, be it a knife in my back, poison in my drink, or any number of things."

"I do not kill my comrades," Zadinn said. "Do you know Isanam? Ask him if he is in danger from me. On the contrary, we are quite loyal to each other."

"Isanam is your servant," Tim said. "You don't have a problem with servants. You have a problem with *equals*."

Zadinn's face changed, losing its smooth contours and morphing into a vicious snarl as he pointed his staff at Nazgar. Tim saw a small black stone, surely a focusing point, atop its handle. A white light blossomed within the stone's depths, and Nazgar clenched his teeth, clearly in great pain.

Zadinn spoke in a low hiss. "Serve me, or the Kyrlod dies. Serve me, or *all* your friends die, and I will make you watch every last one."

Nazgar spoke. "Do not make Timothy Matthias think this is his fault—not when you and I both knew how this would end."

Zadinn turned to the Kyrlod, keeping his staff leveled at the prophet as he stood from his throne. "I do not understand, Kyrlod. You see your own future clearest of all. So why, when you knew this would happen, did you choose to come?"

Nazgar smiled. "Everyone has a job to do."

Zadinn let out a scream of rage, thrusting his staff outward as a brilliant beam of white lightning shot from its tip and slammed into Nazgar. The room shook as Nazgar fell from the air, tumbling past the ledge and landing in a heap, the wall behind him streaked with his own blood. Tim ran over to Nazgar, cradling the old man's head in his lap. Nazgar turned his face to Tim, the back of his head sticky with blood, his eyes dimming.

Tim reached for the Lifesource. He'd never used it to heal anyone's wounds before, but he was about to give it his best try.

Nazgar raised a trembling hand and halted him. "No," the Kyrlod whispered, a trickle of red running from the corner of his lips. "You will drain your energy, and you cannot afford that."

"Don't tell me what I can't afford to do," Tim said. He couldn't finish this without Nazgar in the room. Zadinn was too dangerous.

"Choose," Nazgar said, "and accept the consequences." He smiled, shuddered, and then his body relaxed and went still. Thus died Nazgar of the Kyrlod.

Tim gently lowered the man's body before turning back to Zadinn Kanas, jaw set in a straight line. Anger pulsed through Tim's veins. No more games, no more words—he was here to do his job, to live or die as the Maker saw fit. He pulled his sword from its sheath. Blinding green fire ran along the blade, brighter and fiercer than normal. Tim ran full tilt, leaping to the top of the dais and swinging his sword in a graceful arc. The blade left a trail of smoking air in its wake.

Zadinn moved to the side, twirling his staff in his hands as its black focusing point flared, long tendrils of shadow winding around the length of the wood. Zadinn's staff had shattered swords, and Tim's sword had shattered staves. When the two weapons struck, a blinding flash of lightning erupted between them, and the entire room shook. Warrior of Light and Dark Lord stared at each other from either side of the dais, weapons locked in a crosswise embrace. The final duel had begun.

* * *

Isanam was walking death. He waded through the sea of his opponents, sword flicking from one enemy to the next as he left a trail of corpses in his path. His entire body tingled, both from the excitement of battle and from the river of the Lifesource coursing through him. His mind flashed a warning, and Isanam reacted, slicing the Army of Kah'lash soldier behind him cleanly in half. Without further pause, the Overlord returned to his main course, walking as idly as if he were on an afternoon stroll.

The battle had progressed well. The enemy was smaller than expected, and Isanam's troops had them pinned in the center of the Deathlands. No matter how hard the Army of Kah'lash fought, it would not last long against the superior malichon force.

Isanam pulled his sword from a writhing elion, neatly stepping around the body as it tumbled to the ground. He was not tired, far from it, and the fun had only just begun. He saw that his troops had surrounded the Army ahead, and to the west, more of his malichons engaged in a standoff with the survivors of the Fort of Pellen. Idle amusement at best, he'd leave that to his malichons. It was time to meet Commander Neebra and form one last offensive push to crush the resistance fighters.

* * *

Commander Jend stood with Hugo and Ken. Farther down the line, Garion clung to the standard of the Fort of Pellen as the elions stood their ground against the continual onslaught of malichons. There was no end to the enemy ranks. Wave after wave of malichon troops charged the embattled allies, while the mounting bodies of friends and foes alike covered the slopes of the Deathlands, rivers of blood staining the stones.

Also nearby, Captain Gendar Halion still fought valiantly with a sword in each hand, twin blades spinning in circles as he cut through swathes of malichons. Prince Ladu held his own, making up for his failures on the battlefield two centuries ago. Jend knew it would not be enough. It would be a valiant stand, but it was inevitably doomed as it had been from the start.

A pair of detonations shook the ground to the west, and the malichon formation briefly broke apart. Jend and the elions pressed forward, using this temporary advantage to further weaken the enemy, as a volley of arrows whipped through the sky and buried themselves in Isanam's troops. For a moment, Jend thought reinforcements had arrived, but it was too soon for that. He then caught a glimpse of a stone ridge, where he saw Boblin Kule firing a crossbow bolt from behind the relative shelter of the ridge. Kule had managed to mount an offensive—and a good one, at that—but it could only last for so long.

All too soon, the malichons filled in the gap left by their dead comrades, and a score of the enemy turned their attention toward the elions behind the ridge. Jend knew Kule would not last long, and it made his heart heavy. He'd been leading soldiers to their deaths for too many years, and wanted the burden to end. Today, it probably would.

Garion fell backward against the face of a boulder, and a malichon charged forward, driving its spear through the elion's chest in a spray of blood. Garion's eyes widened in shock, and the banner fell from his nerveless fingers as he hit the ground. An abrupt, awful feeling swept through Jend. The banner must not touch the ground, for if it did, it was all over. A sense of urgency seized him, and Jend leaped forward, cutting down malichons on all sides as he raced toward the falling standard. The flag seemed to descend in slow motion, as if falling through thick jelly. Unless that flag remained firm, upright, and free, all their hopes would die.

The spear-bearing malichon rose up in front of him, but Jend brushed the haft of the spear aside as he jumped and kicked his boot into the malichon's rib cage. As the creature fell onto its knees, Jend took its head from its shoulders. Behind the malichon, the banner journeyed downward. Whatever the cost, Jend could *not* let it touch the ground. He fell onto his knees, catching the pole in the crook of his left arm, and the fabric halted just above the bloodred stone of the Deathlands. Jend hoisted the flag back up, thrusting it high as he regained his footing. "Rally!" he cried. "Fort of Pellen, to me!"

The banner made a lonely sight, an island in a raging sea, a beacon in the night. Jend's remaining allies stood strong, persevering with all their might, refusing to bend, break, or yield, as around them, the enemy steadily closed in.

* * *

Boblin dropped to the ground, back against the stone wall, and slammed another bolt into his crossbow. Beside him, Hedro peered over the edge of their defenses before unleashing a feathered arrow toward the malichons. Boblin wiped grime from his face. Things had been going like this for some time. The malichons held a cautious distance, unwilling to charge the ridge because doing so would allow the elions a clear shot at all of them. But the malichons also had bows of their own, and every time either Boblin or Hedro exposed himself long enough to take a shot, a return volley came.

Right on cue, Hedro ducked to safety as an arrow passed above his head and buried itself in the nearby scrub brush, quivering on impact. Hedro touched his belt. "They're getting more aggressive," he said tersely. "I'm going to give them something to think about."

"Right," Boblin said, peering over the lip of the stone wall. He fired another bolt, but this one did not find a target. Boblin cursed. It wasn't like he had an unlimited supply of arrows at his disposal. Of course, his lack of success did not prevent retaliation. As he dropped back behind the wall to avoid the return volley, Hedro closed his flask and whipped a pouch over the ridge. A satisfying explosion rocked the wall, causing a clatter of dust and pebbles to fall down around them.

Boblin risked a glance over the wall. Bodies lay strewn on the battlefield, and the malichons had scattered.

"That bought us some time," Hedro said, "but probably not enough."

Boblin prepared another explosive, squeezing a few careful drops of juice into the pouch. *Once they're scattered, keep them scattered.* A moment later, he raised himself just high enough to get a bearing on the enemy before throwing the pouch into the air. Boblin saw a malichon leap up, hand outstretched to catch the bag in his open palm, and everything slowed to microseconds.

"Karf," Boblin said.

The malichon threw the explosive back at them. Boblin dove to the side, tackling Hedro out of harm's way. The deadly pouch slammed into the wall above their heads, and the stone ridge erupted, the force of the blast ripping Boblin and Hedro away from each other. Chunks of stone fountained into the sky, and Boblin was thrown several yards before he landed, tumbling underneath the shelter of the tree line. Stunned, he could barely move as shrapnel rained down and his ears rang. Nearby, Hedro was lifted bodily into the air, spinning end over end, before crashing against the ridgeline.

A large boulder hit the ground in front of Boblin, missing him on first impact, but then rolling forward to trap him beneath its bulk. He tried to move, but not fast enough, and the boulder pinned him. He was completely trapped, though the blow was not forceful and he felt no pain.

And it didn't stop him from being able to see what transpired near the stone wall. A contingent of malichons poured through the gap in the ridgeline, coming upon Hedro Desh lying in a crumpled heap. As Boblin watched from a safe distance, unable to move, the malichons surrounded his fallen comrade with swords drawn.

* * *

Hedro rolled over onto his back, eyelids fluttering open. His ears rang from the blast, and his body hurt all over. *By the Maker, that was rough.* Eight malichons stood over him. *Well, this is interesting.* As he willed his mind to focus, his hand groped for his sword at his waist.

"One?" he heard a malichon say. "I thought there were more."

"They fight hard," another replied, "but not hard enough."

Hedro didn't have any illusions about how this would end, but it didn't matter. Hand clenched about his weapon, he set his jaw and dragged himself onto his feet, facing his enemies on all sides.

* * *

Boblin tried to push the boulder away, swearing as his muscles bulged from the strain, but the boulder did not budge. In front of him, he saw Hedro stagger to his feet, sword in hand as he stood against the malichons. Boblin yelled in frustration, giving his all against the stone. "Move, you worthless piece of hisht!"

* * *

Hedro heard the malichons laughing, but he ignored them and unsheathed his blade. Still woozy from the blow, he nonetheless managed to hold it straight in front of him. "Which of you is first?" he asked.

The first malichon didn't even bother to use its sword. It punched Hedro in the gut and Hedro doubled over. Then Hedro came out of his crouch, both hands around his hilt, and beheaded the malichon in one swing.

This only amused the remaining malichons even more. As they laughed harder, two more attacked Hedro. He tilted his body to the left, extending his right leg in a horizontal kick that knocked the first malichon several feet backward. At the same time, he shifted to the left and disemboweled his second opponent. "Can't you do any better?" he said.

* * *

Boblin gasped from the exertion, as at last the boulder moved, if only barely, a mere matter of inches at most. Nearby, he saw Hedro stumbling between enemies as the malichons toyed with him by launching individual attacks on their prey. Boblin placed two hands against the stone. It wasn't going to end like this, not for either him or Hedro.

"*Karf!*"

He screamed as he shoved the massive rock away. He was free but had no time to waste. Using the side of the rock for support, Boblin stumbled into a standing position.

* * *

The malichons decided to end their sport. As one unit, they charged at Hedro with swords held level. Hedro knew it was impossible to fight them all, so he selected just one target. He'd make this one count. As he plunged his sword into the malichon's chest, he felt an excruciating pain as five swords pierced *his* flesh. He tried to stay standing, but it was too hard. He fell to his knees, losing his grip on his weapon.

Strange. It hurts so bad, the pain is almost gone. Hedro grasped his boot knife with his right hand, and with his left hand grabbed a malichon's wrist. Hedro pulled the creature toward the ground with him, slicing into the malichon's neck as he did so.

The tip of a sword at Hedro's throat halted him from any further action. Hedro blinked, momentarily confused. It was becoming more difficult to stay focused as blood ran from countless wounds over his body.

"Answer one question," the malichon with the sword said to him. "Why do you try so hard?"

Hedro reached up with his left hand, grabbing the malichon's blade in his bare palm and pulling it from the startled creature's grip. The pain in his hand was excruciating. Deep red blood ran from a deep gash in his palm, and Hedro cast the weapon away. Hedro did not give the malichon time to recover. He surged to his feet and drove his knife into the malichon's chest.

"Because I want my home back," he answered.

*　*　*

Boblin reached the malichons just as Hedro tumbled. Boblin danced back and forth, blade spinning in all directions. The remaining malichons were so shocked it was almost too easy, and soon their bodies littered the floor of the Deathlands, every last one dead by either Hedro's hand or Boblin's.

Boblin knelt beside Hedro, the rocks of the Deathlands cutting his knees as Hedro looked up at him, eyes dark and glassy. Blood covered Hedro's entire body.

"Hold on," Boblin said. "I'll get you help."

Hedro managed a weak laugh in spite of his injuries. "What help?" he asked.

Boblin's tongue went numb. Even if he did answer, Hedro would know it was a lie. "Just hold on," he repeated. It sounded flat the moment he said it.

Hedro coughed, and flecks of blood spattered from his lips onto his chest. "I need to tell you something, Boblin," he said. "You're the closest thing I ever had to a friend."

"Well, you're a karfing pain in my rear end, and I'm not going to hear talk like that. I'm going to get you out of here. What would Celia say if I let you die?"

Hedro shook his head. "I'm not the one Celia wants to see at the end of this. I *told* you, Kule. I saw you in the Korlan, and I saw you in the caves. I was jealous, because I wanted to rescue her." He paused, taking in several more gulps of air before he could speak again. "But I could have never done what you did."

"Quit wasting time," Boblin said, tearing a strip from his shirt to make a bandage.

"You held me accountable, Boblin, at a time when nobody else did. And now I'll see Triste again, and she'll punish me, because it's what I deserve."

Boblin set aside the bandage, forcing himself to meet Hedro's eyes. The other elion *needed* this, and Boblin owed it to him if nothing else.

"I was *fourteen*," Hedro continued, "but that makes no difference, because I knew better, and I did it anyway. And then Triste died, and I never told her I was sorry. I never atoned, and I've carried that with me ever since."

"Aye, you'll see her soon now," Boblin said. "But she won't punish you. She'll *forgive* you."

"Do you think?" Hedro asked.

"I know," Boblin replied.

A weight seemed to lift off of Hedro. The permanent glower he'd carried about himself—always present, always irritable—pulled back and peeled away, as if the breeze had carried it off. And Boblin knew his comrade, not quite a friend, not quite an enemy, an elion he had both despised and respected, was at long last at peace with himself.

"I have just one request," Hedro said.

"Anything," Boblin replied.

He grabbed Boblin's collar and looked into his eyes. "Keep her safe," he said, voice hard. Boblin nodded, and Hedro's grip relaxed, falling away as he passed into the next life, a fallen hero of the battlefield.

Forty-Three

Quentiin put on chains one last time, a necessary disguise allowing the dwerions to return to the Pit without the guards suspecting anything unusual. After placing manacles around their wrists, the "prisoners" shuffled across the open shaping area, the malichons paying them no heed as they passed by. In the Pit, the slaves labored atop the narrow ledges, chiseling stone from the walls. Guards strode between the workers, mechanically cracking their whips. Quentiin eyed the scene, hoping to catch a glimpse of Veldor, but the Slavemaster was noticeably absent. *What a shame.* Quentiin wanted Veldor in the open, where he would be easy to track down.

Quentiin felt a familiar blast of heat on his face as they approached. The flames appeared more chaotic than usual, swelling as if anticipating the upcoming conflict. The companions paused in front of the bridge leading across the Pit. Its wooden planks swayed in time to the breeze. Quentiin glanced at his comrades, expecting to see fear and hesitation on their faces. After all, they had been cowed and subservient prisoners just this morning, and surely the prospect of battle would make some of them quail. Instead, Quentiin was surprised to see a uniform determination in their eyes.

Jolldo met his gaze. "We started this," he said to Quentiin, "and we're not turnin' back. This place changed me into somebody else, an' I didn't like the dwerion I'd become. Well, it ain't happenin' a second time."

Quentiin smiled. His friend had returned. Not the old Jolldo, for the old Jolldo could never come back just as the old Quentiin could never come back, but neither was he the Jolldo from these last four weeks. Their confrontation with the malichons in the caves had pulled the levees back from the dam, and it had only taken one nudge in a different direction to make everything shift course. The dwerions of Raldoon had remembered their battle spirit, and nothing could turn back wrath of that magnitude. Not for nothing were dwer-ions named the most fearsome opponents on the battlefield, and today they would live up to that name.

As Quentiin led his companions across the bridge, he reflected that he had walked over these planks so many times he no longer noticed the precarious footing. During the last few days, he would have welcomed a fall from these heights, but he had no need for those thoughts anymore. He now had a chance to die in a better fashion, and he was taking it.

A malichon stood at the end of the bridge, monitoring the slaves traveling between the Pit and shaping area. The guard gave the newcomers a brief glance before turning back to watch the other prisoners, but when Quentiin reached the end of the bridge the malichon took a closer look. Quentiin lifted his head to meet the guard's eyes, and the malichon visibly blinked. Every malichon in the Pit knew Quentiin Harggra, for he had made quite a reputation for himself.

The malichon stepped back, looking at the other slaves in confusion as Quentiin gave it a big, broad smile. "Bloody beautiful day, ain't it, laddie?" Quentiin said in an overly cheerful tone as he drew a sword from beneath his robes and shoved it between the malichon's ribs. The guard staggered back, shock spreading across its face as Quentiin ripped his blade free and kicked the malichon over the edge of the Pit. The guard fell halfway to the flames before it finally found a voice to scream.

The other malichons turned toward the commotion, slow to react at first, for they did not expect a battle here in the Pit, where slaves timidly scurried and met guards' eyes only when necessary. It just didn't happen, not here. *But it's happenin' today, mates.*

After a brief moment of confusion, the malichons organized themselves into a tight, defensive formation, swords bared and ready for action. Quentiin and his comrades were already charging forward, consumed with the lust for justice and retribution, and they set upon the guards in seconds. Other mali-chons from farther back in the quarry rushed toward the conflict, but they were not yet close enough to make a difference.

The two forces slammed into each other, weapons flashing. The first casualty came when a malichon raised a spear and skewered Yaavin, the force of the blow throwing the dwerion back several feet. He landed with the thick haft sticking from his chest, dead before he hit the stone. This only fueled the other dwerions' anger, and Quentiin and his companions tore the malichons to pieces.

And then half a dozen new malichons attacked from the sides, surrounding the dwerions in a pincer maneuver and instantly changing the tide of battle. One moment, Quentiin and the others had been standing over their slain enemies, breathing heavily from adrenaline and exertion, and in the next, Kerrill was tumbling, head struck from his shoulders, while nearby, Naalish fell forward with an ax between his shoulder blades. Quentiin growled, clashing blades with a guard, while around him his companions fought for their lives. From the distance, yet another contingent of malichons approached, ready to snuff out this resistance as quickly as it had started.

Things might have gone poorly if not for the other slaves in the quarry. All it took was one man. The prisoner leaped onto the back of a malichon and wrapped his chains tight around the guard's throat. The guard thrashed, trying to throw the slave off, but the man held on with grim determination.

Quentiin slammed an opponent against the wall, putting his sword into the malichon's chest with a *crunch*. He turned to aid the defecting prisoner and saw there was no need. The malichon was already dead, and the prisoner pulled the guard's sword from its limp fingers and raised it into the sky.

"For freedom!" the prisoner yelled.

The rest of the slaves, galvanized by the commotion, took up the man's shout. They swarmed, attacking the malichons with anything and everything at hand. As one, all cried the same phrase: "For freedom! For freedom! For freedom!"

* * *

Sword of green fire clashed against staff of black shadow. Whenever the weapons struck, a white light flashed between them and a clap of thunder shook the room. The Lifesource raged through both men, Warrior of Light and Dark Lord, as the air crackled with energy. Their battle had started atop the dais, but it did not stay there. The two enemies moved in a blur, sword and staff spinning, the power of the Lifesource granting both men unnatural speed. This was as much a battle between swordsmen as a battle between sorcerers.

The two combatants dueled across the length and breadth of the throne room, twisting and turning, jumping and landing, streaks of fire sizzling across the floor. The vents emitted their noxious green fumes with fervent passion. Tim had never felt so *alive* before. And the whole time, Zadinn Kanas never once stopped smiling. The Dark Lord clearly loved this chaos.

Outside the city, above the Deathlands, the red sun beat down on the Army of Kah'lash as troops fought the malichon hordes. However, the skies above the citadel had culminated into an entity of a much darker nature, and a bank of clouds hovered above the Dark Lord's palace, growing heavier and more malevolent as the duel continued. The storm front swirled in tandem with the fight, its underside thick and billowy, filled with sickly hues of yellow, green, and purple. The storm had not yet unleashed its burden, but every so often, streaks of pale lightning separated the masses, which closed themselves afterward with a deafening *clap*.

Inside the palace, the battle moved toward the Cauldron of Souls, where the very air hung frozen and cold. Tim rolled, avoiding Zadinn's most recent attack, and heard a soft moan emanate from within the large vessel. As Tim glanced at the Cauldron, Zadinn struck from the side and Tim ducked, catching the blow on his blade. A streak of lightning shot from the crossed weapons, plowing into a set of sconces. The torches fell in disarray, adding to the other wreckage strewn across the throne room. Zadinn completed his move by slamming the base of his staff to the floor, and a shockwave threw Tim back several feet, his sword flying from his fingertips while he landed.

"Do you like the Cauldron of Souls?" Zadinn asked. Tim did not answer but reached out his hand and summoned his sword, which flew across the room back into his outstretched palm. When he turned to face Zadinn, a hazy green image of Nazgar hovered above the Cauldron.

"I told you the resemblance was striking," Zadinn said. "I send only the best victims to the Cauldron."

Tim looked again, realizing this was not Nazgar at all but his twin brother Ragzan. The spirit remained silent, but his glare spoke volumes.

"They hate me," Zadinn said. "Upon death, most spirits pass into Harmea or Malath, but I like to keep some for myself. As such, those in the Cauldron are bound to me, neither the Maker's nor the Demon Lord's, but *mine*."

In that moment, Tim knew the Dark Lord's depravity had no bounds. When the man spoke of becoming a god himself, it was not mere puffery. Here, the Cauldron served as the ultimate proof of Zadinn's great hubris, for in creating such an awful device, Zadinn had become a grotesque imitation of the

Demon Lord himself, imprisoning souls in his own underworld, a tiny version of Malath where Zadinn Kanas reigned supreme.

The water in the Cauldron parted and an entire legion of howling spirits rose from it, filling the room with the sounds of their torment. Zadinn stood at the vessel's base, moving his staff in a circle to control the vortex of souls. He leveled his staff at Tim, and the spirits flocked toward the Warrior, engulfing him in their midst, the air so cold that ice formed on the floor and his breath fogged. Tim raised his sword, and a ring of coruscating green light emanated from the blade, its pulsating warmth ever so slightly countering the chill. Holding the spirits at bay with the growing light, Tim redoubled his efforts, increasing the blade's radiance to ultimately disperse them as he had done with the Guardian. But when the way parted and Tim could see again, Zadinn was already upon him, striking with renewed ferocity.

Tim deflected Zadinn's blow, knocking the staff aside as a beam of light lanced out from the tip of his sword to strike the Dark Lord in the chest, slamming him against a nearby wall. Zadinn brought his staff back in a diagonal defense, and when Tim struck again, their weapons locked together, the pressure of this blow carried *both* men against the wall. The tip of Zadinn's staff raked against a ledge of skulls, shattering the bones into tiny fragments. Zadinn pressed back, and this time Tim's sword did the damage, consuming the remaining skulls with a wave of green fire. The sorcerers separated as fragments of bleached bone cascaded down all around them.

As both combatants took a moment to regain their breath, a dim part of Tim's mind noticed the pains and scrapes of battle, but he pushed it away. He could not afford distractions.

"You dance well, Warrior," Zadinn said, smiling again, but the light of the smile never once touched his eyes. He pointed to the underside of the domed ceiling above. "But how well would you dance…up there?"

Zadinn leaped into the air, where he hovered as if rooted in place. Tim instinctively followed suit, jumping to stand in midair, the empty space under his feet firm and unyielding.

Zadinn laughed. "You *are* fun." The Dark Lord turned and took three more steps, rising higher as his laugh turned to a screech. An icy sensation lined Tim's insides. He was trapped in a room with a madman, and it would only end when one of them was dead.

Tim jumped to the next level, while Zadinn continued rising above him, and together, the two men raced toward the citadel's far-reaching dome.

*   *   *

The sudden onrush of slaves overwhelmed the malichon guards. For many years, the slave drivers had built a dam of sorts. Behind that dam they had trapped the spirit and willpower of every slave in the Pit. As the years passed, the dam only grew higher and thicker, trapping more and more water. For a long time, those waters remained latent and suppressed, their existence forgotten. Then Quentiin Harggra's arrival weakened that dam, and after the first fissure formed, there was no holding the flood back. Once the slaves found a voice, everything changed.

In the space of an afternoon, the prisoners unleashed years of pent-up rage, seeking vengeance and retribution for the countless atrocities their tormentors had committed. They slaughtered the malichon guards right where they stood, or drove them off the edge of the Pit into the flames. But even as Quentiin watched the remaining guards fall into the fire, a flight of arrows descended upon them from across the chasm, where a new group of malichons bearing longbows had gathered.

"Pull back!" Quentiin yelled as volleys of feathered shafts streaked toward them. Fortunately, they were gathered in a safer part of the quarry. While much of the Pit consisted of narrow ledges, which offered nowhere to run, this main area was favorably larger. The slaves retreated, moving as far from the archers as possible. There was no way they could completely pull out of bowshot, but they could make it harder for the archers to find targets.

"What d'ye think, laddie?" Jolldo asked him.

"Well, we can't afford to sit tight," Quentiin replied. "If we do, we're dead." There was only one way off this rock, via the bridge, and a band of prisoners crossing the walkway would certainly make appealing targets for the malichons. On top of that, the narrow bridge could only fit two or three slaves at a time, making it even easier for the guards to cut them down. They had to move, but the only way out would offer them up for wholesale slaughter.

A surviving malichon in the quarry pushed past Jolldo, running for the bridge, but Quentiin grabbed the guard's arm and halted it. "Where in Malath do *you* intend to head?" Quentiin asked, biting off every word.

The malichon gasped in pain, stumbling as an arrow meant for Quentiin blossomed from its side. As the guard regained its balance, a second shaft planted itself between its eyes.

"Bloody brilliant," Quentiin said, shoving the dead malichon over.

"What?" Jolldo asked.

Quentiin saw three more malichons trying to make it to safety. "Stop them!" he yelled. The slaves needed no urging and took the malichons down in seconds. Quentiin ordered the slaves to bring the guards over, alive. "Tie their hands," he said.

Jolldo raised an eyebrow at him. "I ain't followin', mate," he said.

"Trust me. Ye will." Quentiin took hold of a malichon and ordered the guard in front of him. "We're goin' for a *walk*," he said.

Jolldo finally understood Quentiin's plan and put a hand on each of the other guards. Together, the two dwerions stepped onto the bridge, pushing the malichons in front of them. "Follow!" Quentiin called out. "And *move!*"

The other slaves caught on, climbing onto the bridge behind Quentiin and Jolldo. The wooden walkway creaked beneath their feet, all the more incentive for them to move quickly. Regardless of their malichon shields, this was still risky. The faster they crossed the bridge, the better.

At first, the guards in front dug their heels in, but it was pointless. When the rest of the prisoners stepped onto the bridge, pressing in behind Quentiin, their combined effort pressed the malichons forward. The guards on the other side did not bother sparing their comrades, as the three malichons sprouted quills faster than a trio of hedgehogs. It didn't matter to Quentiin. Alive or dead, the malichons protected them just the same.

Of course, the slaves on their flanks remained unshielded. A volley of arrows flew at them from the sides, plowing into the prisoners with merciless perseverance, and too many of their friends fell into the chasm below. The line of freedom fighters shed dead bodies like a snake sheds skin, while the strain on the bridge continued building. Quentiin pushed forward as fast as he could, driving the slain malichons forward, Jolldo at his side. When they reached the end of the crossway, they shoved the corpses out of the way and sprang back onto solid ground, charging with unsheathed swords at the malichons on that side of the bridge. Jolldo took an arrow in the left shoulder, but it hardly slowed him down. More prisoners streamed off the bridge, and the entire ragtag band slammed into the malichon guards.

Even though the slaves lost many friends crossing the bridge, they still had an edge over the guards. The malichons were fighting as they were trained—albeit very dangerous because their backs were against the wall—but the slaves were fighting for their very right to live, and they prevailed against their captors.

When it was clear the prisoners had won, the last of the malichons turned and fled toward the stone hall. Some of the slaves pursued, but Quentiin held back. His chest heaved, and his muscles screamed from exertion. Cuts and gashes covered his body, so for a brief moment he allowed himself to relax. It wasn't necessarily the physical strain that made him back down, but something more fundamental: he'd accomplished his goal.

From his first day in the Pit, he tried to help the prisoners remember who they were—that they had names, lives, and the right to be free. He'd tried everything he could think of, and at the end he thought he'd failed. He'd given up, succumbing to his own despair—and then, and only then, the slaves showed spirit. Ironic, because then *he* was the one who needed saving, who needed to remember hope, so his friends turned around and handed it back to him, full circle.

Now as he watched the former prisoners run across the quarry, pursuing their captors and winning their freedom, Quentiin stopped and smiled. They could do it now. They could stand up and fight—not with his help, but on their own. He never thought he could feel so much pride as he felt at that moment. Quentiin Harggra stood by the edge of the chasm, alone, the bridge behind him swinging gently in the breeze.

Then Quentiin felt a sudden stabbing sensation as a crossbow bolt struck him in the ribs. The pain was excruciating, and he fell to his knees as his breath left him. He managed to look up to see Veldor the Slavemaster in the middle of the bridge, a crossbow in his hands. The malichon smiled and tossed the weapon aside. The shot had not been meant to kill; it was meant to cripple so Veldor could finish the job with a more personal touch. Quentiin growled low in his throat, and despite the pain, pushed back onto his feet. He grabbed the shaft protruding from his ribs, snapped it off, and met Veldor's eyes with a glare. He seized the pommel of his sword and stepped onto the rickety bridge, where flames raged far beneath them. A dozen strides separated him from Veldor. The time for reckoning was here. *Full circle indeed.*

* * *

Zadinn reached the apex of the citadel's domed ceiling first. Tim saw him raise his staff and strike the dome's roof, and the stones in the ceiling exploded outward, shooting into the sky before curving and plummeting back. Tim had to dart through the air, dodging the rubble as it came down, while Zadinn passed through the hole in the roof and into the black sky outside. A hammering downpour flooded into the throne room as Tim followed through the opening, just as Zadinn rounded on him and attacked again. Tim narrowly blocked the blow, adding an extra burst of the Lifesource for good measure, and the resulting concussion knocked the combatants away from each other. Tim flew across the sloped surface of the outer roof, again using the Lifesource to break his fall.

The storm raged around them, unbelievably fierce, sheets of falling raindrops so thick Tim felt he was staring at a solid white wall. The rooftop was slick and precarious, and hailstones pelted Tim's skin with stinging blows. Savage winds buffeted him and howled over the contours of the building, as the clouds heaved and boiled, erratic bolts of lightning flashing between the masses. The thunderclaps made the stones of the rooftop tremble, the natural world beating in cadence with the duel between light and dark.

An invisible hand slammed against Tim's chest, propelling him toward the dome's pinnacle, where the pointed spire thrust high into the sky. Tim struck the base of the spire so hard the wind rushed out of his body. The monolith jutted into the clouds, making him feel like a sacrifice at the base of an altar. He tried to roll away, but it was no good—chains constructed of the Lifesource held him rooted in place.

Zadinn appeared from the blinding rain, staff leveled at Tim. Tim pushed back, trying to sever the spell holding him captive, but to no avail. The Dark Lord approached, and for once he was not smiling. Grim determination lined his face. The spell was powerful, but it was also taking its toll on the Dark Lord's energy.

A chokehold closed around Tim's throat, cutting off his air. Tim struggled, but again his efforts proved fruitless, and bruises formed on his neck as Zadinn's hold tightened. Black flecks floated in front of Tim's vision.

"An ugly finish, but necessary," Zadinn said.

Aye, and I remember a time when a wise man warned me about the evils of necessity. Tim still held his sword, but he could not so much as lift a finger. Whatever this spell was, it was good. *I can't break the spell with force. I need to use something else.* Tim felt his mind floating. It would be much easier to relax and close his eyes. He was so tired, after all.

No! Tim saw the clouds moving above him and had an idea. He reached out with the Lifesource again, this time toward the storm clouds instead of Zadinn's spell, and he summoned their wrath.

A jagged streak of lightning flashed from the clouds and struck the spire. With a brilliant explosion, the monolith split down the middle. The structure wavered for just a second, gravity vying from every direction for supremacy before it finally toppled. The explosion broke Zadinn's concentration, and the spell around Tim evaporated. At the same time, the force from the blast threw Tim forward, and again he slid across the roof. He twirled, using the tumble to right himself to a standing position.

The remnants of the stone spire crashed down between Tim and Zadinn. The impact opened another enormous gash in the roof. The combatants momentarily eyed each other from across the crevasse, and then they leaped and collided in midair. Their weapons flashed as the duel resumed, sparring atop the treacherous roof. The element of added danger from slick footing and steep drops only made each man fight more fiercely. As time wore on, it occurred to Tim that they were *perfectly matched in power.* Neither possessed a shred of strength more, or less, than the other.

That was when Zadinn surprised him. Tim was accustomed to blocking attacks that came from the focusing point—atop Zadinn's staff—but this time, a stabbing beam of light shot out from the *bottom* of the staff. The black fire plowed into the roof, carving yet another hole into its surface. Tim stumbled backward and felt his heels touch the very edge of the roof. Zadinn struck again, and Tim flew out into the open air, the ground over a hundred feet below him. Here, he hung suspended a brief moment—and then he plummeted.

Forty-Four

Celia spun in a circle, moving so fast that everything around her seemed a blur. She dared not slow down. She had her back in a corner, and she would dig in and not let go, not even if the Demon Lord himself appeared. Celia didn't know how much longer their small company would last, but she intended to make some malichons bleed before she gave up. *And where in Malath are the reinforcements?* She thought they'd be here by now, but no soldiers had appeared on the horizon. Fewer than five hundred members of the Army of Kah'lash remained in the current battle, just a quarter of the number they'd arrived with. The Army of Kah'lash might kill malichons three-to-one, but it didn't matter. Zadinn's army could afford the losses, and the elions couldn't.

The elions of the Fort held their own at the center of the battle. Of them, perhaps a dozen remained. She'd hadn't seen Boblin since the fight began, but she didn't have time to dwell on that, *couldn't* dwell on that.

Celia pulled her sword from a dead malichon and brushed a sweaty strand of hair from her eyes. Looking around herself, she realized she had moved away from the main group and into a shallow cul-de-sac of rock. She couldn't stay long. The others needed her help, and it wasn't safe to be alone. A contingent of malichons would have no trouble wiping out a stray elion. She did, however, pause to catch her breath.

Then she realized the cul-de-sac was not as empty as it first appeared. An elion's dying scream rent the air, and she looked down into the enclosed area to see Kintel collapse in front of a tall, hooded figure. The figure struck with a sword, and Kintel's head flew from his shoulders.

Celia backed up and bumped against another body. It was Borin, dead on the ground, sightless eyes staring up, right beside Maricia, whose body also lay against a sharp rock. Celia's heart quickened. She instantly knew who the tall, hooded figure was. Isanam. And he had killed every elion in this cul-de-sac. She turned to run, to *flee*—it was one thing to dig in, but when a boulder fell from the sky, she knew to run for her karfing life. Before she made it a dozen steps, an invisible finger snagged her shirt collar and yanked her backward. So it was true—Isanam could use the Lifesource. *Wonderful.*

Well, if he wasn't going to let her go, she had no choice but to fight. As the Overlord approached from behind, his rasping breath drawing in and out, she ducked underneath Isanam's incoming blow, retaliating with her own blade. Their swords clashed as Celia set herself against the commander of the malichon army. She dodged back and forth, keeping her movements light. Isanam's motions were fluid and vicious, his blade snaking in and out, coming down with crushing might, one blow after another.

Celia knew she could not keep this up for long, but she had no choice. She was trapped, and her only option was to fight. As Isanam came at her in a whirl of cloak and blade, she slipped past his guard and nicked his forearm. When she pulled her sword back, she saw a fleck of blood on its tip, and smiled. Isanam hissed, part in surprise, part in anger. Celia looked into his red eyes, which smoldered beneath his skull-mask. Few opponents had ever drawn the Overlord's blood, but now Celia had.

Isanam retaliated in an instant, pushing his sword toward her midsection, forcing Celia to parry the thrust with desperate urgency. Completing the attack, the Overlord moved his blade in a flashing arc, slashing toward her head, and Celia only barely managed to block in time. Isanam continued his attack with renewed brutality, his next blow striking her blade overhead and sending an excruciating pain through her arm. Celia staggered back, knowing immediately the bones in her arm were broken. Isanam kicked her in the chest, and she fell facing skyward, sword falling from her now useless grasp. She tried to raise a hand to defend herself, but couldn't move her shattered limb. Above her, Isanam paused for the barest of seconds before bringing his sword down with vicious force.

* * *

Boblin crouched behind a boulder and watched a group of malichons milling on the battlefield. Hedro's body lay on the floor of the Deathlands behind him. Before leaving his friend, Boblin had placed Hedro's remaining explosives along with his into one pouch, which he now held in his hand. He drained the last of the juice into the leather bag. These weapons were devastating enough on their own, but together, combined with every last drop of juice at once…

This one's for Hedro. Boblin threw the explosive cocktail into the sky, and it landed among the malichons. The pouch looked so harmless as it descended through the air; not a single malichon noticed, and Boblin's timing was perfect. He had just enough time to exhale once before the bag detonated on impact.

The ground rocked as a geyser of fire shot into the sky, shredding an entire contingent of malichons. The creatures landed in piles of broken limbs as shrapnel rained down, killing or wounding the rest. Boblin ran across the expanse, cutting down malichon survivors as he moved. He felt neither joy nor fear. Hedro's death had left him blank, and he was more than willing to fill the emptiness with more death. He moved from malichon to malichon, and though a few managed to fight back, leaving their share of nicks and gashes on Boblin, they didn't slow him. He felt the wounds, but pushed the pain to a distant corner of his mind.

A malichon slammed into him from behind. The malichon had no weapons, but a mind to kill Boblin regardless. The malichon wrapped its arms around Boblin, bearing them both to the ground, and both tumbled off the edge of a precipice and down a steep slope. They landed amid a tumble of broken rocks and thorny brush. The malichon climbed on top of him, striking Boblin's wrist against a rock, forcing him to drop his sword.

Empty-handed, Boblin smashed his palm into the malichon's chin, snapping the creature's head back. In response, the malichon placed a steadily tightening grip around Boblin's throat. Boblin grabbed the malichon's wrist and twisted, pulling one of its hands off his throat, driving his knee into the malichon's gut and using his leverage to reverse their positions. He pulled his belt knife free and plunged the blade between the creature's eyes.

Boblin got to his feet, and then froze as he saw Celia and Isanam locked in combat only a few strides away. And Celia was not faring well. She stumbled, dodging Isanam's attacks as the Overlord's cloak moved in a swirl of darkness, his blade dripping with the blood of their elion comrades.

Keep her safe.

This was more than a dying soldier's request—it was Boblin's own mandate, his own directive to himself. Time and again, he'd tried to express his feelings to Celia—and time and again, he'd failed. Because he just wasn't good at the game young couples played, because he didn't know how to tell her he cared, because the Patrol was simple and love was not.

And yet, while Boblin might not be able to do any of those things, he knew that he *could* keep her safe. He'd kept her safe in the Korlan, he'd kept her safe in Malath's Teeth, and by the Maker, he was going to keep her safe now.

Boblin picked up his sword and ran forward. Isanam knocked Celia's weapon from her, and she fell on her back, facing skyward. As Isanam prepared to deliver a killing blow, Boblin leaped through the air and landed in front of Celia's outstretched body, weapon raised overheard, blocking Isanam's blade before it could descend. Isanam snarled and retaliated, knocking Boblin several feet away in one blow. Boblin landed on his side, using his momentum to roll back into a standing position, sword in hand.

Isanam did not charge forward. There was no need; this was just idle fun for him. The Overlord moved toward Boblin with a slow, deliberate pace, stride measured and deadly, holding his sword almost lazily as he advanced. And so Boblin also walked forward, matching Isanam stride for stride, moving neither faster nor slower than his opponent.

Keep her safe.

There was no defense against Isanam, other than running. Those who stood their ground, however brave, died. Boblin gripped his sword, barely concealing the tremble in his hand. "Celia," he said through gritted teeth. "Run."

Heart pounding, sword in hand, Boblin Kule drew himself up and faced the malichon Overlord.

* * *

Quentiin and Veldor met in the center of the bridge, swords crossing. The walkway swayed in the open air, the shaky footing raising the stakes of the combat. Far below, the raging flames of the Pit sent plumes of fire and waves of heat blasting toward the bridge. The arrow in Quentiin's side hindered his movements, causing his sword-arm to falter more easily than it should.

Veldor, on the other hand, remained lithe and vicious, wearing a sardonic smile. He must have had a hiding place while the battle in the Pit played out, and only surfaced when Quentiin turned his back. "You aren't like the others," Veldor said as Quentiin avoided a thrust to his midsection. "You're far more entertaining. I regret having to end things so soon."

Quentiin redoubled his attack, setting his pain aside—no, *crushing* it—and pressing his advantage. Veldor took a few steps back as wind shook the bridge. This was a karfing mess, and no mistake; they'd likely both die up here. "The Pit is too merciful for yer likes," Quentiin said. "I'm the one with regrets, laddie. When ye fall into that fire, it'll be over far too quickly."

Veldor laughed. "I'd forgotten you've only been here a short while." He whipped his blade in an arc. Quentiin could barely predict where he was planning to strike. "The Pit isn't like other fires. It takes *hours* to die."

Instead of trying to follow Veldor's attacks—a common mistake—Quentiin put his mind *ahead* of them. He blocked every blow, though not without increasing effort and exertion. At the same time, he thought of the slaves Veldor had killed in the Pit, the last pair only a day ago. Quentiin steeled himself, swearing to avenge those who had suffered.

Veldor grazed Quentiin's rib cage with a well-placed stroke opposite the arrow, and Quentiin felt a hot flash of pain as this fresh wound, coupled with the original, created twin rivers of bleeding flesh on both sides of his body. Quentiin stumbled back, and Veldor closed in, aiming for Quentiin's neck. Quentiin only barely saved himself, spinning to the side as the blow landed on his shoulder. It cut deep, but missed the vitals in his neck.

Quentiin seized upon a sudden, wild thought, acting on instinct. It was a madman's move, but these were mad times. He twisted to the side, raised his sword, and severed a rope on the bridge. The structure dipped on its horizontal axis, held in place by only the opposite rope. Quentiin, already anticipating the sudden change in balance, grasped a plank in his hand, but Veldor was not as prepared. The Slavemaster pitched over the edge, and Quentiin thought that was the end—but then Veldor managed to grab Quentiin's midsection and clung to him, dangling above the Pit.

Quentiin snarled. *If this is what it takes, so be it.* He raised his sword, slashing the other line, and the bridge split in two. Their end crashed down, slamming against the wall, as dwerion and malichon hung vertically above the flames. Veldor slipped farther down, but still managed to hold onto Quentiin. The Slavemaster had lost his sword, but he wouldn't let it end this soon. He opened his mouth wide and sank his teeth into Quentiin's thigh. Blood streamed down the sides of Veldor's mouth. The Slavemaster wasn't leaving this place without taking some flesh first.

Quentiin didn't mind so much. This scum was as good as dead—because Quentiin, unlike Veldor, still held a sword. "My friend," Quentiin said, "this is one time you *didn't* win." He slammed the pommel of his hilt against Veldor's skull, dislodging the Slavemaster. Though Quentiin could have used the sharp end of his sword to end Veldor's life then and there, he did not. He wanted Veldor alive when he hit the flames, where his punishment would be well deserved.

Veldor's arms flailed in the empty air, hands scrabbling for some kind of purchase, eyes wide open. He issued a long, despairing wail, body dwindling into the distance before disappearing into the blaze, his final cry still hanging on the breeze.

Quentiin dropped his sword. He needed all his strength for the task in front of him. He reached up with both arms and climbed up the bridge toward safety, the going slow and arduous as his muscles screamed for rest. At last— sweaty, bleeding, and exhausted—he pulled himself over the lip of the Pit and lay there for several long seconds, slowly regaining his breath. He put a hand to his side. The arrow stub hurt like Malath, but it sure wasn't fatal. For now, it was probably better to leave it in, as it would do further damage on its way out. After a time, he realized Jolldo was standing over him. Quentiin blinked his eyes, wanting to be sure it wasn't an illusion, and then gave a long sigh. "Are ye just goin' to stand there, or will ye help me up?"

Jolldo helped Quentiin to his feet. Quentiin saw the remaining slaves, now free, gathered in a loose crowd. As soon as he stood up, they cheered his name. "I said it before, an' I'll say it again," Jolldo said, "we're in yer debt...forever."

"Nobody's in my debt," Quentiin said. "Besides, we ain't celebratin' just yet."

Jolldo gestured toward the slave pen. "We're done here. We've won, an' there's no one in the city. Ye said so yerself. They've all left."

"Aye, they left," Quentiin said, raising his voice so the others could hear him, "And d'ye know why they left? The only thing that could make them leave is an army on their doorstep, an' ye can bet yer hide our people are out there right now, fightin' in that army. We might be done here, but the battle's out there." He pointed beyond the walls of the city. "We started this, an' sure as Malath, we're goin' out there to see that it's finished."

* * *

Jend Argul pulled his soldiers in close, the ground beneath him shaking as the two armies hammered each other on the slopes of the Deathlands. He had long since given up on the arrival of the remaining four divisions, and wished he knew where Isanam was. Jend didn't harbor any notions of defeating the Overlord—no one could—but he wanted the chance to spit in Isanam's face before he died. Instead, he had to make do with this.

"Elions of the Fort!" Jend yelled, and the scattering of a dozen fighters responded to his call as quickly as ever. Almost all of the elions had fallen by now. Jend supposed their deaths, more than anything else, lent to his weariness. The standard had fallen twice, and Jend had saved it twice. Now he would carry it into the heart of the malichon army and make an end of things. *And songs will be sung of it, if there is anyone left to sing.*

As always, Hugo and Ken flanked him, always valiant, always strong, always true. Their small company created an arrowhead formation, Jend holding the banner at its head. They would form a spear tip and drive themselves straight into the enemy's side. Jend led the charge as they swept across the battle-strewn ground, cutting through enemy ranks. Before long they passed deep inside the malichon army, elions falling left and right. Jend predicted they'd last a minute at best, but he'd do everything in his power to make it ten.

They lasted for a minute, then two, then three. Soon only Jend and the Rindar brothers remained, and though everyone else had fallen, these last three did not falter, for the Fort of Pellen did not die quietly. They would make the malichons remember why they, unlike anyone else, had remained free these two hundred years.

Then the malichon ranks parted in a ray of sunlight, cloven in two by thick ranks of men in chain mail shirts. The newcomers charged through the lines of malichon troops, the sun glinting off their armor and weapons. These Army soldiers were fresh, clean, and untarnished by battle, their arrival so sudden, so surprising, that the malichons had no time to recover. Jend's company had been a small arrowhead in the enemy lines, but the Army of Kah'lash was now a scythe in a field of wheat. For the first time in a long while, Commander Jend smiled. The reinforcements had arrived.

* * *

Boblin parried Isanam's attacks with desperate urgency, knowing he was almost always a second too slow, blade too low or too high, barely surviving one blow after another as the duel continued. He remained all too conscious of the dead bodies littering the landscape, every last one Isanam's handiwork, and feared he would join them all too soon. Isanam moved with an ease that belied his strength, every attack more likely than the last to break Boblin's arm, just as Celia's had broken. Celia herself, still behind him, crawled across the ground mere inches at a time, trying to reach her sword.

Keep her safe.

Boblin had to find a way to keep her from rejoining the fight. If she returned, she would die the same as he, and he could not allow that. He had to keep Isanam distracted long enough for her to get away. He withstood one, two, and three more strikes from the Overlord, thinking each would be the last. Though Boblin did not have breath to spare, he shouted anyway. "Celia! I said *run!*"

Almost to her weapon, she ignored him and kept crawling forward. He *had* to stop her from taking this sun-baked course of action. She needed to get away, save herself while she still could.

"I've heard your kind believes in a concept called 'chivalry,'" Isanam said, voice grating. "It's touching, but ultimately useless."

Boblin saw the Overlord's muscles clench just so, and recalled the rumors that Isanam could use the Lifesource. Reacting instantly, he used what Nazgar had taught him, looking at the way Isanam's eyes moved, where the Overlord directed his gaze—and then Boblin shifted his stance sideways as the air rippled. The spell slid past Boblin, as if he had found a gap in the stream of magic. He still wasn't quite sure how it worked, but he wasn't about to question it. This tactic had saved him when fighting Tim in Malath's Teeth, and it saved him now. Perhaps Nazgar wasn't such a bother after all; Boblin would have to complain less about the Kyrlod when all this was over.

Isanam's eyes widened as he realized his attack was unsuccessful. He struck yet again with the Lifesource, and Boblin dodged a second time, rolling behind a rock as the ground in front of him exploded.

"Impressive," Isanam said, "but also useless." Lifting his sword, he resumed his former attack. Boblin pulled back as Isanam's blade whisked through the space where Boblin's neck had been. Near the cul-de-sac, Celia at last reached her sword. *Son of a three-legged goat.* He'd hoped she'd be away from here by now.

Boblin's back scraped against a stone wall—he was backed into a corner. Isanam struck again, and Boblin managed to turn away just enough to stay alive. The sword would have penetrated his chain mail, but instead caught him at an awkward angle. Boblin saw sparks as he fell, and didn't doubt he'd cracked a rib, but he lived.

Celia staggered to her feet and threw a knife toward Isanam's exposed back. Isanam raised a hand, and Boblin saw a flash of light as the knife clattered harmlessly away. Even with her left hand, her aim was true—a pity it hadn't finished the job.

Keep her safe.

Isanam turned from Boblin and marched back toward Celia. Boblin got to a standing position, righted his armor, and took a deep breath before stumbling after the malichon. Celia held her sword in her left hand, right harm hanging uselessly at her side, a grim but defiant expression on her face. As he moved toward Isanam, Boblin felt a sudden, crushing blow against his head. The Overlord had used the Lifesource to lift a small rock and strike Boblin from the side. Boblin saw sparks once more as he fell again, blood running from the newly formed gash on his temple.

Keep her safe.

Dazed, Boblin took a few moments to figure out how to stand back up. Dizziness took over as he placed his palms on the ground and pushed himself onto his knees. He blinked, trying to find his sword, clumsily picking it up with fingers that did not seem to cooperate anymore, and climbed to his feet.

Keep her safe.

He could barely focus as the world swirled around him, and he thought he might lose consciousness. *Focus.* He forced himself to take his steps one at a time. *I have to keep moving, before it all ends. Because when I die and stand before the Maker, he will ask me what I did, how I made it worthwhile, and I won't even be able to tell him I kept her safe.*

The world snapped into sudden clarity. Boblin summoned his reserves of strength and crossed the distance to the Overlord. Isanam spun toward the more immediate threat at his back—which was good for Celia, because the second Isanam turned away, she collapsed back to the ground. Isanam easily knocked Boblin's strike away, but then something happened that neither opponent expected.

Isanam made a mistake.

Isanam brought his blade into the sky, but just a fraction too high. Boblin roared, snapping his blade into position and driving it into the Overlord's chest, crunching through chain mail and biting into flesh and bone. Isanam brought his weapon down, trying to defend himself, but Boblin stopped Isanam's wrist in a grip. Isanam's surprise, more than anything else, allowed Boblin to pull the Overlord's weapon from his hand and cast it aside. Unarmed, Isanam sank to his knees. Boblin jerked his sword free, and blood ran without hindrance from the open wound in Isanam's chest.

Boblin flicked his blade, knocking the Overlord's mask away. What he saw made him feel pity—even for Isanam. The Overlord's face was twisted and misshapen, a horrible blend of malichon and human features. His flesh looked like it was rotting right off the bone. For once, Isanam's eyes did not burn with malice, but were wide in disbelief.

"I never believed it possible," the Overlord said.

"Believe it," Boblin replied. "It's possible." And then he struck Isanam's head off. The Overlord's body toppled over, landing in a broken tangle on the stones of the Deathlands.

That was about all Boblin could take. He collapsed onto his knees and struggled free from his chain mail shirt. The thing was so dented and broken, it would be more dangerous on than off. Cuts and bruises covered his entire torso.

Celia stumbled toward him, sweaty, streaked with dirt and blood…and utterly beautiful. She wrapped one arm around him, her broken limb hanging at her side, and Boblin touched her cheek. He drew her face toward him, kissing her as they held each other on the slopes of the blood-drenched battlefield.

"Thank you," she said.

Boblin tried to regain his voice, but had no opportunity before Celia brushed his hair away and kissed him back. After a long moment, they both stood, wind gusting over them. Though the immediate vicinity was silent, they heard the sounds of battle nearby. It would be easy enough to stay here, just the two of them, and find peace in each other while everything else came crashing down, but that was hardly either one's nature. Though they were not fit to fight, not one more duel, it didn't matter.

Their comrades needed them, so they would walk the slopes of the Deathlands anyway, standing side by side until the last. Just before they were about to charge into the field of death to join their friends and allies, trumpets sounded as new soldiers swept onto the fields. The four divisions, eight thousand men in all, slammed into the malichon forces like a wave of white foam crushing a black rock. The enemy troops momentarily disappeared under the surge before reemerging, holding their own and fighting back.

At the same time, a small group descended from the direction of the plateau. It was a ragged-looking band of fighters, but they were a blessed sight. The situation had turned from the certainty of death to a faint glimmer of hope.

Celia touched Boblin's arm. "Look," she said. Boblin followed her gaze to the plateau's forbidding walls. Angry, multicolored storm clouds streaked the skies above Zadinn's city as jagged lightning bolts flashed. It had the look of a storm from Malath, and Boblin could not help feeling a chill. Tim was up there right now, in the midst of a nightmare, and however bad it was here on the battlefield, Boblin knew it was much worse in there.

* * *

Tim broke his fall with hardly a thought, stopping midair as he hovered halfway between the roof of the citadel and the cobblestone streets below. He leaped back up to the Dark Lord and unleashed twin columns of fire from the palms of his hands. In response, Zadinn created a shell of protection around himself, and Tim's flames redirected into the storm clouds around them. Tim rushed forward and slammed into Zadinn, pushing them both back through the massive hole in the roof.

The two men grappled as they fell toward the floor, buffeting here and there on cushions made of the Lifesource, so focused on each other that the magic holding them up grew increasingly erratic. They would fall for a short bit, jerk to a halt, and then fall again. In this odd, jerky manner, they tumbled down a few feet at a time.

As they finally struck the ground with jarring force, the impact made both men lose hold of the Lifesource. They rolled back and forth, hands at each other's throats, each trying to keep the other at bay. In his mind's eye, Tim rushed to retrieve the Lifesource, as he had done so many times before, focusing on the imaginary room with the tantalizing, fluttery veil. This time, however, a black, oily presence was in the room with him, and he did not have the luxury of taking the steps slowly. Tim raced forward in his mind, the shadow hot on his heels. Neither man held the Lifesource yet, but whoever reached the veil first would have a distinct advantage. A fraction of a second was all either man needed to destroy the other.

Tim ran faster, but the room stretched farther as the two enemies matched each other stride for stride in this mental race. The veil came closer, closer, closer yet. Reaching it first meant life, reaching it second meant death. Tim stretched for the veil with his fingertips. All he needed was the slightest touch, the barest advantage, but the dark force matched his movements at every turn. Tim lunged, and the shadow beside him lunged as well—

—and the veil, the veil that had to be opened with the greatest caution, the gentlest touch—

—tore open with enough force to rend apart the cosmos.

A torrential flood of the Lifesource rushed into both of them, ripping the two combatants apart and flinging them to opposite sides of the throne room. Before, Tim had only drawn upon the Lifesource in trickles, streams at best. Now it poured into him with the intensity of an angry river, consuming him with energy and power. Zadinn struck at him from the other side of the throne room, using enough force to turn stone to powder, but Tim deflected the attack and retaliated.

Their previous duel was nothing compared to the raw power they now unleashed. As they struggled, objects around them exploded. Zadinn's throne disintegrated into bony fragments, the walls collapsed, and chunks of ceiling tumbled down. They were like two moths fluttering with a flame between them—they could harness its power for now, but if they strayed too close, it would burn them both to cinders.

* * *

And so it went—but that was not all. The excess torrent of magic, rolling from both men in waves of sheer energy, had to go *somewhere*. While some of it tore at the walls and furnishings of the citadel, most of it returned straight to its source—the earth itself. The violent energies bled into the ground, shedding their excess power. And in response to this unprovoked assault, the earth, mother of the Lifesource, rebelled.

So it was that their titanic duel began to tear apart the world.

Forty-Five

Boblin had taken only a few steps forward when the first jolt ran through the ground. He stumbled and turned to look at Celia. She returned his confused glance, and before either could say anything, a second jolt—stronger than the first—threw them onto their knees while the earth vibrated.

Around them, the fighting came to a halt as the rumblings grew increasingly violent. Sharp, violent tremors rocked the battlefield. Boblin placed an arm around Celia's shoulders, and they struggled to their feet. Fissures, starting as thin cracks that gradually widened into lengthy crevasses, ran across the stony ground while magma spewed from their depths. The hot liquid vaulted high into the sky before raining back down on the two armies. Hundreds of men and malichons, allies and enemies, tumbled into the pits that opened unbidden beneath their feet. The floor of the Deathlands rolled, stones rising high and low to create valleys and ridges. There was nothing gentle or natural about this transformation; the length and breadth of the landscape had become a fuming, deadly beast.

Boblin and Celia rose upward as the ground below them lifted, and the sudden action split them apart from each other, Boblin tumbling down one side of the ridge and Celia falling down the other. As Boblin landed amid a jumble of shifting rocks, the earth folded on top of a score of malichons not a hundred feet away, crushing them and snuffing out their screams.

Boblin struggled to his feet, falling over twice in the process. This was Tim's doing for sure. He doubted Tim was causing the destruction on purpose, but it was nonetheless a result of his sorcery or Zadinn's. *Karfing wonderful.* While Tim and Zadinn were playing Magician's Arm-Wrestling, the rest suffered the consequences. Boblin had had his fair share of bad days on this venture, but this about topped it. They were already as good as dead, and this just poured salt on the whole karfing wound. On the bright side, at least those fissures had stayed away from him…so far.

Boblin grabbed a tuft of grass and struggled up the slope. He had to reach Celia. She was on the other side with a broken arm and in no condition to protect herself. He wasn't going to let her get torn apart by this madness, not after he'd been tossed around by Isanam to keep her safe. *Advocates. Sun-baked lizards, every last one of them.*

Another jolt threw Boblin back to the base of the ridge, while underneath him a telltale crack formed. Boblin cursed, scrambling forward, but he was too slow. A fiery gorge opened beneath his feet, and he tumbled into the gap. *So much for avoiding these bloody things.* He only fell a few feet before landing on a slight outcrop—apparently there *was* justice in the world   and before rolling off the edge into the lava, he grabbed a handhold in the side of the crevasse and pulled himself back up. Beside him, a screaming malichon sailed past into the fires below. Rocks and bodies rained down all around Boblin, but he managed to cling to the wall. All the while, the earth continued to quake and rumble. *Karf, Tim, what* are *you doing?*

Boblin grabbed the lip of the fissure and pulled himself to the top of the ground. He staggered to his feet and began running. A nightmarish world of fire and stone surrounded him in all directions. Rivers of lava flowed across the landscape, devouring victims by the hundreds. In the north, a maelstrom of black clouds completely consumed the citadel. Neither side—malichons or elions, Tim or Zadinn—would survive this. This wasn't a war anymore. It was an apocalypse.

Boblin at last saw Celia, alive and healthy, sheltering at the base of another ridge. As to how long that spot would remain safe, Boblin could not say. The world was in flux, and all one could do was cling to solid ground and pray. He reached her side, and she wrapped her good arm around him. For the time being, all they could do was wait and watch the world fall to pieces.

* * *

In the citadel, the energy continued to crackle in the air around Tim and Zadinn, the heat so intense it singed the hairs on Tim's body. When the quake struck the palace, neither man missed a beat. The danger each presented to the other was far deadlier than anything else they were up against.

As he fought, a vision came to Tim's mind. He saw the Deathlands in chaos, but the destruction did not stop there; it continued in concentric circles throughout the rest of the North. Even the Barricade trembled just a little. Tim realized this battle would, and could, go on for hours. Physical exhaustion was no longer a factor. With this much of the Lifesource running through him, he had no limits. Tim also realized the longer they struggled, the worse the destruction would become. They would all die. *Everyone.* Neither side would have a chance of starting over. Given time, this battle might even touch the South.

Tim brought down a barrier between them. Zadinn threw his powers against it, but Tim held the shield in place, grinding the battle to a stalemate. Zadinn glared at him, pushing harder, but Tim did not yield. The ground rumbled.

"We have to stop this," Tim said, surprised by how flat his voice sounded. "We will destroy everything."

Zadinn only smiled, eyes gleaming. "That's what makes it such fun."

So what now? Tim asked himself. And the answer came, crystal clear: *I am the Warrior of Light. My first responsibility is, and always will be, to the people of the land.*

Zadinn was not about to stop. Tim hadn't expected it—the Dark Lord was insane—but he had needed to try. Because if they continued, the people would die, and Tim would fail them. He only had one option left, one way to protect the people. So he saved them in the only way he could.

He released the Lifesource.

Zadinn's powers slammed into Tim, throwing him across the entire length of the throne room. There was nothing to protect Tim as he crashed into the wall. Pain exploded through his body, and he felt several ribs break. As Tim fell from the wall, Zadinn assaulted him with the Lifesource anew. Tim writhed across the floor, white-hot agony surging through the core of his being. It was sheer torment. The anguish grew so great he barely retained consciousness. The pain was everywhere, in his muscles, his bones, and his mind. He vaguely heard himself scream as his body, surely mangled beyond repair, skittered across the flagstones.

And then Zadinn stopped. Tim's sight returned, but only barely. He was dimly aware of his surroundings as his eyelids fluttered open and shut. He could not even lift his fingers. He saw pools of blood spattered across the ground, and he knew they were his. The Dark Lord stood over the fallen Warrior. Zadinn touched Tim's chest with the tip of his staff, and Tim's back arched. He screamed as the pain blossomed tenfold, but the touch lasted only a moment before Zadinn lifted his staff away.

"Now you die," Zadinn said. "Just like your mother, your father, and the Kyrlod. One by one, you are all mine."

Mother. Father. Nazgar. Those names awoke something inside Tim. The air shuddered, and for a second Tim sensed a world in complete balance. He felt himself tried, tested, and weighed. And then…the balance tipped.

The Lifesource flooded back into him. Vitality coursed through his limbs, washing away the pain as he rose into the air. Rays of gold light formed around his hands. He felt Zadinn attempt to strike him with the Lifesource, but this time Zadinn's powers had no effect. Tim effortlessly cut through the Dark Lord's defenses, lifting Zadinn into the air and shoving him backward. Twin cords of fire shot out from his hands, following Zadinn across the room. The Warrior of Light was in complete control as he raised Zadinn high into the sky, pushing him farther away until the Dark Lord hung straight above the Cauldron of Souls.

Tim dropped him.

Zadinn screamed before splashing into the liquid. The fluid had a viscous, sticky texture. Zadinn struggled to the surface, attempting to climb free, but the murky waters clung to his body. A howling chorus of voices rose into the air as the shapes of men, elions, and dwerions reached forth from its depths. Each soul Zadinn had ever condemned to the Cauldron at last had his or her revenge. Zadinn screamed again, and the torment he had bestowed upon so many others was turned on him a hundredfold. The vengeful spirits swarmed over the Dark Lord, pulling him deep into their embrace, and he disappeared from sight—and from the world.

The earthquake ceased and all was silent. In its wake, the sudden stillness felt surreal. As the Warrior of Light floated to the ground, releasing the Lifesource, the pain returned, consuming him so thoroughly he fell to his knees. His left arm hung useless, and the bones in his right leg felt like they were in pieces.

That was when the Cauldron of Souls exploded. A ring of green light shot outward, passing harmlessly through Tim but turning everything else to dust. A cyclone of whipping wind followed the blast of light. All was silent for several long moments, and then Tim saw that the green energy, which had just passed *outward*, now reversed course and returned to its source, a sphere of light floating where the Cauldron had once been, bringing everything in its path.

Tim had to get away from the sphere. He could almost feel reality bending at its edges. The glowing ball of light was a doorway, a portal to *somewhere else*, and he couldn't let it take him. If he did, there was no escape. The rubble of the throne room blew past him. More than once, debris knocked him back as he tried to get to his feet. His sword flew past him, and he barely grabbed it in time. Tim slammed the sword into the stones beneath his feet, tip first, and wrapped his hands around the hilt, clinging to it, an anchor of support in the chaos.

The earthquake began again.

* * *

Boblin turned north as a massive explosion sounded, raising a hand to shield his eyes from the brilliant light that consumed the plateau. A green ring of energy shot outward, traveling across the landscape at breakneck speed. The stones underneath his feet continued rumbling.

The green wave slammed into the ranks of malichons. The red-eyed creatures disintegrated, their bodies shredding into tiny specks that dissipated on the wind. Boblin winced as the wave approached him and Celia. There was no way to avoid it, so he threw Celia to the ground and covered her with his body. The wave of light, however, passed through them without leaving a mark. Boblin raised his head and saw that the rest of the Army of Kah'lash also remained unscathed.

The wave then turned around and came back, this time bringing a shower of debris with it. *Nothing is ever simple for me. Welcome to a day in the life of Boblin Kule.* Dirt and stone pelted his body, but he maintained his protective cover over Celia. After the energy passed through again, the entire malichon army was *gone*, leaving only the elions and the Army of Kah'lash standing.

They watched as the light gathered at the plateau's center, swirling in a cataclysmic cyclone. A sphere of energy hovered in the center of the vortex, gathering everything to it. The light gradually inverted, dwindling to a mere speck before collapsing atop itself, and the sphere vanished along with the entire plateau, leaving behind only a bare stretch of flat ground.

There was silence for a long while. Then the people collected themselves, picking themselves up and tending to comrades. Everyone knew with undeniable certainty...it was over. At long last, it was over.

"See to the wounded," Commander Jend Argul said, his voice cracking the silence. The Army of Kah'lash was as efficient at battlefield medicine as it was at fighting, and the soldiers immediately knew what to do. The silence gradually ended—a word here, a word there—as everyone found his or her voice again. There was not much talk, but the chatter broke the strange stillness hanging over them. The scene was no longer surreal—grim, yes, but no longer like a waking dream.

Boblin walked to the edge of the Army and stared north. He hoped to spot something, at least a speck, but the landscape remained empty and flat for as far as he could see. Celia stepped next to him and touched his shoulder. "I don't think Tim made it," Boblin said.

"I don't think he expected to."

"No," Boblin agreed, "he didn't."

The sun dipped low in the west as dusk fell on the encampment. A few dried trees and scrub brush remained, not much, but enough to light some fires. They had nothing to eat, but there was no time anyway; the wounded were their first priority. Many of the injured died, but many more were saved.

Boblin formed a bedroll from some clothes and settled on it. Celia nestled underneath his arm, her head on his chest. Her broken arm was in a proper sling now, thank the Maker, and in time it would heal fully. In moments, she fell asleep. As Boblin stroked her hair, a single thought brought a smile to his lips. *She is safe.*

Boblin soon followed Celia into sleep. He dreamed he was standing on the bank of a river with Celia and the other elions from the Fort. Tim Matthias stood on the other side of the river, a peaceful but sad smile on his lips. A bank of mists floated behind him. Tim waved at them before turning and disappearing into the fog. Boblin woke with tears on his cheeks and stood up, letting firelight skip across his face.

He looked north again toward the plateau that was no longer there. The shape of a man stood at the edge of the camp. He took several steps forward, walking with a severe limp, until he stood fully in the light. Boblin opened his mouth to speak, but no words came out.

"The darkness has passed," Tim Matthias said, and then collapsed.

Forty-Six

Tim opened his eyes. He gasped, reaching for the Lifesource to prepare for Zadinn's next attack. The power flooded into him in waves as he quickly raised a defensive barrier in front of himself. Twin balls of green fire danced in his palms before he realized he was merely lying on a cot inside a tent. Sunlight glowed through the fabric, caressing his face with warmth, and the air around him felt still and gentle. At the same time, he became acutely aware of a dull, throbbing agony pulsing through his bones with every breath he took.

Tim paused. Nothing happened. No attack came. He blinked, trying to clear his head. He didn't appear to be in danger, but he didn't know where he was or how he'd gotten here. *Isn't there a battle going on? Or has it already happened?* He tried to seek his last coherent memory. *I need Nazgar.*

Then memories clicked into place like pieces of a puzzle: walking to the citadel, the Guardian's attack, the tunnel of mist…Nazgar killed, the battle with Zadinn, the Cauldron of Souls, the earthquake…What followed after the quake was not so retrievable. He recalled struggling through the chaos, fighting a mad wind he thought would shred his body to pieces, the citadel—the world—disintegrating around him.

Then, silence. He floated in an empty shell but saw lights far ahead—perhaps the lights at the gates of Harmea? He had forced himself to continue walking, to take step after step, and that was when blackness truly took over. He must have fallen unconscious; collapsed on the ground. *But who found me?* Tim didn't think anything could have survived that monstrous maelstrom.

He sat up. Spears of pain stabbed him in the side. Tim looked down and saw bandages covering his waist and his arm in a sling. Surely more ribs were broken than intact. He ground his teeth as the world spun, but this was healthy pain—the pain of *life*. Tim turned to the side of the bed and put his feet on the ground, noticing another bandage, one around his left ankle. He put pressure on his foot and winced. The injury couldn't keep him from walking, but it would give him a glorious limp. He staggered into a standing position and walked with careful tenderness. When he opened the tent flap and stepped outside, he stopped in shock. *This can't be the North.*

The sun brought far too much comfort, and no harsh wind cut his face. But it *was* the North. The familiar jagged landscape rose and fell in front of him, and he recognized the reddish stone of the Deathlands, which had changed beyond measure. It looked like a giant had dragged a rake with iron teeth across the landscape. Enormous crevasses ran across the ground, and in other places the stone had buckled, rising and falling at erratic intervals.

Tim stood in the center of a massive encampment. Men, elions, and dwerions milled around, performing tasks too various to note. Their movements were purposeful, neither frenzied nor hasty, and in that moment Tim knew everything was going to be fine. Nobody had to say anything—their actions said it all. When Tim had last seen the elions of the North, they were marching with implacable purpose toward their doom. That feeling was gone, evaporated like fog at first sign of sunlight. These people were at peace, with joyful if challenging jobs to do.

"Welcome back."

Tim turned and saw Boblin walking toward him. A large bandage covered one side of the elion's head, displaying several brown patches of dried blood. He looked worn, beaten, and utterly content. Tim smiled and held out his left hand. Boblin clasped it and firmly clapped Tim's right shoulder. Sparks shot in front of Tim's vision, and he nearly doubled over.

Boblin stepped back. "Apologies, mate," he said.

Tim straightened and smiled. "I feel like I was crushed by a karfing pile of rocks."

"I don't doubt it. I'll be truthful, I didn't think you were going to make it."

Tim met his gaze. "I'm not entirely convinced I *did* make it. This doesn't look like the place I left."

Boblin patted Tim's shoulder again, and Tim swore at him. Boblin replied with a smirk. "Just proving you are indeed still alive. As for this, I have to blame you." He gestured at the marred landscape.

"I don't even get a thank-you, do I?" Tim asked.

"You will from the rest of them, but from me?" Boblin shook his head. "No. You opened a karfing hole under my feet, and then you made a hill fold over and almost crush me. What in the name of Malath were you thinking?"

"We *are* alive," Tim said. "You're still a sarcastic three-legged goat."

"I won't deny that," Boblin said.

"How long was I asleep?" Tim asked.

"Three days," Boblin answered.

"The truth, please."

"Three days."

"Karf." Tim looked at Boblin. "Food?"

Boblin smiled. "I never thought you'd ask." He led Tim across the camp. Tim followed as best as he could, but he was hobbling more than walking. He wondered if he would carry this limp for the rest of his days. Boblin took him behind the tents instead of in front, a gesture of courtesy for which Tim was grateful. He wanted some privacy while he got his bearings.

"What do you remember?" Boblin asked.

Tim didn't want to say much at the moment. He might talk of it later, but for now he had no desire to relive the experience. "You'll be glad to know I remember the earthquake," he said. "Zadinn and I caused it. We were the stone in the pond, and the earthquake was the ripples. I don't know how I escaped. After Zadinn died, everything fell down around me. It went...somewhere else."

Boblin nodded. "The rest of the Army arrived right before the quake began. Of course, once the ground started falling apart, we didn't have much time for fighting."

"How did it end for you?" Tim asked.

"I'm sure we both saw the same thing," Boblin said. "A ring of green light passed through everything. It didn't hurt any of us, but it destroyed the malichons. They disappeared like smoke, and the green wave returned to the plateau before vanishing. They're all gone."

"To Malath, I'm sure," Tim said.

Boblin looked dour. "Malath? Won't they hold a reception for them there?"

Tim shook his head. "No, Zadinn failed. He was their chance to make this world their world. His welcome will be anything but warm. Besides, Malath is just as bad for demons as it is for anyone else. There's a reason they want to get out. It's not as if they have fun there."

"So there *is* justice," Boblin said.

"I suppose," Tim replied. For the moment, though, he was too tired to feel anything. It was over, and that was enough. Besides, everything seemed so unreal right now. In a way, he was glad for the dull ache throbbing through his body, because it was proof this was actually happening. Boblin stepped toward another tent, lifted the flap, and they both ducked inside.

"By the Maker, it is good to see ye, laddie!" Tim jerked his head up. He barely had time to recognize Quentiin Harggra—*Quentiin Harggra!*—before the dwerion engulfed him in an enormous hug. That did it. Quentiin certainly couldn't be here, and yet he was, and the thousand needles of physical pain shooting through his side would not exist in a dream. The old era was over, and in this new age, dreams could come to life—and the dream that Quentiin Harggra might one day return was given flesh.

"Easy on the man," Boblin said to Quentiin, who scoffed, but he stepped back and released Tim.

"The lad's made of stern stuff," Quentiin said. "He can bounce around on a few broken bones an' be just fine."

Quentiin himself looked like he'd been held under a miller's pestle for a brief turn. Pellen Yuzhar, Commander Jend, and Prince Ladu also stood in the tent. Everyone sported his or her own scars. The arduous battle had taken a steep toll.

"If it's a question of who has the most bones broken, Matthias wins," Jend said. "Well done, Warrior."

Pellen stepped forward, bowing. "Well done, *all* of you." He straightened, looking at Tim, Boblin and Quentiin. "But most especially to you three."

"Aye," Jend said, bowing along with Prince Ladu.

"I feel like I only know part of the story," Tim said, glancing at his two friends.

"To begin with, you went into Zadinn's citadel," Boblin said, "and you killed him—or I assume you did. So we won."

"I thought you'd been taken with the prisoners, Quentiin, but I had no way of knowing for sure," Tim said.

"Aye, laddie," Quentiin replied, "I was there."

Tim shuddered. He'd spent just one afternoon in Zadinn's city, and he never wanted to go back. Quentiin, however, had been there for nearly two months.

Tim realized it wasn't just the scars of battle that made Quentiin look different. Something else had changed, too. Perhaps it was Quentiin's demeanor, or
maybe it was a change in his eyes, or possibly those lines on his face…He was
neither better nor worse, just different, like Tim. Tim hadn't looked in a mirror,
and now he wondered what face he would see. His heart no longer felt heavy,
and his thoughts were far from dark, but the changes remained. There was no
use fussing about it, it just *was*.

As an afterthought, Boblin said, "Oh, and Quentiin freed the slaves."

"I didn't free them," Quentiin insisted. "They freed themselves."

"He downplays his part," Pellen said, "as does Kule."

Boblin scratched his hair, looking left and right as if seeking an opportunity
to leave the tent. "Luck," he muttered. Tim looked at his friend and arched an
eyebrow.

"He killed Isanam," Jend said, "and he still fails to realize this is the greatest
thing any soldier of the Fort has ever done."

Boblin's face turned crimson.

"But enough of this," Pellen cut in. "I'm certain the Warrior would like
some food."

The six of them ate together in the tent. Tim was glad for the privacy, but
he knew it couldn't go on forever. He had to leave, and when he stepped outside, people would see him. They'd talk and point. Nothing would ever be the
same. He had read many tales of heroes in the South. Truth be told, he'd always
thought it would be a grand thing to become one, but now he just wished he
could fade into the background. He hadn't done anything different than the rest
of the soldiers, so receiving honor felt wrong.

The conversation remained surprisingly light. Tim realized this was yet
another elion survival tactic—and it made a world of sense. There would
be time to relive the battle later, to tell their respective tales, but there
was no need to remain rooted in the grim subject when its horrors were
still fresh. They had to remember their humanity first. But he couldn't
avoid telling them about Nazgar's death. Pellen did not seem surprised.
He'd spent a lot of time with Nazgar during the quest for the Army of
Kah'lash, and apparently the Kyrlod knew all along his death would come
in Zadinn's citadel. Tim's respect for the prophet was already deep, but this
only deepened it.

"Well," Pellen finally said, putting down his spoon and looking at Tim. "Are you ready, my son?" Tim nodded. Pellen stepped outside the tent as casually as if going for a morning stroll.

Tim hesitated, but Boblin pushed him forward. "It's you they want to see, mate."

Tim stepped out into the camp. For the first few moments, he actually thought he would escape notice. Then one man turned and, upon seeing the Warrior, stopped. Several more took notice, a slow applause began, and then gradually the cheers started.

"Matthias! Matthias! Matthias!"

Tim stood awkwardly behind Pellen, trying to decide what to do. Boblin again pushed him, and then Tim realized his best course of action was to meet this honor with mutual respect. So the Warrior of Light stepped forward, back straight, and looked into the eyes of those before him. And he bowed to them.

The people went silent. Of course, Tim had no speech prepared. But this wasn't a performance, or anything to be prepared for; it was only the truth. "We've come a long way," he said. "If you want a place to direct your gratitude, then remember you and your comrades were the ones who brought us out of the shadow. The darkness has passed, but that does not mean the work is over. It has only just begun. So today we celebrate. Tomorrow we rebuild."

The cheers came back, multiplied tenfold. The sun emerged from behind a cloud, shining on the small band of survivors. It covered the landscape with its light, on the first free day the North had seen in two hundred years.

* * *

The fires had died down, and the celebration was finished. Boblin Kule decided to walk the edge of the camp, embracing the quiet solitude of the night.

It was over—well and truly over. Boblin felt a satisfaction he'd never felt before. His mind was a whirlwind. He wasn't accustomed to this new feeling and didn't know what to do with it. Oh, there was building to be done, a civilization to be forged, but that wasn't everything. He was free to go anywhere—*anywhere*—in the North without fear of danger. Now that was different...even intimidating in a way.

Boblin's spirits had never been more buoyant, and at the same time he had not ever felt more somber. It was over, yes, but there was a cost. Too many elions were slain on the battlefield, the Frontier Patrol all but destroyed. He could list the survivors one at a time: Jend, Hugo, Ken—those three never would die easily—Celia, Mandar, Jess, Faldon, Tavin, Wayne, and himself. Other members of the Fort who'd been held captive in the Pit also survived, but of the thirty-eight elions who fled into the Kaltu Pass, only these remained. Three out of every four who quested for the Army of Kah'lash lay dead, whether in the Deathlands or in the Mountains. Yes, there was joy but also sorrow.

Boblin sure as Malath expected the elions to look at Tim differently—he was the Warrior of Light, after all—but *him*? Boblin Kule? Yet they did. Hugo and Ken, elions he'd always looked up to, now *they* looked up to *him*! They didn't see Boblin Kule anymore. They saw the one who had defeated Isanam. This war *had* changed many things.

He'd overheard some of the elions, and apparently there was word that Jend Argul was planning to step down as Commander—not that Jend was unfit for the job but because his time was over. Jend's war, the Patrol's war, had been against Zadinn. It was time for the new generation to take command. And then they'd mentioned that if anyone were to be Commander, it would be Boblin Kule. *Nonsense! Just a rumor.*

Boblin stooped near a small outcrop as an unlikely sight seized his attention. A small flower, a whitelily, had pushed itself up from between the cracks in the earth. This made no sense. The whitelily was a spring flower, and summer was almost over. Autumn chill came with every morning now.

"It's confused," Tim said, limping over to stand next to him. The Warrior of Light supported himself with a sturdy cane.

Boblin looked up. "It's confused? *I'm* confused."

"The earth. When Zadinn took over, his presence made the land die, like winter—only this winter lasted for two centuries, and now it's finally over." Tim pointed at the flower. "The land is waking up, but at the wrong time of year."

"Will it always be like this?" Boblin tried to envision a midwinter morning with apples hanging from the trees.

"I don't think so. We'll notice some oddities this winter—a strange growth here or there—but once the North remembers its seasons, things will be all right."

Boblin moved to the edge of the outcrop, looking at the jagged wasteland. "I remember the tapestry at the Fort," he said. "It will look like that again one day, but probably not in our lifetime."

Tim hobbled to the edge of the rock. "No," he said, "I think it will be different." He closed his eyes, and though Boblin could not visibly see it, he knew Tim was seeking the Lifesource. Tim inhaled, exhaled, and his face showed peaceful concentration. His jaw tightened slightly, and the rest of his body tensed. Tim wasn't doing anything violent, but it clearly took effort. Boblin felt a barely perceptible tingle run through the ground underneath his feet, right before Tim relaxed and opened his eyes. "There," Tim said.

"What?" Boblin asked.

"I nudged it—nothing serious, just a nudge. We won't notice anything today or tomorrow, or even the next day, but instead of the trees taking twenty years to grow, they will only take ten. We *will* see this land in a new light before our lifetimes are over." Tim stepped away. "But I'm probably keeping you from something. That's not right of me."

Tim left, and Boblin continued around the encampment. He found Celia right where she said she would be, and they went out into the night together, spending it underneath the stars.

* * *

Quentiin was awake before dawn. It had been several days since the slaves had freed themselves from the Pit, but the habit of rising early had not died. They were moving south today. The elions were going to build a new city, and where better to build it than where the Fort had once stood? They obviously couldn't build it in the exact location—the Kaltu Pass could not contain a city—but they would instead rebuild Galdon on the plains below the hills.

Quentiin wasn't sure what the dwerions were going to do next. Young Matthias was set; the lad was staying in the North, and that was it. The elions were Tim's people now. The dwerions, though, were of the South, and Raldoon waited for them. Now that Zadinn was dead, Tim could open the tunnel again. And for what happened after that—well, Quentiin supposed that sooner or later the two worlds would join. It probably wouldn't happen immediately, but no doubt some settlers would make their way to this new land. It would be a short while before the soil turned fertile, but it would happen, and the North would live again.

Quentiin stepped outside and helped break down camp. These Army types were something else. He wished he could have seen them in battle—they considered three-to-one good odds, and he believed it. Yet though an air of deadliness surrounded every Army soldier, these men weren't bred to kill. They had good hearts—and they certainly knew how to move a camp. However, they would not remain here forever. They would return to their home beyond the Mountains, and after that no living man here would see them again. They were bound to the Warrior, but only for this brief time.

Matthias had told Quentiin about the beauty of the lands beyond the Mountains, of its quiet serenity and placid landscape. It sounded like Harmea. Part of Quentiin wanted to see it, knowing he couldn't, and part of him was glad he hadn't. When Tim told Quentiin about the lands of the Army of Kah'lash, and of the fact that Tim could not return there, such a look of sadness came into Tim's eyes that Quentiin felt like weeping even though he'd never seen the place. The deaths of Daniel and Rosalie cut deep into Tim's soul, and Tim had found the healing he needed in the peace of those evergreen forests and blue lakes.

Though less than a dozen elions remained from the quest northward, several hundred slaves—elions, dwerions, and humans among them—had survived. Except for the dwerions returning to Raldoon, these remaining slaves, now free, would be the first settlers of this new era.

And then there was that Ladu fellow. He was quiet, but that wasn't such a bad thing. Apparently he'd be emperor over these people, and from what Quentiin could tell, the Prince would do just fine. He'd worry if he'd seen Ladu swaggering about, lording it over the rest, but for now he was just another refugee trying to make a new home.

A new home. Raldoon would be a new home, in a way. Old Raldoon was gone, burned to the ground, but Quentiin would see his home village soon enough. And that would be a good day.

* * *

The weeks spent moving south passed quickly for Tim. They had a few horses with them, and his injuries entitled him to ride one. By the time they crested the northern fields of the Durin Plains, Tim could walk again without a cane. His ribs still ached, but they were on the mend, and at least they didn't pierce like arrowheads every time he breathed. His limp was barely noticeable anymore.

He wondered if he could use the Lifesource to heal himself. No doubt he could have, but he didn't have any idea how to go about it and wasn't about to practice on himself. Perhaps he could practice on Boblin sometime. Yes, that seemed like a reasonable course of action. Besides, Boblin never seemed to have the time of day for his old friend anymore. He and Celia seemed to be getting along quite well, and Tim supposed that was a good thing.

Night fell on the company as they settled onto the Durin Plains. Tim left the group behind this evening. He had something he needed to do alone. He set out across the stony landscape, sword strapped across his back, and quiet darkness enveloped him. The air held the cool of autumn but nothing else. The harsh winds were gone, along with Zadinn, the malichons, and their evil city. Tim could grow to like this place. It was as good as any to call home.

Tim reached the foot of the Kaltu Pass and began his climb. It was by no means easy, especially for his recovering body, but he'd survive. He'd passed through worse to get here. The moon hung in the sky, an orb of soft white light, bathing the ground with gentle radiance.

For now, Tim avoided the remains of the Fort. He and the elions would deliver their respects there, but later. Instead he made his way into the Pass to a location he knew well, one that brought him pain but also memories of happiness. He instinctively knew where they were. A misshapen pile of stones marked the place where Rosalie and Daniel Matthias were buried beneath the walls of the Pass. Their sacrifice had been the first on this quest, and many others had followed, but Rosalie and Daniel had set the example—if not for them, everyone would still be under darkness today.

The misshapen mound of stones was the grandest cairn anyone could ask for. Tim knelt in front of it, remaining silent as he relived memories of their times together—sleeping under their roof in the Odow, sparring with Daniel behind their cottage, the warm light in Rosalie's eyes, and Daniel's sharp wit. Tim had thought of many things to say, but sometimes the simplest things were the best.

"Thank you," he said. He unsheathed his sword and summoned forth its green fire. Tim lifted it above his head and then drove its tip into the cairn of rocks. It slid into the ground with no resistance at all. Tim stopped after half the length of the blade was buried. A fitting marker, and there it would keep, wrapped in a spell so it remained untouched by the elements.

Until it was needed again.

Tim made the journey back to camp in complete silence. He knew they were out there somewhere, in the lands of Harmea, waiting for the day when they would be reunited. No doubt they were watching him even now.

He hoped they were proud.

Epilogue

The midday sun shone down on Prince Ladu Jovun IV as he stood atop a wooden dais, elevated five feet above the ground. It was a plain structure, made of sturdy nails and boards, entirely lacking in ornamentation—and it was all the Prince had asked for.

Beside the dais, a square slab of stone rested in the ground. Ladu had laid this stone himself, just this morning, lining it with mortar and setting it into the earth. It was the cornerstone of the city of Galdon, the foundation of the city they were about to build.

The survivors of the Battle of the Deathlands stood in front of the platform, facing Prince Ladu as he faced them. It was thirty days since that afternoon of blood and death. Before holding this ceremony, Ladu had declared one month must pass before he accepted the crown of the North, to properly observe the passing of those who had given their lives for this moment.

Four banners hung behind the Prince. One depicted a broken chain, the symbol of the slaves who'd fought in the Pit. Another displayed the familiar yellow sun on a field of black, the Fort's banner and now a sigil for the elions who'd fought in the Deathlands. The banner of the Army of Kah'lash showed a hawk in flight, crested with five colors for each division. The last banner depicted a green sword of fire, point down, for the Warrior of Light. Today was not to honor only Ladu—it was to honor everyone.

Tim stood at the front of the crowd, Boblin Kule at his left and Quentiin Harggra to his right. Celia Alcion stood next to Boblin, and Tim did not have to look to know the two elions were standing with hands clasped together. It brought a smile to his face. Boblin and Celia represented everything the people of the North had fought and died for; freedom was *wonderful*, but it was nothing without love.

The crowd watched silently as the white-haired figure of Pellen Yuzhar approached the foot of the dais, carrying a pillow with a crown atop it. The man was stooped with age, but his face showed no pain, and his wrinkled, leathery features shone with happiness. Pellen claimed no royal title, but he *was* the leader of the North's free people, and it was only fitting that he crown the new leader. He'd fulfilled his promise to Nazgar, his debt was paid, and after today he was welcome to a long overdue rest.

Pellen walked up the steps of the platform. The people in the crowd did not kneel yet, waiting for Pellen's cue. When the leader of the Fort reached the top of the dais, he turned around to look at the crowd. Even though his voice seemed thin and frail, everyone heard his words. He did not say much, but that made it even better. Excessiveness of ceremony ruined too many good things.

"My friends, it is with the greatest pleasure and the humblest honor that I present the crown of this land to Emperor Ladu Jovun IV." Pellen turned and knelt, raising the pillow and bowing his head. The crowd moved to kneel, but Ladu surprised everyone by waving his hand. Tim hadn't expected Ladu to halt the ceremony, brief as it was, but Ladu was nearly emperor, so it was his prerogative.

Ladu lifted the crown in both hands and held it a moment before taking a deep breath. "I deem this not to be," he said. A murmur of surprise rippled through the crowd, and Tim exchanged a look with Boblin and Quentiin. Both appeared to be just as shocked as he was. Ladu was totally departing from the planned course of events.

"Timothy Matthias," Ladu said. "Please step forward."

Pellen moved out of the way as Tim stepped out of line. *What is this?*

"I am not fit for this position," Ladu said. "You unseated the Dark Lord, not I. By rights and by law, the throne is yours." He knelt to Tim and offered him the crown.

Tim Matthias was numb. For a moment, his mind returned to his travels in the caves beneath the Mountains. He recalled thinking this crown should be his, that it *would* be his by right…and now it was offered to him.

But that was a different Tim. He'd been wrought with grief and anger, done evil deeds and thought evil thoughts. Of course he'd turned the darkness aside. It was gone, and he did not fear its return. But he knew his duty when he saw it before him. He took the crown and held it in his hands. "Stand," he said, and Ladu complied. Tim spoke so his voice carried to the back of the crowd.

"The Warrior of Light is a protector and a defender," Tim said. "He is not a ruler. The throne belongs to the emperor, not to the Warrior. I hereby swear fealty to Ladu Jovun IV, rightful ruler of these lands. As for me, I only wish to serve and protect."

Tim knelt before the emperor and gave him the crown. Ladu paused and then nodded. It was right. Both knew it.

"So it shall be," Ladu said and placed the crown atop his own head. The sound of the crowd's cheers made the steps vibrate. Ladu pulled his sword from its sheath and touched it to Tim's shoulders—right, then left, and right again. "You are the warrior of the people, the warrior of the lands, the warrior at the gates, the warrior of freedom…

"You are the Warrior of Light!"

Author Biography

William Heinzen has been telling stories ever since elementary school, when he discovered the only thing better than reading about sorcerers was writing about them. He holds a degree in English with a concentration in creative writing from the University of Jamestown in Jamestown, North Dakota. William lives in Bismarck, North Dakota, where he enjoys hunting, fishing, being outdoors, and of course, reading and writing. *Warrior of Light* is his first novel. Find him at WilliamHeinzen.com or Facebook.com/WilliamHeinzenAuthor.

Made in the USA
Columbia, SC
04 July 2017